DEDICATION

For my posse people... your support makes these books possible!

LEGACY OF LUCKY LOGAN

OMNIBUS ONE

J. R. FRONTERA

**Published by
TIN CAN**

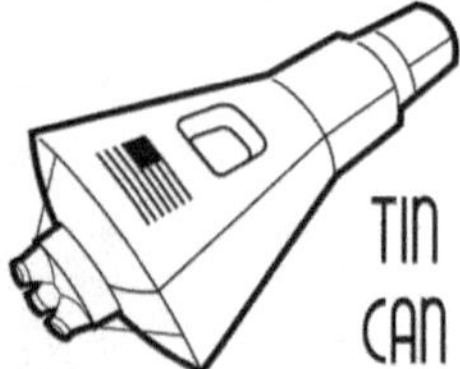

**An imprint of Wordwraith Books, LLC
705-B SE Melody Lane #147
Lee's Summit, MO 64063
http://www.wordwraiths.com**

This is a work of fiction. Names, characters, places, and incidents are products of the author's imagination. Any resemblance to actual events, organizations, places, or persons, living or dead, is purely coincidental or used fictitiously.

Version 1.0

http://www.jrfrontera.com

Cover art by J. Caleb Design
Formatting by Charity Chimni
Maps by renflowergrapx
Chapter Heading Illustrations and page edge designs by Taylor Park

BOOKS BY J.R. FRONTERA

All books available on Amazon.com and most other online retailers, wherever books are sold.

THE LEGACY OF LUCKY LOGAN

(scifi western)

Bargain at Bravebank

Bastard of Blessing

Bones in Blackbird

Demon at Devil's Deep

(and more coming soon)

N'SPACE

(humorous space opera)

Galapalooza

The Starburst Inn

(and more coming soon)

STARSHIP ASS

(humorous space opera)

Of Sporks, Overlords, and Moon Worms

Of Donkeys, Gods, and Space Pirates

Of Donkeys, Dogs, and Rogue Bits

Of Donkeys, Cogs, and Hot Bodies

COMPLETE

For a fully updated book list check out https://jrfrontera.com.

A NOVEL PRODUCED BY

J.R. FRONTERA

PAT STEVENS

VICKY MEYER

BRITTANY STEVENS

ANDREA VIEGAS

TAYLOR PARK

CHRISTINE CHRYSOGONOU

DREW TABB

COVER ART BY
J. CALEB DESIGNS

FORMATTING BY
CHARITY CHIMNI

MAPS BY
RENFLOWERGRAPX

CHAPTER HEADING ILLUSTRATIONS
AND PAGE EDGE DESIGNS BY
TAYLOR PARK

WITH SPECIAL THANKS TO

SARAH HIGGINS
SYDNEY STOKOE
MEGHANN MAUREEN
BETA READERS

JAMIE DAVIS
MEDICAL CONSULTANT

MATT CARLSON
FIREARMS CONSULTANT

BARGAIN AT BRAVEBANK

THE LEGACY OF LUCKY LOGAN

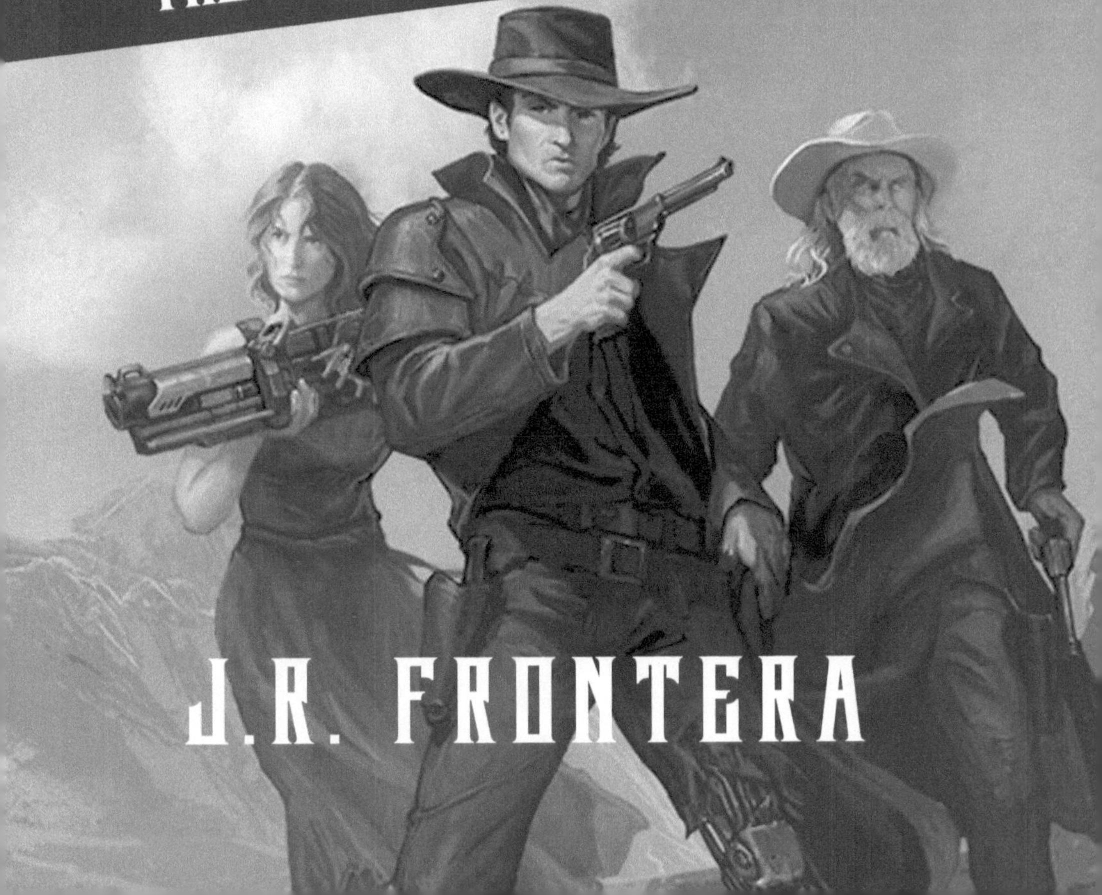

J.R. FRONTERA

THE LEGACY OF LUCKY LOGAN
BOOK 1

WRITTEN BY
J.R. FRONTERA

NORTHERN WILDS
KINGDOM OF CANADA
WESTERN TERRITORIES
CENTRAL COMMUNE
Dakota
Kansas
Iowa
Missouri
EAST REPUBLIC
Pennsylvania
Califia
— rumored
Utah
Purgatory City
Valley of Lightning
Arizona
Blessing
Bravebank
Lesser Texas
Grave Gulch
Redemption
Greater Texas
home
Akansa
SOUTHERN STATES
SOUTHERN WILDS
THE INDEPENDENT AMERICAS

CENTRAL COMMUNE
KANSAS
Califia
—rumored—
WESTERN TERRITORIES
UTAH
Purgatory City
Valley of Lightning
ARIZONA
Sonoita
LESSER TEXAS
Blessing
Bravebank
Nah's hideout
Holding Tank Pool
Peridot
Grave Gulch
GREATER TEXAS
SOUTHERN WILDS
THE INDEPENDENT AMERICAS

A PREDICAMENT

"You've come quite far enough, young man."

The voice, clear and hard as steel and undoubtedly feminine, echoed against the bare rock of the cliff face that loomed ahead on the red dirt path.

I gave a sharp pull on the reins, bringin' my dusty sorrel mount to a halt, stiffenin' in the saddle.

It was her. It had to be her. I drew in a slow, deep breath as my heart quickened. *For Chrissakes, Van, settle down. This is what you've been waitin' for. Don't lose yer nerve now.* I swallowed hard in a suddenly dry mouth and tightened my hold on the reins. "I ain't gone far enough till I find Ethelyn," I called out in reply, keeping the brim of my hat low as I took in the path ahead, squintin' fer a sign of movin' shadows, ears pricked for sounds of shiftin' gravel or the cock of a hammer.

Nothin'. Not a shadow out of place, no sound 'cept the soft breeze whisperin' against the smooth rock face, the far-away shriek of a hawk circlin' for prey.

For a heartbeat I worried my information had been wrong.

I worried Holt had been right.

I worried I'd come all the way out here fer nothin'.

But then a slim figure dressed all in black stepped out from behind the pale, carved rock ahead, abruptly enough to make my horse throw up his head and snort in alarm. I sat steady in the saddle as he shifted uneasily beneath me, never takin' my eyes off her.

Nine-Fingered Nan.

She looked different in person than she did on the posters. Older. Taller. More fierce. Like she could drop you dead with just a nod of her head. And accordin' to some of the stories about her, she could. Long wisps of silver-white hair fell from beneath her black, broad-brimmed hat, floating about her shoulders. She stood straight and proud and seemingly immune to the heat of the noon-day sun beatin' down upon us, her cold blue eyes borin' hard into mine. She had a gun belt over her skirts holding a matchin' set of pistols, a shiny golden buckle that winked in the sun, and a bandoleer across one shoulder.

I tensed. Sweat trickled down between my shoulder blades. My horse gave a nervous whicker.

Nine-Fingered Nan made no move for her guns. Yet.

I was all too aware then of my own pair of irons weighing heavy on my hips. Slowly, gently, I set the reins down over my saddle horn, lettin' my hands sit loose atop it, ready to draw if I needed to.

She tilted her chin up, lettin' the sun splash across her wizened, weather-worn features. Her pale eyes narrowed. "Yer the brother."

It weren't a question. So I didn't answer. Instead I bit off a question of my own, hoarse and rough. "Where is she?"

Nine-Fingered Nan's wrinkled lips twitched. It might have been a smile. It might have been a smirk. "Not here."

I clenched my teeth together hard, resistin' the urge to draw. I was in no mood for games. Not after everythin' I'd done to get this far. "Then *where*?"

"How should I know?"

My heart throbbed in my throat, rushin' in my ears. Somehow I got the words out around the rage. "I know you have her," I snarled. "Hate to tell ya, but yer man Lloyd Renneker squealed. Had to carve him up real good 'fore he'd talk, but talk he did. I know you know where she is. Stop wastin' my time."

Her expression didn't change at my outburst. Didn't even waver at the news I'd cut up and bled out one of her crew. "Your information is bad, boy. Your sister ain't here. Never was. Never will be. You're huntin' a ghost. Your sister is dead."

The words hit like lead, suckin' all the breath outta me. The terrified part of me, the guilt-ridden part that dredged up that night over and over again in nightmares, that hated myself for not getting back to Ethelyn sooner, that urged me to drown myself in whiskey or 'shine or the nearest lake and be done with it, that part of me knew it could be true. But the other part of me, the part that burned for whatever justice I could get, that kept draggin' me on day after day for year after year, chasin' rumors and whispers that a girl named Ethelyn Delano was still alive ... that part of me refused to believe.

Ethelyn was still alive. Lloyd Renneker had said so. And he'd said she was with Nine-Fingered Nan, about to be sold for an exorbitant sum to a wealthy merchant overseas.

"You lie," I rasped. I intended to draw, right then and there, and put a bullet between the eyes of Nine-Fingered Nan.

But the gun blast that roared against the rocks weren't mine.

My horse dropped to the ground like a stone and I hit the dirt path with a grunt, ears ringin'. Disoriented, I struggled to pull my leg from beneath the dead weight of the sorrel as Nine-Fingered Nan crunched across the gravel-strewn ground in her worn black boots, straight at me, one of her pistols smokin' in her hand.

Her right hand. The hand with the missin' trigger finger.

Some people said it'd been my own pa who'd shot off that finger. They said she'd drawn a gun against him, and he'd shot her gun right outta her hand, and taken that finger with it. They said he coulda killed her, but on account of her bein' a young woman and all, he hadn't.

They said he'd meant it to be a lesson to her.

They said it had only made her meaner. Angrier. Deadlier.

I weren't sure if I believed those stories ... until now. I gaped wide-eyed at her as she approached, heart poundin' fit to choke me. *Get up already or you'll be as dead as yer goddamned horse!* I tugged my leg free at last and sprang to my feet, reachin' fast for the pistol at my hip.

It blasted from my hand with a stingin' spark soon as it cleared leather, sendin' a sharp lance of pain through my palm, then a third shot exploded pain through my left thigh. I cried out as I hit my knees. Blood splattered into the dirt. My eyes watered and I ground my teeth, gaspin' at the hazy air in ragged breaths.

My whole left thigh was on fire, pulsin' angrily around the ounce of lead now buried in it, and my right hand throbbed somethin' terrible, too.

Nan stopped a few paces in front of me and leveled the barrel of her gun at my forehead.

I considered the pistol still on my left hip. Considered the point-blank range of the one pointed at my head.

Slowly, I lifted my hands.

My stomach turned. Holt had been right. I was a full-blown idiot for comin' out here. Gone on a death wish. Dead man walkin'. Plenty of men older and wiser and faster and smarter than me had come after Nine-Fingered Nan. And they were all dead.

And Nan was still standin'.

"Call me a liar again," she whispered.

I knew better. I couldn't help Ethelyn if I was dead. I forced myself to look up into those cold, hard eyes, and wondered why I wasn't dead already.

"I just want my sister back," I said, voice gruff with pain. Maybe Nine-Fingered Nan was still human, somewhere down deep in that murderous soul of hers. Maybe she had even had someone else she cared about once. A husband. A child. A sibling of her own. "I just want her back. What do you want fer her? Money? You gonna sell her? Name yer price."

One of Nan's silver-white eyebrows lifted, just slightly.

For a moment a blaze of hope lit through me, dullin' the pain of the bullet in my leg. Nan *did* have her. Or at least, Nan knew where Ethelyn was. That hard, expressionless face had cracked, just a bit, just enough to let me glimpse what Nine-Fingered Nan loved the most: cold, hard cash.

The grizzled old gunslingin' woman took one step closer, sneerin' down at me. "A stupid young fool like yerself could never afford it, that's fer sure."

I ignored the insult. She was right, anyway. I *was* a stupid young fool for comin' here. Or at least, for comin' here alone and thinkin' I could get out alive. But then, she hadn't killed me yet. I took a breath, took a gamble. "I'll owe you," I said evenly.

It was as much a death sentence as lettin' her put a bullet through my head right then and there, but at least it was a chance for Ethelyn to be free. No one wanted to owe Nine-Fingered Nan 'less they were impossibly desperate, so I'd heard. Or 'less they had a death wish.

Well, I *was* impossibly desperate. And I guess I had a death wish, too.

She eyed me for a long, silent moment, the only sound the distant shriekin' of that circlin' hawk. Then she tilted her head to one side, the shadow of her hat brim slidin' long down her shoulder. "The son of the infamous Lucky Logan, willin' to be ol' Nan's little errand boy?" Her face split in a terrible grin. Then she laughed, the sound bouncin' around inside the carved-out cliff face. She laughed and laughed and laughed.

I took it. I stayed quiet. I stayed on my knees with my hands raised, the bullet hole in my leg leakin' blood into the dirt. I let her have her moment.

Pride would get me nothin' but dead when it came to Nan. And not dead quick, neither. She'd made that obvious when she'd shot my horse out from under me. So I waited for her to finish laughin'. I'd waited nine years for this chance. I could wait a few minutes more.

When she finally stopped, she wheezed for air and swiped tears from her leathery cheeks with her gun-free hand. Then she took a deep breath and shook her head. "You got stones, boy, I'll give you that. And maybe, maybe if ya had yer pop's reputation, that'd be a suitable offer. But I don't know that you've proved yerself yet. Least not well enough to rest me assured I'd get my money's worth outta you."

The desperation—that impossible desperation—surged in my chest. She couldn't say no. This was my only chance to get Ethelyn back. After all this time, all the nightmares, all the drink, all the murderin'... there was nothin' else after this. Nothin' but dead ends and death. "Then give me a chance to prove it to you," I said, the words tumblin' out in a rush. "You ain't killed me yet. Why?"

Her gaze sharpened at the question, but I pushed on.

"You coulda killed me three times over already. But you didn't. Why?"

Her lips pursed, the blue glare narrowin' as her pistol arm straightened, bringin' the barrel and its mortal payload closer to my skull. "Testin' the merit of Lucky Logan's get," she said quietly. "So far I have to say I been sorely disappointed."

I swallowed, but held her stare. Tried to slow my breathin', which had gone all quick and shallow. Lookin' down the barrel of a gun had never been a favorite past-time of mine, but doin' it bleedin' and at the mercy of Nine-Fingered Nan was far worse than any of my past experiences with such a thing. In all those cases, I'd still been armed, and the other man dead by my gun 'fore he could get off a shot. "I didn't come here to kill you," I said, just as quietly. It was a half-truth. I'd always planned to kill her if she didn't give me Ethelyn. But as Holt always liked to say, *The best laid schemes of mice and men often go awry, and leave us nothing but grief and pain, for promised joy.* I looked down the barrel of Nan's gun and gulped back the bitter laugh. How perfect was that ridiculous rhyme of his now?

Oh, if only he was here now to see how royally I'd fucked this up. If only he was here now to lend me another gun in this fight.

"I came here to get my sister back, is all," I said. "No other man— or woman—who's drawed against me is still livin'."

I saw her understand. Saw it in the softenin' of her jaw, the slight lowerin' of her gun. She knew it was true. I might not a' had the reputation of my infamous pa, no, but I *did* have one. Or was startin' to. And if she knew who I was, then she'd know what people said about me.

And out here, that was the third best currency to bargain with. Right after cold, hard cash and cold, hard bullets.

I weren't as good as my pa. Not yet. But there was no arguin' I had no qualms about killin' ... not when it needed to be done.

She dropped her pistol abruptly back into its holster. "Fine. We'll see what yer made of before killin' ya outright. You get back to Bravebank alive and with yer wits intact, you'll find my man at the poker table in the Stag Saloon."

I almost didn't hear her. The relief made me dizzy, light-headed. "Ethelyn?" I asked breathlessly. "Where is she?"

"She'll be safe enough. Lest you die in the desert." Nine-Fingered Nan gave an amused snort. "You make it to Bravebank first, boy, then we'll discuss terms."

I nodded, vision blurred with tears despite myself. "But ... you have her? You know where she is?"

Nan rested her gnarled hands on the twin pearl grips at her hips. From my vantage point, the stump of her right index finger was clearly visible. It tapped restlessly against the gleamin' pearl. "Ya said I did," she snapped. "Didn't ya?"

I nodded again. Renneker had said so, yeah. And he'd been one of hers. One of hers for a long time now. Well, till I'd ended him, anyway. Would he have lied?

Would Nine-Fingered Nan lie now?

Of course she'd lie to you, ya dumb sonuvabitch! I could hear Holt screamin' the words even now. Of course she'd lie.

But what I'd told her earlier was true. All my searching had led here, to her. This was it. The end of the trail. If Nan didn't have Ethelyn, then I didn't know where to look next.

Make it to Bravebank first, then she'll discuss terms.

She had Ethelyn. She must have.

I kept noddin' like an idiot. Mostly 'cause I couldn't get any more words out.

And mostly to convince myself Nan had to be tellin' the truth.

"Ya got ten minutes to get the hell outta here, boy," Nan growled. "'Fore I change my mind." And with that she turned and walked away, boots crunchin' on the gravel. She disappeared into the ancient cliff dwellin', and with a start I saw six others emerge from their hiding places as well and follow her. Four men and two women. Likely her most trusted lieutenants. But they'd never even had to announce themselves. Nan had easily dispatched me all on her own, without even breakin' a sweat.

I felt a fool, all right, a colossal fool.

But I was a livin' fool, and that was somethin'.

I'd wanted to leave here with Ethelyn. Instead I was leavin' with a sore hand, a new hole in my leg and a massive debt to Nan that would probably get me killed. But it seemed the only way forward.

For now.

Holt would be furious. Havin' a debt to Nan meant I'd be just what she'd said: her little errand boy. Jumpin' at her beck and call didn't sound particularly pleasant, but if that's what it took to get my sister free, that's what I was gonna do. It'd mess up his plans real good, but, well ... ain't that what his favorite sayin' was all about?

I closed my eyes and sank slowly down to all fours, suckin' in a few deep breaths to settle the fear still coursin' through my limbs. Then I winced and swore; moved my left leg just a bit and cried out at the shock of pain. *Fuck*, it hurt. Blood soaked my pant leg. I wondered if the bullet had sunk into the bone. Wondered if it was broken. Sure felt like it.

I wondered if I might lose the leg. That'd be a sweet sight all right: Lucky Logan's hobbled son.

I shook my head and shoved such thoughts away, then used the body of my poor dead horse as leverage to get to my feet. The pain flared, takin' my breath away. I stood a moment, balanced on my good leg, and waited for it to pass. Breathed through it.

There was surely no way I could put weight on my shot leg. I could tell that much easily enough. So I reached down and pulled my rifle from its scabbard, leanin' on it heavily like a crutch as I looked off the edge of this rocky rise out across the stretch of river below and then beyond, to the mountainous desert that led toward the town of Bravebank.

And my heart sank as I realized my predicament.

No horse. No supplies. A gimp leg. A wound bleedin' like a stuck pig. And miles and miles of desert between me and Ethelyn's freedom.

A GRAVE MISTAKE

I feared I had made a grave mistake.

But it was too late to turn back now. Too late to tell Nine-Fingered Nan that she and her deal could both go to Hell. Too late to decide I should have put a bullet in her brain the second I first laid eyes on her. Too late to take back my willingness to owe her a debt that would probably get me killed.

I stopped in my trek across the burnin' hills. My hat brim shoulda shielded my eyes from the sun's infernal glare, but out here it seemed to hardly help. The unendin' onslaught of light dazzled my vision. Sweat stung my eyes and made my shirt cling to my skin. The throbbin' agony in my left leg had finally subsided into a warm ache, but I wasn't so sure that was a good thing. I'd tied my bandana over the bullet hole; stuck my rifle down inside my boot and tied it to my leg too, to make a crude kinda splint. And I'd cut a length of my saddle girth and cinched it tight around my leg above the wound, but there was a thin trickle of blood still paintin' a long trail of red in the fabric of my pants.

The heat, the distance, these hills, and havin' only one good leg was killin' me, already.

I wouldn't have to wait to die on an errand for Nan at this rate.

I'd die here. Now. In this damned desert without a soul in sight.

Shadows in the shapes of birds slid over me, soundless, and raced ahead, then circled back again. Vultures. Bastards had been followin' me since I'd left Nan's rocky hide-out.

They knew. They always knew.

I lifted my hat from my head briefly to swipe at the sweat on my brow with my forearm. The heat came off the rocks in waves, making everythin' waver. I wavered where I stood, too. Sometimes it was hard to tell what was caused by the heat and what was caused by exhaustion and blood loss.

I blinked hard and shifted my saddle bags on my shoulder. I'd taken what I could manage to carry off my dead horse, sure, but there was only so much one man could hold. And only so far one man with a bullet in his leg could walk.

If only she hadn't shot my horse.

I'd liked that horse, damnit. He'd been my best one yet. Cost me twenty-five dollars. Shakin' my head, I uncapped my one canteen—also rescued off my saddle—and allowed myself a small sip. Not that it would matter.

Wouldn't matter that my horse was dead. Wouldn't matter that I was out twenty-five dollars, plus the cost of that perfectly good saddle. Wouldn't matter that I had half a canteen of water left.

I was makin' slow progress. Too slow.

The birds would have me soon enough. Or one of those mountain lions, maybe. Long before I reached the outskirts of Bravebank.

Damnit, Van. How could you be so stupid?

I closed my eyes, but it seemed the sun still burned there, straight through my eyelids. Burnin', always burnin'. Burnin' away my eyes, my mind, my soul.

I thought of Ethelyn then, and the last time I'd seen her. Nine years ago. In the black of night. Both of us splattered with blood that wasn't ours. And her eyes ... her big green eyes wide in terror, the whites shining in the dark. Her small fingers clutchin' hard at my arm.

She had begged me not to go. *Begged* me.

But we couldn't stay there. So I'd promised I'd be back soon as I could. And I'd gone, anyway. I'd left her there, huddled in some woods a distance out back of our burnin' house. Alone.

Three days I was away, that's all. Three days.

When I'd returned ... she was gone.

Three days away and I'd lost my sister for nine years.

I drew in a sharp breath of air that tasted of furnace. I swallowed though I had no more spit. And I started hobblin' forward again. I trudged onward through that red dirt and rock, mostly draggin' my left foot behind me as I had done for all the last miles.

The sun was steadily droppin' toward the horizon I aimed for, lightin' the way toward the town of Bravebank. Pointin' the way, and blindin' me, too.

Mockin' me.

With every step I heard Nan's voice in my mind: *Get to Bravebank alive and with yer wits intact first, boy, then we'll discuss terms.*

My right hand fell to the pistol on my hip. The pistol with the dent of another bullet in its cylinder now. I suppose it was some small mercy she hadn't taken off my finger, too, in some twisted sense of poetic justice for the finger my pa had taken from her.

But maybe it hadn't been him who'd shot that finger off of her, after all.

My own fingers, all full five of 'em, curled around that worn grip, and I winced as sharp pain stabbed into that palm again. Well, no matter. The fingers still worked, and if I had to draw I could still draw.

I used the grip's familiar feel to bolster my resolve. If I ever saw Nine-Fingered Nan again, I was gonna kill her.

No more talkin'. No more negotiations.

She thought this was a game, fine. I'd play it just long enough to end it. For good. She thought the desert'd kill me? Thought she could dismiss me to go die in the wastes while she sold my sister off, anyway?

Well, I'd show her.

I'd show her just what Van Jensen Delano was made of, all right. I might not a' inherited my pa's luck, but Holt knew as well as anyone else who'd ever spent any time with me that I'd sure as hell inherited his stubbornness. And Mama's, too.

Holt often said I been cursed with a double-barreled shotgun of mulishness.

It almost made me laugh now, half outta my mind with blood loss and heat and sloggin' through the endless desert.

If not for that, I'd'a for sure been dead a long time ago. And probably Ethelyn, too.

And as much as Holt cursed that trait of mine, it'd served the ol' bastard well enough on plenty of our jobs. He'd never complained about it, then.

And so I walked on.

I held the memory of Nan's disdainful sneer in my mind, and Ethelyn's terrified ten-year-old face, and kept on walkin'. Into the shimmerin' fire of the settin' sun. Toward Bravebank. Toward Ethelyn's freedom. Toward Nine-Fingered Nan's eventual end.

Toward my own salvation.

I awoke to harsh whispers and the vague feelin' of hands pattin' at my body.

It didn't take thinkin' to react. I reached for my guns as I surged up sittin' with an angry yell, and the bandits tryin' to rob me jumped back with startled cries of their own.

It took me a good long minute to realize both my hands were still empty.

I blinked hard in the darkness, tryin' to make my swimmin' vision clear. The chill of the desert's night air hit me then and I shivered violently, though my skin was still wet with sweat.

Then one of the robbin' bastards laughed and held up two pistols of his own.

No, wait. They was *my* pistols. The backwater sonuvabitch had *my* goddamn guns!

"Lookin' fer these?" he drawled. He held them forward, lettin' 'em slip down and dangle from his index fingers by their trigger guards.

I gritted my teeth. I wanted to leap up and wrap my hands around his throat. Throttle that smirk right off his sunburned, pock-marked face. But I was only sittin' down, and already the ground was rockin' under me, everything lookin' like the sun was still up, waverin' and shiftin'.

His partner chuckled. "Always disarm those ya gonna rob first," he quipped. "Even if ya think they're dead."

"'Xactly," the man with my guns said, and he grinned like a fool as he tucked 'em into the rim of his pants.

Rage burned in my throat. I was gonna kill 'em. Both of 'em.

The problem was, they had my saddle bags, too, and my canteen. They had everythin' off me already, and I had nothin' left.

"Well, wha' should we do wif 'em now?" the one who didn't have my guns asked his sonuvabitch friend. He held a big revolver, an older model, the kind that sometimes jammed and blew up in yer hand. But the kind that'd punch one big hole in the guy you were amin' at if they didn't blow up in yer hand. The one most folk around here called the Gambler, on account of the fact you took a gamble every time you pulled the trigger. He had it pointed at my chest.

I took a quick look around best I could with my wobbly vision while they debated. I didn't recognize anythin'. I had no idea where I was. The river weren't too far away; I could see the moonlight shimmerin' off it to my right. But then, I'd been followin' the river southwest all day, so its presence didn't help me figure out where I was at all.

I didn't remember passin' out. I didn't remember hittin' the dirt.

But I must have lost consciousness at some point, then dropped in my tracks, right in the open. Right in a prime spot for lazy bastards like these to find me.

My frantic searchin' stopped at the sight of their horses. Two perfectly good horses, standin' patiently not too far away. Loaded with saddle bags of their own, and bedrolls. And more canteens. I tried to swallow. By God was I thirsty.

"Mebee sell 'em?" the one holdin' the revolver suggested to his friend.

But his friend shook his head. "Nah. Lookit 'em. He's mostly dead already. Wouldn't fetch much."

"Shoot 'em, then?" his friend suggested next.

I wished they'd stop talkin' bout me like I wasn't sittin' right there, plottin' how to murder 'em both. But I suppose I couldn't really blame 'em. I surely felt mostly dead. Wasn't sure I coulda got up off the ground anyway, even if my life depended on it.

Which it might.

It was all up to how this debate of theirs turned out.

The one with my guns studied me with beady black eyes that glinted in the light of the full moon. It cast our shadows out long across the sand, as if it were tryin' so hard to live up to the fierceness of its bigger, brighter cousin. But its pale, silvery light didn't burn away your sanity like the sun's did. It only cloaked the scrawny man sizin' me up in hard, silver angles as he spat into the parched dirt. "Nah. Be a waste of a bullet. Lookit that leg a' his. It'll get 'em. We don't need ta do it."

His friend appeared irritated at this assessment. "Well wha', then?"

The man with my guns stared at me for a long, silent moment, and I glared back at him, bracin' myself with both hands against the ground to keep from swoonin' over. Then he smiled, but I noticed he didn't get no closer to me. They were both out of arm's reach, damn it all.

I didn't even have my knife to hurl at 'em. They had that, too.

The skinny, pock-faced fella shrugged his narrow shoulders. "Nothin'," he answered simply. "Leave 'em fer the buzzards. Let's go."

He turned and made for his horse. With *my* guns, and my saddle bags, and the little bit of water I had left.

His friend seemed unsure. He looked from his no-good partner to me and then back again. "You sure?"

"I'm sure." The other man didn't even look back. He was so sure I weren't no threat he couldn't be bothered to waste any more time on me.

I made some sort of growl and lunged toward the ankles of the one still standin' there holdin' a revolver at me. He yelped and staggered backwards, and my reachin' hands grabbed only dust and gravel.

The other fella laughed at his friend and swung up on his horse.

"C'mon, Clint. Stop foolin' around. Let's go 'fore this night gets any older. I wanna get some female company 'fore dawn."

I could see Clint's face darken even in the moonlight, embarrassed at bein' startled by the likes a' me. He grumbled, namin' me foul names, and shoved his revolver back into its holster. Then he scuffed a boot into the ground, givin' me a nice shower of the same dust and gravel that was still gripped in both my fists.

I ducked my head just in time, but my hat was missin', too. I shut my eyes as the grit rained over me, then coughed.

Clint grumbled under his breath all the way to his horse.

I struggled to my feet, anger blockin' the pain of my leg, the throbbin' in my right hand, the exhaustion, the thirst. My vision narrowed, but I could still see the silhouettes of Clint and his sonuvabitch friend. And that was all that mattered.

I swayed and staggered, but somehow managed to keep upright. "Leavin' already?" I husked. My voice sounded like stones in a set of rusty gears. "But we was just gettin' to know each other."

Clint turned to face me just as he was about to mount up, the full moon highlightin' his widened eyes and open mouth.

His friend just shook his head, one hand goin' to rest on the grip of my gun as he leaned forward on his saddle horn. "You wanna die quick, boy? Keep talkin' and I'll letcha."

I widened my stance a bit, plantin' my boots into the ground to steady myself. Felt like the whole world was rockin' somethin' fierce now, but I hoped this sunuvabitch couldn't see that. I hooked my thumbs into my belts. My *empty* belts. "You wanna die slow?" I asked in return.

He straightened in his saddle at my threat and looked to his pal.

Clint, for his part, clambered up on his own mount in a hurry and reined it around to face me. I saw his right hand drop back down to his revolver.

Then the pock-faced thief chuckled. He looked me over again, like he was makin' fer sure I couldn't really deliver on my threat, and sighed. "I kinda like you, kid." His fingers slid off my gun and went back to his reins. "Too bad we won't be seein' ya around again." He tossed me a mock salute. "Adios." He turned his horse and waved for

Clint to follow after, and Clint did so, lookin' over his shoulder at me fer a second longer before turnin' his attention to the trail ahead.

I swore and hobbled after 'em quick as I could, but I hadn't really thought this far ahead.

'Course he hadn't believed my threat ... but I'd had to say it, anyway. I couldn't just let a pair of highwaymen rob me blind without tryin'.

And I sure as hell was gonna try.

I saw a pile of the red, rough rocks that littered much of the land in the Territories off to my left, and a few chipped pieces on the ground 'bout as big as my palm. I stumbled over to 'em and scooped one of the bigger ones up just as Clint and his bastard friend kicked their horses into a trot.

I hurled the rock after 'em with all my strength, aimin' fer the one who still had my guns.

The rock thumped into his horse's rear and the animal startled, jumpin' sideways with his ears pinned and kickin' out with both back feet. It was enough to unseat his thief of a rider, who hit the ground with a grunt.

I ran at him fast as I could manage, half-limpin' and half-lurchin', and tackled him just as he was comin' to his feet.

He gave another grunt as my weight came down on top of him, but I'd already yanked my pistol from his waistline. I pressed the barrel into his middle and fired.

The shot was half-muffled by our bodies, but he jerked as the bullet tore through his gut, and his eyes grew wide and white as the moon, watchin' us impassively from on high with her cold, pale gaze.

Clint gave a yell of mixed surprise and horror, snappin' my attention to him, instead.

I rolled off his pal just as he fired, takin' my left pistol with me, too, and his bullet sent up a spray of dirt right next to his friend. I landed on my back and brought both pistols to bear on Clint, firin' simultaneously.

My twin shots hit him in the chest, leavin' an arc of blood as he went clean off his horse, sprawlin' limp to the ground. His horse swiveled its ears and pranced in place, snortin' nervously. But it didn't bolt.

That was a good horse.

There was movement from the skinny man I'd tackled and I reflexively shifted my guns to him. He froze. We were both still layin' flat out on the ground, only I had loaded irons in my hands, and he was only just reachin' fer his.

Had been reachin'. Till he'd seen my two barrels swing toward him again. "Easy now," I prompted. "I said you'd die slow, remember?"

His face contorted into a scowl, mostly anger, but some pain, too.

A bullet to the gut was a bad way to go, I'd heard.

He glared at me hard, right in the eyes. And his reachin' hand twitched.

I fired again, point blank, tearin' up his left shoulder real good.

His screams echoed out across the distance, overlappin' the noise of my gunshot.

"I did warn ya," I said as he writhed in the dirt. "Twice."

He looked back at me with eyes full of murder and hate and agony.

I drug myself up outta that same dirt and staggered again to my feet, keepin' my pistols aimed straight at him. I was feelin' plenty of agony myself. "Now," I rasped, "you just throw your gun my way, nice and slow." I fought hard to keep my own pain outta my face. Fought hard to keep my hands steady.

"You can go fuck yourself," he spat.

I gave him a smile. What else was I gonna do? The fella was just about as stubborn as me. I shoulda put a bullet in his forehead then, but I'd told him I was gonna let him die slow, and I liked to keep my promises. He wasn't going to talk himself outta that.

I limped around him, bein' careful not to break eye contact. He'd shoot me the second I looked away, no doubt. I went to his right side, and he watched me warily, a sheen of sweat now glistenin' on his brow. His breathin' was harsh and ragged, his jaw clenched tight.

Well, maybe with that shoulder bleedin' out like it was, he wouldn't last as long as I would have liked. But that couldn't be helped now. "Hands up," I ordered.

He slowly complied. At least with his right hand. His left was still clutchin' at the hole in his gut. And I imagined it was suitably useless now, given the state of that shoulder. I also imagined he thought I'd come nice and close to grab his gun fer myself.

But I knew better. I'd learned that lesson years ago. So I focused on his right hand, the one that could still move, and blew another hole straight through his palm.

His screamin' was more like shriekin' now, and I stepped backward as he flopped around bad as a fish tossed outta water.

Clint's horse, steady though it was, shied sideways at all the motion and commotion.

I just stood and watched fer a minute.

Then, satisfied he could no longer shoot me in the back as I left, I turned stiffly and hobbled away from him, over to Clint's horse. I holstered my weapons back where they belonged, then heaved myself up into the saddle. I nearly blacked out as I swung my stiff, splinted left leg over the cantle, but I clutched the horse's mane in my white-knuckled fists and somehow managed to pull myself back from the darkness, settlin' heavy into the saddle seat.

The horse shifted uneasily beneath me.

"Easy," I whispered. "Easy there." I was talkin' as much to myself as to the horse. The night seemed to have gotten darker despite the full moon. No matter how hard or how much I blinked, my vision just wouldn't clear. It took a lot of effort to detangle my fingers from the mane and get them on the reins, and more effort still to nudge the horse forward.

It took a few uncertain steps and then stopped.

The thief I'd shot fulla holes spat curses at me from the ground. Some real bad ones. And some real creative ones.

I twisted in the saddle to look down at him. "Too bad I won't be seein' you around again," I said, echoin' his own words back to him. Poetic justice, that's what Holt'd call it. And that it was. I gave him the same mock salute he'd given me, too. "Adios."

And I forced my heels into the horse's side and closed my eyes, concentratin' on stayin' in the saddle as she picked up into an easy lope. I leaned precariously to one side before draggin' myself upright again.

The thief's screamin' and cursin' was growin' fainter behind me. Good.

He should have just left well enough alone.

I slowed the horse again. I wasn't gonna last long at a lope. It was hard enough to keep my seat at a damned walk. Clint and his sonuvabitch friend were no-good bastards, but they'd been right about one thing: I was mostly dead already.

I lifted my face to the sky, squintin' at the stars and tryin' to orient myself. But the cursed moon's light washed some of 'em out, and the rest kept slidin' and jumpin' all over the place. I shut my eyes again and rubbed at 'em with two fingers.

You ain't never gonna be able to tell where you're goin' in this state. You can hardly keep yerself sittin' up straight!

The horse kept ploddin' along, calm again now that'd we'd left the scene of carnage behind.

I remembered what the pock-faced thief had said about wantin' female company 'fore dawn, and a shred of hope flickered to life inside me. Bravebank was the only town in this desert for a lot of miles. That meant he and his pal Clint had most likely been headed there when they'd found me. And if they coulda got there 'fore dawn, the town couldn'ta been too far away now.

I slumped in the saddle, lettin' the reins go slack. The horse could find the way from here, surely. They always seemed to know the way to the nearest barn.

And this time, that's exactly where I wanted to go.

I let myself relax, one hand reachin' for the canteen looped over the saddle horn.

Approachin' hoofbeats brought me to high alert again and I had one gun out and aimed toward the noise long before my sluggish mind caught up to what I was seein'.

A riderless horse appeared outta the cloud of dust it was kickin' up. Eventually I recognized it. It was the horse of the man who'd taken my guns. The horse I'd hit in the ass with a rock. The horse that'd thrown its rider so I could kill him slow.

I holstered my pistol as the second horse drew up alongside its companion and snorted. It dropped into an easy walk to match our pace. I lifted my brows. Apparently these two had been together awhile now, and one couldn't stand to be without the other. Well, one horse was surely better than none. And two horses was better than one. Maybe I could even make back my twenty-five dollars.

Maybe.

I pulled up the canteen and uncapped it, then took a long swig. It felt like a brick in my hand, and puttin' the cap back on was far more difficult than it shoulda been.

Damnit, Van. Get it together. You gotta make it. Nine years of searchin'... you can't let it end here, not when you're so close. You're almost there now.

I wrapped my fingers in the horse's mane again, hopin' it'd be enough to keep me in the saddle. I was fadin', I could feel it.

Just so tired.

All I wanted to do was sleep. Close my eyes and let it all go. Just fer a minute...

III

MORE THAN ONE KIND OF VULTURE

It was pain that woke me a second time.

Sharp, piercin' pain, shockin' out from the bullet hole in my leg.

I yelled and lurched up before I'd even fully realized I hadn't been awake in the first place. I threw out a hand blindly, the sun searin' my vision. The world was a blur of white and heat, 'cept the few dark shapes lurkin' close. And one was over there near my leg.

It fluttered back a few steps as my hand came at it, and that's when I knew they must be vultures of the animal variety, instead of vultures of the human variety.

Both kinds of vultures were bad news, in my opinion. And one not necessarily better or worse than the other. Not really. Not when you were in my kind of state.

I flung out my hand again. "Get!" It came out a harsh whisper instead of a shout.

The bird only watched me. Unafraid. Patient. Like it knew if it just waited a few minutes more, I'd lie back down and go quiet. Fer good.

I gritted my teeth and tried to conjure up a good swear, but I was too exhausted even for that. I groped for my gun, found it still on my hip. Well, least the birds couldn't take those from me, unlike their human counterparts. I drug it outta the holster and half-rolled toward the feathered bastard. I propped myself on both elbows. Had to hold the damn gun with both hands.

Had it always been this heavy?

A sharp peck on the back of my right calf brought me swingin' round again to the one behind me. "Damn you!" I spat. "I ain't dead yet!"

Not yet. Though I was surely closer to it than I would have liked.

It raised its wings and hissed at me.

"Go to Hell," I growled back. I pulled my trigger.

The others took off with loud cries of protest as their comrade fell, but I lifted the barrel and squeezed off two more shots at 'em, fer good riddance. Got one of 'em, and it dropped like a rock back to the dirt. I was gonna take another shot at the one still flyin', but then I saw that dented cylinder roll upward toward the hammer and I stopped myself. Didn't want to be takin' any more gambles. Lord knew my luck had turned out shit enough as it was, and my right hand was already all hot and swollen.

I swore and fell back into the burnin' dirt myself. Shoulda used the left pistol, instead. Closin' my eyes, I felt for it now, and exhaled loudly when my fingers found it, safe and sound still where it belonged.

And then some clarity returned to my poundin' head.

And I sat up with a start, and looked around at the shimmerin' stretch of desert surroundin' me best I could with that cursed sun bakin' me good as a fish in a pan.

I'd had a horse, hadn't I? And water. And supplies.

But there surely was no sign of any of that now. Not even any hoof-prints in the dirt. I squinted and rubbed at my eyes. But my view didn't change.

I suppose if there had been a horse, its tracks coulda been covered over by the wind by now. However long it had been. How long had I been lyin' here comatose in the open again, tryin' to die?

Long enough for the birds to think I was their next meal, I guess.

Had I imagined Clint and his sonuvabitch friend?

I didn't think so, but then, I wasn't sure of much anymore.

'Cept the fact I was surely gonna die if I didn't find Bravebank soon.

It couldn't be that much further. I had to make it.

I pushed my gun back into its holster and then pushed myself up off the ground, my left leg stickin' straight out in its makeshift splint, stiff as a board. Sweat ran in rivulets down my face and my back. My arms shook, my vision dimmed, and a wave of nausea rocked me. I sat back down hard, the world tiltin' sideways.

I tried to hold myself up, to brace myself, but this time it didn't do no good. I collapsed anyway, the world still rockin'. I wanted to keep goin'. I had to keep goin'. I reached out with one hand, clutchin' at a fistful of dirt and gravel as if it were a hold on life itself.

I crawled forward. Or sorta crawled. More like slithered on my belly, movin' westward still inch by inch. I was glad then that Holt hadn't come. I surely didn't want him to see me like this. And I was even gladder that Nine-Fingered Nan had been left miles behind in her cliff-face refuge. If she ever knew what she'd done to me here, she'd probably laugh until she finally croaked.

I groaned, a bit of dust kickin' up into my face with my breath. *Don't be a fool. She knows exactly what she did to you.*

That's why she'd demanded I meet her man in Bravebank instead of makin' me a deal right then and there. Why she'd shot my horse. Why she'd shot me in the leg instead of the head. Why she'd made my sanity a condition in her agreement to give me a chance to earn Ethelyn's freedom.

All so carefully arranged.

All so expertly manipulated to kill me. After makin' me suffer awhile first, of course.

Damn her to Hell. Damn her straight to Hell. I pulled myself forward another inch. I couldn't let her win. I couldn't let Ethelyn go. Everythin' in me screamed to keep goin', but my body was givin' out. It didn't care what I wanted anymore.

I slumped into blackness.

Somethin' jostled me.

I heard voices again. The damn vultures just wouldn't leave me alone. I made to reach fer my guns with heavy, sluggish arms, and there was an alarmed string of words in response. I couldn't tell what the vulture was sayin'. Whether or not that was 'cause of my own disorientation or 'cause they was speakin' some foreign language, well, I couldn't sort that, either. But that didn't matter. I'd kill 'em either way.

'Cept I couldn't seem to get my hands around my guns.

Another voice answered the first, and this one cut through the haze of my dehydrated, bled-out, sun-dazzled wits. A woman's voice.

I couldn't understand her, neither, but my heart jumped in my chest anyway, thinkin' of Ethelyn. I attempted to roll over, to sit up. Where was I? Who were these people?

Women didn't often travel with bandits of the Territories ... but then, there was Nine-Fingered Nan. She'd been a lady once. Maybe. Now she was the Devil Incarnate.

This woman here could still be a vulture, certainly.

Now there were *two* female voices talkin', runnin' over each other into nonsense. And a boy's voice, too. *What the hell? Who brings a kid out here?*

I tried to drag my eyes open, tried to leverage myself up on one elbow. I felt cool wood underneath me, a stark difference from the hot, dusty ground. *What in—*

Somethin' came down over my nose and mouth. A sweet-smellin' cloth. I reached up in attempts to yank it away just as other hands took my shoulders and pushed me down flat to my back again. My eyes came open at last, but there was only blurry figures around me. My surroundin's were dim, claustrophobic.

Looked like a man sittin' over me, though, the one holdin' the cloth to my face. I grabbed at his arm, but he was damn strong. Maybe if I hadn'ta just spent two days or more walkin' in the desert with a bullet in my leg, I coulda taken him easily.

But not now.

His arm was rigid, the muscles in his forearm hard beneath my clawin' fingers.

"Easy, son, easy now. Calm down. This is for your own good..."

The words filtered through my kickin' and gruntin', but gave me no reassurance. I'd heard such words before, and what followed had never been particularly pleasant. Not to mention this bastard seemed bent on suffocatin' me. And I surely didn't see how that could be fer my own good.

Though maybe there was a few lawmen out there who might've thought puttin' me out of my misery was fer my own good.

Maybe this fella agreed with 'em.

I felt the sleep comin' on, and my beatin' at the man's arm and chest weakened. My arms dropped to the wooden planks beneath me, suddenly heavy as lead. Despite my best efforts, my eyes closed. My thoughts of Ethelyn, of dyin', of Nine-Fingered Nan, drifted off.

"That's it," the man whispered, only now it seemed his words had gained the comfort he'd obviously intended, whether or not it was genuine. I eased into them. "That's it. Just relax. Go to sleep. You're in good hands, now."

Suffocatin' hands, I thought, still breathin' into that sweet-smellin' cloth, slow and deep now. *Damn yer ... suffocatin' hands, you ... no good ... sonuva...*

Next time I came conscious, it was slow and peaceful. No voices this time, no hands on me, no pain. Least, no pain fer awhile. Felt like I was floatin'. No burnin' sun bakin' me. No hot dirt and rock searin' my skin. No sharp peck of vultures tryin' to make me a meal.

Gradually, awareness came back to me. There was somethin' soft under my back and my head. The light through my eyelids was subtle, not blindin'. The air smelled different ... like fire smoke and somethin' savory. And there were sounds, too, muffled but unmistakable: the creak of footsteps on floorboards, quiet conversation, the sound of a knife choppin'. Choppin' what, who knew. Maybe vegetables. Maybe meat.

My gut twisted at the familiarity of it and I drew a sharp breath as memories came floodin' back.

My fists gripped sheets.

I was in a house. I was in a damned house. A house so similar to the one I'd used to know...

My eyes flung open. I stared up at a beamed wooden ceiling. Daylight filtered in through a window to my right, framed in pretty lace curtains. The sight of 'em hit me like a punch in the gut.

Mama'd had curtains like that.

They'd burned up just as nice as everything else in the house.

Includin' her.

A choked noise escaped me and I sat up, then reeled. That's when the pain came back, all at once and somethin' fierce. My whole left thigh felt like it'd been laid open and carved up. I clutched at it and cried out, and that's when I noticed the shape of it didn't look quite right under those crisp white sheets tucked in around me.

Footsteps came runnin' and the door to my left banged open. I jerked my head toward it to see a middle-aged woman gapin' at me. Instinctively I fumbled fer my guns, but I weren't even wearin' my gun belt no more. All I had on was a union suit, and I wondered how that'd happened.

The woman left the doorway, runnin' off yellin' fer someone.

I remembered the women I'd heard talkin' when that man had tried to suffocate me, and figured these were probably the same people. She was probably runnin' off to get the man who'd tried to suffocate me, to tell him he didn't do such a good job of it.

I needed to get out of here. Didn't matter that I was damn near naked, or that I didn't have my weapons. Didn't matter that the room was spinnin' fit to put me right back down into the bed. I'd grabbed the edge of the blankets to throw them back when another person appeared in the doorway; a young woman.

The sight of her stopped me cold. Now it was me who was gapin'. I hadn't expected the other woman I'd heard to be so near my own age.

Then the older woman returned, with a tall, thin man in tow. He wore small, round spectacles and had a well-oiled mustache that pointed upwards on the ends. From that and the spotless condition of his fancy dress shirt and silk vest, I knew right off he was one of those so-called "learned" men. Had he really been the one tryin' to suffocate me?

The bastard was stronger than he looked.

"No, no, no, *no!*" he said quickly, shakin' his head as he came across the room at me. "You cannot be up! Lie back down before you hurt yourself!" He shoved me back down into the pillow with unceremonious force. "You are very, *very* lucky to be alive, son. But if you do not rest now, all of my hard work will be for nothing!"

Well, I understood his words alright now, but he had a heavy, lilting accent. "I ain't lucky," I growled. "And I ain't yer son."

His finely groomed eyebrows lifted above his spectacles. "Perhaps not, but I *did* save your life. You are welcome."

"I didn't say thank you." Even as I muttered it, my eyes shifted from him to the older woman I assumed was his wife, and the young woman I figured was his daughter. Both of 'em looked unsettled, concerned. The wife gripped the choppin' knife in one hand, white-knuckled. So they were the smarter ones in the family, it seemed.

"I am quite aware," the man stated wryly. "But nonetheless, it is done."

Was it? I weren't so sure. Not with the fire that burned in my leg now. It hurt worse than it had in the desert. I turned my gaze back to him. "You shouldn'ta done that," I croaked. "You shouldn'ta brought me here." I'd learned long ago, helpin' people most often just got you dead quicker. And this man had a family. He was even more an idiot for riskin' 'em like that.

The man scoffed, reachin' to the bedside table to retrieve a stethoscope. So what was he, then, some kind of doctor? "Son, if I hadn't of found you and brought you here, you'd certainly be dead, and the buzzards feeding on your carcass."

I swallowed hard, knowin' that was no lie. But that didn't mean I'd wanted the help. Didn't mean I was gonna owe him for savin' my life. I couldn't afford to owe anyone, and I already owed Nine-Fingered Nan everythin' I had left. "I told you, I ain't yer son," was all I said.

He pursed his already thin lips at my response, then stuck the stethoscope into his ears and tried to press the other end of it to my chest like he was gonna listen to my heart. I knocked his hand away.

His wife in the doorway took a step forward, the knife liftin' a bit as if in warnin'.

I met her hard stare over the man's shoulder. As if? No. It was surely a warnin'. Her face spelled out her thoughts clear enough: *Harm my husband and I'll carve you up like a holiday ham.*

"I need to listen to your heart," he said, oblivious to the murderous glare his wife was borin' into me. "Your leg was terribly infected when we found you. I think the infection was stopped at the leg, but I need to be sure."

I looked at him again, tryin' to understand him. Tryin' to figure out why he wanted to help a man like me. Some stranger he'd found half-dead in the desert. His accent marked him as a foreigner. Probably come here from across the sea. Maybe that was it, then. Maybe he just didn't understand how things worked over here yet.

If he didn't sort it out quick, though, the damn fool and his whole family'd end up as dead as I would've been if he'd just left me where he found me.

Just as dead as Mama and Pa.

"Why," I blurted harshly. "Why'd you help me? You shouldn'ta done that."

He blinked behind the thick round glass of his spectacles. "Why? What kind of question is that? I'm a doctor, son. I took an oath. Not only that, but the Good Book says—"

"*No.*" The word tore outta my throat, unexpected tears burnin' in my eyes. I closed them so the man and his family couldn't see. I struggled to keep my composure, a grief fresher than I'd felt in years rakin' at my insides. It had to be this damned house. The lace curtains. The mention of the Good Book, that Mama'd liked to read from every night as she'd knelt and said her prayers.

"No," I choked out again. "Stop. Stop it." I opened my eyes and stared straight into the man's confused face so he'd know how serious I was. "Stop helpin' people. Stop quotin' the Good Book. Forget your oath." I lifted a hand to point at his wife and daughter and then gestured out yonder, out beyond the adobe walls of his house. "Take yer family and go back to wherever you came from 'fore you all end up dead."

He drew back a bit at my words, then looked over his shoulder to his wife and daughter. Maybe he was tryin' to decide if I'd meant that as a warning or a threat. It didn't matter, so long as he listened.

Then the floorboards from the other room creaked a little, and another face appeared between the shoulders of the wife and daughter. A boy's face, maybe ten years old, and I remembered the child's voice I'd heard when I'd been delirious. I'd hoped that'd been part of a dream.

It seemed it wasn't.

His mother noticed him there and scolded him in their native language. I couldn't make out what she was sayin', but her tone and her body language said she was orderin' him away. His wide, dark blue eyes stared straight at me, and his mouth hung open a little.

I glared at him, too.

His mother's words became more urgent, and he finally, reluctantly moved out of sight again. Who knows where he went, but that didn't matter, either.

I wasn't stayin' here, anyway. I couldn't. I shook my head and pushed myself sittin' again. "I gotta go. I can't stay."

The man reached out toward me and opened his mouth to protest my movements, but I threw back the covers before he could stop me.

And froze.

My left thigh ended in a stump. The rest of my leg was missin'.

MACHINE PARTS

Well, there was somethin' there, all right, but it surely weren't my natural leg. It was some kind of mess of metal, all long pipes and gears, and it laid on the mattress where my leg shoulda been, exposed through the cut ribbons of union suit left there.

I stared at it, a horror rushin' through me like I'd never felt. And then a rage. My body trembled, my heart throbbin' wild in my chest. Heat flooded my face as I brought my eyes back to the skinny man. The doctor. The man who had taken my leg.

Murder musta been clear on my face, 'cause he went deathly pale and held up his hands palms out, as if surrendin'. "I was trying to tell you," he said quickly, "your leg was terribly infected when we found you. Infected, and dead. There was no way to save it."

My mouth worked. But the rage was takin' all the words. "You," I finally whispered, then had to swallow. I tried again. "You ... you *took my goddamn leg off*!?"

"As I said, I saved your life!" He was indignant now. "The flesh of your leg was dead. The tourniquet you put on..." He shook his head. "It was on too long. It stopped the infection from spreading it seems, yes, but there was not enough circulation in the leg. I'm sorry. It was all that could be done."

"I ... you ... you sonuva..." The room was spinnin' again. I felt sick. I leaned over the side of the bed and retched.

The man jumped back, but there was hardly a thing in my stomach, and I didn't make much of a mess. His wife was surely glad for that. I spit, my breath comin' harsh and ragged. My left thigh—the half of it left—still pulsed as if it'd been laid open. But now as I looked at it closer, I saw instead that the metal contraption had been attached to it. Flesh and metal fused together.

I retched again and squeezed my eyes shut. I clutched at the sheets and the edge of the mattress, thinkin' I might actually faint. That'd be a good one ... faintin' clean away right in front of the women. I clung hard to consciousness, hangin' on to the anger to anchor me.

"I ... I'm sorry," the man said again in his thick accent. "It is always a difficult thing to lose a limb. But if you had kept the leg, you'd have died. Do you understand?"

I understood, all right. I understood this man had picked me up outta the desert, drugged me, and performed some kinda unholy surgery on me. Some kind of twisted, dark experiment that had fused my body with a tangle of cold, hard, lifeless metal. "You took my leg," I repeated.

"Yes," he said again. "To save your life. It was the only way, I assure you. And I would argue the false leg I have provided you is an advantage, not a disadvantage."

I took a few deep breaths, the anger helpin' to bring me back from the edge of blackness. "An ... advantage?" I lifted my poundin' head to stare at him. "An advantage? You *chopped off my goddamn leg*!" I lunged outta the bed at him, but I was weak and clumsy and minus one leg.

The metal one didn't work like a flesh and blood one, and he stepped easily outta my reach. I crashed to the floor instead, landin' heavy with a cry as a new flare of pain gripped my thigh.

"Please do not exert yourself," the man urged. "You must rest or your body may still reject the false leg and you will die despite my efforts."

"Good riddance," his wife said from the doorway.

"Hanna!" the doctor said, aghast.

I saw her booted feet step toward me and looked up from where I was curled on the floor to see her brandishin' the choppin' knife. She held the point of it at me, aimin' at my forehead, though her husband put his arm out in front of her to stop her advance.

I wasn't sure if he was tryin' to protect her from me … or me from her.

"I told my husband to let you die," she whispered. "I told him you were trouble. That you were not worth it. I could tell it from the looks of you. But he would not listen. My husband is a decent man. A good man. Better than you could ever hope to be. He is too kind. He cares about those he should not care about. And so he saved you. And look what it has gotten him. Nothing." She spit at me, and the wad of saliva fell just short of my face. "No gratitude. No thank you. No kindness. Just curses and anger."

"Hanna," the man said softly, but she would not be silenced.

"Go and leave if you wish. Die alone in the wild like the dog that you are. Like you should have died days ago. I will not mourn for your passing. I think no one will."

She pressed the knife's handle into her husband's hand, gave him a fierce glare, and then spun on her heel and marched out of the room. Her daughter turned and hurried after her, leavin' me alone with the man.

The good, decent doctor who had cut off my leg.

He looked down at me then with an expression I did not expect: sympathy.

I rolled onto my back and closed my eyes against it. Damn fool. He was surely goin' to end up dead. "You should have listened to your wife," I croaked. "I ain't worth savin'."

I was a fool, too. A fool and a failure. I hadn't stopped those men from killin' Mama and Pa, or from burnin' down our house and every-thin' else we owned. I hadn't kept Ethelyn safe; I'd left her and she'd disappeared. I hadn't killed Nine-Fingered Nan when I'd had the chance, and now my leg was gone. I'd finally found the end of my searchin', finally thought I had a chance to get Ethelyn back, after all these years, and instead I hadn't lasted even two days in the desert 'fore nearly bein' buzzard food.

How long had I been here, in this man's house?

How far away was Bravebank from here?

How long would Nine-Fingered Nan's man be waitin' in the Stag Saloon?

After all of this, after everythin', Ethelyn could already be gone. Shipped off. Sold. And Nan laughin' at the both of us as she counted her cash.

"Nonsense," the man said quietly, bringin' me back from the mires of my misery. "Everyone deserves to be saved. Everyone deserves a second chance."

It was my turn to laugh, a choked, bitter sound. "That's the biggest pile a' horseshit I ever heard."

I could think of a few people who surely didn't deserve to be saved. Nine-Fingered Nan chief among 'em. I'd not hesitate to send that woman to Hell if I ever laid eyes on her again.

If I didn't end up there first.

The man gave a heavy sigh. "I understand this is difficult for you. The adjustment will take some time. But please, give it a chance. My wife ... her words are harsh ... but she speaks some truth. If you leave now, you will die out there. Alone. And you might be trouble, but you looked to me like a man who wanted to live. Was I wrong? Are you instead a man who wishes to die?"

I almost laughed again, then pushed the heels of my hands against my eyes to stop the swell of self-loathin'. The right one was still sore.

That was the question I'd been askin' myself since Ethelyn and I had run off terrified into the dark, into the woods behind our homestead that night. Pa's blood still warm where it'd splattered across my face.

I'd wondered then if maybe it would have been better to die with our parents. And I'd wondered again when I'd returned from scoutin' out hideaways to find Ethelyn gone. I'd spent so many sleepless nights frettin' about her. Wonderin' if she was dead ... or wonderin' if she was wishin' she was dead.

And so many times in the years since then, when I was gone hungry another day, or robbed of what little I had, or shootin' another fella in the face 'cause he was tryin' to rob what little I had. Or any of the days Holt and I had taken from the honest folk, or been chased away from another backwater town by the bullets of lawmen and the threat of bein' hanged.

How often I'd wondered if it'd just be better to die.

And yet, despite everythin', despite my wonderin', I just kept on livin'.

I kept tryin'. I kept fightin'. I kept shootin' and robbin' and lyin'.

"I gotta find my sister," I said, and the words surprised me. I hadn't meant to tell him that. I hadn't meant to answer him at all.

"I see. Well, son, it seems to me you cannot find your sister if you are dead. Hmm?"

I ground my teeth. Yes, damn him, such was the curse of my existence. As long as there were rumors of Ethelyn Delano bein' alive, it seemed I was doomed to keep on livin', too.

As long as she was alive, as long as there was a chance fer me to find her … I had just enough hope to keep on goin'. Just enough hope to think maybe I wasn't a complete failure, that maybe I was worthy of still breathin' … long as I didn't give up on her.

"Well." I heard the man's bootsteps move, and dropped my hands and opened my eyes to look up at him. He set the knife down carefully atop the bureau on the other side of the room. "I trust I will not need that, no?" He came back to me and reached down to hook his hands under my armpits. "Come. Let us get you back into the bed."

He grunted as he hauled me up off the floor, and I braced my good right leg under me to help him. I could have used the leverage to knock him off his feet. Could have lurched over to the bureau and grabbed that knife. Could have left the house right then.

But I didn't.

Instead I let him help me back to the mattress and eased down onto it. Sat back against the pillows he propped up behind me. Let him throw the covers back up over my legs to my waist, coverin' up the brace of metal that had replaced my left one.

My body felt numb, my mind strugglin' to accept any of this. Strugglin' to accept his kindness. His understandin'.

His sympathy.

Maybe I was finally dead, after all.

Maybe this was Hell.

"Please, rest," he said. "I will bring you some broth and water. You have been on a liquid diet for a few days ... you will need to work up to solid foods."

He turned to move for the door.

"How long?" I blurted.

He turned with an eyebrow raised. "I beg your pardon?"

"How long since you found me?"

"Oh. Nearly four days now."

I made a noise of despair, sinkin' back into the pillows.

His brows furrowed. "Is something wrong?"

"Yeah," I husked. "I gotta get to Bravebank. Need to meet someone there. Not sure how long they'll stay."

That expression of disapproval came across his face again. "I'm so sorry. You really should not travel for a few more weeks yet. But I would be happy to take the wagon to town and deliver a message to this person for you, to tell them you are currently ... indisposed, but will meet them just as soon as you are well."

I laughed loud and long at that one, makin' him frown.

"Is there something amusing about my offer?"

"Yeah," I gasped, "yeah, sure is. You thinkin' this person is so polite and civilized as to care if I'm indisposed or not. Tell him that and he's just as likely to tail you home and murder us all as he is to spit in yer face at the news."

The good, decent doctor blinked rapidly at this information. "Why ever would you want to meet such a person?"

My amusement died down at last and I shook my head. "You act like I have a choice. I don't."

He was silent at that, as if tryin' to determine what to make of it, or waitin' for me to tell him more. But I'd already told him more than I'd meant to. More than I'd wanted to.

"Well," he said at last. "I will fetch you some food. If you rest up and do as I tell you, you may be able to make it into town sooner."

I said nothin' in reply, starin' out between the lace drapes at the distant clumps of creosote and cacti outside, tryin' to ignore the stranglin' feeling those damned curtains brought to my throat.

He took up the knife on his way outta the room and shut the door softly behind him.

I closed my eyes and leaned my head back against the down pillows, already makin' a plan. It didn't matter what the doctor said; I had to get to Bravebank just as soon as I could. It'd already been five days since I'd met Nine-Fingered Nan in her hide-out. Who knew if her man was still in Bravebank or not, or, if by some miracle he was still there, how much longer he'd stay.

Every day that passed lessened my chances of findin' him, that much I was sure of.

And without that meetin', there was no deal with Nine-Fingered Nan. And without that deal, there was no hope of gettin' Ethelyn free.

Well, there was a few more things I knew now after talkin' with the good doctor who had chopped off my leg, and I was fairly certain it was enough to get me to Bravebank.

I knew this family had a wagon. That meant they had horses or mules to pull it. I could borrow one of those animals to get me to Bravebank.

I also knew it was likely the doctor had set up shop in Bravebank. There weren't no other towns very close, certainly none less than a day's ride, and this climate didn't lend well to growin' crops or raisin' livestock. The only people livin' out here were either into the mines, or into supplyin' and transportin' those who were into the mines.

Or doctorin' those who were into the mines.

And if this doctor had a shop in Bravebank, he wouldn'ta put up his house too far out of the town limits. So he could drive there and back in a day without wastin' too much daylight.

My heart quickened a bit at this realization, knowin' I couldn't be too far off with such speculations. And all of this meant I was closer to Bravebank than I'd thought. All I had to do was wait for my opportunity to relieve the good doctor of one his fine animals.

And find out where he'd hidden my guns and my clothes.

And figure out how this confounded metal leg worked.

THE CONSEQUENCES OF KINDNESS

I had evil dreams and fitful sleep, there in that proper bed with its cotton sheets.

I tossed and turned and woke up in a cold sweat, swearin' I'd heard my mother scream. There was an orange, flickerin' glow cast across the strange room when I opened my eyes, and for a heartbeat my muscles seized in terror, believin' I was gonna have to relive that nightmare yet again.

Then I caught sight of a shadowy figure to my left, sittin' beside the bed, and I nearly jumped outta my skin again as I realized it was a woman. A real flesh and blood person ... not part of my nightmare. And not just any person, it was the doctor's wife.

The orange glow in the room came from the lantern she had lit and set on the bedside table. She sat in a simple wooden chair which she'd pulled up next to the mattress, still and quiet, watchin' me. And in her lap, she turned a knife over and over in her hands.

Not no choppin' knife this time, neither. A huntin' knife. The kind you'd use to dress an animal carcass.

I bolted upright in the bed, scramblin' back away from her to press myself up into the corner. I eyed the window with those damned lace curtains, wonderin' if I was gonna have to throw myself outta it.

But the woman raised a hand and shook her head. "Shhh. Calm down. I am no murderer."

I glanced to the knife still in her lap. The fat blade glimmered in the lantern light.

She followed my gaze, and smiled softly. "This is only a precaution," she said in her heavy accent. "I came here to give you a warning, *idegen*. What I said earlier today; I meant it. My husband is an idealist. I am a realist. If he wants to waste good metal on you, so be it. But do not think you can take anything else from us, understand? While you are here, we will take care of you ... unless you give me reason to doubt my husband's belief in you. Unless you prove to me that *my* impressions of you are correct. In that case..." Her grip on the huntin' knife tightened. "In that case I will not hesitate to defend my family. Do not think our kindness makes us weak. Do not think our kindness makes us stupid. For we are neither."

I studied her face in the flickerin' light, saw the deadly seriousness in her flat stare and set jaw, and swallowed. I knew the look of a person who would kill if they had to.

She had that look.

I gave a nod in acknowledgement. "Ma'am," I said hoarsely, "I don't believe you are either."

Maybe I *had* thought 'em stupid at first ... stupid for takin' in a stranger like me, who coulda robbed and killed the lot of 'em as soon as I was on my feet again ... but it seemed the good doctor's wife at least had already entertained that possibility, and planned fer it.

Which coulda also been why my belongin's—includin' my guns— were nowhere in sight.

"Good." She stood from the chair. "Then if you are to be a guest in our home, you will see that you obey the house rules. No swearing, prayers before dinner, and wash on Sundays. Understand?"

I blinked at her, wonderin' if maybe I was still dreamin'. A multitude of replies ran through my mind, most of 'em impolite, but then, she *was* still holdin' that knife. "Yes ma'am," was all I managed.

"Good," she said again. She moved the chair back against the wall and slipped the huntin' knife into the sash at the waist of her simple cotton dress. "Now that we have an understanding, I will leave you to rest. Pleasant dreams."

And with that, she picked up the lantern and left the room, closin' the door behind her.

I exhaled loudly and sagged back into the pillows.

Almost three weeks later, I was still no closer to gettin' to Bravebank.

Though it weren't fer lack of tryin' ... it was fer lack of havin' two natural legs. As much as I wanted outta that house—and the urgency burned like my own personal Hell in the center of me every damn day—my body weren't cooperatin'.

The pain in the stump of my thigh and the strangeness of havin' all that metal attached to me had me bed-ridden fer a week, and then when I finally forced myself up onto my feet in the second week, the doctor fussed over me like a broody hen over her nest. I didn't want to listen to his multitude of instructions, but it turned out I had to, if I ever hoped to walk normal again. Or if I hoped not to die from another infection.

There were exercises to do to get used to my new leg, which he insisted I perform every day, and I reluctantly did so, though mostly only 'cause his wife was there, starin' me down through narrowed eyes with a choppin' knife in her hand.

And there was washin' and bandagin' to do of the place where my flesh met the metal, every day at first, then every other day, then every few days. Didn't matter how many times I watched the doctor do it, or how many times I did it myself, I didn't understand it.

I didn't understand how he'd done it. I didn't understand how it was possible.

Felt sick to my stomach every time I looked at it. Part of me wanted to demand he cut off the metal leg, too, and leave me be with my stump.

But I wouldn't'ta fared very well out here in the Territories with one leg and a crutch. And payin' off the debt I now owed to Nine-Fingered Nan woulda been a hell of a lot harder, too.

So I kept the metal leg. I kept it and wondered what the doctor imagined I owed him fer it. I kept it and did my best to learn how to use it quick as I could, so I could get outta there and get back to trackin' down Ethelyn. I kept it and tried not to ever look at it. Not unless I really had to.

Now it was goin' on three weeks since I'd first woken up in the good doctor's home, and I was feelin' like my time to go was fast approachin'. I stood outside against his wishes, leanin' heavily on a crutch propped under my left armpit, eyes closed against the bright afternoon sun, breathin' in deep the dry, dusty air. I was in the side yard of the family's house, if it could be called a yard at all, which it could not.

Only dust and rock here, and the surly desert plants that grabbed, scratched and needled you as you tried to pass.

I had been mildly impressed to see a small garden sprouting off the back of the house, which I'd later learned was irrigated by a deep well and some complicated length of plumbin' the doctor had engineered himself, and all powered by a windmill that rose up off the roof of the house.

I opened my eyes and squinted down at the toe of my boot stickin' out the bottom of my left pants' leg. Inside of that boot was a metal foot. Maybe the doctor shouldn'ta been called a doctor at all, but more an engineer. I still couldn't fathom how the false metal leg he'd attached to me could work on its own, either, and he said that's why I was havin' so much trouble controllin' it.

"Walk as if you still had both natural legs," he'd urged me.

But that was hard to do when I couldn't feel the ground under my left foot. All I could feel was the metal where it met the flesh and muscle of my left thigh. I felt it pressin' there, shiftin' and movin' when I swung my leg and took a step, and it was still mighty sore.

And I was still mighty weak. Not nearly myself.

And that wouldn't do if I was gonna be owin' Nine-Fingered Nan.

I heard footsteps aproachin' from behind, light and quick.

It could only be the boy. Radley, he was called. Probably slipped away from his mother's watchful eye again. She didn't like us talkin' much, and truth be told, I didn't like it much, either. I wasn't so good with kids. I never quite knew how to act around creatures so innocent.

He stopped beside me.

I said nothin'. Just kept studyin' the toe of my boot. At least they'd given my clothes back. All cleaned and pressed, too. And gifted me an old, beat-up hat to replace the one I'd lost. My guns, however ... my guns were still missin'.

And I surely still felt naked without those belts around my hips.

"Are you really a gunslinger?" Radley asked abruptly, almost like he could read the thoughts in my head right then. He hardly had an accent at all.

I sighed and took my time to answer, shiftin' my weight experimentally to the metal leg. It held me well enough, but a little shock of pain flared again in my thigh. I winced and transferred my weight back to the crutch. "Who says I'm a gunslinger?" I asked finally.

"Fanni says," he answered simply. "And Mama, too. Well, Mama says you're an outlaw, mostly. She says 'gunslinger' is just a fancy name for 'murderer'."

The corner of my mouth pulled upward at that statement. Good ol' Hanna was more right than she knew about that one.

"Papa doesn't help outlaws, though," the boy went on. "He turns 'em over to the sheriff. So I don't think you're an outlaw. Anyway, Papa said there aren't any posters with your face on 'em hanging in town."

No, there ain't, I thought wryly. *Not here. Not yet.*

"I bet Fanni six penny candies that you weren't a gunslinger. So, are you?"

I turned my head finally to look over at the boy, archin' an eyebrow at him. "Ain't ya a little young to be gamblin'?"

His brows came down to hood his dark blue eyes and his hands balled into fists. "It's only candy, mister."

"Okay, all right." I shrugged. "Take it easy. Just thinkin' yer mama wouldn't approve."

"Mama don't know."

"Of course she don't." I switched my gaze out to the westward horizon, rollin' with the desert heat. I'd discovered where this family kept their wagon and mules easily enough; the barn behind the house was hard to miss. My guns were the only thing left to find.

There was a moment of stony silence between us. "Well?" he prompted. "Are you or aren't you? I wanna tell Fanni who wins the bet!"

I cleared my throat and swiped at the sweat that beaded on my upper lip. "Now why would yer sister—or yer mama—think I was a gunslinger?"

The boy scuffed the toe of his boot into the dirt. "I dunno. Well, I mean, you got two guns. They say a man lookin' to protect himself carries a gun ... and a man lookin' to kill some folk carries two guns."

A snort of amusement escaped me.

"What?" the boy asked suspiciously.

Hanna, the good doctor's wife ... more fulla truth than I gave her credit for. But I surely didn't wanna confirm his mama's worst fears. So I only shook my head and said, "What about the man who travels across a lot of bad land? The man who'd like to reload after twelve shots instead a' six when a buncha bandits come out of the rocks?"

The kid was silent for another minute, presumably thinkin' it over. "I dunno," he said again. "I guess that makes sense."

"And what about you?" I asked, suddenly curious. I turned slightly to face him, my boot and my new metal foot crunchin' in the gritty dirt. "What makes you think I *ain't* a gunslinger?"

He looked up at me, right in the eyes. "On account of your leg, mister."

I frowned. "My leg?"

He nodded. "Sure. You were shot in the leg, bad enough Papa had to take it off and give you a metal one."

"Gunslingers get shot sometimes, too, ya know," I said.

But Radley shook his head. "Nah. Gunslingers shoot folk dead, or get shot dead. I've never heard of a gunslinger who crawled away into the desert after getting shot in the leg. At least, that's never what happens in those books Fanni reads."

My eyes narrowed at the way him sayin' it like that made me sound like a coward. At the way he so casually compared the romanticized tale in a dime novel to my daily Hell of a life. But the rise of anger sputtered out nearly as quick as it came.

He was only a kid. He didn't know. I prayed he'd never know.

It didn't matter what he thought of gunslingers, anyway. Or what his mama or sister thought of gunslingers, neither.

I was no gunslinger either way.

I was just a man lookin' fer the only family I had left. Lookin' fer a way out of the grave I'd been diggin' fer myself since the day Ethelyn had disappeared.

"Well, yer right," I muttered. "I ain't no gunslinger." Maybe if I had been, I'd of got the draw on Nine-Fingered Nan, and she'd be dead now, and Ethelyn'd be free, and I'd still have my leg. I mighta been pretty damn good at shootin' guns, but out here, anythin' short of the bein' the best eventually landed you dead.

Hell, if Nine-Fingered Nan hadn'ta wanted to fuck with me, I'd be dead already. I wouldn't be here now, talkin' to this kid.

"Ha! I knew it!" Radley exclaimed triumphantly, breakin' me outta my broodin'. "I gotta go tell Fanni! She's gonna owe me next time we go to town!"

He turned on his heel to make off for the house, but I called out to him before he could get too far. "Hey, kid!"

He drew up short and turned to face me again, shieldin' his eyes against the sun with his hand. "Yeah?"

I glanced around the yard, and didn't see none of the other family about. But still, I didn't want to take any chances of bein' overheard. I hobbled carefully toward him, leanin' heavy on the crutch, my metal foot half walkin' and half draggin'. I stopped about an arms' length from him, where I could talk quiet. "Look," I said, "you know I ain't no gunslinger. And I ain't no outlaw, neither." Well, that weren't entirely the truth. But it weren't entirely a lie, neither. I weren't an outlaw in this state. Yet. "Yer pa said himself, there ain't no posters of me up."

The boy shrugged. "Yeah."

"And I appreciate what yer family's done fer me and all ... but I got business to attend to in Bravebank. Business that can't wait. Business that requires I go in with my guns. Understand? You wouldn't happen to know where yer ma or pa hid my guns, would ya?"

He only stared up at me from beneath his hand. "I thought you said you weren't an outlaw? Murder's against the law, mister. Unless ... are you a lawman?" his voice rose a bit at that last part, as if he were suddenly comin' to a realization. "Is that why you have two guns?"

"No ... no," I said, signalin' hastily for him to quiet down. I glanced around again to make sure his mama wouldn't come out and catch this conversation of ours. She mighta used that knife she'd threatened me with if she knew what I was askin' of her youngest. "Not a lawman, kid. But the people I'm supposed to meet ... they're bad, bad men, see? I ain't goin' there to murder 'em, but they might try and murder me. And if that happens ... well, I need my guns. To defend myself."

He pursed his lips and dropped his hand from his eyes, lookin' around like I had done to see if any of his family was close by.

"Please, kid," I said, and I let some of the desperation clawin' around in my chest into my voice. It was embarassin' to be at the mercy of a ten-year-old boy, but so I was. His sister wouldn't come near me, and neither of his parents were gonna hand me back my weapons till they were good and sure I was healthy and healed and headin' out far away from their homestead, I was sure of it.

"If I got your guns for you, would you leave?" he asked at last.

It wasn't the response I'd been expectin'. But I answered honestly. "Yes. My business is urgent. I've already been here too long."

He looked me up and down then with a scrutinizin' eye I didn't much like. "I'm not sure that's a good idea, mister. Papa says you need to—"

"Yer papa don't understand," I bit off, and then at the widenin' of his eyes, checked myself and exhaled slowly. "I'm sorry. But like I said, my business is urgent. I can't afford to waste any more time. If it makes ya feel any better, I'll come back when it's done. Yeah? Let me go take care of my business, and then I'll come back here and heal up nice just like your pa would want."

Now that ... that was a full-out lie. But I'd gotten pretty good at lyin' in my lifetime. It sounded like the truth.

Radley was silent for a long moment, chewin' at his lip.

I wanted to say more, to push him for an answer quick-like, but it wouldn'ta helped. He had to make the decision for himself. So I waited in the dusty yard, quiet and still on the outside and jumpin' with nerves on the inside, sweat slidin' down my neck.

"Okay," he said finally.

I blew out the breath I'd been holdin'.

"But don't tell no one how you found 'em, okay? Else Mama'll give me a whooping and..." he looked me up and down again, "well, I don't know what she'd do to you."

"I have a pretty good idea," I muttered. "My lips are sealed, kid. You have no idea how much yer helpin' me, here."

He nodded, resolute now that he'd made a decision. "Yeah, sure. I'll get 'em for you tonight. But you'll need to be gone before morning, and get back quick as you can. Otherwise Papa might organize a search party for you. He worries a lot about his patients."

My eyes lifted from Radley to rest on the barn in the back. "I can see that he does," I said, but my mind was already gone, thinkin' ahead to tonight, makin' up my plan to escape.

We had dinner in awkward silence, per usual, with Dr. Balogh—as I'd learned was their family name—attempin' and failin' to make small talk. Then Hanna read to her children from the Good Book by lantern light, and I excused myself into the small spare bedroom and closed the door, unable to bear the sound of those verses.

The Good Book hadn't saved my mama, despite her readin' from it daily.

It hadn't kept our home from burnin' down, neither. Nope, the Good Book itself had burned up with everythin' else ... reduced to nothin' more than a pile of ash, indistinguishable from any of the rest of it.

I did not undress for bed this night, but propped my crutch against the wall and eased myself under the sheets fully clothed. I had to grab my false leg under the knee and drag it up onto the mattress, and I winced at the throbbin' in my thigh.

Perhaps the doctor had been right about not wantin' me to travel so soon.

But I didn't really have a choice now, did I?

I settled back against the pillows and waited, watchin' the play of the lantern lit in the corner against the walls and ceilin'.

Despite myself, I must have dozed. I jerked awake at a soft creakin' noise, and looked over toward the door to see the boy tip-toein' in. And, bless his innocent little soul, he had my gun belts in his hands.

I sat up and scrubbed my hands over my face, shakin' off the sleep. The lantern in the corner was burnin' low now, barely givin' off enough light for the boy to see as he crept across the room. He set my belts and my two holsters, complete with both revolvers, on the end of the bed. "Here," he whispered.

"Thank you," I whispered in return. I wished I had somethin' to give him for his help, but all my belongin's—what I hadn't left with Holt back in Grave Gulch, anyway—had been lost to the desert. "I'll bring ya back somethin' nice from town," I offered instead.

I threw back the covers, swung my feet to the floor, and pulled the belts toward me.

"How you gonna get there?" the boy asked, still in a whisper. "I don't think you should walk, not with that leg. And the wagon's too noisy."

"Just gonna borrow one of the mules," I said, bucklin' on my first belt. A part of me questioned the wisdom in tellin' him so much of my plan. But then ... he had almost as much to lose in this as I did now. He wouldn't tell no one.

He shook his head. "Oh. Papa won't like that."

"I imagine yer parents won't like any part of this plan, kid."

"He can't drive the wagon with just one mule."

Guilt weaseled its way into my gut, workin' up toward my throat. I tried to swallow it down and buckled on my second belt. Damn this family and their cursed kindness.

What did kindness get 'em, anyway?

Another mouth to feed and a stolen mule, that's what.

And what did their kindness get me?

A whole wagon-load of guilt, damnit.

I shook my head and stood from the bed, reachin' for my crutch. "I'll bring it back," I said. "Won't be long. Promise." I hoped he couldn't see my face in the dyin' lantern light.

I was surely gonna go to Hell fer lyin'.

VI

DEAD MEN MAKE NO DEALS

In the end, I took more than the mule. I took one of their saddles, a pair of their saddlebags, a canteen of water, a mutton steak wrapped in brown paper, a bit of bread and cheese, and the bottle of laudanum the doctor had put on the bedside table for the pain in my thigh. I stuck my crutch in the saddle scabbard made fer a rifle.

Radley was an accomplice to all of it, which didn't make me feel no better. In fact, it made me feel worse, considerin' the fact he thought I was comin' back. At least he didn't see me off. I made him go back inside to bed before I mounted up, partly because then he could honestly claim he hadn't seen me ride off, and partly because I didn't want him to see me try to get that tangle of metal that was now my left leg up over the saddle.

But I did it, finally, after a lotta gruntin' and cursin' and sweatin'.

The mule wasn't too happy about it, neither, swivelin' its ears around and chompin' the bit, dancin' in place.

"Just calm down, ya edgy bastard," I growled as I gathered up the reins. I urged it off at a lope, wantin' to put as much distance between me and the Balogh homestead as quick as possible.

The moon was up, no longer full, but bright enough still to light my way.

Far as I could tell, it was near midnight. And the kid had said Bravebank was only four miles away. I could make it there in no time at this rate.

I set my sights on the path ahead, the non-existent road, and resisted the urge to kick the mule into a full-on gallop. It wouldn't do to go tearin' off into the dark, even if this were a mostly flat piece of arid land. Last thing I needed was for the animal to go down, or to go lame.

And anyway, just ridin' at a lope was makin' my thigh ache bad enough. I ground my teeth against the pain, tryin' to ignore it.

I remembered what the doctor had said, about my body rejectin' the leg if I didn't rest up enough, and whispered a curse that was lost beneath the mule's drummin' hooves.

Maybe I could rest when I was dead.

My heart leapt when I saw the lights of Bravebank.

It was a big enough town to have a few street lamps, and these glowed yellow against the night, throwin' weak circles of light on the ground below as I finally turned down its dusty main road.

Most of the shops were dark at this hour, but down the street a-ways I saw the lighted windows of the sanctuary for any weary traveler: the saloon, the hotel, and the brothel. I dropped the mule into a walk as I approached, the boisterous piano music spillin' from the saloon growin' louder with each step.

There were a few people out on the street, mostly drunks or saloon girls hopin' to catch a late arrival and steer 'em inside, but I ignored all of 'em as I reined up my mount at the hitchin' post. I fished out the bottle of laudanum right quick and took a little swig, hopin' it would dull the fire that now ate away at my left thigh after my ride.

I couldn't go in there with the crutch. Couldn't risk Nan's man—or anyone else, for that matter—thinkin' I was an easy mark. I swiped suddenly sweaty palms against the grips of my guns. Least I had those back, and plenty of bullets.

That would have to do.

I swung down off the mule real careful, but the shock of pain was still enough to make me suck in a sharp breath. Sweat prickled under my collar. I took a minute to compose myself, leanin' against the animal.

"Long ride, my love?" a woman's voice asked. "Need me to take care a' ya?"

I glanced up to her, saw her leanin' over the hitchin' rail and battin' long lashes at me from above the rim of her fan. Her corset had been pulled tight, her ample bosom nearly spillin' out the top, and her skirt was short. Her long hair was pinned atop her head, spirals of curls fallin' down around her bare shoulders.

I swallowed hard, cursin' the lust that stirred despite everythin'. I wondered if The Stag's girls were actually sportin' women, or if she just wanted to get me inside so I'd spend all my money on drink. "Nah," I husked. "Not now."

She feigned a pout. "Aww. You sure? You look tense. I could help ya relax..."

So maybe she *could* offer more than a drink. But it didn't much matter. I didn't have the coin or the time for such things. She sauntered in my direction, but I waved her off and shook my head. "Maybe another time." It took a mighty load of concentration to stay standin' without a woman hangin' on my arm, too.

To my relief, she accepted my second refusal with grace, steppin' back to take up her post again at the hitchin' rail. She fanned herself and shrugged. "All right, then. You know where I'll be."

"Sure." I took a breath, and took a step with the metal leg. It hurt. I grimaced and wavered there fer a minute, thinkin' I was about to go down into the dirt. Well, they'd probably think I was just another drunk.

The girl watched me stagger there with a raised brow. "You ain't even gone inside yet," she commented.

I tossed her a glare, but made no retort. It took too much focus to keep my balance. But somehow, miraculously, I made it to the boardwalk, and thanked what shit luck I had that this saloon didn't have no stairs out front. And then I reached the door and drew another deep breath, shovin' the pain down deep as it could go.

I pushed through into the noise and light of the place.

The late hour had not slowed the business of The Stag Saloon, certainly. There were plenty of girls busy makin' the rounds, the bartender was busy pourin', the piano busy playin', and a whole lotta folk busy drinkin' or dealin' cards.

My God, did I want a shot a' whiskey all of a sudden—maybe more than one—but I had no coin fer that, either. I kicked myself for not swipin' a few of those off the good doctor too while I had the chance.

Guess I'd have to do this sober. My eyes swept the floor, lingerin' on the poker tables. Nan had not given me a description of the man I was supposed to meet, nor his name, but I'd figured he'd probably know I was comin'. And my face weren't on any posters in this town, no, and I might not of had a hole in my leg anymore ... but the metal one did give me a limp that was painfully obvious no matter how much I tried to hide it.

I limped now, slow and careful, over toward the left wall, plannin' to plant myself there and watch till I identified the fella I was lookin' fer. I leaned back against the wall and crossed my arms, wantin' nothin' more than a chair. But the place was full. There weren't no more chairs available.

So I stood, ignorin' the pain, and watched.

My heart throbbed in my throat, and the very real worry that I'd come weeks too late rubbed at my nerves. Or maybe he'd retired early. Or maybe he was a day gambler.

Or maybe Nan had played me fer a fool entirely, and there was never no man a' hers to meet here.

Anger burned in my ears at the thought, knowin' it was surely possible.

There was so much I didn't know. Too much.

And I'd been so distracted by my dead horse and the bullet in my leg and the revolver pointed at my head and a chance at earnin' Ethelyn's freedom that I hadn't thought to ask more questions.

As if Nan would have answered 'em, anyway. So I stood. And I waited. And I watched.

And the time ticked by on the pendulum clock across the room.

Saloon girls came to see if I were interested in a dance or a chat or a nice, warm bed, but I declined 'em all.

Then they came to see if I would at least buy a drink or some food, but I declined that, too.

I started gettin' a suspicious side-eye from the bartender, so then I told 'em I'd order once the man I was meetin' here showed up. They left me alone for awhile after that.

My leg ached somethin' awful. Sweat gathered under my collar. My skin felt hot, and all I could think of was the doctor, and how mad he'd be if I ended up droppin' dead out here.

Then the laudanum kicked in, and the pain dulled for a bit.

Then the laudanum wore off, and the pain came back, worse than before. A cold sweat broke out all over. Exhaustion pulled at my body, my mind, my eyelids. People came and went in The Stag Saloon, the moon trekked across the sky, and I still stood there, watchin', tryin' my damnedest to stay awake, and to keep from swoonin'.

I needed somethin', anythin', to keep my strength up and dull the fire eatin' away at my thigh. So I started lookin' fer marks, instead of my contact. Plenty of the men here now were blind drunk. They'd never notice a missin' coin purse. Not till they sobered up, and then it'd be too late.

One such man was staggerin' toward the doors now. He tilted, wavered, and stumbled sideways into a table, jostlin' the drinks and elicitin' angry protests from the men seated around that table.

I moved quick as I could manage—which wasn't quick at all— toward the fella and grabbed the back of his vest, haulin' him back upright just as he was shoutin' threats at the seated men. "Okay, mister," I muttered. "Think you've had enough. Time to go."

"Git yer 'andsoffame!" he slurred, swingin' around with a fist, which I easily dodged.

The men at the table he'd stumbled into laughed, which only made the drunk's face get redder.

I ignored his curses and the new threats he was now directin' at me and dragged him toward the doors, cursin' my heavy limp and the eyes he'd drawn toward us. But his fumblin' and staggerin', while nearly knockin' me off balance and onto my ass myself, gave me enough cover to snatch the small purse at his belt in the dimness of the saloon's entrance. I shoved it into my own pocket, then threw him out the door.

He went sailin' and landed with an *oomph*, rollin' out into the dusty street.

Where he pushed himself back to his feet again and turned to face me, hand goin' fer his gun.

The grip of my own weapon was in my hand in an instant, but I didn't even have to draw. The drunk swayed, starin' at me, then his eyes rolled up into his head and he fell face-first into the dirt, out cold.

I released my own gun and turned back to face the interior of the saloon, which had considerably hushed since I'd laid my hands on another patron. I gave those who was lookin' at me now, and that was most of the saloon, a rueful smile and held my hands shoulder-high, shruggin'. I surely didn't want any of 'em to think I was here lookin' fer trouble.

Well, if Nan's man was here and hadn't noticed me yet, he couldn'ta missed me now.

To my relief, it seemed the drunk I'd booted was not a particular favorite here. The other patrons merely blinked at me, then went back to their business. A few of 'em whistled or clapped.

And then everythin' went back to the way it was, and I let out a long, slow breath.

There was an empty chair at a table to my right now, so I limped over there and sat heavily, unable to hide the grimace at the flare of pain in my thigh.

Two old men sat at the table I had joined, with plates of biscuits, beans, and bacon. Miners, judgin' from the state of the grime dug into the creases of their skin and clothes. They had a bottle of whiskey set between 'em, and two glasses. One of the men poured a finger of whiskey into one of the glasses, and pushed it toward me.

I raised an eyebrow.

He nodded at me and swiped at the beans stuck to his grizzled gray beard with the back of his hand. "Ya done us a favor, boy. Tha' Jake, he's a right ol' blowhard, he is. Always in here full as a tick, causin' trouble. Ain't no one like 'em. Go on, drink up. Ya deserve it."

I grunted. Seemed I'd picked the right man to rob and toss. I downed the whiskey and closed my eyes at its burn, willin' it to cool down the burn in my damned leg.

"Jus' you be careful tomorrow, though," the second miner said then, gesturin' at me with a greasy finger. "Jake, he likes ta pick fights. If he remembers ya tomorrow, he'll be lookin' fer ya."

I sighed. Or I'd picked the wrong man to rob and toss.

The first old miner poured me another finger, and chuckled as he did so. "Here. Here's ta hopin' he don't remember ya." He pushed the glass at me again.

I shook my head and threw the whiskey back. "Here's to hopin'," I muttered.

Despite the scene I'd caused, no one approached me to talk business. No one took any particular notice of me.

Folk in The Stag Saloon just kept drinkin' and eatin' and gamblin' and flirtin' with the girls.

I ordered my own whiskey with the coin I'd lifted off the angry drunk, and helped myself to some hard-boiled eggs and cold-cuts off the back table, now that I'd ordered myself some alcohol and satisfied the narrow-nosed bartender, who'd been givin' me a hard glare now and then up till that point.

I sat with the miners till they bade me farewell and retired for the night, then sat with some other folk I ignored. And they ignored me, in turn.

Just the way I liked it.

Gradually, the patrons of the Stag thinned out. They went upstairs to their rooms, or out to their residences or the other hotels, some with a girl on their arm, some alone.

But I stayed.

The sky I could glimpse through the saloon's front windows above the buildin's across the street began to lighten. My eyes burned. My body wanted nothin' more than to sleep.

That urgent desperation I'd felt when facin' off against Nine-Fingered Nan was back, that feelin' of bein' so very close ... and yet not bein' quite close enough.

I'd missed him. I must have missed him.

My heart beat hard in my throat, and I swallowed more whiskey to try and drown it.

Damn it all to Hell, I couldn't let it end like this.

I slammed the glass back hard to the table, but the only one sober enough to disapprove of my recklessness was the bartender himself. I ignored the fresh glare he tossed me, squeezin' shut my achin' eyes. I rubbed at my face with my hands.

How long could I stay here?

Not forever. Not long at all, in truth.

Soon enough the doctor and his family, well, all of 'em except Radley, would find out I'd gone. They'd discover a mule was missin', and I'd told 'em I had business in Bravebank. They'd know where I went. Doctor Balogh would come lookin' fer me here, I was sure of it.

And when he found me ... what then?

Would he try and force me to return to his homestead with him?

And if I went back with him, what would his wife think? How would she handle my stompin' all over her family's good will and tenuous trust?

And would they accuse me of stealin' their mule?

I grimaced at the thought. At least I hoped it wouldn't come to that. I was in no state to outrun or fight off any law who might come after me fer such a thing. And I most certainly didn't want to hang over a mule.

I swallowed more whiskey. Surely Radley would tell 'em I was only borrowin' the animal. Maybe it was a lie, but they only had to believe it was the truth long enough fer me to make the deal with Nan's man and get outta town.

Course, that was the catch, weren't it? I couldn't get outta town till I made the deal, and I couldn't make the deal till I found Nan's man. And he was provin' to be harder to find than I'd hoped.

Anxiety crawled all over me like a livin' thing. My skin itched with restlessness and I glanced again out the window.

He's not here. I missed him. I came too late.

But I shook off the thought soon as it went through my head.

No. No. He has to be here ... maybe he's just upstairs, havin' a good time with one of the girls. He'll be back. He's got to be back eventually...

I kept tellin' myself that. And kept nursin' the whiskey, hopin' the drink would soothe my nerves and numb the pain in my leg.

I couldn't leave now. Not after I'd finally made it here. Not until I was absolutely certain.

And I couldn't stay, neither. Not unless I wanted to face a very disappointed Dr. Balogh, or chance runnin' into an angry, sobered-up Jake, or possibly encounter a lawman come to get me fer rustlin' a mule.

Outside, the sun crept closer and closer to the horizon.

Inside, I did my best to drown all my hopes and fears in whiskey.

"Well, well, well."

I jerked awake and sat up straight, then winced and caught my breath at the shootin' pains that raced up my spine. And my legs were goin' numb. I squinted in the light, liftin' a hand to shield my face, blinkin' hard to clear the blur in my vision.

"Look what the cat dragged in, boys."

I blinked some more, tryin' to find the source of the voice. A silhouette in the shape of a man moved across my field of view, followed by another. And another.

I closed my eyes and rubbed 'em. Moved my toes around in my boots.

No, wait. I couldn't feel my left foot.

My eyes shot open, and I grimaced again in the sudden onslaught of light. A headache stabbed in my temples and I groaned. I supposed I might have tried a little too hard last night to forget my worries—*shit!* And that's when I remembered. That's when I remembered all of what my worries the night before had been.

My hands dropped to my guns—both of 'em—but in the morning silence the sound of five pistols clearin' leather might as well have been loud as a herd of stampedin' cattle.

I froze.

The silence held. No one fired.

I forced myself to breathe slow and deep, though my heart had quickened, and blinked again in the dazzlin' mornin' light. I cursed the cloud of stupid the whiskey had brought down upon my head. The risin' sun had broke above the buildin's across the street, and I'd picked a table dead-set in the middle of its blazin' rays. *Stupid. Stupid, Van! You shoulda stayed sober. And awake.*

"Whew, boy!" the voice said, the tone of mock relief. But I heard a thread of truth in there ... the barest of trembles to the man's tenor. "Better watch it, fellas! This one's quick. So they say. This is Lucky Logan's brat. Ain't you?"

I tried to focus on the fella who kept talkin', the one who clearly thought he was the leader. He was at least smart enough to stand directly in front of that damned blindin' sun, so that no matter how hard I squinted, I couldn't make out none of his features. He was only a shiftin' silhouette, a blur of black against the bright.

Well, he thought that made 'em smart, anyway. Sure, I could hardly peel my eyes open to get a look at him, but what I did see of him was outlined real nice against such a shiny background.

"Depends on who's askin'," I said. I kept my hands restin' on my guns, real light. I didn't move 'em, didn't so much as twitch. Those five naked guns hadn't found their five empty holsters yet. And even I didn't like those odds.

But I moved my focus to my hands, then. Away from my achin' back and legs and waterin' eyes and that bastard of a silhouette. Just to my hands. The feel of the metal warmin' beneath my skin. The texture of the grips beneath the slight curl of my fingers.

"I told Nan you were dead," the man said.

My focus shattered at those words, and the world became a blur of light and shadows and pain once more. "What?" I strangled out. All I could think of was Nine-Fingered Nan then, tellin' me Ethelyn would be safe enough till the deal was made ... lest I died in the desert.

"I told her you was dead," the man repeated, louder and slower.

"I ain't dead," I snapped.

"Not yet," the man drawled. "But Nan said to watch fer ya weeks ago. Ya didn't show up. Thought for sure that bullet she put in ya killed ya."

"It didn't. And I'm here now." My heart throbbed in my throat, pulsin' wildly. So this was the man Nan had told me to meet. I'd found him at last. Or rather, he'd found me. But if he'd already told Nan I was dead … was it too late? *Please don't let it be too late. Please.*

I lifted my hands from my guns, slow and careful, and set them flat on the table in front of me. "So we gonna make a deal or what?"

He laughed, and then a brief silence followed, and I listened to the poundin' of my own heart in my ears.

"Maybe," he said. His shadow moved around the table, closer, and I heard the click of a hammer bein' pulled back, closer. "But I already told Nan you were dead. And I'd hate to be made a liar."

I shook my head, choosin' my words carefully. "Somethin' tells me Nan wouldn't like it much if anyone killed me but her."

"She'd never know. She thinks she killed you already."

I chanced a glance away from him, away from the sun's glarin' light, first to my right, then to my left, to the rest of his group, tryin' to judge where their loyalties lie. More with him, or more with Nan?

Their expressions were hard, unwaverin', their gun hands steady. I glanced around the rest of the saloon, searchin' to see if there might be any witnesses. There were a few men asleep as I had been, folded over the tables, even a few sprawled on the floor, but no one currently conscious. And the bartender was conspicuously absent.

I sighed, bringin' my eyes back down to my own hands, still flat against the table, and nodded. "All right. What do you want?"

"I want a percent of whatever you get fer Nan."

"Ain't that somethin' you should work out with her?"

He laughed again. "Nah. You just add my percent on top."

I rubbed at my throbbin' temples and closed my eyes against the light. "And what are Nan's terms, then?"

"Ah. Glad to hear yer willin' to be reasonable." I heard his hammer ease off and his weapon slide back into its holster. The scrape of the chair he pulled out was loud to my achin' head and I winced. The chair creaked as he settled down into it, and then there was a thump and the jingle of spurs as he set his boots up on the edge of the table.

The other four men he'd brought with him did not holster their weapons, nor did they sit down. I waited. And listened.

"Well, ya see, Nan's been offered a lot o' money for yer sister," he said.

Revulsion roiled in my gut at the words and I tensed. So help me, soon as I had Ethelyn back, I was gonna end everyone involved in this...

"So the only way yer gettin' her back is to pay Nan at least what she's been offered already, if not some more just to make it worth her trouble of entertainin' ya in the first place."

Entertainin'? Is that what she called shootin' my horse dead and nearly shootin' me dead?

"How much?" I asked.

"Twenty-five thousand."

I barked laughter, pushin' my chair back away from the table and squintin' at him into the sun. "You're outta yer goddamned mind!"

"And if you wanna stay alive long enough to earn that twenty-five thousand," he said evenly, "you'll add another five thousand fer me and my boys here."

I swore, havin' half a mind to just draw then and there and take my chances in the rain of bullets that would surely follow. But before I could decide one way or another, someone walked into The Stag Saloon.

All eyes turned to him, and he paused just inside the door. He looked toward us. I imagined our little group made quite a sight. But then I blinked again. Even with my sun-dazzled vision, he looked familiar.

"Van?" He sounded surprised.

And I was just as surprised to hear his voice as he must've been to see me here, in this predicament. Or maybe that part wasn't what surprised him. Maybe what surprised him was that I was still alive. "Holt?"

For a heartbeat no one moved, no one said a thing.

My seared vision cleared a bit, and in that second of clarity I saw on Holt's face what he was gonna do.

Holt was fast—you didn't get to be an old bastard like he was by bein' slow—and two against five were much better odds, but I wasn't tryin' to kill these men, not yet. I was tryin' to make a deal fer my sister's freedom. And you couldn't make a deal with dead men.

I opened my mouth to tell him not to do it, but too late. He drew and fired before any of Nan's men could react. The one standin' nearest to my right jerked and hit the floor in a spray of blood.

Then I hit the floor, too, but on my own accord, just as the inside of The Stag Saloon filled with bullets.

VII

THE BARGAIN AT BRAVEBANK

"Stop!" I yelled, throwin' my hands up over my head as splintered wood showered over me. "Cease fire! Cease fire, damnit!"

My words were drowned by the noise of gunfire, the crack of bullets punchin' into wood and shatterin' glass. I rolled as one of Nan's men pushed the table over and barely dodged it landin' on me. The fella crouched down behind it and I crawled over to another table, pushin' it over and doin' the same. I drew a gun of my own, the undamaged one, and swore some more, cursin' Holt's timin'. If only he coulda given me a few more minutes. Or if only he coulda found me weeks ago, when I was facin' Nan herself.

"Cease fire!" I roared. "Holt! You bastard! I'm tryin' to make a deal!"

One of the guns—the one nearest the saloon entrance—stopped firin'. After a long moment, the others fell silent, too.

My ears rang. Cautiously, I lifted up onto my knees and looked out above the edge of the table. Three of Nan's men were dead on the floor, their blood soakin' into the floorboards. The leader and the one other fella left were still ducked behind the other table, far as I could tell.

I saw Holt pressed up against the doorjamb at the entrance, his revolver still held at the ready, but quiet. From that angle, they'd never get a clear shot at him.

The other patrons passed out across other tables or on the floor hadn't so much as stirred. Which was good fer them, otherwise they mighta ended up dead. I dropped back down behind my cover.

"What kind of deal?" Holt said from the doorway.

"A deal ta buy his sister back," Nan's man called out. "But ya just shot up three of my boys. Nan ain't gonna like that. Good help is awful hard to find these days, ya know."

My fingers clenched hard around the grip of my gun, then I winced as the soreness in my palm turned sharp again and loosened my hold a bit. Somethin' in there still weren't quite right since that day Nan had shot the gun outta my hand. But at least it was healin'. Slowly. "Yeah, well, look at the bright side," I said. "Five thousand split two ways is better than five thousand split five ways, ain't it?"

"Five thousand!?" Holt shouted from the door. "Yer out of yer damned mind, kid! How do you know they even have yer sister? Eh? Did ya even think to ask?"

"Five thousand?" Nan's man repeated, not givin' me time to answer Holt. "Oh no. The price is gone up now. On account of the emotional trauma you's caused me by murderin' half my crew."

I ground my teeth and knocked my head back against the underside of the table I leaned against. I breathed a long string of swear words. "Fine," I spat. "How much?"

"Whaddaya mean, 'How much?'?" Holt demanded from the doorway. "Don't be stupid, Van!"

I ignored him, listenin' for Nan's man's answer instead.

He ignored Holt, too. "Make it a nice, even ten thousand and ya still got yerself a deal."

"Ten thousand!" Holt exploded.

"Deal," I said. I didn't have the faintest idea where I was gonna get my hands on thirty-five thousand dollars ... but I was gonna find it, one way or another.

"No deal!" Holt said. "They're playin' ya fer a fool, kid. How do ya know they even have yer sister?"

I shifted to glare at him from over the battered table edge, but he just shook his head in that infuriatingly disapprovin' way of his. He'd never believed my insistences my sister was still alive, not since the day he'd met me.

Nan's man laughed. "Oh, we got her, all right. Purty little thing, she is. Couple of us wanted to keep her fer ourselves, but Nan wanted the money. Oh well. Guess we can buy a whole lot of whores with ten thousand dollars, eh?"

I lurched to my feet and shoved my table to the side. It crashed against a chair as I limped across the floor to their sideways table and lowered my gun over the top of it, straight at the leader's head.

His and the other man's weapon came up quick, hammers cockin'. "Ah ah ah," he warned, "careful, boy. Kill me and I can guarantee ya, there'll be no deal at all."

My heart pulsed in my throat, and my headache pulsed with it, red seepin' in around the edges of my vision. I wanted nothin' more in that moment than to pull the trigger, to freeze that slimy smirk under that black, droopin' handlebar mustache in place so he could show it to the Devil when he woke up in Hell.

"Van..." Holt said uneasily, but I hardly heard him.

There were people shoutin' out in the street. Surely they'd heard our gunfire and were callin' for the sheriff. But I didn't move. Didn't blink. Just stood there with my gun leveled at his head, rage hummin' in my blood.

"Here," Nan's man said, and his free hand slowly lifted to a small pocket in the breast of his shirt. "Ya want proof?" His fingers slipped down inside and fished around, then pulled out a delicate golden chain. "Nan gave me this ta show you. Said you'd know what it was." He extended his arm outward, the chain danglin' from his closed fist.

I risked lookin' away from his face to glance at the necklace. Hangin' from the chain was a small, oval cameo of a white rose.

My breath hissed out between my teeth. I suddenly felt too light. Woozy. My gun hand wavered.

"Van," Holt called again from the doorway. He'd leaned around the frame of it, watchin' us warily. "That don't mean it's yer sister's. Plenty of women got necklaces like—"

"Not like this one," Nan's man interrupted. His dark brown eyes were locked on me, glitterin' with a cruel glee. "There's an engravin' on the back. With a date and a name. Think you'll find it mighty familiar."

My breath came short and ragged as I stared at it.

After so long ... sometimes even I had believed she was a ghost.

After so long ... to know I had been right all along ... to know I had finally found her...

I snatched the necklace from him. My gun hand steadied. "Where is she?" I husked. I remembered what I'd done to Lloyd Renneker to get him to talk. Nan didn't want this one of hers dead? So maybe I wouldn't kill him. Maybe I'd do so much worse....

His long black mustache twitched as he grinned. "Don't ya worry about her none. Nan's keepin' her safe and cozy fer ya. Long as you get us that money, anyway. When ya get it, come find me here again, and I'll tell ya the spot to meet Nan. And get yer sister."

Holt scoffed, and from the corner of my eye I saw him lean out toward the street briefly before duckin' back inside the saloon. "Back here? We done shot up the place!"

Nan's man shook his head once. "Me and the sheriff have an ... understandin'. You two, though..." He clucked his tongue in admonishment. "Well I can't speak fer you two. He probably won't take too kindly to yer murder and destruction of property. Guess that ain't my problem though, now, is it?"

The shoutin' outside was gettin' louder.

"Van, we gotta go," Holt said. "Like *now*."

I hesitated. There was still so much yet I wanted to do. I wanted to shoot the bastard at the end of my gun and the other man with him, too. Or I wanted to *hurt* them. Hurt them until they told me where Ethylen was, and the thirty-five thousand be damned.

"Van," Holt said again.

The man at the end of my gun lifted an eyebrow. "Well, boy, what'll it be? Ya wanna get that money and get yer sister back? Or you wanna hang fer murder? I gotta admit, I wouldn't mind watchin' ya swing."

I took another step forward and thumbed my hammer back.

He didn't so much as flinch, starin' me down, his gun still ready too, pointin' at my middle.

More voices from outside filtered through the silence.

"Van, *now*!" Holt barked.

"*Damnit*!" I lowered my pistol and eased the hammer down, then shoved it back into the holster, spinnin' away from Nan's men and hobblin' fast as I could manage toward the door where Holt waited all fidgety like.

"They're gonna see us leavin'," he muttered as I approached.

"We'll just have to make a run fer it," I said. And hope they wouldn't get a good look at our faces, or the good doctor and his family would see mine on a poster in town, after all.

"Yeah, that's right," Nan's man called from where he still crouched behind that table. "Ya better run, boy. Run, boy, run!" He cackled a laugh.

I swore again at my shit luck, wishin' I had the time to do somethin' about his arrogance. But I didn't. So I followed Holt out of the saloon and squinted in the bright mornin' sun.

The mule was there, right where I left him.

I shoved Ethelyn's necklace deep into my pants pocket and struggled up into the saddle from the right side, suckin' in a sharp breath as my left leg went over the cantle. It hurt almost as bad as it had when there'd still been a bullet stuck in it.

"Come on, come on, let's *go*!" Holt urged. He was already kickin' his horse up into a gallop, and I followed suit, grindin' my teeth against the pain in my thigh as it jostled against the mule's side.

"Hey!" someone shouted behind us. "Hey! Stop in the name of the law! Stop, I say!"

But the voice fell behind quick, drowned in the noise of our thunderin' hooves as we hauled ass toward the edge of town.

A rifle cracked, and I ducked low over the mule's neck, Holt and I both jerkin' our mounts quick around the nearest corner. Then there was empty street ahead of us, a wide stretch of dirt road, and I supposed maybe my luck was good enough at least to have us leavin' early enough in the mornin' to give us a clear path outta town.

We raced side by side, Holt and I, the town blurrin' by around us, until we broke out clear into the wild desert and left Bravebank behind in a cloud of dust.

We spent the rest of the day runnin'.

Well, runnin' and then takin' turns doublin' back to make sure we weren't bein' followed. And then coverin' our tracks.

By the time the sun was dippin' low to the horizon, we still hadn't caught any sign of pursuit.

"I think we're clear," Holt said, comin' back from checkin' our trail again.

"Think so," I agreed. Surprisin', considerin' we'd left three dead men in our wake. But maybe the sheriff of Bravebank weren't too fond of Nan's men, either, no matter their *understandin'*.

We looked for a place to camp for the night then, and settled on a little patch of dirt in between some big boulders. It weren't too tight, so we could get out in a hurry if we needed, but the bulk of the rocks would also hide our silhouettes and those of our mounts from any casual passersby. We were still in the valley, the land mostly flat, spotted with scraggly bush, mesquite trees and tall cacti. Two men and two horses woulda stood out pretty clear, even in a dark night.

On account of the fact we didn't want to be found, this spot seemed the best we could manage given the circumstances. We made a cold camp, too. No fire. The blaze woulda been a beacon fer all sorts of unwanted attention from all sorts of vultures.

It wasn't until we'd unsaddled, hobbled our mounts, and rolled out our bedrolls that Holt finally said what I'd known was on his mind all day.

"Ten thousand!" he blurted. "Christ, Van. Thought I raised you smarter than that! This ain't a game of cards, kid. You can't bluff yer way outta this one. Where you gonna get that kind of money? And how do ya know they have yer sister, anyway?"

The fingers of my right hand went to my pocket where I'd tucked the necklace. There was an engravin' on the back, just as Nan's man had said. I'd studied it good and hard while Holt had been off scoutin'.

And it *was* mighty familiar. Pa had given it to Ethelyn for her tenth birthday, just weeks before he'd been killed. It was the most expensive thing she'd ever owned, and she'd worn it every day. Even slept in it.

"They have her," I said. "Renneker said so. And I saw it on Nan's face when I offered her money. And ... that bastard in the saloon had her necklace."

Holt rolled his eyes and scoffed. "That ain't proof, kid. Renneker weren't no lieutenant. And with what you did to him, well, any man woulda said anything to end it. Of course Nan ain't gonna say no to money, not if yer stupid enough to offer it to her. And that necklace ... yer sister coulda pawned it off fer a hot meal, fer all you know."

"They have her," I snapped, glarin' at him through the darkenin' twilight. The sun had dropped below the horizon now, and the moon was only a thin crescent creepin' up to take its place, but it was more than enough to see by. I saw his hard, level gaze, silvered by dusk, and his mouth turn down in disagreement. "They have her," I repeated, but more for myself than fer him. He didn't understand.

If Nine-Fingered Nan didn't have her, I'd have to go back to bidin' my time, waitin' fer another clue to follow. And I'd already spent nine years doin' that. This was the best, most solid lead I'd had yet by far.

Whether or not it turned out to be real, I'd never be able to live with myself if I didn't pursue it.

"Fine," Holt spat at last. "Then where you gonna get that kind of money? Nan ain't gonna give her to you without it, and I ain't sure she's gonna give her to you *with* it."

"I'll get it," I grumbled. I didn't think now was exactly the time to tell him I needed thirty-five thousand, not ten thousand, or that I had not the faintest idea how I was gonna get that thirty-five thousand. "And I won't be leavin' there without Ethelyn, one way or another."

Holt grumbled then, and shook his head. "You ain't gonna be leavin' there at all, at this rate. Yer gonna end up dead. You and yer sister both, if they've got her."

I eased down to the dusty ground, my left leg stretched out straight in front of me, and leaned back against my saddle. "Maybe," I admitted. But at least she'd know I hadn't abandoned her. I'd come back fer her, just like I'd promised.

"Hell, I thought you was dead already when you didn't come back to Grave Gulch!" Holt said. "Looked fer you fer weeks. Thought I was seein' a ghost when I walked into that Bravebank saloon."

"Near enough," I said. I fished in my saddle bag for the laudanum. My head was still throbbin' from my overindulgence in whiskey the night before and a day in the sun. My whole body ached from the hard ridin', my thigh on fire again.

I was sweatin', but shiverin' too. I didn't think that was too good. "How'd you manage to find me, anyway?"

He shrugged. "Luck. Like I said, I been searchin' fer you fer weeks. Goin' anywhere people said Nan had business. Bravebank happened to be my next stop. Figured if you wasn't there, least I'd probably be able to rustle up a score of some kind. That saloon ... she owns it, ya know."

"I didn't know that." But it made sense, now, lookin' back. Her man bein' there, the bartender gettin' scarce this mornin', the understandin' with the local sheriff....

I took a rather large swig of the medicine.

Holt was watchin' me, his gray brows low over those suspicious blue eyes. "What's that?"

"Medicine," I croaked, and shuddered at the bitterness of it. I corked it and shoved it back into my bag.

"Laudanum?" he asked. "How long you been on that stuff?"

I closed my eyes and leaned my head back on the saddle. "Not long."

He grunted, clearly not believin' me. "I got whiskey. You take that next time instead, ya hear?"

I didn't answer. I didn't think there was any amount of whiskey that could take away the pain I was feelin' right now. Felt like needles stabbin' into my skin where the metal started, hookin' the flesh, burnin'. The pain went down deep into the muscle, to the bone where it'd been sawed off. It throbbed. And sometimes I swore I could still feel my natural leg there down below, but of course that was a lie. An ugly lie my mind told my body, a phantom hope that was shattered over and over again every time I tried to move it.

The doctor had said the metal leg had advantages. Like some medicines built into it to help me heal. I didn't understand any of it, but I was hopin' now that was true. I was gonna need all the help I could get, 'specially judgin' from the way I was feelin' right now.

Maybe I shoulda asked the kid to grab me the schematic of the leg along with my guns. The doctor had mentioned he was gonna give me such a thing when it was time fer me to be on my way. Along with even more instructions. But I hadn't waited around fer those, and now I was kinda wishin' I had.

"What happened to yer horse?" Holt asked abruptly.

A pang of regret hit me. I'd really liked that horse. "Shot dead."

I heard him sigh. "Nan?"

"Yeah."

"And yer limp? That curtesy of the ol' hag, too?"

I smiled. Smiled like a mad person and opened my eyes, sittin' up. "Yeah. More than that, too." I rolled up my left pant leg to expose the metal rods that made up my lower leg now and the gears that made up my knee.

Holt stepped backward at the sight of it and spat a string of curses, his hand droppin' down to his gun like maybe he thought I was some kind of abomination.

Maybe I was.

Then he looked back to my face, his eyes wide and face paler than I'd ever seen it. "What in the Devil is that?" he hissed.

"My new leg." I covered it up again and resumed my reclined position on my saddle.

"Wha ... what ... *how?*"

I shook my head and shrugged. "I dunno. Nan shot my horse, then shot me in the leg. She woulda killed me outright then, but I made a deal she liked, and she let me live. Fer a little while longer, at least. I tried to make it to Bravebank. Couldn't. I woulda died in the desert, but this doctor found me. This doctor ... he ain't from around here. He said my leg was dead, so he sawed it off. Then ... gave me this one. Said it has *advantages*."

Holt still stared, mouth open, hand restin' on his gun. "*Advantages?*"

"Yeah. That's what he said. I ain't found no advantages to it yet, though. All it is, is trouble. And pain."

A long silence stretched into the night. I waited for him to comprehend, if he could. I wasn't sure I did, still. And I'd had the damn thing for weeks now.

"Is it … is it Old World tech?" he asked slowly.

"I think so."

"And he just … he just gave it to you? Fer free?"

"Like I said, he ain't from around here." Though he'd probably at least expected me to repay him and his family with kindness and respect. I hadn't even done that much. My eyes shifted to the mule, standin' quiet and tired to my right. I wondered if Radley suspected I wasn't comin' back yet. I wondered if he regretted givin' me back my guns yet.

I wondered if there were posters of my face up in Bravebank yet.

I closed my eyes against the wash of guilt. I'd make it right, someday. After I got Ethelyn back, I'd atone for all my sins. It was a promise I'd made myself a long time ago.

It helped me sleep at night.

Holt muttered more curses. "Christ, kid. I told ya. I told ya! Never shoulda started down this road. Yer gonna get yerself killed."

That was a very real possibility, sure. No arguin' that.

So I didn't argue.

Instead I reached back and pulled my hat down over my face, the hat that had come from the doctor, too, easin' into the warm embrace of the laudanum as it finally soaked into my blood and took the edge off the hurt.

Maybe this road only led to my death … or maybe it finally led me to Ethelyn.

Either way, I supposed I'd be atonin' fer my sins one way or another soon enough.

Hoofbeats woke me, fast and loud.

I sat up with gun in hand still blinkin', groggy from the opium. Damnit, I'd taken too much of that, too. It took a minute to remember where I was, what had happened, and by that time Holt was already crouched up against one of the boulders, guns drawn.

Our mounts were still in place, still hobbled, though both of 'em now had their heads up and ears pricked in the direction of the oncoming hooves, keen on seein' who of their kind might be approachin'.

I scrambled to join Holt behind the nearest boulder, wincin' as I dragged that confounded metal leg behind me. "Who is it? Can you see?"

He peeked beyond the edge of the rock, then shook his head. "Nah."

"The law?"

He gave me a look that said I should know better. "The law wouldn't come chargin' in here like a herd a' terrified cattle. They'd come in slow and quiet, try an' catch us asleep."

I frowned, concern tightenin' in my belly. "Who, then? And how'd they find us?"

"I don't know. And I don't know that they're after us, yet. They might not know we're here."

"Sounds like they're headed right for us," I whispered.

"Maybe. Just stay quiet. Don't fire till we know fer sure, understand?"

I nodded, but he didn't have to tell me. Gun shots were louder than thunder out here. They'd draw more trouble than a fire even, in the end.

I glanced to the mule again. He looked awfully eager about these new arrivals. I hoped he wouldn't try and run off to join 'em with those hobbles still on, or I'd be out another mount. I also hoped he wouldn't call out to 'em. *Stay quiet*, I urged him silently. *Please don't—*

He opened his mouth and let out a terrible warblin' sound, some bastard cross between a bray and a whinny that properly reflected his unnatural heritage.

I flinched.

Beside me, Holt swore a blue streak. "Goddamnit, Van—"

"I didn't have a choice," I hissed. "It was the mule or walk!"

I wasn't sure the riders out there in the dark had heard it, anyway, not over the sound of so many gallopin' hooves. Who was stupid enough to race through the desert like that in the night, makin' so much noise?

Either stupid ... or good enough and mean enough they don't have to care.

My mouth went dry at the thought. I pulled my second gun from its holster, the damaged one. I didn't wanna have to use it and risk it explodin' in my hand, but maybe just the presence of it would be enough.

We waited.

They came straight for us, all right. Maybe they'd heard the mule call out, maybe they hadn't. But they came straight for the boulders without slowin' down, and even if they couldn't see us, there weren't no way they didn't see those loomin' rocks. They veered around 'em at the last second, and fer a heartbeat I thought they'd ride on by.

But they didn't.

They circled round.

And round and round.

The damn mule gave another bastardized whinny, and if they hadn't heard it before, they'd heard it now. I couldn't tell how many there were, but they sure outnumbered us.

Their circlin' kicked up a lot of dust that thickened the air and clouded the once-clear moonlight. I squinted my eyes against it and coughed, and next to me, Holt readied a few quick-change cylinders.

"Van Delano!" one of 'em shouted, a woman, and my stomach clenched.

Through the dim, murky moonlight, Holt looked to me sharply.

"We know you're in there! And that no good ol' cur Haggerty too! Ain't no one passes through Nan's land without her knowin'."

I looked to Holt. The expression on his face then couldn'ta been more clear:

You gone and got us both killed, kid.

"She knows about yer mess in Bravebank, too," the woman shouted. "You killed three of her men, Delano. She really ain't happy about that. That weren't part of the deal!"

This time I glared at Holt, well sure he knew exactly what I meant: *I told you not to shoot those men!*

He grunted in reply and shoved the pre-loaded cylinders back into his belt.

I didn't bother to shout back that it hadn't been me who'd killed those men at all. It didn't matter to Nan who had pulled the trigger. It only mattered that I had been there, and the one who had murdered her men was an associate of mine. That was enough.

"Such things got consequences, Delano! Nan ain't gonna stand fer that! From now on, you get an itchin' to kill someone, you kill someone Nan wants dead, ya hear? In fact, from now on, till yer debt is paid up, you don't so much as spit 'less Nan tells ya to, understand?"

I ignored Holt's look this time, though I could feel his stare burn hot as a brand into the side of my face. But I didn't need his reprimandin'. I'd known what I was gettin' myself into the day I'd ridden away from Grave Gulch to confront Nan the first time.

"We'll be watchin' you, Delano. Don't think we won't be. Nan's got eyes and ears all over this country. Ain't nowhere far enough you can run now."

"I ain't runnin'!" I barked, then coughed again from all the dust.

The bastards out there were still circlin'.

Like vultures.

"Glad to hear it," the woman said. She, at least, was stationary, planted on the other side of the rock Holt and I crouched behind. "In that case, you just keep yerself outta trouble till Nan calls upon you, got it? And remember ... you lay a finger on any more of her men ... the deal's off. And more than that, we'll be comin' fer yer head."

I said nothin'. I didn't need to.

An object sailed through the swirlin' dust and thumped to the rocky ground near our boots. Nan's men—and at least one woman—wheeled their horses and took off with a few partin' yells.

Holt and I didn't move, not even as the whoopin' and hollerin' and hoofbeats faded.

It wasn't until the night had fallen silent again, and my damn mule let out another lonely whinny, that Holt shoved his revolvers back into their holsters and swore again. Loudly.

I did the same. Well, I holstered my guns. And I swore, but my swearin' was silent. I threw an arm over my nose and mouth to breathe through the dusty air and reached out to pick up the thing they'd thrown at us. It was a square of burlap tied with twine.

I checked on Holt, but he'd wandered back over to his bedroll and was rummagin' around in his saddlebags, still mutterin' and grumblin' and shakin' his head.

I untied the twine, and realized then that my fingers were wet. Frownin', I held them up to the dusty moonlight.

Blood.

My breath hitched. I stared down at the folded burlap, and pulled back the layers with tremblin' hands. Fold by fold, the dread crawled up my throat to choke me, until my breath was harsh and ragged, and then stopped, and I couldn't breathe at all.

Fingers. Three fingers.

A woman's three fingers.

Some kind of noise escaped me.

There was a note tucked in alongside the fingers, marred with blood, the ink smeared. I plucked it out and blinked hard, tryin' to clear the black spots dancin' in my vision. I read the words without seein' 'em, then read 'em over and over again until their meanin' finally sunk in.

"Careful, boy. There's plenty more where this came from."

My hands shook violently. I dropped the bloody bundle back to the dirt.

"Van?"

I looked up to see Holt standin' near. His eyes went to the burlap square. The severed fingers. "Holy Mother," he breathed.

I hardly heard him. There was a rushin' in my ears soundin' like a freight train. "I ... I ain't..." I stopped and swallowed. "I ain't gonna be her errand boy."

Holt cleared his throat. "Van—"

"I'm gettin' Ethelyn back. *Right. Now.*"

"Van, ya heard what they just said! If you try an—"

"I'll get Nan the damn money," I growled. "I'll get the money and I'll buy her back outright. And then I'm gonna even the score." I pushed myself to my feet, the rage singin' hot through my limbs. "I'm gonna put a bullet right between the eyes of that old hag."

"Van, I know yer upset—"

I shoved past him and limped to my own bedroll; started gettin' my stuff ready to ride.

He followed me. "Kid, don't do this again. Last time you stormed off in a rage Nan killed yer horse and nearly killed you. Remember? It weren't even that long ago! You got a metal leg now, fer Chrissakes! You need to stop and cool down, *think*!"

"I'm thinkin'," I spat. And I was. I was thinkin' of all the ways I was gonna lay the hurt on ol' Nine-Fingered Nan, and any of her cronies who got in my way.

"And where you gonna get that kind a' money, anyway? Ten thousand is gonna take time, you gotta plan—"

"It ain't ten thousand," I said. "It's thirty-five thousand."

"Thirty-five ... *thirty-five thousand*?! Van Jensen Delano, you have certifiably lost yer goddamn mind! No. No way. Where you gonna find that kinda currency?"

I already knew. I'd already decided. I'd done a lotta bad things in my life, had a lotta sins to atone fer, but there were still a few things I hadn't done. There was still a line I'd refused to cross.

Until now.

"I'm gonna rob a bank," I said.

VIII

A BLESSING OR A CURSE

That got Holt's attention.

He'd been itchin' to rob a bank fer years, sayin' we could stop sleepin' in the dirt and livin' day to day if we just got one big score.

'Cept he always forgot he'd told me once that he and Pa and the others they'd run with when they were young and stupid had robbed a bank.

More than one, in fact.

And it seemed to me, from the stories Holt told, one score was never enough, no matter how big. There would always be "just one more job" on the horizon. And no matter how much you robbed, no matter how far you ran, you just couldn't reach that horizon.

You didn't stop till you took a long drop on a short rope ... or till you took a shotgun blast to the face from some old acquaintance who didn't appreciate the fact you'd tried to go straight.

"A ... a bank?" Holt repeated.

"That's right." I shoved thoughts of Pa outta my mind. There wasn't nothin' I could do fer him anymore. But Ethelyn ... I still had a chance to save Ethelyn. I buckled up my saddlebags and hefted my saddle, limpin' over to the mule, who nickered at me. I scowled at him. He'd caused enough trouble fer me already. "Ain't that what you always wanted?"

"Well ... yeah."

At least the man was bein' honest.

"But Van ... not like this. We hit a bank now and all that money'll go to Nan."

I shook my head. "I'm only usin' the money to get the meetin'. Then I'm gonna kill her. And then we can keep the money fer all I care. Long as I have my sister." I tossed the blanket onto the mule's back, then the saddle, and cinched it up.

"Ya can't spend money when yer dead, kid. And havin' yer sister back won't matter if yer dead, neither."

I whirled to face him. "And what else am I supposed to do?" I demanded. "Keep livin' like this? Give up on her? Leave her to be sold off to some slaver overseas?" I waved at the piece of burlap still on the ground and the three severed fingers, turnin' gray now. "Look what Nan did! I ain't leavin' Ethelyn with that monster a day longer than I have to. So you can do what you want. But I'm gonna go rob a bank and get myself thirty-five thousand dollars. And if I happen to get more than that, I'll keep it, sure. Unless I'm dead, in which case, you just keep it all fer yerself. That's what you want most of all anyway, ain't it?"

Holt's expression soured, but he stayed silent. He just stood there starin' at me, hands planted on his hips right above the grips of his guns.

I turned away from him then, undoin' the hobbles and puttin' on the bridle. Then I rolled up my bed mat in a hurry and tied it to the back of my saddle with more force than necessary. I hauled myself up onto the back of that mule with effort and settled my seat, glarin' down at Holt, who still hadn't said a word.

"Well?" I prompted. "You comin' or what?"

He frowned and sighed heavily. Then scuffed the toe of one boot into the dirt. "Which bank?"

"I dunno yet," I snapped.

"You honestly think you could pull off a bank job of that size all by yer lonesome?"

I kept his level stare, but swallowed. "If I had to." Truth be told, I didn't want to have to. But I was also too angry at the moment to admit that.

He grunted in response and shook his head. "Christ, kid. Fine. Wait up a minute, I'll saddle up."

"Yeah well hurry up," I growled. "I want that money by sundown tomorrow."

Holt let out a noise that made it clear he didn't think there was a chance in Hell we'd have that money by sundown tomorrow. "Wish you woulda had this kinda enthusiasm for robbin' a bank a long time ago," he muttered as he threw the saddle on his black gelding. "Maybe if you had, we wouldn't be where we are now."

"Yeah, you're right. We'd be hanged already."

He tossed a glare at me over his shoulder. "And if you try and rush this job, kid, we'll end up hanged now. Fer sure."

"I ain't gonna rush it."

"Sounds to me like you are." He bridled his horse, checked his saddlebags, and mounted up, gatherin' the reins as he pulled the gelding around to face me. "Robbin' banks takes careful plannin'. Took us weeks sometimes to set everythin' up, and there was lots of us."

"We're gonna do it with two," I said, and I pulled my own mount around and gave him a kick, sendin' him out between the boulders and into the cool desert night at a lope.

Holt caught up to me and matched the mule's pace.

"And we got from here to Blessing to plan it."

"Blessing, huh? That where you wanna pull this job?"

"Yeah." I'd just decided that, too. But it made sense. It was north of where Nine-Fingered Nan had her strongest influence, and was one of the richest towns in the territory, owin' to the massive cache of Old World metal some miners had found buried there awhile back. Thus the town's name. Some considered such a stash to be a blessin'.

Others, namely those enslaved by the metal merchants and made to go down into the ruins to gather the stuff, and those who often got murdered so someone else could steal their share of the stuff, considered it to be a curse.

But the town of Blessing had a bank. And the bank of Blessing held a lot of rich people's money. It'd take the rest of the night and a good part of tomorrow to get there, but if any town within a day's ride would have the thirty-five thousand I needed, it'd be that one.

Holt was quiet a minute as he contemplated. "Makes sense, I guess," he finally agreed. "But the security there is gonna be tough. Those metal barons don't like partin' with their coin. Not even to give it to a bank. It'll be locked up tight and guarded well."

"Yeah," I said again. I knew that, too. "That's why I have you. You said you'd done this kinda thing before. So come on. What's yer plan?"

Holt laughed then and shook his head, adjustin' his hat as we rode along under the moon, weavin' through the brush and cacti. "I can't make a plan till I see the place, kid. And anyway, this is yer rodeo. Or maybe yer funeral. You should take point on this one."

I grunted. He was probably right. But all I could think of then was those three severed fingers, and the necklace still tucked in my pocket, and Ethelyn still in the clutches of the monster Nine-Fingered Nan and her demon minions.

Disfigured ... and who knew what else.

I kicked the mule on faster, ignorin' the pain that was steadily buildin' again in my left thigh and the rocks that littered the path ahead, threatenin' to trip up my mule. To Hell with the pain. To Hell with the metal leg. To Hell with Holt and his doubts, and to Hell with Nan and her threats.

I was gonna get the money. And I was gonna meet with Nan. And I was gonna get Ethelyn back and kill Nan and as many of her people as I could, and then we were gonna run, Ethelyn and I.

Together. Far, far away. Maybe even all the way to the East Republic. And start over again.

The town of Blessing was gonna be my blessing, all right.

And I was gonna be its curse.

We plodded into Blessing in the afternoon the next day, hot and sore and tired, and hungry and thirsty, too. Holt was proper mad by then, 'cause I hadn't let us stop to rest or eat anythin' outside of what was absolutely necessary to not kill the horses.

After all, I surely didn't want to be stuck in the middle of the desert with no horse again.

I'd told him he could stop and rest and do whatever he liked if he wanted, but I was gonna get to Blessing before nightfall the next day.

He'd thought about stoppin' without me, I could tell, but in the end he'd kept up, though with great reluctance and a whole lotta curses. Most of 'em aimed at me.

I'd ignored him and rode on, thinkin' only of that money.

Thinkin' of how in the hell I was gonna get that money.

But by afternoon, when we finally made the turn and went under the archway of patchwork metal that marked the town's main entrance, my thoughts were all runnin' together, and I wasn't really thinkin' much at all anymore, 'cept for about how much I wanted some food and drink. And sleep.

The mule's hooves were draggin' now, his head sunk low and ears droopin'. He was lathered up and breathin' hard, and I felt a little bad for pushin' him so much.

But we were here now.

I'd let him rest up and cool down, get him some good quality feed. He deserved that much.

And me and Holt, we deserved somethin' too, while we were makin' up this plan fer the robbery. I urged the mule up the main street toward the nearest saloon and took note of the townsfolk starin' ... and those who didn't stare. Blessing was a busy place, sure enough.

The street was wide, but crowded enough to make it slow goin' even if we weren't spent and tired. Horses and carts and loaded wagons of all kinds clogged the way, and foot traffic, too. And here and there on the street corners perched a lawman or two, their stars rough-hewn and hammered outta rusted scrap.

Well, there weren't really no *official* lawmen out here in the Western Territories, but each town generally had its version of 'em, fer better or worse. Whether or not the so-called lawmen upheld the law or just took advantage of it, though, was always a gamble.

I studied these particular lawmen of Blessing as we passed 'em by, but didn't look too long. Lookin' too long at anyone in these parts was a good way to get yerself a bullet in the gut.

They watched Holt and I hard enough in return, fer certain, which didn't bode well fer the chances of our robbery bein' a success. I cursed my shit luck again as the saloon came into view. Of course. The town with all the money had the lawdogs who actually wanted to uphold the law.

But then ... maybe I could find a way to convince them to look the other way. This town liked money, after all. Maybe these lawmen wanted more of it.

I stopped the mule outside of the saloon; the wooden one. Down the street a ways I saw another one, but that one was made outta metal, gleamin' in the sun like some sort of unnatural jewel. My left thigh flared, as if the metal attached to it could sense its long-lost cousin down the road.

I scowled at both of 'em. I'd never liked much made outta metal. Not much except my guns and the lead they fired. In my experience, metal was meant to kill.

Not to make a roof over your head.

Or a leg for walkin'.

The people comin' outta the metal saloon looked different, too. Their clothes were fancier and less full of dirt, and the chains of pocket watches glinted on their breasts. And the women on the arms of such men didn't look like prostitutes, neither. They were all dressed up in frills and lace and bustles. There were lawmen posted at the door of that one, too, rifles already in their hands as if they were expectin' some kind of trouble.

Holt was lookin' at it too as he pulled his gelding up next to me. "Now what do you suppose that is?"

I tore my eyes away from the thing and shrugged. "I dunno. A place we don't belong, fer sure."

"I'd say."

I took a breath and eased myself down outta the saddle, keepin' myself upright mostly by my grip on the mule's stiff mane. I closed my eyes and took a minute again to gather myself.

"Come on, kid," Holt said, suddenly at my elbow. "You look like death. Let's get you some whiskey."

I nodded mutely and pulled the crutch from the rifle scabbard. It didn't matter now what people thought of it; I had Holt to back me up. And anyway, after such a long ride, I wouldn'ta been able to walk straight—or at all—without it if my life depended on it.

I glanced around at the busy street again, and at the lawmen at the nearest corner, and hoped my life wouldn't depend on it.

We tied our mounts at the hitchin' post and walked on in.

Well, Holt walked. I limped and hobbled, every bone achin'.

We found a place at the bar with only a few curious looks our way. Most folk didn't seem to care, though. Not about my limp and my crutch, nor about the state of ourselves, sweaty and dusty from the long hours in the saddle.

To my surprise, the barkeeper was a woman. Tall and slender, her complexion a warm, mellow brown, she slid our way with a grace like no other barkeep I'd ever seen. Not surprisin', since she was the only woman barkeep I'd ever seen.

"What'll it be, boys?"

"Whiskey," Holt answered, diggin' in his pockets for some coin.

"Hrmm." She looked at him, then at me, her dark eyes sweepin' me up and down, then glancin' to the crutch I'd leaned up against the bar's edge. I tensed on my stool, but she only inclined her head in my direction. "I can see that one needs the medicinal variety. But what about you?" She swung her gaze back to Holt. "You paying for the same, or you just wanna get drunk quick?"

Holt glanced at me, then sighed. "Just give me the same." He fished out more coin and tossed it to the counter.

She nodded and swept the money away with one hand, the other hand procurin' two shot glasses, which she set in front of us. Then she was pourin', and I found myself mesmerized by the preciseness of it, how she spilled not a drop.

But maybe that was just the exhaustion and the pain workin'.

"You boys gonna stay long?" she asked, pushin' the full glasses toward us. "Need rooms for the night? I got some."

I shifted on my stool. So she was the barkeep and the saloon keeper, too.

"Depends on how much," Holt said. He brought the glass up to his nose and sniffed, and his thick gray brows lifted.

I glanced down to my own full glass. Holt was mighty picky about his whiskey. This musta been good stuff, indeed. I'd have to enjoy it, then. Wouldn't be able to afford any more of it.

The woman watched him, her mouth quirked in amusement. "Half dollar a night, each."

Holt pursed his lips, paused, then swallowed back his drink.

"We'll take two," I answered for him. My hopes of havin' the thirty-five thousand by sundown had been checked by the sheer number of people in this town.

And the sheer number of lawmen in this town.

Holt was right, damn him. This was gonna take more careful plannin' than I'd wanted. Better to hole up for the night, get some rest, and have a place where we could discuss a strategy without no other nosey eyes and ears around us.

And anyway, we needed our mounts fresh for the job, too, so they could get us outta here real quick once it was all done.

I reached into the pouch on my belt and gave her the coin myself this time. Ol' drunk Jake's money was comin' in handy, all right.

She swept that away too and smiled at me. "How about baths? Or girls? Though I have to insist, if you want any of my girls, you're gonna have to bathe first. We have standards here, you know. Maybe not as high as the Iron Jewel's standards, but we do have 'em." She gave a nod as if to motion down the street, and with a name like *Iron Jewel*, I guessed she probably meant that metal monstrosity of a saloon that squatted down the road.

Self-consciously, I looked down at myself. I supposed I probably did look a mess, and Holt weren't much better. But he always had some scraggly mess of beard on his chin, and dirt rubbed into all the creases of his skin. Me, I usually preferred to be clean-shaven and mostly washed. A consequence of growin' up with a roof over my head and a wash basin at my disposal, I suppose.

Though neither myself nor my clothes had had a good cleanin' since the Sunday before I'd left Dr. Balogh's homestead.

I cleared my throat and swallowed my whiskey, then closed my eyes to appreciate it. It was the good stuff, all right.

"We're all right fer now," Holt said.

"If you say so," the woman said. "But if you change your minds, you know where to find me." She smiled again. "Feel free to help yourselves to the spread at the back." She nodded toward the back of the central room, where a long table was set with a bigger variety of food than I'd ever seen, too.

Seemed Blessing was full of surprises.

My stomach growled.

"If you want anything special, you come see me. I got a chef who can make almost anything from any region. You get a hankering for anything specific, I can get it made for you."

"For a price," Holt muttered.

Her smile widened to show white teeth. "Of course, darling. Everything comes at a price in Blessing. But it's the same everywhere else too, really, ain't it?"

"I guess."

"Most certainly it is. Now, I'll have Ginger make up your rooms for you. They'll be upstairs, numbers five and six. You boys make yourselves at home here in the meantime, but don't cause no trouble." She folded her hands on the bartop then and leaned forward, as if she were gonna tell us a secret.

I leaned toward her instinctively, catchin' a whiff of her perfume.

"They call me Seven Knives Sally around here," she told us, lookin' at us each long and hard. "I bet you can guess why that is. And I bet you can also guess why I'm still running this place, despite the fact there's a mighty lot of greedy bastards out there who'd love to take it from me."

Her gaze shifted over my shoulder, and I twisted on my stool with my hand halfway to my gun, expectin' to find someone unfriendly comin' up behind me. But there was no one.

In fact, now that I took the time to look around this place a little better, I noticed it was clean and well-kept, and the patronage less rowdy and raucous than what could be found in most other saloons I'd visited.

I turned back to Seven Knives Sally and lifted an eyebrow. "Awful nice place you have here," I said.

"Yes," she agreed. "And I plan to keep that way. So you two will be causing no trouble, ain't that right?"

"Of course, ma'am," Holt said, all sugar, tippin' his hat to her. "Wouldn't dream of it."

"Glad we have an understanding," Sally said. She started to slide away, to help the next set of thirsty customers down at the end of the bar.

"Wait," I spoke up, stoppin' her in mid-step, "we're needin' a place to stable our horses. Someplace good."

She flashed me that white smile again. "Why of course. Best horse care is Abbott's Livery. Head north two blocks, then west three blocks and you'll run right into it. Tell him I sent you."

And then she left us.

Holt watched after her, then exhaled a long breath and shook his head. "Whew-boy!" He gazed down into his empty whiskey glass. "I'm kinda startin' to like this town."

I scowled at him. "Well don't. We ain't stayin' long."

"Right." He eased off his stool. "You stay here. I'll bring ya some food, see if we can't get the color back in yer face."

He headed off toward the back table, and I glanced to my reflection in the large oval mirror behind the bar. It was etched with gilded, flowin' letters that spelled out the name of this place—Seven Knives, right enough—but between all the shiny flourishes I could see myself.

And he was right. And so was Seven Knives Sally.

I looked like death.

The sun was settin', and I was stretched out on a bed in the upstairs of the Seven Knives saloon. It was a nice bed, too. I leaned back into the pillows, feelin' the effects of a full stomach, that whiskey—it was some-thin' special, all right—and the laudanum I'd sipped soon as Holt had left.

He'd gone to take our mounts to the stable and to do some scoutin' of the town, he'd said. We'd learned the bank weren't too far from the Seven Knives, just a few blocks north. Holt had insisted on walkin' by it, maybe goin' inside it, checkin' to see the specifics of its layout and security.

At first I'd wanted to go with him, but he'd insisted I stay here and rest up, get my strength back, 'cause we were surely gonna need every bit of our wits to pull off this job.

Now, as I marinated in the brief comfort provided by the food and whiskey and opium, I saw the wisdom in that decision. My thigh was finally startin' to feel a little better, and the rest of me, too.

I'd stopped shiverin' and sweatin'. And sure, got some color back, too.

The room was decent; the wallpaper only a little faded and a little ripped in places, only one bed post missin'. Seven Knives Sally had a nice place, indeed.

I looked down to my left boot. The foot I couldn't feel. With my pants and the shoe, you couldn't tell that leg weren't natural. It looked completely normal from the outside. I stared at that boot and tried to move that foot.

I could hear the gears and pistons of the metal leg movin' and turnin'. And my boot twitched.

I tried to bend my left knee. Well, it weren't really *mine* no more. It was the machine's knee. But I tried to bend it, anyway.

There was more whirrin'. And then the leg jerked.

I rolled my eyes and sighed, leanin' my head back against the pillows. *Just walk normal*, Dr. Balogh had said. Sure. That was workin' out real fine, all right.

A soft knock sounded at the door and I bolted upright, hand goin' to my gun. "Who is it?"

"It's Ginger, love. May I come in?"

Ginger. The older woman Seven Knives Sally employed to keep the place tidy. I swept a gaze around the room to be sure nothin' incriminatin' had been left out in the open—but then, we hadn't robbed the bank yet —and I had precious little to my name anymore. "Sure," I said warily.

I still couldn't fathom why Ginger'd be payin' me a social call.

I kept my right hand near my holster as she swept open the door and paraded into the room, a wooden tray balanced on one hand. She came straight to the bedside and set something down on the night table.

Another shot glass of whiskey.

I lifted my eyes to her in question. "I didn't order—"

"Oh I know, love." She turned and smiled at me over her shoulder, givin' me a wink. "It's on the house. Sally says so herself." She lowered her voice, though it was still a great deal louder than a whisper. "I think she might fancy you." Her round figure sashayed toward the door, but drew up short just before passin' through it. "Oh, and I'm supposed to ask if you want us to call a doctor? We know a real good one."

"No. No, I don't need a doctor."

She lifted one sculpted, painted eyebrow and tilted her head to the side. A few of her graying curls fell against her face. "You sure, now?" She looked to the crutch I had propped up against the wall and then at my left leg. "You get shot? That can fester, you know. Better to get it looked at then die later from infection! I should know. My cousin Louisa, her good friend—"

"I'm fine," I blurted. Then, seein' her aghast expression at bein' so rudely interrupted, sighed. "I already got it looked at by a doctor. It's fixed up." *In a matter of speakin', anyway.* "Just gotta heal now. It takes some time."

Her expression softened. "I understand. Well, glad to hear it. We don't like folk dyin' under our roof, if you know what I mean."

I didn't.

She gave me a nod. "G'night, mister. Remember, you change your mind about a bath or some women—or men, mind you, we gots those, too—just go downstairs and tell me or Sally, yeah?"

"I'll remember."

"Good." And with that, she slipped out and shut the door behind her.

I looked down to the whiskey on the night table. Damn. Maybe at another time in my life I woulda gone downstairs right away and shown Sally some appreciation for her kindness. Woulda at least gone down to see if Ginger was right ... find out if Sally really did fancy me.

But not now. Not this time.

There were too many other things needin' my attention right now.

Like the Bank of Blessing.

And thirty-five thousand dollars.

And Ethelyn.

The sight of those three severed fingers flashed into my mind again and I squeezed my eyes shut, rubbin' at 'em like maybe I could scrub that memory away. Then I groaned and opened my eyes again.

I took the whiskey and pushed myself off the bed, limpin' carefully to the window. I opened it to let in the fresh air, relishin' the fact this air weren't full of dust like all the towns further south.

The sun had sunk low, and the buildin's on the street below threw out long shadows over all the people still bustlin' about, goin' about their business.

I wondered if this town ever really slept.

My eyes went north, toward the so-called Iron Jewel, and I sipped at the whiskey, savorin' it this time. Just beyond that somewhere was the bank.

I was feelin' pretty confident now that by the time Holt came back this evenin', he would have some kind of a plan in place.

We'd have the money by this time tomorrow and be outta here, well on our way back to Bravebank to arrange the meetin' with Nan.

And get Ethelyn back.

I was about to turn away from the window and get back to the comfort of the bed when a commotion broke out on the street below. I stepped over again to see what was goin' on.

A group of lawmen on horseback were clearin' the streets, trottin' up fast and nearly runnin' over a few folk. Shouts of offense and indignation welled in their wake, but they drew up short in front of the

Seven Knives, right below my window. They milled about restlessly, scannin' the crowds nearby, who were quickly dispersin'.

My right hand drifted down to my gun, restin' easy.

The group below looked almost like a posse. And I didn't much like posses. Especially when they were comin' after me. I wasn't sure who this group was after, exactly, but they were surely after someone. I didn't think they could be after me or Holt, but it was always better to be safe than dead.

I eased my pistol a little out of the holster, quietly and carefully pullin' the hammer back.

"Where is she?" one of the men in the posse bellowed, his voice echoin' out across the street. "I know one of you saw where she went! Failure to aid us is a crime, you remember that! Speak up now or face the justice of the law!"

Oh. *She.* I eased the hammer down again and settled my gun back into leather.

Wait. She?

"*Where is she?*" the lawman demanded again. But now there was hardly anyone left in the street to hear him. They'd all scattered at the sign of trouble.

The doors to the Seven Knives opened, and I saw Sally herself exit the saloon and calmly walk down the front steps to face the group of lawmen. They all turned their horses to face her. In turn, she put her hands on her hips and shook her head. "Now, now, gentlemen," she scolded. "Pray tell, why must you make such a ruckus in front of my saloon?"

"We're looking for a slave that run off," the lawman snapped. "One of Baron Whittaker's. Young woman. Red hair. About your height. You seen her?"

Sally crossed her arms. "I have not. But I will certainly alert the sheriff's office if I do."

My hand tightened again around the grip of my pistol, and a sour taste rose in the back of my mouth. Slavers. Like the ones who'd caught up to Ethelyn. I'd kill 'em all myself if I could.

But killin' all those lawmen down below wouldn't be smart. Not now. Not yet.

There was a heartbeat of silence, and I could tell the lawman didn't believe Sally hadn't seen the woman they were after. "We tracked her here," he said finally. "She's around here somewhere. Probably trying to hide in one of these buildings, I imagine. Maybe trying to hide in your saloon."

Sally shrugged. "Maybe. Why don't you put up a poster of her with a nice reward?"

"We already did," the man snarled.

"Well then I imagine the best thing to do would be to wait. Give it some time. There's a lot of people in this town, mister. Someone's bound to find her."

"We ain't got time," the lawman said. "Baron Whittaker wants her back. Now."

The door to my room flung open behind me and I spun, gun drawn. But it weren't no thief or bounty hunter comin' after me, it was a woman. She slammed the door shut again behind her, latched it, and turned, then froze at the sight of me and my revolver, eyes going wide.

I blinked, takin' in the sight of her dirt-streaked trousers and blouse, her skinny frame, the red hair a mess and fallin' down over her shoulders and face. It was *her*. The escaped slave.

Through the open window I heard Sally say, "Seems to me Baron Whittaker could stand to learn some patience."

"I have money," the woman in front of me blurted. Then she squeezed her eyes shut and shook her head, snapped them open again. "I mean ... my family has money. Help me escape. They'll pay you twice as much as Whittaker would."

I lifted my eyebrows. I didn't even know how much this Baron Whittaker was offerin' fer her return. It didn't much matter. I wouldn'ta taken her back to him, anyway.

But the offer of money didn't sound too bad, neither.

"Search these buildings!" the lawman roared to his men below. "Every single one of them. Every single room. Find that girl!"

Shit.

Across the room, her dark blue eyes grew impossibly wider.

And that's when I realized there was only one way out of this.

IX

PROPER MANNERS

"Take off yer clothes," I ordered.

"I beg your pardon! *What* did you just say to me?"

I'd never heard a woman sound so offended. I limped to the wardrobe, throwin' it open. Course there weren't nothin' suitable for a woman in there, but I weren't lookin' for clothes. I was lookin' for somethin' else, and prayin' Sally kept some of it stocked in her rooms as a service. Usually the nicer places did, and Sally had a nicer place. "Take off yer clothes," I repeated. "You want those lawdogs to find you or not? We ain't got much time. Wash yer face in the basin, strip, and get in the bed."

She let out a little laugh, high and airy.

I heard some of the posse stompin' around downstairs, and my heartbeat quickened. I pulled open the wardrobe drawer, rummagin' through shavin' supplies and—finally! Boot polish. I pulled it out.

"You think I'm going to bestow my *charms* upon you just because I asked you to help me escape? No way, mister. No way." She'd backed up against the door, hands clutched to her breast, shakin' her head.

I stared at her fer a minute, then grasped her meanin' and realized my instructions had sounded all wrong. "No," I said. "No, lady, I ain't tryin' to take advantage of you. I'm tryin' to help you escape! But they're gonna recognize you unless we change up yer appearance, you follow? We can make it look like yer one of Sally's girls, but we gotta act fast."

Comprehension dawned on her face.

I heard some of the posse stompin' up the stairs now. We were *really* runnin' outta time. "Quick!" I snapped. "I'm gonna smear some of this in yer hair to cover up the red, yeah?" I held up the boot polish.

She grimaced in disgust, but nodded.

I got to work on her hair best I could as she splashed water on her face, scrubbin' off the dirt. Then I scrubbed the polish off my hands best I could and threw the dirty basin water out the room's side window. By the time I'd done that and replaced the basin, she'd taken off her dusty clothes and shoved them beneath the sheets at the end of the bed, and crawled under the covers herself.

I heard heavy bootsteps comin' down the hall.

I tossed my hat to one of the bed posts and pulled my shirt up over my head, havin' no time to mess with the buttons, throwin' it to the floor.

She watched me with terrified eyes as I unbuckled my gunbelts and let 'em thump to the floor, but within easy arm's reach of the bed. Better to be safe than dead.

She didn't fully trust that I wouldn't take advantage of her, that much was plain on her face. I stepped out of my boots, hearin' doors bein' busted in now and the loud protests of the other rooms' occupants.

"You try anything, mister, and I'll yell," she whispered as I moved toward her. "I'll tell the law who I am and tell Whittaker what you did and he'll—"

"I ain't gonna try anythin'," I hissed back. "I ain't even takin' off my pants!" And I wasn't. For more reason than to prove to her my honest intentions. I also didn't want her to see my metal leg. I slipped under the sheets, avertin' my gaze from her nakedness, and rolled over on top of her just as our door got kicked in.

I scowled and swore, feignin' anger at the interruption, and twisted half-around to glare at the two men who'd barged in. "Hey! Ya mind? Can't ya see I'm a little busy?"

"Shut it, you," one of 'em growled. "We're looking for an escaped slave." He stepped into the room and opened the wardrobe, then looked behind it.

"Well they ain't in here," I said, lowerin' down over the girl as the second of 'em came closer to the bed, then bent down to look under it. "Pretty sure we woulda noticed." I hoped they wouldn't look at her too close. The polish in her hair was rubbin' off on the pillow. Her naked breasts pressed into my chest and I felt her rapid breathin', the poundin' of her heart.

I swallowed. Maybe this hadn't been the best idea. It'd been a long time since I'd been in bed with a woman. I cleared my throat and refocused my attention on the two lawmen. "You boys about done? I'd like to get on with it..."

They were makin' a show of checkin' the room, lookin' behind the single chair and wash basin stand, even though it were obvious there was no one hidin' there.

"Oh, no, take yer time," the girl drawled, surprisin' me. She'd made her voice higher and inflected a southern accent. She lifted one hand to stroke my cheek and smiled up at me, puttin' on a show. "I charge by the hour, after all."

Despite the fact she weren't no real whore and I'd never really hired her, my frown was a real one.

It made one of the lawmen chuckle and one of 'em scoff. To my relief, they both headed toward the door. One turned back just before leavin'. "You see a skinny redhead girl with the Whittaker brand, you tell the sheriff. One thousand dollars to you if you bring her in yourself. Got it?"

I nodded. "Sure thing, officer."

He touched the brim of his hat, eyes slidin' toward the lady.

I held my breath.

"Enjoy," he said, and then he stepped out and pulled the door shut behind him.

Of course, it didn't latch no more, seein' as they'd busted it. But it stayed mostly closed, only a thin crack lookin' out into the hallway.

Then I heard 'em thump back downstairs. My room was the last room in the hall.

I breathed out a long, slow breath.

The woman planted her hands against my chest and gave me a shove that knocked me clean outta the bed. I went sprawlin' to the floor, takin' most the sheets with me, and hit with a grunt on my left hip and elbow, wincin' as pain shocked through my leg.

She yanked the sheets back toward her to cover up her nakedness, scootin' me a foot or so along the floor. She was damn strong for bein' so skinny. "Ow," I complained, rollin' free of the twisted sheets and crawlin' toward my discarded shirt. "No need fer that. I was gettin' up."

She didn't answer, already diggin' around in the bed in search of her own clothes. "I have to get out of here," she muttered.

"That wouldn't be too smart," I said.

She lowered the sheets from over her head, and I saw she already had her shirt back on. It was streaked with black shoe polish now, her black-streaked hair an awful mess, and her dark blue eyes blazin'. "Excuse me?"

I shrugged into my own shirt and then used the edge of the bed as leverage to push myself to my feet. "They're still out there. They'll be searchin' this block fer awhile. Best to stay here. Maybe fer the night."

She gave me a look.

I chuckled at her resolute suspicion and shook my head, pickin' up my gun belts to buckle 'em back on. "Look, lady, if I was gonna take advantage of you, I woulda done it just then. You asked me to help you escape. You want help or not?"

Her expression softened, and I saw the unmistakable fire of hope light in her eyes. It twisted my stomach.

Hope.

The killer of souls.

But I suppose hope had also been what hadn't let me give up on Ethelyn, even after all this time. And now I had a chance to save her. Hope had gotten me this far, so maybe it weren't all bad.

I looked away from her to grab my hat and pushed it back onto my head.

"If you take me back to my family," she said breathlessly, "they'll pay you handsomely."

"How much?" Maybe takin' this woman back where she belonged would be easier than robbin' a bank. I hobbled to the open window and shut it, drawin' the shades. The posse might've already searched this room, but no need to take unnecessary risks.

"Ten thousand, at least."

I sucked a breath through my teeth. Well, that was sure somethin'. But not enough. Not nearly enough. "Where is this family of yers?"

"The East Republic. Pennsylvania."

I swore and turned to face her. "Pennsylvania!? That's a whole country away!"

The burnin' fire came back to her eyes, her full lips thinnin' into a hard line. "Yes. And I was dragged all that way by dirty bandits who sold me to Baron Whittaker! Take me back to my parents and they'll pay you well, I promise."

I swore some more and paced the room, or at least, paced as well as I could with my lame leg. I rubbed a hand over my mouth, stubble scratchin' at my palm. As an afterthought, I grabbed the wooden chair set in the corner and used it to push the door closed and hold it there. Releasin' a heavy sigh, I shook my head. "I'm sorry. I ... I can't."

She lurched off the bed and threw back the sheets, fully dressed now. "You ... *can't*? What do you mean you *can't*?"

"I can't go that far. I'm sorry. I have someone near here who needs me, soon. I can't take the time to escort you all the way to the other side of the country. Maybe if yer parents were closer I could ... but no. Not that far."

Her mouth opened, but her words seemed lost. She stared at me for a long minute, and I saw emotions play across her face, everythin' from fury to terror to hopelessness, and then comin' back around to anger. "So everything you just said about helping me escape was a lie, then?" Her voice trembled now, and tears shone in her eyes.

I let out an exasperated breath and eased down into the chair I'd pushed up against the door. Guilt tightened in my chest again. I'd done a lot of stuff I shouldn't have in my search for Ethelyn ... and *not* done a lot of stuff I probably should have, too. "No. I helped you avoid those lawmen, didn't I? I just can't take you cross country. I have ... other people who need me here right now."

She made a show of lookin' around the empty room. "Really? And where are these people?"

I met her angry gaze evenly. "Kidnapped. Enslaved. Just like you." I fished around in my pocket and pulled out Ethelyn's necklace, holdin' it out so she could see. "My sister."

Her stiff stance sagged a little and she blinked rapidly, the tears streakin' down her cheeks.

"Nine-Fingered Nan has her," I said, though I wasn't sure exactly why I was tellin' her more. Surely she didn't want to hear about mine or my sister's problems. She had plenty of her own. "I'm going to buy her back."

She swallowed visibly. "The bastards who took me," she said quietly. "They were Nine-Fingered Nan's crew."

I straightened on my chair at this news. Nine-Fingered Nan's gang ... all the way in Pennsylvania? I remembered what her woman had yelled at me just the night before. About how there was nowhere far enough away I could run to now. Maybe that was truer than I had been willin' to accept. *Shit.*

"And she sold me to Baron Whittaker," the girl finished. She sat down abruptly on the edge of the bed. She wasn't angry now. Just exhausted. Sad. Hopeless.

Hope.

That soul killer.

I watched her and swallowed hard, thinkin' of how Ethelyn must be feelin' pretty much the same right now. Only probably worse, if Nan had really knifed off three of her fingers. The thought made me sick.

"He wanted me to be a part of his harem," the girl currently sittin' on my bed continued, and the words made my stomach lurch again. She stared across the room at the wardrobe, eyes unfocused. "But I fought him so hard he decided he'd try and break me first. Thought he'd show me how much worse life could be so I'd beg him to come back. He sent me down into the mines with the others." Her blue gaze slid back to me, hardenin'. "Six months I've been in the mines.

Collecting scrap for twelve hours a day, barely eating, barely sleeping, and I'd rather do that till I die than share his bed."

Then she dropped her eyes to her hands, folded in her lap. "But ... this isn't the first time I've escaped ... and if he catches me again ... well. I don't want to think about it."

I sighed and dropped my head into my hands, then rubbed at my face again. I couldn't help her. Not like she wanted. But the thought of doin' nothin' turned my stomach more than even the horrors this poor girl and my own sister had experienced.

Doin' nothin' was out of the question. "How many slaves does Baron Whittaker have?"

She frowned at the question. "Nearly a hundred. Why?"

I let out a low whistle. That was a lot. "All of 'em itchin' fer freedom as much as you?"

"Many of them. Some of the older ones have given up. Some of the older ones are even loyal to the bastard."

I nodded. That happened sometimes. "I still can't take you back to yer parents. But there might be somethin' else I can do."

She looked at me in question, but didn't let herself hope this time. Not fully.

I rose from the chair and lit the room's lamps, then went to the side window and pulled the shades there, too. I faced her, then, and considered what I was about to do.

Holt was gonna be mad. Again.

"What if we give Baron Whittaker a lot of other things to think about besides gettin' you back? That would give you time to clear the area, get a big head start toward Pennsylvania."

She swiped at the tears on her cheeks and sniffed. "What do you mean?"

I hooked my thumbs into my belts, thinkin'. "What if we set 'em all free? All Whittaker's slaves. And set his house on fire. And ... he keep his money at the bank?"

She tilted her head to the side. "Yes. Most of it..."

"And we rob the bank. I take what I need to get my sister ... you take what you need to fund yer trip back to yer parents."

She stared at me as if I'd gone mad. Maybe I had. But I was bettin' she weren't gonna go runnin' off to tell the law my plans, seein' as she was wanted by the law herself. And truth be told, we could use another hand for that job, if she was up fer it.

"Well?" I prompted.

Her mouth opened. Then shut. She stood from the bed, but then hesitated. "I ... I don't know. What you're proposing ... if we're caught ... they'll hang us for sure."

"Is that any worse than what Whittaker will do to you if he catches you again?"

Her eyes dropped to the floor. "No."

"Would you rather go back to him and live out the rest of your life in his bed? Or the mines?"

Those dark blue eyes flicked up to meet mine again. This time her voice was hard, resolute. "No."

I spread my hands. "Then why not make his life hell for a bit? Don't he deserve it after what he's done to you and all those others?"

"Yes." She straightened, throwin' back her shoulders and liftin' her chin, and through the black shoe polish smeared in her hair and the dusty state of her clothes, I saw clearly for the first time the young woman she must have been, before all this tragedy befell her. A young woman of proper breedin', most like, with manners and money and everythin'.

The adjustment to life out here as a slave musta been rougher on her even than most.

"All right," she said. "Let's do it."

I smiled. Holt hadn't even come back yet with his scoutin' report or his plan, but I was already well on my way to makin' my own. A hundred escaped slaves and a baron's house on fire would make mighty good cover for a bank robbery. "Good. Well then, Miss, if we're gonna be workin' together, I suppose I should properly introduce myself." I tipped my hat to her. "Name's Van. Van Delano. Pleasure to make your acquaintance."

She arched one eyebrow. "I'm sure it is, considering you've already seen me without my clothes on."

Heat rose to my cheeks. I cleared my throat. "For what it's worth,

Miss, I never looked. I would never ... I mean I only made the suggestion to keep you—"

"I know," she cut me off, wavin' away my words. "And I suppose it worked. So ... thank you, I guess. But never again, understand?"

"Of course not."

She gave a little nod, another gesture reminiscent of the few ladies of high society I'd ever seen in my life, and stepped forward, holdin' out a hand. "Charlotte," she said. "Charlotte Harrison. Pleased to meet you, Mr. Delano."

I momentarily panicked at her formal tone, havin' not the slightest idea about proper manners. But I'd seen a gentleman or two kiss the hand of a lady before, so I did the same now, takin' her hand in mine and brushin' my lips against her knuckles and hopin' that's what she'd been expectin'.

Seemed it had been, 'cause when I straightened she was lookin' at me with both surprise and somethin' like pleasure.

I stepped back then and exhaled a quiet breath, feelin' awkward and my face burnin' worse than before.

To Hell with all these manners. I needed to get back to things I knew. Things like shootin' and robbin' and settin' things on fire. I cleared my throat again and limped to my half-glass of whiskey. I scooped it up and offered it out to her. "To the end of Baron Whittaker," I said.

She eyed the glass fer a second, then took it. Half her mouth quirked into a humorless smile, and her fair features hardened. It was a look I knew well.

It was the look of anticipated revenge.

"To the end of Baron Whittaker," she said, and threw back the rest of the drink.

It was then someone knocked on the door.

SMOKE AND FIRE

Charlotte gasped and spun to face it, droppin' the whiskey glass, which thankfully didn't shatter as it hit the floorboards, only thumped, bounced, and rolled underneath the bed.

I drew my gun and stepped in front of her, shovin' her behind me and aimin' at the door. "Who is it?" I called.

"Who ya think it is?" Holt grumbled from the other side. "It's me, Holt! What the hell happened here? The place is a mess!"

I exhaled in relief, holsterin' my pistol. "It's my partner, Holt," I said to Charlotte, and went to move the chair. "He's all right. No friend of slavers, that's fer sure." Or the law, but I wasn't entirely certain how much of that to tell Charlotte just yet. Generally the folk of the East Republic tended to frown upon livin' a life outside the law even more so than the folk of the Western Territories did.

I stepped aside to let Holt in and then shut the door quick again behind him, movin' the chair back into place.

"Fer Chrissakes, Van," Holt complained, stompin' into the room, "I leave fer a few hours and the place we're at gets—" He stopped and drew up short, his eyes finally fallin' on Charlotte. "Oh. Errr. Hey, if you have company, we can talk about this later." He turned toward me, stickin' out one of his thick fingers and shakin' it in my face. "But she better be one of the cheap ones, Van, cuz we ain't got much more coin to be wastin' on—"

I slapped his finger outta my face. "She ain't a whore, Holt."

His bushy gray eyebrows furrowed. "Eh?"

"She ain't a whore."

He turned to look her over up and down. "Well then what the blazes is she doin' in here?"

"She, uh ... she needs our help."

Holt rounded on me again, givin' me that look. That disapprovin' look. That look that said, *Van, we have enough problems to worry about right now without tryin' to help out strangers, too.*

And that was true enough.

'Cept in this case, her cause could help out our cause.

And anyway, maybe a part of me felt like doin' some good fer Charlotte would make up fer what I'd done to the Balogh family by stealin' their mule.

"Van—"

"It'll keep the law busy while we rob the bank."

His eyes widened and he motioned fer me to quiet down. He glanced at Charlotte, clearly uneasy with her bein' included in this discussion.

"She knows," I said. "And she's in."

His lips thinned into a hard line. He tried to bluster some protests.

Charlotte crossed her arms. "I know how to shoot a gun," she said, as if that were the only criteria needed to convince Holt of her trustworthiness and usefulness.

Well, she weren't too far off.

He grumbled some more and shook his head, stickin' his thumbs in his belt. Then he sighed, and shrugged. "Fine. Fine. You wanna drag a nice lady into this mess, and she's crazy enough to jump into it, fine."

"I'm in a big enough mess myself already, mister," Charlotte said. "Adding a little bit more now surely won't make any difference. And anyway," she looked to me over Holt's shoulder, "like your friend told me, I think this might be the best way to both get what we want."

"I hope so, missus. I surely hope so." Holt sighed again. "Well then. I suppose we're gonna do this. Shall we make a plan?"

We did.

Long into the night we talked, and spent more of our dwindlin' coin on some drink and a meal fer Charlotte. And some more drinks fer us, too.

Holt told us what he'd found out about the Bank of Blessing. It weren't too different than most other banks in the Territories, 'cept with a few extra armed guards. But it had a teller same as the others, and from what he'd been able to see from the lobby, safes like all the others.

But the teller hadn't seemed timid or shy. Wasn't likely we'd be able to bribe or threaten him into helpin'. So we'd have to deal with the safes directly.

Holt laid out a few sticks of dynamite on the bed, and I shook my head.

"Not very subtle. They'll hear us robbin' that bank fer miles."

Holt snorted. "Thought you said we had somethin' in line to occupy the law?"

"We do. But the sound of dynamite might make 'em look back toward the bank awful quick."

"You got an ear fer openin' safes, then?"

I scratched at my chin and shook my head. A regular lock I could pick, sure. But not those combination safes. All those little clicks sounded the same to me.

"Then I guess we'll wait till the law is good and distracted, and then we'll have to get outta that bank when the job is done right quick, too."

"Yeah…"

Charlotte was silent. She looked nervous, her pale face even paler now.

"It's all right," I told her. "We'll get you a fast horse." I surely didn't know it was gonna be all right, and we'd have to *steal* her a fast horse, but there was nothin' much else to be said.

This had to work. It *had* to. Ethelyn's freedom depended on it.

And now, Charlotte's too.

She gave me a nod in return, but I could tell she weren't convinced.

Hell, I don't think any of us were. But we were doin' it, anyway.

"All right," Holt said. "Tomorrow we find the girl a horse. Tomorrow night, you two get to the baron's manor and light it up, get those slaves free. Meanwhile, I'll be waitin' on the bank to close up, get inside all quiet like. When you two are done at the manor, *hustle* it back to the bank, understand? I don't want to have to hold it all by my lonesome long. I won't blast anythin' till you two show up ... 'less you get yerselves killed beforehand. In that case, I'm takin' all the money myself and high-tailin' it outta town. Got it?"

Charlotte and I nodded in unison.

"Give us an hour," I said. "An hour after you hear the fire alert go out ... we'll be there. Unless we're dead." I glanced to her. "But I don't plan to be dead."

She met my eyes. "Me neither."

"All right, then, it's a plan." Holt pushed himself standin' from where he'd been sittin' at the edge of the bed, and the springs squeaked. "Now you two be careful at that manor, ya hear? I heard a few things about Baron Whittaker while out today, and none of 'em were particularly pleasant."

"I know my way around that place," Charlotte said. "Trust me, the last thing I want is to be found by any of his men. We'll be careful."

Holt gave her a grave nod. "Let's all get some rest. We're gonna need it." He looked at me one last time, and I knew what he was thinkin'.

This is your show, kid. Or maybe yer funeral.

"Good night," was all he said aloud. He tipped his hat to Charlotte as he made for the door. "Miss."

Then he was gone, and I stood from my seat on the bed too and slipped my boots back on. We'd rented a third room from Sally, and I was gonna take that one so Charlotte could have this one. I bid her good night as well, and left her alone on the bed, huggin' herself, as I slipped out into the hall and shut the damaged door best as I could behind me.

She was gonna move the chair under the knob once we were gone to secure it. That's what we'd agreed. I hoped she'd remember.

I considered our strange meetin' and mutual goals as I shuffled down the hall to my own room. I also hoped all this would go accordin' to plan.

Most of all, though, I hoped she wouldn't try and sneak off on us durin' the middle of the night.

I didn't sleep well, and was up with the sun the next mornin'. To my relief, Charlotte hadn't run off. We took breakfast in her room, not wantin' to risk any greedy folk downstairs recognizin' her. Those lawmen who had so courteously searched the saloon's rooms had left a poster of her face up on the wall right next to the bar.

Sally was still put out by the damage done to her property, but there weren't much she could do about it 'sides complain and apologize to her patrons. Which she did. Profusely.

I assured her we had experienced worse, and slept in worse, and to not trouble herself over concern fer our comfort. Then I took our plates of food and rushed back upstairs.

Sally gave me a funny look as I left with three plates instead of two, but didn't ask no questions, fer which I was grateful.

The three of us ate quick and light, not much in the mood fer food.

Nerves were already gettin' to me.

Sure, Holt and I had done plenty of robbin' and stealin' since I'd first met up with him eight years ago, but nothin' on this scale. And maybe he'd done somethin' like this before, sure, but it had been a long time ago.

Back before I was born.

Back when he was a lot younger and quicker, and still ran with my pa. Back when my pa still ran with Paul Johnson, better known in most parts now as Kill 'Em All Paul. Back when they'd had a much bigger crew than just two. Back when the Territories were even wilder and more lawless than they were now.

We didn't talk much, and after we'd eaten what we could, we spent the rest of the day makin' the last few preparations and gettin' the rest of our needed supplies. Holt and I did, anyway.

Charlotte didn't like havin' to stay hidden away in the room, but she didn't want to be recognized by the law or anyone else wantin' that thousand dollars, neither, so she reluctantly stayed behind.

We managed to bribe one of Sally's girls into givin' us an extra pair of women's clothes, at least, so she could change and get herself cleaned up a bit while we were out.

Holt picked up more dynamite and I got myself a good huntin' knife to replace the one I hadn't got back from those bastards who'd robbed me when I was passed out half-dead in the desert. I'd have preferred throwin' knives, to be honest, like the kind I was pretty sure had given Sally her name, but I was no good at throwin' knives. Those took a skill I had yet to figure out.

And I surely couldn't afford to be missin' any throws tonight.

We also went on the lookout fer a fast horse for Charlotte, but didn't have any luck.

There were plenty of horses in Blessing, all right. Plenty of mighty fine steeds. But there weren't many good opportunities fer stealin' any of 'em. Especially given the fact we wouldn't be leavin' town till nightfall.

It was too much of a risk the animal would be reported stolen and found again before we were gone.

So we left it. She'd have to ride double with either me or Holt. Not ideal.

Not ideal at all.

"Wish you woulda just left it," Holt grumbled as we made our way back through the crowded streets toward the Seven Knives. "Don't know why you always gotta do this kinda thing. I've told ya once and I've told ya a million times, ya gotta start *thinkin'* 'fore you go rushin' off into things."

I shook my head. "I didn't rush into anythin'." I'd had nothin' to do with Charlotte burstin' into my room, certainly. "And anyway, I don't know why yer complainin'. Torchin' Baron Whittaker's place gives us good cover. Without it ... we'd almost be sittin' ducks."

Holt spit from the side of his mouth. "Maybe. But we could torch the baron's place well enough without the girl."

"Maybe," I echoed. "But we wouldn'ta even known about him if not fer her. And anyway, I'd rather have her there to show me around. Don't wanna be wanderin' around blind in a place like that. Not if the baron is really as *wonderfully pleasant* as you heard he was."

Holt grunted. "I guess. But now we got another body to worry about. She'll slow us down."

I rolled my eyes. "She don't weigh that much. It'll be fine."

"Whatever you say, kid."

Dusk came slow.

Or so it seemed.

By the time we were ready to head out, I felt as anxious as one of those ol' seasoned quarter mile race horses, pawin' and chompin' at the bit at the startin' line, ready to explode onto the track.

Holt headed off toward the Bank of Blessing on his black gelding, leadin' my mule behind him.

Charlotte and I went the opposite direction, toward Baron Whittaker's manor, arm in arm. Fer now, we played the part of a young couple in love, meanderin' along and window shoppin'. I'd had a wash and a shave, myself, and Charlotte looked different all right, all shined up and with her hair pinned atop her head. She'd borrowed a clean green blouse and dark brown skirt from one of Sally's girls, and a lace parasol, too. The parasol threw patterned shadows across her freckled face, and I hoped her change of clothes and a bit of cover fer her head would make her less obviously the wanted, escaped slave she was.

Just in case, we made sure to pass wide around those law officers stationed at some corners. But fer the general public, our idea seemed to be workin'.

Fer now.

We kept on mosyin' along, and the sun kept settin'. The crowds were thinnin' out now though, finally, now that it was almost dark. Along the main streets, a few street lights had been lit. Eventually, the buildin's of the town became fewer and further between. Ahead, the dirt street turned to cobblestone, and it seemed the town itself just stopped. There was a large stretch of empty land carpeted by lush green grass, and then a massive residence at the top of a small hill, all lit up with electricity. The cobblestone road led right up to its expansive porch and front door. It was surrounded on all sides by a makeshift metal fence, lookin' like it had been patched together with pieces from the Old World ruins itself. The front gate of that patchwork fence had two men standin' on either side of it, armed with rifles.

I frowned at the looks of it.

"That's it," Charlotte whispered to me. "The baron's manor."

I could feel her tremblin' through the arm she had entwined in mine. I wasn't sure if she was tremblin' from fear ... or rage. "Come on," I whispered back. We ducked into the next alley, a narrow space between a tailor's shop and a gunsmith's. "The bank'll be closin' up soon. We need to light that place up."

"Going around back is best," Charlotte said. Her fingers were clenched around the parasol handle so tightly now her knuckles were white. "That's where the slave barns are, anyway. They'll have some guards, of course, but I think the dynamite will distract them."

"I'd think so." I opened the small satchel hooked to my belt, checkin' on the sticks of explosive. They were still there, right where they were supposed to be. The matches I'd put in Jake's coin pouch on the other side of my belt. "All right. Let's do this. You ready?"

She stared at me with wide eyes, then swallowed. Her breathin' was fast and shallow, but she nodded.

"Okay. Stay close. I'm gonna try not to shoot anyone on account of the noise. Least, not till there's some other noise to cover it up. But no guarantees. Still ... if things go south ... you just run. Understand? Just get out of here and don't look back. Head fer yer family. Got it?"

Again the wordless nod.

"Okay. Here we go."

Charlotte closed the parasol and pulled the long, slender knife that had been cleverly hidden in the handle. Those prostitutes had to be as resourceful as anyone, I figured. She set the rest of the parasol against the shop's wall, and then we both moved out from the shadow of the alley, stickin' to other shadows, instead.

We crouched and moved as fast as we could, which wasn't too fast on account of my leg. I'd left the crutch holstered in my saddle scabbard, and as such, the best I could manage was a lurchin', fast walk.

Interestingly, Charlotte never asked any questions about my limp. Not before, and not now, despite the fact it slowed us down somethin' awful.

At least it wasn't hurtin' quite so much anymore. And it seemed maybe even the metal foot was sorta goin' where I wanted it to go.

But there was no time to properly test it. We had to keep movin'.

So we did. Excruciatingly slowly, it seemed, bein' real careful to stay far enough away from the house that no one gazin' out the windows might spot us. There were a few perimeter guards, but we stayed far away from them, too. We reached the back at last, where there was another gate in the fence, this one guarded, too.

Only the two of 'em, though, and they weren't payin' much attention.

I pulled my left pistol and held it out toward Charlotte, butt-first.

She only stared at it.

"Just in case," I said, and nodded toward the gun. "Try not to shoot on account of the noise, like I said. But if you gotta, you gotta."

She took it gingerly, then tucked it into the waistband of her skirt, next to the knife from the parasol.

I took out two sticks of dynamite, then, and handed one to her. Then divvied up the matches. "One should do it. But make it a good throw. Soon as this first one goes off, you make a run fer the house. I'll go straight to the slave barns, like we talked about. When yer done, meet me there. Got it?"

"Got it." Her words were hardly a whisper.

"All right." I lit a match, then lit the fuse to my dynamite. I stood, took aim for a nice open spot in the baron's extensive back yard, and hurled the thing with all my might.

I covered my ears and braced myself, and Charlotte did the same.

A long, silent minute passed.

Then ... *BOOM!*

I flinched despite myself, my heart nearly leapin' outta my chest. Charlotte, too, cringed away from the blast, duckin' her head as a few clumps of grass and dirt rained down around us.

The two guards by the fence fair near jumped outta their boots, squawkin' and shriekin' and fallin' all over themselves as they scrabbled fer their rifles and turned in the direction of the explosion.

Charlotte and I both moved fer the gate, then.

She went through it, and I went right up behind the nearest guard and slit his throat with my new huntin' knife. His partner didn't even notice ... till I did the same to him. I side-stepped the fallin' body and grimaced, wipin' the blade on my pants leg before sheathin' it again. I woulda rather shot a man any day over bleedin' him out like that, but in this case I surely didn't want all of Baron Whittaker's loyal men pinpointin' my location from my gunshots.

I kept in a crouch and moved across the back yard through the shadows. There were shouts comin' from inside and around the house now, women soundin' scared and men yellin' fer someone to go out and see what the hell was goin' on.

It sounded like a lot of them. A lot of people in that house.

I wondered if it had really been a good idea to send Charlotte up—

BOOM!

The second explosion nearly knocked me flat. Instinctively I covered my head with my arms and threw myself back against the side of the nearest buildin'. A hole opened up in the back of the house, the wall fallin' inward on itself with a tumble of plaster and wood and shattered glass.

I blinked. That had been a good throw, all right.

Now there was a lot of screamin' and wailin'.

BOOM!

I ducked and swore, ears ringin' good now. A second blast to the house had never been a part of the plan. Where had she even got more dynamite?

I felt absently at the satchel on my belt, but I hadn't really counted the number of sticks. Maybe I shoulda.

I looked up to see the wood timbers of the house, the wooden furniture with its highly flammable lacquer, and the curtains all on fire. That second blast had opened a crater inside the house, and apparently upset a candle or an oil lamp or somethin', 'cause the flames were spreadin' fast now.

Well, that's just what we'd wanted, all right.

Charlotte had sure taken care of the house, so I refocused on my own job. Turned around to see the barn I was leanin' against was probably one of the slave barns. I heard runnin' footsteps comin' in the grass and pressed myself up against the wall again just as several more men with rifles rushed past.

But they weren't payin' no attention to me. They were all gapin' at the house.

I turned quick around the corner of the barn and went to the doors, still standin' open. Maybe that's where the men with the rifles had just come from. I ducked inside and took a quick look around the dim interior.

A lot of confused, wide eyes stared at me.

This was one of the slave barns, all right. Looked like they were all bedded down fer the night on mounds of straw, a lot of 'em crowded into a single, wide open space. A few had pillows or blankets, but that was all the belongin's I could see. Which was good, 'cause I was about to burn it all down.

"Go!" I hissed at them, wavin' toward the door. "Go! You're free! Quick!"

They looked to each other, then back to me.

And didn't move.

"Go, damnit!" I drew my gun, and that got their attention. I waved it at 'em. "Go! Get out that door and run! Go, go!"

A few of the ones nearest to me scrambled away from my weapon as I advanced on 'em, and I acted like I might shoot 'em if they didn't run.

That they seemed to listen to, that and watchin' some of their fellows go, because soon they were all jumpin' up and runnin', pourin' out into the night. I chased 'em out of the barn and made sure they all kept runnin', over the fence and through the gate and across that carpet of grass. Then I marched back into the barn, took down a few of the lanterns from the walls, and smashed 'em into the straw.

It caught fire quick.

I limped outta that barn and headed fer the next one.

Rifle fire barked behind me and I ducked again, throwin' myself into the nearest shadow.

There was shoutin' everywhere now, and it took me a minute to figure out where the rifle shots were comin' from.

Behind me.

I turned. Some of the guards who'd been starin' at the house had now realized that some of the baron's slaves were escapin'. They were aimin' into the dark, takin' shots at the fleein' people.

My hand tightened around my gun, still in my hand. "Shit!" I hissed. I could get a few of 'em, sure. And then the rest of 'em would turn right around and see me, and those odds weren't good.

I stood for a second in indecision, heart hammerin' in my throat.

They took a few more shots. Some of the slaves dropped mid-run. Some were dead. Some were wounded, addin' their cries to the rest now fillin' up the night.

My revolver lifted and I clenched my teeth. Braced myself.

My finger wrapped around the trigger, but still I hesitated.

I couldn't help Ethelyn if I was dead.

The flames in the barn next to me roared up, lightin' up the night. The men with the rifles saw it and turned, and I jumped around the side of it hopin' they hadn't seen me. My metal leg tripped me up and I hit the ground with a grunt, then belly-crawled a few feet before gettin' back up and hobblin' to the side of the next barn, thankful the light of the fire hadn't reached its shadow yet.

"Fire!" one of the men yelled. "Fire! Get the fire wagon! Get the fire wagon *now*!"

That was our signal to get out of there and head toward the bank. But I had three more barns to burn. And I hadn't seen Charlotte yet.

I swore under my breath as I reached the second barn. "Come on, come on, girl. Where are you?" A part of me wanted to go to the house and find her. *No. Just stick to the plan, Delano. Stick to the plan.*

So I kicked open the door to the second barn with my good foot, ready to shoot if I had to.

Only terrified eyes met mine. No guns. Just like the last barn, it seemed any guards there might have been had run off to investigate the explosions and the fire. Better fer me.

I had to run these slaves out same as the first group, only this time I was swearin' all the while. Charlotte shoulda been here by now.

Somethin's wrong.

I smashed some lanterns into the straw again and limped toward the third barn. We still had to get back across town to the bank...

Somethin's wrong...

A barrage of gunfire erupted from inside the house, bringin' me up short just as I was about to kick in this next set of doors. I looked toward the back of the ruined manor and increased the intensity of my curses. That was most definitely *not* a part of the plan, neither.

The sporadic bursts of gunfire from the house were abruptly drowned in the roar of somethin' else, somethin' that was unmistakably a gun, but like nothin' I'd ever heard before.

It was firin' at an inhuman rate.

Dread settled like an anvil in my stomach.

I almost didn't notice all the people runnin' all over around me ... from Baron Whittaker's guards and staff tryin' to organize a water brigade to put out the house and the barns, to the slaves I'd just freed dartin' their way through the chaos to freedom, to more guards now mounted and tryin' to chase 'em down.

And no one else seemed to notice me, neither, standin' there in the middle of it, gawkin' at the house.

Some people came out of the manor, then, from the side doors and some even climbin' over the rubble, lookin' wild-eyed and scared. Men and women both, well dressed and covered with a fine layer of white dust. They ran, too, joinin' the mess of it all, quickly lost in the flurry of bodies and horses and smoke and fire.

The roar of the strange gun fell silent.

There were no other shots that came after.

I swallowed hard in a dry mouth. Took in a deep breath of air choked with acrid smoke, then coughed. And then I tore myself away from starin' at that ruined house and went back to the barn. One more. I was gonna free one more barn fulla slaves, and set it afire, and then it was time to go.

Even if I had to leave without her.

She's probably dead already. Damnit, Charlotte. Why didn't you just stick to the plan?

I shouldered through the third set of barn doors, expectin' no resistance.

And came face to face with three rifles. I froze.

The man nearest to me eyed me up and down and spit onto the straw-covered floor. "Who the fuck are you?"

I glanced over his shoulder to the slaves in this barn, lookin' much the same as all the others. Dirty. Bedraggled. Their clothes tattered, faces gaunt, and eyes wide and fearful. I brought my gaze back to the three men pointin' their guns at me. And said the first thing that came to mind. "Fire! Didn't ya hear? The other barns are on fire! The house, too!"

They looked to each other. Then at me.

"The fire wagon'll take care of it," one of 'em said.

"And you didn't answer us," another of 'em said. "Who the fuck are you?"

I opened my mouth to answer. But I wasn't sure what to say. They surely showed no signs of concern over the fire, nor any inclination to leave this barn. My gun was still in my hand, the weight of it temptin' me to shoot 'em all down.

But three against one ... at point-blank range ... I wasn't sure I was that fast.

Turned out it didn't matter, anyway.

Pain exploded through my head at just that moment, and all the chaos of the night got swallowed into blackness.

THE WONDERFULLY PLEASANT BARON WHITTAKER

I came back to consciousness slowly.

My head ached somethin' terrible, especially around my right temple. The pain was sharp and pulsin' there, and judgin' by the wetness spread down that side of my face, I guessed I'd been hit pretty hard.

Hit by who or what didn't matter.

All that mattered was that I was pretty sure I was fucked.

I tried to open my eyes. Managed to pry 'em open a crack, but all I saw was darkness and a dim orange glow. I blinked and groaned. My skull felt like it was gonna split open.

I tried to shift my arms, but they were stuck. Slowly, I moved my awareness to the rest of my body and away from my throbbin' head. Pulled on my arms again.

They were tied. Tied at the wrists behind my back, around the back of a chair. A wooden chair, by the feel of it. And a damned uncomfortable one at that.

I tested my feet next, already knowin' what I would find, and not bein' disappointed. My ankles were tied, too, presumably to the legs of the chair. Even my metal leg, which I could only guess was tied same as my natural leg, since I couldn't feel no rope around that ankle. But the thing didn't jerk out uncontrollably when I tried to move it, either.

My boots were missin'.

Yep, I was pretty fucked.

I sighed and forced myself to lift my head. The movement sent shocks of pain stabbin' into my eyes and I grimaced, but kept my head up. I squinted through blurred vision and a smoky haze to see a man standin' in front of me. He was dressed fancy in a suit, which looked odd considerin' he was standin' in the middle of the ruins of one the burned-down barns. A bit of ash or maybe plaster powder from the house explosion dusted his shoulders. His graying hair had only a single piece fallen loose from the rigorous hold of his pomade, and it fell across a stern brow above a pair of severe eyebrows.

He must have been Baron Whittaker.

And he was glarin' at me like any wealthy man who'd had his house blown up and slaves freed and barns burned might.

There were six other men with him, three on each side of him, all givin' me murderous looks. They held weapons of various types: rifles, revolvers, crowbars, knives. But what I found most concernin' were the other, unarmed people present.

They were kneelin' in front of the baron's six men with their hands on their heads, eight of 'em, and from their clothes and their physical state I knew they had to be some of the slaves. Recaptured, maybe. Or maybe these hadn't even had the chance to run in the first place.

I swallowed. I was fucked, all right. Really, really fucked.

I glanced to either side of my lone chair, set in the middle of the burned out hulk of one of the barns. The other barn I'd set on fire had also mostly burned down, but the third was still standin'. Looked like all the flames were out now, though, and there was no sign of the fire wagon. The moon had moved to the other side of the sky.

Looked like I'd been out fer awhile.

Well hell. Holt woulda had the money already, then, and been long gone away from Blessing. And Charlotte ... least I didn't see her kneelin' in the ashes there in front of me.

Maybe she'd escaped.

Or maybe she was already dead.

Either way, I was on my own here. On my own and facin' down a very pissed off Baron Whittaker. I cleared my throat. "Looks like you had a bad night," I croaked.

Without hesitation, one of his men stepped forward and cracked the butt of his rifle into my face.

It hurt. A lot. But I swallowed back the cry, not wantin' to give him the satisfaction.

The man stepped back, and I made myself look up again, glarin' through waterin' eyes. The left side of my face was throbbin' too, now, and that eye would probably swell up closed 'fore too long.

Baron Whittaker held up a hand. "Easy there, boys. I want him to be conscious for what comes next." He spoke quietly, each word carefully pronunciated. Then he took one step forward, his shiny shoes swiftly coated in ash as he did so. He directed his next question at me. "Where is she?"

My heart quickened. So maybe she wasn't dead. "Who?"

He smiled. "The girl. The redhead."

I scoffed and shook my head. "Mister, you know how many redheaded women I know? Yer gonna have to be more specific."

His smile thinned. "Her name is Charlotte. She ran away from me yesterday, and yet I know she was here tonight. She nearly killed me in my own house. Now, it seems, she has vanished, leaving only you."

"Sounds like a smart girl," I said.

Now his smile vanished, just like Charlotte seemed to have done. "Did she put you up to this? She give you some sad story to pull at your heart strings and convince you to come here and risk your life? And for what?" He turned slightly to glare down at the kneelin' slaves, his lip curlin' in a sneer. "For these poor wretches?"

I said nothin'. Sayin' nothin' was usually best in these types of situations.

Baron Whittaker held out a hand toward his men, palm up. One of 'em handed over a revolver. The baron pointed it toward the head of the nearest slave.

I tensed. It took everythin' I had to stay quiet, to seem like I didn't care. But inside, my heart thundered in my temples, puttin' my head in a vice of pain.

"You one of those freedom fighters, then?" Baron Whittaker asked. "Come to set these poor souls free? Well, I can help you with that." He fired.

I yelled, tryin' to come up outta the chair. But the ropes held me fast, and I only succeeded at nearly tippin' myself over.

Baron Whittaker looked at me, one eyebrow raised. "Oh. So you do care. Perhaps we are getting closer to the truth, then." He aimed at the head of the next slave, a woman, who was now tremblin' and cryin'. All of 'em were.

I stared at him, strainin' against the ropes, breath comin' fast and hard.

"Well," he said, voice maddeningly calm, like those people didn't matter to him at all. "Let me show you what you have done for these people." He fired again, and the second slave in the line of eight fell backward with a bullet hole between her eyes, a cloud of ash risin' up around her like a shroud when she landed.

He took aim at the third.

"Stop!" I shouted. "Stop, please!"

He drew back the pistol and turned to face me. "Where is she?" he asked again.

"I don't know."

He shot the third slave without even lookin'.

"Stop, goddamnit!" I pulled hard at my wrists, the rope rubbin' the skin raw, but I'd been tied tight. Not that it'd do me much good to get my hands free, anyway, as they'd taken my gun belts. But I couldn't stand to just sit there and watch this. I had to get free. I had to do *somethin'*.

Course, *doin' somethin'* was what had landed me—and the poor sods now dyin' and kneelin' in the ash—in this spot to begin with.

Maybe I shouldn'ta agreed to help Charlotte at all. Maybe I shoulda just left her to chance escapin' the law and the baron on her own. Maybe Holt had been right all along.

"We split up," I blurted. And I was glad I didn't know where she had gone, then. I had a feelin' this Baron Whittaker woulda been able to tell if I were lyin'. And if I'd known where she'd gone, I'd have to lie, now. As it was, I could be honest. "We split up and I don't know where she went. She was supposed to meet me back here at the barns, but she didn't. I thought she was dead."

The baron tilted his head to the side fractionally. His blue eyes narrowed, and I could tell he was weighin' my words, decidin' whether or not he believed me.

I kept my eyes locked with his, both to sell the truth of my words and to keep my gaze from slippin' to the five slaves still alive. I couldn't look at 'em. Couldn't stand the thought of them dyin' just so the baron could get at me. If I looked at 'em, he would see that.

And I couldn't let him see that.

"What does it matter, anyway?" I went on at his continued silence. "You have me. This was my idea, not hers. I talked her into it. She wanted to just run ... I convinced her to come back here and show me the way in."

My voice caught. Because it was true. It *had* been my idea. I'd used her and her desperate situation, risked her life, all to cause a distraction so we could get our money.

My money. For Ethelyn.

And now here I was. Guess I'd be atonin' fer my sins sooner than I'd thought.

Baron Whittaker lowered the hand that held the gun. "Why?" was all he said.

I kept my gaze away from the cryin' slaves only with difficulty, and swallowed again. That, I didn't want to tell him. The truth, whether about Ethelyn or Charlotte, he'd only use against me, and there weren't no suitable lie he wouldn't see through in a second. I shoulda learned more about the wealthy barons of Blessing. Maybe then I coulda claimed to have been sent to sabotage him by a rival or some such.

But as it were, I knew nothin' about Baron Whittaker's rivals. So I said nothin'.

He nodded, as if my silence itself were some kind of answer. "I see. Let me give you a piece of advice, young man. The next time you decide to go after one of the barons of Blessing ... you be sure you kill him. First thing. And you raze his house and everything he has to the ground. You should probably be sure to kill the rest of his family, too." He gestured to one of his men who held a crowbar, and the man walked around behind me.

I braced myself for a blow, but none came.

The baron made a show of openin' the cylinder of his revolver and reloading the three empty chambers. "You see," he went on, clickin' the full cylinder closed again, "we don't forgive. And we don't forget. You leave us alive, and we're going to be sure we get back what you took from us."

I worked on the ropes around my wrists, but all I managed was to send them into a fire of pain, too.

"So let's see. What have you cost me tonight?" Baron Whittaker paced slowly along the line of five slaves, some of whom had started to quietly beg him for mercy. Some of whom threw themselves at his feet, grovelin'.

It made me sick to watch. I tried to get up outta the chair again, but it only rocked at my efforts.

The baron paid me no mind, pacin' back and forth between me and the slaves, gun in hand. "You've cost me a lot of money, certainly. A lot of trouble. And a good night's rest. But I can tell from the looks of you that you don't come from money. So I won't bother demanding monetary retribution. Nor can your one body replace the number of slaves I've lost tonight." He stopped pacin' and turned on his heel to face me. "So, I shall take it in blood, Mr. Freedom Fighter. And I think it will take a good long while to make all of this up to me." He lifted his hands, pistol and all, and waved around at the smokin' destruction that surrounded us.

I gave a little laugh despite myself. "That's ... that's very melodramatic of you, Baron."

He smiled at me again, that thin, humorless smile. "Perhaps I do have a weakness for theater," he conceded. "I always do like to put on a good show." Then his smile went away with chilling abruptness. "Which is why they are going to watch what happens to people who try and steal my property," he nodded toward the slaves, "and then you are going to watch them die."

The man with the crowbar reemerged from behind me, and the

end of his crowbar was now glowin' orange. There musta been some embers still smolderin' somewhere.

"Hey hey hey, *wait*," I said, eyin' the crowbar as the man stepped close to me. Heat shimmered off it and I pressed myself back further into the chair. "They don't need to die. They had nothin' to do with any of this!"

"Oh, I know," the baron said. His voice was gentle, sympathetic. Terrifyin'. "Do you think I enjoy destroying perfectly good slaves? Of course not." He shook his head. "It's a loss to me as well, in more ways than one. But *you* did this. You condemned them to death as soon as you barged onto my property and tried to spirit them away. As soon as you encouraged them to betray their master, and as soon as they decided to attempt such a thing. Their deaths are *your* fault, Mr. Freedom Fighter. And the others will learn from their mistakes. From *your* mistake."

He waved his man forward.

I opened my mouth to argue further, but then the end of that glowin' crowbar pressed into my right bicep with a hiss, and all my words were lost in a blaze of white-hot pain. My scream echoed up outta that ruined barn, up into the night, up to the glitterin' stars that watched us all with their cold, impassive stare.

The crowbar drew back, then bit again. And again.

I lost track of how many times that bastard branded me with that pry bar. The pain all ran together, lightin' up the whole of my right arm like they'd put it in the fire itself. I struggled against the ropes, tried to pull away from it, tried to escape its relentless advance.

Tipped myself over once and got a face full of ash, only to be pulled upright again by unseen hands.

Then the fresh pain stopped.

I waited, braced for it to come again, hunched in the chair and gaspin', my face wet with traitorous tears. My right arm still screamed, waves of pain runnin' from shoulder to fingers.

"Ah," Baron Whittaker said in his calm, quiet voice, "don't worry, Mr. Freedom Fighter. We're only just beginning. Soon we will move to more ... *sensitive* ... areas."

I peeled my eyes open to give him what glare I could muster, blinkin' through a blur of tears and ash and agony.

He was smilin' again, but a real smile this time, truly enjoyin' my sufferin'.

I wanted to kill him, then, even more than I'd wanted to kill him before. I wanted to kill him fer what he was doin' to me, and fer what he'd done to the people enslaved to him, and fer what he'd done to Charlotte.

Unfortunately, it seemed unlikely I'd get the chance.

"But first," he said, and waved at another of his men with a crowbar, who advanced on me.

I wondered why these men seemed to have such a fascination with pry bars. But I shouldn't have. I got my answer in the next second, when he drew it back two-handed and then smashed it with all his might into my left knee.

If it woulda been my right knee, the blow woulda surely shattered my kneecap, and I woulda been sent into a world of hurt that made the brandin' seem trivial, indeed.

But it was my left knee, instead, made up now of metal and gears, and the pry bar bounced off it with a clang, makin' me jump in surprise and the man weildin' it stagger backward.

He lowered the crowbar and stared at me.

I stared back. And I thought of what Dr. Balogh had said about the metal leg havin' *advantages*. I'm sure this wasn't what he'd meant. But I was thankful fer not havin' a shattered kneecap just then, certainly. Though I also had the impression that Baron Whittaker findin' out about my metal leg wouldn't lead to anythin' more pleasant in the end, anyway.

"What was that?" the baron asked.

"I dunno," his man with the non-heated crowbar answered. He stepped forward again and tapped on my shin experimentally with the end of the bar. It made a little *tink tink tink* sound.

Unmistakably metal against metal, even through the fabric of my pants.

Shit.

"What the Devil...?" Baron Whittaker handed off his revolver and took one of the big huntin' knives instead. He came up to me himself now, and I wished more than ever I could get even just one of my limbs free from the damned ropes.

But I couldn't.

I kept tryin' anyway, even as he stabbed the knife down hard into my leg, right above the knee. Least he hadn't tried it in my thigh, where I still had flesh and bone.

The knife's edge jarred off the metal pipin' of my leg.

The baron looked at my knee fer a minute, then looked up at me.

I said nothin', but I could feel my heart throbbin' in every part of me they'd hurt. I didn't know what he'd do when he saw my leg. The town of Blessing was famous for its Old World ruins.

Baron Whittaker was wealthy 'cause of his expeditions into those ruins.

Was my metal leg Old World tech? And workin' Old World tech, at that?

I didn't know. I didn't even know if Dr. Balogh knew, really.

But it sure seemed similar. And people had killed fer a lot less when it came to Old World tech.

Baron Whittaker returned his attention to my leg, slidin' the knife blade into the hole it'd made in my pants, then cuttin' down all the way to my ankle. He tore the pants leg open, and there was my metal leg, all right, gleamin' dully in the light of the moon.

"Well, well, well," he mused, standin' back to study it, "would you look at that?"

The man who'd hit me with the crowbar muttered and signed himself.

The one with the heated crowbar only stared, seemin' to have forgotten to re-heat his tool, because the end of it was no longer glowin'. Course, that was just fine with me.

The baron's four other men glanced at each other, some swearin' and some prayin' under their breath.

And the five slaves still left alive somehow looked even more terrified. They huddled together in a bunch, their eyes so wide I could see the whites, even in the dimness of the night.

Baron Whittaker clucked his tongue. "Now where oh where did you get that, Mr. Freedom Fighter? You steal it?"

I barked a laugh. "It don't even work," I rasped. "It might look fancy, but it's just a crutch. A crutch made outta metal in the shape of a leg. That's all."

"Where did you get it?"

I shook my head. "Doesn't matter."

"Oh, it matters." Baron Whittaker grabbed a fistful of my hair and pulled my head back so I had to look up at him. "You see, I don't know of anyone in the Territories who can do such work. And that's a problem. Because I make it my business to know everyone who has such talents. It's not fair their gifts be *wasted* on people such as yourself, you see."

I grinned at him through the blood and tears. "Well shit, Baron. Life ain't fair though, is it?" I worked up a nice bit of phlegm and spit at him. It landed on the front of his fancy suit.

He released his grip on my hair and pulled a handkerchief from the front pocket of that fancy suit. He wiped the hand he'd just had in my hair, then wiped up the wad of spit from his jacket. Then he tossed the silken square into the ashes and sighed. "All right. You just let me know when you're ready to talk. I can wait. As I said, we're only just beginning."

He left me, exchangin' his knife for a gun again and goin' to stand behind the cluster of five slaves this time. He clasped his hands in front of him, the pistol pointin' at the ground, I was happy to see, instead of at anyone's heads.

I let out a breath. I'd expected that to go worse.

But then I saw the fella with the heated crowbar come up beside me, and the damn thing was glowin' again.

Fuck me. I wondered how long Baron Whittaker would find torturin' me entertainin'. I wondered how long he'd wait fer me to tell him all about Dr. Balogh. I wondered how long I'd be able to stay quiet, or if eventually he'd break me.

And I wondered what he'd do to the good doctor if he found him.

I didn't want Baron Whittaker to find Dr. Balogh and his family. I'd already stolen their mule. I didn't want to get them killed, too.

I'd gotten enough people killed already.

The red-hot crowbar pressed into my inner left thigh this time and I started and yelped, then clenched my teeth against the scream. Hands caught the back of my chair and steadied it as I almost tipped again.

He held the shimmerin' metal to my skin longer this time, probably tryin' to get some noise outta me, but I swallowed it back with every ounce of my willpower till he gave up, pullin' it away.

I dared to breathe again, suckin' in air in harsh, ragged gulps. Fresh tears wet my cheeks. I could stop the screamin', sometimes, but I couldn't stop those. Nausea rolled in my gut, and my whole body was shakin'.

Somewhere in the distance, across the silence of the night, I heard a horse whinny.

"Looks like he's got regular flesh there, Mr. Whittaker," said the man holdin' the hot crowbar.

"Good." The baron's cold blue eyes shifted to me. "And what about your other leg, Mr. Freedom Fighter? Is it metal, too? Or just flesh and bone?"

"Only one way to find out," said the fella with the second crowbar. He walked around to my right side, kickin' casually at the piles of ash in his way as he did so.

I swore I could hear hooves in the grass, comin' from somewhere. But maybe it was just my throbbin' heart, rushin' blood through my achin' head, tickin' down the final hours of my life.

The man with the second crowbar positioned himself to take a nice hard swing at my right knee.

This one wasn't gonna bounce off metal.

This one was gonna hurt like hell.

I sucked in a breath and closed my eyes, bracin' myself.

Another whinny, loud and piercin', and close.

I snapped my eyes open and looked.

A horse galloped by us, no rider and no saddle, whinnyin' again. An answerin' whinny sounded from a little ways away, across the baron's yard. And then a few more horses came gallopin' by, followin' the first.

We all stared after 'em, not one of us understandin'.

Baron Whittaker rounded on his six men, currently all gathered around me in my lone chair. "Those are *my* horses! How did they get out?"

The men looked to each other, but it seemed none of them had any answers.

"You said all the escaped slaves had been recovered, yes?" the baron asked.

"Well, most of them, sir," one with a rifle answered. He had no hat, and his brown hair was long and greasy. "Some of them were shot while escaping. And a few we couldn't find. But John's already talked to the sheriff's office—"

Baron Whittaker's face reddened, his fists clenchin', even the one around the gun still in his hand. "Maddox, Russell, you go get those damn horses and put them back where they belong. The rest of us will stay here and deal with this thieving bastard. Got it?"

Two of the six—unfortunately neither of the men currently holdin' crowbars—nodded and ran off into the darkness.

They were just passin' by the third slave barn, the only one left standin', when it exploded.

The blast sent wood shrapnel and both men flyin'. They landed amid a rain of wooden splinters, and neither of 'em got up again.

I hoped they were dead.

It was then I realized there didn't seem to be anyone else inside the barn that had exploded. There weren't no screamin' and wailin', no bodies.

Baron Whittaker seemed to realize this at the same time. "What in the Devil is going on here?" he shouted. "I thought you men told me the perimeter was clear!"

"It—it was, sir," one with a knife said.

The baron swore. So he wasn't so much better than the rest of us, after all. Funny how all that money and learnin' didn't seem to matter much in the face of danger. "Does that seem *clear* to you?!" He jabbed a finger toward the third barn, now only a heap of broken timbers. Then gestured toward me, toward the slaves huddled before him. "Get them inside! All of them! And one of you go tell McCormick to double—no, *triple*—security out here! I will not stand for—"

The sound of more hooves cut him off.

He turned with a scowl, clearly expectin' another of his horses runnin' free.

And it was another of his horses, I suppose, but this one wasn't runnin' aimlessly. This one had a saddle and a rider.

A rider carryin' a very big gun. A gun that looked more like a cannon.

Baron Whittaker's mouth fell open, makin' a nice, round O.

Hell, my expression probably looked somethin' of the same, because that's when the rider came close enough fer me to recognize her.

Charlotte.

She opened fire.

XII

BEHOLD A PALE HORSE

The cannon of a gun she carried roared and spit fire, and I realized it made the same sound I'd heard earlier, comin' from inside the house. The gun that had silenced all the other guns.

Her horse threw up its head and pinned its ears at the flash and the noise, wild-eyed and jumpy, but she drove it onward with her heels, her finger never comin' off the trigger.

Baron Whittaker was just bringin' his pistol up toward her when a wild spray of slugs punched into his chest and sent him sprawlin' into the ash. Blood splattered across his slaves. They shrieked and flattened themselves against the ground.

The baron's four men around me scrambled fer their guns, too. Only one of 'em had his ready, the one with the rifle. He'd just sighted down the length of it when she mowed him down, and I shoved myself over sideways just as the storm of bullets filled the air where I'd just been.

The three remainin' men dropped heavily all around me, big, gapin' holes punched through 'em. I coughed in the cloud of ash they stirred up.

Heard the hoofbeats circle around, then come to a stop.

I lifted my head and looked through the haze to see Charlotte had dismounted, looped the reins of her nervous horse over a charred two-by-four still stuck in the ground, and was now stridin' in my direction, the cannon still gripped in both hands.

I couldn't rightly tell by the look on her face if she meant to rescue me ... or kill me, too. I opened my mouth to ask, but the words got stuck.

She ignored me fer the moment and propped the giant gun back against one shoulder, then bent down to retrieve the heated crowbar, still glowin' a faint orange on one end.

Fer a second I was afraid she planned to use it on me again, but then she turned away and went to the baron's body.

No ... he weren't dead yet.

I could see him twitchin', hear the rattle of his breath as he gasped fer air.

Charlotte marched right over to his side, standin' over him with the cannon-gun in one hand and the hot crowbar in the other, her skirt and blouse streaked again with dirt and soot, her wavy red locks, once neatly pinned atop her head, now in disarray and fallin' down around her shoulders.

"Y-you..." the baron gurgled.

"Me," she said. And then she jammed that hot crowbar up between his legs, right into his goods.

I grimaced.

The baron screamed, high and terrible.

The nervous horse whickered and rolled its eyes, dancin' in place.

Charlotte jabbed the crowbar at his face then, into his eye.

His shriekin' raised the hairs on my arms. And yet, it was the kind of justice a man like him deserved.

She took his other eye, too, lettin' him scream and blubber and choke and rattle, hands weakly flailin', tryin' to find her, or tryin' to find his gun. Then she threw the crowbar away and drew my pistol from the sash at her waist. Her face was hard and expressionless and pale in the moonlight as she aimed. And pulled the trigger.

His screamin' abruptly stopped, his body goin' still, and the sudden silence rang in my ears.

She stood there fer a minute, lookin' down at him. A tendril of smoke trailed from the barrel of my gun. Then she tucked it back into her sash, and looked down to the five slaves still flattened against the ground there, all of 'em now gapin' at her with open mouths.

"Go," she said quietly. "Get out of here. You're free now. Go back to your families."

They didn't move.

She didn't prod them. She looked toward me, instead. Then carefully stepped around them to make her way back to my sideways chair. She picked up my gun belts from where they'd been tossed into the ash and buckled them around her own waist, though they were too big and slipped down low around her hips. She grabbed up my boots next, then pulled the parasol knife and crouched, sawin' through the ropes that bound me.

One by one, my limbs fell free, and I rolled away from the chair and onto my back, starin' up at the stars, gaspin' myself. My head still felt as if it might split in two, my right arm as if it were on fire, and the branded spot on my thigh was worst of all. My left eye had swollen up, all right, leavin' me with half a view.

Charlotte's face eclipsed that half a view of the stars.

At least it seemed she had no intention of killin' me. I didn't think. "What..." I winced, my throat raw from screamin'. "What took you so long?"

"I was freeing the others," she said. "And taking care of some of the perimeter security. How did you know I would come back for you?"

"I didn't."

She leaned down to help me sit, and I winced again at the movement. "You thought I would leave you here? For the baron?"

I prodded gingerly at the swollen places on my right temple and left eye. My fingers came away sticky with blood. "That woulda been the smart thing to do."

She hissed a noise of dismissal. "No. I've seen enough people suffer at his hands. And anyway ... you helped me back at the Seven Knives. It was the least I could do to return the favor."

"Except this was my idea," I mumbled. "I coulda got us both killed."

"Could have," she agreed. "But didn't."

"Close enough."

"Hardly. You'll be all right." She gave a little grunt as she helped me to my feet and steadied me as I swayed. She set my boots upright for me and held me as I shoved my feet down into 'em, nearly swoonin' from the pain. "I'm sorry. But you made a very good distraction. I had to be sure I got as many out as I could."

She used her massive rifle like a walkin' stick on one side and wrapped her other arm around me, helpin' me limp toward the horse.

"Was that your plan all along, then? Use me as a distraction?" I felt a fool. I felt used. And yet there was a kind of justice in that, too, weren't there? After all, I'd arranged this whole business as a distraction fer the bank robbery in the first place. The irony of it almost made me laugh despite the pain. *Who used who, I wonder?*

"No," Charlotte insisted, and she even sounded a little offended. "My only plan was ... well, our plan. The plan we made at the Seven Knives. But when I got here ... once I was inside ... my plans changed. I only wanted to kill Baron Whittaker. But he got away from me in the house. I came back out to meet you at the barns, like we said, but by then they'd found you and knocked you out cold. So I improvised.

"I got them all out, Van. All the slaves except those five." She looked over her shoulder to them, and they seemed to be recoverin' a bit from their shock now, sittin' up and talkin' in whispers, pointin' and gesturin' first toward Charlotte and then out at the land beyond the fence. "Well, and except for some of the house staff. But they'd run when the dynamite blew out the house wall. And anyway, most of them were loyal to the baron."

I only managed a grunt, concentratin' too hard on not blackin' out.

"And I found myself a fast horse."

It looked fast, sure enough, but it also looked awful hot, nostrils flarin' and eyes rollin', pawin' at the dirt. It was a tall, sleek blue roan with a mane and tail black as night. And Baron Whittaker's brand on its left hip.

We'd have to fix that right quick, or we wouldn't get far at all. Not after the sun rose on all the death and destruction we'd rained down on this place tonight.

"Gotta get outta here," I muttered.

Charlotte scoffed. "What do you think we're doing? Here, let me mount up first, then I can give you a hand up."

I clutched a fistful of mane to keep myself standin' as she let go of me, then clumsily scrambled up into the saddle. That damn cannon-gun of hers was heavy and unwieldy, and she had nowhere to holster it, neither on herself nor on the horse.

"Leave it," I said.

She looked down at me in surprise. "I beg your pardon?"

"That gun. Leave it. Too big. It'll just slow us down."

She laid it over the front of the saddle with one hand and reached her other hand down toward me. "I will do no such thing. As far as I know, this is the only gun of its kind in the Territories. Baron Whittaker never shut up about it. And as you saw, it's quite useful. I'll be keeping it, thank you very much. Now, are you coming or not?"

I eyed her and that ridiculous gun, sittin' proud upon that tall horse, and thought suddenly of one of the verses from the Good Book Mama had sometimes read to us. The one about the pale horse and the rider that was Death.

Well, with that horse and that gun, Charlotte could be Death fer a lot of people, certainly. And bring Hell followin' after her, all right.

I steeled myself for new pain as I gripped her forearm with my left hand and managed to stick my metal foot in the left stirrup.

"On the count of three," she said. "One, two, *three!*" She pulled and I mustered a hop off my right foot, barely managin' to get myself over the back of the horse without either blackin' out or slidin' right off the other side.

I clutched the back of the saddle as the horse danced around.

Charlotte spoke soothin' words to it, though I wasn't sure they did much good.

"Hold on to me," she instructed.

"I'll take us both down if I fall off," I warned.

"Just do it."

I did so reluctantly, slidin' my arms around her slender waist. The feel of her was strangely comfortin', and I had a sudden impulse to lean into her, to rest my head on her shoulder and close my eyes.

But I didn't.

That wouldn'ta been appropriate.

She kicked the horse up into a canter and the comfortin' thoughts all went away with the sharp reminders of all my pain. I sucked in a breath and ground my teeth against it.

"Hold on," she called back to me. "Stay with me. We'll get someplace safe."

Someplace safe. As if that existed anywhere in the Western Territories. And after hearin' Charlotte's story, I wasn't sure even the East Republic was so safe anymore.

But safe didn't much matter, anyway. All that mattered was that money.

"Grave Gulch," I managed to choke out. "Get to Grave Gulch."

Holt woulda left Blessing without us by now, sure, but our fallback meetin' place had always been Grave Gulch. He'd wait there a month before movin' on. That had always been our agreement if things ever went to Hell on a job: go back to Grave Gulch. Wait a month. If the other of us didn't show up by then, we were most likely dead.

"Grave Gulch," Charlotte mused. "That's a pretty far ride."

"Yeah."

"I haven't been here that long, but even *I've* heard the stories about those who live in Grave Gulch. You sure it's the best place to go right now? In your condition?"

"Yeah. We got a camp there. It's fine."

A long stretch of silence, broken only by the horse's quick hooves on grass, followed my statement. I could tell Charlotte didn't like that idea none. But it was as close as I had to a home. As close as I had to somewhere safe. And Holt was as close as I had to any kind of family anymore.

"All right," she finally said, reluctant. But she turned the horse in the right direction.

Of course, there was a chance Holt had taken that money from the Bank of Blessing and decided to strike off on his own without waitin' fer me. He coulda decided to keep it all fer himself.

That kinda money woulda been a mighty strong temptation fer anyone, much less a man like Holt Haggerty, who'd never spent a day of his life on the right side of the law.

My stomach turned at the thought.

If Holt had taken off with the money ... well. I didn't want to have to track him down. I didn't want to have to try and take back that money. I didn't want to have to kill him. Not after everythin' he'd done fer me these past eight years.

But then ... maybe he was already dead. Maybe he hadn't pulled off the bank job at all. Maybe the law had gunned him down, and I'd be the one waitin' at Grave Gulch with no money at all, a massive debt still owed to Nine-Fingered Nan, and a lot more scars.

"Hold on," Charlotte reminded me, and her soft voice jolted me back to the present.

I realized my hold on her had been slippin', that my vision had dimmed. I fought back to consciousness, tightened my hold around her waist.

"I'll head toward Grave Gulch," she said. "But we're going to have to camp a few times between here and there. I don't suppose you have any supplies stashed anywhere?"

Supplies. All my stuff was packed on my mule. And Holt had taken the mule. "No," I said.

She said nothin' in reply. She was probably regrettin' her decision to rescue me. Probably wonderin' how we were supposed to make a few days' ride with one horse and no supplies and me in my current state, hardly able to keep myself upright on the back of that pale horse.

I was wonderin' the same thing.

I drifted in and out of awareness as we rode, the rhythm of the horse's hooves lullin' me into a semi-conscious state. Any time I'd dip too deep into the welcomin' darkness and start to slip, Charlotte's warnin' would snap me back awake, just in time to grab hold of her again and right myself.

The situation was disturbin'ly familiar, really. It hadn't been all that long ago I'd been atop that vulture Clint's horse, ridin' toward Brave-bank with a bullet in my leg and a fever in my blood. Only I hadn't had anyone else with me at the time to wake me up when I passed out.

I'd only come to later, sprawled out on the ground, minus my canteens and minus my horse.

Wasn't sure I was all that much better off currently ... but at least I had Charlotte fer the moment. And at least she was on my side.

Fer the moment.

She brought us to a stop in the late mornin' beneath a thick grove of trees. We were several miles south of Blessing now, and these kinda trees wouldn't be commonplace anymore after a few more hours of ridin'. But fer now I was thankful fer their shade, and fer the softness of the grass as I eased off the horse and collapsed down into it.

Charlotte dug around in the saddlebags, then came to my side with her arms fulla stuff. She knelt down next to me. "Take off your clothes."

I turned my head to look at her. "What?"

She set down the stuff in her arms, arrangin' it in a neat semi-circle on the grass. "Take off your clothes," she repeated. There was a hint of humor there in the way the corners of her mouth quirked, the glint in her dark blue eyes. But then she sobered. "I need to treat those burns. You're not the first person I've seen the baron do this to. If we don't get them taken care of they could get infected. So." She gestured with her hands. "Come on. Off with it."

I grunted and complied. Or tried to. It was hard to work my right hand with that arm still blazin' in pain. The fingers were swollen, even though that hellish crowbar had never gone past my elbow.

Charlotte watched me fumble at my shirt buttons fer a minute, then sighed and reached forward to help me.

I eyed her. "I hope you don't think I'm going to bestow my *charms* upon you just 'cause you helped me escape?"

Her fingers paused on the buttons, mouth twistin' into a wry smile as she looked at me. "Hah. Very clever, Mr. Delano. Maybe I would, if I thought you had any *charms* to bestow in the first place."

I gave a rough chuckle and shook my head. "Fair point."

She finished with the buttons and helped me shrug outta the shirt, sweat-soaked and stained with ash and charred in several spots along the right arm. "There we go. Now, just hold still."

That was easy enough to do. Mostly. 'Cept fer the few times I'd wince or flinch as she cleaned the blistered skin and gently spread a salve over it, then wrapped it with clean bandages. "Where'd you get all that?" I asked, tiltin' my chin toward all the stuff.

We didn't have no campin' supplies, no food, but it looked like she'd managed to bring a whole doctor's medicine cabinet along with her.

She tied off the bandage on my arm and moved to investigatin' my face, holdin' my chin in one hand while carefully wipin' at the dried blood with a damp cloth. "Mm? Oh." She took a deep breath and let it out slowly. A heavy sadness fell over her face and she shook her head. "I knew what he was going to do to you soon as I saw they'd found you. I made a trip back inside the house to get these before it all burned down. Everyone had cleared out of it after the dynamite, anyway."

"You didn't get any food, though?"

She rolled her eyes. "No. But I did grab a few other valuables, too, while I was there."

That piqued my interest. "Like what? And how much?"

"Enough to pay for supplies, if I can find a place to sell them."

I would have liked to have known more about the stuff she'd grabbed from the baron's house, but then she pulled out a spool of stitchin' thread and one of those ugly hooked needles and my attention went to keepin' quiet while she sewed up the gash on my head.

By the time she was ready to fix up the burn on my thigh, I was plum wore out.

And I was grateful she didn't require me to shuck off my pants entirely while she doctored that burn, too. Instead, she just ripped 'em a little more, and I tried to think of other things while she cleaned and applied ointment to that one, both 'cause of the deep, burnin' pain that still radiated from there ... and 'cause of the nearness of her hands to my groin.

I suddenly became quite aware of the sight I musta been. A sorry one, indeed.

She finished wrappin' the thigh burn and tugged the two halves of my torn pants leg back together, back over the burn and the bandage, back over the unnatural seam where flesh met metal, back over the rest of the metal contraption that made up the rest of my leg.

Her eyes lingered on it, even after it was covered. "Well, I didn't get any thread for mending clothing," she said, "but I'll add that to the list of supplies I'll try and buy. We'll get those sewn up so they'll be good as new."

Still her eyes didn't leave my leg.

I wanted to say somethin' about it, but I wasn't sure exactly what. I opened my mouth to fill the widenin' silence, but then she turned her face to me abruptly and I closed it.

"Where *did* you get it?" she asked.

I swallowed, shrugged. "Some foreign doctor. I didn't ask fer it. I was unconscious when he ... when he took my leg. And then when I woke up I had this one." I twitched the metal foot, then startled as the toes actually moved like I'd intended. Maybe, after all this time, I was finally startin' to understand the thing.

"It's a dangerous thing to have," Charlotte said softly.

I nodded toward her cannon-gun, the fat barrel propped up against a nearby tree. "So is that."

She followed my gaze and smiled. "Except I don't need that thing to walk."

"Well, half the time I don't need this thing to walk, either," I grumbled. "It mostly don't work, just like I told the baron."

Her smile faded. "He would have cut it off you, eventually."

I grimaced at the thought, but had no doubt it was true. I reached out and took her hand, surprisin' myself as much as her. But there was somethin' that needed said. "Thank you. Fer comin' back fer me. And fer doctorin' me up. You shouldn't have ... but thank you."

Color rose to her cheeks, tryin' to cover up the freckles there. "Like I said, it was the least I could do. I appreciate you not handing me over to the law as soon as you saw me. A thousand dollars would have swayed a lot of people."

I shook my head.

"And thank *you* for giving me the opportunity to end Baron Whittaker," she said then, her voice turnin' hard. "I never could have done it without you. Those slaves wouldn't be free without you, either." She squeezed my hand. "I'm just sorry for what you had to go through to achieve it."

My mouth was dry and I tried to wet my cracked lips. All I could think of was those three slaves Baron Whittaker had gunned down. And the others shot down with rifles as they'd fled into the night, too.

And everythin' else I had done and hadn't done in all my years of searchin' fer Ethelyn.

I deserved worse, in truth.

But I was close now. So close. Closer than I'd ever been.

Long as Holt had managed to get that money.

I pulled my hand from hers and cleared my throat.

She blinked and looked away, then began to gather up all her stolen medical supplies.

The thought occurred to me then that those supplies were worth quite a bit of money by themselves. Maybe we weren't so bad off on this journey after all. If she could find anywhere to sell them.

I wanted nothin' more at that moment than to close my eyes and sleep, right there in the grass where I lay. But we weren't far enough away from Blessing yet to rest comfortable, so I swallowed down a few gulps from the single waterskin Charlotte had taken, and struggled up behind her onto the stolen horse again.

We rode on.

We stopped again in the late afternoon, mostly 'cause I couldn't seem to stay on the damn horse. Exhaustion took me soon as I settled back against a young birch. I was vaguely aware of Charlotte headin' down toward the bank of the river we'd been loosely followin', but then slipped gladly into blackness.

I started awake some time later and groaned as consciousness brought back the dull ache of pain, everywhere. Especially in my head. Night had fallen, and I blinked in the glow of a nearby fire. I squinted, fuzzy shapes and colors slowly resolvin' into things familiar.

Charlotte crouched there by the fire, warmin' somethin' in a small pan. She noticed I was awake and came over, bringin' me more water, some jerky and beans, and whiskey.

I drug myself up sittin', thinkin' I'd never seen anythin' more wonderful in my life. "You found a place to sell the baron's stuff," I croaked.

She smiled. Nodded. "Well, traded, more like. But yes. I found a place."

We made little conversation as I ate, for which I was grateful. My head was poundin' too hard fer words to come easy. I ate quickly and gladly accepted the bedroll Charlotte offered me ... only after assurin' myself she had her own.

I eased my battered body onto the thin woolen roll, and slept again.

We rode once more at dawn's first light. At my urgin', Charlotte kept our pace steady, but not too fast. I didn't want to lose the horse. And carryin' two instead of one was burden enough.

Hour by hour we rode.

She stitched up my pant leg when we stopped to rest that afternoon under the thin shade of a mesquite. And went scoutin' off around our camp with her ridiculous cannon-gun, leavin' me to fret over every minute of her absence, my hand always waitin' on the pistol in the belts she'd now returned to me.

But she came back soon enough and claimed she hadn't seen no one followin' our trail.

Still, when we headed out again, we kept off the roads.

The landscape had changed over the course of the day into what I'd known for so long now: clumps of creosote and mesquite, cacti, and those red rocks. Gone were the trees and lush grass carpet of the north.

We made cold camp that night.

And carried on the next dawn. Little by little, the pain in my burns eased to somethin' tolerable. My headache calmed, too. I got some of my strength back.

And then at last, mid-morning, appearin' upright as we rounded a bend, was a human skeleton.

The horse threw up its head and snorted.

Charlotte let out a gasp and reined it in sharply.

"It's okay," I said. "Just markin' the edge of the town. We're close."

Charlotte said nothin', her eyes fixed on the bleached bones, hung as if the person was still alive and standin'. You almost couldn't see the sticks that held 'em up, not till you got good and close, anyway. It made fer a rather alarmin' effect. Which was, of course, the intention.

The horse whickered and pawed at the dirt.

"It's fine," I said. "Go on, it ain't gonna hurt you. They've been dead a long time."

Charlotte hesitated a moment more, then reluctantly pressed her heels to the horse's side. It went wide around the skeleton, eyein' the thing the whole time, same as Charlotte.

I couldn't help but feel amused by their mutual suspicion. Regardless of the stories about this town, I'd lived here a long time, and never yet had the dead risen to haunt me.

No, they did that plenty well already from my dreams.

We headed in toward Grave Gulch at a trot, leavin' the silent skeleton with its baleful, hollow eyes to its eternal watch behind us.

DISAGREEMENT IN GRAVE GULCH

I instructed Charlotte to ride around the town proper and head up into the hills behind it. Our "home", such as it were, was a small cave hollowed out in one of the pale bluffs there. It was nearly midday by the time we finally closed in on it, and up ahead I saw Holt's black geldin' and my mule tethered to some low brush outside the mouth of the entrance.

The mule perked up his ears at our approach and nickered.

Soundin' the alarm again, the bastard.

But I didn't even care this time. The relief at seein' our mounts there and waitin' far outweighed any annoyance at the mule's overly social nature. If the horses were here, that meant Holt was here.

And he was, sure enough.

He came barrelin' outta the cave with both pistols drawn and ready, squintin' in the sun despite his hat.

"Hold up," I said quickly as Charlotte brought the horse to a stop and dropped a hand toward the giant gun across her lap. "It's us, Holt. It's me."

His eyes widened, his mouth droppin' open. He slid his guns back into place and outstretched his arms. "Ho-lee *shit*, Van! Thought fer sure you were dead this time."

"Me too."

He scrambled forward to help Charlotte down from the horse. She surely didn't need it, but accepted his hand, anyway, usin' it to help steady herself as she drug that cannon-gun down with her.

Holt let out a low whistle at the sight of it. "My, oh my. Never seen anythin' like that before."

"No one has," she said, layin' it back over one shoulder. "I don't think." She turned toward me and offered her free hand up, as if to help me down.

Holt laid a hand on her shoulder and gently nudged her backward. "Here, let me do that, Miss." She obliged, and instead Holt stepped up to take my arm as I slid off rather ungracefully, wincin' the whole time. "Well, well," he said. "Don't you look like you took a trip to Hell itself."

"Almost did," I said.

He clapped me on the shoulder and I grimaced. "Shit, kid. You musta got some of yer pa's luck, all right. Ain't seen no one else but you and him come through so many scrapes in one piece."

I shot him a glare. "He didn't come through that last one in one piece, though, did he?"

They may have called my pa Lucky Logan fer most his life, but in the end he'd still died same as everyone else. That was the problem with luck.

It always ran out.

The smile faded from Holt's face and he cleared his throat. "No, I guess not."

Charlotte looked from one of us to the other, watchin' in silence.

"Well," I prompted, not wantin' to talk about pa anymore. That familiar tightness was already closin' in around my throat. I focused instead on the present. On the urgent matter at hand. On those who were still livin'. "We did our part. Blew up the baron's house, burned his barns, freed his slaves. You get that money?"

Holt looked at me fer a minute, then burst out laughin'.

I wasn't sure exactly what kind of answer that was, so I waited fer him to finish bein' amused, impatient. Charlotte glanced to me in confusion, but I only shrugged.

Holt walked between us, back toward the mouth of the cave, still laughin', and shook his head. "Whew, boy!" he finally gasped. "You did yer part! Ha! Oh, that's rich, all right. That's rich."

I followed after him, wincin' as I limped along. Anger at his dismissal stirred in my belly, but I tried to ignore it. "Holt," I said flatly. "I woulda been there if I coulda been."

He turned to face me, his clear blue gaze sharp. "Sure." He crouched at the edge of the small fire he had goin' at the cave's entrance and poked at it with a stick. "But you weren't."

It was my turn to laugh, half disbelief, half anger. I turned to show him the burns along my right sleeve. "You think this was an accident? No, it weren't. Holt, I was gettin' treated to Baron Whittaker's famous hospitality. I got to see his kinda manners up close and personal."

"It's true," Charlotte said, steppin' up beside me. She still held that massive rifle, cradled in both arms. "Van was captured. I managed to get him free ... but we were delayed."

"Clearly," Holt muttered.

"You know I woulda followed the plan if I could have," I said, steppin' closer to the fire.

"Right." Holt tossed his stick into it and stood. "Except we had a plan before, Van, a perfectly good plan." He glanced toward Charlotte and tipped his hat to her. "I am sorry fer yer situation, Miss, I really am." He turned back to me, all the softness fer Charlotte goin' hard again. "But we shouldn'ta brought her into this. We shoulda stuck with the plan we had. Yer the one who wanted to complicate all of it by actin' the hero, and look where it landed ya! Nearly dead! Both of ya coulda ended up dead!" He waved at me and Charlotte both, but then focused his frustration back on me. "Meanwhile, there I am at the Bank of Blessing, tryin' to pull off a robbery all by my lonesome! I told ya it wasn't an easy job, Van. I told ya we needed more people! 'It'll be fine,' ya said. Freein' the slaves'll be a good distraction, ya said. Sure. Horseshit! *Horseshit*, Van!"

He spun away from me and paced angrily back and forth in front of the cave. Took off his hat and swiped at the sweat on his forehead.

I only watched him, feelin' more guilt now than anger. And worry. A deep, gnawin' worry that he hadn't gotten the money at all. That it'd all gone wrong, just 'cause I'd wanted to act the hero, so he said.

But it wasn't about actin' a hero. I glanced to Charlotte.

Was it?

I wet my lips and swallowed, bracin' fer the worst. "You didn't get the money?"

He shoved his hat back on his head and rounded on me. "Yes, I got the blasted money!"

My heart soared. I exhaled a gust of relief.

"But not nearly as much as I coulda got if you'd have been there, too. And I had to shoot more people than I would have liked. And it still weren't no Sunday stroll, no matter what distraction yer antics at the baron's house mighta generated."

The relief was a better salve against the aches and pains in my body than even Charlotte's ointment. My shoulders slumped and I closed my eyes, breathin' in and out, deep and slow, into the reprieve.

"Thank you," I whispered. *Ethelyn, not long now. I'll be there soon.*

"Don't thank me yet," Holt grumbled. "'Cause, kid, I'm sorry ... but I'm keepin' it."

My eyes opened, starin' straight at him. "*What?*"

He stood there in front of me, legs splayed and hands planted on his hips, just above his gun grips. "I said, I'm keepin' it."

Anger blazed hot and full. "Like hell you are." My hand dropped fer my pistol, but he'd known it was comin' and had his drawn before mine cleared leather.

"*Don't!*" he barked, the word echoin' out over the hills.

I froze, fingers still wrapped around my pistol grip, the gun halfway outta the holster, the burns under the bandages screamin' as my muscles flexed and stretched the blistered skin. I stood there waitin', teeth clenched and breathin' hard, glarin' across the flat six feet or so that separated us.

From the corner of my eye I saw Charlotte slowly back away from me, step by step, huggin' that big gun to her chest.

I couldn't quite decide then if I wanted her to use it to mow down Holt or not.

"Don't," he repeated, this time in a whisper. He held his gun level at his hip, but it was aimed at my chest. "I don't want to shoot you, kid, but so help me ... you draw against me and I *will* shoot you dead. Understand?"

I said nothin' fer a long time, heart racin' and rage buzzin' in my ears, rekindlin' my headache. He couldn't do this to me. He couldn't. Not when I was finally so close. Not after all these years. He knew how much findin' Ethelyn meant to me. He *knew*.

I let go of my gun. Let it nestle back down into the holster. Slowly lifted my hands. "Don't do this, Holt. Please."

"It's fer yer own good," he said. "Now take off yer belts and throw 'em over here. Nice and easy."

I glanced to Charlotte. She was still inchin' away, closer to her stolen fast horse. Holt didn't seem to care if she was gonna leave or stay. He was focused on me.

So I focused back on him. "You can have whatever's left," I reminded him. "That was always the agreement. Just give me the thirty-five thousand—"

"See, that's the problem," he said. "Like I said, since you weren't there, I couldn't get as much money as I'd hoped. And boy, was there a lot of money in that bank." He whistled and shook his head. "But I had to leave most of it behind, all because you wanted to go play Good Samaritan." He shrugged. "Which is fine, sure, but now, if I give you that thirty-five thousand, that don't leave so much fer me. And considerin' I was the one who did all the work to get the money in the first place—"

"*All* the work?" I scoffed. "Holt, if it hadn't been fer us you woulda had the law all over yer ass soon as you showed that teller yer gun!"

He gave a nod. "Maybe. But ya put me in a real bad spot leavin' me to do that robbery alone, Van. And I told ya ... I tried to tell ya we shoulda picked somethin' else to occupy the law. But you insisted. Well, ya risked yer life, her life, my life with this one, and like I said, you were damned lucky to get out of this one this time. We all were. But I'm tired of this. I'm tired of watchin' you run head-first into tryin' to get yerself killed, and stickin' my neck out along with ya, and all fer chasin' a ghost!"

I stepped forward at that, but he lifted the gun in warnin' and I stopped again. "Ethelyn is *alive*," I hissed. "How many times I gotta tell you that? How much proof you gotta see before you believe it?"

"Nine-Fingered Nan is fuckin' with you, Van." He tapped at his own temple with a finger. "She's fuckin' with you! Jerkin' ya around like a puppet on strings, and yer playin' right into her hands! She's gonna take this money from ya and then she's gonna *kill you*. You understand? Even if she does have yer sister, there ain't no way she's gonna hand her over. She's gonna take the money and then whether she has yer sister or not, kill you! You forget ... I was there fer a lot of the times she tried to kill yer pa. She hated him probably more than she hated anyone else, and that woman hates a lotta people. She ain't gonna let you walk away, Van. Why can't you understand that?"

"She had my sister's necklace," I husked.

"Which coulda been pawned off to who-knows-where a long time ago," he countered.

"And the fingers?"

"Coulda come from any poor woman they'd got ahold of."

I swallowed, shook my head. "If there's a chance she has Ethelyn, I have to take it. If there's a chance she'll honor her deal, I gotta try. Holt, please. You know I have to do this. It's all that matters to me."

He grunted. "Yeah, and that's why I have to do this. This obsession of yers ain't healthy. I've watched it go on long enough. Now, do as I said and throw over yer gun belts."

"Holt. Please. Please don't do this."

"*Now*, Van."

I swore. Unbuckled my belts. "Holt, goddamnit, you take that money and I swear ... I *swear* I'll come after you and take it back."

He sighed and shook his head. I saw the disappointment etched in the lines of his face. "No you won't. I'm gonna make this easy on you, kid. Just come with me. Come with me and we'll take that money and go far away, put this whole mess with Nine-Fingered Nan far behind us. Live out the rest of our lives in luxury."

"You know I can't do that."

"Damnit, Van! Yes, you can. You *can* do that! It's as easy as puttin' down yer gun and ridin' off east with me! We'll even give the girl some cash, just like you wanted, so she can get home, too. Hell, we could escort her back!"

That gave me pause. I glanced to Charlotte again, saw her standin' near her horse, but still watchin' both of us. She'd positioned herself in the middle of us, so that all together we made up the three points of a triangle. I wondered if she was waitin' to see who won this argument ... or if she was tryin' to pick a side.

With that gun of hers, whichever side she chose would be the winner.

I turned back to Holt. "I'm going to free my sister. With or without you."

His lips pressed into a thin line. "Yer gonna ignore the livin' fer a chance to save the dead?"

"*She ain't dead!*" The words bounced around the rocks.

Holt sighed again. "Fine. You wanna walk into that hell, that's yer choice. But I ain't gonna sit around and watch you. Throw over yer belts."

I did so, with more force than necessary.

They thumped into the dirt at his feet and he stooped to pick 'em up, loopin' 'em over his shoulder. His pale blue eyes locked on mine. "Don't come after me, kid. 'Less it's to apologize. Let me be clear: I see you comin' at me with a gun in yer hand, and you'll be just one more foolhardy idiot I gotta gun down. Got it?"

"Don't worry, you won't see me comin'."

A little smile curled his lips. "Sure."

Again that dismissal. The fire in my gut raged anew, but he still had his pistol trained on my chest, and his eyes never left my face.

That was somethin' he'd taught me early. A person's face would tell you what they were plannin' to do. Get good at readin' people's faces, and you could predict their actions. You could throw a punch before they did. You could draw before they did. You could shoot before they did.

But you couldn't watch two faces at once.

A heavy whine from Charlotte's direction heralded the warm up of her big gun.

Holt and I both looked at her in surprise.

She was aimin' at him. I guess she'd picked her side.

And I saw in his face the instinctive reaction. He reached fer his second gun.

He wouldn't escape her storm of bullets. But then, she wouldn't escape his shot, either.

I realized in that one breathless second I didn't want either of 'em to die.

XIV

SWEET GOODBYES

I launched myself across the six feet of ground between me and Holt and slammed into him, takin' us both down into the hard-packed dirt. He grunted as I landed on top of him. "Don't shoot!" I yelled.

But there were already bullets whizzin' by overhead and punchin' into the rock of the bluff behind us. Shards of stone and bullets both flung off the sheer wall in all directions, stingin' where they grazed skin. "Don't shoot! Stop! Don't shoot!"

My words were nearly swallowed by the roar of that massive rifle.

Holt scowled somethin' terrible, then tried to bring the butt of his right gun into my temple. I managed to partially block the blow, but the edge of the grip still smacked into my face hard enough to send a white flash across my vision. The cut where the rifle butt had smashed into my eye only two days ago was still fresh and swollen and I ground my teeth as a sharp pain flared.

I wrestled with him in the dirt, grabbin' fer his guns and my guns both.

The roar of Charlotte's rifle wound down and stopped, and so did the rain of stingin' shrapnel.

Holt bashed his left gun into the burns on my arm and I gave a cry, my grip on his wrists loosenin'. He lurched sideways and threw me into the dirt, then rolled over the top of me and sat on my chest.

I looked down the gullet of his two twin guns, and couldn't rightly tell if he meant to shoot me or not. "I just ... I just saved yer life!" I spat out, gaspin' under his weight.

He opened his mouth to say somethin' in return, but Charlotte loomed behind him and brought her giant rifle down hard across the back of his head.

He slumped sideways, both guns droppin' from his hands. Out cold.

I shoved him off me with a growl and rolled to my hands and knees, then struggled to my feet. Swayed and staggered as all the pain of all that movin' finally registered with my senses.

Charlotte grabbed my elbow to steady me. She looked from me to Holt's unconscious form, pale and wild-eyed. Her horse was the same, dancin' around again. That big gun of hers had even unnerved my mule and Holt's geldin'. They were all watchin' us with the whites of their eyes showin', their ears flickin' all directions.

"Why didn't you let me shoot him?" she asked, breathless.

I looked down at him, too, and muttered a curse. I bent stiffly to pull my gun belts outta the dust, shook 'em out, and put 'em back where they belonged around my hips. "He's ... he's a friend." *A friend who might have shot me.*

She frowned at me, creases formin' on her forehead. "He said he was going to shoot you."

"He wouldn't have." But I took his guns, too, and stuck 'em into my own belt. *He wouldn't have. Not after everythin' we've been through together. Not after eight years of watchin' out fer me, all that talk of pa bein' his best friend....*

"He sounded serious to me," Charlotte said softly.

"Well, he's surely gonna be serious mad when he wakes up. We'll need to tie him. So he can't follow us. Then find that money."

Charlotte only watched me as I limped into the cave and went to some of the supply crates stacked along the walls. "But what if ... what if Nine-Fingered Nan does kill you?" she asked.

It was a reasonable question. I didn't look up as I rummaged in search of some rope. "Then I guess he was right all along."

"But won't he starve if you leave him tied up here? If you don't come back to free him, I mean. Wouldn't it be better to just shoot him?"

I did look up at her then, quirking an eyebrow and then wincin' as it pulled at the bruise around my left eye. "No. I can't ... I can't shoot him."

"But you said—"

"I know." I found what I was lookin' for and slammed the lid of the crate shut again. "I know what I said. But he's been my partner fer eight years now. Saved my hide more times than I can count. Found me when I was cold and starvin' as a kid ... gave me food and shelter." *Taught me how to rob and kill. Taught me how to survive.* I scowled and shook my head, walkin' over to his prone form. "He's a right ol' bastard, but I can't shoot him. Not even fer wantin' to take that money." I rolled him onto his stomach and pulled his wrists behind his back, bindin' 'em together, tryin' to ignore the headache wantin' to split my skull. "I'll leave him a way to get free in case I don't come back. And leave him a trail to follow fer his part of the money. That should keep him busy fer awhile. Long enough to let me get to Ethelyn before he comes after me to murder me fer this."

The rifle lowered in Charlotte's hands. "So ... he *would* shoot you, then?"

"Naw." I tied his ankles next. "Maybe. Possibly. I dunno. I wouldn't put it past him to put a bullet in me fer this. Nothin' mortal ... just a flesh wound to make his feelin's on the matter apparent."

Charlotte blinked, clearly not understandin'.

"It don't matter," I assured her. "All that matters is I get my sister. I can deal with whatever he brings my way later." I finished the last knot and stood. "Thank you." It seemed all I did these days was thank her. "Fer helpin' me there." In case he woulda shot me.

At the very least, he woulda taken all that money from Blessing and left me back at needin' to find thirty-five thousand dollars.

She swallowed and nodded. Tucked a strand of wavy red locks behind her ear. "Sorry I almost killed your friend. I think."

A smile twitched at my mouth. "Well, like I said, he *is* a bastard."

Her gaze drifted down to him, then to her horse. "If there's a chance Nine-Fingered Nan still has your sister ... you need to go to her." She nodded resolutely, as if she had to convince me. Or herself. "You're right. You can't just leave her with that monster."

I nodded, too. I didn't need no convincin'. "I know."

Her eyes found mine again. "You'll go to her now?"

"Almost. Need to set things up fer Holt here. And see to that brand on yer stolen horse. And see you safely off toward home. Then I'll go to Bravebank to arrange the meetin' to buy back my sister."

She nodded again. "Thank you. For all you've done in helping me get free. And the others, too."

"It weren't nothin'." That weren't exactly true. But I hadn't really had a choice in this one. I'd done a lotta stuff over the years I weren't proud of, things that woulda made Mama roll over in her grave if she knew. But leavin' Charlotte on her own back in Blessing to face the law, or worse, Baron Whittaker, woulda been unforgiveable, even fer me.

I grazed the stitches in my right temple with my fingertips. "Think I owe you a little more, truth be told. Fer gettin' me outta there and doctorin' me up so good."

She smiled. "Well. Maybe you can repay me by not getting yourself killed by Nine-Fingered Nan."

I grunted and shook my head. "That ... I can make no guarantees."

It was nearly evenin' by the time I was ready to send Charlotte off.

We'd dragged Holt inside the cave, left a knife fer him within reach, found the money and taken our part of it, hid his part of it with a note of cryptic instructions on how to find it again, and modified Baron Whittaker's brand on Charlotte's horse.

I felt sorry for the poor beast. Gettin' branded were a particular form of painful.

But it were necessary if we hoped to get very far without bein' too much noticed. I didn't think the authorities of Blessing would have expanded their search this far south yet, but it was only a matter of time.

The Barons of Blessing had a lot of reach, all right, and I didn't think the murder of one of 'em would be forgotten all that easily.

Charlotte needed to head east soon as she could.

And I needed to head west.

There weren't no stagecoaches or trains that left outta Grave Gulch, considerin' no sane person travelled there by choice, so we'd headed up northwest a bit to the town of Peridot. It was small, but on account of Grave Gulch not havin' a coach stop, at least had that, and a saloon, and a general store. Weren't too bad of a town, really. Certainly one of the quietest and cleanest around these parts, and next to a mesa that got carpeted in gold poppies in the spring.

I kinda wished it were spring now.

Woulda been a pretty send off.

As it were, we only had the scrub brush and cacti and dust surroundin' us as the sun sank further into the west.

We'd arranged a ride fer her on the last coach outta town fer the night. It'd stop over the border in Redemption, Lesser Texas just after dark, and she'd stay the night there, then head out east on the first train in the morning. She'd cleaned up in Peridot, bought a new pair of clothes from the store, and looked again like a completely different woman from the one I'd seen kill Baron Whittaker.

This Charlotte Harrison, I imagined, looked like the one she had been back in Pennsylvania. She had a proper dress now, deep purple, the bodice huggin' her top half, the high collar fastened with a cameo brooch, and a ruffled hem on the skirt. Her new boots even had little heels on 'em, and she had a black handbag now, too, where she'd tucked away the money she'd need fer the rest of her journey.

We stood a ways from the stagecoach headquarters, sayin' our goodbyes.

Or tryin' to.

I was havin' a hard time findin' the words.

She cleared her throat and blessedly broke the silence. "I want you to keep the horse. And the gun."

I instinctively looked back over my shoulder, where the blue roan and Holt's geldin' were tied. I'd left Dr. Balogh's mule in Grave Gulch, not knowin' whether or not it mighta been reported as stolen in Bravebank. We'd rigged a makeshift scabbard for that ridiculous cannon-gun off her saddle, and it hung bulky off to one side.

She musta seen the protest formin' on my face. "I have no use for either. The horse will only make my journey home more expensive, as I'd have to pay for its place on the train, and we have plenty of horses on my family estate. And the gun..." She sighed. "It's too obvious. I don't want to draw any more attention to myself than absolutely necessary. I'm sure you understand."

I did. But I didn't like the thought of her goin' on such a long journey unarmed. I pulled one of my pistols—both of 'em undamaged now, as I'd lifted one of our spares from camp to replace the one of mine Nan had shot—and held it out to her. "Then take this, at least."

She looked at it fer a long minute, hesitatin'.

"Look, if you woulda had one of these on you when Nan's men hit yer coach in the first place, you never woulda ended up out here, sold to Baron Whittaker."

She glanced up at me, held my stare. "All right." She took the gun, her fingers brushin' mine.

My breath hitched, and I cleared my throat to cover it. "Will you ... uh, will you send me a letter when you get home, let me know you made it safe?" I asked.

She smiled and slipped the pistol into her handbag, then withdrew a folded piece of paper from it. "I was going to ask you the same thing. Will you write me? Once you deal with Nine-Fingered Nan and get your sister back? It would mean a lot to me to know you're both safe." She held the piece of paper out toward me. "This is the address you can send it to."

I took the paper and turned it over in my fingers. Swallowed. Gave a nod. Wondered why my mouth suddenly felt so dry.

"Where should I send my letter to you?" she prompted.

"Oh." I hadn't thought that far ahead. Hadn't written anything down on a convenient note. *Stupid.* "Just ... address it to me ... Van Delano, and send it to the Grave Gulch post office."

Her eyebrows lifted. "They have a post office?"

I shrugged. "Worshippers of the dead still get mail, it seems."

"And you go *into* the town to check your mail?"

"Like I said ... the stories aren't all entirely accurate."

Her smile widened. "If you say so. Okay. I'll send something there once I'm home."

"Thank you. I'm ... I'm sorry I couldn't take you back myself."

She shook her head, reachin' out to put a hand on my arm. "Your sister needs you more. You've already done more than enough for me."

"Last call!" the coach driver yelled, startlin' us both. "Last call fer those headin' to Redemption, Lesser Texas! All aboard!"

"You'd better go." I put my hand over hers, still on my arm, and squeezed. "And please, be careful. Be ready to use that gun if need be."

"I will. And again, thank you. For everything."

I touched the brim of my hat. "It was the least I could do, Miss."

She rolled her eyes at my formality and leaned up to kiss my cheek. "You be careful yourself, Mister."

Then she turned, her hand slipped from under mine, and she went to board the stagecoach with the others. I watched her, heart in my throat.

But she would be fine. The coach had two shotgun riders and a team of six mules. It'd make good time and be well-protected. And Charlotte had my gun now, besides. She'd be on the first train in the mornin', steamin' toward the east.

She'd make it.

She'd be all right.

She was free now ... and Ethelyn weren't free yet.

And if Nine-Fingered Nan had her claws reachin' out all the way to Pennsylvania ... well, I planned to deal with her, too. Soon. Soon I'd cut the head off the beast, and the rest of it wouldn't live too long without her.

Charlotte took the offered hand of the stagecoach driver and climbed the step to duck inside. But she paused in the doorway and looked back to me.

I met her eyes one last time, and it seemed in that one last moment I relived the whole of our brief, whirlwind acquaintanceship. I hoped she would write.

I hoped I would see her again. Somehow.

I tipped my hat to her.

She sent me one last smile and then climbed inside, and I couldn't see her anymore.

But I waited there and watched till the rest of the passengers got on board, and they closed up the coach, and the driver and his protectors settled themselves in their places, and the driver twitched the reins.

"Gee-up!" he yelled, and slapped the reins again.

The mules jerked into motion, the stagecoach wheels creakin' as it gained speed and headed outta town. Eastward.

I watched till its retreatin' cloud of dust faded, then sighed and turned back to the horses. I stuck Charlotte's note with her address down deep into my belt pouch, the one I'd lifted off drunk Jake. I drug myself up atop the blue roan, then winced as the saddle chafed the burn on my thigh. It woulda been nice if I coulda waited till those were healed up more before meetin' with Nan ... but Ethelyn couldn't wait that long.

Neither could I, in truth, not with an angry Holt soon to be comin' after me.

So I ponied his geldin' from the roan, and we headed off toward the settin' sun. Westward.

Toward Bravebank.

XV

MORE STUBBORN THAN IMPATIENT

I traveled till the sun went down that night, made camp, and was up again with the sun the next mornin'. Took me a little more than another half day of ridin' to reach Bravebank, and I entered town in the afternoon feelin' anxious.

The blue roan twitched her ears and nickered. I patted her neck and shook my head. "Easy, girl." I tried to relax, as much fer her sake as my own. Didn't need her gettin' skittish now. Holt's geldin' plodded along behind, not carin' in the least about what was happenin', or about what might happen.

But no one gave me any trouble as I headed down the main street toward The Stag Saloon. No one seemed to look at me over-long or give me a second glance. Still, I made sure to study the walls of the buildin's I passed, just to see if I saw mine or Holt's face lookin' back at me from any of the posters hung up there.

I didn't see anyone recognizable, least of all my own self.

I exhaled a long breath. I'd fully expected the bastard I'd made a deal with here to have given a full description of me to the town's sheriff. Just to make my life more difficult. But I guess that ten thousand dollars he'd demanded of me was more than the sheriff could offer in reward fer my head.

Well, that was fine by me. He could have his ten thousand dollars.

Long as it kept my face off a poster.

Long as I got Ethelyn.

I tied the horses to the hitchin' post outside the Stag. It was easier to dismount this time ... the leg seemed to be cooperatin' more these days. Now it was just those damned burns protestin' my every movement.

I made sure I had the money stashed right where I'd left it in my saddlebags, threw 'em over my shoulder, checked my single remainin' pistol, and pulled the massive rifle stolen from Baron Whittaker from its sheath, wincin' as the raw skin on my right arm started screamin' under the bandages again.

My arm didn't like draggin' around the weight of that gun.

It *was* too obvious of a weapon. Charlotte was right about that. But then, I was also hopin' the sight of it might keep Nan's man from double-crossin' me.

At the very least, it would make sure he died if he did.

The door to the saloon had been propped open on account of it bein' mid-afternoon, and I stepped through it like I owned the place. My gaze swept the floor in search of the man with the droopin' handlebar mustache. The place was fairly full, and the general buzz of banter and conversation dimmed as eyes fell on that giant gun.

The hush rippled outward, startin' with those closest to me and the door, and travelin' all the way to the back of the joint.

The barkeep stopped polishin' his glass.

Several hands dropped toward their weapons. Ready, just in case I was gonna start trouble.

But there was only one man in the vicinity I wanted to start trouble with.

I noticed the place seemed all put back together from our gunfight here a week ago. All you could see of it now were some fresh bullet holes in the walls. "I'm lookin' fer the man who answers to Nine-Fingered Nan," I said.

The bartender gave an amused snort. "Ain't that everyone in the Territories?"

I glared at him from under my hat brim. "No. It ain't."

"He's lookin' fer me," came a voice from the back.

Everyone sober enough to grasp what was happenin' turned to look at him.

And it was him, all right.

Sittin' at a poker table with his legs stretched out in front, ankles crossed, slouched in the chair like he had not a care in the world. He studied me fer a minute, then studied his cards. Then he heaved a sigh and threw his cards to the table.

"You save my seat, hear?" he told the man to his right.

The man gave a grave nod, and Nan's man took his time in standin' up, pushin' his chair back so that the legs screeched on the wooden planks of the floor. He stretched. Then waved me over. "Come on, boy. Come to my office and let's talk business."

My fingers tightened around the rifle. If I didn't need him to set up my meetin' with Nan ... if I thought I could find her without him ... I'da shot him down right then.

But instead I walked across the saloon, slow and deliberate so my limp weren't as bad, never takin' my eyes off him, though I surely felt all the other sober eyes in the saloon followin' me.

His eyes watched me, too. And then, as I got closer, they slipped down to the rifle briefly before comin' back up to my face. His expression didn't change, but I saw his hand go to casually rest on his own gun grip. "This way," he said. He turned and led me through a door at the back of the saloon, then up a creakin' staircase to another door, which he opened and gestured me through.

I did as he beckoned, but went sideways, so as to still keep an eye on him.

That made him smile.

I did not return the sentiment.

He came in after me and shut the door behind him, then strolled over to a table set toward the far wall. A single window let in the light of the afternoon, throwin' bars of white gold on the floor. He went around the table and then turned to face me, crossin' his arms. "Well?" he prompted. "Ya got my money?"

"You got my sister?"

He lifted a black eyebrow. "Not till I see that money."

I walked closer to the table, then set the rifle down, proppin' it up against the table's edge. I pulled the saddlebags from my shoulder and opened 'em, grabbin' up the stacks of cash. I made a pile toward the left side of the table. "That's the ten thousand fer you." Then I made another stack, a much bigger stack, on the right side of the table. "And there's the twenty-five thousand fer Nan. Fer my sister."

Both his eyebrows lifted now. He stared down at the money, one hand strokin' his mustache. Then looked up at me. "What happened to yer face?"

My left eye was still bruised and swollen, that gash still fresh and the other one in my head still fulla stitches. But none of that were his business. "Doesn't matter," I snapped. "I got the money. Now go tell Nan I want my sister back."

He pursed his lips and looked back down to the money. "You got all thirty-five thousand dollars in a week?"

I hooked my thumbs into my gun belts. "What can I say? I'm resourceful."

He grunted. "Well, a course I'm gonna have to count it before I take it to Nan. You just make yerself comfortable. That's a lotta cash. Might take me awhile."

The grin he flashed me then made me wanna put a bullet right in his teeth. I resisted the urge ... barely. I still needed him to set up the meetin' with Nan.

There was only one chair in the room, which he pulled up to the table and settled down into. Then he pulled one stack of bills toward him and began to count.

Very slowly.

There was nothin' else in the room. No other decoration, no other furniture, and I realized with a flash of irritation and dismay that his invitation to 'make myself comfortable' was just him fuckin' with me. Again.

I ground my teeth, my fingers twitchin', itchin' to draw my pistol.

But instead I drew in a slow, calmin' breath and exhaled evenly. If he wanted to play that game, then fine. I'd waited nine years fer this. This was the closest I'd ever been to gettin' Ethelyn, and I wasn't gonna quit now on account of him wantin' to jerk me around.

I could wait a little longer. I picked up the giant rifle, makin' a show of it fer his benefit, and settled myself against the opposite wall. I stared him down, unwaverin', unrelentin', holdin' that rifle at the ready.

Two could play at this game.

I didn't know how long he counted that money. Didn't know how much time had passed. I watched that patch of white-gold sun move across the floor, and said nothin'. He took as long as he could possibly take, I was sure, hopin' to test my patience. Maybe hopin' to break me. Maybe hopin' I'd swing that rifle around in his direction so he'd have a chance to gun me down. Have a chance to keep all that money fer himself.

I wasn't generally a patient man, true enough.

But he'd underestimated my resolve. Holt coulda told him I was more stubborn than impatient any day. I wasn't gonna let this bastard win this one.

So eventually he gave up, with a great, theatrical, disappointed sigh, and finished countin' that money. "Looks like it's all here," he said. "All right. She said if you actually brought the money to tell ya to meet her up in the Bone Spur Mountains, near the holdin' tank pool. Ya know the spot?"

I straightened from the wall, shiftin' the rifle in my arms. The muscles were startin' to tire after so long, the burns still afire beneath their bandages. "Not particularly."

"Guess you'd better figure it out, then. That's where she'll meet ya fer the trade. Tomorrow, high noon."

"I'll be there."

"I'll tell her to expect you." He reached a hand out toward the money again, and that's when I swung the rifle in his direction. He paused, his other hand droppin' to his own gun. "Don't do anythin' stupid now, boy."

"Put the twenty-five thousand back in the bags," I ordered. "I'll take it to Nan myself." Holt thought me a fool fer makin' this deal in the first place, and maybe I was, but I weren't *that* big of a fool to trust this cur with that kinda money. It'd never get to Nan. And I'd never get Ethelyn. I knew that much.

He hesitated, eyein' my rifle again.

"This thing'll chew up this whole room and you with it," I warned. "You can't spend that ten thousand if yer dead."

He smiled. "And ya can't get yer sister back if *yer* dead." His finger tapped against his gun.

"How good's yer aim when you got a chest fulla lead?" I pulled back on the trigger, just a bit. Just enough to start that signature heavy whine, that unholy sound that heralded an incomin' storm of bullets.

His smile widened into a yellow-toothed grin, and he lifted his hand from his pistol, holdin' it up in surrender. "Ya know, I'm kinda startin' ta like you, boy."

"Can't say I feel the same about you."

"All right. All right. Take it easy. You can take the twenty-five thousand yerself. Nan'll still kill ya if she feels like it."

I had no doubts about that, so I only shrugged.

He chuckled and swept Nan's large pile of cash back into the saddlebags. He buckled 'em up, then tossed 'em over to me.

I bent to pick 'em up and settled 'em on my shoulder again, never lettin' the rifle barrel lower from aimin' square at his chest. Then I backed toward the door. "See ya around," I said, though I had no intention of ever seein' the likes of him again. Not if I could help it.

He gave me a salute, still with that sly smile plastered beneath his mustache. "Maybe," was all he said.

I opened the door and backed through it, too, then turned and headed quick as my metal leg would allow down the stairs and back into the saloon proper.

The conversations hushed again as I went through, and all the eyes followin' me bored into my back. But I paid them no mind. All that mattered was gettin' outta there before the mustached man—or anyone else—decided to stop me.

But they didn't. Yet.

I mounted up in a hurry and turned the horses down the street toward the post office.

I didn't intend on stayin' around Bravebank fer long. There were too many people here I didn't want to run into again. I planned to head out toward the meetin' place just as soon as I could.

There was just one more thing I had to take care of first.

I handed the post master a small package I'd wrapped in brown paper and tied tight with twine. Didn't want anyone gettin' greedy. "For Doctor Balogh," I instructed him. "Will you see that he gets it?"

The man shrugged as he took the parcel from me. "Sure. The doc comes here to collect his mail regular enough. He'll get it."

"Thanks. And tell him ... tell him that's fer what I owe him."

"All right. Sure." He tucked the brown-wrapped rectangle in one of the mail cubbies behind him and pulled a piece of paper and pencil toward him, preparin' to write. "And who should I say the package is from?"

That gave me pause. My name weren't on no posters here, but that didn't mean there wouldn't be other people lookin' fer me. There was always someone out there somewhere lookin' fer me, it seemed. "No name," I said. "He'll know who it's from."

The man rolled his eyes and pushed the paper and pencil away. "Suit yourself. I'll tell him."

I tipped my hat to him. "Thanks, Mister."

"Don't mention it."

"Oh, uh ... you happen to have a map of the state on you?"

He lifted an eyebrow. "Sure. I got a map." He reached down under the counter and produced a large, folded paper map. He spread it out in front of us and turned it around to face me. "Wanna take a look?"

"Yes. Thank you." I perused it fer a minute, findin' Bravebank easy enough. Then my eyes went outward, searchin' in ever-widenin' circles fer one of the many nearby mountain ranges to be labeled *Bone Spur*.

To my relief, it weren't too far. Westward again.

I tapped my finger on the Bone Spur Mountains. "You know where there's a place here they call the holdin' tank?"

The post master leaned his elbows on the counter and cocked his head to look at the upside-down map. "Up in the Bone Spurs? Sure. The stagecoaches sometimes stop there for water. It's off the main road that goes up through there. Should be easy enough to find. It's the only standin' pool of water in the area. Can't miss it."

I nodded. "Good. Great. Thanks again, Mister."

"Sure." He pulled the map toward him and started to fold it up again. "But listen, if you're fixin' to head up that way, be careful. Lots of bandits and thieves in the area, waitin' for the coaches to stop at the pool. Lots of good nooks and crannies they can shoot at you from 'fore you even know they're there."

I sighed. Of course. "Thanks. I'll keep that in mind. You have yerself a pleasant evenin'."

"And same to you, sir."

I turned from the post master and caught a glimpse of the evenin' sun out the window. I'd been too long here already. But at least now the guilt over that damned mule and saddle were eased. Holt had a little less money fer it, since I'd taken the cost of the animal and saddle outta his share ... but still, makin' out with almost fifteen thousand dollars weren't no small thing, neither.

Dr. Balogh and his family could get another mule to pull their wagon and replace the saddle I'd taken, Holt would still get most all his share of the money, and I could stop feelin' like I'd betrayed that poor kid Radley.

Though I had a feelin' that money wouldn't make that kid feel any better. At the least I hoped his parents hadn't figured out he'd been the one to bring me back my guns. And if they had, I hoped he hadn't gotten whooped fer it. I hoped in that case they'd put the blame all on me ... the no-good drifter who'd sweet-talked their innocent child into becomin' an accomplice to mule rustlin'.

I sighed again as I stepped out from the post office into the evenin', then turned toward the horses—and ran straight into a fist.

IN THIS TOGETHER

The blow hit me in the jaw and knocked me back against the wall of the post office. I staggered, caught completely off guard, and then hands grabbed the front of my shirt and hauled me around the corner into the alleyway, tossin' me to the ground.

I rolled and came up again almost immediately, but my metal leg was still sluggish and I tripped on it, nearly goin' right back down to the dirt. I stumbled, reachin' fer my gun. Another fist landed in my jaw, then one to my right wrist knocked the pistol outta my hand, my fingers numb. I got shoved back into another wall, and my curse was cut short by the forearm that landed across my throat.

I groped fer my left pistol, only to remember I'd given it to Charlotte. So instead I sent a fist of my own hard into my attacker's gut.

He grunted and doubled over a bit, and as he did my left hand went to his right hip, aimin' to relieve him of his gun.

That was when I felt the barrel of another gun shove hard into my ribs, and the forearm pressed harder against my throat. "Hands off the pistol," he growled. The one shoved into my ribs twitched in warnin'.

I choked and gagged, abandonin' my attempt at freein' his second gun to use both hands on his arm, tryin' to pull it away so I could breathe.

"Insolent, ungrateful bastard," he whispered harshly, "I oughta kill you where you stand."

That voice. I knew that voice. I blinked, focusin' on the face of my attacker fer the first time since runnin' into his fist. His clear blue eyes were narrowed beneath the bushy gray brows. Glarin' like I'd never seen.

I tugged at his arm, suckin' in a thin gasp of air. For an old, angry bastard who was thickenin' around his middle, he was stronger than he looked. "Holt," I choked out. "Let ... let me explain..."

"*Explain?*" The gun in my ribs pressed in harder and I grimaced. "You already done explained things, boy. You *explained* you was gonna take the money I got ... the money I'm *owed* ... and give it to that shriveled up cunt Nine-Fingered Nan on some fool's quest to get yer sister back!"

"I left ... yer share..." He wasn't makin' it easy on me to talk. Every word, every breath was a struggle, raspin' through the little space I could make with my efforts to lighten the weight he leaned on my throat. "Didn't ... didn't you get ... the note?"

He leaned on me harder, his face inches from mine, his glare fierce. "I ain't no child to be placated with riddles, Van. What'd you think, I was gonna go off on some half-assed treasure hunt? No ... I *earned* that money, and I ain't gonna go wanderin' around lookin' fer it, yer gonna take me straight to it."

Black spots danced in my vision. I could have gotten to his gun still, maybe we woulda traded shots into each other and both died there in that alley.

But I didn't want to have to kill him. I wondered if he really wanted to kill me.

"Holt." I couldn't rightly tell if I were speakin' aloud or not; all I could hear in my ears now was a rushin' sound and the frantic, panicked beatin' of my heart as it starved fer air. "I ... I didn't ... let her ... shoot you."

He just stood there fer a second stranglin' me, and the blackness slowly closed in on the alley until I could hardly even see his face.

Then, suddenly, his arm let up and I could breathe again.

I fell to my hands and knees, gaspin' and gaggin', suckin' in air so greedily I choked and fell into a coughin' fit.

Holt picked up my dropped pistol and stuck it into his waistband. "Take me to my money, Van. All of it."

I was still breathin' hard, my heart still racin', my head throbbin', but I sat back on my heels and looked up at him. I swiped at the blood runnin' down my chin now from the split in my lip and shook my head. "You know I can't do that."

He shifted on his feet, his lips formin' a hard line. "Why?" he demanded. "Why do you insist on doin' this? We could take that money ... live out the rest of our lives on that cash!"

I looked straight at him, knowin' full well that weren't true, not with the way he spent money when he had it. But that weren't the point of this argument, either.

"Look at you!" he went on, not givin' me a chance to reply. He paced back and forth in front of where I knelt in the dirt. "Look at you! You've nearly killed yerself already in pursuit of this idiotic venture ... several times over now. How much longer you think yer luck'll hold? Huh? You said yerself ... yer pa weren't so lucky there in the end, was he? Why you so eager to fall into the grave after him?"

I shook my head. "I don't care what happens to me. Long as I get Ethelyn free first."

Holt threw up his hands in exasperation. "Always about yer sister, and you don't even know if she's—"

"I promised her!" The words belted out loud and desperate in the narrow confines of the alley. I shoved myself to my feet and faced Holt square, hands balled into fists. "I promised her, Holt. I promised I would come back fer her, and I don't care how long it's been, I ain't gonna abandon her now."

"But you don't even know if she's—"

"I have to try." I cut him off. I couldn't bear to hear him insist she was only a ghost any more. Not when I was so close. Not after I'd already sacrificed so much to get this far. "If there's even the smallest chance, Holt, I have to go. I have to try."

"And what if Nan takes all the money and still don't give you yer sister, or don't even have yer sister?"

"Then at least I'll have the satisfaction of killin' Nan."

Holt gave an amused and skeptical snort. "I don't think even yer pa could beat Nan's draw these days."

I remembered how she'd downed my horse, shot the gun clean outta my hand, put a bullet in my thigh. All before I'd registered what was happenin'. I swallowed. "Well. Then at least I'll die knowin' I tried. I can't go off and try and live a life knowin' my sister might be out there somewhere, made a slave—or worse. I can't. And you should know that, Holt. You should know that."

He sighed heavily and shoved his drawn pistol back into its holster. "Yeah. Guess I do. Guess I just hoped maybe after all these years you'd wise up."

"I ... I can't give you the whole fifty thousand we—*you*—got from Blessing. If you need to shoot me fer that ... you'll just have to shoot me." I hoped I'd read his bluff right. If not, well, I wouldn't get the chance to try and free Ethelyn or kill Nine-Fingered Nan at all.

He looked at me fer a minute, contemplatin'.

And fer a heartbeat I thought I'd guessed wrong.

But then he sighed. Rubbed a hand over the short gray beard on his chin and shook his head. "God damn it all, kid. I don't wanna shoot you. Never did."

I exhaled quietly.

"But my money ... I *am* real pissed about my money..."

"We can rob another bank," I offered. "After I have Ethelyn. Do it together from the beginnin' this time. Get yer money."

He rolled his eyes and started pacin' again. "Naw. Soon as you get yer sister back, you'll go straight. I can see it in ya. You've never been a natural killer. That's why I was able to get the jump on you so good just then." He gestured lazily back toward the post office porch.

I clenched my jaw against the retort and felt the ache of the bruise that would be darkenin' there 'fore mornin'. "Lloyd Renneker might not agree with you on that point," I muttered.

Holt grunted and shook his head. "I didn't say you were against killin', Van. I know you can do it ... I seen you do it plenty of times.

What I'm sayin' is that yer choosy about yer killin'. And once ya get yer sister back, you won't have much reason to go about it no more."

Well, maybe that was true. But what did it matter, anyway? I didn't need to be no natural killer. I'd done just fine like I was. So instead I said, "One last job. I'll stay fer one last job, fer you. To get you the money yer owed."

He stopped pacin' and faced me. "What if Nan kills ya?"

I shrugged. "Well, then … I guess you've proven you can pull off a bank job yerself, in that case."

A smile pulled at one corner of his mouth. "Well … maybe I woulda had a harder time of it if I hadn't of had a partner to distract the law fer me."

Some of the tension in my coiled muscles relaxed at that admission. If he was willin' to admit that now, maybe it was true he didn't really want to shoot me. Maybe he'd finally realized him gettin' that money wasn't truly a one-man job, and I was entitled to it as much as he. Maybe he'd finally get it through his head that I was gonna meet with Nine-Fingered Nan to trade twenty-five thousand dollars fer my sister, no matter how it all worked out in the end.

"So," I said, "we'll do one more job then? After I get my sister. Together."

He pursed his lips and exhaled a long, slow breath through his nose. His hands were on his hips again, the fingers tappin' on the sides of his double holsters. "That means you gotta stay alive through another meetin' with Nan, kid. I told you the first time you went off to see her … I didn't spend all that time lookin' fer ya and raisin' ya just to watch you charge off to die."

"So maybe meetin' Nan ain't a one-man job, either," I said.

He tilted his head fractionally to the side. "Meanin'?"

"Come with me. Give me another gun in the fight." I'd asked him to come with me the first time, too. He'd refused, sayin' he weren't gonna watch me throw my life away on somethin' so foolhardy. Nor was he gonna risk his own neck fer a ghost. I wasn't sure this time would be any different, but I had to try.

Maybe if he'd been backin' me up that first time I'd confronted Nan, things would have ended up different.

Or maybe they'd have ended up the same, except with him dead.

It was hard to know. All I knew is that I'd feel a lot better going into those mountains tomorrow with another gun on my side.

"The meetin' place is up in some mountains not too far from here," I said when he stayed silent. A kind of plan was formin' in my mind now ... a plan I thought he might approve of. "The post master said there's a lot of hidin' places up in there. So we get you a rifle. A sharp-shootin' rifle. And we put you up high somewhere where you can see the meetin' spot. You can cover me. And give 'em hell from on high if things go south."

He scratched at his bearded chin and grunted. "You got any idea how expensive those rifles are?"

"You can take Baron Whittaker's rifle, too."

He looked surprised at that. "You still got that monstrosity?"

"Yeah."

He glanced around the darkenin' alley, as if lookin' fer someone. The sky over the tops of the surroundin' buildin's had turned a navy blue, night comin' on quick now. "Speakin' of, where's the girl? She didn't come to save you this time."

I straightened, choosin' to ignore the jab. Choosin' to ignore the anger that stirred in my gut. "She's on her way home. Sent her off last night."

"Ah, well, good riddance." He spit into the dirt.

"She helped us," I said stiffly, not likin' his disregard fer Charlotte. *And if not fer her, I woulda suffered a helluva lot more hurt at the hands of Baron Whittaker. And probably be dead.* I wondered how painful that death woulda been, too. From the way it'd been goin', I imagined it woulda possibly been one of the worst ways to go in this world.

"She also tried to kill me," Holt said flatly.

"She thought you were gonna shoot me."

"I was thinkin' about it."

"Then it seems her actions were justified."

He looked steadily at me. "Yeah. Maybe so."

"Yer welcome, by the way."

He frowned then. "Fer what?"

"Fer savin' yer life. When she tried to kill you."

He barked a short laugh and shook his head. "Kid, if you think that makes us even, you've got a long way to go yet. Fer all the times I've pulled you outta scrapes ... fer gettin' you off the streets and gettin' food in yer belly—"

"And that's why I didn't let her kill you," I cut him off before he could continue his list. I didn't need to hear it again. I'd heard it all before. Many times. "I'm grateful fer everythin' you've done fer me, Holt, I am. Yer an insufferable, self-centered bastard—"

"And yer a reckless, hard-headed fool."

"—but I am grateful. So. We in this together, or not? What do you say?"

He grumbled somethin' and spit again, hookin' his thumbs in his belt. Then he heaved a sigh and pulled my pistol from his waistband, holdin' it out to me butt-first. "Guess we'd better make a proper plan."

Course, I wasn't sure how proper of a plan it was, really, considerin' there was only the two of us, and who knew how many Nan would bring with her. I remembered clear enough those lieutenants of hers she had hidden in the rocks durin' my first encounter with her.

I suspected somethin' of the same this time, too.

But at least this time I'd have Holt.

We sold the baron's fancy horse and got a fair amount fer her, to my surprise. The hostler didn't ask no questions; he barely even glanced at her brand. I was beginnin' to understand a lot more about Bravebank now.

I was beginnin' to understand it was a town loyal to Nine-Fingered Nan.

The realization made me uneasy, no matter that it had worked in our favor this time, and we left the livery in a hurry. Then we got Holt a sharpshootin' rifle just before the gunsmith closed. It weren't the best on offer, but it was the best we could afford. It would do just fine. Holt took his geldin' back, givin' me another glare fit to flay a man— he'd been real sore about havin' to ride that mule into town—and we made what time we could that night, ridin' even after dark.

I kinda would rather have kept the baron's horse, truth be told, but it was still a risk, even with the modified brand. And she seemed to run kinda hot, which weren't necessarily a good thing when you were out and about in the wilds where there was always the chance somethin' bad could jump out at you.

And anyway, the mule was mine now, bought and paid for.

He plodded along slow and steady under me, and we rode on till the moon was high, cold camped, and went on again at dawn.

We saw 'em long before we reached 'em, the rocky hills those around here called mountains. They rose up outta the surroundin' flat scrubland and climbed up toward the bright blue, cloudless sky.

The Bone Spur Mountains.

We angled to approach them from the south and enter along the road there, like I'd seen on the map. The coolness of the mornin' was burnin' off by the time we reached the foot of 'em, and then we reined up our mounts.

Holt took off his hat and swiped at the sweat startin' to glisten on his brow. "Well," he said. "Guess this is it."

I peered up at the side of the nearest one. They looked like most other mountains in the area I'd seen, only in these, some of the big rocks up toward the top were a lighter color. Not red or black, but a grayish white.

Like bones.

"Guess so," I said. I took a moment to breathe, settle my nerves. This was it. This was what I'd been waitin' fer for nine long years. I closed my eyes and opened them again. Readjusted my hat. Cleared my throat. "Well, let's go." I kicked the mule, and he moved forward obediently.

Holt trailed after me, the sharpshooter rifle in its scabbard glintin' in the late mornin' sun.

XVII

BODIES AND BONES

The road gradually sloped upward as we went, deeper and deeper into the mountains. The rock walls on either side of us grew higher and higher, until we rode mostly in shadow. Shadow that slowly shortened as high noon approached.

We picked up our pace as much as we could manage.

The pale rocks surrounded us now, tumbled and jagged, makin' plenty of good hidin' spots, just like the post master had said. Some of those rocks had drawin's on 'em. Ghostly images of animals and shapes, near lost to time, but still visible if you looked close enough.

And I couldn't help but look close enough. It was eerie, to see those pictures suddenly appear amidst so much wilderness, no other trace of civilization around for miles and miles.

I heard Holt mutter a curse behind me. "What is this place?"

I could only shake my head. I didn't know no better than he.

We pressed onward, and came upon the pool close to noon. The post master had been right about that, too. You couldn't miss it.

Though it weren't much of a pool. There hadn't been a rain for some time, and as such there weren't much water left for the pool to hold. But it was there, all right. Greenish and tepid in the growin' light of day.

Holt grunted. "Good spot fer an ambush."

I raised my eyes from the pool to look at him. He, in turn, was studyin' the cliffs around us. I followed his gaze. The area here by the pool was relatively large and open, flat. A good spot fer stoppin' coaches to get water, sure. But the road in and outta here was narrow, and the walls on all sides sheer and tall.

It'd have been easy enough to block the ways in and out, and anyway, there surely wasn't enough room even here by the pool to turn a coach. Lucky fer us, we weren't in a coach.

It still woulda been a good spot fer an ambush, though. Even just on horseback. Unease prickled at my skin. "You'd better go," I said, lookin' up at the sun. "Plant yerself atop one of these walls. Should give you enough height."

Holt craned his neck back to look up at 'em. "I'd say."

"There was a side trail a little ways back that looked like it'd take you up there."

"I saw it." He blew out a breath through his teeth and looked at me. "All right, kid. This is it. Don't fuck it up. And ... be careful, damnit. You hear?"

I nodded. "I'll do my best."

"Mm-hrm." He looked at me a second longer, as if thinkin' of sayin' somethin' else. But then he only reined his geldin' around and headed back the way we'd come.

When he'd disappeared around the bend, I walked my mule around the clearin' a few times and back down the trail a ways before comin' back to the pool to confuse the tracks a bit. The floor of the area was mostly bare rock, but there were a spot or two of dirt and gravel that would show a horse print, and I preferred Nan and her company to think I'd come alone ... or with a little hidden army of my own, maybe.

Then I waited beside the pool. Alone.

I stayed atop the mule, nerves hummin' with restless energy. I kept one hand on the reins, one hand on my gun, watchin' the road ahead and the rocks around me, listenin' fer any sound.

These mountains were quiet. Far too quiet.

Beside me, the surface of the small pool was still as glass.

Above me, the sun moved higher into the sky, until it beat down upon me full force, shinin' squat in the middle of that great ring of bone-colored rock.

That's when my mule perked his ears and lifted his head, and I tensed.

Far away, faint, I heard the approachin' clip-cloppin' of hooves. Lots of hooves.

My heart quickened, throbbin' in my throat. My fingers tightened around the grip of my gun, already slick with sweat. I fought to control my nerves, my anticipation, my relief, my rage ... too much feelin' threw off yer aim. Made you sloppy. That's what Holt always said, and experience had proved him right more often than not.

The cleanest kills, the easiest kills, always came when the killin' was instinctive, a reaction, a muscle-memory response to a threat.

That, or when the rage went on long enough it settled into somethin' hard and flat and numb.

So I waited and breathed through all the things jumpin' around in my gut ... waited fer one of those two things to happen. Either I'd have to react, or the rage would settle. I wondered which might happen first.

Horses appeared on the path ahead.

My mule gave his signature bastardized whinny in greetin'. Sounded like somethin' was killin' him. Here in this quiet place, among the bones of the earth and so many ghostly drawin's, the unnatural sound seemed to strangely belong.

But the horses didn't deign to answer him. They entered the clearin' two by two, which was all that could fit abreast on the road at a time.

Two women riders came first, and my heart jumped fer a second, then fell again as I quickly realized neither of 'em were Ethelyn. They split as the road opened up into the pool's clearin' and went alongside the rocky walls, past the pool, to take up positions behind me.

Blockin' the way out.

I swallowed and took another breath. It didn't matter. In truth, I'd never expected anythin' less.

And I still had Holt, hidin' up there somewhere, watchin' all this through his scope.

I hoped.

Four more riders came then, all men. They took up positions on either side of me, reinin' up their horses near the sheer walls. The two on my right had their horses' hooves nearly in the water. They turned their mounts to face me, hands restin' casually atop the pistols at their hips.

My attention was pulled away from glarin' at 'em by the single rider who came next.

It was the bastard from the Stag Saloon with his handlebar mustache. He eyed me as he rode in and smiled, touchin' the brim of his hat.

I glared him down.

But it was the shaggy chestnut pony he led after him and the figure sittin' atop it that made my breath catch. It was a woman, her wrists tied in front of her, one of the hands that gripped the saddle horn missin' three fingers. She had a burlap sack over her head, but long black hair spilled out the bottom of it.

Long black hair like Ethelyn's.

Fire leapt up in me then, nearly blindin'. I laid the fist grippin' my reins on the saddle horn to hide the tremblin' in my body and fixed my eyes on the mustached man.

It was all I could do not to shoot him down right then.

But there were an awful lot of hostile eyes on me right now, and an awful lot of fingers ready to pull triggers. If I drew now, we'd all die. Me and the man with the mustache would die first, but the rest Holt would get with his rifle, or they'd get hit in the crossfire of ricochetin' bullets, I had no doubt.

This mighta been a good spot fer an ambush, but it weren't such a good spot fer a gunfight.

So I waited. I waited and watched fer my chance.

Behind him came two more riders, one man and one woman this time, and they halted in the mouth of the road there, rifles already drawn and laid across the fronts of their saddles. Blockin' the way ahead.

And that was it.

No one else was comin'.

There was no Nine-Fingered Nan.

But as long as I got my sister, I could settle with just killin' the mustached bastard in front of me.

"Howdy," he said cheerfully, grinnin' from ear to ear. "Guess I'm seein' ya around again sooner than we thought, eh?"

I kept my hand on my gun and my eyes on him, no matter how desperately I wanted to look at my sister, who I hadn't seen since she was a scrawny girl of ten. And I spoke only to him, too, though everythin' in me wanted to call out to Ethelyn and tell her everythin' was gonna be all right, that I was here now, that I was sorry—*so sorry*—fer leavin' her alone all those years ago, even if it was only supposed to be fer one night.

"Where's Nan?" I asked flatly, swallowin' back all those feelin's.

Now wasn't the time.

Too much feelin' threw off yer aim. And I was gonna need all my wits about me fer this one.

He shifted in his saddle. "Ah, you know. Somewhere else. Doin' more important things."

I swallowed again. *More important things.* Well, it didn't matter. I'd find her someday. I'd find her someday and make her pay, too.

"So?" he prompted. "Ya wanna make this trade or what? Ya got that money with ya?"

"Of course I do," I snapped.

He pushed up the brim of his hat with a thumb. "Well, let's see it, then."

"Hand over my sister first."

He chuckled and looked over his shoulder toward Ethelyn. Then turned back to me and shook his head. "Boy, you ain't in no position to be makin' demands. Yer lucky I brought yer sister at all. What's to stop me from just tellin' my crew here to shoot ya down? Then I could take the money *and* yer sister. Come to think of it, that's probably the better deal. Fer me."

His lewd grin turned my stomach, but I held his gaze. Resisted the urge to look up at the rocky walls. Resisted the urge to try and pick out any sign of where Holt mighta perched himself. "Yeah, but yer forgettin' somethin'," I said hoarsely.

"Am I?" His right hand slid over toward his gun.

"Sure."

"And what's that?"

I let go my reins and lifted my left hand slowly. And prayed Holt was settled up there, watchin'. I was countin' on him to be my angel, here. "Yer forgettin' ... I got friends, too."

The mustached man laughed. Or started to.

Until I gave Holt the signal.

The sharpshootin' rifle cracked like lightnin' hittin' an old tree, and the bastard sittin' in front of me went clean off his saddle, his left shoulder explodin', nearly severin' his arm. He hit the ground screamin'. His horse reared.

My mule threw up his head, eyes rollin'.

Fer a second, none of those ready trigger fingers surroundin' me moved, frozen in startled confusion.

I jumped off the mule in that split second and swung to my right, workin' my own trigger, fannin' the hammer.

Two bodies fell from their horses and hit the water with a splash.

Holt's rifle cracked again, near ear-splittin' in the bowl of those rocks.

Another body hit the ground.

And that was all the time we had before the rest of 'em woke up from their surprise.

I ducked behind my mule as the first one of 'em fired. Least they weren't shootin' wild—they knew the danger of a ricochet same as me. And thankfully fer my mule, it seemed they didn't want to waste their bullets on an animal, neither. They were makin' their shots count.

Holt fired again, and the head of one of the women ridin' toward me just plain disappeared in a spray of red mist.

I turned away as the headless body slid from her horse, wincin'. And glad Ethelyn couldn't see none of this. Least, I hoped she couldn't see anythin' through that burlap sack.

My mule took off, the traitor, barrelin' through the chaos to disappear down the road, and I threw myself to the ground just in time to avoid the fire of three of the five left. Their bullets missed, some of 'em pingin' back again against the rocks before finally stickin' in somethin' or breakin' apart.

Riderless horses shrieked and galloped wildly around the pool's clearin', stirrin' up the ones that still had riders, and one of 'em headed right for me. I curled myself into a tight ball as the hooves thundered at me and they only barely missed, ringin' against the rock only inches from my head and then runnin' off down the road after my mule.

Holt shot again, and then there was only three left ridin'.

I uncurled myself with a curse and looked fer that shaggy chestnut pony carryin' my sister. It was still in the clearin', prancin' wild-eyed and draggin' its lead, half-buckin' now and then as my sister clung to the saddle horn with white-knuckled hands.

One of the riders still livin' was tryin' to catch it. Another of 'em was aimin' his pistol at Ethelyn.

I pushed to my knees and fired, hittin' the one aimin' at Ethelyn in the side. He yelled and reined his horse around to face me instead, his pistol quickly followin'.

I fired again and got him in the throat.

He went off his horse backward.

"Tell your man to stop shootin'!" barked the only man still left standin'. "Stop shootin' or I'll kill her!"

I swung around to face him, still on my knees, pistol outstretched. But my finger stilled on the trigger.

He'd dismounted his horse and pulled Ethelyn off the pony, and now held her with an arm hooked around her neck, his gun pressed against her temple. She whimpered, but the sound was muffled. Sounded like she might be gagged.

That's when all the rage inside me settled. It went all flat and numb. My harsh breathin' slowed. My nerves stilled, a strange, detached calmness comin' over me.

The other rider still livin', a woman, fought to control her frantic horse, but she kept her seat well enough and kept her gun trained even, too. On me.

"Put your gun down," the man ordered. "And tell your man up top to stop shootin'. Or I swear I'll—"

The crack of Holt's rifle ate the rest of his words, and half his head, too.

I didn't wait fer his body to drop. I fired two quick shots at the woman remainin' even as I dove fer the ground again. Her bullet grazed my right shoulder as I ducked, but both of my bullets hit home.

She jerked in the saddle as blood painted the front of her vest, then wheeled her horse around to flee. Guess she'd decided—too late—she'd had enough of this mess. The horse tore off northward with her leanin' sideways in the saddle, barely stayin' on.

I let her go, pretty sure I'd got her through the heart. She wouldn't live fer long.

And anyway, I had Ethelyn. That was all that mattered.

A gunshot echoed from behind me.

Fer a minute I didn't understand. It didn't make sense. There weren't no one left standin' to shoot. And anyway, at this range, I surely woulda felt the bullet.

My fingers tightened around my own grip, but I'd emptied the chamber. Frownin', I turned.

The mustached man still lay where he'd fallen, his mangled shoulder leakin' bright blood to stain the bone-colored rocks, his face ashen gray. He writhed there, moanin' and groanin', but laughin', too. Cacklin'. Manic. He held his pistol in his right hand. And he laughed. And laughed and laughed.

From the corner of my eye, I saw Ethelyn fall.

XVIII

LAND OF THE LIVING, LAND OF THE DEAD

Everythin' in me shattered.

I ran to her, horror in my throat, my empty pistol clatterin' to the rock as I dropped it, forgotten.

I hit my knees at her side, gatherin' her up into my lap.

Holt's rifle fired one last time, silencin' the mustached man's cacklin' laugh.

But all I saw was the bloom of crimson spreadin' across the breast of Ethelyn's dress; all I heard were the short, choked gasps comin' from under that sack. "No," I whispered. "No no no."

Tears blurred my vision, streaked down my face. I yanked the blood-splattered burlap off her head and threw it away. Pulled the tied cloth outta her mouth. Cradled her face.

Blood trickled from between her lips. She looked up at me with wide, terrified eyes.

Eyes that were the wrong color.

Ethelyn had always had our mama's eyes. A sea-green shade. The color of jade, our pa used to always say.

This woman had dark eyes. A warm, soft brown. Kinda like my own.

But my sister and I had never looked very much alike.

I stared down at her. Stared down at this girl I held in my lap. This dyin' girl. This girl who weren't my sister.

This girl who weren't Ethelyn.

I couldn't comprehend. Couldn't understand. My body felt numb again. My head too light.

She tried to speak. Coughed and choked. Blood bubbled up in her mouth.

I shook my head, tried and failed to speak myself. Tried to swallow down the sickness risin' in my insides. *I'm sorry*, I wanted to say. *I'm so sorry*. I wanted to comfort her somehow, this poor girl who'd suffered and was gonna die fer nothin', but the words were stuck. I was findin' it hard to breathe ... much less talk.

If this weren't Ethelyn ... then where the hell was my sister?

Was all this a trick? A double-cross?

Or was this the girl Nine-Fingered Nan had had the whole time, and all this just a terrible case of mistaken identity?

It all made me sick. All of it. My heart beat too hard, too fast, pulsin' out in my ears a frantic, desperate rhythm.

There was nothin' else I could do 'cept hold her as she exhaled a long, rattlin' breath and then went still, her warm brown eyes goin' cool as they stared past me to the sky.

Fresh tears ran trails down my face as I eased her off my lap and laid her down against the warm rock. Tears fer her, whoever she was, and a life wasted fer no reason, and tears fer my sister, who was still out there somewhere.

Maybe still with Nine-Fingered Nan.

Maybe not.

The idea of startin' my search for her over fresh was almost too much to bear.

I closed my eyes against the surge of panic and forced myself to breathe. *Focus. Focus, Van.* First, I needed to figure out what had happened here. First, I needed to figure out who else was gonna die fer this.

Anger sparked again in my chest, slowly buildin' back up into that familiar rage, burnin' away all the numbness of the shock at not seein' my sister under that burlap sack. I stood and backed away from the girl who weren't Ethelyn, lettin' that rage warm my limbs.

I turned to face the flat space of the holdin' tank pool, suddenly hopin' someone had lived. Bodies lay everywhere. A few of the horses had stayed and were mostly settled now, snortin' at the ground and lookin' to me curiously.

I stalked forward, hardly limpin' now, and scooped up my pistol. I reloaded quickly, studyin' each body in turn, lookin' fer breathin'.

There were two.

"Holt!" I barked. My voice echoed up against the cliffs. "Holt, get down here!"

Maybe he was already on his way. But if not, now he would be.

We had some business to take care of.

I went to the nearest body still breathin', a man, lyin' face down and bleedin' somethin' terrible from a big hole in his gut curtesy of Holt's sharpshootin' rifle. I dug one toe under his shoulder and kicked him over onto his back. He was unconscious.

Well, if he thought he was gonna get to go so peacefully, he was sorely mistaken.

I caught a fistful of the back of his shirt, drug him over to one of the cliff walls, and propped him up sittin' against it. I freed him from all his weapons, tossin' 'em into the pool, then slapped him. Hard.

He stirred, but didn't wake.

I slapped him again.

His eyes fluttered open. Then he choked and cried out in pain. His hands went to the ragged hole in his belly, his face deathly pale. His gray eyes found my face eventually, glassy and unfocused.

I gave him a smile. "Howdy, mister. Welcome back to the land of the livin'. Fer a little while, anyway. We need to have a talk."

His eyes left my face and wandered around the scene of death spread out behind me. They paused fer a bit on the body of the girl, then stopped altogether on the body of the mustached man.

"Yeah," I said. "He's dead. But that ain't my problem. My problem..." I pointed to the body of the girl, "my problem is that she ain't my sister."

His eyes followed my finger, then came back to my face, a little more focused now. A grin split his lips, showin' off bloodied teeth. "I know," he gurgled. Then he chuckled. And choked, coughed, and winced.

I straightened, glarin' down at him. The pistol was heavy in my hand, warm against my palm. "That amuses you, does it?"

"Yeah." He choked out a few more chuckles. "You thought it was her, though, didn't ya? Thought it was yer sister?" He coughed and cried out, then spit a wad of blood in my direction. "Wish I coulda seen yer face when she went down. Or did ya already know it weren't yer sister by then?" He could hardly keep his eyes open, his breath wet and labored, but that didn't stop him from grinnin' up at me.

I put a bullet through his right knee.

His scream got amplified by our rocky surroundin's, ringin' up into the sky, bouncin' back over itself. He sagged against the wall, and fer a minute I thought he might pass out on me again.

I stepped forward and leaned down to slap him again to keep him awake, then took a fistful of his shirt to hold him upright against the rock. "Where's my sister?" I growled through my teeth. "My *real* sister? Does Nan have her?" I shook him. "Does Nan have her or was this a ruse from the beginnin'?"

He rolled his head up to look at me. His eyes wouldn't focus, and he blinked slowly. But he was still smilin', damn him. "Nan ain't gonna ... give up ... yer sister," he said weakly. "Deal's ... deal's too good. And ... and anyway ... Nan thinks yer dead." He tried to laugh again, but it came out a wheeze.

I let go of his shirt. I remembered what the mustached bastard had told me durin' our first meetin' in the Stag Saloon ... that he'd told Nan I was dead. But I wasn't dead. And I'd paid him ten thousand dollars extra to go back to Nine-Fingered Nan and tell her he'd been wrong about that. I swallowed hard, all the pieces startin' to fall into place.

Humiliation crawled up under my shirt collar and burned worse than the noonday sun beatin' down upon us. "He never told her I showed up in Bravebank."

The man bleedin' out in front of me grinned all the wider. "Desperation ... makes a man ... a fool, Taggert said. Guess he was right." He choked out another chuckle.

My mind was racin', goin' back through everythin' I had done to get to Bravebank, and to get that thirty-five thousand dollars. All of that and thirty-five thousand dollars I thought would get my sister back. Instead, it had all been fer nothin'.

A fool's errand set upon me by one of Nan's crew who'd decided to use me to make himself and his closest allies rich.

I'd been played all right, jerked around like a puppet on strings, just like Holt had said.

Only it hadn't been Nine-Fingered Nan doin' the pullin'.

Unless ... unless the man bleedin' out in front of me now was the one lyin'. Unless *he* was the one fuckin' with me now, tryin' to get in one last stab before headin' off to Hell. I squinted down at him. "The fingers," I said. "They had a note from Nan."

He shook his head and tried to spit more blood at me, but it missed. By a lot. "Did it? Funny. Don't remember ... there bein' a signature."

He was right. There hadn't been a signature. In truth, anyone coulda written that note. Hell, anyone coulda written that note even if there *had* been a signature. I'd never seen Nine-Fingered Nan's writin' before. I had no way to know. I'd just assumed it had come from her, given the circumstances.

I spun away from him and paced a few steps, runnin' a hand over my face, careful fer the swollen lip Holt had given me the night before. *You fool. You goddamned fool!*

"Taggert ... just wanted to ... to dissuade you ... from killin' any more ... of his guys. And said ... said it would ... motivate you. Guess he was ... right about that, too."

The wheezin' laugh came again, but this time in short, hard gasps. He weren't gonna last much longer.

"Sure, Nan woulda ... woulda done the same ... if she'd known about it."

He thought it all real funny, laughin' even though it musta hurt somethin' awful. Takin' great pleasure in these last few moments of his life lettin' me know just how big of a fool I'd been.

Well, I figured I should make his last few moments more comfortable fer him in return. I turned and put a bullet in his other knee.

This time he didn't have enough air to scream. He only grunted, his face goin' even more pale, chokin' and gaggin' as his eyes rolled back in his head. I holstered my pistol and went to him, slappin' him around to consciousness one last time. "Wake up, you no good sonuvabitch."

He did, but there weren't much of him left by now.

"Yer gonna meet the Devil with yer eyes open, mister."

His glassy gray gaze found my hard glare. His lips tried to smile one last time, but in the end he couldn't do it. Between the hole in his gut and his ruined knees, he was down too deep in a world of hurt.

And he was still there when the life went outta him, the expression frozen on his face in death not smilin' at all, but instead a grimace of pain. Pain, and some fear, too. That fear men feel when they die slow and have the chance to count their sins before takin' their last breath.

I had a feelin' this man had a mighty long list of sins.

Maybe I shoulda given him a little more time to count them.

Maybe then he woulda been a lot more scared to leave this land of the livin'.

I wouldn'ta minded seein' him realize what he'd have suffer there in the depths of Hell. Wouldn'ta minded seein' him realize that poor girl they'd kidnapped and tortured and brought here to die would get her justice ... whether in this life or the next.

But fer now I supposed I'd have to be satisfied by what justice I'd given her in this life.

I left him there and made my way toward the second one still breathin', grabbin' the reins of one of the horses on the way and leadin' it after me.

Hoofbeats gallopin' up the south road behind me rose into the silence and I turned to train my pistol on the narrow opening between the cliffs, ready fer whoever might be comin'.

Holt exploded into the clearin' on his black geldin' and reined it up into a hard stop, his pistol pointed at me in turn before we both took fingers off triggers and lowered our weapons. "Van! You all right? I heard shots…" He circled his horse, lookin' fer anyone else with a pistol in their hand, but found none. He stopped cold at the sight of the girl's body and then turned to me with a look of distraught alarm on his face.

Ah, so he did care. All that talk about not wantin' to go after a ghost, but it turned out he didn't much like the thought of bein' right about that.

"Yer … yer sister," his words came out a strangled whisper. "Is she … is she…?"

"That ain't her." I resumed my walk to the single remainin' survivor of our shootout, this one a woman lyin' face up, sprawled out near the pool. She had a nice big hole in the right side of her chest. She was unconscious, too, her shallow breaths already quick and raspy.

"Wha?" Holt asked from behind me.

"That ain't her," I repeated, louder. "I was had by that mustached bastard from the Stag Saloon. Nan don't even know about this deal. She still thinks I'm dead. She…" I shook my head, waited till I could bite back the bitter surge of feelin's. "She still has Ethelyn."

Unless it was too late now.

Unless that deal had already been done.

All this time I'd wasted…

I sucked in a shudderin' breath and pulled the lasso off the saddle of the horse I led. I couldn't think about any of that now.

All that mattered was that I didn't waste any more time.

I left the raspin' woman where she lay. She wouldn't last more than three or four hours with a hole like that in her chest, not long enough to be any use to me. I coulda put her outta her misery, I suppose, but then, she had sins to pay for, too.

And who was I to interfere with the work of the Devil?

Instead I went over to the dead man with the mustache. Taggert, I guess his name was.

Holt was just starin' at me. "That … that ain't yer sister?" He looked back to the girl's body.

"No."

"Who is it, then?"

"I don't know." I blinked hard, shovin' down those goddamned feelin's again. "She died before she could say anythin'."

"Maybe ... maybe they got the wrong girl by mistake?" Holt ventured.

"No they didn't." My voice was hoarse, rough. "They knew exactly what they were doin'. They used her to use me to get their money. They were never gonna trade. This was a trap. Fer all of us." I pulled my knife and went to work on the the dead Taggert, dressin' him out like he were the carcass of an animal I'd just killed in a hunt.

"What the hell are you doin'?" Holt asked.

"We got a ways to travel," I said. "And this desert sun is hot. Don't want him gettin' too ripe 'fore we get there." I finished my grisly work, wiped my knife and my hands on Taggert's shirt tail, sheathed the knife, and leveraged the body up onto my shoulder, ignorin' the way it made all my burns flare up into sharp agony and the nice red stain it left on my own shirt. Then I threw him over the saddle of the horse I'd caught, a dapple gray, and tied him there.

By the time I was done, sweat was drippin' off my nose.

Holt was still starin' at me. "Before you get where?"

I walked over to grab the reins of another abandoned horse, a chestnut with tall white socks, trailin' the one holdin' Taggert's body after me. I swung aboard the chestnut and pulled it around to face Holt. "I'm goin' to pay Nan a visit," I said. "And get my sister back."

Holt looked at me as if I'd gone ravin' mad.

And maybe I had.

"And just how do you plan to do that?" he demanded.

"I'm gonna make her a new deal."

He tilted his chin downward, sendin' me a warnin' glare from under the brim of his hat. "Van, damnit, last time you said somethin' like that and rode off to find Nine-Fingered Nan she all but outright killed ya!"

"But this time I'll be bringin' her a gift." I swept out my hand toward the dead Taggert.

Holt's eyes went wide.

I swung the chestnut mare around and kicked her into a trot, headin' northward in hopes of findin' my mule and all that cash he carried.

"Van!" Holt yelled out in my wake. "Goddamnit! All this and you ain't learned nothin'! You ride in there with the corpse of her man on yer heels and—"

"Be sure you bury the girl," I called back over my shoulder. "Leave the rest of 'em to rot."

"Van! Van, goddamnit, *get back here*!"

I ignored him, lettin' the sound of my horses' hooves drown out his shoutin' and cursin' as I went on down the road, weavin' through the towerin' rocks with my grisly caravan. I needed to find that mule and that cash and head fer Nan's rocky oasis of a hideout, and fast.

I wondered if Holt would follow and try to stop me.

Let him, if he wanted.

I weren't gonna stop. Not this time. Not any time. Not till I got back to Nine-Fingered Nan.

Not till I got Ethelyn back.

ALL THE CARDS ON THE TABLE

My mule hadn't gone too far, turned out.

His social nature wouldn't let him stray too far from his fellows. And they were all there, all the horses who had bolted in terror once the shootout started and their riders fell, all clustered in a group where the road curved around to the northeast and opened back out into the gentle, slopin' hills that were the feet of the Bone Spur Mountains.

I dismounted the chestnut mare and retrieved my mule, walkin' him back to my borrowed mounts. The saddlebags on him were still intact, the cash still buckled up safe inside.

I let the other horses be, leavin' the mare to join 'em, knowin' they'd eventually find their way back to wherever they called home ... or at least back to whoever tended to feed 'em most. Then I climbed back aboard my mule, leadin' the gray behind us. I pointed him east and kicked him into motion, pickin' up into a canter.

I had a long way to go, and I didn't want Taggert's body gettin' too ripe before we got there.

Three days ridin' under the sun was makin' me feel pretty ripe by the end of it, and I weren't even dead.

On the outside, at least.

I'd stopped along the way in Bravebank to get a few supplies fer the journey, but then I'd headed off again. I pushed the mule and the gray as hard as I dared, workin' 'em up into a lather before slowin' down to let 'em cool off.

The ride coulda gone faster if not fer all the damned mountains that littered this part of the Territories. There weren't no straight road to be found fer more than a few miles at a time. I went east sure enough, but then had to pick my way north and then south again to get around the biggest peaks in this particular cluster, which the locals had dubbed the Superstition Mountains.

Superstition. Maybe those worshippers of the dead in Grave Gulch shoulda settled in these mountains, instead. Woulda suited them just fine.

As it were, maybe it was just fittin' enough that Nine-Fingered Nan had chosen this place to be her home. There were some mighty interestin' stories circulatin' about her, too.

If this really was her home, anyway.

Truth be told, I didn't know if she'd still be at this particular hideout of hers or not. But I had a feelin' someone would be, and that someone could take me to Nan, wherever she might be. Surely. And if they were reluctant to do so, I was fully prepared to persuade them, one way or another. Whatever it took.

On the evenin' of the third day, I topped a ridge and saw the river snakin' out below me, nestled down along the craggy feet of the Superstitions. The sun was already droppin' in the west, makin' the water shine like liquid gold.

My mule was blowin' hard, the gray the same. I patted his sweaty neck. "Easy there, boy. You done good. We'll go down in the mornin'."

I mighta been ravin' mad, but I weren't stupid enough to walk into Nan's lair in the dark.

I made camp there on the ridge, but had no fire. Nan's people mighta spotted me already. But if they hadn't, I didn't wanna make it any easier on 'em.

I didn't sleep much that night, on account of several factors:

Part of me still expected Holt to show up blusterin' mad in efforts to stop this latest affront to his cautious self-preservation sensibilities.

Part of me expected some of Nan's crew to manifest outta the darkness and either try and kill me, or truss me up to drop me like some neatly delivered parcel at Nine-Fingered Nan's feet.

And part of me expected some kind of vulture of the animal variety might take a sudden interest in the pounds of slightly aged meat I carried with me. The buzzards had followed me most the way here, hopin' fer an easy meal. I wondered how much longer their patience would last.

Though, the birds were a manageable annoyance.

Considerably less manageable would be the big mountain cats that prowled this area. If one of those were to take an interest in Taggert's overripe remains ... well, that fight would be quite a bit more hazardous to my health than a disagreement with the buzzards.

So I settled back against my saddle to wait through the long night and pulled my hat low over my face, though I kept my eyes uncovered. And half-open.

And I kept my hand on my gun.

At last, mornin' came.

Holt, Nan's crew, and the lions did not.

Some mighta called that luck. But I didn't believe in luck. So I packed everythin' back up, saddled up, hauled Taggert's carcass back onto the dappled gray, and then took a minute to catch my breath and let the agony in my angry burns fade again.

Least my metal leg was farin' better now. And the nick across my right shoulder I'd gotten in the shoot-out at the pool wasn't hurtin' so much anymore. But Charlotte had said those burns would take a few more weeks to heal up. Guess I couldn't ask fer too much.

I climbed aboard the mule, and we went slow and careful down the side of the mountain toward the river.

Last time I'd met Nan here, it'd been right outside an impression in the cliff face that resembled a cave, only it weren't a cave at all. There'd been buildin's carved outta that rock. Nan hadn't done that herself, of course. No, those rock dwellin's had been there a long, long time, long before us. Maybe done by the same people as had done those drawin's out in the Bone Spurs.

Or maybe it had been someone else.

Either way, the makers of those cliff-carved buildin's had long since gone. Some of the walls were crumblin' now, some of the stairs worn away to nothin'. But that didn't stop murderers and thieves like Nine-Fingered Nan from usin' what was left of 'em fer shelter.

I picked my way down the same path as before, until about halfway between the ridge I'd camped on and the river, I saw ahead the big hole carved outta the cliff and the pale face of those crumbled walls.

I drew the mule up short. Studied the brush and cacti and boulders that littered the land around me. But nothin' moved. The mornin' was still and quiet.

The mule blew a snort and shook his head, jinglin' his bit.

There were hoofprints in the soft red dirt of the path. Fresh ones. Someone was here, all right. They just weren't wantin' to show themselves. Yet.

I loosened my pistol in the holster, kept my fingers wrapped around its grip. I settled my seat in the saddle and drew in a slow, calmin' breath.

This was either gonna be the day I got my sister back ... or the day I died.

As soon as I opened my mouth now, there'd be no goin' back. I'd be puttin' all my cards on the table.

Well ... I'd always been shit at poker.

"Nan!" I bellowed out. "Nine-Fingered Nan! I got somethin' fer ya!"

My words carried up loud and clear to those crumbled buildin's and echoed away out over the river. Both the mule and the gray perked up their ears and lifted their heads at the sudden noise in the quiet.

The only thing that answered me was the heavy drone of flies buzzin' around Taggert's body.

Swearin', I nudged the mule into a canter, makin' my way up the narrow path as it switched back and forth toward the carved-out dwellin's. "Nan!" I yelled again. "Get out here! I got business to talk with you!"

And then she appeared at the top of the hill, Nine-Fingered Nan, her horse standin' across the path. He was a tall, lean bay with a white star in the middle of his forehead, watchin' us approach with bright eyes.

Nan watched us approach, too, her double pearl grips glintin' in the sun.

I pulled the mule to an abrupt stop, the gray slidin' up behind me. But I didn't draw. Didn't even try. Not this time. I was here to make a deal, not to die.

Her eyebrows lifted in the shadow of her wide-brimmed hat. "Well, well, well," she drawled. "Look who's still breathin'. Taggert told me you were dead."

I yanked my knife from my belt and leaned over to cut the body free of the gray's saddle, then gave it a push. The lifeless corpse thumped to the ground in a cloud of dust and the dappled horse side-stepped away from it, bumpin' into me and the mule. "That Taggert?" I jerked my head in the direction of his body.

Nan's eyes narrowed as they went to him, then came back to me. "Yes. That Taggert."

"He lied," I said harshly.

"I can see that."

"He double-crossed you. Lied to you and made a deal with me himself fer the return of my sister. Had a couple of yer other guys and gals with him, too. Wanted me to get him a lot of money. I don't suppose he meant to share it with you."

Two of her lieutenants rode up behind her then, two men armed with rifles. They took up positions to either side of her, squintin' glares at me.

Nine-Fingered Nan eyed me coolly with that pale gaze of hers. Her weathered face was shadowed by her hat, her hands restin' light on her reins. She weren't concerned at all. "How much money?" Her voice, as clear and hard as the first time I'd heard it, rang against the cliff face.

How much money. There was that thing she loved most again. Cold, hard cash. A flicker of hope rekindled in my chest. Maybe this was gonna work. "Thirty-five thousand," I said.

A grin split her wrinkled lips. She chuckled. Looked back over each shoulder to her two lieutenants in turn. Then she faced me again and shook her head. "I always knew Taggert was an under-achiever. So? What of it? Did ya get the money?"

"Yeah. I got it."

"Let's see it, then."

I swallowed. Forced myself to ask the question. "You got my sister?"

"What, you mean Taggert didn't have her?"

"No." I couldn't tell if she was bein' serious or just fuckin' with me. "He didn't."

"Imagine that."

She was fuckin' with me. I ground my teeth. I looked to each of her lieutenants, countin' my odds. I wanted desperately to draw and put a bullet right into that calm, smug face of hers, but I surely wouldn't be gettin' out of that alive.

Of course, stayin' alive only mattered if I had Ethelyn. "Where," I repeated, slow and gruff, "is my sister?"

Nan spit off the side of her horse. "I told you before and I'll tell you again. She's safe enough fer now. Long as you do as I say. Long as you show me that money."

I stared at her and she stared at me, and my breath came too fast and my heart beat too hard. But I couldn't just take her word fer it. Not after what'd happened with Taggert and that poor girl he'd killed. "So I give you the money and you give me my sister, then?"

"Sure."

I want to see her," I blurted. "Show me Ethelyn and I'll show you the money."

Nan smiled. "No."

A sick feelin' crawled into my gut. I shifted in the saddle, and the mule shifted, too, chewin' at his bit. All I could hear in my head then was Holt, screamin' at me fer the fool I'd been twice over now, ridin' straight into this trap. "How do I know you have her, then?" I managed to choke out. "How do I know she's still alive?"

Nan shrugged. "You've seen the proof. If that ain't enough fer you ... well, then ... I guess you got to make a choice. But, I gotta tell ya," her right hand, the one with the missin' index finger, slid smoothly to her right pearl grip, "I ain't the most patient of women. So make yer choice quick, boy."

I *had* seen the proof. What little there was of it. And half of it had already proven to be false, just like Holt had warned. But what was the greater gamble, here? Believe it to be true, believe Nan did have Ethelyn, and bargain fer her freedom? What could I lose by believin' such a thing, aside from twenty-five thousand dollars? Or I could believe it to be false, decide Nan didn't have Ethelyn, and leave here empty-handed or stay here and die bleedin' out into the dirt, and risk bein' wrong and doomin' Ethelyn to a life of slavery overseas in a foreign land.

There really was no choice at all.

I growled a foul curse and dropped my reins, then picked up the saddle bags holdin' the cash and tossed 'em at her. They hit the path about mid-way between us, stirrin' up their own cloud of dust.

Nan looked at 'em, then arched an eyebrow. She clucked her tongue in admonishment. "Well now. You won't get too far with those kinda manners. Pick 'em up and bring 'em to me, boy. On yer feet."

I glared at her, but her even stare didn't blink.

A pair of clicks echoed out into the mornin' as Nan's lieutenants thumbed back their hammers and aimed at me, just in case.

Scowlin', I dismounted carefully, though that was mostly 'cause of my burns and metal leg more than from a fear of gettin' shot. I limped up to where the bags had landed and pulled 'em outta the dirt, then went to the side of Nan's tall horse and held 'em up toward her. "Here," I spat. "Here's your damn money."

She smiled down at me. A horrible, triumphant smile. And took the saddle bags. "Thank you." She laid them over the front of her own saddle and proceeded to open 'em, riflin' through the contents. "There's only twenty-five thousand here," she said after a while. She counted a lot faster than her man from the saloon. "I thought you said you got thirty-five thousand?"

"I did. Taggert took ten of it earlier. Don't know what he did with it."

She grunted and closed up the saddle bags. "Well. Twenty-five thousand ain't near enough to get back yer sister."

"Then how much?" I demanded. "Name yer price."

She looked down at me again, sizin' me up.

I pushed on. "You told me if I made it to Bravebank alive and with my wits intact you'd discuss terms. Well, I did. I got to Bravebank. I made a deal with Taggert and delivered what I promised. He didn't follow through on his end of the deal, and now he's dead. He was double-crossin' you. I did you a favor cuttin' out that rot from yer gang ... now I'm here to make a new deal. A legit deal. With you. Directly. When I came here before, you said I hadn't proved myself yet. Well, I have now. So we gonna bargain, or what?"

Nan was quiet fer a long minute. The only sound in the silence was the drone of the flies around Taggert's body. Her gaze dropped down to my left leg. The leg she'd put a bullet in. "Looks like that leg healed up all right."

I shifted on the metal foot, glad she couldn't see what most my left leg was made of now. "Well enough," was all I said.

"Musta found yerself a real good doctor."

Somethin' in her tone I didn't like. My mind went to thoughts of Dr. Balogh and his family, a spike of worry lancin' into my heart. But she couldn't know. She couldn't have known he'd been the one to find me in the desert. The one to fix me up. She'd thought I was dead. Taggert had said so. She'd said so. And anyway, what interest could she have had in a doctor?

Old World tech.

That damned doctor was gonna get himself killed flauntin' that stuff around. "Good enough." I made it sound casual, dismissive. Didn't let my eyes slide back in the direction of Bravebank. Kept 'em on her. "My sister," I said again. "You want that other ten thousand? I can have it to you in three days."

"Yer face, though," she said, squintin' down at me. "That doesn't look so good. Run into some trouble gettin' this money, did ya?"

I ran my hand over my chin, feelin' the start of somethin' near a proper beard now under my palm. Sweat prickled under my hat brim and between my shoulders. "Somethin' like that," I said. "But I got it."

"So you did," Nan mused. "Thirty-five thousand dollars in the space of ... how long it'd take you to get Taggert's money?"

"From the time we made the deal to the time I delivered it? A week."

"And you say you can get me ten thousand more in three days?"

"That's right." Might mean Holt wouldn't hold back in shootin' me, after all, but she didn't need to know we already had extra cash stashed away fer ourselves.

She gave a low whistle. "Well, Mr. Delano ... it seems I may have underestimated you. When I shot you last time ... well, I never expected to see you again. Least, not alive. Thought maybe bein' raised in a nice, warm, lovin' home woulda made you soft. Thought maybe up to this point in yer life, you'd just been lucky. Like yer pa. And yet ... now here you are. Not dead. And with twenty-five thousand dollars."

"I just want my sister back. Like I told you before."

She nodded. "Sure, sure. Seems you wantin' yer sister back is a mighty powerful motivator."

I had nothin' to say to that, so I only stood there glarin' up at her, fists balled at my sides.

She looked away from me to gaze down along the path I'd come in on as if ponderin' somethin'. "Ya see, I'm just sittin' here thinkin' to myself ... well, hell, if Lucky Logan's boy is gonna be so eager to please ... so resourceful and efficient ... why waste such potential?" Her eyes came back to me then, hard and glitterin'. "You still willin' to owe me, Mr. Delano?"

I didn't like the look on her face. Not at all.

But I'd already given her the twenty-five thousand dollars. Already told her I was here to make a new deal. Already put all my cards on the table. So I forced myself to hold her greedy stare and gave a nod. "You set my sister free and I'll owe you whatever you want."

A slow smile spread across her face. "Very noble of you, Mr. Delano. But I think I'll hold on to yer sister fer now ... fer safe-keepin'. And to be certain you stay *properly motivated*, ya understand."

An image of those severed fingers flashed into my mind. Those hadn't been Ethelyn's fingers, no, but I also remembered what Taggert's man had said about 'em. *Nan woulda done the same thing.*

I swallowed back the bile that rose in my throat, tried to breathe through the fire burnin' in my chest. "I want to see her," I said again. "I want proof you got her."

"And I told ya no. Look, you've lasted this long, boy. Don't push yer luck. This money," she patted at my saddle bags, "and the body of that traitor over there," she nodded toward Taggert, "bought you another chance. Bought yer sister more time stayin' off the boat. But you want to see her? Yer gonna have to make it worth my trouble to get her here, understand? You do a few things fer me and manage to live through 'em, I'll consider it. Till then, don't ask again. Them's my terms. That's the deal I'm willin' to make. You can take it or leave it."

There was rushin' in my ears again, my chest too tight and my head too light. I held her stare fer as long as I could while I considered my greatly limited options. Then I tore my eyes away from her and glanced at her two lieutenants. They were both still sightin' down their rifles at me.

But no one had shot me yet.

Not even Nan.

And I'd already been willin' to make this deal before, a horse and a leg and a month ago.

Why not now?

"Daylight's wastin', Mr. Delano," Nan prompted. "What'll it be?"

I stepped back from her horse and gave a nod. "Fine. I'm in."

"Very good." Her maimed gun-hand slid off her pearl grip and went back to her reins. "Good to see yer finally usin' those smarts of yers. Musta got those from yer mama, yeah? She were a smart woman, weren't she? 'Cept fer the fact she married yer pa, of course. That didn't get her very far, did it?"

I took a few more steps back from her horse, heart poundin' and fingers itchin' at her goadin'. *Don't do it. You just made a deal. This is your best chance yet ... don't ruin it.*

How many times had I said that, now?

Maybe this one would finally come through fer me.

Or maybe it was all another lie. Another trap. I had no real way to know. But I was still almost certain Nine-Fingered Nan had Ethelyn. Somewhere. If she was gonna let me do some business fer her, maybe I could do some pokin' around of my own and see where she might be holdin' my sister.

And if I could find that out, I could take things into my own hands.

No more payin' debts. No more playin' games.

"Just tell me what I owe you," I growled.

"Oh, I'll think about it. In the meantime, why don't you make yerself comfortable in Bravebank. I'll put in a word with the sheriff that yer to be granted ... *permissions* ... to conduct my business. Now, a'course I can't promise the same kind of leniency in all other towns in the Territories—yet—but that'll be somethin' we'll work on. So see that you don't get yerself arrested durin' the conductin' of my business. You do, and ain't no one will come to save you from the noose." She nudged her horse forward till she was beside me once again, loomin' over me. "Unless you go sayin' things to the law you shouldn't, of course. Then we most certainly will come to save you from the noose. And deliver you into somethin' a great deal more unpleasant. Understand?"

I remembered well what I'd suffered at the hands of Baron Whittaker, and wondered if there could be much else worse than that. I didn't think so. But then, I surely didn't feel like findin' out, neither. I lifted my hands, slow and careful so as to not prompt her lieutenants' trigger fingers into firin'. "Sure."

"Good. Then I look forward to seein' what else you can do fer me. I'll have someone fetch you when I decide what that's gonna be. Till then..." she tipped her wide-brimmed hat to me, a corner of her mouth quirkin' in a smirk, "pleasant day to you, Mr. Delano."

She kicked her heels into her horse's side and he leapt forward into a canter, headin' down the path toward the river. Her two men holstered their rifles and followed after her, thunderin' by me on either side and startlin' my mule and the gray, makin' 'em trot off a ways.

I was left alone, coughin' in the swirl of red dust they left behind.

Alone, with no money and no sister and only a dead body and its flies fer company.

All I had left now was hope.

Hope that Nine-Fingered Nan was actually the one holdin' my sister in the first place. Hope that she weren't lyin' to me about that.

Hope that if all that were true, she'd keep her end of the bargain better than Taggert had and set my sister free.

Hope that Ethelyn was truly safe enough fer the time bein', fer however long it took Nan to feel we were even.

Hope that I'd survive any of this.

I hung my head, blinkin' away the grit in my eyes, then turned my face toward the sun, still risin' in the east. I trudged toward the mule and took his reins, then gathered up the dappled gray, too. If they were gonna leave me the horse, I could at least get a little somethin' out of all my troubles here.

I mounted the mule and led the gray behind, and pointed us back west.

Toward Bravebank.

I didn't want to wait in Bravebank as a lackey fer Nine-Fingered Nan, millin' about aimlessly till she came to fetch me. But I supposed I didn't have much other choice. At least, not fer now.

The mule ambled back down the switch-back path, and I thought I'd have felt a lot happier about makin' a solid deal fer my sister. After all, if everythin' worked out, I'd be gettin' exactly what I wanted.

If everythin' worked out.

I sighed heavily, suddenly feelin' every place on my body that hurt. And there were a lot of places that hurt. I glanced over my shoulder to the sun as it warmed my back, then closed my eyes against its light.

Hope.

That soul killer.

EPILOGUE

A BARON'S BASTARD

Charles Miller paced a slow circle around the man hanging from the ceiling.

He'd been hanging down here for three days now. Alone, in the dark. No food, no water. He squinted now in the dim light created by the lantern Charles had set on the small wooden table to his right. The air reeked of excrement, still and damp, moisture seeping through the cracks in the stone-brick walls.

The man looked terrified. He was so pale. His breathing fast and haggard.

Charles shook his head. Clucked his tongue in admonishment. He had hoped this man would be harder to break. He'd seen his father do this kind of thing plenty of times ... he'd been looking forward to trying some of the same strategies. He was sure he could have equally as satisfactory results.

Except ... he wasn't sure now he'd get the chance to hurt this man.

He looked ready to talk again. Unprompted.

Charles stopped in front of him and sighed heavily. He clasped his hands behind his back.

"I ... I told you," the man gasped. "I already told you everything I know, I swear!"

Charles frowned, sucking on his top teeth. "Mmm."

The man's dangling feet hung only inches above the floor's damp cobblestones. The skin of his wrists showed raw and bloody in the lamplight. He'd been struggling to get free these last three days, it seemed.

Alas, no one had ever escaped from this cellar. Not in Charles' lifetime, at least.

"I see," Charles said quietly. Patiently. "So you're telling me it was just one man who did all of that?" He pointed upward, up through the yards of earth that blanketed them, toward the surface. Toward the three burned-out husks of barns, and the once-splendid manor with its now-charred beams and ruined furniture, and the horse barn that was still half empty, the rest of the highly bred and very expensive animals still missing.

Stolen, most likely. Or kept by whoever had chanced to find them, more likely.

Anger kindled deep within, and Charles drew in a slow breath.

"Yes!" the man blurted. His voice cracked. He must have been so thirsty. He struggled in the chains, and his body swung gently back and forth. "And a woman, like I said. I swear, I'm telling you the truth!"

Charles nodded. He knew about the woman. She had been identified easily enough by some of the household staff, as well. A known trouble-maker. A rebellious soul.

If it had been up to him, she would have hanged months ago.

But his father had always had difficulty letting go of his prettiest possessions.

Charles would not make his father's mistakes. "I know the woman," he said curtly. "I'm not concerned with her. If I know her, I can find her. And trust me, I will find her." He began his slow circling again, hands still clasped behind his back. "No, what concerns me is this man you speak of. No one seems to have gotten a very good look at him. No one who is still alive, anyway. No one seems to know who he was."

The man now hanging from the ceiling shook his head vigorously.

Long, lank strands of dark hair fell across his face. "No, I didn't know him, neither. Never seen him before."

"And you're *sure* it wasn't another of my father's slaves?"

"Yes. Yes, sir. He surely wasn't!"

Charles stopped in front of him again and shook his head. He went to the table where the lantern sat, and studied the tools lined up neatly atop it. He picked up the crowbar. One of his father's personal favorites. "It's just ... I find it terribly disappointing that so many of my father's slaves were so eager to abandon him ... to betray him ... after he did so very much for them. The Territories are such a dangerous place." He tested the crowbar's weight and balance in his hand. Gave it a few half-hearted, experimental swings. "Do you think any of you would have survived for long out here without his protections? Without all the things he provided you?"

The man shook his head again, his eyes growing wide. "No, of course not, sir. That's why I came to you first! I didn't abandon the baron! I didn't betray him! Please, you must believe me!"

"Yes," Charles said. "Yes, you did the right thing, coming to me and telling me about these people ... these *murderers*. I will see justice done for my father's death." He set the crowbar down gently, and lifted a knife. He studied the fine edge of its blade in the lantern's light. "It's just, well, I *really* need to know more about this mystery man."

"I'll tell you," the man hanging from the ceiling blurted as Charles stepped close. "I've already told you! I swear, I told you everything! You don't need the knife. Don't need anything. Just ask! I'll tell you again! Ask whatever you want to know and I'll tell you!"

"Mmhmm." Charles leaned down to slice away one of the man's tattered trouser legs. He always liked to start with the tendons in the legs and work his way up from there.

"He—he was not from any of the other families," the slave babbled on. "I think he was one of those freedom fighters. He wanted to free the baron's slaves, certainly. He was working with the woman!"

"Mmmhmmm." Charles had already heard all of this.

The man tried to jerk his leg away from Charles' grip, but three days of no food and water had weakened him considerably. Not that he'd been in spectacular condition to begin with, anyway. Charles tightened his hold on the grimy ankle. "Now, now. Hold still, would you? Don't want this blade to slip…"

"Please," the man gasped, "please, you don't have to do that. I'll tell you anything you want to know!"

Charles rolled his eyes. Just as he'd suspected. This one had no spine. And would therefore be no fun at all. Oh well. He'd do what he could, anyway. The slave had come to him voluntarily, yes, and supposedly told him all there was to know about that horrible night, and yet Charles still felt there was something missing from the man's story.

People didn't just show up out of the dark of night to set a baron's house on fire and free his slaves … not even those blasted, bleeding-heart freedom fighters would have had the stones to make such a direct attack against his father.

There had to be some other motive at play here. Either this man who had helped that troublesome woman slave was a brilliant mastermind playing at some game Charles didn't yet understand, or he was just colossally stupid, led by a pretty face into something that would guarantee his death.

Charles snorted in amusement at the thought as he set the knife's sharp edge against pale skin, made all the more pale by so much time spent underground in those Old World ruins. *Certainly wouldn't be the first time a young man followed the pull of his loins into death.*

"He—he musta been demon-touched!" the slave shrieked.

Charles paused. The skin beneath his knife blade remained unbroken. He straightened and stepped backward. That part was new. "*What* did you say?"

The man trembled in terror. His wide eyes gleamed in the lamplight behind strands of greasy hair. He tried to wet his cracked lips, but had no spit for it. "He musta been demon-touched, sir."

Charles cocked his head to one side, intrigued. "And why is that?"

"B—because, sir … on account of his … on account of his m—metal leg, sir. His metal leg."

Charles bit back an impatient sigh. *Oh, of course.* The metal leg. The thing he personally found most interesting about this whole affair. After all, it wasn't every day you saw a man walking around with a metal leg.

It wasn't something you saw in general. Ever.

No one had ever used Old World tech in such a way before. No one had even *considered* using it in such a way before. But if this was really true ... if there was someone out there who had succeeded in fusing that kind of tech to their own body...

The thrill of the potential, the possibilities, took his breath away. Which was exactly why he needed to find this mystery man who had murdered his father.

To exact justice ... and to claim such a thing for himself.

"It..." The man hanging from the ceiling swallowed visibly. Or tried to swallow. His throat nearly spasmed. Poor man desperately needed a drink. Too bad he wouldn't be getting one. "It ... it ain't natural," he husked at last.

Charles resisted the urge to roll his eyes this time. If he had a nickel for every time he'd heard someone in these parts mutter those words, he wouldn't have needed the rights to his father's fortune to live a comfortable life. "Now, now, Mister...?"

"George," the man answered breathlessly. "George Gillham."

"Mr. Gillham. Of *course* it ain't natural. It's *metal*."

"Sir ... but ... please ... that tech ... it's the Devil's work. We shouldn't be messin' with it. And he ... he had it ... *attached* to himself. Sir..." The man's eyes were wild, his already extremist beliefs fueled by delirium, most likely. "What if he comes for me, next? Or—or *you*, sir?"

Charles gave a short huff of impatience. "George, you said my father captured this man for a time."

He nodded.

"And did he bleed?"

George blinked. "Well ... y—yes. Yes he did."

Charles stepped closer. "And my father had him branded?"

"Y—yes, sir. Several times."

"And did his flesh burn same as everyone else's?"

Again the rapid blinking. "It ... it seemed so."

Charles took another step closer. "Exactly. He is not a demon. He is not demon-touched. He is a *man*, George. A mortal man who dared to attack my family, who helped to murder my father. And I will see to it that he is properly repaid for the atrocities he committed here that night. And you are going to help me, George, aren't you?" He hooked his hand around the back of the man's neck, holding him steady as he brought the knife's edge to rest against the gaunt cheek. "You want to tell me every single little thing you can remember about this man so I can hunt him down and send him straight to Hell, don't you?"

George Gillham trembled in Charles' hold, taking short, shallow breaths. He dared not nod again, not with the knife pressed so firmly against his skin. His dark eyes didn't blink now. They were wide, wide open, begging Charles silently for mercy. "Yes," he breathed, in a voice hardly louder than the guttering of the oil lamp in the darkness. "Yes, I'll help you. I told you, sir. I told you everything I know!"

Charles granted the man a friendly smile. "Well. Let's just be sure about that, shall we?"

George's face went so pale as to look positively sickly in the dim lantern's light.

Charles released him and stepped back again, but allowed the blade to pull across the man's cheek as he did so, leaving behind a bright line of blood.

George gasped.

Charles ignored him and resumed his circling. "So. This metal leg. Which leg was it, again?" He remembered which leg it was. He remembered every detail this slave had recounted to him about that night, in fact. But he still wasn't entirely convinced the man was telling him the truth. That he hadn't been making up stories in attempts to gain himself a better position within the estate. Or, if all of this *was* true, that the slave wasn't holding back some vital piece of information out of fear ... or spite.

"The left one!"

Well, that was what he'd said the first time, too. But no harm in being absolutely certain. "I see. His left leg was made out of metal? The whole leg?"

"No, j—just from the knee down. Like I told you before."

"And you believe it was Old World tech?"

"L—looked like it, sir. Your father thought so."

Charles considered this, as he'd been considering it since the moment this man had first come to him. With something so rare as a metal leg, and *working* Old World tech, surely someone, some-where, had to know something about it ... had to have seen this man around... "You're absolutely *sure* this man didn't say where he'd gotten that metal leg?" he asked. "My father never got it out of him?" That seemed hard to believe. For as long as Charles had known his father, there had never been a man—or woman—he couldn't break.

Eventually.

But George shook his head vigorously again. "No, sir," he rasped. The blood from the cut on his cheek made red lines down his face and dripped off his chin to splatter the stones beneath his feet. "Your father ... he tried. But the man ... wouldn't say. Then—the woman—she came. She came and killed them all."

Charles stopped pacing at that, fury flaring in his chest and burning up his throat. Yes. The woman. Charlotte Harrison.

But she would pay. He'd see to that. He already had some of his most loyal people tracking her down. And she shouldn't be that hard to find. He knew her name and her face. He knew she'd come from the east. And he knew she'd had proper breeding. That had been quite clear as soon as she'd arrived.

That's what had endeared his father to her so completely.

But it would also be her undoing. Charles was sure of it. There were only so many proper ladies from the east named Charlotte Harri-son. He would find her, all right. It was only a matter of time.

As for this man, however ... the mystery man with the metal leg ... the man who had resisted his father's interrogations for just long enough ... well. Charles would be damn sure he was found, too. What-ever it took.

He turned toward George Gillham and lifted the knife once more. "Isn't that a shame? You see, Mr. Gillham, I really must find out where this man is now, and where he got that leg." The man's eyes got real wide again as Charles stepped close once more. "Let me just see if I can't help you recall any details you might have forgot..." He grabbed George's ankle again.

"No," the man whispered, kicking and struggling. "No, please, I swear! I swear, I t—told you all I know! P—please, sir!"

Charles ignored George's pleas and went to work, calm and sure, just as he'd seen his father do so many times before.

George's begging turned to shrieks and screaming.

More blood ran down to paint the cobblestones.

And still, relentless, Charles carved on.

It went on for hours, long into the night.

George Gillham desperately babbled his whole story again and again, and sometimes, Charles would ask more questions. To which he would receive the same answers as before, only less and less coherent, of course.

Eventually, George wasn't making any sense at all, lost in a haze of pain and blood loss.

Charles stopped his work then, and set the knife back on the table. He picked up the white linen towel and wiped the blood from his hands, even more disappointed now than he had been when he'd started this process.

Mr. Gillham had been telling the whole truth about the night of Baron Whittaker's murder from the start.

There'd been no lies, no omissions, after all.

Charles grunted and tossed the soiled towel to the table.

How very rare.

How very ... *disappointing*.

"Fire..." the slave muttered. He hung limp from the chains now, too weak to struggle, too weak to even lift his head. "Fire and thunder..." His greasy hair hung in a curtain around his bloodied face.

Fire and thunder, yes. The weapon that red-haired bitch had stolen from his father had often been described as thus by the household staff, on the rare occasion the baron would deign to fire it. The staff was terrified of it. The slaves were even more terrified of it.

And Charlotte Harrison had taken that from his family, too.

Charles ground his teeth and picked up the lantern. Just another thing to recover and reclaim for his family—for himself—once he found Ms. Harrison and ended her.

"Demons!" George gasped suddenly. "Demons ... comin'. They're ... d—demons! Comin' fer us ... comin'..."

Charles lifted the lantern to take one last look at the pathetic mess of a man who hung before him. "Yes, Mr. Gillham," he said softly. "Demons, indeed."

Then he turned and made his way out of the cellar, leaving the dying man in darkness. Not that he'd notice, most like. He'd finish bleeding out soon enough.

Charles would have to send someone down to clean up the mess later. But for now, he had some organizing to do. He climbed the stairs up toward the surface quickly, already forming a plan.

If the folk around here wanted to think a man with a metal leg was a demon, why, Charles Miller would let them. The masses were quick to turn on a person perceived as evil, after all, and their hatred and suspicion got ugly in a hurry if that person could be said to be doing the Devil's work.

Superstition could be a very useful tool, indeed. It was a tool his father had often used to keep his staff and slaves in line. It had proven quite efficient.

Charles might not have gotten as much information as he would have liked out of George, but he'd gotten enough. Enough to have some wanted posters drawn up. Enough to start spreading whispers about a demon-touched man with a limp and a metal leg, set loose upon the Earth to slake his bloodlust on the innocent. That should stir up the locals, all right.

And he'd make the reward for the capture of this demon high enough everyone in the Territories would be looking for him.

Didn't matter that Charles didn't have access to the family's fortune ... yet. Once he got his hands on that metal leg, and recovered his father's Old World rifle, he'd have enough. He'd exact his revenge on his father's murderers. And then he'd take care of his meddling half-brother, and finally take his rightful place as head of the Whittaker family.

It was all just a matter of time.

He came to the cellar's door and threw his shoulder up against it, swinging it open, then stepped out into the night. He turned to push the heavy slab of wood shut again, then set off across the yard, past the ruins of Whittaker manor toward his own, much more humble abode.

Even still, there was a spring in his step as he marched across the grass, and he inhaled the night's fresh air deeply. Anticipation swelled in his chest.

It's time to do some demon hunting...

THE END

FREE BOOK ALERT!

Before he was a rancher and a family man, Logan Delano was a 15-year-old orphan, running in an outlaw gang led by the ruthless Paul Johnson. In the wilds of the Independent Americas, under the merciless eye of Kill 'Em All Paul, having any kind of conscience just might land you dead.

Unfortunately for Logan, it seems he's still got part of his...

Was Van's pa really the one to shoot off Nan's finger? Only one way to find out! Download your free copy of LUCKY LOGAN right here:

https://jrfrontera.com/posse-up/

BASTARD OF BLESSING

THE LEGACY OF LUCKY LOGAN

J.R. FRONTERA

THE LEGACY OF LUCKY LOGAN
BOOK 2

WRITTEN BY
J.R. FRONTERA

ACES HIGH

The sonuvabitch was cheatin'.

I may have been shit at poker, but I'd learned enough about it in the last few weeks to know when a man was cheatin'. And the sonuvabitch sittin' across from me at the table right now was cheatin', sure enough.

So when he laid down his winnin' hand with a cocky grin and made to grab for the stash of money in the middle of us, I put my hand over the top of it first. His grin slid fast into a murderous scowl, and the other four men sittin' with us pushed their chairs back a mite, not wantin' to get caught in the middle of this. They glanced to each other, then toward the barkeep, but I paid 'em no mind.

This here was the Stag Saloon, under the ownership of none other than Nine-Fingered Nan, the oldest and most feared outlaw in the Territories, and around here, I was Nan's man.

No one had much wanted to pick a fight with me before, and they certainly didn't want to do so now. So I kept my glare on the man across from me, my hand atop his money, and he glared right back. His left hand was below the table, but I happened to know he only wore one gun, and it was perched on his opposite hip. If he tried to draw, I'd beat him easy.

"I don't much like cheaters," I said.

His face reddened.

The other four sittin' with us pretended to look surprised, but I had a hard time believin' they hadn't suspected somethin'. I was shit at poker, and the room was on the verge of spinnin' on account of all the whiskey I'd downed since sun-up, but even I had seen it.

Maybe I was shit at poker, but this fella was even more shit at cheatin'.

"Yer drunk, Delano," he said. "You should mind the words comin' outta yer mouth. Might getcha into trouble."

"Might," I agreed. "But I still don't much like cheaters. And yer a cheater. And a bad one, at that. If yer gonna do it, you should at least get good at it before you come in here tryin' to rob me and the rest." I tilted my head toward the others at our table. "So why don't you go ahead and get outta here. Before yer cheatin' gets *you* into trouble, yeah?"

His face got even redder, and his eyes darted from me to the other fellas sittin' round. They were watchin' him, tense on their chairs, ready fer him to try somethin'. Or fer me to try somethin'.

His eyes finally came back to me, glarin' somethin' fierce. "I ain't no cheat," he hissed. "You shut yer lyin' mouth 'fore I gotta teach you some manners!"

The conversations nearest to us faltered at his shoutin', people turnin' to see what the commotion was about.

I smiled at him. Truth be told, I was itchin' fer a fight. But then, it seemed I was always itchin' fer a fight these days. Three weeks I'd been holed up in Bravebank now, waitin' on word from Nan over what she wanted from me in exchange fer my sister—beyond that twenty-five thousand dollars I'd already given her.

Three weeks of waitin' with nothin' to do but drink, sleep, and gamble. And avoid goin' near Dr. Balogh's shop, which I'd discovered was set up over on the east edge of town.

All that time, and not a word yet from Nan.

Holt were convinced no word would come. He figured she'd said such things just to get me outta the way. Just to fuck with my head while she sold Ethelyn off, anyway.

That coulda been true. But if that's what she'd wanted, it woulda been easier for her to just gun me down three weeks ago when I'd showed up at her cliff-side hideout with the gutted body of one of her men in tow.

She coulda just ended it all then.

But she hadn't.

I had to believe she wanted more from me. I was bankin' on her greed. Bankin' on the fact that would be enough for her to keep her word, enough to save my sister.

But there was always that doubt in the back of my mind, made manifest in Holt's conviction of Nine-Fingered Nan's dishonesty, and his certainty she was only manipulatin' me.

That, and the fact no one in this damned town seemed keen to talk when I inquired as to the details of Nan's operations, was enough to drive a man to madness. So I only smiled at that cheatin' sonuvabitch across the table, and stood slowly from my chair. I rocked a bit as the room tilted, but reached out to steady myself on the table. Well, maybe I'd had more whiskey than I remembered.

"I'm gonna give you one more opportunity, Mister," I said slowly. "You can leave now on your own two feet, quiet-like, or we can make a nice scene and I'll throw you out."

He stood then, too, but fast, knockin' his chair over.

More people turned to look now, and I saw his right hand dip toward his sixgun.

I coulda drawn then and put him down, even drunk, but there was too much fierce anger roilin' around inside me, and it wanted out. So instead I grabbed the edge of the poker table and flipped it over toward him just as his gun was clearin' leather.

He had to jump back to keep from bein' hit by it, throwin' off his aim. Cards and money went everywhere.

The other four men sittin' there yelled and dove fer the money, likely tryin' to recover their share of it before anyone else could claim it.

Someone somewhere shouted out in alarm.

And then the cheatin' bastard recovered his balance and took aim again. I launched myself at him, tacklin' him just as his gun went off.

It was loud, right in my damn ear, but I still heard the barkeep swear and yell for us to take it outside.

Too late.

We crashed to the floor, and a commotion erupted all around us. Seemed the other patrons were quick to pick sides in this fight ... or quick to get the hell outta there.

The cheater's pistol jarred out of his hand as he hit the ground and went spinnin' off across the floor. And all his aces fell outta his sleeve. But I ignored all that, rollin' over the top of him to land a few good fists into his face before he could bring up his forearms to block my pummelin'.

He struck out with a fist of his own and caught me on the chin, ringin' my bell pretty good. I fell sideways and caught another fist to the jaw, then I was the one on the floor. He made a grab for my left gun but I twisted away outta his reach, and then the other four fellas we'd been playin' cards with found him and hauled him up to his feet.

From the beatin' they proceeded to lay on him, seemed like they'd sided with me.

Hands found me then, too, grabbin' my upper arms and draggin' me upright. I winced as their fingers dug into the mostly healed burns on my right bicep. The burns were mostly healed, sure, but the skin there was still kinda sore, and I didn't much like people diggin' into it.

Too bad fer me, they weren't friendly hands. Seemed the cheatin' bastard had some people on his side, too.

A fist landed in my gut and I doubled over, the breath goin' out of me. Then another cracked into my face and I staggered sideways before bein' caught again by more hands.

I ducked the next blow and sent my own fist into someone's middle, then reached out fer a half-empty bottle on the closest table and came up swingin' it, catchin' the nearest man on the side of the face.

The bottle shattered. The man howled and spun away as blood painted his cheek.

His friend stepped up to take his place, and another fist sailed at my face.

I dodged that one, too, but stumbled. Damn the whiskey. I'd drunk more than I thought. The room was spinnin' now, and I caught the back of a chair to keep from pitchin' over onto the floor again.

Someone was yellin' fer the sheriff, and the barkeep was cursin' all of us.

A blow landed in my right kidney and sent me down to my knees, but I let myself roll with the momentum even as I gasped in pain, and took the chair with me to use as cover.

The next fist punched the solid wood of the chair back instead of me, and then that man was the one cryin' out in pain as he shook out his hand. I kicked at him with my left boot, the one that had a metal foot in it, and made solid contact with his right shin.

It knocked his leg out from under him and he fell forward. His face smashed into the chair on the way down and I grimaced. *Ouch. That had to hurt.*

Sure enough, he wailed and rolled away with his hands over his nose.

It was probably broke.

Well, at least my metal leg was cooperatin' better these days. It almost even acted like a real leg now.

Three men loomed over me then, one of 'em a big, burly fella with a bushy beard. He didn't look friendly, neither.

I threw the chair at 'em, but the big guy knocked it away easy and it bounced off his meaty forearm to crash into another fella and knock him sprawlin'. Then the big guy reached down and grabbed the front of my shirt.

Well shit.

He pulled me up as easy as he'd knocked away the chair and grinned into my face. "Hey there, Delano," he drawled. "Remember me?"

I frowned at him as the fightin' went on all around us, the sounds of yellin' and shoutin' and shatterin' glass makin' a real ruckus. I had a feelin' I shoulda remembered him, and he had the kinda build that was hard to forget, but I couldn't recall crossin' paths with him before. "No," I admitted.

But then, I *had* been awful drunk lately...

Maybe the swill was startin' to affect my mind.

Maybe I needed to lay off a bit.

"Well then, let's see if we can't refresh your memory," he said.

He drove one of his big, meaty paws into my middle hard enough to send black spots burstin' across my vision, and then I was on the floor on hands and knees, retchin' and gaggin' fer air.

He didn't give me time to catch my breath.

He caught the back of my shirt and lifted me again, then threw me at the nearest table.

I crashed into it and knocked it over, and what food and drink had been left atop it clattered to the floor, addin' to the mess. I landed myself in a tangle of chairs, but I still couldn't breathe. I rolled onto my side, gaspin', tryin' to blink the black from my eyes.

A pair of boots stomped up next to me, but they didn't look like the big fella's boots.

Then a shotgun roared out over the noise of the fight, and I flinched at the closeness of it. I fumbled fer one of my own guns, but all the damn chair legs was in the way.

"All right, that's enough!" a familiar voice boomed into the little hole of quiet the shotgun blast had bought him. "All of you, that's enough! Party's over!"

I shoved some chairs outta my way and rolled over onto my back, a hand over my achin' stomach and feelin' like I might vomit. I looked up into the angry face of Sheriff Earl Jennings, the man who passed fer the law around these parts. So those boots had belonged to him.

He stood over me with his shotgun ready, three of his deputies fanned out behind him.

The sound of people runnin' quick out of the saloon marked the hasty retreat of several of the fight's worst offenders, and the sheriff motioned fer his deputies to go after some of 'em. I hoped that blasted cheater wouldn't get away.

I wasn't quite sure what to hope for that big, burly fella. On the one hand, I wouldn't mind him spendin' a few days in a cell while I recovered my wits. On the other hand, if the sheriff had scared him off now, maybe he wouldn't chance comin' around again if he managed to escape this time.

Least, I was pretty sure Sheriff Jennings had scared him off. He weren't comin' fer me anymore, anyway. And fer that, I was grateful. I smiled up at the lawman standin' over me and ignored his scowl. "Howdy, Sheriff. Mighty nice timin' you got."

His frown deepened beneath his gray mustache, and his dark eyes glittered. He looked awful angry this time. "Delano," he growled. "You start this again?"

"No, sir." I touched gingerly at my jaw, already feelin' a spot swellin' up. "I didn't start nothin'. Only called out a man fer cheatin' at cards, is all."

"He started it, all right," the barkeep called from across the room, and I pushed myself up sittin' to glare at him.

He was glarin' back at me, and his slicked-back hair and hooked, narrow nose sure made him look somethin' like a vulture, waitin' to pounce on a meal.

"He was *cheatin'*," I said again. "You wanna harbor cheats at your establishment? I thought you wanted to be a respectable place of business?"

He scoffed, throwin' up his hands as he looked around the saloon. "Respectable place of business? Delano, look at this place! You've trashed it!"

I gave the room a glance-over. Everyone else able-bodied had cleared out now, leavin' only me, the barkeep, and the sheriff. It *was* quite the mess. Tables overturned, chairs broken, glass and shattered bottles all over the floor, and some bodies, too. Looked like they was all breathin', at least, though they'd likely have some awful bad headaches in the morning.

It seemed things had escalated, sure enough. But I hadn't been the one to cause such a mess. I'd only called out one man fer cheatin'. "What was I supposed to do?" I asked. "Let him rob me and the others? That don't seem smart. All I did was call him out, give him a chance to leave quietly." I prodded at a new split in my lower lip. "He refused my offer. But ya can't say I didn't give him a chance."

"This is the third time I've had to come in here 'cause of brawlin' in just as many weeks," the sheriff said. "And every time it seems I find *you* in the center of it."

He was lookin' at me.

I lifted my hands and shook my head, then winced as that made the room start spinnin' again. "No, sir. I ain't at the center of nothin'. Seems there's just an excess of cheats and swindlers in this town. Maybe you should work a little harder on cleanin' them up, yeah? Then we wouldn't have so much of a problem."

One of his thick gray eyebrows lifted up into his hat brim. "All right," he said. "We're gonna go have a little talk."

He grabbed the collar of my shirt before I could protest the notion, and I found myself once again hauled to my feet. Sheriff Jennings was an older man, but he'd lived in the Territories all his life, and the sun and the heat and the outlaws he'd been chasin' most that time had whittled him down into a hard, unyieldin' man.

It made me wonder what Nine-Fingered Nan had on him, to bend such a man to her whim.

I had no such leverage, least not yet, and so he was none-too-gentle as he dragged me across the mess of the saloon floor to the back door and shoved me through it.

I tripped across the threshold, partially 'cause of too much whiskey, and partially 'cause of that damnable metal leg, and landed hard in the dirt on the other side. All the places I'd been pummeled in this most recent tussle started to make themselves known, and I groaned as I picked myself up onto hands and knees.

I was gonna be one sore mess soon enough.

But for now ... for now I had to decide what to do about Sheriff Jennings.

He rounded on me in the back alleyway behind the Stag, and I noticed he kept his shotgun in-hand, as if unsure whether or not he might need to use it.

Smart of him, 'cause I wore both my own sixguns, and I weren't sure whether or not I might need to use those, neither. I sat back on my heels and regarded him through a haze of alcohol and a deep, throbbin' pain that was startin' up in my temples.

"Listen here, you cocky little shit," he snarled. "You might be in Nan's fold now, but that don't mean you have free rein to go around causin' trouble whenever you damn well please!"

I scoffed. "Don't it? Thought you and her had an *understandin'*." I remembered clearly the sneering face of Taggert, the handlebar-mustached bastard who'd double-crossed Nan and me both the first time I'd tried to make a bargain in this town. He'd also been the first to clue me in to the fact Bravebank was ruled by Nine-Fingered Nan.

And now, he was dead.

"Yeah, we got an understandin', all right." Sheriff Jennings stepped up closer to me. "We got an *understandin'* that this town is gonna run business as usual. None of her crew goes around shootin' up folk or causin' trouble, and we let some of her questionable business practices go unnoticed, let her use the place as a base of operations for her industry expansion out further west."

"Industry expansion?" What the hell was he on about? The only industry Nine-Fingered Nan seemed interested in was robbin' and murderin' and the sellin' of innocents as slave labor, and that was an industry I was keen on bringin' to an end.

"Yeah," the sheriff said. "And you're givin' the Stag a bad reputation, Delano. Word's startin' to spread that it's a good place for bad men, and that's just what we *don't* want. Word like that scares away the honest folk and brings in people who might be lookin' to move in on Nan's territory. You startin' all these fights and wreckin' the saloon every week is *bad for business*, got it?"

I only scowled at him. Frankly, I didn't give a damn about the success of his business, or the Stag's business, or Nan's business. Far as I were concerned, they could all go to Hell. But I was stuck here, bidin' my time, until Nan sent word on what she wanted next from me.

And if most of the town was loyal to Nan, it wouldn't do much good to make enemies out of 'em all. Not yet.

Maybe this Sheriff Jennings was the one I shoulda been tryin' to talk to about Nan's operations these last few weeks. Seemed he knew an awful lot about 'em. I wondered how loyal he really was to their *understandin'*, given he was a lawman and all.

He was at least loyal enough to be upset over my recent public disturbances, I supposed. I wondered if he'd tell me anythin', either, in that case.

"If there's one thing Nan hates most," he said now, "it's people gettin' in the way of her business. You best watch yourself, Delano. She ain't got no qualms about cuttin' loose dead weight. You best make yourself of more use and less trouble, else..." He broke open his shotgun and made a show of pullin' out the spent cartridge, puttin' in a new one, and snappin' it closed again. "Else she's gonna cut you loose, and then there won't be nothin' between you and the law. Nothin' between you and me. Understand?"

I grumbled and scrubbed at my eyes. It all made sense, sure. Made sense I'd backed myself into a nice, tight corner, and I didn't much like that feelin'. "Yeah," I growled. "Sure."

"Glad we have an understandin' now too, then," Sheriff Jennings said. "Cause I'm gonna need you to come back to the jailhouse with me. Take a little time to cool off and sober up."

I stared up at him, pretty sure I'd heard him wrong. "You wanna lock me up?"

"That's right."

He was starin' down at me steadily, shotgun in hand. Close-range. Real close. If he wanted to take me in, there weren't much I could do about it. But even still, that restless anger flared again inside, heatin' up my blood. Why should he go after *me*? I weren't the one cheatin', or tryin' to kill a man over cards. And I'd had nothin' to do with what anyone else did in that saloon. "Like hell—"

He didn't give me time to finish.

He whipped that shotgun around and cracked its butt into my skull, and I went out cold.

II

MORNIN', SUNSHINE

Consciousness came back slow, and the pain came back quick.

I groaned and rolled over, feelin' a thin mattress underneath me. My head was splittin', my jaw achin', and bruises all over my body throbbin'. My middle was especially sore, and I put a hand over it as I forced my eyes open.

The place I were in was dim, lit only by a single lantern sittin' across the way on the corner of a desk. There was one window, high up and small and barred, but not much sunlight came through it.

Barred?

Shit.

I brought my focus back to my more immediate surroundin's and found a whole wall of bars right there not three feet from my face.

The jailhouse. That damned sheriff had got me here, all right. I muttered foul words and shoved myself up sittin' on the cot, then grabbed for the bucket meant as my chamber pot as nausea rolled up my throat.

I emptied out what was left in my stomach and sat there fer a minute gaggin', then grimaced and spit, and shoved the bucket away into the far, far corner of the cell. Then I lurched back to the cot and collapsed down atop it, pushin' myself back into the corner of the wall to keep me upright.

Fer Chrissakes, I felt like I'd been ran over by a whole herd of cattle.

The door to the jailhouse opened then, spillin' in a bright beam of light, and I winced and threw up an arm to shield my eyes.

"Well," came the sheriff's deep, resonant voice. I imagined it probably made the ladies around here swoon. "Look who's finally awake. Mornin', Sunshine."

The door shut and mercifully closed off the light, and I squinted toward his voice.

He clomped across the room to his desk, spurs janglin'. He had a folded newspaper under one arm, and a steamin' cup of joe in the other hand. He eased himself down into his chair and sipped at his coffee, and I realized that's what I very much needed right now: a good, strong cup of joe.

He smiled over at me and put his boots up on the corner of his desk. "Thought maybe you'd sleep all day."

I growled at him, fingers brushing my left temple where his shotgun butt had come into contact with my skull. The spot was tender to the touch. A fine match fer the place on my right temple I'd had to have stitched not too long ago after my run-in with Baron Whittaker. Still had a scar there from that one, still pink. "Didn't have to hit me so hard," I muttered.

The sheriff shrugged. "Couldn't take any chances. I gave you an opportunity to come quiet. You refused my offer. But you can't say I didn't give you the chance."

I peered through the bars at him, wonderin' if he was usin' my own words against me on purpose. Who was bein' a cocky little shit now? I sighed and rolled my eyes, leanin' my head back against the brick wall behind me. "Where's the rest of 'em?" I gestured weakly to the other two cells in the place, which I'd noticed were empty.

"Gone already," the sheriff said. "Had a few in here overnight for all that ruckus you caused at the Stag, but I think they got the message. Let 'em free this mornin'."

"Yeah? You get that cheatin' bastard?"

"He got ran outta town. But after that beatin' he got, I don't think he'll be back."

I grunted. Not exactly what I'd wanted, but good enough, I supposed. "What about the big guy with the beard?"

The sheriff's brows lifted at that one. "Thomas Withrow?"

"Don't know his name. But he's a big, ugly fella with a beard that could use a trim."

Sheriff Jennings shook his head and chuckled. "Sounds like Tommy. You get sideways with him, too?"

"I dunno. Maybe. Seems so. I don't rightly remember."

The sheriff let out a low whistle and set down his cup. "Good luck with that one, Delano. Tommy's a mountain man, tough as they come."

"Mountain man?" That didn't make no sense. "What the hell's he doin' down here, then?"

"Came to visit his sister awhile back. She lives close by. Married to a railroad man, though last I heard he'd taken pretty sick. Guess that's why Tommy showed up. Maybe to help her out for a spell."

Huh. Somethin' about all that seemed kinda familiar, but I couldn't quite place it.

"But no," the sheriff went on. "Tommy weren't in here. He didn't do nothin' wrong, far as I could tell."

My hand still rested on my stomach, and I could almost feel the shape of that man's fist in the bruise there. It ached every time I breathed. "I think he wanted to kill me," I said. "Or else come real close to it."

"Well. Maybe if you'd stop stirrin' up trouble, you'd stop makin' yourself so many enemies."

"Real helpful, Sheriff," I drawled. "Thanks."

"Just statin' facts, Delano."

"And what about me? You gonna let me free now, too?"

He sighed and pulled his boots off his desk, leanin' forward in his chair. He tossed the newspaper to his desktop. "I dunno. You gonna stop causin' trouble 'round here?"

"I said so, didn't I?"

"Yeah, well, sayin' and doin' are two different things, ain't they?"

"This is a strange town you run, Sheriff. Gotta say I ain't never been jailed fer callin' out a cheater before."

"That ain't why you're here and you know it." His voice turned sharp. "You're scarin' the townsfolk and interruptin' business. I had to bring you in here to give 'em a little reassurance. Let 'em know there's still law and order in this town."

I laughed despite myself. "Law and order? That's rich, comin' from a man under Nan's thumb."

His face went all stormy at that, and he pushed his chair back and stood, leanin' over the desk to glare at me. "And just where do you think you're at, Delano? Right there with me, ain't you? Only I heard you volunteered for the job, which makes you one of the worst kinda people. Either that or stupid. Or maybe both."

I glared at him through my bars, heat risin' up under my shirt collar and makin' my head hurt even worse. *Volunteerin'* was a funny way of puttin' it. But I didn't feel like explainin' myself to him. So all I said was, "I have my reasons."

"Yeah? Bet you do. Same as me. So why don't you cut the shit? Least I know my place ... least I *have* a place outside of Nan's arrangements. What do you got outside of that, Delano? Huh? An appointment with a noose somewhere? How many towns in the Territories got bulletins up with your face on 'em, I wonder?"

I managed to hold his glare, but I had nothin' to say about that.

It was true enough. Outside of tryin' to save Ethelyn, I didn't have much else. I had Holt, if that could be counted fer anythin', considerin' we hated each other most the time. And I had our little camp in Grave Gulch, the closest thing to a home anymore. And my two guns, and a mule that'd been stolen once, but was now bought and paid fer.

None of that mattered much. And it didn't matter at all if I couldn't get Ethelyn back.

"Yeah, you can go," Sheriff Jennings said abruptly. He fished a heavy ring of keys off his belt and sorted through 'em till he found the one he wanted. "For now. But I'm tellin' you ... watch yourself. No more brawl-in', no shootin' no one—"

"What if they try to shoot me first?"

He paused mid-step on the way over to my cell and pursed his lips under his neatly groomed mustache. "Then you'd better hope you got witnesses. Otherwise I swear to God, Delano, I'm gonna try you for murder."

"Awful biased operation you got goin' on here," I grumbled as he turned the key in the cell door's lock.

"You ain't given me any reason to trust you," he snapped back. He pulled the barred door open with a horrific screechin' of hinges, and I winced. Then he turned on his heel and marched back to his desk, where he retrieved my gun belts from a hook on the wall behind it.

I grabbed up my hat from the floor and shoved it back on my head, then made my way slowly off the cot and stood unsteadily, rocked a minute, then stabilized. I was stiff and sore, all right, and my head pounded somethin' terrible. I limped toward the sheriff as he held my belts out toward me.

"Your rig," he said. "Just remember what I said."

"Yeah, yeah. I'll remember." I took my belts from him and buckled 'em both back around my hips, then checked both guns to be sure everything was still in place. They looked fine, and, satisfied, I slipped 'em both back into their holsters. "One more thing, Sheriff."

His eyes narrowed, his hand goin' straight to his gun grip. "What's that?"

I lifted my own hands, not wantin' him to get the wrong idea. "Just wonderin' what you can tell me about Nan's operations, is all," I said. "You mentioned she was lookin' to expand her industry out further west. What industry is that, exactly?"

He raised his eyebrows. "She didn't tell you?"

"No."

"Well then," he gave me a smile, "that means she don't want you to know. And that means *I* sure as fuck ain't gonna tell you."

I sighed. But I was too tired and too sore at the moment to push the subject, or to do anythin' about his reluctance to share, so I only rolled my eyes and turned away from him, then hobbled toward the door, grimacin' with every step. Maybe we could resume this conversation later. When I felt more myself. "Can't wait to leave this godforsaken town," I muttered.

"Can't wait till you're gone," he said from behind me. Then he stalked past me and yanked open the door to the outside, blindin' me with that sunlight again. "Now get the fuck out of my jailhouse."

He didn't have to tell me twice.

A jailhouse was the last place I wanted to be, though the irony of my situation weren't lost on me, neither. Any other day, before I'd made a deal with Nine-Fingered Nan, I likely wouldn't have had the chance to be *walkin'* out of a jailhouse, not unless I was walkin' out to make my way to the gallows. Most certainly I wouldn't be walkin' out free. Least, not if the sheriff took any time to investigate my background properly.

Course, I never woulda stayed in one town a whole three weeks, neither. And likely wouldn't have downed so much whiskey, or been itchin' so much fer a fight, or played enough cards to be able to know when a fella was cheatin'.

I sighed again as I made my way slow and careful out of that brick buildin' and into the street. Sheriff Jennings slammed the door behind me and I cringed again. Goddamn. He have to do everything so goddamn loud?

I squinted in the daylight despite my hat, and swept a look down the street both ways. It was late mornin', thereabouts, and most folk were on about their daily business now. The streets were quiet, mostly empty.

I had nothin' to do still, seein' as Nan hadn't seen fit yet to retrieve me.

The anger flared up again, hard and bitter, but I tried to shove it back down, somewhere deep where it'd stay buried and stop gettin' me into trouble. Just like the sheriff had said.

What I needed was coffee. Coffee and food. Maybe that'd improve my mood. But I figured I'd better stay away from the Stag fer awhile. Had a feelin' that barkeep was mighty tired of me by now.

No matter. There were plenty of other saloons in Bravebank. I turned in the dusty street toward another of 'em, this one called, amusingly, First Chance, and ambled that way, instead. I was just passin' the tailor's place when a shadow moved in the alleyway between the buildings and came right at me.

AN ESPECIALLY BAD DAY

I swung around toward the shadow with a yell and went fer my gun, only to stop mid-draw as I saw it were Holt.

I swore at him somethin' awful and shook my head, then leaned against the nearest hitchin' post and waited fer my heart to slow. "*God damn*, Holt. Yer fixin' to get yerself killed, sneakin' around like that."

The old man scoffed. "I weren't sneakin'. You weren't payin' attention."

"Why you always gotta be lurkin' around in the shadows, anyway?"

Holt looked both ways down the street, same as I had just a few minutes ago. "Cuz I don't like towns. They ain't nothin' but trouble waitin' to happen."

Well, that certainly seemed true enough. Least fer people like us. Funny how when I was a boy, livin' with Mama and Pa, towns hadn't seemed to be much trouble at all. "Seems all right to me," I lied. I pushed off the hitchin' rail and resumed my walk toward First Chance, and Holt joined me, though his eyes kept dartin' around all fidgety like.

"Yeah, sure," he said. "That why you spent the night in the jailhouse?"

Damnable nosy old man. I'd been hopin' that had escaped his notice. "Yeah," I said. "Wanted a sample of the sheriff's hospitality. That Sheriff Jennings, he's a real friendly gent."

Holt snorted. "Sure he is. You just be careful, Van. I heard what trouble you've been causin'. Yer the talk of the town, pretty much, and it ain't nothin' good. I know Nan's got some kinda agreement with that lawdog, but I don't like the look of him."

"You don't like the look of no one. Not even me."

"Yeah, and that's why I ain't the one bein' locked up."

"It weren't nothin'," I insisted. "Just a misunderstandin'. Sheriff and I got it all worked out now."

"Uh huh."

We walked in silence fer awhile, and I turned my attention to nursin' my multiple bruises. A covered wagon rattled by at a trot, and the driver and his missus gave the both of us condescendin' looks as they passed.

We ignored 'em. Weren't nothin' we weren't used to.

"By the way," Holt said at last, reachin' to the inside pocket of his duster. "You got a telegram from that girl. Charlotte."

My stomach lurched at the sound of her name, and my heart picked up pace again.

Holt pulled out a folded piece of paper and held it toward me. "Was at the Grave Gulch post office when I went back there last week. Post master said it'd been waitin' there awhile."

I took it from him and swallowed hard. I gave a nod, suddenly findin' no words, and shoved it into my back pants pocket.

Holt looked at me funny. "Ain't you gonna read it?"

I shook my head, then cleared my throat and managed to speak. "Naw. Later." I already knew what it would say, anyway. If she'd sent me somethin' in the first place, it meant she'd made it home safe, and that was all that really mattered.

I didn't want to read the rest of it. She'd be askin' about Ethelyn, most like. Wantin' to know if my sister was home safe, too. Wantin' to know why I hadn't written her myself yet to tell her so.

But of course I hadn't written her myself yet.

I didn't have nothin' to write about. I still didn't have my sister. And I didn't need any more reminders of that.

"Suit yerself," Holt muttered.

There was another long minute of silence between us, and truth be told, I was happy fer the quiet.

Too bad it didn't last.

"How long you gonna stay here, Van?" Holt asked abruptly.

I sighed. We'd already had this conversation. More than once. "I told you. I'm stayin' here till Nan says what else she wants fer my sister."

The muscles in Holt's jaw flexed, visible even under his scraggly gray beard. "Fine. Let me say it a different way. How long you gonna stay here 'fore you give up on hearin' from Nan?"

I stopped walkin' and faced him. "If you need to move on, you just go ahead and move on. I ain't stoppin' you."

"Like hell." He tossed back the sides of his duster coat and stuck his hands on his hips. "You still owe me a job."

"I ain't forgot that."

"Good, cuz I got somethin' lined up." He dropped his voice. "Another bank."

I shook my head and wet my dry lips, feelin' at the place where a fist had bloodied 'em. It was all dried and scabbed over now. "Not now, Holt."

"See, kid, that's the problem. You wanna wait here fer who knows how long, maybe forever, and I ain't got that time to just sit around. You still owe me a job, and that job needs doin'!"

"After I get Ethelyn, I told you."

"And what if you never get her?"

I said nothin' fer a long minute, just starin' at him as we stood in the oppressive heat of that dusty street. *What if I never get her?* I couldn't think about that, so I hadn't. And I wouldn't. "After I have her, I'll do the job. I swear."

Holt threw up his hands, pacin' away from me angrily. "Goddamnit, Van. Yer swearin' don't mean shit to me. I don't got time fer this nonsense!"

"Then leave," I shot back. "But I ain't goin' nowhere, Holt, not till

I hear from Nan. You do what you gotta do, and I'll do the same." I turned away from him and strode off toward the saloon, but he weren't gonna let me go so easy.

He caught up to me and grabbed at my shoulder, yankin' me around.

He caught me on a bad day. Hell, I hadn't had a good day in a long, long while. But this day was an especially bad day.

I weren't in no mood for his shit, and that anger I'd tried to bury deep turned out to not be buried so deep, after all. It came roarin' back up at his man-handlin', and I lashed out with a fist and got him good in the left eye.

He stumbled backward and I saw the surprise go quick across his face. Holt and I had had our share of spats in our years travelin' together, sure, but I'd never started nothin' before. Not like this.

He straightened, and the surprise got replaced by fury.

This time I hadn't been so much itchin' fer a fight, but it seemed I'd be gettin' one, anyway. 'Less I could make amends real quick. "Holt—"

He came at me like a rabid dog, and I cursed the impulse that had made me want to deck him in the face. I weren't in no condition for another fight so soon after the last one, least of all with a mean old bastard like Holt. But I weren't gonna let him beat on me without defendin' myself, neither, so I dodged his rain of blows as best I could and landed a few of my own, too.

If only I hadn't already felt like I'd been trampled by a herd of cattle, or that my skull was splittin' open. I staggered as I blocked one of his fists with my left forearm, exhausted and just wantin' him to stop already, but in doin' so I left my already much-bruised middle wide open, and he took advantage of it.

He didn't hit me that hard, in truth, but he got the spot big ol' Tommy Withrow had hit the afternoon before and it was enough to draw a yell outta me and send me down to my knees, folded up with an arm over my belly.

Holt grabbed the back of my neck soon as I was down and dunked my head straight into the nearest water trough.

It weren't cold, and it weren't pleasant, and I weren't sure he didn't intend to drown me right then and there. We'd nearly shot each other a time or two before ... him drownin' me wouldn't be much different.

I braced my hands against the edge of it and tried to leverage myself upward, but he had a hold of me good and was leanin' his weight on me, and I couldn't budge him from that angle. I struggled, kicked, flailed, but I couldn't find nothin' of him to grab onto. My hands slapped against the sleeves of his duster and I took fistfuls of 'em and tugged, tryin' to loosen his grip.

Nothin'.

I kicked out with my metal foot, hopin' to find one of his legs, but he weren't stupid. He was standin' close, too close fer me to get any good force behind my struggles.

My lungs burned, everything in me screamin' for me to open my mouth and take in a big ol' gulp of air. But there weren't no air to be had. It was all I could do to fight that urge ... and the burnin' in my chest got worse, till I realized it was gonna happen whether I wanted it or not.

My mouth opened, lettin' out bubbles, and my chest spasmed as I sucked inward, bracin' myself to drown.

But instead I got air.

Mostly air. Some water.

I choked and coughed, gulpin' at the hot, dusty air like it were the sweetest thing I ever tasted. And right then, it was.

Holt threw me sideways and I fell into the muddied dirt and just laid there, relishin' the act of breathin'. So he still couldn't bring himself to kill me. Well, that was somethin'. I supposed I still didn't want to kill him, neither.

Maybe.

"Fine," he spat down at me. "That's it. I'm done. You want me to leave? I'm leavin'. Good luck, kid. Yer gonna need it."

I watched his boots turn and walk off, but I didn't have enough air yet to call out after him. Not that I had anythin' to say, anyway. I had no right to make him wait here with me, or to ask him to accompany me on any errand Nan might eventually have fer me. I was the one who'd made the deal, and the deal'd had nothin' to do with him.

If he couldn't have patience enough to wait till my deal was done ...

well ... like I'd said ... I wasn't stoppin' him. He had to do what was right by him. Same as me.

Even still, there was a strange sorta melancholy in my burnin' chest as I watched him stalk off down the street and turn the corner out of sight. Sure, he mighta just almost killed me, but in the end, he hadn't. And we'd been runnin' together fer a long time now. He'd been the one to keep me from starvin' after Mama and Pa were killed.

I wondered if he'd really be gone fer good this time.

Swearin' and scowlin' and breathin' hard, I shoved myself up sittin' and sat back against the side of the trough I'd almost drowned in. I fished my hat out of it and tried to shake the water off best I could. "Ain't ... ain't no such thing as luck," I husked.

I stuck the drippin' hat back on my head, and that's when I noticed several folk in the street, all starin' at me. I wondered if they'd been drawn outside by the noise of the fightin', or maybe by all my splashin' around.

I wondered if they was the real reason Holt had spared me.

Well. Guess I'd never know, now.

I glared at 'em all. "Whatcha lookin' at?" I snapped. "Go on back to yer business. Show's over."

They milled about, some havin' the grace to at least look sheepish. Others of 'em didn't seem to have no shame.

I ignored 'em. I didn't have the strength left to yell anymore. Didn't even have the strength left to get up from where I sat. So I just pulled my damp hat down over my face to block out the light, block out the folks starin' at me, and let my head rest back against the lip of the trough.

I closed my eyes and let myself relax, not carin' what happened next.

Surely this day couldn't get no worse.

Someone kicked at my boot and I startled awake, pullin' my hat down off my face and then squintin' in the sun. Seemed I'd been out awhile. Looked like afternoon now, and the heat of high summer was swelterin'. No one sober or sane was out and about at this hour, but there I was, still sittin' next to that trough.

My head still throbbin' and my bruises still achin'.

Someone kicked at my boot again, and I forced myself to focus. There were three silhouettes standin' in front of me. The one front and center had a familiar shape. Tall and thin, with a wide-brimmed hat and two pearl-gripped pistols, one on each hip.

She had her thumbs hooked into her belt, and she was starin' down at me with those hard, pale eyes. "Didn't realize I'd hired the town drunk," she said flatly.

Fuck.

Nine-Fingered Nan.

The outlaw boss herself. Come all the way to Bravebank. And here I was passed out in the middle of the street.

"I ain't drunk," I rasped. Least, not anymore. I could use a drink right then, though. Preferably of somethin' like coffee. I reached out to grab the edge of the trough and used it to pull myself up sittin' straight, then struggled to my feet.

And anyway, *hired* wasn't what she'd done to me. Forced, extorted, ransomed ... one of those descriptors woulda been far more accurate.

"Sheriff Jennings tells me you've been causin' him a lot of trouble," she said.

I glanced down the way toward the jailhouse, a squat brick buildin', and scowled. There was two ways to approach this situation, but there weren't no way I was apologizin' to Nan fer anythin'. So instead I brought my gaze back from the jailhouse and put it right on her, lookin' her square in the face.

Ignorin' the two lieutenants flankin' her.

"I was bored," I said.

To my surprise, a corner of her mouth quirked upward at that statement, almost smilin'. "That so?"

"Yeah."

"Good."

I hadn't expected her to say that, neither, and I didn't know what to say in reply. Besides maybe somethin' like, *Fuck off, ya old cunt*, but I didn't think that'd probably get me very far in gettin' back my sister, so I kept my mouth shut.

"Well," she said then, "I've had a nice, good think on what I want from ya, Mr. Delano. You ready to talk business, or ya wanna continue yer nap there in the mud?"

I swallowed back the swell of anger at her derisive tone and shook my head, then brushed futilely at the dirt crusted to my clothes. "Naw, I'm ready. Let's talk."

"Fine. This way, then." She nodded at her lieutenants, then turned and headed straight fer the Stag.

Shit. But this time I had no choice in the matter, so I went after her, limpin' and wincin'.

Her two lieutenants fell into step behind me. I didn't like 'em there. The hair on the back of my neck prickled, but there weren't nothin' I could do about them, neither.

So I walked quiet in the shadow of Nine-Fingered Nan, and tried not to dwell on the fact I felt an awful lot like a steer bein' driven off to slaughter.

IV

IF THE MATH ADDS UP

She marched into the Stag Saloon like she owned the place.

I suppose that's 'cause she *did* own the place.

The barkeep snapped to proper attention as he realized it was *her* walkin' in, only sparin' me a quick, annoyed glance. He'd made a lot of progress in cleanin' up the place since yesterday afternoon. Except fer a few new stains on the floor, and a missin' table or two, the place looked pretty much same as it usually did.

Weren't many people in there, though, for this time a day.

Nan seemed to notice the sparse patronage, a flicker of somethin' passin' over her face before it went neutral again. But I saw it. Saw it, and noted it.

"Get out," she snapped, wavin' at the barkeep, then sweepin' her glare across the rest of the place. "All of you. Out."

No one said a word in protest. No one argued. The barkeep marched straight out the back door, and the few other fellas in there just stood and filed past us toward the front door, givin' Nan a wide berth, and not one of 'em makin' eye contact.

That didn't make me feel no better.

Nan went to a table in the middle of the room and pulled out a chair, then sat down, facin' the front door.

One of her men went to that door, too, and posted himself just inside it. I guessed to be sure no one else wandered in durin' our discussion.

The other of her men went back behind the bar and poured a few drinks.

Of whiskey.

Nine-Fingered Nan nodded at the chair across the table from her and pushed it out with one boot. "Sit," she commanded.

I did so, slow and stiff. I didn't like my back to the door, or to her fella over there. But then, I didn't like a whole lot about this situation. Didn't like the situation as a whole, altogether.

Her second man came to our table and put the drinks down in front of us. One fer Nan. One fer me. One fer himself. He downed his and set the empty glass on the table, then moved around to stand behind Nan's right shoulder.

As if she needed him lookin' out fer her.

Even at my best, I weren't sure I could beat her.

And I most certainly weren't at my best today.

Nan reached out with her left hand, the one with all the fingers, and picked up her glass. "Well, Mr. Delano. You sure yer up fer this? Yer lookin' a little worse fer wear."

I surely felt worse than even that. But I'd waited three long weeks fer this. I weren't gonna wait any longer, not if I'd been at Death's door, itself. "I'm up fer it." My voice was all hoarse, and I cleared my throat. Reached fer the whiskey and stared down into it.

If only it were anythin' but whiskey.

"Good to hear." She took a long, deep drink from her glass, savored it, and set the glass back to the table. "In that case..." Her left hand went up again, the fingers gesturin'.

The man behind her reached into the satchel he had slung over one shoulder and pulled out some documents. He put them into her waitin' hand.

She put them on the table between us, pullin' off the top paper to unfold it—with both hands this time, and I couldn't help lookin' at her stump of a finger.

Least it weren't a stump of a leg, like she'd given me.

'Course, missin' a leg didn't much matter to my shootin' abilities. Losin' the trigger finger of yer dominant hand, though, weren't no small thing. But she'd managed. More than managed.

She'd built a whole terrible empire out here in the Territories. An empire that seemed to be stretchin' awful far to the east, if Charlotte were right about Nan's crew bein' the ones who'd grabbed her out of the Republic.

And an empire Nan seemed awful keen on stretchin' out further west, too, based on what Sheriff Jennings had told me. And I didn't like the thought of either of those things bein' true.

She smoothed the paper out, and I saw it was a map. A couple routes had been marked along it to the north of us, comin' down from Utah and goin' toward Blessing.

That was a town I surely had no wish to return to any time soon.

"What I need from you, Mr. Delano," Nan said, tracin' the marked routes with the gnarled middle finger of her right hand, "is to intercept a stagecoach that'll be along one of these roads here, goin' south. I'll need you to get to it, and stop it, before it comes anywhere near its final destination."

"All right. Where's it headin', then?"

"Blessing."

My breath hissed out between my teeth before I could catch it.

Nan looked up at me, then sat back in her chair. "There a problem, Mr. Delano?"

"No." I shifted on my own chair. "No problem. Just don't much like that town, is all."

"That's good, 'cause if that stagecoach gets to Blessing, then ya didn't do the job, did ya? And then we're gonna have a problem."

"We won't have a problem," I said. "I'll stop it before it gets there." I wasn't gonna step foot in Blessing again if I could help it, that's fer sure.

"See that you do. Yer sister will be countin' on ya."

A shot of somethin' went through me at the mention of Ethelyn. A shot of somethin' like fear. Anticipation. Hope. All the things I couldn't afford to feel. I straightened on my chair and fought to keep my voice even. I didn't want her to see any of those feelin's. Didn't want her to hear the desperation clawin' around in my belly. "So I stop a stagecoach. Make sure it don't reach Blessing. That all?" It almost seemed too easy.

"Not quite."

Of course not. I shouldn't have asked.

"Stop the stagecoach. Kill everyone aboard it, and be sure they're dead." She pulled another piece of paper from her pile of documents and slid it over across the table toward me. "It'll be carrying a lockbox that'll look something like this. Fetch that from the coach—might be on one of the people ridin' in it, or maybe in the coach's treasure box— and bring it back here to me."

I picked up the piece of paper. It was a pencil sketch of the item in question ... but it only looked like somethin' you might see in any someone's home who had a bit of money, protectin' their valuables. I raised my brows. "A lockbox in a lockbox?"

"That's right."

"Must be some mighty fine valuables in there."

"You could say that."

"But it looks like any other lockbox," I said. "How will I know if it's the one you want?"

"Not like any other lockbox," she said, sittin' forward in her chair and givin' me a look of disapproval that woulda rivaled Holt's. "Look-it." Her middle finger jabbed the paper in my hand. "Lookit the lock."

I squinted at the sketch. Sure enough, it weren't *quite* like any other lockbox, after all. This one didn't need a key to open it. Instead, there was a row of small dials across the top, each with their own set of numbers, kinda like one of those combination safes. "Ah."

She plucked up a third paper and pushed it at me. "And this is the coach yer lookin' fer. Seems like a hired coach, same as all the rest, but it ain't. It belongs to Baron Haas and his family."

My stomach turned at the mention of another of those metal barons.

"It ain't much, but if you look close, you can see the difference.

There's no company name across the top. The rear boot is smaller'n most. And it won't be loaded up with passengers. You find this coach, and it'll have that lockbox I want in it somewhere."

I put down the sketch of the lockbox and considered the picture of the coach. This was a real picture, an actual photograph. It showed a nice-lookin' stagecoach pulled by four tall, glossy horses. Well, that in and of itself woulda stood out. Most public coaches had seen their share of miles. They were roughed up a bit, the paint chipped and faded, and the horses more of the workin' variety.

This one had a sharp-dressed gentleman and his similarly sharp-dressed lady standin' in front of it. Baron Haas and Lady Haas, I reckoned. I swallowed hard. "Will the baron be aboard?"

Nan shook her head. "Nah. He wouldn't risk such a thing. Just be some of those he employs on-board. The driver and a few armed guards."

I looked up across the table at her. This was gettin' more and more complicated by the minute. Don't know why I was surprised. "How many armed guards, exactly?"

She shrugged. "Fer anythin' transported by the barons? Three to five marshals is pretty standard fare fer their types."

I muttered a curse and tossed the photograph back to the table. "So all I gotta do is stop the stagecoach, kill the armed, angry men accompanyin' it, the driver, and whoever else is aboard, grab that lockbox, and bring it all the way back here to you. That sound about right?"

Nan smiled, then picked up her whiskey and took another long pull. "Precisely, Mr. Delano. Must be those smarts you got from yer mama at work."

I glared at her fer a long minute, but before I could think of a proper retort that wouldn't also get me shot, she leaned forward again and spoke.

"Just one other thing."

"What now?"

"See that you don't open that lockbox."

"Shouldn't be a problem, seein' as I don't know the code to open it."

"Some might try and open it usin' other means," Nan offered.

"Well, *I* won't."

Her pale eyes stared at me, flat and even. "Good. If I see that lockbox has been tampered with, or opened, the deal is off."

I had no intention of tryin' to open that lockbox. But my mouth went all dry at the finality in her tone, anyway. "I ain't gonna try the lockbox," I growled. "You'll get it, safe and sound. And then I want my sister. In the same condition, safe and sound, understand?"

She gave me that bland, disturbin' smile again. "Of course."

I got the feelin' she mostly didn't expect me to live through this escapade.

Well, that was fine. She hadn't expected me to live through the last one, neither. That time she'd left me stranded in the desert with no horse and a bullet in my leg. Yet here I was. "Good," I croaked, then cleared my throat again. Why did my insides feel so jumpy?

I'd run down stagecoaches before.

I'd murdered more folk than I liked to remember.

Hell, I'd even dealt with those bastard barons before ... and this one weren't even gonna be aboard his own coach.

None of this should be much trouble, really. Especially once I got my hands on one of those long rifles Holt liked so much. All I had to do was this one more job, and I'd have Ethelyn back. A small price to pay.

I pulled the map toward me and looked it over again. "When exactly are you expectin' this coach to be comin' south?"

"Accordin' to my source," said Nan, "it should be passin' through Sonoita in about six days or so. Should give you plenty of time to head up north and get situated afore it comes by."

"Sonoita?" I squinted down at the map, searchin' fer such a town. "Never heard of it."

Nan thumped a finger down on a particular spot, then tapped at it forcefully. "Right here, Delano. You *can* read, can't ya?"

"Yeah," I grumbled. Course I could read, with Mama havin' been a schoolteacher and all. But Arizona was a big place. It helped to know the general area to look in, first. I found the town easy enough after she pointed it out. Then frowned. "Why Sonoita? That don't make much sense if they're headin' to Blessing. You sure yer source is reliable?"

Nan's gaze went cold at my question. "They're reliable," she snapped. "I ain't the only one after this stagecoach. And Baron Haas knows that. He's got it runnin' all over the country, tryin' to confuse those lookin' to steal from him. And he's got a few decoys out there, too. So you be sure the stagecoach you stop matches that one in that photograph, got it? That's the one we want. That's the one that'll have the lockbox."

I slumped in my chair and rubbed at my burnin' eyes with one hand. A nonsensical route, decoys, armed guards, a disguised coach ... what in the hell could possibly be in that lockbox? I didn't ask. Certainly she wouldn't tell me, of that I had no doubt. So I only said, "Sure. Got it. Can I take the map?"

She waved her hand as if shooin' me. "Yeah, yeah. Take the lot of it. That's what it's for."

I refolded it, then tucked it into my shirt pocket. The sketch of the lockbox and the photograph of the coach followed it.

Nine-Fingered Nan watched me, then sat forward and leaned her elbows on the table just as I was about to stand and take my leave. "You know," she said, "I heard the Bank of Blessing got robbed 'bout a month back. Was all over the papers. If I recall correctly, that was right about the time you managed to show up with thirty-five thousand dollars for that swindlin' sonuvabitch Taggert, weren't it?"

I sat back in my chair. So maybe I weren't goin' nowhere yet. But I also weren't about to freely admit to Nan where I'd got that money. "Dunno. Maybe. I don't keep much track of the days, to be honest. They all kinda run together after awhile."

Her eyes narrowed. Clearly she didn't believe me. "You by chance get all that money from Blessing, Mr. Delano?"

I shrugged. "Don't matter where I got it, does it? It all spends the same."

She smiled a little at that. "Sure. Yeah. Guess it does." She leaned away from the table, and her chair creaked as her weight shifted. Her left hand turned her whiskey glass around in circles as she kept starin' at me. "But a lot of those metal barons had their money in that bank.

They sure are sticklers about their money. Boy, that robbery got that town all in a fuss, all right. *And* it seems one of those barons got murdered. His house burned down and all his slaves freed and everythin'. Same night as the bank robbery." She shook her head. "The town of Blessing had a bad night that night."

"Sounds like it," I agreed. I'd had a helluva bad night that night, too. I eyed my own glass of whiskey and contemplated downin' it. She was wearin' on my nerves, and I didn't like the feelin' of sittin' so on-edge.

"How long you been here in the Territories, Mr. Delano?"

The question made me look up from the whiskey and I frowned across the table at her. "Awhile."

"How long?"

I did some rough estimations in my head. "'Bout four years. Maybe five. Like I told you, I don't much keep track of time."

She grunted. "You ain't learned much about the barons of Blessing in all that time, have ya?"

"Can't say I have." Unless, of course, you counted the time I blew up Whittaker's house, burned down his barns, freed his slaves, and then got treated to his very special *brand* of hospitality.

My right arm twinged with a phantom pain just thinkin' about it.

She fixed me with a full-on grin, then, and it was truly the most terrifyin' expression I'd ever seen her wear. "You should know better than to lie to me, Mr. Delano."

I tensed, but she only lifted her left hand again, gesturin' to her man who stood there behind her.

He pulled another folded piece of paper from his satchel and handed it to her. She took it from him and unfolded it, and her steady stare never left my face. She slid it toward me. "Seems you'll be just as popular as yer sister 'fore too long, at this rate."

Frownin', I dared to tear my eyes away from her to look down at this new document.

And my throat closed up at the sight of the face that stared back at me.

It was mine.

Or ... real close to mine. Not a photograph, but a sketch. And a fair good one, too. Across the top of the bulletin were those bold, fat letters: WANTED. And below the drawin' of my face was my price: *fifty thousand dollars*.

All the breath went out of me. Felt like that brute Thomas Withrow had buried his fist in my gut again. I kept starin' down at the paper while the rest of the room went to tiltin' like it had on me yesterday afternoon after all that whiskey. The rest of the words printed there all ran together, but a few of 'em stood out clear enough:

Murder. Arson. Theft.

The bounty had been posted by the Whittaker family. Whatever was left of 'em.

And they wanted me *alive*. At least there was that.

Maybe that's why Nan hadn't shot me yet.

But then ... this poster didn't make no sense. All those who'd seen my face—or Charlotte's face—were dead. I was sure of it. Couldn't say the same fer Holt, of course, since I hadn't been there when he'd robbed the bank. Not fer sure. And maybe that's why he was so keen on movin' along and stayin' out of Bravebank in general. Maybe he knew someone had got a good look at him.

But that seemed doubtful. That woulda been sloppy of him. Holt knew better than that. He hadn't lived to be so old by bein' sloppy.

Guess I couldn't say the same about me. Who could have escaped my notice that night? Who could have escaped with a good look at my face and also been a person strongly inclined to go tell the rest of Baron Whittaker's family just who exactly had murdered their patriarch?

"Looks an awful lot like you, wouldn't ya say?" Nan quipped.

Slowly, I lifted my eyes from the poster to look at her.

She still had that horrible grin on her face.

"There's no name," was all I managed.

"Indeed there ain't," she agreed. "But it does mention a lame left leg." Her head cocked to one side. "Which, coincidentally, you got. It also mentions that lame left leg is made outta metal. And that, Mr. Delano, is what I find of *particular* interest. There may be other famil-iar-lookin' stupid young fools out there wanderin' the Territories with lame left legs ... but I'm willin' to bet an awful lot there'll only be *one* of those legs that's made outta metal."

I didn't say nothin', didn't so much as twitch, but I was sure calculatin' just then what I would do if she decided she wanted to hand me over to the Whittakers. Or if she decided she wanted to know more about my metal leg, or even wanted to take it fer herself, as it seemed so many others had been wantin' to do of late. Calculatin' who I'd need to shoot first, and tryin' to figure out what she might find more valuable—the offer from the baron's family, or the possibility of workin' Old World tech.

She must've seen somethin' change on my face despite my best efforts, 'cause she held up her hands and shook her head. "Now, now, don't you worry yer pretty little head none. I just gave you a job to do fer me, didn't I? Why would I do that if I planned to hand you over to those barons?"

I could think of a few reasons, but then, I didn't want to encourage her none. So I kept my silence, not hardly darin' to blink, havin' no idea what kinda plans she mighta had in her head right then.

"Hell, if you wanna know the truth of it, Mr. Delano," she went on, "*I'm* the reason the people of this town ain't killin' each other fer the chance to truss you up and cart you off to Blessing to get that reward fer themselves. These posters came down maybe a week after you showed up and planted yerself here. I instructed Sheriff Jennings not to post them. He burned the lot of 'em, in fact. All except this one, of course, which I saved special just fer you. Don't know what other bounties you might have on yer head in other places, but it looks like you done pissed off the Whittaker family somethin' awful. They've sent these out all over the Territories. And with a price that high..." She shook her head again and gave a low whistle. Her pale gaze gleamed.

She sure loved talkin' about that cold, hard cash.

Either that, or she sure loved twistin' that knife in me just as often as she could.

I remembered what Holt had said about her hatin' my pa more than anyone else she'd ever hated. Had she possibly hated him so much she could now hate his son just as much?

I swallowed hard at the thought, wonderin' if maybe ... maybe this was a game I couldn't win, after all. But then, she didn't know how stubborn I was. If she thought any of this was gonna scare me off, convince me to stop tryin' to free my sister, she was sorely mistaken. And anyway, neither she nor anyone else had managed to kill me yet. Seemed I had some tricks up my sleeve, myself.

She reached out and plucked up the poster, then rolled it. "Just consider this a friendly warnin', Mr. Delano. Ya see, I did the math. Turns out that lockbox I'm sendin' ya to fetch is worth more to me than the fifty thousand the Whittakers are offerin' fer you." Her pale blue gaze dropped to the table, and she nodded toward my left leg, currently tucked safely underneath it. "Worth more to me then that leg of yers, too, even if it really *is* made outta metal." Her eyes came back up to my face. "So fer now, I'm doin' what I can around the Territories to keep this poster out of circulation. *But*," she pointed the rolled up paper at me, "if I don't get that lockbox, then the math don't add up. And in that case, I'll take the next best thing. Meanin' I'll be keen to learn all about that leg of yers, especially concernin' where you managed to get it. Then I'll go ahead and take it off you. Then I'll hand you over to the barons and let them do whatever the hell it is they're plannin' to do with you. Do I make myself clear?"

I glared at her steady, but every muscle in my body was all coiled up, braced and ready in case she changed her mind. In case this was all another trap. In case she was lyin' about not wantin' to take me to the barons. It was makin' all my bruises ache even worse, and the headache pulsed in my skull. "I'll get yer damned lockbox," I whispered.

As if it weren't enough she was already holdin' Ethelyn over me.

Now there was the goddamned barons and their bounty to worry about.

And Dr. Balogh and his family and the consequences of their foolish, misguided kindness.

"I should hope so," Nan said. "I hafta admit, Mr. Delano, you *do* keep surprisin' me. And that ain't an easy thing to do these days." She handed the rolled-up poster back over her shoulder to her lieutenant. He jammed it down into one corner of his satchel, and Nan's eyes narrowed at me. "Ain't never heard of anyone gettin' away from Baron

Whittaker. Much less gettin' away from him and burnin' down every-thin' he owned. And ... *murderin'* him, to boot..." She shook her head again, then blew out a breath and caught up her whiskey glass.

I didn't bother to mention it hadn't really been me at all who'd murdered Baron Whittaker. Charlotte had done that. Hell, it hadn't even really been me who'd gotten away from him, neither. That had been Charlotte's doin', too. If not fer her, that night woulda turned out a whole lot different, all right.

But I kept my mouth shut. Nan hadn't mentioned Charlotte yet, and if by some miracle the old hag didn't know of Charlotte's involve-ment in all that, I sure didn't want to be the one to tell her. She didn't need nothin' more to add to her extortion of me. That list was growin' long enough all on its own.

"You might be just the man to pull off this job," Nan said. She leaned back in her chair. "Long as you don't let that coach get to Bless-ing. That's a town I got no jurisdiction in. Be plenty of people on the hunt fer the likes of you around those parts."

"I got no intentions of settin' foot in Blessing, or anywhere near it," I said, and that was the whole truth. "Much less entanglin' myself with any of those barons." And that was even more of the truth. I surely didn't want to meet another baron of Blessing so long as I lived.

"Good. Guess you really are smarter than ya look."

I scowled and shoved my chair back away from the table. If she weren't gonna shoot me or collect the bounty on me, I was done sittin' here and takin' her insults.

"Somethin' wrong with my whiskey, boy?"

Her sharp tone stopped me. I looked up to see her man's hand on his gun. Nan was glarin' at me now. She stuck her chin out in the direc-tion of my glass, still full. I hadn't touched it.

I hesitated, then twisted to look over my shoulder at her second lieutenant. He had his hand on his gun, too. And was blockin' the door.

I faced Nine-Fingered Nan again and cleared my throat. Guess I still weren't goin' nowhere. I shook my head. "No," I croaked. "No." Of course there weren't. I'd downed enough of the stuff in the last three weeks to last me months. And the headache throbbin' in my skull reminded me well enough how much I'd had of it yesterday. I hadn't drank so heavy since before I'd had a good lead on the whereabouts of my sister.

If only Nan coulda served me coffee now instead.

I picked up the glass and raised it as if in a toast, then took a breath and downed it. I set it empty back to the table between us, and Nan gave a nod.

She raised hers in turn and finished it off, then set her glass next to mine. "Well then. Seems we've got ourselves a suitable arrangement." She stood and touched the brim of her hat. "I shall be eagerly awaitin' yer return from this errand. As will yer sister."

A whole swell of feelin's rushed up inside me at her mention of Ethelyn, all the things I'd been feelin' and fightin' since the day I'd come back to find her missin': anger, desperation, fear. But I swallowed it all back, kept my gaze hard and even.

Kept silent.

"Good luck to you, Mr. Delano," Nan said then, a hauntin' echo of Holt's last words to me. "Yer gonna need it." She smiled again and nodded to her two lieutenants.

Then she went toward the Stag's front door, and as she passed me she clapped a hand down hard on my shoulder. I recoiled at her touch, but her grip was strong, sharp and bony, diggin' into my flesh. Then she let go and went on, her two lieutenants trailin' after her, and I turned in my chair to watch her leave ... mostly to convince myself she was actually goin'.

She was.

Her tall, black-clad figure stepped through the door and out into the white heat of the afternoon, and then she turned right and was gone. One of her men shut the door after them, and I was left all alone in the middle of the Stag Saloon.

I heaved out a long breath of relief and dropped my head into my hands, rubbin' at my achin' temples.

Truth be told, that coulda gone a lot worse.

And the job coulda been a lot worse, too. A whole lot worse.

In the end, it really weren't so bad. All I had to do was stop a stage-coach and steal a lockbox. That bounty would complicate things some, sure, but I didn't plan to get too close to any kind of civilization. I'd need to hit the coach before it reached the town of Sonoita, anyway. The bounty wouldn't change that fact. If I played my cards right, all this shouldn't really be that hard.

And I was gettin' better at cards, at least.

The sound of a door openin' and shuttin' from somewhere in the back made me lift my head with a grimace. I heard footsteps across the floor, and soon enough the barkeep reappeared. He stopped short at the sight of me, a look of clear disgust twistin' at his features.

I ignored his distaste as a spark of hope lit in me. "Hey ... you got any coffee?"

OVER THE EDGE

Turned out that barkeep disliked me more than I'd thought.

He'd had coffee, all right. He'd even brought me some. And then he'd spit in it.

I'd thought about shootin' him fer his trouble. I was far too tired and sore to suffer such nonsense. I wondered if Nan would care any.

Most likely not.

Sheriff Jennings, though, he probably woulda cared. And he'd seemed awful serious this mornin' about not wantin' me to shoot no one. If I was too tired and sore to suffer havin' my coffee spit in, I was surely too tired and sore to suffer bein' tried fer murder.

And so the barkeep of the Stag Saloon got to live another day.

I'd left him standin' there, holdin' that cup of joe he'd spit in and givin' me a look like he dared me to shoot him fer it, and I'd limped on down the street to the First Chance and got myself a fresh cup there. And some good grub.

Spit-free.

I pulled out the map Nan had given me and studied it as I ate, makin' plans. There was a decent spot to plant myself with one of those long rifles, looked like. The coach was takin' a path southwest out of Utah, accordin' to Nan, then cuttin' back eastward to hit Sonoita before goin' south again toward Blessing.

I could catch 'em easy enough on that eastward leg. Get my own sharpshootin' rifle and take out the driver and as many guards as I could from a distance. I weren't as good with those rifles as Holt, but I weren't about to take my chances up close and personal with a group of armed marshals, that was fer sure. Not when I was havin' to do this job all by my lonesome.

Briefly, I wondered if Holt might try to pull off that new bank job of his all by himself, too.

But then I shook my head and grumbled, took another swig of my coffee. I didn't have time to be worryin' about Holt. He was a mean old bastard. He could take care of himself. I had plenty to worry about on my own here.

Stoppin' that coach. Gettin' that lockbox. Killin' those marshals.

Watchin' fer anyone comin' after that fifty thousand dollar bounty.

Freein' my sister.

And I only had six days till that coach was scheduled to arrive in Sonoita. That was ... if Nan's *source*, whoever that might be, could be relied upon. I sure hoped this person was more trustworthy than her man Taggert had been, anyway.

In any case, I figured I'd better head on up that way just as soon as I could manage. It'd be a few days ride to reach the spot I wanted. And with no time to retrieve any more supplies from Grave Gulch, I'd have to buy anythin' else I needed here. To include that rifle.

I sighed, folded the map, and stuck it back in my shirt pocket.

It'd be a long ride, indeed, in my current condition, but the coffee and the food *was* helpin'. A bit. Still had the headache and the bruises, but those would pass too, in time.

Well, I'd stay one more night in Bravebank. Buy the rest of what I needed once I finished here. Get a proper hotel room and sleep in a real bed. Get proper rested up so I had a clear head startin' out tomorrow.

There was an awful lot ridin' on this little errand.

I surely didn't want to fuck it up.

We headed outta town late the next mornin', me and my mule. He weren't such a bad animal, really. Overly social, sure, but generally steady. He didn't spook easy, and mostly did what I asked.

I was workin' on teachin' him to ground-tie and to come when I whistled. And I'd named him Joe. Holt had always insisted namin' yer mount was a surefire way to get 'em killed ... but that had only happened to me once ... and had only happened recently.

The horse Nine-Fingered Nan had shot out from under me the first time I'd come across her. The one I'd called Ace. Despite his name, his luck had turned out even worse than mine.

I'd really liked that horse.

But Joe ... I was pretty sure he was safe with a name like that. It weren't considered lucky or unlucky, it just was.

So we went, Joe and me, and we kept a consistent and steady pace northward. I stayed well off the roads, and didn't stop to camp that first night till after sunset. I braved a small fire, bein' as I was off the beaten path and not yet too near Blessing, but truth be told I only wanted it fer a little light to see by.

I pulled Charlotte's telegram out of my back pocket as I sat cross-legged on my bedroll in the cool desert's night, and wondered why I was nervous to read it. The plan had been fer her to write me when she got home safe, and fer me to write her once I had my sister and had ended Nine-Fingered Nan.

If Charlotte had sent this ... it meant she was home.

It meant she was safe.

That surely weren't nothin' to get worked up about.

I shoulda been happy about the telegram. Relieved.

And I guess I was. But there was somethin' else there, too. Somethin' that was tyin' my stomach up in knots as I sat there starin' down at that paper.

Was it only 'cause I hadn't been able to write her myself, yet? 'Cause I didn't have Ethelyn yet? Not only that, but I hadn't ended Nine-Fingered Nan yet, neither. Nope, instead here I was, actin' as her errand boy, headin' straight back toward the wasps' nest Charlotte and

I had kicked up real good those weeks ago, hopin' I weren't about to get swarmed and stung.

I drew in a breath, then let it out long and slow, and tilted the telegram toward the glow of the flames:

DEAREST VAN

AM HOME SAFE STOP HOPE AND PRAY YOU AND SISTER ARE THE SAME STOP EVER SO GRATEFUL FOR YOUR AID STOP PLEASE CALL UPON MYSELF OR MY FAMILY IF YOU NEED ANYTHING STOP WILL SEND PROPER LETTER VERY SOON STOP PLEASE WRITE AS SOON AS YOU CAN

I let out another long exhale, feelin' as if I'd been holdin' my breath, and blinked hard. I read it over a few more times, mostly to convince myself she'd really made it, that she was really home safe. Then I rubbed a hand over my mouth and sighed, and slipped the note back into my pocket.

Well, she was safe. That was all that mattered.

Fer now. I wondered again if there was a bounty out on her for what had happened to Baron Whittaker. I wondered if I should write her now, after all, and warn her that such might be the case. The Republic didn't usually honor bounties posted by the Territories—hell, they mostly didn't honor those posted by the Commune, even—but if the reward fer her was anythin' like the reward fer me, there'd be more than enough greedy types out there who might be determined enough to track her down ... even all the way out to Pennsylvania.

Maybe that's what had me all worked up; concern she'd made it all the way back home just to be hunted again by more lowlifes. Concern they'd catch up to her eventually, and she'd be brought right back here to face whatever unpleasantness Baron Whittaker's family had in mind.

I stood at that thought and paced in front of my small fire.

Joe was hobbled behind me, already dozin'. He felt no concern at all over my predicament, nor Charlotte's. The sky was black overhead, a thick carpet of stars visible in the absence of any moon.

I had to warn her. She seemed to come from money; maybe her family could just pay off the Whittakers. The baron himself had mentioned somethin' about monetary retribution before proceedin' to torture me ... if I'd had enough money, maybe it woulda saved me all that pain.

Maybe Charlotte had enough money to spare her any of that.

My fists clenched and I paused in my pacin', lookin' up at the stars.

Even if she didn't, even if the Whittakers wouldn't take her money, I wasn't gonna let them—or any bounty hunter—get their hands on her again.

After I got this lockbox fer Nan, after I freed Ethelyn, we'd head east. We'd find Charlotte. And we'd get ready fer anythin' they sent after us.

It weren't enough—weren't nearly enough—but it was the best I could do.

Fer now, I'd write her that letter I'd promised. Only it wouldn't have the news she'd been hopin' to hear.

I reached the place I'd wanted on the fourth day, in the late afternoon.

By then, I had a pretty good idea of what I was gonna write to Charlotte. Once I got back to a town with a telegraph station, anyway. Maybe I could pass through Sonoita myself on my way back to Brave-bank and send it from there.

After I took care of this coach and got that lockbox.

I pulled Joe to a halt at the top of one of the numerous hills that marked this area, then took off my hat and brushed at the sweat runnin' down my face with a sleeve. Squinted down at the road that ran below us.

This spot would do just fine.

The road ran along the side of the hill here, with a steep incline on one side and a steep drop on the other side. I could set up my camp here and get a good shot at 'em with the rifle as they came eastward. And they'd have nowhere to go but straight backward or straight forward, and my bullets would be waitin' fer 'em either way.

I was high enough they shouldn't be able to get too good a shot at me, in return, and there was some brush around I could lay behind to help hide my location and the glare of the sun off the rifle.

All I had to do now was wait.

There was another day and a half or so, maybe two, before that coach was due to come through here. So I made myself comfortable. Found a tree a little ways away to tie Joe to, and set myself up under its shade to keep an eye on the road. I kept my binoculars handy, too.

Anyone comin' down this way now was worth a good look at, just in case.

I settled back against the trunk of the tree and took out the photograph of the coach. Studied it long and hard, till I had all its features memorized. There was bound to be more than one such vehicle pass through here in the next day or two, and I didn't want to be shootin' up the wrong people.

Then I occupied myself by draftin' up my message to Charlotte, scribblin' it out on the edge of the brown paper my cheese was wrapped up in with the little stub of a pencil I kept in my pack. And checked over my new sharpshootin' rifle; made sure it was ready fer shootin' on short notice. Took a few practice shots at a rock far down the road when I sure there was no one comin', just to get a feel fer how it handled.

And kept on waitin'.

Night fell, and I wished suddenly I weren't doin' this job alone, after all. That coach could come by at any hour. If I missed it 'cause I was asleep ... that wouldn't be no excuse Nan would accept, I was sure of it.

So I moved myself down the hill aways, takin' my binoculars and my rifle with me, and rolled out my bed closer to the road. Where I could hear anyone comin' through, and I only dozed off in fits and starts, joltin' awake at every rustle and snort from Joe.

It weren't a restful night, fer certain.

The next day passed in much the same way as the remainder of the first, only now I were more tired. A few riders came by, and I checked 'em all through the binoculars, but no sight of any coach, yet.

Not till nearly dusk, when one came thunderin' down the road and made me jump to my feet, heart racin'. But then I saw it was pulled by six horses instead of four, and my heart fell again. Still, I made sure to get a closer look at it, just in case ... but the build of the coach was all wrong. Older and bigger and with a lot more missin' paint. A mail coach, looked like.

I scowled in disappointment. Blew out a breath and eased back down to sit against my tree. I knocked my head back against its trunk and scrubbed a hand over my eyes, really hopin' Nan's source hadn't gotten their timin' wrong.

Really hopin' this wasn't some elaborate game Nan was playin' with me...

Holt's incessant warnings about that woman kept ringin' in my head, but I did my best to ignore 'em. She'd come fer me in Bravebank, after all, hadn't she? She'd said she would send fer me, and she had. That hadn't been a lie. Why would this be?

Especially somethin' so complicated and involved as this particular coach robbery. Why invent somethin' so complex? If she was gonna send me off after somethin' that didn't exist, why not make it somethin' a lot simpler?

And so another restless night came and went, and I was awake again at dawn, sittin' there watchin' the road, my eyes burnin' now.

Today was the day. If it didn't come today...

No, I weren't gonna think about that. Not yet. One problem at a time.

I shook my head and set about makin' another small fire. I wanted coffee, damnit. And it just so happened I'd brought some with me.

I'd brought whiskey, too, of course, but I still had the remnants of a headache hauntin' my temples, and the thought of drinkin' that stuff right now made the pain flare up again. I'd really overdone it that day I'd gotten in that fight in Bravebank. I hadn't been that drunk in a long, long while.

And I didn't want to be that drunk again fer a long, long while, neither.

I was sittin' there, sippin' at my cup of joe as the sun climbed into the sky and began to warm the day, when a cloud of dust rose on the horizon. I didn't let myself get excited this time. Just kept sippin' at my coffee as I lifted the binoculars and focused on the bend in the road. They'd be comin' around it any time now…

Four horses in harness came into view, movin' at a brisk trot. They pulled a coach … a mighty familiar coach.

I set my coffee down quick, sloshin' some on my hand. I scowled and shook my hand off, wiped it on my pants, and stood, grabbin' up the rifle. I left Joe at the tree and moved down the hill a bit to the bush I'd picked out to be my cover. I flattened myself behind it, layin' out on my belly, and propped myself on my elbows. I slid the end of the rifle barrel through the bush's sparse branches, and put my eye to the sight.

I tracked the coach as it came right at me, and double-checked its features. The horses weren't the same four glossy ones I'd seen in the photograph, but that weren't unusual. The rest of it looked right enough. No company name. Smaller boot. Shiny paint. The shades were drawn, so I couldn't see who was inside, but that didn't matter so much. There was one shotgun rider in front, next to the driver, and another in the back. That meant there'd be another two to three marshals ridin' passenger.

This was the coach Nan wanted. Had to be.

I aimed fer the driver first. Needed to slow 'em down so I could shoot 'em all from afar before they had time to pass me by. I took a few breaths to try and calm my nerves. Remembered what Holt had told me about shootin' these rifles. Be still. Be patient. Exhale.

I did so, breathin' out long and slow, and squeezed the trigger.

The crack of it echoed out loud as dynamite, rollin' back and forth between the hills.

The driver jerked, blood sprayin' out from his chest. He slumped on the bench, and the reins dropped from his limp hands.

I watched through the sight as the marshal next to him sprang into motion, reachin' over to try and catch the reins before they fell out of reach. I pulled back the rifle's bolt action, expellin' the spent cartridge, then pushed it forward, loadin' a fresh one. Took aim again, this time fer the marshal scramblin' fer the reins.

The rifle barked a second time, the bullet catchin' him in the right shoulder and throwin' him back against the coach's cab. Shoutin' rose up into the mornin', though faint at this distance. Some of the shades rolled up. The sun glinted off gun barrels as they poked from the windows, searchin' fer a target.

But I paid those no mind; focused again on the marshal in front. He cradled his injured arm against himself and shoved the dead driver off the bench. The body hit the dirt and rolled. The marshal took the vacated seat and struggled to gather the lines with his one good hand.

I buried another bullet in him and ended him. He, too, slumped, and this time the reins dropped free, bein' as there was no one else to catch 'em. The horses slowed, confused and unsure of all the ruckus. They tossed their heads and chomped their bits.

The marshal at the back of the coach had started to make his way toward the front, goin' around the far side of the cab so I couldn't get a clear shot at him.

Smart.

But he'd have to come out into the open eventually.

So I waited and watched through my scope. Stayed still. Stayed patient. Anticipation ran hot through my blood, and I took another few deep breaths in efforts to calm it. I saw his hand grab the back of the driver bench and braced myself, finger wrapped around the trigger.

What emerged next, though, weren't a body. It was what looked like a big piece of metal. Rough and pitted, but big enough to cover him from knees to head. He kept it angled in my direction as he clumsily clambered around the corner of the cab and up onto the driver's seat.

The hell was this?

Nan had never mentioned anythin' about no metal shields. I'd never seen anyone with anythin' like that before, neither. Not on any coach.

I laid there fer a minute on my belly in the dirt behind that bush, tryin' to decide what to do now. Would it really save him from my bullets? I squeezed off a shot, just to test it.

The *ping* of the bullet ricochetin' off that metal sheet reached me even from my hidin' spot, and the force of it knocked the man back onto his ass. But he didn't fall off the bench, damn him. He only struggled back up to his feet and hunkered down behind his shield as he groped for the fallen lines.

Their horses had picked up their pace again now, and, swearin', I switched my aim to the coach's windows. Maybe I could get at some of the bastards inside, at least, while I figured out what to do about that man in front.

There were two gun barrels pointed at me, and I only barely had time to recognize that fact before the muzzles flashed, and the shots rang out into the hills, and a double spray of dirt kicked up right in front of my bush.

I flinched back despite myself and spat more curses, then steadied myself and resumed my flat-out position, cradlin' that rifle again as I looked back down the scope. I tried to even out my breathin', tried to focus, and honed in on one of the dark shapes I could just barely make out inside the cab. His barrel was pointed up toward me, but I resisted the urge to scramble away from my cover. No way could they have a good shot at me from down there. If I moved now, I'd only give away my position fer certain, and make myself a much clearer target. So instead I stayed put, and made the last shot in my first clip count.

One of the guns hangin' out the window jerked and fell away, and a splatter of blood painted the window edge. I'd got one of 'em, at least. Couldn't be sure if I'd killed 'em, but at least I'd hurt 'em awful bad.

The second gun re-positioned itself in the absence of its fellow.

I dropped the rifle to reload it, and in the time it took me to slide in another five cartridges, the man in the front with the metal shield had pushed the dead marshal off the bench and gotten control of the horses. I heard him shout at 'em as he slapped the lines and urged them up into a canter.

So they were gonna try and run.

At that pace they'd pass me by right quick, sure enough.

And me and Joe coulda caught up to 'em, yeah, but I weren't fool enough to face down two or three armed marshals all by my lonesome. Especially not with that armor of theirs.

I took one more shot at the cab's window, but their speed made it harder to track 'em with the rifle, and the bullet buried itself in the back corner of the coach, sprayin' out wood splinters.

They cracked off another shot at me, and this time their bullet whizzed through the branches of the bush only a foot or so above my head.

Instinctively, I ducked, and my swearin' turned truly vile. They musta had a rifle in there somewhere themselves. One with a scope. Or some binoculars, maybe. In any event, they'd managed to pinpoint my position with more accuracy than I would have preferred.

And that man in front was workin' the horses up into a full-on gallop.

I was runnin' out of time. Runnin' out of chances.

I scrambled to adjust my aim again, this time fer one of the front horses. I hesitated, then, as they charged up the road straight toward me, and gritted my teeth. That horse hadn't done nothin' wrong. Animals usually didn't. Only their no-good masters usually deserved the killin'.

But I *had* to stop this coach.

I had to get that lockbox.

For Ethelyn. And Dr. Balogh and his family. And myself.

"*Shit*," I hissed, rememberin' my own horse, Ace, gunned down by Nan. "I'm sorry. I'm sorry, I'm sorry..."

I pulled the trigger.

The front left horse dropped in the harness, and the other three, still gallopin', stumbled at the sudden dead weight that dragged 'em down and tripped, then went down themselves, fallin' onto their knees. The coach lurched into almost a dead stop all at once, and the marshal in the driver's seat was thrown forward, his metal shield goin' flyin', and him landin' on the wagon shaft, right in-between the two rear horses.

They didn't like that none. They staggered back to their feet and tried to shy away from him, but they were still in their harness, and tied to their dead fellow, to boot. The third horse wasn't too happy, neither, and was tryin' to jump sideways ... away from the dead one. But in so doin', he was gettin' awful close to the edge of the road where it dropped away into nothin'...

"*Shit*," I hissed again.

Forgettin' caution, I slung the rifle over my shoulder and jumped up from my cover, pullin' one of my pistols as I headed down the hill at a run. Or half-slid down the hill with all the gravel, more like.

Don't you do it, I willed that horse. *Just stay put, stay calm, it'll all be over soon...*

But he didn't listen. Not one bit.

The marshal in the front was flailin' around, tryin' to untangle himself from the traces. He'd just managed to right himself and sit up as his companions inside the coach also appeared to regather themselves, because that gun emerged from the window again.

I saw it from the corner of my eye as I raced toward 'em, and saw the man sittin' between the horses grab fer his gun, too, his eyes goin' wide as he spotted me comin' at him.

I drew my second pistol and shot at both of 'em simultaneously, not even breakin' stride. My left gun's bullet hit the front man's left shoulder and he yelled and swore. My right gun's bullet went into the dimness of the coach's interior, but I heard a grunt. That gun fired anyway, but the shot just missed me.

The marshal in front brought his own gun up and took aim, but I already had him in my sights again.

Didn't matter, though.

The horses were all riled up, and that's when the one in the lead stepped a little too close to the edge of the road. The ground of that steep incline gave way under its hoof, and it slipped and fell, jerkin' the coach along after it ... just enough to unbalance the horse behind it, who also slipped and fell, and then the whole coach tipped precariously to the side, all of it bein' dragged inch by inch toward that drop.

The man in front had abandoned his gun now, clingin' to the wagon shaft, tryin' to climb around the flailin' horses to get free of the coach entirely. There was a commotion comin' from inside, too, and the side door started to open.

I stumbled down at last onto the flat of the road with my guns at the ready, just in time to see the terrified expression on the marshal's face as him, the coach, and all its horses disappeared over the edge.

ONE PROBLEM AT A TIME

"Fuck."

I stood there in the road with no company save the two dead men lyin' a ways back, at a loss, and grimaced at the noise of that coach and its horses and its passengers all tumblin' down that slope.

I shoved my guns back into their holsters and rubbed a hand over my face, the sweat tricklin' down my neck. I glanced back over my shoulder, up the hill I'd just come down, back toward my bush and beyond that, my makeshift camp and the tree Joe was tied to. Couldn't even see it from down here.

Well, I didn't want to take Joe down the slope. He'd be fine up there fer now.

I didn't want to go down the slope, neither, but I didn't have much of a choice. I had to get that lockbox. At least maybe the fall woulda killed the rest of those marshals fer me. Though I was hopin' it hadn't killed all the horses.

I'd feel awful bad if that were the case.

'Cept you weren't the one who killed 'em. They did that all on their own. You can only take the blame fer the one. I shook my head, shovin' the guilt

down where I kept all my feelin's, and waited till the commotion of the rollin' coach stopped. Then I took a breath and stepped up to the edge of the road myself. Looked down over it.

And grimaced again.

It was a mess, but mostly intact. It had landed on its side, and one of the wheels had come off. The marshal that had been in the front was dead fer sure, but I couldn't tell what had happened to the men inside. The horses had come unhitched from the coach in the tumble and looked, miraculously, mostly fine. Looked like maybe they'd managed to just slide down instead of roll like the coach. The three alive were still harnessed up together and staggered around a bit, then shook themselves, seemin' dazed.

Good, let 'em stay that way fer awhile ... maybe they'd stay quiet long enough fer me to get down there and unharness 'em before they could try and kill themselves again.

But I had to hurry. There'd be more travelers along this road before long, and the bodies lyin' along it would be a clear sign of trouble. Any curious folk, whether vultures themselves lookin' fer an easy score, or Good Samaritans lookin' to involve the law, might stop to investigate. And we weren't that far out from Sonoita. If anyone *were* inclined to go and get the law, it wouldn't leave me much time to get clear of this whole disaster. And if anyone stopped lookin' fer an easy score, well, *I* had to get to that lockbox first.

So I sighed and took the rifle off my shoulder to hold it. Didn't want it gettin' caught on anythin'. Then I grumbled and eased myself over the lip of the road. The slope was steep, all right. Too steep to do much walkin' or runnin' down it. Mostly I just went down on my ass, lettin' the loose dirt and gravel carry me down, usin' a hand now and then to keep my semi-controlled descent from turnin' into an uncontrolled fall.

I got to the bottom soon enough and without much trouble, just covered in dust now and with a few scrapes on the hand I'd used to steady myself. Goin' up, on the other hand ... that was gonna be a whole 'nother problem. But I couldn't worry about that right now.

One problem at a time.

Sure seemed I was sayin' that an awful lot these days.

I jogged over to the horses first and cut 'em free of their harness. They snorted at me, but seemed content to stay put. Of course. *Now* they weren't keen on dancin' around and bein' stupid. If only they'd have kept their heads while up there on the road, we wouldn'ta been in this situation.

I waited, then, and listened fer any sound of life comin' from inside the sideways coach. But things stayed quiet. There was only the soft noises from the horses shiftin' and snortin' around, and the buzz of flies that had found the nearby dead already. I crouched, anyway, and moved up quick and quiet-like to take cover right behind the cracked driver's bench. Then I waited again, and listened again.

Still nothin'.

So I propped my rifle up against the broken bench and helped myself to the front boot, slicin' it open with my knife and rippin' the canvas apart. Then I sat there and just stared into it. It was empty. Completely empty.

All right. Well, Nan had said it would be *somewhere* around here ... didn't mean it had to be in the front boot. So I stood and moved to the rear boot. Did the same there; sliced it open and ripped it apart.

This time there *was* somethin' there, and my heart did a little jump as I realized it was a lockbox. But not the one I was lookin' fer. This one was too big, and had a regular padlock keepin' it shut. But it coulda been holdin' the one I wanted. So I pulled it out into the sun, into the open, and shot off the padlock. The lid creaked as I swung it open, and despite myself, I held my breath as expectation sparked through me.

But then all the anticipation soured, and I snarled and spit into the dirt.

Empty again.

I stepped back away from it and chewed at my lip. I rested my hands on my gun grips, the fingers drummin' restlessly. A very bad feelin' snaked its way through my gut just then, and I didn't like it. Didn't like it one bit.

My eyes went to the cab itself. Guess it was time to see if anyone was alive in there. Time to see if any of 'em was carryin' that lockbox on their person.

And what if they ain't?

The thought shot through my mind before I could stop it, and I took a deep breath against the dread that rose in my throat. Tried to swallow it down. It had to be here somewhere. *Had* to be.

Nan had said so. Her source had said so.

If whatever was in that lockbox was valuable enough to garner decoy coaches and routes wanderin' all over the map, they was probably just makin' it right difficult to find.

Though why there weren't nothin' else at all in either boot, and why they had a locked lockbox that was empty, didn't add up right. But then, not much about those metal barons seemed to add up right.

I hissed out my frustration in a long breath and clambered up atop the side of the coach. I peered through the windows; saw a tangle of limbs and splattered blood. Didn't look like no one was movin', but I wouldn't take no chances. I pulled at the door, but it was locked, too. Another shot from my pistol made short work of that, and I yanked it open while keepin' it between me and anyone on the inside.

I waited a second, but no one came out shootin'. No one so much as moved or made a sound. I peeked cautiously around the edge of the door and down into the mess of bodies below. Stared at 'em fer awhile. Couldn't see no one breathin'.

Satisfied they were dead, I swung my legs over the side of the doorway and hopped on down, tryin' not to step all over 'em, but only partially succeedin'. I winced at the look of the place. Some limbs were clearly broken, bent at odd angles. The two I'd managed to shoot through the window had gotten blood all over the place. One was missin' part of his face. The other had taken a slug to his chest. There was a third man in here, too, and he didn't look like no marshal. He was sprawled underneath the body of one of those armed guards, but he weren't wearin' no guns, himself.

And he was dressed fancy. Even had a monocle danglin' out from his vest pocket, the lens shattered.

Fer a minute I worried it might be Baron Haas aboard his coach after all, but his suit weren't as nice as the one Baron Whittaker had been wearin'. Maybe not all barons dressed the same, sure ... but this man's outfit reminded me more of Dr. Balogh, instead.

Maybe just another learned man, then.

But why was he on Baron Haas' coach?

And why hadn't Nan mentioned him?

Maybe she'd known he didn't carry and hadn't deemed him a threat, seein' as how he weren't wearin' no guns.

Well, none of that mattered. I shook off the questions, the curiosity, and refocused on my job. It didn't matter who that man was, or why he was aboard this coach. All that mattered was that I found that lockbox with those coded dials and got it back to Bravebank. To Nan.

A cursory glance around the grisly interior revealed no lockbox.

Of course it wouldn't be that easy.

Reluctantly, I bent down and started movin' bodies and limbs around, tryin' to see if maybe the box was loose in here somewhere and had ended up buried by one of these gents.

I'd just shoved the man missin' part of his face aside to check under him when a gunshot blasted from behind me, deafenin' in that small space. My hat blew off my head as I flinched away and spun, drawin' and firin' almost without thinkin'.

To my surprise, a shriek of fear answered my return shot instead of a cry of pain, and I found myself starin' down at the man in the fancy clothes.

So he weren't dead. Coulda fooled me.

He was still under the body of the other marshal, and it seemed my shot had gone into the dead guy instead of the live guy. He was usin' that body as a shield somewhat, and pointin' one of the marshal's guns at me.

Though from the way his gun hand was shakin', I weren't too worried about him hittin' me, even at this range.

I kept my gun trained on him, anyway.

And my hand weren't shakin'.

"D-don't shoot!" he yelped. "D-don't shoot or I'll … I'll … I'll shoot you back!"

I blinked at him. Did he not understand how these things worked? But as long as he was alive, I figured I should take advantage of the situation. "All right," I said. "I won't shoot you then. Long as you tell me where the lockbox is."

His face scrunched up in confusion. "L-lockbox?"

"Yeah. You know, it's a box with a lock on it? Usually holds expensive stuff inside?"

"That's what this is? All this murder, all this pain ... for a ... a robbery?"

I gave a huff of impatience. "Look, Mister, I don't got all day. Start talkin' or I'm gonna start shootin'."

He tried to steady his hand, bravado hardenin' his features. "You shoot and I'll shoot back, I told you!"

I rolled my eyes and stepped forward, snatchin' his gun before he had time to blink. I shoved it into my belt and stepped back again. "There. Now you don't have to worry about it. Let me ask you again: where is that lockbox?"

His mouth dropped open, and his eyes got real wide.

I waggled my own gun at him. "Mister? You'll want to be talkin' right about now ... my trigger finger is startin' to get real itchy..."

"It's ... it's in the back," he blurted. "In the back!"

My shoulders slumped. I really didn't have the patience fer this right now. I scrubbed a hand across my eyes and sighed at him. "No, not that one. I already found that one. It's empty. I want the other one. The one with the dials."

His eyes got wider. His breathin' quickened and he swallowed. "How ... how did you know about that one?"

"A little bird told me. Just like yer gonna tell me where it went to. Right now. Ain't you?" I thumbed my hammer back for emphasis.

He went very pale. Silence stretched out between us for a heartbeat, and his eyes darted around like he hoped to find some way out of this predicament.

But he was stuck under a dead body in the cramped sideways space of a turned coach, and there weren't no more guns within his reach. His scared eyes eventually came back around to me. He opened his mouth.

The creak of wood sounded from outside, like a boot climbin' up the side of the coach, and I twisted quick toward the open doorway.

Just in time to look down the barrel of a sixgun.

The man behind it smiled lazily and touched the brim of his black hat with his free hand. "Howdy there," he said. "You the one who made all this mess?"

I swallowed, hesitated, lookin' him over, tryin' to judge how fast he was. I still had my own pistol in my hand ... pointin' in the wrong direction. And my left hand had come up to my left grip, but stopped at the sight of that barrel in my face.

"Now, now," came a new voice, a woman's voice, and I looked over my shoulder to the other side of the open doorway. She was lyin' on the side of the coach on her belly, all casual-like, her dark hair spillin' over her shoulders as she smiled down at me. She had a pistol, too, silver-plated and bright in the sun, leveled at my head. "Don't even think it. You won't beat him. Won't beat me, neither."

"That's easy to say when you sneak up on a fella," I growled.

Her smiled widened, and she shrugged. "You wanna square off? Who's it to be? Me or him?" She nodded toward the man in the black hat. "Moses has been real bored lately. I'm sure he'd take you up on it."

"Sure," the man agreed.

I turned back to him.

"Just say the word."

And I could tell from his tone he'd shot down plenty of men. His eyes were mostly blue, squinted under his hat brim, and they'd gone all flat and cold.

I cleared my throat. "No. I don't wanna square off. I wanna finish up my business here and ride on, understand? I got no quarrel with either of you. I don't want no trouble."

"Hrm," the woman mused. "Seems a man who don't want no trouble probably shouldn't go around robbing stagecoaches."

"I ain't robbin' it," I snapped. "I found it like this."

"That's not true!" the man in the fancy clothes blurted. "You were just asking about the lockbox!"

I closed my eyes and exhaled quietly. He didn't have no foreign accent like Dr. Balogh, but clearly he weren't from around here, neither.

"A lockbox, you say?" the man called Moses drawled.

I opened my eyes again at his question. He was starin' straight at me.

"There's a lockbox out here," the woman said. "But it's empty."

"There another one around here somewhere?" Moses asked, and his tone had switched from cold-blooded killer to all kinds of curious.

My stomach tightened at his interest, and suddenly I prayed the man in the fancy clothes had more spine than I had judged him to have.

"N-no," he practically squeaked. Seemed he had realized right quick now these two newcomers weren't exactly on his side. "No others. We're not carrying any valuables. None at all!"

"You're just carrying around an empty lockbox?" the woman asked. She sounded mighty skeptical. "Locked up for nothing?"

The man in the silk vest craned his neck sideways in an attempt to look up at her. "I don't know, I suppose? This isn't my coach! It belongs to Baron Haas. Maybe they were carrying it for whatever they were supposed to pick up later in the day."

Moses grunted. "Seems highly unusual to me."

"I'm telling you, I don't know anything about any other lockboxes or any other valuables," the man in the fancy clothes insisted. "I swear!"

Relief flickered through me. At least he hadn't mentioned the box with the dials.

"So it was just you and four armed escorts on this here coach?" the woman asked. "What the hell were they protecting, then? You?"

The man had the courage to look affronted at the question. "Yes!" he blustered. "Of course! Is that so hard to believe?"

"Maybe," Moses said. "Who are you, then? Someone important?"

I turned to look at him too, curious despite myself. He glanced between all of us, and tried to push the dead marshal off of himself. But his leverage weren't so good, and he only barely managed to budge the body. He gave up, pantin' from exertion, but puffed up his chest as best he could from his undignified position, anyway. "Yes, in my own way," he said. He reached for his monocle, frowned as he saw it was shattered, and sagged back against the coach wall. He let the monocle drop again. "Name's Professor Christopher Morton. I'm Head Curator of the Royal Museum for Her Majesty Victoria the Third, Queen of Canada."

Moses let out a low whistle. "The queen, huh?" He snorted a laugh. "I don't buy that fer a minute. You?" His gaze shifted over my shoulder, presumably to his lady partner.

"Nope," she said. "Canada is a real, real long way from here, Mister."

"Yes, well..." the man tried to shove the body off again, and again, failed. "It's true. All of it. And if you'll just be so kind as to get me out of here, and safely escort me to the residence of Baron Haas in Blessing, I am quite sure he would be most pleased. Probably offer you a nice reward to show his appreciation."

"That so?" Moses looked again to the woman behind me.

He mighta been the killer, but it appeared she was the boss.

"That so?" she echoed. "Well, we didn't come all the way down here for nothing. Let's get you boys out of all that blood and gore and have a *proper* chat about all this, shall we?"

I remembered then how Nan had been quite explicit in wantin' me to kill everyone aboard this coach. But then, she hadn't ever said nothin' about no museum curator from Canada. Was he included in her kill order? And even if he was, if these two new folks decided to take him to Blessing, I didn't think there was much I could do about it. "Look," I said, "I told you, I don't want no trouble. I ain't a part of any of this. You let me ride on now, and I'll leave you to whatever you get from here. From him. Ain't no business of mine what happens after I'm gone." I glanced to the man still trapped beneath the dead marshal.

He gave me a look like he weren't quite sure if I'd meant that in a good way or a bad way.

But I hadn't meant it in any particular way. I only needed to get myself clear of Moses and his lady boss so I could watch from a safe distance and see if they ended up makin' the deal with Professor Morton. Then figure out my next steps fer how to find that damned lockbox with the dials, dependin' on whether or not that deal was made.

One problem at a time.

But Moses shook his head and somehow managed to look genuinely sympathetic. "Don't think so, partner. You'll be stayin' put fer awhile. And I'm gonna need you to hand over yer piece." He paused, his eyes shiftin' between all three of the guns currently on my person. "All of 'em."

The click of a hammer sounded from behind me.

"Go on now," the woman prompted. "Do as he says."

I gritted my teeth, fingers tightening around the grip of my pistol. But there was nothin' to be done fer it. They had me dead to rights.

Seemed I was gonna have a whole lot more problems to work through, after all.

Fuck.

VII

IF

It was almost high noon now, and the blisterin' heat made the sweat roll down my face even under the brim of my hat, which the woman had so kindly returned to me. It had a brand-new bullet hole in it now, but better it than my head.

I sat cross-legged on the dusty ground, my back against a big boulder. And my arms tied behind me, around the boulder's bulk. The so-called professor sat on the other side of the rock, his arms tied as well in a similar fashion.

And he wouldn't shut up.

He shouted relentlessly at Moses and the woman as they turned the coach inside out, very thorough, indeed, in their search for valuables. At first he'd been pleadin' with them to take him to Blessing, promisin' rewards and treasures. But they didn't seem to believe him. So then he'd tried threatenin' 'em with the queen's justice ... but they'd paid even less attention to that. Even laughed at him a few times. So now, he'd resorted to insults. Callin' 'em all sorts of foul names.

They were ignorin' those, too.

Professionals, these two.

"Would you *shut up?*" I finally hissed. "Please, for the love of God, *shut up.*"

He went silent for a blessed moment, then directed a string of muttered insults at me.

I twisted best I could toward him, but couldn't see him around the curve of the boulder. "Look, Mister, you want them to come over here and put a bullet through yer forehead? 'Cause I gotta admit, if I was them, I'd have already done that. They ain't killed us yet, and I'd like to keep it that way. Yeah? So please, if ya wanna stay alive ... *shut it.*"

Stony silence answered my plea.

Maybe he'd realized I'd made a good point.

Well, I'd take it. I breathed a sigh of relief, closed my eyes, and leaned my head back against the rock behind me. It was hot as fuck out here. And I was wishin' fer a drink out of my canteen about then. But all my supplies—and Joe—were up at my makeshift campsite.

I kept quiet, though. God hadn't ever seemed real keen on grantin' me favors, but by some kinda mercy, it didn't seem Moses or his lady partner had seen the bounty posters with my likeness on 'em yet. At least, I was prayin' that were the case. And if it was, I wanted to keep it that way.

I wanted 'em to forget about me. To leave me be. I wanted to show 'em I weren't no trouble. Maybe convince 'em they could untie me and let me go on about my way.

A cry of triumph from the woman made me snap my eyes open and sit up straighter, heart jumpin' with fear they'd found that other lockbox. But when I looked toward the coach, they were only draggin' out two trunks.

Must have been a hidden compartment in there somewhere.

Still ... one of those trunks could have the lockbox with the dials inside it...

I tugged at my wrists again. Tied tight, damnit. The skin already raw, and my arms achin'. If they did find that lockbox ... well, I didn't have a plan fer that yet.

I watched as they jimmied both trunks open with their knives and started sortin' through the contents.

Clothes. It was all a bunch of clothes.

From the noise of despair that came out of the professor, I guessed those trunks had belonged to him.

That was sure a lot of clothes fer just one man.

Moses and the woman rifled through it all, tossin' pieces here and there, to the growin' frustration of Professor Morton.

"So that's all you are, then?" he finally growled, unable to hold his silence any longer. "Nothing more than a pair of scavengers!"

"Hardly," the woman scoffed. She pulled out a pair of nice, polished boots and raised her eyebrows. She held 'em down by her own feet, checkin' to see if they might fit her. "I'd call us ... *opportunists*."

Professor Morton gave a disgusted grunt. "If you were true opportunists, you'd see the benefit in taking me to Blessing! You wouldn't be rummaging around through my baggage and throwing my wardrobe all over the desert!"

"Yeah, there's just one problem with your offer, there, Professor," the woman said. She set the boots aside and held up a white dress shirt so clean it hurt to look at it in the sun.

"Pray, do tell," Professor Morton quipped.

"You see..." She paused as she put the shirt up against Moses and tilted her head to one side, clearly considerin' what a man like him might look like in such a garment. His current get-up was a standard button-up that may have been white once, but was now more a beige color, with faded blue stripes.

Moses, fer his part, gave her a glower.

She only raised an eyebrow and threw the white dress shirt over her shoulder, then returned her attention to the trunk and cleared her throat. "You see," she said again, "the problem is that Moses and I got no love at all for those metal barons. Can't stand 'em, if I'm to be honest. So we ain't going to Blessing, I'm afraid."

"Not even for a reward of thousands of dollars?"

The professor sounded truly confused. But I understood well enough. I wouldn'ta gone to Blessing fer thousands of dollars, neither. Not after meetin' with Baron Whittaker up close and personal.

"Nope," the woman said.

"But ... but if you like my wardrobe so much, you could buy a whole trunk-full of similar clothes for yourselves with the reward money!"

"No thank you," the woman said again. "These'll do just fine." She collected a few more shirts and a pair of trousers while the professor continued to bluster on, appalled.

I started to relax, finally, after they'd emptied out both trunks with still no sign of that dialed lockbox.

But then a shout echoed out from up on the road and made me tense up again.

Moses and the woman twisted around to look up the slope, both of 'em pullin' iron faster than I could see.

Shit. Good thing I hadn't tested 'em. Either of 'em.

Up on the road, the small figure of a person could be seen leanin' over the edge, peerin' down at us. I imagined we made quite the sight. At least at the moment I looked like one of the victims ... instead of like the murderer I was.

But the person up there only turned, talkin' to someone else, and then he disappeared from view, only to reappear a second later on the back of his horse, goin' on down the road. Another man rode with him, and they both took off at a gallop.

Toward Sonoita.

"That's our cue to leave," Moses said. He pushed his pistol back into his holster and went quick to gather up the things they'd deemed worthy of keepin'. He threw 'em over the back of his horse, a tall, shiny black gelding. Woulda put Holt's gelding to shame.

The woman did the same, tyin' stuff to the back of her own saddle. Her horse was a white mare. And a true white horse, at that, with a pink nose and everything. Didn't see those very often.

Moses finished loadin' up his saddlebags, too, then grabbed up my long rifle from where I'd propped it against the turned-over coach.

Now it was my turn to make a noise of despair. I'd just bought that damn thing! "Hey," I blurted. "Come on, not the rifle. Please?"

He paused, lookin' at me dubiously from under his hat brim. "I'm doin' you a favor, boy. You want this weapon here when the lawdogs arrive? Anyone can see this rifle is what put those holes in those marshals ... and you want me to leave it here, lyin' right next to you?"

I considered his point. Though I had no plans to still be here by the time any law arrived, that was fer sure. We were close enough to Blessing they could have seen that poster. And even if they hadn't, they'd be askin' questions I surely didn't want to answer.

But before I could say anythin' further, he'd shouldered it and swung up onto his horse. "And anyway, we're leavin' you yer irons." He nodded toward my gun belts, rolled up nice and neat next to the coach. Far out of my reach. "I'd say that's mighty generous, wouldn't you?"

"Like I said," the woman chimed in as she also mounted up and reined her mare around to face me and Professor Morton, still tied around that boulder, "we're opportunists, not savages." She grinned at me, and turned her mare away. Kicked up into a trot, leavin' a little trail of dust behind her.

Moses touched the brim of his hat again, like he had when he'd first caught me unawares in the coach. "Pleasure doin' business with you gents." He turned to follow after the woman, and as he caught up to her, they both spurred their horses into a nice, easy canter, ridin' off into the desert.

And just like that, they were gone as quick as they'd come.

And I was stuck here, tied to a boulder, like a snared rabbit waitin' on the return of the hunter.

This job was really not goin' my way.

I sat there fer a minute thinkin', tryin' to figure out how I was gonna get myself free before someone *less generous* came along and found us ... or until those men got back with the law.

If that's even where they were goin' in the first place.

If.

That's when the idea came to me. I twisted around toward the professor again. "Hey, Mister ... Professor ... help me out, would ya? I think we can get free if we work together."

He'd been mutterin' somethin' about wishin' he'd never come here—I couldn't fault him fer that sentiment—but he paused in his lamentations long enough to scoff at me. "Oh, is that so? And just what makes you think I'd want to help out a man like you? You *murdered* those men! You robbed me! And you might have murdered *me!*"

I winced at his accusations. I was afraid he'd feel that way. "Now, now ... I didn't rob you. Those other two did that."

"But you *would* have. If they hadn't come along!"

"Look, all I'm interested in is that lockbox with the dials. I wouldn't have taken any of yer other stuff like those other two did. And now ... well, now we're both in trouble, ain't we? We're both in a right predicament, meanin' fer now, we're on the same side. So let's get out of these damned ropes, yeah?"

"I'm not in any predicament," he protested sullenly. "I have no reason to fear the law. I'm perfectly content to wait here till they arrive to cut these ropes. And then I'll be giving them a *full* account of what happened here. And don't think I'll leave out *your* part in all this. Oh no. You're the one who started it! I was having a perfectly fine day until you started shooting up my escorts!"

I winced again. I was afraid he'd feel that way, too.

But that's where the *if* came in. Uncertainty could sway a lot of folks.

So I gave a little laugh. "You think the law is comin'?"

"Yes. Why else would that man called Moses and that woman have taken off so quickly?"

I scoffed at him now. "Because when you're a thief, it ain't smart to stay put in once place too long." I shifted against the hard, rough rock pressin' into my back. "Look, Mister, two men ridin' off in the direction of a town after seein' a turned coach and a buncha dead bodies ain't no guarantee they're goin' to retrieve the sheriff. More likely they run off scared. More likely they wanted to make it clear they didn't want no part of this. I guess you couldn't see Moses and his lady friend draw, bein' as you were facin' the other way, but I can tell you, friend, they were lightnin' fast. And I've seen a lot of people draw, mind you. Anyone with any sense woulda high-tailed it outta here at seein' their speed ... maybe that man up there on the road saw it, too. And he and his friend did the sensible thing and made a hasty exit."

He was silent after my speech, and hope stirred in my chest. Maybe I was gettin' to him.

A shadow slid across the ground in front of me and I looked up to see a vulture glide overhead. It circled around over the coach, no doubt quite pleased to see such a feast laid out beneath it. Where there was one, more would follow.

Damned buzzards. Seemed they was like my own shadow ... always there and waitin' when I turned around, no matter where I went or what I did.

"And that's another thing," I said, watchin' the vulture circle. "See that buzzard, there? He ain't the only kinda animal out here. There's others, too. Like those mountain cats. You ever seen one of those?"

"No..."

"Yeah well they'll be attracted to all this meat same as the buzzards. Except they're not just scavengers. They like live meat just fine. And here we are, all trussed up nice fer 'em. One of those finds us ... they may not even kill us before they start eatin' on us. That's if, of course, we ain't dead already from thirst or exposure to the sun."

I paused then, but the professor still said nothin'.

So I went ahead and made my closin' argument. "Sure, Mister, yer right ... we *could* just sit here and do nothin' and wait fer the law to show up ... and sure, that wouldn't be too good fer me ... but if I gotta be honest ... it's probably not gonna happen. Or if it does happen, they'll come too late. Some other *opportunist* will find us first, and they might not be so generous as Moses and his lady friend. They might decide we're both better off dead so we can't go around describin' their deeds to the authorities."

The vulture finally landed on one of the bodies. It looked right at us and raised its wings, lettin' out a screech, as if challengin' us to take away its prize.

"Or one of those cats will find us first," I said. "Or the desert will kill us first. And I don't know about you, Professor, but I don't much like those odds. I don't much want to take that kinda chance. Maybe none of those outcomes are particularly favorable fer me, but only one of 'em is favorable fer you. You willin' to take that kinda chance? You willin' to bet yer life on it?"

More silence.

This time I let it stretch. Let him think it over.

The vulture started peckin' at the body.

One of the harness horses snorted at the dirt. They'd wandered a bit, but hadn't gone too far yet. I wondered why Moses and the woman hadn't taken the extra horses with 'em. Maybe they'd figured it was too much trouble. Maybe that was part of their "generosity", leavin' us some kind of mounts.

The professor cleared his throat. "If I help you get free ... how do I know you won't just shoot me afterward?"

The flicker of hope in my chest solidified. This might just work... "Didn't you say Baron Haas would reward anyone who brought you safe to Blessing?"

"Well ... yes. That's what he paid those marshals for. But now that they're all dead, I imagine those funds could go to someone else. To whoever ended up fulfilling the job they were meant to do."

"All right, then. So that means yer worth more alive than dead, Professor. If I killed you now, I'd be throwin' money away, wouldn't I?"

"That's an awful way to put it."

"But it's true, ain't it?"

"So you're saying that if I help you get free, if we both get free of this rock, you'll escort me all the way to Blessing? Safely? Even though you already tried once to rob and shoot me?"

I shrugged as best I could with my arms wrapped backwards around the bulk of that boulder. "What can I say? Circumstances have changed, Professor. Like our friends who left us like this ... I consider myself an opportunist. But *unlike* them, can't say *I* can pass up such an opportunity. Like you said, thousands of dollars is a lot of money. So, yeah, that's what I'm sayin'."

Again, a long stretch of silence.

More vultures arrived on the scene, circlin' over us.

"All right," Professor Morton said at long last.

I breathed a quiet sigh of relief.

"All right, fine, I'll help you. But I want to get free first. And I want to keep hold of your guns for the journey."

A snort of laughter escaped me. "Professor, just how do you expect me to protect you on the way if I don't have my—"

"You can have them back if we run into trouble."

"*If?* No sir, it'll be *when*. And if I have to get 'em off you before I can shoot, it'll be too late to do anythin' about the trouble!"

"Then I suppose we'll just take our chances here."

I ground my teeth and rolled my eyes. Why'd I always have to get stuck with these kinda bull-headed idiots? "Fine," I spat. "Fine. You get free first and hold onto my guns. That agreeable to you?"

"Quite."

"Wonderful. Thank you. Let's get free of these ropes then, yeah?"

"And just how do you plan to do that, anyway?"

VIII

WHEN

I explained to him another of the "generosities" left by Moses and the woman. Maybe they hadn't done it on purpose, but it seemed a pair of professionals like them probably woulda been more thorough with the method of tyin' us if they'd wanted to leave no chance at all of us freein' ourselves. As it was, they'd tied each of us to the boulder with a separate rope, and there was just enough slack in it to let us move around it, if we wanted. Weren't easy, but it could be done.

So I grabbed my rope on either side in my fists to take some pressure off my wrists, and slowly, bit by bit, shuffled myself around the rock until my right hand met with Professor Morton's left. Then I worked at the knot around his left wrist one-handed, pullin' at it with my fingers.

"You really come all the way here from Canada?" I asked. I didn't really care all that much if he had or hadn't, truth be told, but I was hopin' he'd get comfortable enough with me to answer the questions I was gonna ask him later. And also to not leave me here to rot once he got free himself.

"Yes. I really did."

"Huh. So why in the hell are you here, then? And why go to Blessing, of all places?"

"I'm here on business for Her Majesty, as a matter of fact. As I said, I am the Head Curator for the Royal Museum, and Her Majesty is very interested in acquiring some of Baron Haas' antiquities for her collection. I'm here to make an offer on her behalf. Not only that, but the baron himself is quite interested in my appraisal of his most recent finds." He puffed out his chest like he had before in the coach. "My expertise and advice regarding Old World artifacts is sought the world over, you know."

"Uh huh." I didn't really understand what any of that meant.

"You must know that Blessing has one of the best-preserved Old World ruins on this continent?"

"Sure." My left leg—the leg made outta metal itself—twinged, but I ignored it. I didn't much want to talk about Old World ruins, or Old World tech.

"And many of the barons there have pieces that belong in a museum for all to enjoy ... not hidden away in a private collection."

"Whatever you say, Professor." I thought of the giant cannon-gun Charlotte had stolen out of Baron Whittaker's manor and wondered what this man would think of that if he ever saw it. Charlotte had left it with me when she'd headed home, but I didn't use it myself. It was far too obvious of a weapon. And unwieldy. And ... I didn't really understand how to work it, anyway. I mostly just left it packed away in a crate at our camp in Grave Gulch.

Professor Morton turned to look at me as I continued workin' at the knot. "Clearly *you* are not the one interested in that dialed lockbox."

My fingers paused in loosenin' that knot as my focus abruptly sharpened.

"Someone hired you to get it for them, didn't they?"

I squinted at him. "What makes you think that?"

"Young man, I've spent my entire life studying Old World technology. And most of my life around others who are ... shall we say, *highly enthusiastic* about the subject. You strike me as someone who is anything but. And yet, you murdered those marshals and nearly killed me hoping to get that lockbox. So, you must have been hired."

I swallowed hard and met his curious gaze, only one fact out of his whole speech catchin' my attention. "The lockbox with the dials ... it's ... it's Old World?"

The professor nodded. "That's right."

My mouth went dry. So Nine-Fingered Nan *was* interested in Old World tech. And interested enough in this lockbox and whatever was inside it to ignore my metal leg and whoever had given it to me. Fer now. Unless I didn't bring her back that lockbox. Then I guess she was gonna take the next best thing.

"The person who hired you didn't tell you that?"

I cleared my throat and went back to workin' at the knot around his wrist. "No."

"Who was it that hired you, anyway? Was it another one of those barons? You weren't the first one to try and ambush us, you know. Those men who were escorting me said the barons are always trying to murder each other, steal from each other. I thought perhaps they were exaggerating ... but now I'm beginning to think they weren't exaggerating at all."

I shook my head, rememberin' Baron Whittaker's cruelty clear as day. "I don't think they were exaggerating."

"So it *was* another baron who hired you?"

"I didn't say that."

"Really? Who was it, then? I haven't found many in this country very knowledgeable about the Old World except those barons ... and I'm sorry, but if I'm to be frank, even they really aren't much more than thugs dressed up like gentlemen."

"I'd have to agree with you there, Professor."

"Are there other collectors besides them around here somewhere?"

I stopped tuggin' on the knot again and looked at him. "I'm not at liberty to say." That weren't exactly true, I didn't think, but Nan *had* said she'd wanted everyone aboard the coach dead, so I figured that was close enough.

He frowned at me. He was quite pale, and I imagined all this time in the sun was gonna give him a nice burn, seein' as he had no hat. Sweat trickled down his face.

"What's in that lockbox, anyway?" I asked, tryin' to change the direction of the conversation and also sound casual. "Seems a lot of people want it." Nan mighta instructed me not to open it, but she hadn't said anythin' about askin' questions.

He shrugged. "No one knows."

I barked a laugh. "*What*? All these people after a lockbox and no one knows what's inside? That don't make no sense!"

Disappointment etched his sweaty features. He looked pointedly to his wrist, then, the wrist that was still tied.

"Oh, right." I started pullin' at that knot again.

The professor sighed. "The fact that it is an Old World artifact gives the item value in and of itself to some people," he told me then, as if it should have been obvious. "But there is a widely held belief among Old World scholars that that particular lockbox just might contain a key to navigate through the Valley of Lightning safely."

I chuckled again and shook my head. I'd heard of plenty of crazy people over the years believin' this or that would get them through that death-trap ... but they'd all ended up just as dead as all the others who had come before. Once, as a boy, I'd been fascinated by those stories. But now ... now that Mama and Pa had been murdered, our homestead burned down, my sister kidnapped, and every day since become its very own struggle to survive ... it all just seemed a bunch of nonsense.

My concern at Nan's interest in this Old World lockbox eased a bit. If she were fool enough to buy into that madness, too .... let her spend her time chasin' fairy tales. Might keep her occupied while I worked on bringin' down her empire and found my sister.

"Laugh if you want," Professor Morton grumbled. "But if it's true, it will be the greatest discovery of our time."

"Sure," I said. "Sure. And yer tellin' me this super important lockbox ain't on that coach?" I jerked my head in its direction. "Any-where? Not in another hidden compartment or anythin'? 'Cause the person who hired me sure thought it was. And if you were ambushed before, seems they weren't the only one under that impression."

But the professor shook his head vigorously. "Oh no. No, no. Baron Haas knows it's a piece Her Majesty is particularly interested in. And he's a suspicious sort. He wouldn't trust me to ride with it, certainly."

I wanted to laugh again. Of course. I gave a hard tug on the knot in my frustration and the professor gave a cry of joy as his arms dropped, free at last. He pulled his hands into his lap with a wince and rubbed at his wrists.

"Where is it then?" I rasped.

He looked to me sharply, and I realized my tone had not sounded casual at all. And I was still tied to that rock. Couldn't afford to scare him off now...

I swallowed, tried to keep my frustration in check. "Just curious, is all. Wonderin' how so many people could be wrong about its whereabouts."

His eyes narrowed, and he scrambled up to his feet, still rubbin' at his raw wrists. "You still want to find it." He didn't seem too pleased about that fact.

Fer a second I just stared up at him, and the urge to lie warred with the urge to just tell him the truth. Which would he be more inclined to trust, I wondered? I tried to wet my lips, but I was even more thirsty now than I had been before. "Look, Mister ... the person who hired me is just about as bad as those barons. If I don't get that lockbox fer 'em, if I don't try like hell to get it, at least, a lot of people are gonna die. A lot of innocent people. I don't want that to happen, understand? If you know where it is ... I'll escort you to Blessing and all, keep my end of our bargain ... I just need to know where it is."

All right, so I'd given him half the truth and half a lie. Maybe he'd believe 'em both.

"So you can steal it?" His eyes were hard.

"Like I said, Professor ... innocent people will die if I don't get that lockbox. You want that on your conscience?"

His expression darkened. Maybe that had been the wrong thing to say. "Oh no," he said, shakin' his head, his voice harder than it had been all day. "No. You don't put that on me. Innocent people have already died because of that lockbox, and one of them was almost me!" He pointed back at the bodies of the marshals, now attended by several vultures. "*They* were innocent, weren't they? And you didn't seem to have any problems gunning *them* down! So no, you don't put that on me. That's on *you*, young man, and only you. Understand?"

I opened my mouth to protest his accusation, but he didn't give me a chance.

"You want to know where that lockbox is?"

I shut my mouth abruptly. If he was gonna tell me without further promptin' on my part, I'd let him tell me. What he thought me guilty of or not guilty of didn't matter.

"As far as I know, it's already at Baron Haas' estate!"

All the hope in me died at those words.

But the professor didn't seem to notice. "I'm going there to negotiate for its purchase, among other Old World pieces, as I said. That kind of discovery should be handled with care, studied judiciously, treated with the significance it deserves! Not displayed as a show of arrogance and power ... or sold off to the highest bidder who might destroy it and whatever's inside of it in their eagerness to open it!"

Clearly this was a subject he was passionate about, indeed. But all I could think of, sittin' there tied to that boulder in the afternoon desert sun, was how much I didn't want to go back to Blessing. How much I didn't want to ever see any of those barons again.

"You think you'll just stroll on in to his house and steal it out from under his nose?" Professor Morton scoffed and spread his arms, the rope danglin' off his right wrist. "Then be my guest. But I will not be an accomplice to your crimes!"

I blinked up at him. The cloudless blue sky was dazzlin' in the heat. Maybe the sun was gettin' to him. Maybe the sun was gettin' to me. "I never asked you to—"

"You think I believe you won't kill me as soon as I set you free?"

Oh no. No no no...

"You think I believe you'd take me to Blessing and I'd ever get there alive? When you've made it abundantly clear what you'll do in efforts to find that treasure?" He waved again toward the marshals' bodies. "I don't think so, young man. You'd kill me first chance you got, and then kill who knows how many more trying to get that lockbox. And *that's* what I can't have on my conscience." He turned away from me then, and marched over toward the remains of the coach.

"Professor..." It was hard to find the words. The true realization of how dire my situation would be should he leave me here kept chokin' off my air. "Professor ... we had an agreement!"

"One I am quite certain you had no intention of keeping." He bent down to pick up my gun belts, and fear cut through me like a knife.

But the anger came after it, as I watched him buckle my belts around his own waist, drownin' out the fear, leavin' only that buzzin' rage. "Professor. You don't even know how to handle those things. You run into any trouble on the road, you'll be dead before yer hand even starts to drop! You think you can make it to Blessing by yourself? After you've already been ambushed more than once along the way?"

"I'm not going to Blessing," he said calmly. "I'm going to the nearest town. What'd they say it was? Sonoita, I think. Said it was only a few miles further. I'm sure I can manage that far."

My heart beat faster, crawlin' up into my throat. I pulled at the rope still holdin' my arms to that rock, but it wasn't goin' nowhere without outside help.

Professor Morton surveyed the mess of his trunks and wardrobe and sighed, then picked up the canteen left sittin' there and uncapped it, takin' a few big gulps.

I wanted some of that myself, real bad. I tried to swallow, and tried again. "Professor ... all that stuff I told you before, about the mountain cats and the sun and other *less generous* souls wanderin' by ... all that is still true. You leave me here like this and I'm as good as dead."

He turned to look at me, then walked back in my direction, and I hoped against hope he'd had a change of heart. He held the canteen down fer me, and tilted it so I could take a few good gulps of my own.

"I'm not going to leave you here to die," he said.

Relief flooded my limbs. Maybe I wouldn't kill him when I got free, after all.

"I'll get to Sonoita fast as I can, and then I'll send the sheriff back for you. I'll be sure he hurries."

All that hope inside me died again. Shriveled up into somethin' dry and hard and bitter. I stared up at him, wishin' my hands were free so I could wrap 'em around his throat. Pull *my* guns off him and put him out of his misery. I tried to surge to my feet, but I didn't have enough leverage with that rope holdin' me to that rock, and all I managed was a futile little lurch.

Professor Morton jumped back with a yelp, anyway, givin' me a little satisfaction, and then he glared at me in indignation as he recapped the canteen and slung it over his shoulder. He cleared his throat. "Well. Like I said ... you *did* free me, even if I suspect you planned to murder me later, so I won't leave you here to die. I'll send the sheriff back to rescue you."

"Some rescue," I spat, and the burnin' ball of rage and frustration and loathin' livin' in my chest made my voice sound not my own. "They'll hang me fer sure."

He looked down at me in silence fer a long minute, but there was no remorse on his face. No sympathy. Just the flat conviction of a man who believed he was unquestionably in the right. "We all make our own choices in life," he said finally, quietly. "Perhaps you should have considered where yours were taking you before you acted on them."

He turned from me again then, takin' my guns and the water and goin' to retrieve one of the harness horses.

"You don't know nothin' about my choices," I growled after him. "Nothin'!"

He didn't reply, concentratin' on fashionin' some proper reins from the harness lines. Then he gripped fistfuls of the horse's mane and swung up on its back like he'd been doin' such a thing his whole life. So he was better at horses than he was at guns, clearly.

And he really *was* gonna leave me here.

"Professor," I choked out, strainin' to see around the curve of the boulder as he kicked his chosen horse into motion. "Professor! Please —she has my sister!"

That slowed him up. He reined the horse back around to face me.

"She has my sister," I repeated. "And she's gonna sell her off unless I bring her that lockbox."

"Who?"

"Nine-Fingered Nan."

A pause. He walked the horse a little closer.

Yes. That's right. Please come back... I just needed him to get me free of this rock....

"And you think that justifies the murder of countless others?"

The question took me by surprise. Did I?

Yes. No? I suppose I didn't rightly know. I'd never stopped to do the math. I didn't much care fer math. The math didn't matter much anyway when her face kept hauntin' my sleep. When all I could remember was how I'd promised her I'd come back just as soon as I could ... but I hadn't come back soon enough. "She's all I have left," was all I said in answer. Guess he was gettin' the real truth outta me, after all.

Another pause. "Then I suppose you should tell the sheriff about that too when he arrives. Maybe they can do something about it through proper means."

I closed my eyes. Slumped back against the warmth of the rock behind me. *Proper* means? Maybe where he came from the law might do somethin' about every poor kidnapped soul ... but not here. Not here.

Especially not against someone like Nine-Fingered Nan.

"I'll have someone back here as quickly as I can," he said, and then I heard him take off at a gallop. The other two horses followed for a bit, but it didn't matter.

None of it mattered.

If he didn't make it to Sonoita, I was gonna die out here.

If he *did* make it to Sonoita, I was gonna die there.

Weren't a question of *if* anymore. All that uncertainty had turned certain awful quick.

The only question left to answer now was when. *When* was I gonna die ... sooner or later?

I supposed I wouldn't have to wait too long to find out.

IX

SOME LUCK

By the time I heard hoofbeats approachin' again, I didn't care who was comin'.

I didn't know how long it'd been, exactly. Long enough fer Professor Morton to have reached Sonoita, I figured. Long enough fer him to have told his whole story to the town's sheriff. Long enough fer the sheriff to have gathered a few more men and headed out this way. Long enough fer that posse to be arrivin' right about now.

The vultures were still feastin' on the dead, lots more of 'em here now and sometimes fightin' amongst themselves fer the best bits. A few of 'em had a peck or two at me, but I yelled out and kicked at 'em, and that dissuaded 'em from tryin' too hard to eat me.

The sun had moved across that dazzlin' blue sky some, and I'd managed to slide myself into what little bit of shadow the boulder was throwin' out now. It weren't much, but I would take it. I'd take any kinda small mercy at this point.

My shoulders ached, my wrists rubbed raw from the rope, and I was hot and thirsty as hell. I didn't move as the hoofbeats came closer, didn't look up, didn't open my eyes. I just listened and tried to count the number of horses. More than a few, sounded like.

Coulda been the sheriff and some others. Coulda been a gatherin' of vultures of the human variety. Either way I hoped they'd just put me outta my misery quick. I'd had plenty of time now sittin' out here in silence, alone, tied to a rock, thinkin' of all the ways I'd failed my family. All the ways I'd failed Ethelyn.

"Holy Mother," someone breathed as the horses came to a stop next to my boulder.

"Get those buzzards out of here," another voice ordered. "And start gathering up the bodies."

"Yessir."

If they were concerned about the bodies, they surely weren't scavengers themselves. Must be Sonoita's sheriff, then. Guess the professor had made it, after all.

I heard 'em all dismount, several of 'em, and start about their business. The vultures weren't none too happy about it, protestin' loudly as they flew off, reluctant to give up so much meat.

Slow bootsteps approached me then, spurs janglin'. Then someone kicked at my foot, and the voice that had given the orders spoke up again. "Hey. You still alive?"

I sighed and roused myself, openin' my eyes to squint up at him. He was the sheriff, all right. A badge glinted on his chest in the sunlight. Looked all shiny and new. He was an older man, with skin deeply tanned and weathered, but younger than Sheriff Jennings. Had a moustache himself, but also a thick carpet of gray stubble across his jaw. He'd pulled his duster back to show the grip of the revolver at his hip. As if he'd need it with me tied like this, and the professor havin' taken my guns.

"Does it matter?" I asked.

He smiled a little. "Depends. You do all this?" He turned to look out over the bodies and the sideways coach and the trunks with their contents strewn all over the place.

When he turned back toward me, I shook my head. "No, sir."

One of his eyebrows lifted. "That a fact? We got a man back in town who says otherwise."

I grunted. "You believe every story you hear?"

"Only those that sound sensible."

"And that man's story sounded sensible to you?"

He shrugged. "As sensible as a tale of murder and robbery can sound, I suppose."

"I guess he told you I murdered these men?"

"Sure did."

I saw his crew pass behind him, carryin' the dead marshals to the extra horses they'd brought, but I kept my focus on him. They'd sure come prepared. "And what if I told you a different story? If it sounded sensible enough to you, would you consider believin' me instead of him?"

It was always a gamble out here in the Territories if the lawmen would bother to uphold the law. I usually assumed they wouldn't, since that was most often the case, but the fact this sheriff here had gone through all this trouble to retrieve the dead spoke to him havin' a conscience, which meant he weren't likely to be swayed away from proper justice.

But I had to try.

His eyes narrowed. They were an unusual mix of brown and green. "Don't matter what *I* believe, really. You can tell your story to the judge and jury if you want. They'll be the ones you gotta convince."

My eyebrows nearly lifted off my scalp. "A *jury?*"

"Yeah, that's right. You'll get a trial." He glanced at his men, who were tyin' the bodies to saddles now. "Even if you don't deserve it."

"My, my, Sheriff." I clucked my tongue and shook my head again. "A trial! Ain't you all such civilized folk up here."

He turned a glare on me and motioned for two of the posse he'd brought with him. "Cut him free, but then tie his wrists again. In front so he can get on a damn horse." He pulled his pistol and thumbed the hammer back, then aimed it at me fer good measure. "And you," he said, lookin' right at me. "You don't try anything or you'll be gettin' fulla lead instead of gettin' that trial, understand?"

"Sure," I muttered. "I got it."

Maybe he weren't convinced, or maybe his men weren't convinced, because two more of 'em came over and pointed their guns at me, too.

Maybe Professor Morton had talked me up into bein' some terrifyin' monster.

But the truth of it was my arms were mostly numb now from bein' stuck in such an awkward position fer so long. And the days of waitin' on that coach, the nights of little sleep, the hours under the sun, had sapped most my energy. So when they cut me free, I only winced as my hands finally thumped to the ground, and didn't protest at all as one of 'em roughly grabbed my arms and pulled 'em around front to tie my wrists again.

Then they hauled me up to my feet and escorted me toward one of their waitin' horses. I stumbled a bit, stiff from hours of sittin' cramped against a boulder, and struggled some with gettin' the metal leg to cooperate. By the time we reached the horse, though, most the stiffness had worked out, so at least I didn't make a fool of myself as I mounted up under the watchful eye of no less than five guns.

"I got a mule," I told the sheriff as one of his men proceeded to tie my bound wrists to the saddle horn. "Up the hill from the road there." I nodded in that general direction. "And the rest of my supplies with him. Will you get 'em fer me? The mule, at least? Take him to town? He's tied, so ... well, if I don't come back he won't fare too good."

The sheriff holstered his weapon and gave a nod. "Sure." He signaled out two more of his crew. "McGregor, Belmont, you go on up and get that mule."

"Sure thing, Sheriff."

They mounted up and headed off, and then the rest of the posse took to their saddles, goin' in turns so there was always a gun trained on me, just in case. I wondered just what exactly Professor Morton had told 'em about me.

Then we headed off at a trot, my horse ponied behind the sheriff's mount. There were two each of the posse on either side of me, and they led the horses holdin' the bodies behind 'em. The sheriff had come prepared, all right.

We rode in silence. Had to follow the narrow valley for quite a ways before the slope that shouldered the road to our left evened out enough for our horses to go up it without too much trouble. Then we followed the road the rest of the way into town.

We caused quite a commotion as we passed down the main street with our parade of dead, headin' toward the jailhouse. Most the townsfolk stopped their business to stare wide-eyed. Some of 'em started mutterin' and whisperin' to each other. Some of 'em signed themselves and started prayin'. Lots of 'em looked at me in horror ... and anger ... and disgust.

I tried not to look back at 'em. Me bein' tied to this saddle sure made me look guilty, all right, and if that jury was gonna come from these townsfolk, I didn't want to see their judgments already bein' made.

The sheriff instructed his men with the bodies to go on toward the coroner's, and he and I stopped outside the jailhouse. He untied me from the saddle and ordered me to dismount, which I did obediently enough. Still, he took my right bicep in a grip like iron and steered me quickly inside the building, where he showed me to a cell in the back corner.

He pushed me inside and swung the door shut after me. The lock clicked as I turned back around to face him, lookin' over the place. This jailhouse was bigger than the one in Bravebank. Had six cells instead of three, all currently empty except fer mine. And no windows at all. The inside was dim, lit with a couple lanterns. The sheriff's desk was across the way, along the wall opposite the cells ... along the wall lined with bulletins of people's faces.

Wanted posters.

I shifted my eyes away from those quick as the sheriff pulled his knife from his belt and gestured fer me to hold my hands out between the bars. I didn't want him to follow my gaze. Didn't want to remind him to check his collection to see if my mug was up there. I hadn't seen my own face there, yet, but I'd only barely managed a glance at 'em.

He cut the rope from my wrists and I sighed in relief, rubbin' at 'em. "Appreciate it."

"Sure," he said. He tossed the cut rope into the corner and then crossed the room to a sideboard just behind his desk. He grabbed the pitcher sittin' on it and a tin cup and brought it over to me. Poured the cup full and offered it to me.

Water.

I took it and gulped it down, then wiped my mouth with the back of my hand. "Thank you."

"More?"

"Please." I handed the cup back to him, and he refilled it fer me. I drank down three more cups before the thirst finally seemed satisfied.

He took the pitcher then and put it back where it belonged, and I eased myself down onto the bench and thin mattress that served as the cell's cot. I sat back against the wall and watched him. He weren't like other sheriffs I'd met. Even Sheriff Jennings, who claimed to be an honest lawman despite his arrangement with Nine-Fingered Nan, hadn't offered me nothin' when I'd woke up in his jailhouse with my whole body achin'.

"You hungry?" this sheriff asked.

I nearly fell right off the cot in surprise. "Yeah."

"All right, I'll get ya some grub." He headed fer the jailhouse door, but paused with his hand on the doorknob and turned back to me. "Don't think of trying nothing, though. I'll have armed men in here in just a minute to keep an eye on you."

I held up my hands in a gesture of innocence. "I ain't goin' nowhere, Sheriff."

He only grunted and stepped out, and the door shut firmly behind him.

I sank back against the wall and closed my eyes, pullin' my hat down over my face. Behind bars fer the second time in a week ... my luck had never been good, no matter the things people said about me, but it had sure taken an especially bad turn of late.

And this time ... this time I weren't sure if I'd make it out alive. Hell, maybe I *had* been lucky up till now. Maybe this was just what shit luck I'd ever had finally runnin' out. Like I always told Holt, that was the problem with luck. Eventually, it just ran out.

Could I somehow convince a judge and jury I hadn't murdered those marshals? That man called Moses was right—at least I hadn't had that rifle on me when the sheriff had found me. That left the murder weapon missin'. And the professor had taken my pistols, so now I didn't even have those. I was entirely unarmed. And how could an unarmed man rob a stagecoach, or murder anyone?

Of course Professor Morton could tell 'em all what had really happened, but if I could manage to fashion a story just good enough to make that jury start doubtin', start questionin'...

Maybe they wouldn't hang me.

Weren't likely. But maybe.

Maybe my luck hadn't entirely run out just yet.

I heard the door open and shut again and some more bootsteps cross the dusty floor. Musta been those men the sheriff had sent to keep an eye on me. They came over toward my cell, but I didn't bother acknowledgin' 'em.

They didn't seem to care.

"You the one that killed those men?" one of 'em asked.

"Nope," I answered, loud enough to be sure they could hear me from under my hat. The darkness was awful welcomin' after so many hours out in that sun.

There was a grunt. Then the other one said, "Why don't you get that hat off yer face and talk to us proper?"

I sighed. "I've had a long day, boys. I just wanna enjoy some peace and quiet fer a bit. Yeah? Ya mind?"

My answer was the horrific clang of metal bangin' on metal. Sounded like one of 'em was probably draggin' the barrel of his gun across the bars of my cell, back and forth.

Back and forth.

I tried to ignore him, knowin' he was only takin' advantage of my situation, tryin' to rile me up, but it *was* an insufferable racket, and I weren't exactly the most patient sort, even on the days I hadn't spent chasin' down a stagecoach only to get robbed and tied up and betrayed myself.

I put on my best murderous glare and pulled the hat down off my face.

Sure enough, the one of 'em had been pullin' his gun barrel across the bars. He stopped as my eyes met his and grinned at me, showin' off yellowed teeth. "Oh lookie there. That's better, ain't it?" He was about a foot shorter than his companion, but they both looked to be the rougher sort: badly sunburnt, generally unwashed, their clothes thread-bare in places. A far cry from the crew the sheriff had brought with him to retrieve me, in any case.

Maybe all the decent folk were seein' to the final arrangements fer those marshals.

Or too scared of me to come in here, maybe. Depended on what Professor Morton had been tellin' people.

The taller one of the two was squintin' at me, leanin' close to the bars.

I switched my glare to him. "Somethin' wrong with yer eyes there, Mister?"

Both of 'em were close enough I could probably make a grab fer one of their weapons...

"Nah," he said, and stepped back.

All right, maybe I'd go for the other one's gun, then...

"It's just that you look mighty familiar." He pulled a rolled-up piece of paper from out of the back of his belt and unfurled it, lookin' back and forth from it to me.

Uh oh. I considered slappin' my hat back over my face, but, well, that woulda made it even more obvious. So I kept still and tried to look innocent, holdin' his stare.

"Ha!" He said, and he slapped his friend's shoulder and held the poster up in front of his face. "Look! I told ya! That's him, that's gotta be him!"

Fuck.

The shorter one peered down at the paper, then did the same thing as the other fella, glancin' back and forth between it and me. "You sure?"

"A 'course! Lookit! Looks just like him!"

I scowled. It was a fair enough sketch, sure, but sayin' it looked *just like me* was goin' a bit too far. The ears were too big, fer one thing, and the eyes too squinty.

"Shit," the shorter one said. He pushed the poster out of his face to look directly at me again. And his gaze dropped to my left leg. "You gotta metal leg there, pal?"

I scoffed. "A *what*? You been drinkin', friend? Ain't no one got a metal leg."

"All right then, prove it."

"Prove what?"

The shorter one grabbed the poster out of his companion's hand and shook it at me. "Prove you ain't got a left leg made outta metal! Prove you ain't this fella here!" He rolled it out and held it at me so I could see.

It was my poster, all right. This particular one was well-worn, the creases deep, the corners tattered. At least one of these men had been lookin' fer me since that bounty had first dropped, seemed like.

I swallowed and shook my head. "I don't know who that Charles Miller fella is, but he's a swindler. Playin' desperate people fer fools. There ain't no such thing as a man walkin' around on a metal leg." I never woulda believed it myself, not ever, if I hadn't been livin' it.

"Then you'll have no problem showin' us yer leg, will ya?" the taller one put in. "Go on ... just roll up that pant-leg and let's see it."

"No thanks." I settled back against the wall again and pulled my hat back over my face. "I ain't gonna jump through hoops just to prove to a pair of idiots some tall-tale ain't true. Of course it ain't true. It's horseshit to begin with."

"Who ya callin' idiots?" one of 'em snarled.

I lifted the hat just enough to peer out underneath it. "You two. Clearly. And anyone else who believes such nonsense." I dropped the hat. There was silence fer a minute. I thought maybe I'd convinced them. Then there were steps movin' away from my cell, and I hoped they were leavin'.

But no such luck, after all.

The footsteps came back in my direction, accompanied now by the sound of jostlin' keys, and then a click as my cell door unlocked.

I sat up quick at that, and pushed my hat back onto my head just in time to see both of 'em step inside the cell, blockin' the doorway, with their guns drawn. The space was cramped with all three of us in there, and I had to admit they both looked a lot bigger at such close range, made of hardened muscle from some kind of manual labor. Their forearms bulged as they clenched their fists.

Well, I'd managed just fine before against worse, I supposed. Though my middle was still sore from the barfight in Bravebank ... and these were mighty close quarters for a tussle.

"You wanna say that again now that you don't got bars protectin' ya?" the taller one growled.

I held up my hands and stood slowly from the bench. They were less than two feet from my face. And they mighta just handed me my opportunity to get out of here ... if I could get past 'em first. "Now, now, gentlemen. I don't want no trouble."

I kept sayin' that, and yet it didn't seem to make no difference.

"Then stop insultin' us," the shorter one hissed through his teeth, "and show us yer left leg is made outta flesh." He lifted his pistol and thumbed the hammer back. "Else we'll figure it out through *other* means."

"I believe that poster specifically says the reward is only fer the target bein' delivered *alive*," I reminded 'em.

"Who says we're gonna kill ya?" the taller one said. "We're just gonna make you bleed some."

I smiled at him, but was also plannin' out my first move. Their throats were in nice, easy reach. I could probably throat punch 'em both before they got off a shot. "I'd prefer it if you didn't," was all I said.

He leaned forward a bit, comin' nose to nose with me. "Then show us yer leg. 'Fore this gets ugly."

I bit back the urge to tell him it was already ugly enough from where I was standin' and sighed instead. Nodded. "All right. All right. No need fer violence, boys. You wanna see my leg, I'll show you my leg. Fine. But I'm tellin' ya, that's all nonsense."

"Just get on with it already," the shorter one snapped.

I sat back down on the bench and bent over like I was gonna roll up my pant-leg. They both leaned forward eagerly, wantin' to see it up close, I suppose.

It was just what I'd hoped they'd do.

LOST AND FOUND

I sent my right fist into the throat of the shorter one and kicked out with my left foot at the taller one, gettin' him in the knee. The shorter one gagged, droppin' his gun as both hands went to his throat. The taller one yelled somethin' awful and crashed to the floor, flailin' around as he clutched at his leg.

I snatched up the short one's pistol and vaulted over the one on the floor. He reached out fer me as I landed on the side of freedom, and his fingers hooked my ankle just enough to trip me up. I went sprawlin' to the floor myself, but scrambled back to my feet quick.

And got tackled from behind by the short one. All the air went outta me as he landed on me, but I managed to twist around and pistol-whip him across the face even as his hands clawed fer my throat. He sagged sideways, dazed, and I shoved him off me.

I rolled over and pushed to my hands and knees just as the jail-house door opened again, and a third man stepped in. He didn't look familiar, but he weren't no ruffian. His clothes were new and well-tailored, his complexion smooth and dusky brown, and he had a pair of pistols on his hips. But his boots and his coat were dusty. Fer a second we just stared at each other, him and I, while I tried to decide if I wanted to up my murder count.

He decided for me, goin' fer his piece.

I grabbed up my stolen gun, too, but a fist hit me like a brick in the side of the face and sent lights flashin' in front of my eyes. It knocked me spinnin' and then I was flat out on the floor again.

That short bastard pounced on me before I could recover my wits and got his hands around my throat good this time. He started squeezin' like maybe he didn't care about that fifty thousand dollars no more. I gagged and kicked, tryin' to throw him off, but he didn't budge. Blood trickled down his face from where my blow had split the skin of his temple and he looked real, real mad.

"That's enough!" the third man barked, his boomin' voice like thunder through the jailhouse. "Get off him. *Now.* I need him alive."

That loosened the grip around my neck. The man sittin' over me twisted around to look at the one givin' orders. "Too late, friend," he coughed. His voice was all rough and hoarse from that fist I'd landed in his throat. "If yer after that bounty, my brother and I got here first."

The third man strode across the jailhouse and leveled his drawn pistol at the short man's head. "Then it looks to me like you can't read. Mr. Miller wants him *alive*."

The hands tightened again, chokin' off my air, and I tried to dig my fingers down under 'em to loosen the grip. "I ain't gonna kill him," the man chokin' me growled, but I didn't much believe him at this rate. "Just gonna hurt him. I think he broke my brother's leg!"

"That's too bad," the third man said, though his tone weren't sympathetic. "But I suppose that's what you get for openin' his cell. I'll say it one more time, *friend*. Let go of his neck. And get off him."

Through the rushin' in my ears I heard the click of the hammer goin' back.

The short man scowled somethin' terrible and gave my throat one more squeeze I thought would crush my windpipe, but then he released me and rolled off, gettin' to his feet to face the stranger with balled fists.

I coughed and choked and rolled onto my side, gulpin' air greedily and wonderin' why so many people seemed to have a problem with me breathin'.

"That's better," the third man said, and he kicked the gun lyin' on the floor over into the far corner. Well outta my reach. Well outta reach of the brothers.

"We found him first!" the taller brother yelled from where he laid in the cell's doorway.

"Looks to me like you were tryin' to lose him," the stranger drawled.

The taller brother's face reddened, and he reached out fer his own gun, but the third man had his second pistol out in a second, and his shot made my ears ring. The taller brother yelped as the bullet buried itself into the floorboards just short of his hand.

"Why don't you just leave that?" the stranger said. "Go get that leg looked at. Go on." His dark gaze flicked from one brother to the other, and he emphasized his instructions with the barrels of his guns, flickin' 'em toward the door, which still stood open.

I pushed myself up sittin' and rubbed at my achin' throat. "No need fer all this fightin', gents," I coughed. "That ain't even me on that poster. Yer goin' through an awful lot of trouble fer nothin'."

"Sure," the third man said. "Hear that, boys? He ain't even that fella on the poster. So you can go on home now. Let me sort this out."

The short one's face went pale all of a sudden, all the anger meltin' away. "Wait ... are you ... you that bounty hunter? Duster, is it?"

I looked up at that man myself, then, just in time to see him smile in a way that didn't reach his eyes. I'd never heard of a bounty hunter called Duster, but it was clear these two brothers had. And apparently he had a reputation. If I managed to get out of this new predicament alive, I'd have to educate myself. There were plenty of bounties out fer me floatin' around the Territories ... and if there was a bounty hunter good enough to have a reputation out here, too, I needed to know about him.

I needed to know *a lot* about him.

He held his pistols aimed at the brothers, one fer each of 'em. "That's me all right."

The shorter brother backed away slowly, but the anger came back to his face. "Look, Mister ... we were here first. Don't matter who you are, that bounty is ours by rights."

The man called Duster shrugged. "Only if you can deliver this outlaw to Mr. Miller ... and it don't seem that was goin' very well for you boys. But I'll tell you what. Why don't we settle this outside in the street at twenty paces? Last one standin' gets to take him in?"

I lifted my brows. Damn, this Duster fella was serious. I eyed the gun in the corner. Could I possibly edge over to it while they were all conversatin'?

The two brothers had both gone pale now. The shorter one glanced to the one on the floor. Then he swallowed visibly and went to help the taller one to his feet. "He may not even be the fella on the poster," he muttered.

"That's right," I said. "I told ya, I ain't that man. All this trouble fer nothin'."

"You shut up," Duster snapped, "and don't even think about goin' fer that gun." He lowered one of his pistols toward me and I frowned. Had I been that obvious? But he kept his eyes on the two brothers. "So? What'll it be, boys?"

"I'm takin' my brother to the doc," the shorter one scowled. His eyes blazed hatred as he glared at the bounty hunter. "But don't think we're done here."

"I should hope we ain't," Duster quipped.

The brothers limped away like kicked dogs, tossin' hooded glares over their shoulders as they left the jailhouse.

They passed the sheriff as they went out, who stepped inside quick, a bowl in one hand and his gun in the other. He took in the sight of my open cell door and me on the floor and the man standin' over me with guns drawn, but then, to my surprise, holstered his weapon. "What the blazes happened in here?" he demanded.

The man called Duster put away his right gun and reached down to grab my arm and pull me to my feet. "Greed makes some people stupid," he said. He nodded back to the sheriff. "Shut the door, would you?"

The sheriff did so, and Duster dragged me back into my cell and shoved me down onto the bench. I opened my mouth to protest his manhandlin', but that's when he drew his knife and slashed it downward at my left leg, so fast I didn't have time to react.

"Hey!" the sheriff barked, clearly as surprised as me.

But then that blade was at my throat, and instead of comin' up to my feet and punchin' that Duster fella right in the chin like I'd been plannin', I only froze, still sittin' on the bench, glarin' at him eye-to-eye.

He gave me one of those cheerless smiles. "Careful, Delano. I'd like you to stay alive probably as much as you'd like to stay alive."

Alarm went through me at the mention of my name, and his smile widened. "That's right. I know who you are." He straightened, but kept the knife at my throat. Glanced down to my left leg and the slash he'd made in my pants, right over my shin. "Well, would you look at that? No blood."

"Duster," the sheriff said, "you better tell me what the hell is going on here or I'm locking you up too, understand?"

"Sure thing, Sheriff." The man called Duster withdrew his knife and sheathed it, but kept his left pistol trained on me while he backed out of my cell. Then he swung the barred door shut and locked it, tossin' the key ring to the sheriff, who caught it mid-air.

I gave 'em both my best glare, but I didn't like the way things were shapin' up here. Not at all. My heart beat too fast, too hard, and I'd lost my appetite. The sheriff slid the bowl of stew through the small openin' in the bottom of the cell door, anyway, givin' me a curious look, but I ignored both it and the food.

He turned to the bounty hunter as he stood, who had gone over to the sideboard and poured two glasses of whiskey. Duster held one out to the sheriff as the older man crossed the room.

"All right," the sheriff growled as he took a glass. "Start talking."

"Came out here to start askin' some questions and caught sight of you paradin' down the street with a mighty familiar face in tow," Duster said. "You found a real prize there, Sheriff." He threw back his whiskey and nodded toward me.

Clearly these two knew each other. Clearly they had some kinda history. Great.

The sheriff glanced over at me, then downed his own whiskey and poured them both another glass. "That so? He worth something?"

"You could say that." Duster reached into the inside pocket of his coat and pulled out a whole stack of folded papers. He set 'em on the corner of the sideboard and pulled 'em off one by one, unfoldin' 'em and layin' 'em out in front of the sheriff as he explained. "This one's got posters in several states. All the way from Alabama to Dakota. Everything from murder and robbery to cattle rustling."

The sheriff perused the stack of posters, then glanced over his shoulder at me and lifted an eyebrow. "Looks like you've been mighty busy—" he checked the topmost poster—"Mr. Delano. You still wanna tell me you didn't kill those marshals?"

I slumped back on the bench and crossed my arms. So this Duster fella was a professional, trekkin' across the whole country lookin' fer the next face that might bring him his next payday. Well, that didn't mean I was gonna freely admit to another crime. "I didn't," I insisted.

Duster actually laughed. He shook his head and threw back his second whiskey. "I've had all these for awhile," he waved his hand at my stack of bulletins, "but there's been worse folks out there worth more money. However ... I happened to come across *this* one the other day." He set one last poster atop the stack. "Caught my attention right quick. Not many folk out there worth *that* much, Mr. Delano. Not no one, in fact."

The sheriff squinted down at it, then muttered a curse. "*Fifty thousand?*"

"That's right," Duster said. He started foldin' up all the posters again. "And I aim to collect."

"There ain't no name on *that* poster," I reminded 'em both.

Duster turned to smile at me. "There sure ain't. But it sure looks like you ... and coincidentally, you got a left leg that don't bleed when cut. I ain't never found a leg made out of flesh that don't bleed when it's cut."

The sheriff stared at me like maybe he'd seen a ghost, then threw back his own second whiskey. When he spoke again, his voice was rough. "You're ... you're telling me he's actually got a leg made out of metal?"

"That's what I'm telling you," Duster said.

The sheriff poured himself a third whiskey, and his hand shook, just a bit. "That's ... that's something I coulda done without knowing. Look, I'm real sorry, Duster, but I can't let you take him. Metal leg or not."

The bounty hunter swung around to face the sheriff, the smug expression on his face wipin' clean off. "What now?"

I straightened on the bench and unfolded my arms, though there surely weren't nothin' I could do from inside this cell. But I hadn't been expectin' this turn of events, fer certain.

Sonoita's sheriff straightened from the sideboard and cleared his throat. He was several inches shorter than Duster, but he stood his ground, anyway, and I saw he'd flicked back his coat to show the grip of his revolver again. "I can't let you take him."

Duster drew himself up, too, but didn't draw his weapons. "And why the hell not?"

"He committed murder in *my* jurisdiction—"

"Allegedly," I grumbled, but they both ignored me.

"And *I* got him. He's here, in *my* jailhouse. I got to prosecute him here, for the crimes committed in my town. Whatever he did anywhere else ain't my concern. You understand."

The man called Duster drummed his fingers against the top of the sideboard. "Prosecute? Damn it all, Longley ... you still insisting on holding those trials?"

Least I weren't the only one thinkin' this sheriff were out of his mind fer such a thing.

"That's right," Longley said, soundin' defensive. "I've already sent someone out to fetch the judge. This man will be tried for murder here, in Sonoita. And if he's found guilty, then he'll be hanged here. In Sonoita."

I swallowed despite myself. I could almost feel that noose around my neck already.

Duster let out a dry chuckle and shook his head, then grabbed up the whiskey bottle and took a swig direct. "God damn, Longley. You sure don't make my job easy. So you're tellin' me you're gonna take that *fifty thousand dollars* right outta my hand ... you're gonna pass up splittin' it with me, even ... you're gonna say *fuck you* to Charles Miller ... just so you can pretend there's some semblance of civilization out here in the Territories?"

"Somebody's got to try and bring it out here, don't they?" Longley countered. "Might as well be me."

Duster muttered more profanities and slammed the whiskey bottle back to the countertop. "Damn fool is what you are," he scowled. "And you're gonna end up a dead damned fool, too, if you ain't careful. Don't you know who Charles Miller is?"

The sheriff shrugged. "Sure. But the only reason those damned barons got so much influence in the first place is because we let them. 'Bout damned time someone stands up to them."

The look on my face just then musta mirrored Duster's. We both looked at Sheriff Longley in disbelief, highly skeptical that he really had any good idea of what exactly it might mean to "stand up" to one of those barons. I'd tried it, indirectly, even, and it hadn't turned out so good.

I couldn't imagine what might happen if a person tried to do so more directly. Not unless they had a whole army at their disposal, maybe. And I didn't see no army at Sheriff Longley's disposal. I only saw one old man who liked the idea of tamin' the wilds of the west.

A damned fool old man, just like Duster had said.

Before the bounty hunter could manage to explain to the sheriff just what a terrible idea that was, Longley spoke up again. "And anyway, Mr. Miller ain't even a baron by rights. Ain't he just a bastard? They got what, dozens of those running around out here between all of them? Hard to keep track of them all."

I frowned at the mention of a bastard and remembered Charlotte sayin' Baron Whittaker had a harem. How many children did he have, exactly? And how many of 'em might be considered legitimate or illegitimate? I also remembered how Baron Whittaker himself had told me I should have killed him first thing, and all the rest of his family, too. But if he had dozens of children around these parts, and bastard children to boot, that seemed just about as possible as diggin' out a colony of fire ants without gettin' stung.

"Yeah," Duster said. "He's a bastard, all right. In more ways than one. He's even crazier than his father, if you ask me. Awful bitter about bein' cut off from the family fortune and all. Likes to take it out on other people."

Sheriff Longley picked up his third whiskey. "That so? If he don't have access to the family fortune, how's he fronting this bounty?"

Duster shrugged. "Guess he got backed by some of the other family members. But trust me, he's the one drivin' for Mr. Delano, there. And you don't want to get on his bad side."

Longley tossed back his drink and set down the glass with a heavy *thunk*. "That's just too bad. Civilization's got to start somewhere, Duster. I'm keeping Mr. Delano here, and he's gonna have a trial here, and that's the end of it. Got it?"

Duster stared at the lawman fer a good long minute, and I braced myself fer a shootout.

Honestly, I was rootin' fer the sheriff at this point. A trial woulda given me at least some kinda chance at goin' free, however small. And even if I ended up swingin', that sounded much preferable to meetin' any of Baron Whittaker's family, legitimate or otherwise.

But then, at last, Duster exhaled a long, hissin' breath, and his shoulders sagged. "All right. All right, Longley, fine." He rubbed at his face, like all of this was suddenly so exhaustin'.

I rolled my eyes. Surely his day hadn't been nearly as awful as my own.

"Have it your way," he said. "But if your jury sets him free, he's mine. Agreed?"

The sheriff pulled the whiskey bottle from the bounty hunter's grip and poured them both yet another shot. Then he held up his freshly filled glass, and Duster lifted his in turn. "Agreed," he said.

They made a toast to my fate, sealed either way now, like it was nothin' more than another business transaction, and all I could do was look on. Helpless.

Guess what little luck I'd had was up, after all.

I groaned and dropped my head into my hands, scrubbin' my palms over my eyes.

"But look," Duster said then, "if you're gonna insist on keeping him here for a trial, you'd better get it done just as soon as you can—"

"Judge can be here in a week," Longley said.

"—and you'd better keep him under heavy guard until it happens." Duster jabbed a finger toward me. "And only by those you *really* trust, Longley. Like I said, greed makes people stupid. There were two idiots in here who nearly let him go when I first came in. They were after that bounty, too."

The sheriff spat a string of curses. "So much for my volunteers," he muttered.

"If it's gonna be a week till the judge arrives, you need to keep him in here, unseen as much as possible, and don't go around talkin' about who he is. Keep it all as quiet as you can manage. That bounty's high enough you'll have *everyone* goin' after it. And I've heard some other things circulating recently."

Sheriff Longley let out a frustrated growl, then left the sideboard with the whiskey bottle and walked over to his desk, where he collapsed heavily into his chair. "Let me guess, more good news?"

"Some folk are sayin' Mr. Delano here is a demon."

The sheriff barked laughter at that, shakin' his head. He pinched the bridge of his nose and squeezed his eyes shut, then snapped them open again, lookin' over at me. "Well? What do you think of that, Mr. Delano? You some kind of demon?"

I raised my head and lifted my eyebrows, sittin' back on the bench again. This was news to me, but I was already wonderin' if I could somehow take advantage of it. "Not that I know of, sir."

Sheriff Longley gave a snort and took a good long swig out of the whiskey bottle.

Duster crossed the room to stand in front of the desk, leanin' forward over it. "You know how those people get," he said, voice pitched low so I could hardly hear him.

"Sure," the sheriff scowled.

"His metal leg has them all up in arms."

"That's ... ridiculous," the sheriff spluttered. "No one should take that claim as serious without seeing it for themselves!" His gaze flicked up to Duster, then shifted back to me, and that look went over his face again, the one like he might have seen a ghost. He swallowed, and I got the sense that somewhere in his head he might be entertainin' the idea that I *was* some kind of demon.

On account of my metal leg, maybe.

Funny how that whole stack of posters hadn't seemed to convince him of such a thing. But a leg made outta metal ... well now *that* he found downright unsettlin'.

He cleared his throat and turned back to the bounty hunter. "So what you're telling me is that I gotta guard this man against greedy idiots *and* the devoutly religious, both."

"That's right. If you want your trial." Duster spread his arms to the side. "Unless, of course, you'd like to just hand him over to me. Make him my problem." His grin flashed white teeth.

But the sheriff was not amused. He narrowed a glare up at Duster, then slammed the whiskey bottle onto his desk and stood fast from his chair. "Damn it all to Hell. You stay here and watch him. Don't let anyone in here till I get back. I'm going to go round up more *trustworthy* men." He turned toward me as he stomped toward the door. "And you. You'd better eat that stew before it gets cold. It's gonna be a long week."

XI

TROUBLE

Turned out bein' locked up was all kinds of borin'.

At this rate it was gonna be a long week, all right.

Least I weren't the only one stuck here against my will. Turned out that good-fer-nothin' Professor Morton was still in town, and it seemed the sheriff weren't gonna let him leave until after my trial, bein' that he was the only key witness and all. He weren't locked up in a cell, no, but the sheriff had assigned some men to watch him, to be sure he wouldn't go nowhere without permission. And apparently the professor was real sore about it, yellin' about how he worked for Her Majesty the Queen and had important business to see to that he couldn't be late fer. It was the best news I'd heard all day, and I had a good laugh at his expense.

I hoped he *would* miss out on his *important business*. I'd had important business, too, damn it all, business a lot more important than acquirin' some rusted old relics fer a monarch, and he'd sure put a wrench into my plans good.

Sheriff Longley had rounded up lots more people, sure enough, men and women both, and I hoped they were trustworthy. There was always a few of 'em inside the jailhouse with me, and he posted more of 'em outside around the building. The bounty hunter called Duster took on a few shifts, but the sheriff insisted on takin' point himself that first night.

I'd managed to choke down the stew ... it weren't a bad stew, it's just that I weren't much in the mood fer eatin' anymore. But I managed it, and later that evening the sheriff brought me another plate of roast chicken and greens, and I managed to eat that, too. He even passed me a cup of whiskey, though he eyed me in a suspicious way as he did so, like maybe he thought I was gonna use some kind of demon magic to spring myself from my cell.

If only I had such magic.

But I took the whiskey with a nod of thanks. Maybe this town weren't really so bad.

I didn't sleep much, though, on account of several factors. Mostly I weren't convinced Sheriff Longley's new crew were as honest as he thought they were. I kept expectin' one of 'em to try and break me out and take me to Mr. Miller. Or I expected Duster to try it, maybe when his good friend the sheriff fell asleep.

But he didn't.

And neither did any of the others.

There was also the troublin' thought that I wouldn't get out of this one, no matter which way the trial went. If I even made it to the trial at all. Longley said the judge was supposed to be here in a week ... but that was a long time fer me to be trapped here like a sittin' duck, waitin' fer greedy folk to make their move.

Holt was way back in Bravebank, or Grave Gulch by now, most like, or maybe wherever that bank was he'd wanted to rob. He didn't know where I was ... probably didn't even care. Charlotte was nearly a whole country away, but I didn't want her here anyway, certainly. I didn't want to chance her gettin' mixed up with any violent idiots or devoutly religious types. And I really didn't want her to see that stack of posters featurin' my face. Didn't want her to see all those bad things I'd done.

Let her go on thinkin' I was a good person.

It was a small comfort I could take, lyin' there on that bench and starin' at the flickerin' shadows of the lantern light on the ceilin'. A small comfort to know she didn't know the whole truth of it. That she only knew I was tryin' to free my sister, and didn't know any of the other things I'd done to get this far.

But then ... this Mr. Miller fella could have been after her, too. I needed to send that message. To warn her. That worry kept me up most the night, tossin' and turnin', that and wonderin' what would become of Ethelyn if I didn't get back to Nine-Fingered Nan.

She'd be sold off to who knew where.

She'd think I'd abandoned her. Left her to that horrible fate.

The agony of it ate me up from the inside, and what little sleep I did get only brought me bad dreams.

In the mornin', bleary eyed and groggy, I asked Sheriff Longley to send a telegram to Charlotte fer me. I'd looked over all those bulletins on his wall durin' the long hours of the night, and I didn't see her up there. It was another small comfort I could take from this whole nightmarish situation, and I'd take whatever I could get.

This bull-headed fool of a man who'd rather hold a trial than take half of a fifty thousand dollar bounty was probably the most honest person I'd ever met, except fer my own mama, of course, and maybe Charlotte herself, so I figured he'd be my best chance at gettin' the warnin' out. I figured he'd relay my message to the telegram operator without readin' it, himself. Though I supposed even if he did read it, it wouldn't much matter. He'd already promised me a trial ... was riskin' his own life to hold it, and had already said whatever I'd done in other places didn't matter to him.

Even still, I tried to be vague in the wordin', but get the meanin' across. And the urgency. I wrote it out on a scrap of paper the sheriff provided me, then folded it up nice and tight and handed it to him through the bars. He nodded as he took it from me and tucked it into his shirt pocket.

He left right then to get it sent off, leavin' me under the watchful eye of some of his other people.

I sat back down on the bench and sighed. Well, that was Charlotte taken care of best I could. And the sheriff had told me last night his men had retrieved my mule and my supplies, and settled Joe into the livery and kept my stuff safe. Fer now. Till it was decided what was gonna happen to me.

Then they'd probably auction it all off, includin' Joe.

Maybe I shouldn't have named him, after all.

Least he weren't gonna get shot, I supposed. He'd go on to be useful to someone else.

Which was more than I could say fer myself. I stretched out on the bench and resumed my starin' blankly at the ceilin', turnin' over the whole of my life again and again in my mind.

Lots of regrets, there. Not much I was proud of.

If only I'd managed to find Ethelyn ... all of it might have been worth it.

The day passed slow, with me takin' stock of all my sins, and workin' on the story I was gonna tell that jury. I dozed on and off a few times despite myself, but everything stayed quiet. I started to wonder if maybe that Duster fella had been exaggeratin' in an attempt to convince the sheriff to hand me over.

But it turned out he weren't.

Trouble came on the second night.

And it started with a fire.

All the shoutin' made me sit up, lookin' in question to those in the jailhouse with me. They'd set up a little table along the back wall and were deep into a game of poker, but they abandoned the cards right quick and readied their weapons at the sound of the ruckus.

There weren't no windows, so we couldn't see nothin'. But one of 'em went to the door and opened it a crack, peerin' out. Duster had left a few hours ago, claimin' he was off to the saloon and the brothel, but Sheriff Longley was still here. He'd been readin' the paper with his boots propped up on his desk, but dropped 'em to the floor at the commotion and looked to the man at the door, too.

A gunshot rang out on the street, and the man at the door jerked back, blood flingin' across the walls. He sprawled to the floor, a hole through his head.

Then the outside erupted into a whole hail of gunfire, and I guessed it was all those people the sheriff had recruited to guard me goin' after whoever was tryin' to spring me.

I came up to my feet along with the sheriff, who ran at the door and shouldered into it just as someone on the other side tried to open it. It slammed shut again, and he dropped the bar across it to lock it good.

The other men and women in the jailhouse hurried to take up defensive positions, all aimin' at the door.

That's when the back wall of the jailhouse exploded.

The force of it threw me back into the corner of my cell and then I crumpled to the floor, ears ringin' and coughin' in the haze of dust that billowed out from the hole. Half the lanterns in the place had been blown out or blown up, and the shapes of three men stepped through the resultin' gloom. The muzzle flashes of their guns lit up their eyes, their hat brims, the bandanas coverin' the lower half of their faces.

Those in the jailhouse guardin' me—those not killed or knocked unconscious by the blast—scrambled to return fire. But they didn't stand much chance in all the confusion.

I stayed on the floor with my hands coverin' my head, deafened by the dynamite and all the shootin'. Saw my hat lyin' there only a foot away, all covered in dust with its new bullet hole curtesy of Professor Morton, and snatched it up, stickin' it back where it belonged.

The shootin' stopped.

My ears were still ringin', but I risked a glance upward to see who'd won.

Someone was stickin' a key into my cell door. And it weren't the sheriff.

I hadn't seen what had happened to Sheriff Longley, but there was a part of me that hoped he was still alive, somehow.

Another shadowed person came up to my bars, and he pulled down his bandana as he glared at me. I only caught a glimpse of his face in what weak lantern light was left, but it was enough to recognize him.

The shorter brother.

Certainly not a person I wanted to see right now. He grinned down at me, teeth gleamin' in the dim lantern's glow.

The other fella yanked open my cell door and stepped aside, and I jumped to my feet in a hurry, plannin' to make a run fer it. Or a fight fer it. If they thought they were draggin' me off to that Mr. Miller easy, I was gonna change their mind right quick.

I charged at the brother, but then somethin' bright and blue flared in the darkness, and it hit me in the chest.

My whole body seized, my teeth snappin' together as I crashed back to the floor. It was a sharp, hot, clenchin' pain, everywhere, takin' away all my breath. The place where the flesh of my thigh met my metal leg burned like a ring of fire eatin' at my skin, but I couldn't scream. My mouth was locked shut, my lungs crushed.

Then it was gone.

I gasped, relaxed, saggin' into the floor. Hands grabbed me, rolled me over onto my stomach, and yanked my arms behind my back. I heard the clink of metal, felt the cold touch of iron against my wrists. If I was gonna get out of this, it had to be now.

My muscles were still half-numb, but somehow I managed to twist myself around sideways, yankin' my wrists out of the one man's grip. The manacles clattered to the floor and he swore, and I kicked upward with my metal foot as he was bent over and caught him right in the face.

There was a crunch and he staggered backward with a cry, hands over his face and blood seepin' through his bandana.

The other masked man gave a yell and brought up his gun as I rolled to my feet, but then that blue light flared again and I finally recognized what it was: a cattle prod. Pa had had one of those to help move the cattle sometimes. The shorter brother jabbed it at his partner, sendin' *him* down to the floor this time. "Don't shoot him, you idiot!" he snapped.

I took the chance and charged him again, and he didn't have time to swing that rod back around before I crashed into him. It flew out of his hand and bounced across the darkened room as he hit the ground, but the hotshot didn't concern me.

I only wanted his gun.

I grabbed it out of his holster just as he seemed to realize my intentions. His fist cracked into my face and I saw stars again, but rolled off him with the momentum of the blow and came back up to my feet. I staggered, head spinnin' as I tried to orient myself. Goddamn, that man could throw a punch, all right.

He and the man he'd zapped both scrambled to their feet, and out of the gloom I saw the third man had recovered himself enough to come lurchin' at me, eyes waterin' somethin' fierce. He had his gun in-hand, bringin' it upward.

I fired three times, the muzzle flash searin' my vision.

Everything still sounded like it was comin' from underwater, but I heard three vague thumps and blinked. It took me a minute to realize those men weren't comin' at me no more. To realize nothin' in that jailhouse was movin' no more.

'Cept me.

Three good shots, and they were all dead.

I stumbled over to the corner of the sheriff's desk and sank down onto it, feelin' light-headed and dazed. But I didn't have time fer this. Didn't have time to recover my wits. There was still shoutin' outside, that fire down the street still ragin'. But it wouldn't last forever. And I didn't think all the men and women the sheriff had recruited to guard me had been killed by these three men ... didn't know if these three were the only ones involved in this scheme, neither.

And Duster was still out there. Wouldn't be long before more people turned their attention to what was happenin' at the jailhouse, and I needed to be gone long before that.

I shoved myself off the desk and unbuckled the nearest man's gun belt, cinchin' it around my own waist, though I kept that brother's gun, too, and tucked it into my waistband. Then I grabbed an unbroken whiskey bottle from the floor—it'd been knocked from the sheriff's sideboard by the blast—and moved fer the hole in the wall. I glanced back as I stepped through it, surveyin' the bodies, and caught a glimpse of the sheriff's star shinin' dully in the remainin' light.

Fer a second, I hesitated.

But then I gritted my teeth and went on through the hole and out into the night. He mighta been a fair and honest man, but that still meant he'd have been happy to see me hang. And I didn't have time fer that.

I still had work to do.

There was an old buckboard wagon waitin' out back of the jail-house, probably what they'd been meanin' to transport me to Mr. Miller in, and a few more dead bodies. Looked like most of those who'd been set up out here to guard me had gone to help put out that fire, though. And the rest shot down.

Didn't see anyone else out here left alive to take me to Miller, either, so I figured the three who had made it inside musta been the only ones to survive the part of Longley's crew who'd stayed behind.

I stepped over 'em all quickly, and left the wagon. It was too big and too noisy fer my purposes.

I couldn't risk goin' to get Joe, neither, nor any of my stuff.

I crept around back of the buildings, movin' away from the glow of the fire and all the commotion around it, stickin' to the shadows, till I reached one of the saloons. There were several horses hitched out front, and all those sober enough to notice a stolen horse were preoccupied by the flames roarin' down the street, most runnin' to help with the water brigade.

I chose the horse nearest to me, a short bay with a scruffy coat, and stuck the bottle of whiskey into one of its saddlebags. Then I swung up into the saddle with only a little wince. That spot on my left thigh where the metal and flesh met still stung, and my jaw ached from the force of that brother's blow, but the rest of me felt all right, considerin'. I urged the horse into a trot and went off down the street, reinin' it around the nearest corner before headin' outta that town at a canter.

We rode off into the night, but I had no idea where I was goin'.

All I knew was that I needed to put as much distance between me and Sonoita as I could, as quick as I could. Unfortunately, the land around here didn't offer much in the way of cover. Weren't many good spots to hunker down and lay low. And as soon as that fire was put out, and the townsfolk realized what'd happened at the jailhouse ... what'd happened to their sheriff ... I imagined they'd be real angry. I imagined they'd blame me fer all of it.

I imagined they'd send out search parties and a big ol' posse.

I imagined Duster would be ridin' out soon, too, and awful keen on findin' me himself.

So I kept that bay horse at a canter longer than I should have, till he was lathered up and blowin' hard, and then I only let him walk with great reluctance. And I realized I'd been headin' south without even really thinkin' about it.

South toward Blessing.

South toward Bravebank.

But I couldn't go back to Bravebank yet. I couldn't go crawlin' back there to Nan like a dog with my tail tucked between my legs, empty handed and beggin' fer her protection. Just like that first time we'd met, when she'd sent me off into the desert to die, it was clear now she'd given me a task she figured I couldn't survive.

She was probably back at her hide-out now, laughin' about it all. Part of me wondered if she really even wanted the lockbox, or if she just enjoyed makin' threats and settin' tasks to see if I'd jump through her hoops.

A puppet on strings... Was that all I was now? Just like Holt had said?

I sighed heavily and scrubbed a hand over my face. I was too tired to sort any of this. In the end, it didn't matter, anyway. Didn't do no good to ponder any of it, neither. I was gonna jump through Nan's hoops as long as it gave me a chance to free my sister. Long as it bought me time to find her myself, or to buy her back.

And that was that.

So I weren't goin' back to Bravebank without that lockbox.

I wondered if Professor Morton was right about it already bein' at Baron Haas' estate. But if that were the case ... I'd have to go back to Blessing. I'd have to walk right back into that viper's nest. Into the heart of the place I was most wanted right now. Into the home town of Mr. Miller himself, Baron Whittaker's unstable bastard son.

And I'd have to do it all by myself this time. No Holt. No Charlotte.

I twitched the reins, aimin' my tired mount in the general direction of Blessing. I cut across country, stayin' well away from the roads, and didn't dare stop to make any kinda camp. Not that I had any supplies, anyway.

I rode on through the night, keepin' my eyes and ears open fer trouble best I could around the exhaustion steadily buildin' in my mind, and prayed I'd come up with some kinda plan by mornin'.

XII

ON THE SAME SIDE, MAYBE?

I didn't.

I watched the sun come up from atop a small rise to the southwest of the town of Blessing, and still had no idea how in the fuck I was supposed to go in there and find out if Baron Haas had that lockbox.

I'd circled around the town from a distance most the night, mostly to try and keep myself awake in the saddle. And mostly because I was afraid that if I stopped fer too long, someone would find me. That bounty hunter Duster, or someone else from Sonoita. Or maybe just any other folk goin' about their normal business who had just happened to have had a good look at the bounty posters recently and wanted to take their chance on ringin' in a mighty good payday.

Of course, I was armed now, and I'd started makin' a decent reputation fer myself as a gunslinger around these parts, so maybe there wouldn't be as many folk as I feared willin' to risk dyin' to bring me in.

Like Duster had said, though, greed made people stupid. I couldn't afford to lower my guard on account of hopin' folk would know better than to pick a fight with me.

And anyway, I couldn't shoot no one if I were asleep when they found me.

So I tried not to sleep.

I just kept my horse pacin' a real big circle around Blessing, and kept tryin' to think of a plan that wouldn't land me killed or dumped at the feet of Mr. Miller. And I kept lookin' fer a good spot to hide. I was gettin' tired ... real, real tired. I was gonna have to sleep soon.

But all the cover was too close to Blessing fer comfort. Down in the valley by the river, where it was all green and fulla trees. Woulda been a real good spot to hide out. 'Cept I didn't want to get that close.

Which meant I was stuck out here, in the blazin' sun and the rocks and sparse brush and the cacti. None of which woulda done much to hide me and my mount from curious onlookers.

So we stood up there on that ridge, and I looked down at the green of the valley and the bustle of Blessing and the gleam of what remained of those Old World ruins above the surface, and I muttered a lot of foul words. Maybe I *should* just head on back to Bravebank. Maybe I could at least tell Nine-Fingered Nan her contact from up north had been just as fulla horseshit as her man Taggert, and suggest that maybe she be more selective in who she took on as part of her trusted circle. Suggest that maybe if she wanted to send me off on an errand fer her, fine, but she could at least give me good information to do it on.

But then I remembered her threat about takin' my leg. And about findin' out where it had come from. And I remembered Dr. Balogh and the boy Radley and the girl Fanni, who'd been terrified of me, and the doctor's wife Hannah with her ever-present choppin' knife.

No ... if I went back to Nan now, without that lockbox—whether or not she actually wanted it—I had no doubt she wouldn't bother to hear my suggestions, or my excuses. And I had no doubt she'd follow through on her threats.

I sighed and slumped in the saddle. Urged my scruffy stolen horse onward again. I went southward, but I weren't goin' back to Bravebank. I'd head a little further that way, sure, maybe get closer to Nan's circle of influence, where maybe more people hadn't seen that poster of my face worth fifty thousand dollars. I'd dare to venture a little closer to the river then, where I had better cover, and find a spot to get some rest, and maybe hunt somethin'. Even a stringy jackrabbit woulda been a welcome catch at this point.

My stomach was growlin' awful loud now, and all I had was that bottle of whiskey I'd swiped from the sheriff, and some jerky I'd found in these saddlebags.

So I went south, and then I went toward the river, and both the horse and me were mighty happy to finally pass under the shade of those cottonwoods. The horse fell to grazin' almost immediately, and I had to fight him fer every step until I found a suitable place to make my camp. Then I let him drink and graze all he wanted, makin' a picket line to tie him to. I settled into my spot up against a small bluff, back behind some thicket.

It was late afternoon now, and I was still hungry, but I couldn't hold off the sleep no more. The huntin' would have to wait. I dropped down onto the ground, pulled my hat over my face, and let myself slip away.

Voices woke me, and I came up sittin' with strange guns in my hands. I blinked hard in the darkness as I oriented myself. Behind the thicket, against the bluff, near the river. South of Blessing. That's right.

It was night now, and dark under those trees. The moon's light hardly reached me despite bein' almost full, though I could see it up above, turnin' some of the leaves silver. Damn, I'd slept hard. Musta been more tired than I'd thought.

The voices came again and I held my breath, glancin' out through the underbrush toward the horse I'd stolen. He lifted his head and pricked his ears fer a second, but then went right back to grazin'. I exhaled slowly, fer once grateful I hadn't had the chance to get Joe from that livery. He woulda surely called out to these newcomers, whoever they were, and given away my hidin' spot.

This horse didn't seem to care in the least.

But I used his momentary curiosity to help pinpoint where the voices were comin' from. Up above me, atop the bluff I leaned against. I kept still, kept quiet, and listened.

"You gotta piss every goddamn hour, we ain't never gotta get there!" a voice hissed.

"Ah, shuddup," another voice snapped. "You in some kinda hurry?"

"Yeah, matter of fact I am. I'm tired of listenin' to all the cryin' and whinin', and the wagon is startin' to smell."

Cryin' and whinin'? Just what kind of business were these men dealin' in, exactly?

"Just hit 'em a few more times with that rod. That'll shut 'em up."

The first man scoffed. "I'd like to shut 'em all up *permanently*. But then we wouldn't get paid, would we?"

"Guess not." There was a short pause, then, "Ya mind? I'd like to take a piss in peace. Why you followin' a man who's tryin' to take a piss?"

"To press upon you the urgency of our journey," the first man growled. "To make you hurry the fuck up. I want a drink and a goddamned bed. This is the last time we're stoppin' till Blessing, got it?"

The second man only grumbled, and I heard the first stomp off through the undergrowth.

I relaxed a bit, but only a little. So these weren't any kind of bounty hunters. Nor anyone from Sonoita. There *was* a road up there, a ways off, I'd seen it from atop that ridge earlier. It led into Blessing, sure enough, comin' in from the east.

The second man relieved himself, mutterin' and grumblin' the whole time about how he weren't gettin' paid enough to deal with all this shit, then I heard him turn and move away, back toward the road.

I exhaled long and slow, and crept out from behind my thicket. I checked on my horse again, but he weren't payin' me any attention. So I made my way quiet as I could along the bottom of the bluff until it tapered off and I could move up on top of it. I went quicker now, hearin' the second man's footsteps fade, but didn't get too close.

I weren't exactly known fer my stealth, and even if these men weren't bounty hunters, that didn't mean they wouldn't be if they happened to see me and recognize me. So I went from tree to tree, flattenin' myself up against the trunks, until I could just make out the wagon on the road.

As much as I'd been missin' Holt back in Sonoita, now I was glad he weren't here. He'd be complainin' somethin' awful about me comin' to take a look at this wagon. He hated when I got *nosey*, as he called it. Nosey, or playin' Good Samaritan. Or sometimes it was *actin' the hero*. He liked to call it all those things. Said it only got me into trouble.

That coulda been true. Gettin' involved in Charlotte's plight had nearly got me killed, after all.

I mighta done a lot of bad things myself in my life, sure ... but that didn't mean I was gonna turn a blind eye to other atrocities committed out here in the Territories. Even I had my limits. Lines I wouldn't cross.

No matter those lines seemed to be gettin' blurrier of late...

Still, there was somethin' about how these men had been talkin' that had set me on edge.

And now that I could see that wagon, I knew why. It was fulla *people*.

They were crammed in tight, and lots of 'em were cryin' and whinin', all right. The wagon itself looked like one giant cage, and there were six armed and mounted escorts along with it, three on each side. Four men and two women. Every now and then, one of those mounted escorts would stick a prod through the wagon bars, and I saw the familiar blue flare, heard the snap, and someone in the cage would yelp, and the wailin' would escalate.

The man who'd been takin' a piss climbed back up onto the driver's bench.

Anger flooded heat through my blood. My heart quickened, beatin' hard in my ears, and I thumbed my hammers back. They outnumbered me by a lot. But they also didn't know I was here. And it was dark. I could probably shoot down half of 'em before they even figured out what was happenin'—

I heard somethin' sounded like a whisper, and one of the armed escorts on the side facin' me gave a little grunt, then slid off his saddle and thumped to the ground.

Behind the trunk of the tree I was usin' fer cover, I straightened. Squinted at him. *The hell?*

More whispers, and more of the guards on horseback fell off their saddles. Finally, the two on the bench and the two remainin' escorts realized somethin' was goin' on. The driver yelled and slapped the reins, and the two guards fired wildly into the woods on both sides of the road. I ducked back behind my tree as bullets went whizzin' by.

Then ... the shadows beneath the trees around me *moved*.

I swallowed back a yelp and hunkered down. Thought at first I was seein' ghosts, or maybe even demons. Shapes like people formed outta the ground and the trees, black as the night itself, and slid forward toward the wagon.

I stayed behind my cover, not wantin' to risk bein' caught in the hail of bullets, or bein' seen by the movin' shadows ... whatever they were.

The wagon picked up pace, the horses whipped into a frenzy by the driver, but a knot of those shadows surged after it, and the two guards went down next. One of 'em was in a patch of moonlight brighter than the rest, and I saw what looked like the shaft of an arrow go right through his throat and halfway out the other side.

I didn't see what got the other fella, but by the time I looked back to the wagon again, the driver and his pal were dead too, slumped over each other on the bench. And I hadn't heard a single gunshot, hadn't seen a single muzzle flash from the trees.

Despite my initial horror, I stepped out from behind my tree to watch, mouth hangin' open as one of the black shadows caught up to the back of the wagon and leapt up onto it, then scurried over the top of it to drop down into the driver's seat and rein up the horses.

They snorted and pawed and danced around, but more black shadows clustered around them and seemed to be soothin' 'em.

So ... not ghosts, then. Or demons.

"Who are you?" a quiet voice demanded, and I fair near leapt out of my skin. I whirled around to see a person-shaped shadow loomin' right there, right in front of me, and instinctively brought up my guns.

There wasn't a sound—was hardly a flicker of movement—but my left pistol jumped outta my hand like it was alive with the ring of metal strikin' metal, and my right arm got jerked backward and trapped against the tree. I tried to yank it free, but my sleeve was stuck, and stuck good. Just as I was movin' to grab my right pistol with my left hand, that shadow stepped up real close, and the point of a knife pricked the side of my neck.

And there was another blade at my gut, its sharp point bitin' into my skin through my shirt.

I stopped tryin' to reach fer my gun. Stopped movin' at all.

"Shhh," the shadow whispered. "Stay quiet. And drop your piece."

Their hooded head nodded fractionally toward the gun in my right hand. All I could see of 'em was their eyes, glintin' in the dim moonlight. The rest of their face was swathed in black, and their whole body, too. Couldn't tell if it were a man or a woman, but I guessed it was a woman, bein' as they were several inches shorter than me, and their frame lighter than most men.

The knives pokin' at me poked harder. I winced and let go of the pistol, and it thumped into the undergrowth.

Knives. That would explain why I didn't hear no gunshots. This person was also wearin' a bow over their shoulder, and a quiver fulla arrows on their back, though it was all hard to make out, since the weapons were entirely black as well, all of 'em.

They whistled suddenly, sharp and shrill, but kept their eyes and blades on me.

I heard murmurin' from back at the wagon, and the people inside of it were still cryin' and whinin'. They sounded awful scared. I couldn't turn to see what was happenin' over there, though, as I didn't want this person in front of me to decide to slit my throat.

"Who are you?" she demanded again, still in a whisper.

I swallowed. "No one important."

Her eyes narrowed, and her blades pressed a little harder. "What are you doing here?"

"I was just ... camped nearby. Heard a commotion. Came to investigate."

"Investigate. You mean rob?" She said it like she was some kinda lawdog tryin' to get me to confess.

I snorted a laugh despite my situation. "No. But even if I *was* plannin' to rob those men ... you people *murdered* 'em. Which is a good deal worse than robbin'."

The knife in my gut twitched and I sucked in a breath, pretty sure I was bleedin' now.

"Not that I care any," I blurted quickly. "If you—if you wanna know the truth of it, I was thinkin' about murderin' 'em, too. And not to rob 'em. Just took issue with people bein' caged and hit with hotshots is all. So really … don't that make us on the same side? Maybe?"

Unless these shadow folk were plannin' to cart off the wagon-load of people fer themselves. My stomach clenched at the thought. If that were the case, I sorely needed my guns back.

"Are you alone?" was all she said.

That gave me pause. Which answer would let me live, I wondered? Or maybe she planned to murder me no matter what I answered.

Before I could decide on what exactly to say, more black-robed people appeared next to her. And behind her. And all around me. They formed a circle around the tree, watchin' me through the narrow slits of their hoods. They moved under the trees with hardly a sound, and everything on them was black. Made 'em almost impossible to see clearly. But now that they were closer, I noticed they were all heavily armed. No guns, though. Just arrows and knives. Lots and lots of knives, sheathed all over their bodies. Across chests, arms, legs...

Not the big knives, though. The little ones. Throwin' knives.

"Who is this?" one of the new arrivals asked. Sounded like another woman.

"Found him sneaking around," the one holdin' her blades to me said.

"I weren't sneakin'—"

"Watching our business."

"Which matters to me none at all," I reminded her.

"Wait, wait … hold up a minute," another voice spoke up from within the circle. One of the shadows moved, makin' her way through the others till she stood at the front. "I think I might know this cowboy."

I couldn't turn my head to look at her, but I moved my eyes her way. Didn't matter any, though. She was robed in black same as the others. Her voice sounded mildly familiar, but I couldn't place it, and so couldn't be sure if her knowin' me might work for or against me here.

"That so?" the one with the blades on me asked. "Well then ... he trouble or not? Do I cut his throat or let him go?"

The casual way she asked the question made me swallow. My heart quickened again, pulsin' against the point of that knife pressed to my neck. I started makin' plans fer how I was gonna escape this knot of knife-laden shadows should the answer come back unfavorable ... though I suspected I wouldn't get very far before havin' enough blades in me to look like a porcupine.

Didn't mean I wouldn't try.

The woman who had claimed to maybe know me fumbled at her belt, and the rasp of a strikin' match sounded before the little tongue of flame brought a glow of light to all the shadow. She held it up toward my face and I squinted.

And held my breath. Waited fer her answer.

"Hey," said another shadow. Another woman. Were they all women? "I recognize him now. Ain't he the one who—"

"Yeah," the one with the match said slowly. "Yeah, that's him, all right." She shook it out as the flame neared her fingers, and plunged us all into an even deeper darkness than was there before. "He's the one who helped that redhead slave who escaped about a month back. And who wrecked Baron Whittaker's estate."

Numb confusion raced through me even as more murmurs passed around the circle of shadows, and I forgot I'd meant to try and escape myself right about then. Instead I only stood there, frownin' into the dark, tryin' to piece together how she could have known about Charlotte. Baron Whittaker's estate, sure, that was all on that damned wanted poster. But Charlotte ... that didn't make no sense...

The knives pokin' at me withdrew, and I blinked.

Not what I'd been expectin', considerin' most others who knew about the baron's place so far wanted to bring me in fer that fifty thousand dollar reward.

The one who'd recognized me first lit another match and pulled back her hood to reveal familiar features, though the night's darkness deepened the rich sepia tones of her skin. She flashed me a grin. "Well howdy there, Mister," she said. "So nice to see you again."

She looked a lot different than the first time I'd met her, no matter how brief that had been, but now that I could see her face, too, it all came rushin' back to me. "Sally?!"

XIII

FREEDOM FIGHTERS

"That's right." She extinguished her second match, then stepped across me to put one boot up against the tree trunk, bracin' herself to yank out one of the blades that pinned my sleeve to it. She handed it back to its owner, then did the same for the second blade, handin' that over, too.

Then she reached down to pluck my guns up off the ground and gave 'em a little twirl before holdin' 'em out to me, butts-forward.

I took 'em from her, but then just stood there, starin' at her and the rest of the black-clad gang that surrounded us. "That's, uh ... a lot more than seven knives," I husked. She was fair near bristlin' with 'em.

She laughed and gave some kinda signal to the others. They dispersed, gradually, meltin' back into the natural shadows, until only a few remained.

"Sure," Sally said, turnin' back to face me. "I carry seven at the saloon and most everywhere else. It's all I usually need. Except for this business." Vague shiftin' of her silhouette indicated her gesturin'. "Then I usually need a few more."

I shut my mouth with a click. I blinked and then also realized I was still standin' there with my guns in hand. So I stuck 'em back into their holsters and cleared my throat. Looked around at the woods, and saw some of her group had re-materialized back at the wagon. I lifted my fingers to brush at the trickle of blood slidin' down my neck. Those blades had broken the skin, all right. I felt gingerly at the stingin' spot in my middle. Well, it coulda been worse. A whole lot worse. "What ... what exactly *is* this business?" I asked.

To my surprise, she hooked her arm in mine and turned us toward the wagon, then led me in that direction.

"We're in the business of rescue, Mister..." She paused. "Hrm. I don't think I ever got your name."

"You didn't."

"I see. Well that's a shame. I believe we're on the same side, after all. This wagon-load of folk was headed to the new Baron Whittaker's estate. To replace all the slaves you helped set free."

I drew up short, my arm reflexively clampin' down on hers.

"Easy there, cowboy," she drawled. "Don't get your dander up. If we'd wanted that reward, I wouldn't be here strolling through the trees arm-in-arm with you, would I?"

That was true enough, I supposed. I relaxed a little. But then the full meanin' of what she'd said finally registered and a cold dread slithered through my gut. "Wait. The *new* Baron Whittaker?"

She huffed a sigh, and pulled me onward toward the wagon again. "That's right. His eldest son took over the estate. He is now the new Baron Whittaker, picking up where his father left off. Trying to rebuild what you ... destroyed."

I lifted my free hand to rub at my eyes, then pinched the bridge of my nose. "Great. He as *wonderfully pleasant* as his father?"

Sally gave a little grunt. "If you are referring to the former baron's penchant for torture, this new baron seems to be a little saner, truth be told. Certainly better than some of his siblings."

"Like Charles Miller."

"He's probably the worst of them."

I rubbed at my eyes harder.

"Unfortunately," Sally continued, "the new Baron Whittaker still prefers slave labor to mine his ruins. So he's not all that much better than his father. And still leaves us with plenty of rescuing to do."

I opened my eyes and dropped my hand, and we came to a stop at the wagon's side. Sally's pals had unlocked it, helped people climb out of it, and were busy distributin' canteens and some scraps of food to the newly freed folk. There were all kinds of 'em ... young and old, men and women, in varying states of physical condition. My stomach rolled at the sight of all of 'em, then growled at the sight of the food.

I ignored it. "You said all these were meant to replace the ones I freed?" The ones *Charlotte* had freed, in truth. But if she weren't on any posters, I weren't goin' to implicate her, even if Sally and her folk seemed friendly. Couldn't risk word gettin' out, gettin' around. Not if this Charles Miller fella was as bad as he seemed.

The stories about his pa had turned out true enough ... I didn't doubt the stories about the bastard son were similarly accurate.

"Yes."

"So ... the new baron never found the others? They all escaped, free and clear?" Despite all the trouble I'd endured the last few days, all the agony I'd endured at the hands of the old Baron Whittaker, my heart lightened a bit at that thought. Maybe somethin', *somethin'* had finally gone right.

Sally's face sobered somewhat then, and my brief hope faltered. "Well, most of them," she said quietly. "There were some that were re-captured. And some ... *examples* made in the town square." She winced, and again that anger warmed in my belly, flarin' up to burn in my chest.

As much as I never wanted to lay eyes on another of those damned metal barons so long as I lived ... another part of me wanted to ride into Blessing right that moment and burn everything they had to the ground.

Sally turned toward me before I could get words around that anger and took my hands in hers, givin' 'em a squeeze. "But most of them did escape, yes. Free and clear. We helped those of them we found, set them on their way back to wherever they came from, or to start new lives somewhere else."

I looked down at her, strugglin' to comprehend everything she was sayin'. She made it sound like they had a whole operation here. My eyes lifted to look over her shoulders, to the number of black-robed folk goin' about with quick, efficient movements. They ushered those from the wagon off the road, into the trees, and in the dim, dappled moonlight there I saw horses waitin' now where there hadn't been before. I wondered where they'd stashed the animals. Wondered who had gone to retrieve 'em.

They *did* have a whole operation here. That was clear enough. Sally's gang knew what they were doin'. They had a plan, a plan they'd practiced a great number of times, from the looks of it, and they went about it with a unity and precision I hadn't seen many other folk able to execute.

Certainly their plan was a great deal better than mine had been. I hadn't really thought any further ahead than just killin' the drivers and the guards.

Holt was always yellin' at me fer that, too. Not thinkin' my plans all the way through.

"So," I said, shovin' Holt's reprimands outta my head, "that's what you'll do fer these folks, too, then? Help 'em get back home? Or somewhere safe?"

I thought of Ethelyn, then. Like these folks, only worse-off, probably, bein' directly in the clutches of Nine-Fingered Nan. The one person I wanted to free more than any other ... and I couldn't seem to get to her. Couldn't seem to find her...

"Yes," Sally said, turnin' back to watch her people work and pullin' me from my worry. "We may not be able to act so boldly as you did— not yet, anyway—but we do what we can when we can." She extended an arm outward to indicate the wheeled cage. "Like this. We hit their transports as often as we can. Disrupt the trade. Stay a thorn in their side. Rescue as many of these poor souls as can be managed."

My brows lifted. They had a whole operation, all right. And were either very brave or very stupid. Another realization hit me, then.

Freedom fighters.

These were the people Baron Whittaker had thought I was allied with, that night he'd caught me burnin' down his barns. It all made a lot more sense now...

The sound of another wagon approachin' on the road snapped me from my musin's and Sally gave a surprised yelp as I shoved her around behind me and spun to face it, pullin' my right pistol, ready fer it to come around the bend.

"Stop," Sally hissed. She grabbed the wrist of my gun-hand and pushed it downward. "That's *our* wagon."

I glanced to her over my shoulder. "How do you know?"

She pursed her lips. "We have lookouts stationed down the road in both directions. If someone else was coming, we'd have already heard the warning."

"You sure? What if they got ambushed? Overpowered? Gunned down?"

She tilted her head to one side. "You hear any gunfire from down the road lately?"

I frowned. Let my arm drop under the pressure of her grip. "No."

"Then I'd say that's unlikely."

"Better safe than dead," I muttered.

"True enough, Mister." She stepped up beside me and put a hand on one of those throwin' knives tucked into her belt. "Let's be ready, then, but not shoot on sight, yeah?"

"Fair enough," I agreed.

So we waited, side by side, me with my gun and Sally with her knives, alone in the road now. The emptied cage stood open behind us, but all the others had moved into the trees, out of sight.

The second wagon came around the bend at last, a big buckboard pulled by a pair of horses, and Sally gave two high-pitched whistles.

The driver of that wagon gave an answerin' whistle, long and low, and two short trills.

Sally dropped her hand from her knife and put it on my arm. "That's them, all right. They're fine. No ambush."

I shook my head and rolled my eyes. A whole language made of whistles. All right, then. But I waited to holster my iron till the wagon reined up to a stop beside us, and no one tried to shoot us. The others emerged from the trees then, too. The situation was explained to the freed folk: some of 'em would go on horseback, some of 'em would go in the new wagon, all of 'em escorted in some way by a few in the black robes to wherever they wanted to go.

Some of the freed folk nodded and seemed grateful and relieved, but some had been tricked or misled into captivity, and now didn't trust Sally's gang any more than they trusted the bastards who'd gotten 'em into such a predicament. There was some shouted, angry words, and they ran off on their own into the darkness, either on foot or by horseback, but Sally's friends didn't stop them.

I asked Sally if that was a wise idea, but she only shrugged. "We can't force them to stay. They each have to make their own choice. If they want to go it on their own, that's their decision. Some are plenty capable of taking care of themselves."

"And what about those who ain't?"

She shrugged again. "Least we gave them a choice in things, which is more than they had before."

I pondered that as I watched 'em all ride off in different directions, and the wagon disappear on down the road, where I was told it would turn back east again before runnin' too awful close to Blessing.

The bodies of the slavers were dragged away into the underbrush, the wagon with the cage in back was driven off the road and into the trees, and its horses unhitched and led away. And then the night was quiet again, no evidence of what had happened here remainin' except fer a few new blood stains in the dirt.

Only me and Sally were left now. I turned to her and was startled to see her already lookin' at me, and lookin' at me in much the same way she'd looked at me that day I'd first walked into her saloon and taken a stool at her bar.

I shifted under her scrutiny and cleared my throat, hopin' I didn't look quite as much like death as I had that day. "Well?" I ventured. "Ain't you gonna escort anyone to safety?"

She smiled slyly. "Sure. *You*."

I barked a laugh that echoed out into the night. "I beg yer pardon?"

She crossed her arms, and those dark, shinin' eyes of hers ran me up and down again. "What are you doing out here, anyway? The Whittaker family is *furious* about what you did ... and that price on your head is obscene. The town is all up in arms over it. Lots of folk just up and left their professions to go on the hunt for you."

My heart sank right down into the pit of my stomach, and all I could manage was a grunt.

"I would have thought you'd have cleared the area by now. That would have been the wise thing to do. Unless ... you gonna go after another baron? Because I'm not so sure that's a great—"

"No," I blurted. "No. No more barons." Not if I could help it. "It's just ... I got ... I got some other business I need to take care of here before I can go." I didn't exactly want to give her any more specifics. I'd just told her I weren't goin' after another baron, after all. And maybe I wouldn't be. But I *did* need to find out if Baron Haas had that lockbox, or if it were still out there somewhere else.

"Hrm." Her eyes narrowed. "Other business. In Blessing?"

"Unfortunately."

"The very town where your face is right under one of the highest bounties I've ever seen?"

I hissed out a breath through my teeth. "That's right."

"That's risky, Mister. Real risky."

As if I didn't know that already. "And if the business weren't urgent, and important, I wouldn't risk it. But I don't got no choice in this."

"That so?"

"That's so."

She tilted her chin upward, gazin' at me from under long lashes. The moonlight splashed silver across her skeptical expression. "And you think you should just walk right on in to Blessing to carry out this other business of yours?"

I shook my head. "No, ma'am. No I do not."

"All right, so what's your plan, then?"

I looked down to the dusty toes of my worn boots and rubbed at the back of my neck. "I ... well I don't exactly have one yet."

"Sounds to me like you need that escort, then."

That brought my gaze back up to her quick.

"You got a ride around here somewhere?"

"Yeah ... down on the other side of the bluff ... wait, you sayin' you'll help me get into town without bein' seen?"

"Getting *into* town ain't the hard part, cowboy. It's not being seen once you're there for ... however long you'll need to do your business.

You can hole up at the Seven Knives, if you'd like. I've got ways in and out of there a person can go secret-like." She smiled. "For use in my own business, you understand." She held out her arms to encompass the now-empty road and the blood stains in the dirt.

"I see. That's ... that's mighty kind of you, ma'am—"

Her smile soured.

"—but I wouldn't want to impose. Or endanger you, if someone were to find out you were harborin' a fugitive."

She rolled her eyes and snorted. She hooked her arm in mine again, rather forcefully this time, and marched us off the road and under the trees, headin' back fer the bluff. "First of all, Mister," she said, "no more ma'amin' me. My name is Sally, so use it, would you?"

Her brisk tone and brisk pace left me a bit bewildered, and I nearly struggled to keep up with her despite my longer stride. She moved through the dark as if she had eyes like a cat, and in the absence of an urgent need to run, my metal leg liked to lag behind my natural one somewhat. The limp was less pronounced these days, sure, but it weren't gone entirely. Not by a long shot.

Sally hardly seemed to notice. "Secondly, *I'll* decide what company I'll keep in my own saloon, thank you very much, fugitive or not. You think I haven't kept wanted folk in there before? Ha! Been doing it for years. After all, no one found out you were hiding that redhead in there, did they?"

I stopped walkin' at that and grabbed her arm, pullin' her around to face me. Her eyes flashed dangerously, one of her knives comin' into her hand seemingly of its own accord, but I paid it no mind, only carin' that she answered my next question. "Yeah, about that redhead. How did you know I helped her?"

Sally's rigid stance relaxed at the question. Her knife slipped back into its sheath. "Oh. That." She gave a little laugh and shook her head. "You weren't very subtle about it, were you?"

I frowned at her.

Her eyebrows lifted. "You didn't think it might be suspicious you booked a third room later in the same evening? Why would two men need a third room? The next morning you took three plates. And some of my girls were talking ... said you'd traded them various things for some women's clothes. They thought it all quite amusing ... thought maybe you were the type of man who sometimes enjoys dressing up in women's things, but I suspected a different reason."

I only stared at her, runnin' back over all of it my mind, heat growin' in my face as I realized she was right. We hadn't been very subtle at all.

She shrugged. "Of course I went on letting them think what they wanted. Better than having the truth get out. But if you would have tried that at any other place, Mister, you and her and your other friend would have all ended up hanged. So. I *insist*. Hole up at the Seven Knives while you're in town, yeah?"

I swallowed, wonderin' if she was right about the hangin' part, too. Probably.

"All right," I said finally. "Sure. If you insist."

She grinned at me. "Very good. Now, my horse is just right over yonder. You go and fetch yours and meet me back here, and I'll take you in to Blessing and over to my saloon safely."

I touched the brim of my hat. "Much obliged."

She nodded and stepped away from me, then melded seamlessly back into the shadows in a way that made the hairs on my arms prickle.

I shuddered as I turned away to head back down fer my own horse, more thankful than ever she and the rest of her crew were on my side. I'd been in a lot of scrapes in my life, but I couldn't imagine tryin' to fight folk who were so good at bein' nothin' more than shadows, who could move and kill so silently.

Whose faces you couldn't see at all, unless they wanted you to.

I usually just stuck a bandana over half my face when I was gonna do somethin' unsavory. And sometimes I didn't remember to even do that. These people took hidin' their identities to a whole new level. I imagined the law wouldn't ever get any kind of report from a witness they could follow up on. It was hard to pin down just who or what a livin' shadow might be, after all.

My fingers drifted up to my neck again and the little spot of blood there, now dried, but sore. I'd had enough of nearly dyin' these last few days. I really *was* gonna have to be more careful ... with Nan's information all wrong, a sky-high bounty on my head, and every shadow possibly a pair of ears and eyes and fulla knives, the Territories were gettin' to be a mighty interestin' place.

My stolen horse was right where I'd left him, grazin' on that picket line. No wonder he was so fat. My own stomach growled somethin' awful as I saddled him up quick and rode on up to meet Sally; found her waitin' just where she'd said she'd be.

Her neutral expression twisted into confused horror as I approached, her eyes locked on my scruffy mount.

"He ain't mine," I said in defense, but then at the flash of alarm that crossed her features, felt a stab of panic myself. "I mean, he ain't my usual mount, is all," I tried again. So maybe horse thieves weren't among the fugitives she tended to hide. I suspected stagecoach and bank robbers might also not be on that list, nor murderers of innocents. "Got a mule," I muttered. "Back at ... well, I had to leave him behind. Fer now. I'll go back and get him later."

Sally squinted at me, either in confusion or suspicion, or maybe both, and I decided I should stop talkin'. I shut my mouth and fell in beside her as we headed toward Blessing, weavin' through the trees and stayin' off the road.

To my relief, she only grunted at my ramblin'. "Well cowboy, if I'm going to be hosting you at my saloon, I should probably have something proper to call you. Mister...?"

"Van De—" I stopped myself abruptly, swallowin' back my real name. It'd nearly come on out without me even thinkin'. I hesitated, warrin' with myself over whether or not to tell her the truth. A reputation like the one I was gettin' could open some doors, sure. But it could close plenty of other doors, too. And I didn't want this particular door to close. Not yet.

"Er ... Lynd," I said instead, fallin' back to an old alias I'd used before. Slightly modified to accommodate my previous blunder. "Van ... Der Lynd."

"Really? That a Dutch name?"

I shrugged, tryin' to look casual. "Maybe."

"All right, then, Mr. Lynd. Let's get you to the Seven Knives. And

I'm guessing you wouldn't be opposed to a hot meal once we get there?"

"Not at all, ma'—Sally." My stomach agreed wholeheartedly with another loud rumble.

"And a bath," she added. "You could most definitely use a bath as well."

I weren't so sure about that part, but I weren't gonna argue with someone who was willin' to show me any kinda hospitality at this point. "Sure. I suppose."

"No supposin' about it, cowboy. We'll get you a meal and a bath and a good sleep in a bed, and then you can tell me all about this other business of yours in Blessing."

I winced at those words. I didn't much want to do that. Maybe I woulda been better off stayin' out here on my own, after all. Maybe I shouldn't have accepted this invitation of hers.

Or maybe I could just keep lyin'.

I'd done it plenty of times before. And done it plenty of times to get just these things: a roof over my head, a bed, a hot meal ... wouldn't be nothin' new.

So I made no protest to the notion, and only followed Seven Knives Sally silently into the dark.

XIV

THE RIGHT KINDA TROUBLE

We got into Blessing easily enough, all right.

Left the horses at the edge of town—Sally promised she'd have someone retrieve 'em soon—and went the rest of the way on foot. It was an unconventional route from there, mostly back alleys and rooftops, until we reached a general store a few buildings removed from Sally's saloon.

She unlocked the back door and waved me inside, then locked it again behind us. She took an oil lamp from the wall and lit it, then showed me the way to a trap door in the floor, behind the cashier's counter.

"Norman is a good man," she whispered as she pulled it open. "We have an arrangement." Then she climbed down inside the hole on a short set of rickety stairs, and I followed her down and shut the trap door behind me.

The room beneath was small and pitch black save for the light of Sally's lamp. The weak circle of yellow light illuminated the edges of some shelves, stocked with extra wares for the store above. The air was still and muggy from the day's leftover heat, but Sally kept movin'. She ducked into a tunnel at the back wall, and I fair near had to double over to pass through it myself, fightin' with my metal leg to maneuver in the cramped space.

I tried to keep my breathin' slow and even, though I felt the edges of that panic come back, closin' in around me like these packed dirt walls. I didn't much like tight places. I tried to focus on the bobbin' lamplight, on the slender curve of Sally's gloved fingers around its handle, on her lithe, shadowed form glidin' effortlessly in front of me … on anythin' but the nearness of this ceilin' and these walls. Anythin' but the thought of us bein' underground, with a whole town on top of us. Anythin' but the feelin' that this muggy air was thickenin', that it was gettin' harder to breathe...

A ladder appeared out of the gloom, then, and I exhaled in relief. Sally stepped up to it and knocked at the trap door at the top, another pattern, like all her whistles.

The sound of a bolt bein' drawn back came muffled through the thick planks, then hinges creaked and a square of light spilled down over us. We squinted upward at a girl.

A woman, rather. But young. Couldn't be much over eighteen. My face flushed as I realized she was only wearin' her undergarments, and I hastily found somewhere else to fix my gaze. But she only looked sleepy and bored. Dark, messy ringlets of hair framed her face as she yawned and waved us up.

"Thank you kindly, Nora," Sally said as she climbed the ladder and stepped out into the room above.

I followed her up, studiously avertin' my eyes from the half-naked Nora, but I needn't have bothered. There were more women in the room just like her, loungin' or sleepin' or smokin', all in various stages of undress. And some of 'em I recognized as those Holt and I had traded with fer new clothes fer Charlotte. Rememberin' what Sally had said they'd thought of me regardin' that, the burn already flamin' in my ears burned hotter.

These were Sally's whores, then. And this room a room most folk never saw.

I decided now would be a good time to study the stolen gun belt around my hips, maybe count the cartridges stuck in its loops. Might be a good thing to know, anyhow, in case I ran into trouble later.

"And how's business this evening?" Sally asked conversationally as she re-locked her side of the underground passage.

Nora shrugged as she resumed a spot on a red velvet chaise lounge and sprawled with legs spread and feet danglin'. "Lighter than usual. On account of the Whittaker upset and that bounty, I figure."

Her brown eyes locked on me, and I realized all at once I was starin' at her, instead of countin' the bullets in my belt like I'd been meanin' to. I dropped my eyes again in a hurry, goin' back to the countin'. Except I didn't remember how far I'd got. I started over.

"Still?" Sally sighed impatiently and straightened, brushin' gloved hands against her snug black pants. Now that we were in better light, I saw she'd wrapped herself in black from head to toe, and all of it hugged her close. Better to sneak around the wilds at night, I reckoned, without snaggin' sleeves or trousers on brush.

The handles of all her knives glinted in the room's electric lights. She extinguished the lamp she'd brought from the general store and set it atop a nearby cabinet. "Well, be patient. Men'll be back here soon enough. They always come back. Not even treasure chasing will keep them away forever."

For some reason she looked at me when she said that, and I remembered again I was supposed to be takin' stock of my ammo. Except I couldn't seem to drag my eyes away this time. There was a lot of exposed flesh in this room, pale and rosy, bronze and tawny, smooth and ochre brown, thighs and breasts and slender necks, and it was all beginnin' to properly trample my focus.

"Why, Mr. Lynd," Sally said, givin' me one of her sly smiles, "you're blushing like a virgin bride on her wedding night!"

The girls around the room giggled at that and I scowled, shiftin' uncomfortably on my feet. Heat bloomed up my neck now, too, and I only wanted to get out of this room, clear my head. I'd never really figured out how to act around whores. Always been taught to treat a woman like a lady, no matter her station ... up till the day Mama and Pa were murdered, anyway, and I guess fifteen years was long enough to get somethin' stuck inside yer head so solid another nine years weren't long enough to make it fade away.

Holt had always found it amusin', and the whores usually did, too. Those that didn't find it off-puttin', at least.

Another reason I tended to seek the sportin' women only on occasion ... only when it became a powerful need ... when it was startin' to cloud my judgment and take my concentration away from other things. Away from more important things.

Maybe it was all the stress of the last few days, or the overly long interval since last I'd visited a brothel myself, or maybe it was the memory of the last time I'd been in this saloon, upstairs, disguisin' Charlotte as one of these whores, bracin' myself over the top of her while her nakedness pressed into my bare skin, but that need surged up in me now hot and urgent, its intensity catchin' the breath in my throat.

I gulped it back and grumbled somethin', turnin' away from her, from all of 'em, to search frantically fer the door.

"Now, now," Sally said, "don't get yourself all bothered, Mr. Lynd, I'll get you taken care of. Everything's on the house while you're here." Her voice shifted away from me, so I could tell she was talkin' then to her whores. "Girls, this is Van Der Lynd. He might look familiar, yes. That's because he's the one on that bulletin. The bulletin that turned a lot of Blessing's folk into bounty hunters."

I stiffened, questionin' the wisdom of her tellin' so many others that information. And yet, if she brought those she chose to shelter in her saloon through that tunnel and straight into this room with all these other eyes, well, I supposed she must have a mighty powerful trust between her and these other women. So maybe it was all right...

"And yes, he's the one who killed Baron Whittaker and freed all those slaves—"

Charlotte, I thought again. *Charlotte did that, not me.* But I clenched my teeth against sayin' it out loud. All I'd done that night was get the shit kicked outta me by the baron's men. Though Charlotte had said that was the distraction she'd needed to free the others, so maybe I'd played a necessary role in some sense.

The old pains flared up again at the thought of that night. The burns on my arm and my thigh, not-quite-healed yet, pulsed dully. The scar across my right temple ached and I brushed my fingers across it absently. But it had doused the eagerness of my lust somewhat, fer which I was thankful. A bit of clarity returned to my thinkin'.

"—he's the one who helped that redhead that posse was looking for when they came through here and busted things up," Sally continued.

At least that part was fully true.

A round of whispers and mutterin' circled the room at that.

I'd found the door, but I didn't exactly want to march out of here without my host, especially considerin' I weren't exactly sure what lay beyond. Would the faces on the other side be friend or foe? Would they have seen that poster too, or not?

"He'll be staying here for a little while," Sally told them. "So you know what to do. And like I said, thanks to the service he's done us regarding the Whittakers and helping out that poor young woman, whatever he wants during his stay should be considered bought and paid for." She paused. "Within reason, of course. Everyone understand?"

A chorus of "Yes, ma'ams" answered her. Seemed she didn't mind *them* ma'amin' her.

I kept my attention focused on the door in front of me with its worn brass handle and the blessedly woman-free space around it, and not on the other thoughts now creepin' into my head at Sally's mention of my stay bein' entirely free.

"Glad to hear it. Now ... Nora, Nettie, would you go get a bath ready for Mr. Lynd while I fix him up some grub? In the suite. Give him the Double Special. He seems tense."

"Sure thing," Nora answered, echoed by another soft voice that must have been Nettie.

The aches and pains leftover from my night at Baron Whittaker's weeks ago were fadin' again now, but the heat in my face blossomed anew as hands touched the small of my back and I startled, whippin' around to see Nora smilin' up at me.

"Pardon me, Mr. Lynd," she said, and she slid around me to move fer the door, steppin' closer than was necessary so that her front brushed up against mine.

That need raged up again full force, damn her, and Nettie stepped around behind me, trailin' a hand lightly up my arm and across my shoulders as she did so. Then they both slipped out the door, and I made to go after them.

A hand on my arm stopped me.

"Mr. Lynd."

I pulled my stare away from the retreatin' forms of Nora and Nettie only with great difficulty and found myself lookin' down at Sally. I blinked hard. Her form weren't much less distractin' at the moment, but the shine of all those knives gave me somethin' else to look at, too. "Yeah?" I managed to croak.

"Not quite yet. You want some food, don't you? I could hear your stomach the whole ride here."

"I..." Truth be told, food had suddenly become much less of a priority. I coulda waited a bit longer fer grub. I weren't sure how much longer I could wait to catch up with Nora and Nettie. My eyes drifted from Sally to look back down the hallway where the two had disappeared.

Sally gripped my elbow and guided me through the doorway, but then pulled me in the opposite direction.

I might have whimpered in protest.

"Come on now, Mr. Lynd. The bath won't be ready yet, anyway. Remember those standards I mentioned to you when you came here last? They haven't changed."

Standards? What did that even mean? Vaguely, I remembered some mention of standards and a place called the Iron Jewel, which I'd taken at the time to be the metal-made saloon down the street.

"And you've got the stink of a long time in the wilds about you, currently."

My driftin' focus narrowed into an acute self-awareness at her statement. Did I smell? I'd hardly noticed.

She took me through another door, and we ended up in the kitchen, where a flurry of scents more pleasant than my own made the hunger come back right quick. My stomach gave another loud rumble as we passed a long counter spread with meat and vegetables, attended by no less than four cooks.

They hardly glanced up as we went around 'em.

I wondered what they could possibly be cookin' this late at night. But the fire in the hearth was hot, and there was a big black pot over it simmerin' with somethin'.

A small, rickety table sat in the corner, complete with two stools, and Sally led me to it and pointed. "Here you are. Have a seat. I'll get you something."

"Thank you kindly." I took the stool facin' the cooks and another door which I suspected led out onto the floor of the saloon proper.

Sally moved off to inspect the spread of food on offer, and at just that moment, another woman pushed through the other door. Plump and round, gray curls fallin' over her face, she carried an armful of empty plates.

I recognized her just about the same time she saw me, and she stopped short on her way to the wash basin already fulla dirty dishes.

Ginger. She'd brought me that second shot of whiskey up in my room last time I'd been here. Asked if I'd needed a doctor.

Surprise, then confusion, crossed her face, but then Sally appeared at my tableside with a heapin' bowl of stew and a chunk of bread, and Ginger's features smoothed into understandin'. She resumed her march toward the wash basin.

And I dropped my attention to the food Sally had set in front of me, mouth waterin'. It was thick and savory, heartier and of better quality than the stew I'd been offered in Sonoita. I dug into it eagerly as Sally next set a mug and a pitcher of sour beer on the table, then took the stool across from me.

Ginger dropped off her load of dishes and sauntered toward us, wipin' her hands on her apron. "Well, well," she said. "Look who's back." She glanced to Sally. "He's our special guest now, is he?"

Sally nodded. "For the time being. Has some business to take care of here before he can move on. And clearly he don't want to be just moseying on down the street in plain sight these days."

Ginger's eyebrows arched, and she turned toward me. "Awful brave of you to come back here so soon, Mister. Town's already in quite a stir from yer last visit. Here to cause more trouble, are you?"

Sally shot Ginger a look, but I was too grateful fer the food and hospitality at the moment to take any offense.

I swallowed before speakin'. "Not if I can help it."

"Glad to hear, then. Business ain't picked up again yet from all that mess. Hate to see a return to normal prolonged any further by more shenanigans."

"Ginger," Sally began, but the woman waved her off.

"Just sayin' what needs to be said. You got a soft spot fer trouble-makers, Sally, don't pretend you don't."

I glanced up from the stew to Sally at that, and saw her shift on her stool.

She scoffed. "Only if they're making the right kinda trouble," she said. "The rest of them I poke holes in." She pulled one of her knives again, spinnin' it around in her fingers like it mighta been made of fluid instead of metal, then tucked it away so smooth and quick I almost didn't see it.

She handled those knives like I'd seen the best handle their guns.

I swallowed another mouthful of stew and wondered again what kinda trouble she defined as the "right kind". Hoped it was my kind.

"Speaking of those I poke holes in," Sally said. She turned on the stool toward Ginger. "You had any trouble tonight while I was out?"

Ginger shook her head. "Nah. Been quiet. Got the usuals at the tables still, though ... guess they think their luck is better in here than out there, lookin' fer that bounty."

Her eyes drifted to me again, but I ignored her, stuffin' a hunk of bread into my mouth.

"They'd be right," Sally said. "Good you ain't had any trouble, though. Guess I'd better get changed and make the rounds one more time before calling it a night."

"Sure thing, boss. I was just doin' another round myself before turnin' in."

"Thank you, Ginger."

The older woman gave Sally a nod and whisked off again, lookin' over the cooks' shoulders and peerin' into the bubblin' pot before movin' on again.

Sally turned back toward me. "You can have the suite tonight, but just tonight. After that you can have the cot we've got set up in my office."

I nodded. "Appreciate it. But yer sure my bein' here ain't an ... imposition? Don't wanna cause you any trouble after what you've done fer me."

She smiled. "Not at all, Mr. Lynd. We have guests like you all the time. It's no trouble at all."

"All right, then. Well ... thank you. Again."

Her smile widened. "Think nothing of it."

Across the kitchen, Ginger musta been listenin' to our conversation, 'cause she called out suddenly, "Should I get the suite ready then, boss?"

Sally glanced to the woman, brief annoyance crossin' her features. "No need, Ginger. I got Nora and Nettie making Mr. Lynd a bath in there as we speak."

Ginger rounded to face us, one arm wrapped around a big bowl of boiled eggs, and a pot of somethin' that looked like oatmeal in her other hand. "Eh? Nora and ... but I thought you said last time you wanted to give him a ride yerself?"

I choked on my stew.

Across from me, Sally stood abruptly from her stool, face flushin' a rosy, russet brown. She cleared her throat and sent Ginger an awful accusatory glare. "That will be quite enough, Ginger, thank you."

I reached fer the mug of sour beer and gulped it down, tryin' both to clear my airway of food and mask the fresh occurrence of heat once again crawlin' up under my collar.

Sally smoothed at the hips of her snug-fittin' pants, palms runnin' over the multitude of knives sheathed there. "Excuse me for a moment, Mr. Lynd ... I'll just go and ... change ... be back right quick. You finish up there, and let the cooks know if you'd like more..." She turned abruptly and strode across the kitchen to exit out the back door we'd come in through, tossin' Ginger another glare as she did so.

Ginger, fer her part, only looked highly amused as she watched her employer leave. Then she turned back to me.

And I turned back to the pitcher of beer, pourin' myself another mug-full.

"Well," Ginger muttered, passin' close to my table as she moved fer the door that led out into the saloon, "it ain't no lie." Then, louder, she said, "Do enjoy yerself, Mr. Lynd. And don't worry, Sally's quarters are right off her office, so if you two do decide to get to ruttin', you don't gotta do it on that cot."

I coughed into my beer and then I choked on that, too, but Ginger only tossed me a grin and pushed on through into the saloon, leavin' me to attempt to recover my air on my own.

I thumped at my chest and rocked back on the stool, then glanced furtively toward the cooks through waterin' eyes to see if they'd paid any attention to that conversation.

If they had, they surely showed no interest nor concern over it. Acted like they hadn't heard nothin' at all, though I couldn't imagine they'd not. Oh well. Nothin' to be done fer it now.

The coughin' finally quieted and I took in a few deep breaths before clearin' my throat and turnin' back to the food. At this rate, this place was gonna be the death of me, instead of some noose or gunfight somewhere. I poured myself yet more beer and struggled to scrape together what was left of my wits.

And my dignity.

Sally returned a short time later, seemingly much more composed herself now, and clad in a simple white blouse, brown corset, and layered skirts. I'd finished my bowl of stew and the bread by then, and she asked if I wanted more, but I declined.

It weren't so good to gorge yerself after a long time of little food, I'd learned. Better to ease into a more normal meal schedule gradually. And anyway, I was satisfied enough, fer now.

"Glad to hear it," Sally said. "Then if you'll come with me, I'll show you to the suite. Got a back staircase that goes up to it, for ... *discreet* business. Just checked on the room myself and it's all in order. Should be fine to head up now."

"Sure." Now that the food and beer were settled in my stomach, the exhaustion had kicked in again. It had been an interestin' few days of late, fer certain. Hard to believe just the night before I'd been in a jail cell awaitin' trial, and then sprung and nearly carted off to meet the Charles Miller I'd recently heard so much about.

I followed Sally out the kitchen's back door once more, and down the softly lit hallway and up a narrow staircase to another, wider hallway lined with doors. Looked mildly familiar, but we were on the opposite side of the building from the room I'd taken last time I'd stayed at the Seven Knives.

There were double-doors set into this end of the hallway, and they were carved all fancy with flowers and vines windin' around the edges and over toward the brass knobs.

"Here we are," Sally said. "The suite. Usually reserved for our most distinguished guests. All yours for tonight." She unlocked it with an iron key, then handed the key over to me. "I suggest you stay hidden away within as much as you can, and keep it locked. I'll retrieve you in the morning to get you moved into the other, less extravagant arrangements for later."

Her mention of the "mornin'" made me grunt, and I looked around fer windows, but there weren't none in the hallway. "Mornin'? Ain't it already almost daylight now?"

She shrugged. "Perhaps. But I'll give you the equivalent to a night's stay in hours, anyway. Now..." She turned toward the double-doors and pushed them open dramatically, then gestured grandly into the room. "Make yourself at home, Mr. Lynd."

It was the biggest room-for-rent I'd ever seen, and certainly the biggest I'd ever gotten to step foot in, myself. It was richly appointed, the wallpaper not peelin' like in the other room I'd stayed in here. The bed was also the biggest bed I'd ever seen, and had all four posts. Drapes hung from it, and heavy curtains covered the windows, so I suspected there'd be no way to tell what hour it was anyway so long as they were drawn.

A small desk and velvet-upholstered chair rested up against the wall to my left, and to my right, a small alcove set with a copper, claw-footed tub.

There was that bath Sally kept talkin' about, all right. The water steamed, the air heavy with the scent of lavender and rose. Across the tub lay a wooden tray set with soaps, sponges, and a bottle of whiskey. The good kind. Her *medicinal* variety.

And then, from behind the changin' screen in the corner, emerged

Nora and Nettie. Both pale, with dark hair and dark eyes. And they wore nothin' at all on their top halves, and even less than before on their bottom halves.

The breath pushed out of me at the sight of 'em. That need roared to life again full force, blazin' white-hot and burnin' away any thoughts of anythin' else.

"Mr. Lynd," Sally purred from beside me, "I'll leave you in their capable hands. I'll see you in the morning."

I hardly noticed as she stepped backwards, out of the room, and shut the doors behind her.

XV

AHEAD OF THE STORM

Nora and Nettie padded across the floorboards toward me on bare feet, each offering soft smiles. I weren't quite sure what to do, then. I'd only ever hired whores who'd turned out to want to rob me, or who just wanted to get things over with as quickly as possible.

It'd never been anythin' like this, with all this set up, and build-up, and women who seemed keen to do more than just lay there.

"All right, Mr. Lynd," Nora said, comin' close and hookin' her fingers into my gunbelt. "Let's get you washed up."

Fuck. I hadn't felt the pull of it like this in a long, long time ... maybe not since that first time.

She flicked open the buckle with expert hands and pulled the belt loose.

Another pair of hands slid around either side of me from behind, pressin' into my stomach ... and slidin' downward. Nettie.

But the fallin' away of my guns' weight from around my hips sent off a faint warnin' in my mind. Small, and strugglin' hard against the nearly overwhelmin' flood of lust, but enough to drag some sense back into me, kickin' and screamin'. I pulled back a bit from Nora's attempts at the buckle of my second belt, the one that held up my pants, and forced my eyes away from the roundness of her breasts to assure myself she'd put my pistols in a conspicuous spot. Somewhere within easy reach. Somewhere safe.

And that she'd actually put them *down*.

Wouldn't forget that lesson so long as I lived.

Yes, she'd put them down. On the floor next to the—

Nettie's right hand reached my groin and I gasped. And then I didn't give a damn about those pistols. Didn't give a damn if these two wanted to rob me blind. Didn't give a damn if they saw my metal leg and decided they wanted to turn me over to Charles Miller, even.

So long as they let me finish this first.

My second belt came unbuckled, then Nora started on my shirt buttons. I weren't real sure what all happened after that, but I was stark naked soon enough, and lost in a haze of agreeable sensations I hadn't felt in far, far too long.

Made me wonder why I didn't do this more often.

Truth be told it was over faster than I would have preferred, though I suppose that was to be expected given my recent bout of rather lengthy abstinence. And once it was, and I stood there wrung out and pantin', my clarity of thinkin' came back. And I realized abruptly I was standin' there naked in front of two women strangers, my metal leg in its entirety in full view, from toes to thigh. The edges of panic fluttered in my gut, and I glanced reflexively to my gunbelt, coiled on the floor next to the bed.

"Itchin' for those again already, Mr. Lynd?" Nora asked. She'd grabbed a linen towel from a stack folded on the floor and wiped herself with it, but now followed my gaze toward my pistols. Fear etched lines into her face before she obviously tried to wrestle it under control and glanced back at me. "Whatever would you need them for, currently?"

She tried to sound casual, but the fear lurked there, under her words. Her voice shook just slightly.

And my own panic dissolved under the horror of causin' her to feel such a thing. Under the horror of realizin' her profession could often put her at the mercy of unsavory or violent types, and my stomach turned at the thought. Clearly, Sally tried to run a high-quality establishment here, likely thanks to those standards she'd mentioned earlier, but that didn't mean things didn't occasionally get out of hand. I wondered if that had ever happened directly to Nora or Nettie, or if their fear was only from hearin' stories second-hand.

Either way, at that moment all I wanted was to assure them they had no reason to fear me ... and to end anyone who might have hurt them before.

"I ... I don't need 'em," I croaked. "Just ... well, there's been a lot of folk interested in ... in this, of late." My left hand dropped down to my left thigh, grazin' against the lower half of it. The half of it made of gears and rods. It felt strange to have it exposed like this. Felt strange to have it exposed and yet not be fearin' fer my life. "Usually tryin' to cut it off me."

Nora's dark eyes widened, and Nettie stepped up beside me and took my right hand in hers.

"Don't usually let people see it, is all," I muttered. I shifted on my feet, feelin' awkward and lost again now that that ragin' desire had abated. I kinda wished they'd just leave, like all the whores I'd hired before.

But it seemed they had no intention of doin' so.

"Come now, Mr. Lynd," Nettie said, wrappin' my arm in both of hers. "We ain't got no interest in that. We see Old World tech all the time. Ain't no matter to us."

Nora came to take my left arm, and I blinked at both of 'em, but let 'em guide me toward the tub. "You ... you seen other people with metal legs?"

"Well, no," Nettie said, "not that, exactly. But a lot of gadgets you wouldn't believe 'less you saw them yourself."

"Some of the area prospectors sometimes get lucky," Nora explained. "Find somethin' out in the wilds, outside of the barons' claims."

"And they can't wait to come in here and brag about it, show off their finds," Nettie finished. "Especially to us. Makes them feel all big and important, I suppose."

We'd reached the tub. The water still steamed, and dried rose petals and lavender leaves floated atop it.

"Won't you step in, Mr. Lynd?" Nettie gestured to the water.

"Can it get wet?" Nora asked, lookin' at my leg.

I hesitated. "I ... don't rightly know." Another thing I hadn't chanced to ask the good doctor before high-tailin' it away from his place. I'd washed up a few times while stayin' at his homestead, of course, and I hadn't gotten it too wet, then. I'd kept the thing propped up on the side of the tub. It was more healed now, hurt less and worked better, sure, but I still weren't certain if it should go under water. So I figured I'd just do the same now as I'd done then. "Probably shouldn't get too much wet. I'll just rest it up on the side of the tub."

"All right," Nettie said. She picked up the tray holdin' the soaps and sponges and whiskey so I could climb in, and I tried to do so as gracefully as I could, given that I didn't want to submerge my left leg.

But eventually, I got myself eased down into the hot water, restin' my metal calf and ankle along the tub rim and leanin' back with a sigh. The water was deep enough it covered the seam where the doc had sawed off my natural leg and attached this one, but I thought that probably didn't matter, since that seam had been washed plenty of times before durin' my healin' process.

And anyway, it felt good there, surrounded by the water's warmth.

It all felt good. All of this. Better than I'd felt in a long, long time.

Nettie replaced the tray, and Nora poured me a generous dose of that good quality whiskey. She handed it off to me and then went around to kneel behind the tub, her hands slidin' over my shoulders and diggin' into the muscles there, but in a good way.

Nettie picked up the chunk of soap and a sponge. "You're smart to not let most people see that leg, though," she said quietly, also kneelin' beside the tub. "Those prospectors who brag about their gadgets ... a lot of times they end up talking too much. The barons hear of their finds. And it usually don't end so well for those folk. One way or another."

I only grunted. I could imagine. But I didn't much want to consider the barons or their oppressive nature right now. Right now I only wanted to enjoy this bath, and this whiskey, and the way Nora's hands seemed to be unknottin' months of tension from my shoulders.

And the way Nettie's hands had now plunged underwater, and were currently workin' that sponge along my right thigh.

"But none of that matters here," Nora offered, as if she could read my thoughts. "You ain't got nothin' to worry about from us."

"That's right, Mr. Lynd," Nettie whispered. She leaned over the side of the tub for better access to my submerged lower half, her breasts nearly full in my face, and I swallowed as I felt the vestiges of that desire rouse again. She glanced at me from beneath dark lashes, wisps of hair fallin' across her face, and smiled coyly. "You just relax," she said. "Enjoy yourself. We got *all* night."

I slept the sleep of the dead.

Couldn't remember the last time I'd slept so sound, the last time I'd passed a night without a single nightmare.

Woke to the sound of hard poundin' at a door, and groaned in frustration at havin' such a nice slumber interrupted. My limbs were warm, languid, my eyelids heavy. I tried to pull 'em open without much luck.

The poundin' on the door intensified. A woman called out, "Mr. Lynd? You awake? You all right in there?"

She sounded vaguely familiar. I muttered somethin' and rolled in the bed, draggin' a heap of quilted bed sheets along with me.

The combination of unusual sensations finally pierced through my groggy contentment. Soft mattress. Softer linens. Quilted bed sheets.

And I was naked. Not a thread of clothes on me.

The last bit jolted me full awake in a hurry, just as I heard the turn of a key in the door, and it swung open. I sat up quick, disoriented, blinkin' the heavy press of sleep from my eyes even as I searched frantically fer my guns. The room was dark ... unnaturally dark ... only a thin sliver of white light slicin' through a crack in the drawn curtains at the window to my left.

I squinted in its searin' brightness and followed its line across the floorboards, only to see the vague shape of a woman—presumably the woman who had been shoutin' outside and who had unlocked my door —stride in with purpose, a tray set with tea service for two balanced on the hand which did not hold the key.

And that's when I finally saw my gunbelt. It was looped over the back of the chair at the desk against the opposite wall.

Far, far out of reach.

The woman drew up short at the sight of me sittin' there and exhaled a long, loud breath. "Mr. Lynd! You gave me a fright. Thought maybe those girls had been too hard on you, made your heart give out, or something. I know, I know ... wouldn't think it'd happen to a strapping young man like yourself, but I've seen it a time or two."

I blinked hard, and my blurry vision finally cleared enough fer me to recognize it was Sally standin' there in the near dark.

Those girls...

Slowly, the memories came back, piecin' together the hours before my dreamless sleep bit by bit. I swallowed.

Nora and Nettie. And the bath. And that whiskey.

And ... everything else.

The whiskey bottle sat on the bedside table, empty. The tub was still half-fulla water, what I could see of it, anyway. The rest we'd splashed out, mostly. But that mess had all been cleaned up, looked like. And the pile of used towels was gone, too.

And ... and my clothes appeared to be missin', as well.

I adjusted the sheets around my waist as Seven Knives Sally crossed to the lone desk and set the tea tray carefully atop it. Then she turned and went to the window, the one with the cracked curtains, and threw 'em wide open.

I cried out as the light stabbed into my skull and threw up my arm to shield my eyes. "Blast it all, woman, you make a habit of bargin' into people's rooms and blindin' 'em?!"

"Only if I think they might be dead."

"I ain't dead!"

"I can see that ... now. In that case..." She marched back to the desk, fussin' over the tray. "I brought you some tea."

I scrubbed the palms of my hands into my eyes, tryin' to clear both the fog of such a long, hard slumber and the dazzle of the light. Then I opened one and peered across the room at her. "Don't you got any coffee? Or whiskey?"

She snorted. "I'm afraid there's a limit on the quantity of that whiskey you can imbibe without paying for it in real currency, Mr. Lynd. And as for coffee, most certainly I got some, but I think you'll find this tea beneficial for clarity of mind. It's rather invigorating, if I do say so myself."

I opened my mouth to tell her I didn't much like tea ... didn't like it at all, if I were to be honest ... but then changed my mind and shut it again. Probably weren't polite to say such a thing after all the kindness she'd shown me recently. And probably weren't a *wise* thing to say, neither, considerin' my gunbelt was across the room and out of reach, and my clothes had gone mysteriously missin'.

So I kept quiet as she brought me a cup and offered it out. "Here you are."

I took the delicate piece of dishware from her reluctantly. It felt awkward and small in my hands. To my surprise, the sides of the ceramic were cool to the touch instead of warm. Perplexed, I sniffed at the pale liquid within, then coughed.

Peppermint. And very strong.

"Go on, drink up," Sally instructed, pourin' herself a cup.

I gritted my teeth and forced myself to take a sip. It was cold, all right. That, combined with the mint infused within it, sent a shock through me, sure enough. It cooled my mouth instantly, and went up through my nose into my head.

I coughed again, but there was a subtle sweetness beneath the powerful coolin' mint that made it not an entirely unpleasant experience to drink. I took another cautious sip.

"See, not so bad, eh?" Sally came to my bedside with teacup in one hand, then gathered up her skirts in the other hand to perch herself next to me on the edge of the mattress. She smoothed her skirts back out, arrangin' 'em neat and proper over her slender legs.

I lowered my right hand from the teacup to clutch a fistful of sheets myself, makin' sure they stayed in place while she situated herself. Makin' sure they kept me as decent as could be managed in my current situation.

Sally's brown eyes dropped down to that hand, and then she smirked behind the rim of her floral-patterned teacup. "So suddenly modest, Mr. Lynd. You are an enigma of a man, I'll give you that."

I frowned behind my own teacup. "How's that?"

She shrugged. "Just don't often see an outlaw that's got any manners. Or any modesty. Or that knows what the word *enigma* even means."

My heart quickened a bit at her use of the term *outlaw*, though I told myself that could merely apply to what I'd done at Baron Whittaker's manor. And that was somethin' she'd already more than shown her approval toward. Was, apparently, the "right kinda trouble".

Sally sipped at her tea and squinted at me while I tried to figure out what to say. My mind felt sluggish, disoriented. Maybe it'd been all that whiskey. Or the particular attentions Nora and Nettie had given me fer hours on end. Or the fact I was sittin' here unarmed and naked within arm's reach of a woman I was fair certain could be bad fer my health, if she so chose.

And there was also what Ginger had said about Sally last night. About her wantin' to have a go at me, herself. I hoped she weren't entertainin' the idea of doin' that now. Didn't think I had anythin' left in me fer that kinda business at the moment.

"You almost even act like a real gentleman," Sally said abruptly. "Sometimes."

I gulped at my tea. Maybe that clarity of mind would get here quick. I felt I was gonna need it soon.

Sally's teacup lowered to rest gently in her lap, cupped by her other hand. Her head tilted to the side as she studied me. "Almost like someone taught you once how to be a real member of society. But then you got those reflexes ... survival reflexes. Gunfighter reflexes. And some rough edges ... like those fine manners you once had got all worn away over time. Like after awhile, you started to forget. Except sometimes, now and then, you remember again. It all comes back to you. Just now and then. Here and there. Making you, like I said, an enigma of a man."

I cleared my throat, shiftin' my gaze away from her toward the door. Least she'd shut it behind her. My eyes went next to my gunbelt, and I wished it were closer. That's not where it'd been when I'd fallen asleep, that much I knew fer sure. "Manners ain't worth shit out here," I muttered.

But even as I said it, I thought of Charlotte. And how I'd panicked at not knowin' how to act in the presence of a lady with proper breedin'. So maybe manners were worth a little somethin' out here. Sometimes. If you met the right kinda person.

Sally smiled at my declaration. "Now, now. That ain't true. They're worth something in some places. *Quality* places. They're worth something in my joint, I can tell you that."

My gaze went back to the empty whiskey bottle on the night table. "They worth more of that whiskey?"

Her smile widened into a grin, and she arched an eyebrow. "More like they're worth not getting a knife in the gut or swift boot to the ass sending you right back out into the thoroughfare."

"Ah."

"But maybe if you're especially sweet, I could rustle up another bottle for you."

"Mm. I'll think about it."

"You do that. In the meantime, I've got the cot all ready for you in my office. You can have that for the duration of your stay. Which will be ... how long, would you say?"

"Hard to say, exactly."

"I see. Well, as a business owner in this fair town, I am particularly sensitive to its ups and downs, as I'm sure you can imagine."

"Sure."

"So, if you *were* to be stirring up trouble here at some point during your visit, I would much appreciate being forewarned. In order to ... stay ahead of the storm, you might say."

I shook my head. "I don't plan to be stirrin' up any trouble."

She squinted at me again. "And yet, something tells me things don't often go your way." She reached out to pat the shape of my metal leg beneath the sheets, and her eyes drifted pointedly to the thick bars of shiny pink scars lined down my right bicep.

I shifted in the bed, uncomfortable with the truth of that statement. "Yeah, well..."

Well shit. Seemed I had nothin' else to say about that. If my pa had ever had any real luck in his life, it surely hadn't passed to me when he'd died.

"More tea?" Sally asked, and I realized I was starin' down into my empty cup.

"Please." I handed the little cup over to her, relieved at the interruption to that path of conversation, and hopin' she'd drop it. That clarity of mind she'd mentioned hadn't come yet, and I wished it'd hurry up.

Sally took both teacups and stood from her seat on the bed, then moved over to the desk to refill 'em both. "Let me get straight to the point then, Mr. Lynd," she said, and her conversational tone turned all business.

Reflexively, I looked toward my gunbelt again. It hung right next to her and that tea service. If I didn't much like her point, there'd be no chance I could reach it before her, or before she could plant any of her seven knives in me.

She seemed unconcerned, her back to me as she poured. "Being a business owner in this fair town," she said, "and being particularly sensitive to its ups and downs, as I told you before, I've taken measures to protect my own interests here." She dropped a brown sugar cube into each teacup, and lifted a tiny silver spoon to stir them.

That would be the sweetness, then.

"Understandable," I said, curious as to where she might be goin' here.

"One of those measures is to extend a network of eyes and ears throughout Blessing, so as to report back to me the happenings and moods of the townsfolk regularly. To help me stay ahead of any oncoming storm, you see. If I have word of what's brewing before it breaks, I can take measures to ensure my establishment and my employees are protected."

"Smart of you," I offered. I wished she could have waited to have this conversation till I was more awake, and preferably fully clothed.

She finished stirrin' the tea and set the tiny spoon back on the tray. The memory of those manners she'd spoken of filtered back to me then, somethin' about not clinkin' the spoon against the side of the teacup. I had never paid much attention to those lessons, preoccupied more at the time with the things Pa was teachin' me about ropin' steers and shootin' rifles.

But I remembered the bit about not makin' the spoon clink when you stirred.

And Sally's stirrin' had been utterly silent.

She turned back to me, a teacup in each hand. "I am glad you agree. And so my point, Mr. Lynd, is that if your business here should require a network of eyes and ears about the town, or even, maybe, any eyes and ears within the barons' estates themselves, I should be happy to lend you the services of mine. It might prevent you falling into further trouble, is my thought. Being as it's not exactly wise for you to be wandering around the streets at the moment. And being as many of us business owners would prefer no further upset to our commerce ... at least not for a time ... as Ginger said in so many words last night."

She offered me the refilled teacup, and I took it from her, considerin' both her offer and what I suspected was the real meanin' behind it. She'd help me out, sure, on her own terms. And so long as my business didn't interfere with her own best interests.

I didn't think stealin' a lockbox from Baron Haas would do much to interfere with her interests, but neither did I feel particularly inclined to get her involved. Didn't want her to end up like Charlotte, too, hunted by the likes of Charles Miller.

She resumed her place at the edge of the mattress and looked at me expectantly, takin' another sip of her tea before speakin' again. "Or does your business here require more direct action? I have some in my service who could be employed for just such a thing, as well."

I looked at her fer a long minute, tryin' to judge her intentions. Did she suspect that by helpin' me out here, I'd feel inclined to owe her some kinda favor later, in return? I was already movin' quickly toward bein' in her debt, if I weren't there already three-fold, and I didn't feel much like owin' anyone else any debts.

I had more than enough already with Nine-Fingered Nan.

I dropped my gaze down to the full teacup restin' in my lap. It still felt awkward and small in my grip, and all kinds of wrong. "Will you ...

let me think about it fer a space? Truth be told, I'm not exactly sure what kinda action would best suite my business here just yet."

She nodded. "Of course." She sprang up standin' again, and went back to the desk and the tea tray. She finished off her second cup and set it down, empty, then faced me again, smoothin' at her skirts. "You just let me know when you decide, and we can go over the details then."

"All right." I had no intention of givin' her details. But if I owed her anythin' at this point, it was politeness and gratitude fer her kindness, at least. So I'd keep up the pretense as long as I could manage.

"I'll leave the tea for you. Please help yourself. And if you'd like a midday meal, take the back stairs to the kitchen. The cooks will have something for you."

"Midday..." I squinted toward the window, saw the slant of the sun anglin' across the street, and groaned, rubbin' at my eyes again.

"Indeed, Mr. Lynd. Now you know why I came to check on you. But I've other business to attend to for now, so I'll leave you be. I'll have Ginger come soon to show you to your new arrangements. Till then, do try to stay generally out of sight."

"Right," I said.

She headed for the ornate double doors, and that's when I remembered I had no clothes. "Wait," I called out.

Sally paused, one hand on the knob, and looked to me in question. "Something else you need, Mr. Lynd?"

"My clothes ... seem to have gone missin'."

"Ah, that." A spark lit in her eye, and one corner of her mouth drew up. "I'm sure there are some who would not object to you wandering these halls just as you are, but we do have those standards to uphold. Yes, the girls took your clothes to be laundered. Should be fresh and clean for you by now. I'll have Ginger bring them up."

"I'd much appreciate it."

Her smirk widened into a genuine smile. "Most certainly, Mr. Lynd."

XVI

DON'T NEED NO NANNY

Ginger brought my clothes, indeed, not long after Sally had departed, and I clutched the sheets around my waist again as she bustled about the room, settin' the neatly folded stack of garments on the desk's chair and sweepin' away the tea tray.

She told me she'd wait outside the door while I dressed, then show me to Sally's office and my cot. I nodded to her, and she stepped out, pullin' the door shut behind her.

It took me a bit longer than usual to rouse myself outta that bed. Still felt I was movin' slower than usual, too, and didn't seem my head was much clearer than it had been before. Maybe I'd get some coffee down in the kitchen when I got some food.

I dressed quick as I could, grumblin' at the stiffness in the freshly washed fabric of my shirt and trousers. Then I grumbled at the strangeness of the stolen gunbelt and its irons as I buckled it around my waist and checked the guns, just to be sure everything there was all in order.

It was, so I pushed my hat down onto my head and went to the doors, exitin' that fancy room with more reluctance than I'd ever anticipated leavin' a room like that.

Ginger spun at the sound of the doors openin', the tea tray balanced on one hand. She smiled at the sight of me. "Well, lookie there! Ain't you just a vision of a man when you get all cleaned up!"

I halted, blinked, feelin' all sorts of awkward again.

"Come on, then." She waved me onward with her free hand. "Follow me. This way."

She led me down the narrow stairs and through the hallway that passed the kitchen's back door and the whores' room, and my eyes lingered on that door as we went by it and on down to the other end of that hall. Ginger opened the door at the far end and showed me in.

"Here we are."

It was a cramped space, mostly filled with a desk and a chair in the middle of the room and a cabinet on the back wall. There was one window, its curtains drawn, and a simple cot rested along the right wall. On the left wall was another door.

"There's the cot," Ginger said, pointin' at it. "Just make yerself at home. Sally'll be in to chat with you when she can." She started to retreat back out into the hallway, then paused. "And don't think of stealin' nothin'. Sally's got this whole room inventoried."

I turned to her in surprise. "I weren't gonna—"

She lifted her free hand to cut me off. "Just gotta say it, regardless. All right, then. I'll leave you to it." She stepped out then and again shut the door behind her.

Leave me to what, I wondered?

I didn't have nothin' to do, 'cept have a nice, hard think on how I was ever gonna figure out where that lockbox was. And maybe get some grub. My stomach growled at the thought, but I decided to take a quick poke around the place first. Weren't gonna steal nothin', not from Sally, not after all she'd done fer me, but I couldn't help myself. If I was gonna stay here fer the next few days, it wouldn't hurt nothin' to get a better idea of just who Seven Knives Sally was.

She seemed awful young to be a saloon owner. Couldn't be more than a few years older than me. But then, from what I'd seen of her abilities last night, and the quality of this establishment, I figured she had just the kind of steel personality and deadly skill with those knives to get her this place ... and to keep hold of it.

I browsed through the room, quick and careful, takin' note of the valuables, though there weren't much. Probably on purpose, considerin' she hosted guests in here on the regular. Standard fare in the desk: paper, pencils, ink, whiskey, a ledger book fulla numbers, but I'd never been so good at numbers. A kettle fer boilin' water, a tin cup, a box fulla tea leaves ... all right, that part weren't so standard, but it fit with the more refined part of her I'd seen earlier this afternoon. I put everything back where I found it.

One of the desk drawers was locked.

I decided not to pick it. Felt wrong to go that far.

I crossed the room and tried the door on the left wall. It weren't locked, so I pulled it open a crack and peeked through. A small, simple bedroom. The lights were off in there, so I couldn't see much, but I shut the door again, anyway, rememberin' Ginger's mention of Sally's quarters bein' off her office.

Felt wrong to go snoopin' around in there.

And so concluded my search of the place. I had no belongin's to stash, so I went ahead and slipped on out of the office, goin' to the kitchen fer that midday meal Sally had talked about.

I ate fast at that rickety table, helpin' myself to some beef roast, onions and beans, applesauce and fresh peaches, and coffee. Couldn't remember the last time I ate so good, or tasted anythin' so good, either, and I had the thought that if it weren't fer that sky-high bounty on my head and nearly everyone in this town wantin' to collect it ... I might be tempted to stay here fer a good long while.

As it were, I had business to see to, and no time to waste.

So I left the kitchen soon as my meal was done and checked the office, but Sally still weren't in there. I glanced both ways down that back hall. It was currently empty; patrons weren't allowed back here and the girls were occupied or restin', I figured. There was another door to my right, at the very end of the hall.

A door that led out back of the saloon, if my sense of space was correct.

I ran my fingers over the tops of the cartridges tucked into my gunbelt. I hadn't ever got around to countin' 'em, but there were enough. I pulled my hat down low, lifted the collar of my duster, and went fer the exit door.

Sally had said lotsa people had left Blessing to go on the hunt fer me. That meant they wouldn't be around town. And anyway, who would ever think I'd be crazy enough to be walkin' around the town I was most wanted in? I'd stick to the alleys and back streets, have a look around Blessing myself. I weren't plannin' to do anythin' ... yet. Just watch and listen, like she said her people did. Maybe try to find out where Baron Haas kept his residence. Maybe lurk around there a bit.

Wouldn't draw no attention to myself.

Would beat sittin' around doin' nothin' in Sally's office all day, anyway. And would keep me from feelin' inclined to tell her any details about why I'd really come back here.

So I stepped quietly out the back door of the Seven Knives, drew it shut silently behind me, and slipped away into the afternoon shadows.

I lurked. Listened. Watched.

But kept on the move.

Seemed to be even more lawmen out and about on the streets now than there had been the last time I'd been here, and I wondered if that was because Baron Whittaker had been murdered. Nan had mentioned that seemed an unlikely feat ... maybe it had got all the other barons rattled.

The thought brought a grim smile to my face as I stalked down one back alley, skirtin' wide around a pig pen.

Good. Let 'em be rattled. Let 'em realize they were mortals just like anyone else.

I went from one end of Blessing to the other. There mighta been more lawmen around now, but the town was emptier of other folk than it had been before, that was fer certain. Though the regulars were still busy enough. Still plenty of saloons open fer business. And the livery. And the bank.

The ruins of Baron Whittaker's manor sat up on that hill, and I paused briefly in my walk to stop and take in the sight of it. Despite my sufferin' there, it brought me a great satisfaction to look upon the place now. The house was missin' its roof, and a good part of two of its walls near the back. Charred beams poked up into the hazy blue sky like the ribs of some great beast.

Some of the barn remains could be seen too, just over the hill's rise.

Too bad it looked like they were already rebuildin' it. There were fresh new beams up now in the places where the walls had burned, and several men hammerin' and sawin' at more.

I gave a grunt and moved on, circlin' around the outskirts of the town now. There were more fancy houses out a distance on the perimeter, lookin' much like Baron Whittaker's place, and I wondered if one of 'em might be Baron Haas' residence.

I saw one in the distance, on the west side of town, that had big blue and yellow banners draped over its wooden front fence at intervals. That was different. So I aimed fer that one, gettin' as close as I could without leavin' the cover of lengthenin' shadows. I planted myself behind one of the less reputable brothels and leaned against its back wall, where I could have an unobstructed view of the big house and its banners.

Now that I was closer to it, I could see the bustle of activity goin' on around and within it. A wagon had pulled up at the end of the drive, and a buncha folk were unloadin' crates and sacks from it and carryin' 'em into the house. And there were more people out and about brushin' the place up, looked like. Trimmin' the hedges, sweepin' the porch, wipin' the windows.

Looked like they were gettin' ready fer somethin' big.

Curious.

A well-dressed older man stood amid a cluster of armed individuals at the base of the porch steps, one of 'em a woman with a long brown braid, clearly givin' some kind of instructions. He gestured to various places around the yard, and then over his shoulder toward the house. I could only barely hear some of what he was sayin', but I gathered from what I could make out that the group of armed folk were his security.

"...don't give a toss what that bastard thinks or what he says to you, you are *not* to let him step foot into my house, understand?"

Well, that part I heard clear enough. The folk around him nodded gravely.

I could only wonder if he meant Mr. Miller, the bastard I was so familiar with by now, or a different one. Or maybe he weren't referrin' to an actual bastard at all, but instead usin' the slur in a more general sense, aimed at someone he particularly didn't like.

Whichever way he meant it, his group of hired guns seemed to get the message. After a few more, less passionate orders from the older gent, they dispersed to go on about their business or take up their assigned positions.

The well-dressed fella had turned and was about to ascend the porch steps when a coach rattled up the road and pulled to a halt just behind the supply wagon, its horses all lathered up. He paused and turned back to face it.

I watched, too, curious about who might be in such a hurry to arrive at this estate. Curious about who this older fella was, and what he could possibly be preparin' for with all this stuff and all this security.

I couldn't see who came outta the coach at first, since the vehicle itself blocked my view of its occupants. But the older man's face changed at the sight of whoever it was. He seemed almost glad, his face lightin' up, and he threw his arms open as he made his way down the long front walk to greet the newcomer.

"Professor!" he nearly shouted.

And that's when the new arrival finally came into my view, havin' gone down the walk far enough himself to emerge from behind the bulk of the coach.

And I straightened abruptly from where I'd been slouchin' against the brothel's wall, my right hand goin' immediately to my gun, but then stoppin' there with my fingers curled around the grip. There were far too many witnesses around here fer that. Wouldn't do to murder a man in broad daylight in front of all these folk in a town I was already most wanted in.

But boy did I sure want to murder him.

Professor Morton.

He shook hands heartily with the older gentleman, and I noted he weren't wearin' my guns no more. I wondered if he still had 'em some-where, or if he'd sold 'em off or some such. He better have still had 'em somewhere ... as I fully intended to get 'em back. Somehow.

My fingers tightened around the strange pistol-grip currently sittin' on my hip, but I resisted the urge to draw. Barely.

"So sorry I'm late..." the professor said, but the rest of his words were lost to me as he was ushered toward the big house.

I ground my teeth as I watched 'em go, talkin' enthusiastically amongst themselves, until they stepped inside and out of sight.

So the professor hadn't been lyin' about his Old World knowledge. Or about the fact he'd been expected at Baron Haas' place. Maybe he weren't lyin' about workin' fer Her Majesty, neither. He musta managed to slip away from Sonoita after my jailbreak. Guess if there weren't no outlaw left there to judge, there weren't no need fer a trial, and there-fore no need fer a witness.

This must be the Haas residence, then. I'd found it after all. Still didn't know what all the fuss was about ... but at least I knew which house it was. And if the professor was here, I might just manage to get my justice fer what he did to me along the way.

I stayed there in the brothel's shadow as long as I dared, hopin' to catch some driftin' piece of conversation that might tell me what they were gettin' ready fer, or to come up with some decent excuse to wander closer and maybe find a way in.

But there was just too much activity at the place fer me to feel safe enough venturin' any closer. And all I heard was some complainin' about the heat, and complainin' about how the town's best butcher had gone off in search of that bounty.

At that, I scowled and tugged my hat lower. But I didn't think any of 'em could see my face well enough from that distance, anyway. If they even noticed me here, in the first place.

The sun dropped low to the western horizon, silhouettin' that big house and all its activity, and I figured I'd probably better start headin' back to the Seven Knives. The wagon of supplies had left, and another wagon shown up in its place. This one fulla flowers. Fresh flowers.

And ones I'd never seen before. Where in the world had they found *those*?

Maybe I could ask Sally if she knew what was goin' on here.

I sighed and straightened up from the wall, stretchin' out my stiff muscles. An afternoon of waitin' and listenin', and I hadn't learned much. Maybe I *should* take Sally up on her offer of help...

I turned away from the wagon load of fresh flowers and ambled around the corner of the brothel, grimacin' at the thick stench of urine in the alley there. I made my way quick as I could back toward the more respectable parts of Blessing. It was easier now, as the twilight grew more shadows fer me to hide in and the streets gradually emptied, the more respectable residents headin' home for their supper.

I was only a few blocks away from the Seven Knives when I realized I had a few shadows of my own, tailin' me. A sigh hissed out between my teeth, and I switched directions. No use bringin' 'em to Sally's place.

At least that poster made it clear I was wanted alive. That would buy me some time.

I led 'em around to the back alley by the pig pen, and then stopped. It was as good a place as any. Buildings on four sides, with only narrow paths between leadin' in or out. Nice and removed from the sight of any of those lawmen prowlin' the wider streets.

It was near full-on dark now, only a touch of light showin' over the roofs that surrounded me. I hoped I was in enough shadow to cover the motion as I slid my hands down to the grips of those strange irons in my stolen belt. "I know someone's back there," I said. "Might as well come on out and tell me why the hell yer followin' me."

Fer a minute I got no answer.

Then came the sound of boots in the dirt. A couple pairs of 'em.

They approached from behind, and went around either side, but didn't come too close.

I didn't move. Kept my eyes straight ahead, my hands on my grips, and just listened.

Somewhere far off, a dog barked. A wagon rattled by on the main street. The pigs grunted and snuffled about in their pen.

"We were just hopin' for a chat," a man said from directly behind me.

"Hard to chat with a fella when you don't announce yerself," I commented. From the corner of each eye I could see two of 'em. One to either side of me, both about my age. Both holdin' a pistol already bare, but lowered toward the ground.

"Well," the man behind me said, "wanted to make sure you were the fella we wanted to chat with, first."

"And?" I prompted. "What did you conclude? Am I the man you were lookin' fer?" I shifted just slightly to look back over my shoulder.

An older man stood there, blockin' the way I'd come in from. He had both a rope and a gun on his belt, and a hand poised over each. He shrugged. "Ain't quite sure yet. But the way you've been skulkin' around in the shadows makes you look mighty suspicious. And I couldn't help but notice your limp."

I resisted the urge to scowl down at my left leg. "Yeah. Twisted my knee up real good ropin' steers once as a kid. What about it? Ain't nothin' unusual about that."

"Maybe not," he admitted. "But the man we're looking for would have good reason to skulk around in the shadows. And he has a limp, too. You maybe wanna step out of this alley? Into the light so we can get a good look at your face? And a good look at that lame leg?"

"Why would I want to do that?"

The two young men on either side of me glanced to the older man behind me, but kept their guns lowered.

The older man sighed. "So we can make sure you ain't the man we're lookin' for. He's worth a lot of money. I'm afraid we can't let you be till we make sure you are or you ain't him, Mister. If you step on out here into the light so we can check real quick, we can all go on about our business."

I let my shoulders slump. "You know how many times I've been mistaken fer that man? Might go on the lookout fer him myself ... and if I ever find the bastard, shoot him fer the trouble."

"He's only worth the money if he's alive," one of the young men said.

I scoffed. "Lucky fer me, then." I drew both pistols and fired 'em as one, one to each side, one bullet fer each of the young men. They both staggered backward as my shots hit 'em in the chest, their expressions morphin' into shocked surprise.

The man behind me yelled out, but I'd already dropped to one knee and twisted, and my two bullets hit him in the chest, too, just as he was raisin' his own gun.

I didn't wait to see him fall. I turned back around, lurched to my feet, and took off down the alley straight ahead, then pivoted down another to my left. The reports of my gunfire rolled away into the dusk, and there was already shoutin' and yellin' fer the law.

I needed to get away from there, and quick.

Unfortunately, my limp was only more pronounced the faster I tried to move.

I twisted and turned down the alleys and back streets blindly, not really knowin' where I was goin', and not carin'. As long as I put as much distance as I could between me and those men I'd just shot, I could work out what to do next later. Part of me wanted to run back to Sally's, all right, but I didn't think that was such a wise idea. Not yet. Not till I was certain there weren't no one else suspicious of my identity followin' me around.

I was so intent on listenin' fer sounds of pursuit and watchin' fer shadows on my tail that I failed to see the one that stepped out in front of me. Not till a hand caught my shirtfront, yanked me into a narrow side alley, and threw me up against a wall so hard all the breath crushed out of me.

"*The fuck you think yer doing?!*" an angry voice hissed.

My instinctive scramble fer my guns paused at the tone ... I didn't recognize the voice, or the hulkin' shape currently holdin' me against that wall. But they sure sounded like they knew me. I squinted at the man who'd grabbed me, but his face was all in shadow under his hat.

"Huh?" It was all I could manage to get out in my confusion and bewilderment, and considerin' his huge paw of a hand pinned me to the wall and made it hard to breathe.

"Sally told me to keep an eye on you," he said, voice pitched low and soundin' an awful lot like Pa had used to sound when he'd caught me doin' something he didn't like. "And I thought, 'Nah, he ain't stupid enough to go wanderin' around outside the saloon, surely.' And yet, here we are. And you firin' off your guns, to boot. So I'll ask again: what in the fuck do you think yer doin'?"

I didn't much appreciate his tone. He weren't my pa, and I weren't no child. I shoved his hand off my chest and straightened from the wall. "I'm a free man," I spat back. "I can do as I damn well please. And I don't need no *nanny* to keep an eye on me."

"You ain't a free man," he shot back. "Yer a *wanted* man. And you'll be a dead man soon enough, too, if you keep on bein' so stupid."

"Fuck you," I snarled. "I was doin' just fine, till you stopped me. Anyone with any smarts knows we shouldn't just be standin' here, waitin' on the law to find us."

"Yeah, yer right."

He took a step back, and I took a step forward, anticipatin' movin' off into the dark again to get lost in the town's maze till the commotion over my shootin' died down some.

But instead, that big giant of a man clipped me on the temple with his big, giant fist, and I fell into a whole different kinda darkness.

XVII

THE CURSE OF CARING

"Those girls fuck all the sense out of you?!"

I winced at Sally's outburst, mostly 'cause my head was poundin' from where her man had hit me and knocked me clean out. I sat on the edge of the cot in her office, where I'd woken up groggy and disoriented only a few minutes ago. Sally had been there already, seethin', waitin' fer me to open my eyes. I had no idea how I'd gotten back here.

Now, Sally paced furiously back and forth in front of me, skirts swishin'.

And that giant goon of hers was there too, blockin' the door that led into the hall with his arms crossed. He was big, all right, but not exactly all muscle. Still, he was glarin' down at me, lips set in firm disapproval, and I got the sense he was the kind you didn't want to cross.

Of course, Sally weren't the kind you wanted to cross, neither.

"What in all blazes were you thinking?" she demanded as she rounded on me. "Taking an afternoon stroll through town when you're currently the most wanted man in the Territories?"

I groaned and dropped my head into my hands, scrubbin' my palms over my face. "I needed to take a look around. No one saw me."

"Oh, someone saw you," the man over by the door said.

"And then you *shot them*!" Sally hissed.

"Well…" I looked up at 'em, both of 'em, one to the other. "It was either that or let 'em take me to Mr. Miller, I guess. What the hell else was I supposed to do?"

Sally straightened. "Hrm, let me think. Perhaps *stay put*! Stay here, perhaps? Perhaps let me send my people out to take a look around *for* you like I'd already offered? Perhaps not go strolling about town in plain sight like an idiot!"

"I weren't in plain sight," I snapped. "I was careful enough."

"*Not* careful enough," the man muttered. "You got seen."

"Not fer most the day," I said. "And I handled it."

Sally put her fists on her hips, her eyes narrowin' to slits.

I hadn't seen that expression aimed at me from a woman in a long, long while. I swallowed and shifted my seat on the edge of the cot, droppin' my gaze to my hands. Goddamnit. Why was I feelin' guilty over this?

"You didn't make sure those fellas you shot were dead," the man by the door said into the resultin' silence. "Livin' fellas can still talk. You want them tellin' the law who shot 'em?"

"They don't *know* who shot 'em," I countered. "Not fer sure. I shot 'em before they could *be* sure. That's the whole point. And anyway, why would they do that? If they want to collect that money, they gotta get me themselves, not send the law after me."

It was good enough reasonin', but neither the big brute nor Sally seemed to think it acceptable. Their stormy expressions didn't lighten at all.

I released a heavy sigh and prodded at the new lump on my left temple. "Why do you care what happens to me, anyway? My life ain't no concern of yers."

"I guess it ain't," Sally admitted. "But unfortunately, Mr. Lynd, as I've told you before, some of my business is in rescuing people. Which means, even more unfortunately, I have to live with the curse of caring what happens to strangers." She paused, then clarified. "The ones who ain't complete bastards, anyway." She turned away from me, goin' to her desk and pullin' out the drawer that held the whiskey bottle and two glasses. She uncorked the bottle and poured a finger into each glass. "And," she went on, "I live here. My livelihood is here. And if, Heaven forbid, you *were* to get carted off to Mr. Miller now, well ... certainly he'd be asking you some questions before he executed you."

"Lots of questions," said her man by the door. "Under *extreme duress*, mind you."

Sally nodded and threw back one of the whiskeys before immediately pourin' another. She handed the second glass to the goon, who took it with a touch to his hat brim.

I couldn't help but notice she did not offer one to me. That guilt squirmin' around in my gut intensified.

"And under such conditions," Sally said, lookin' to me again as she leaned back against the desktop, "you might be inclined to tell him all about what you saw last night."

"Which wouldn't be too good," her man said. He tossed back his own drink.

"Not good at all," Sally agreed. "So. Please understand now the importance of keeping yourself safe while you're here, if you have to be here at all. Please understand the importance of *listening to me* in this regard, considering I know this town and its residents backwards and forwards and inside out. I realize now I should have been more to the point when we talked earlier today."

I lifted an eyebrow at her. I'd thought she'd been quite to the point already, myself.

She set down her second glass of whiskey and straightened off the desk, lookin' me square in the eyes, her face deadly serious. "So I will be as clear as I can possibly be now, Mr. Lynd. While you are here as my guest, under my protection, you will not leave the Seven Knives Saloon again unless you come to me first and arrangements are made for you to do so. If this proposal is distasteful to you, I will have someone retrieve your horse, and you can take your leave of this establishment and this town. Agreed?"

I looked at her steadily fer a minute, but her glare didn't waver. She didn't even blink. I didn't much like the thought of leavin' here, and not just because of her good whiskey and good food and good whores. And I most certainly couldn't take my leave of Blessing. Not yet. So I hissed out another breath and nodded, shiftin' my gaze over to the room's single window, which still had its curtains drawn. "All right," I muttered. "All right." My hat was sittin' over on the end of the cot, and in its absence, I raked my hand through my hair and then over the stubble on my jaw. I'd been so preoccupied with Nora and Nettie last night I'd completely forgotten to shave. "Fine."

"Then you agree to these terms?"

"Yes," I spat. "Yes, goddamnit, I agree."

"Good." She stopped starin' me down and turned to her man by the door. "You're the witness to Mr. Lynd's agreement of these conditions."

"Absolutely," he said.

I scowled and pushed myself up standin', then grabbed up my hat. "Don't need no witness," I said. "I'll do what I say I'm gonna do."

"I'm sure that's true," Sally said, and I noted some of the steel had gone out of her voice. She picked up the glass of whiskey from her desk and handed it out toward me. "So let's start again, Mr. Lynd. Let's start with *why* exactly you felt it necessary to venture out about town when you're currently the most wanted man in the Territories?"

I eyed the glass in her hand, aware that if I took it, she'd expect full honesty outta me. Not that I had to meet those expectations, of course, but I was already feelin' awful bad about slippin' out of the saloon and I weren't even entirely sure why. And she still didn't even know my real name.

I hesitated. Put my hat back on my head.

"He was watchin' the Baron Haas residence, mostly," the man by the door supplied at my continued silence, and I shot him a glare.

"I can speak fer myself," I growled. I snatched the glass from Sally's hand, mostly to cover my alarm at the fact he'd clearly followed me all afternoon and I hadn't seen him even once. He was awful stealthy fer such a big fella. "And who the fuck are you, anyway?"

He drew himself up, as if he needed to be any taller or bigger, and hooked the thumb of his empty hand into his belt. That's when I noticed the huge knife hangin' there. Sally and her people sure had a thing fer knives. He lifted his chin, lookin' down his nose at me. "Name's Bill. Bill North."

"He's my right-hand man," Sally said.

"Yeah?" I swung my gaze back to her. "He always go around knockin' out yer guests?"

Now Sally crossed her arms, and one of her eyebrows arched. "Only the difficult ones."

I grunted. Shot another glare over to Mr. Bill North, then threw back the whiskey Sally had handed me. "Yeah, I was watchin' the Baron Haas residence. He's got somethin' goin' on there soon, looks like."

"He does," Sally said, her tone suspicious. She uncrossed her arms now and glanced over to her right-hand man. "A showcase of his Old World finds, and an auction ... for interested parties..." She turned toward me again, her dark eyes bright. Intense. "You an interested party, Mr. Lynd?"

I shifted under that sharp stare of hers and handed her back my empty glass. Then I paced over toward the far wall, toward the window. This room was too small, with too many bodies in it. It was startin' to feel claustrophobic. "I might be," I admitted. "He might have somethin' I need in there. In his house, I mean." I tucked my fingers under the edge of the curtain and pulled it back, just a sliver, peekin' through to the outside. The window looked out onto a narrow street. It was full dark now, though I couldn't quite tell the time. Yellow light from a few electric street lamps illuminated the far end of the alley. "I'll need to get in there. Somehow. Have a look around."

Bill gave a snort.

I let go of the curtain and stepped back from the window, glancin' over at him and Sally. They were both watchin' me, skepticism written all over their faces.

"I thought you said you weren't going after another baron?" Sally said.

"I ain't. I'm goin' after somethin' he's got. And I ... I don't..." I paused, considerin' the cost of bein' fully honest. Maybe I could just keep on bein' *mostly* honest. "I don't exactly have the means to pay fer it."

I left it at that. Let 'em figure out the rest of it fer themselves.

Sally and Bill glanced to each other again.

Then Sally grabbed up the whiskey bottle and poured herself some more. She sat back against the edge of her desk and studied me. "You want to steal from Baron Haas?"

I shrugged. "If he's got what I want."

"*That's* your urgent business here? *That's* why you risked your life coming back here?"

I supposed it didn't sound too reasonable when you put it like that. But they didn't know about Ethelyn. Or about Nine-Fingered Nan. When you considered those two factors, it all made a lot more sense. But I didn't exactly want to share that part of it, so I only nodded. "That's right. There's a deal I made ... a trade I've arranged... fer this thing Baron Haas has got. And in return, I'll get back somethin' real important to me."

Sally's eyes narrowed.

Behind her, from his station at the door, Bill shook his head.

I stood under their scrutiny, lettin' the silence stretch, and forced myself not to fidget. I hoped Sally wouldn't ask fer more details.

She didn't. Instead she stated flatly, "Someone's blackmailing you."

It was the last thing I'd expected her to say, but her words hit me nearly as hard as Mr. North's fist, and I felt like she'd somehow knocked all the wind out of me. I stood there gapin' at her like a fish, and couldn't find no words to say in return.

Unease prickled up my arms and under my collar at bein' so easily read. Denial flooded up my throat, but Sally lifted her hands and shook her head before I could speak.

"No, no, it's all right. You don't have to tell me. I've seen enough of it to know how it goes. I've seen that ... look ... on people's faces more times than I care to count. I know it ain't easy. I'm ... I'm sorry." She swallowed her second whiskey and sighed. "All right. So you want to steal from Baron Haas. Can you say what, exactly, you're hoping to take?"

I breathed out long and slow, tryin' to slow my heart, relief washin' through me at her understandin'.

And now I felt even worse about sneakin' off this afternoon ...

about betrayin' her trust. She'd already done so much fer me ... and was continuin' her kindness even still. She hadn't deserved my previous brusqueness. Didn't deserve my unhappiness with her conditions of my stayin' here. Didn't deserve my mistrust.

My throat felt like cotton as I tried to swallow and wet my lips. "A lockbox," I croaked. "A specific lockbox. Old World."

"Hmm." Sally twisted around to look at Bill, but he only shrugged.

"Don't look at me, boss. That old stuff is your wheelhouse, not mine."

"Hmm." Sally turned back to me. "And it's one of the pieces on display at his auction, then?"

"I ... don't know fer certain."

She managed to look both surprised, dismayed, and discouraged all at once.

"It weren't where it was supposed to be," I clarified. "Weren't where I was told it was at first. But then I heard it was supposedly back here, at the baron's estate." That's what that Professor Morton had said, anyway. And he'd said it was a piece he and the Queen of Canada herself were interested in, too. And I'd seen him there, at the Haas residence, just today. It had to be there, surely. Ready fer this auction the baron was havin'.

"Hard to plan a robbery if you don't know the location of what you're trying to steal," Sally said.

"Yeah," I growled. "Yeah..." I paced again, back and forth in front of the window. And then it occurred to me I knew someone who had been inside that house, and just today.

I stopped pacin' abruptly and swung around to face Sally and Bill, a plan coalescin' in my mind all at once and dullin' the headache pulsin' in my temples. "I know someone who would know," I blurted. "And he's here, in town. Saw him this afternoon at the baron's place. I'll get him to tell me where it is."

And then I'd pay him back fer all the trouble he'd caused me. Pay him back fer leavin' me tied to that boulder. Fer gettin' me arrested and thrown in jail and nearly hanged. Fer takin' my guns.

Satisfaction warmed my insides at just the thought of it.

"Hmm," Sally said again. She straightened from her desk. "We'd best be quick about it then. That auction is happening tomorrow evening. Doesn't leave a lot of time to plan." She put the whiskey bottle and the glasses back in their drawer as she glanced to her right-hand man. "You take care of those fellas Mr. Lynd shot?"

"And left alive?" He looked pointedly at me, but I only scowled back at him. "Yeah. I took care of 'em. They won't be doin' any talkin' to no one."

"And no one saw you bring him here?"

"Nope. Put him in the wagon, covered over with canvas. No one was the wiser."

Well, that explained how I got back to the saloon, as undignified as it was. My scowl deepened.

"Good," Sally said. "What's the name of this fella you have in mind, Mr. Lynd?"

"Morton. Professor Christopher Morton."

"Do you know where he's staying?"

"No. But he shouldn't be too hard to find. He's a foreigner. Come all the way from Canada. Dresses fancy. Thinks himself awful important."

"All right." Sally moved over toward Bill and put a hand on his arm. "Go find this professor, would you? Bring him back here. And keep it *quiet*."

"You got it, boss." He turned fer the door.

"Wait." I stopped him as he reached fer the knob.

He looked over his shoulder at me and lifted an eyebrow in question.

"If he's got a pair of gun belts on him, or in his room, will you bring those, too? They're mine."

Now both his eyebrows lifted. He looked to Sally, who frowned, but then nodded. At his boss's approval, Bill shrugged. "All right." He stepped out and shut the door behind him.

That left just me and Sally in that cramped room. She stood over there by the door, lookin' across at me like she wanted to say somethin', but she weren't entirely sure what. In the quiet, the piano music carried over through the walls from the main room, and the general murmur of voices. Sometimes a shout or a burst of boisterous laughter.

I rubbed at the back of my neck and cleared my throat. "Thank you. Again. But I hope you ain't doin' all this just fer me."

She gave me a soft smile. "No, not *just* for you, Mr. Lynd. Don't you worry your pretty self none, I got my own reasons, too."

I nodded. "All right, then. And … I'm sorry. Fer … slippin' out. I just ain't very used to gettin' other folks involved in my business." 'Cept Holt, of course. He'd been involved in enough of it. And complained about all of it enough. "Don't like it much, to be honest. Involvin' other folks, I mean."

"We all have our flaws, Mr. Lynd. But I don't got no love for those barons, you know that by now. So I surely don't mind helping you rob Baron Haas. But we're going to have to be careful about it." She tilted her head to one side, lookin' me over. "You got any money on you?"

I dropped my gaze and sighed, suddenly afraid my wanderin' off had gotten my free stay privileges revoked. "Naw." What little I'd had before startin' off on this venture was still in my saddle bags in Sonoita.

"Well, you can do some work for me around here then to pay me back. You're going to need some new clothes."

XVIII

BY INVITE ONLY

Sally had Ginger bring us more whiskey and some supper, and we stayed holed up in her office while she laid out her initial idea fer pullin' off this robbery. She suggested goin' in herself, as an interested party, lookin' to buy some of Baron Haas' pieces.

"I think we can get you in, too," she said. "Now that you've cleaned up, and with a change of clothes."

I eyed her doubtfully across my emptied plate. "You want me to just ... walk in the front door?"

She sat back in her chair. "Both of us. Yes. Baron Haas surely doesn't care about Baron Whittaker's murder. If anything, it helps his own position in town. He won't care about that bounty on you, if by chance he's studied those posters hard enough to think you familiar. Though I'd be willing to bet he hasn't paid those posters any mind at all. And the only reason anyone else around here is interested in that bounty is because they want that money. The people who will be at that auction, though ... they won't need that money. Even a reward as high as the one on your head right now won't catch their interest."

I leaned forward in my chair, pulled up in front of her desk. "*Fifty thousand dollars* won't catch their interest?"

Sally shook her head.

I let out a low whistle. "Goddamn."

"So, yes. I propose we walk in through the front door. I'll pose as the interested party, and you can accompany me as my manservant."

"Yer ... what now?"

"My manservant." She poured me more whiskey. "My servant."

I straightened in the chair.

"I'd suggest you could pose as my husband," she said, cuttin' me off as I opened my mouth, "but those manners of yours are a little too rusty to pass for that, I'm afraid."

I opened my mouth again.

"Unless you happen to know the proper way to address someone of greater or lesser social standing than yourself? The acceptable and unacceptable subjects of casual conversation? And possibly, how to waltz?"

I shut my mouth and sagged back in the chair.

"Didn't think so." She pushed the refilled glass of whiskey toward me. "We should probably say you're mute, as well."

I pursed my lips and growled in displeasure as I reached fer the whiskey.

"I thought you'd be relieved. Useless small talk is unbearably boring." She rolled her eyes and picked up her own glass. "This way, all you have to do is stay by my side and play dumb. Least until we spot that lockbox you want."

I mulled that over, and decided she was right. She was right about all of it. I didn't have the manners or the etiquette to fit in with a crowd of people who couldn't be bothered to take an interest in fifty thousand dollars. Didn't have a hope of even pretendin'. I sighed heavily and nodded. Scraped a palm over the stubble on my chin. "All right. Fine. I play dumb till we find that lockbox. Then what?"

She shrugged. "That ... we'll have to figure out once we have more information from that Professor Morton you mentioned."

"You think your man will find him?"

A slow smile pulled across Sally's lips. "Oh, absolutely. Don't you worry about that."

And so we waited for her man Bill North to return with the professor. Sally excused herself to her quarters to rest while she could, and suggested I do the same. But there weren't much chance I'd be able to sleep, nor did I much feel the need, so I occupied myself by pacin' around the office some more, studyin' again the various items Sally had stashed there, and worryin' about steppin' foot in a baron's house.

It was nearin' dawn, by count of the pocketwatch on Sally's desk, when a hushed commotion sounded from outside in the hall. Anticipation jolted through me and drove out the weariness that had started to weigh down my eyelids. I turned from the window, where I'd been peerin' out, watchin' fer the rise of the sun, just as I heard someone knock on the door of Sally's quarters that faced the hall.

I held my breath. Heard her footsteps cross the room, the door creak open, muffled voices. Then the door shut again, and her footsteps came toward the joinin' office door. I straightened as it opened.

Sally swept through, clad now in a cream-colored dressin' gown with ruffles at the end of the sleeves and a low neckline. She'd loosed her hair, and it fanned out around her face wild and full, little ringlets fallin' toward her eyes.

I had opened my mouth to confirm Bill had found the professor, but my words got lost at the sight of her.

She didn't seem to notice, pausin' just inside the door to look right at me. She opened her mouth too, but then paused, takin' in the sight of me, I supposed, fully dressed with my hat and boots and gunbelt still on and everything. She huffed a sigh, but then said, "Bill found him. Got him in one of the boarding rooms meant for the girls' business. I'll..." She glanced down at herself. "I'll get decent and show you where."

I nodded, and she stepped back into her room.

Didn't take her long to get decent, and she emerged a few minutes later in her customary blouse and skirts, though I noticed she hadn't bothered with a corset. She led me out of her office and down the back hallway to another row of doors. Bill stood outside one of 'em, arms crossed and lookin' smug.

He nodded toward the door as we approached. "He's in there. All trussed up for ya."

"Thank you, Bill," Sally said. She turned to me. "I suspect you'd like to be the one to question him?"

"Yes." The word hissed out with more force and enthusiasm than I'd intended.

"Oh yeah," Bill said. He uncrossed his arms and held one huge hand out toward me. Coiled in his fist were my two belts, with my two pistols in the middle of 'em. "Found these in his room. They yours?"

"Yes," I said again, and relief eased some of my coiled muscles to see somethin' so familiar. I took off the borrowed belt right then and there, in the middle of the hall, and put on my own, and havin' 'em back brought a strange sort of peace down around me. They fit just right, and the weight was balanced proper again, and I knew just how many bullets were tucked into those loops.

...unless the professor had fired any. I checked 'em over at that thought, doin' a quick count, and pulled the guns from their holsters to give 'em a careful look-over, too. If he *had* tried to fire 'em, who knew if he'd taken proper care of 'em after.

But they looked just the same as the last time I'd seen 'em, and none of the cartridges were missin' from the belts.

"You done?" Sally asked.

I startled, havin' almost forgot her and Bill were standin' there. Then I cleared my throat, heat risin' up under my collar, and nodded. I handed off the stolen belt to Bill.

He took it with an annoyed expression. "The hell am I supposed to do with this?"

I shrugged. "I don't care. Sell it if you want."

He muttered and grumbled at me, but I ignored him, squarin' off to face the door.

Sally stopped me from bargin' in with a hand on my arm. "We'll need to know if Baron Haas has what you're after in the first place, of course," she said softly. "But also, where it is inside the house. And how many the baron has employed to watch over his valuables while his guests are there. And the layout of the place, if possible."

I frowned. "That's a lot."

"If you want me to do it—" Bill started.

"No," I snapped, glarin' at him over my shoulder. "No. I got it."

He shrugged. "I'm just sayin' I got lots of experience with gettin' people to talk."

Somehow I didn't doubt that. Or the fact he also had lots of experience knockin' people out. But I was gainin' plenty of experience askin' people questions myself of late. I moved my right hand to the knife on my belt and drummed my fingers against its sheath. "So do I," I said, and then I swung open the door and stepped into the room before either he or Sally could say anythin' else.

And I closed the door behind me. Locked it.

And turned to see Professor Morton tied to a wooden chair in the middle of the room.

Or ... there was a man tied to a chair in the middle of the room, but he had a burlap sack over his head. So I couldn't exactly tell if it was really Professor Morton or not. The room didn't have much else in it 'cept a small bed and a night table, and it was lit only by two oil lamps ... one hangin' by the door, and one on the little table.

At the sound of my entrance, the man struggled against the ropes and tried to say somethin', but I couldn't understand him. Clearly, he'd also been gagged.

Rollin' my eyes and scowlin', I crossed the room and yanked the sack off his head, tossin' it to the floor.

The man blinked, pale and sweatin', and his eyes got real, real wide when he saw me.

It was Professor Morton, all right.

He yelled somethin', but all his words were muffled into the neckerchief that had been shoved into his mouth and tied around the back of his head. He struggled more, makin' the chair creak. He had no shoes, and wore only a long, white nightshirt. A puddle of wetness spread in his lap as he pissed himself.

Well. Maybe this would be easier than I'd thought.

I ignored the pool of urine collectin' on the floor at his feet and pulled my knife.

He yelped, strainin' at the ropes.

"I ought to kill you here and now," I growled.

He shook his head vigorously, again tryin' to voice his protests through his gag. His eyes pleaded with me, wild and desperate.

"We had an agreement," I said, low and dangerous. Made it sound like I fully intended to carve him up real good. And a part of me wanted to, fer certain. I'd nearly ended up hanged because of him. Certainly come closer to it than ever before, even in all my years runnin' and robbin' with Holt. No one had ever gotten as close to bringin' me to justice as that Sonoita sheriff. "We had an agreement, and you just left me there. Left me to die."

He protested that statement, too, and I was sure he was tryin' to say he *didn't* leave me to die, he'd sent that sheriff back to retrieve me. But it was as much a death sentence as havin' just left me tied to that boulder, so I ignored his efforts to explain himself.

"*And* you stole my goddamned guns." I circled around behind him and took a fistful of his thinnin' gray hair, pullin' his head back and lookin' down into his terrified face. "And that ... that makes me real, real sore, especially. Last people who tried that ... well, I murdered 'em. Left 'em to rot in the desert." And so I had. A man called Clint and his sonuvabitch friend. That seemed like a long time ago now, though it hadn't quite been two months since, in truth.

I brought up my knife, and the blade glimmered in the lamp light. The professor stiffened in the chair, his face gone deathly pale, hardly breathin'. He squeaked a little whimper.

"You want to die today, Professor?"

He squeezed his eyes shut, tears leakin' through his lashes, and shook his head as well as he could with my fist in his hair. He mumbled more nonsense.

I made a show of considerin', lettin' the silence draw out till he started tremblin'. "Well," I said finally, "there *is* somethin' you might be able to do fer me. Somethin' that might convince me not to murder you."

His eyes shot open.

"I need that lockbox, Professor."

He slumped in the chair and closed his eyes again, and whatever he tried to say next came out all high and whiney.

"What was that? 'Fraid I couldn't understand you. I know you were over visitin' with Baron Haas today. Saw you go into his house, I did. So? He got that lockbox like you thought he did?"

More mumblin'. Frantic. Clearly wantin' that gag outta his mouth.

"All right, Professor. I'm gonna take that gag out fer you. Then yer gonna answer my questions, or I'm gonna make you bleed. Understand?"

He stared wide-eyed at me, and sweat slid down his temple. But then he gave a nod.

I released his hair and pulled the neckerchief out of his mouth.

"Please don't kill me!" he blurted immediately. "I didn't leave you to die, I sent that sheriff back right away, and he got you to town before—"

I slapped him, good and hard across the face, and he cried out as the chair rocked. Truth be told, I wanted to punch him right in the nose fer what he'd done, but I got the sense he didn't have the strongest constitution, and I didn't have time to be sittin' around waitin' fer him to regain consciousness.

"Stop talkin', Professor. Unless yer answerin' my questions. I told you, I ain't gonna kill you if you tell me what I want to know. Got it?"

He nodded weakly, head hangin', hunched in the chair, and tears dripped off his nose.

"Good." I grabbed the back of his chair and turned him to face the bed, then sat down on the edge of the mattress. I kept my knife bare, turnin' it around in my hands as I glared at him. "Does Baron Haas have that lockbox? The one I want, with the dials?"

He made no answer.

I sighed. I didn't want to have to get blood on Sally's floor. "Professor." I slapped the flat of the blade against the top of his knee and he jumped as if I'd gone ahead and stabbed him. "Thought you said you knew how this worked?"

Silence. He stayed bent over with his eyes squeezed shut.

"Professor. Look at me."

Slowly, he cracked one eye open. Lifted his head incrementally.

I stared evenly into that one open eye of his. "I will bleed you out right here and now if you don't answer me. You think I won't?" I pointed at my own self with my knife-free hand. "Look at my face. You see how serious I am? I swear to God I'll do it. So I'm gonna ask you one more time. And you better fuckin' answer me. Does Baron Haas have that lockbox?"

He was heavin' now, maybe tryin' to hold back sobs. But he gave the slightest nod of his head.

Relief surged through me, almost makin' me light-headed. I closed my eyes and exhaled a long, slow breath, lettin' myself soak in that feelin'. Lettin' myself appreciate somethin' goin' right fer once. But then I shoved it all away, back down deep with everything else, and opened my eyes again to glare at the professor. "All right. Good. That's better. Next question. Where's he keepin' it? Where's he gonna put it durin' that auction of his?"

Professor Morton opened his other eye, and his throat bobbed as he swallowed hard. "That piece … that piece is critical to scholarly pursuits. Isn't there anything else you'd rather take, instead? Anything? Baron Haas has some very nice pieces … I can give you an inventory of everything I remember…"

I shook my head. "Just want that lockbox, Professor."

He hesitated again, glancin' toward the door. He worked at his wrists, tied together around the back of the chair, but that Mr. North was experienced with knots, too. Morton gave an exasperated huff. "But … but like I said … it could be the greatest discovery of our time. You can't just … you can't just *take* it…"

"Sure I can."

He lifted his head a little more now, squintin' at me through the glow of the nearest lamp. "Is it money you want? If you're just looking to sell it … I have the Royal Treasury backing me, you know. I had intended to buy it from Baron Haas. Tell me what you're being offered for it. I'll match that price and add ten percent more."

I snorted laughter.

"Twenty percent more, then."

I tried to swallow back the laughin' and shook my head again. "Professor, there are plenty of other, easier things I could be doin' to get money, if that's what I wanted. But no. This ain't about money." *Fer once.* "This is about that goddamned lockbox. So I need you to tell me where the baron is keepin' it."

There was another short silence, and I could almost see him thinkin', strugglin' fer a way to save both the subject of his scholarly interest and his own skin. "Who do you work for, then?"

I groaned and scrubbed a hand over my face. Fer a man who'd been blindfolded and gagged and dragged out of his room in the pre-dawn to end up here, tied to a chair, and who'd pissed himself at the first sight of me, he sure was persistent about protectin' that lockbox.

"Arrange a meeting for me with them," he went on. "I'll offer *them* the money. Then you can keep whatever other arrangement you've got with them. I'll make it worth your while," he insisted. "I'll make it worth *their* while. I swear it."

I'd had enough of this. Time was wastin'. I stood from the bed and he shrank back into the chair. "I'll just cut off a few fingers, then," I said. "You don't need all ten anyway, do ya?" But even as the words left my mouth, I remembered those fingers Nan's crew had thrown at me in the desert outside of Bravebank, and felt suddenly sick.

I braced myself against the back of the professor's chair, not hearin' whatever pleas he was currently babblin'. A sour taste rose to my mouth and I had to swallow back bile. Three fingers they'd thrown at me. One fer each of the three men I'd killed in the Stag Saloon. Three fingers I'd thought at the time were Ethelyn's, but instead they'd belonged to some other poor girl. Another young woman who'd died needlessly because of Taggert's cruel treachery.

She'd died in my arms, and I'd never even known her name. She was buried out there now, at the base of the Bone Spur Mountains. Nothin' more than a pile of rocks. Nothin' more than a nameless grave.

I sucked in a harsh breath, strugglin' back to the present, strugglin' out of the memory of her warm dark eyes goin' cold, starin' up at the sky.

And then I didn't want to maim Professor Morton anymore. Didn't want to make him bleed. Not even fer leavin' me fer Sonoita's sheriff, or fer stealin' my guns.

"Surely we can talk this out!" he nearly shrieked, unaware of the fact I'd just lost my motivation to murder him. "We can come to some kind of arrangement, some kind of agreement!"

I took another minute to regain my composure, still standin' behind him like I meant to follow through on my threat of choppin' off some fingers. Maybe I didn't have the stomach fer that anymore, but I *did* still need that lockbox.

If I had to do it...

I hoped I wouldn't have to do it.

"Why would I want to make another deal with you, Professor?" I forced out the words before I could lose my resolve. Wrestled down the tangle of feelin's jumpin' around in my gut as I reached down and tried to pry one of his fingers free of his tightly clenched fists. "Nope. No more deals, Professor. You just decide if your scholarly pursuits are worth dyin' for ... and decide quick-like, mind you."

I managed to wrench out the pinky finger of his left hand and held it fast.

He struggled hard, rockin' in the chair, yammerin' in a panic, talkin' so fast I could hardly sort what he was sayin'. Wasn't nothin' I wanted to hear, anyway. So I brought my knife blade to the base of his pinky, but only gently touched the edge to his skin. "How many fingers is it gonna take, Professor?"

I pressed just a little harder. Clenched my teeth against the wave of nausea. Braced myself to cut through that little bone.

"All right!" he barked. "All right, all right! Stop! Stop, God damn you, I'll tell you!"

I let out my sigh of relief slow and quiet, so he wouldn't hear it. But didn't remove the knife from his finger. Not yet. "Well?" I prompted. "I'm waitin'."

"It's ... it's in his safe! Where else would he keep it?"

"What about the auction? He gonna keep it in his safe fer the auction, too?"

"Yes!" He twisted, tryin' to look at me over his shoulder. "For most the time, anyway ... he's not putting that piece up for sale with everything else! He's holding a private auction for it later in the evening, by invite-only ... I went to his residence today to try and work out a deal for it myself. Alas, his greed has blinded him. He refused my offer, said I had to bid on it like everyone else!"

I scowled at this news, and Professor Morton yelped as the knife pressed into his finger a little too hard, drawin' a line of blood. Wincin', I lifted the knife a space.

"I'm telling you the truth!" he said. "I swear to God that's the truth!"

"So ... yer tellin' me he's keepin' that lockbox in his safe until it goes up fer sale itself?"

"Yes!" He was almost sobbin' now. "Yes, that's exactly what I'm saying!"

"And this invite-only auction ... where's that gonna happen?"

"In his cellar! But no one can go down there unless they've been personally invited by the baron!"

I contemplated this development. Maybe it weren't all bad ... Baron Haas would have to take it out of the safe eventually, after all. And move it down to the cellar where the auction would be takin' place. "And these invites you mentioned," I said, "you got one?"

"Yes! Of course! Baron Haas knows I am the envoy for Her Majesty, and he knows I'm backed by the Royal Treasury! Like I said, he is blinded by his greed. It wouldn't surprise me at all if he arranged this auction just to force me to pay through the nose for it ... much more than I could have offered him for it without such stiff competition ... and he also knows the queen will pay almost anything for it. He may have wealth and power here ... but he's a damn thief just like the rest of you!"

I grunted at his assessment. He'd meant it to be an insult, I was sure, but that didn't mean it weren't the truth. "Well, Professor," I said, and I sheathed my knife, movin' around to the front of him again. I hooked my thumbs in my belts as I looked down at him. "I might have a deal fer you, after all. You give *me* that invite of yours. And you pen a nice letter to Baron Haas, and you tell him you've been indisposed, but are sendin' along those you trust to act in your stead as far as acquirin' that lockbox, and those you trust are them that's holdin' that letter. You do those things, and I won't murder you. Agreed?"

He only looked up at me with wide, terrified eyes, and shuddered in revulsion.

Well, I felt the same about him.

XIX

DRESSED LIKE A TURKEY

I put the gag back in the professor's mouth and left him there, tied to the chair, while I stepped out into the hall again and told Sally and Bill what he'd just told me, about the private, invite-only auction and all. Then I told 'em my thoughts about gettin' the professor to give me his way in, and havin' him write a letter to explain it.

Sally looked thoughtful fer a minute. "Did he happen to say how many were invited to this private auction?"

I shook my head. "Naw. But I think I've softened him up. Sure he'll answer any other questions we got, if you want me to ask."

She pursed her lips, arms crossin' over her body like she were tryin' to hug herself.

"Boss," Bill said quietly, "you don't gotta go in there. You got no obligation."

His words took me by surprise, and I realized then her stance coulda surely been one of discomfort rather than contemplation. I didn't want to press her, not when she'd not demanded to know more about my own business here ... but I also weren't gonna ask her to go

403

into Baron Haas' place if she didn't want to. She'd done enough kindness fer me already, and I'd gotten enough people hurt by draggin' 'em into my trouble.

"He's right," I said. "You don't owe me nothin'. If anythin', I'm still in debt to *you*. I can do this myself."

Sally gave a little laugh. "No offense, Mr. Lynd, but I don't think so."

I straightened. "I can do it my way. With my guns and some dynamite. Forget all that invite nonsense."

She looked at me, her eyes shiftin' briefly to my right bicep, where she'd seen those scars earlier. "And what did I say before, Mr. Lynd? When Mr. North here had to knock you senseless and bring you back in the wagon to clean up your mess? I know this town. I know these people. That ain't the way to do this ... not if you want to live through it. Subtlety is better here, trust me. And I might not have an obligation to you, true. But I *do* got an obligation to ... others. I'll go." She straightened her shoulders and smoothed at her skirts, liftin' her chin. "*We'll* go. I'm overdue to call upon Baron Haas, anyways."

"You ... wanna do more than just take that lockbox?" Bill asked. "Maybe burn his house down like Baron Whittaker's?"

Sally seemed to consider the notion, and I remembered her organization of black-clad, knife-wieldin' associates. If she'd wanted to do somethin' like that, surely she could ... and have better success at it than I had, likely.

But she shook her head. "No. Not that. They'd put the town under lockdown if another baron got attacked so soon after the Whittaker incident. All of us would suffer. No, I'm thinking something more subtle. Maybe take back some of what should be mine in the first place."

Bill nodded, like he knew exactly what she were talkin' about.

I hadn't the faintest idea what she might be referrin' to, but again, I didn't want to press. So I pushed down the feelin' of bein' left out of a conversation and tried to contribute to the plannin'. "The private auction will be in the baron's cellar," I said. "Which is gonna make it harder to get in and out of. Seems the entrance will be guarded. Only those with invites let down."

Sally shook her head. "The private auction's no good. Not enough exits, and not enough people. We take the lockbox from there and Baron Haas will question everyone who was present till the end of time, or until he gets his treasure back. Such an exclusive event would mean he'd know exactly who was there, which would make his pool of suspects much too small for my liking."

Bill nodded in agreement.

I frowned. "Well then ... how we gonna get it? Professor says it'll be locked in a safe till that auction, and if you don't want me blowin' stuff up..."

"We'll have to grab it while he's moving it," Sally said. "While it's going from the safe toward the cellar."

I considered the notion, but that didn't seem no better than the close confines of the cellar. "Won't there be more people around who might see us grab it, then?"

Sally shrugged and glanced to the lamp on the wall behind me. "Not if we make it hard to see in general."

Bill and I both followed her gaze, but it was Bill—again—who caught her meanin'.

"Electricity," he said.

My frown deepened. "How's that gonna help us get the lockbox out?"

The giant man smiled. "The baron's house runs on electricity. It's all wired."

I still didn't see how that could help. Lotsa wealthy, fancy folk had electric houses. "So?"

"So..." He shoved that stolen gunbelt back into my hands and then started to pace, one big hand fisted on his hip and the other in the air, index finger extended, wavin' around with each point. "Electricity is all connected to a central point. We cut that connection in the right spot, all the lights go out. Everywhere, all over the house."

"That ... just might work," I admitted.

"When the lights go out, we grab the box," Sally said.

"What about us?" I asked. "We gonna be able to see to grab the lockbox in the first place? And find our way out? And what about his security? I saw an awful lot of armed individuals gettin' instructions over there."

"The dark won't be a problem for us," Sally said. "I got a way around that."

"A way around it?" I repeated, incredulous. "The dark ain't somethin' you just ... get *around*."

Bill snorted, and Sally gently patted my cheek. "It is for us, Mr. Lynd. You'll see soon enough."

I frowned at that statement, but then remembered how she'd slipped around in those dark woods like it was the middle of the day, and figured that was true enough, indeed.

"As for his security..." she began.

"We need a distraction," I said, seein' the glint in Bill's eye and wantin' to beat him to it this time. Of course. Of course that's what we needed. Seemed there was always need fer a distraction with this kinda thing.

"Yes, that would do it," Sally agreed.

"Dynamite?" I suggested.

Bill snorted. "That yer answer to everythin'? Blow it up?"

I glared at him and crossed my arms, shruggin'. "It's worked fine enough before."

"Not dynamite," Sally said gently. She put a hand on my arm, as if tryin' to ease the sting of Bill's derisive tone. "Too destructive. We'll need something disruptive, but that won't cause too much damage. Like I said ... we don't want the barons getting *too* cautious. Things are already hard enough around here after Whittaker's murder." She paused, then added, "As much as I appreciate his absence from this world, we need to be careful about how this plays out."

Bill paced again, both hands on his hips now.

I considered. Disruptive, but not too damagin'? That meant no fires, and no dynamite. Which were generally the most disruptive things you could get 'round these parts. Outside of that ... maybe a buncha loose horses or cattle? Weren't a lot of cattle around here, though. Horses could work, I supposed...

"I got it!" Bill said, loud and sudden enough to give me a start. He clapped his hands together with his epiphany. "Firecrackers!"

I grunted in amusement. "Thought you were against explosives?"

His enthusiasm dampened at my question and he frowned. "Never said I was against explosives ... this just ain't the time to be blowin' stuff up, is all. Firecrackers make a lot of noise. They'll draw attention, but not destroy nothin'."

"*If* you know how to use 'em," I countered. "You know how to use 'em?"

"Damn straight I do." He drew himself up and puffed out his chest, hookin' his thumbs in his suspenders. "Fair near an expert with 'em, I am."

Sally smiled at him, then turned to me, confirmin' his boast. "I do have Bill set some off every year, on the anniversary of the Seven Knives opening."

"We have a whole celebration," Bill added. "Whole town loves it. Well ... most the town, anyway."

"True enough," Sally said. "And it's a good idea. It will sound enough like dynamite to cause concern, bring people running to see what's happening."

I nodded and did a little pacin' of my own. "So ... we cut the electricity, grab the lockbox, set off the firecrackers, and get out while everyone's flounderin' around in the dark in a panic. That about right?"

"That's about right," Sally said.

"Sounds like a good time to me," Bill said.

I stopped pacin' and faced the two of 'em. "All right, then. Now we just gotta figure out when he'll be movin' it, where his safe is, where the cellar is, and what path he'll be takin' in-between so we know where to be."

"The *when* will be on that invitation," Sally said. "And I'm willing to bet he'll wait to move it till real close to auction time. But we'll want to be ready early, just in case."

"Leavin' the *where*," I said.

Sally and Bill looked to each other.

"Rose," Bill said.

"Rose," Sally agreed.

I was startin' to get real tired of feelin' left out. "What the hell does a rose got to do with this?"

"Not *a* rose," Sally said.

"A person," Bill offered. "Rose is a person. The Haas' housekeeper."

"Rose is my contact at the Haas residence," Sally said.

I blinked at her. "You ... you got a person in there?"

Sally granted me a smile. "Well, *I* didn't put her there. She was already there. I only took advantage of an opportunity and created a mutually beneficial arrangement. As I said before, Mr. Lynd, I got eyes and ears all over this town. Rose will know where that safe is, and where the cellar is. I have a good idea she'll also hear wind of the route Baron Haas plans to take that lockbox in-between."

I straightened, tryin' to absorb the implications of this information. "And yer sure you can trust her?"

"Oh yes," Sally said without hesitation. "Absolutely." She stepped past me to lock the door of the professor's room and then looked back to Bill. "Could you head on over to the Haas residence? Check things out yourself and speak to Rose so we can straighten out all the particulars before tonight?"

Bill gave a nod. "Sure thing, boss." He touched the brim of his hat, then ambled off down the hall, toward the saloon's back door.

Sally looked to me then, and I stared down at her. "He's just gonna go over there and have a chat with the housekeeper? And the baron won't think that odd?"

She let out a little grunt. "He won't even know. He doesn't keep track of all his servants' daily doings. That's Rose's job. She makes daily morning rounds around his grounds, anyway. Her and Bill have chats on the regular. And the baron is none the wiser."

"Huh."

"As for you," she said, lookin' me up and down, "we'll need to get something for you to wear. They'll never let you in looking like that, washed or not. I'll have Ginger fetch something. In the meantime," she took the extra gunbelt out of my hands, "there are dirty dishes in the kitchen that need scrubbing. If you'd be so kind? High fashion don't come cheap."

The notion didn't sound appealin'—scrubbin' dishes *or* wearin' high fashion—but I surely weren't gonna let Bill and Sally go to that auction by themselves, and I owed Sally more than a few hours of scrubbin' dishes by this point, anyway. So I only nodded myself, and gave her a wry smile. "Sure thing, boss."

I would rather have scrubbed dishes fer days than wear what I was wearin' now.

Ginger slapped my hand away from tuggin' at the collar. "Stop that. You're gonna get it all folded over!"

I didn't think that was possible, not with how heavily the shirt had been starched. The high collar hugged my neck uncomfortably close, its top edges cuttin' into the underside of my jaw if I moved my head too awful much. "I can't breathe," I muttered sourly.

"Nonsense." She moved to the front of me and straightened the gold bowtie from where I'd knocked it askew.

That was too tight, too. Felt like a noose. Felt like I was standin' on the gallows, about to be hanged. Instead, I stood in front of a full-length mirror that had been brought into Sally's office, bein' dressed and attended to by Ginger, while Sally was off gettin' ready herself in her quarters, attended to by another of her saloon staff. Bill had done his scoutin' and come back with a full report, then gone and retrieved the professor's things, so we could fish out that invitation. He'd been left in charge of Professor Morton then, usin' his intimidatin' figure to convince the man to do as we instructed.

It was approachin' evening, approachin' time to leave fer the baron's fancy auction, and I was wishin' I'd gotten more sleep than the few hours I'd managed earlier in the afternoon, after scrubbin' all those dishes. And I was wishin' I could think of a different way to get that lockbox now, too.

Goin' in with guns and dynamite blazin' sounded like a mighty good plan right about now. Anythin' would be better than sufferin' the torture of spendin' hours in this ridiculous outfit.

Ginger fussed about me, tuggin' at the jacket's hem, brushin' out its long sleeves, adjustin' the lay of its tails, givin' the toes of my shiny new shoes one last polish.

That was another thing. The shoes pinched my natural foot somethin' awful. Fer once I was glad that metal left foot couldn't feel nothin'.

The shoes sure were shiny, though. Shiny and black.

The navy blue trousers were pressed into crisp lines, the vest pale gold with a paisley pattern, and the jacket navy blue too, with a satin gold linin', and the same satin gold trim on its edges. It was embroidered with flourishes in gold thread at the cuffs, around the standin' collar, and over the shoulders. Its two tails went down to my knees in the back, and it had three big, gold buttons in the front, which Ginger was now fastenin'. Or tryin' to.

"Would you hold still?" she grumbled.

"It's too small." It was all I could do not to rip it all off. Felt like it was squeezin' me. Couldn't bend my joints properly. Couldn't look around properly.

"Oh it is not. It's just that it's tailored to fit you proper."

"Well it don't fit. I can't fuckin' move. Can't fuckin' breathe."

"You come up with a different plan fer gettin' this thing you want, then? 'Cause I wouldn't object to Sally not goin' into that place, I have to say."

I glared at my reflection in that tall mirror. "Sure. Shoot 'em up, blow open the safe. Sounds good to me."

Ginger scoffed and shook her head. "Don't think so, Mister. That'd end bad fer all of you. And I don't want the boss to end up dead."

I only grumbled more.

"Just be thankful you ain't a woman," she said as she finally finished with the buttons and straightened. "How'd you like to be put into a corset and a bustle?"

"I wouldn't."

"All right then. So shut yer trap." She took a step back and admired the results of all her fussin'.

I looked over it, myself, in my reflection. I stood stiff as a board, scowlin' heavily, but admittedly, the costume made me look almost like a whole different person. I'd had a fresh shave, and they'd put pomade in my hair to make it all shiny, too, and slicked it back. The gold of my vest and jacket almost matched its dark blonde color, and without my hat to shade 'em, my eyes stood out more, lookin' an even darker shade of brown against all the shine on me.

"My my!" Ginger exclaimed. She nodded her approval. "If you ain't careful tonight, you might just come home with a wife!"

"Ha." I tried to shake my head. "That's the last thing I need."

Ginger arched one grayin' eyebrow. "On the contrary, Mister, I think that's the exact thing you need."

I was gonna argue with her further, but she turned away and moved fer the office door.

"You just wait here," she said. "I'll go see if the boss is ready yet."

She took her leave, and then I was left alone, standin' in front of the mirror in those awful clothes.

It took awhile longer fer Sally to get dressed, but when she was, Ginger came back to retrieve me, and we all met in the narrow confines of that back hallway. And I nearly choked when I saw Sally now.

If Ginger thought I'd find a wife dressed like this, well then, surely Sally would be comin' home with a husband. Or at least, any available man would be trippin' over himself to gain her notice. And maybe even those men who *weren't* exactly available.

She stood straight and regal, shoulders back, chin tilted slightly upward, clad in a dress of black and white. The bodice looked almost to be a black jacket worn over a white blouse, with sleeves to her elbows that ended in ruffles and black-and-white striped pleats, and a row of tiny black buttons all up her front. The buttons that should have closed the high collar of the dress up tight had been left open ... exposin' the hollow of her throat. And despite the fact her regular-worn blouse often left more than that visible, my gaze stuck there at the base of her throat, unexpected feelin's rousin' in me.

Maybe it was the way the corset and bustle flattered her figure, which I supposed musta been the purpose of 'em to begin with. But she made a sight, all right, the striped pleats along the bottom half of her gown creatin' a mesmerizin' pattern as she walked. The main skirt of it was black, but all the layers of her bustle were striped like the pleats, and my eyes kept goin' there, too.

She wore a woman's black top hat, pinned slightly askew atop her oiled, ironed curls, and white gloves on her hands.

She paused when her eyes found me, and despite the intense displeasure I felt at bein' dressed up like a turkey, I didn't mind at all the way her gaze brightened at the sight of me. Or the faint flush I saw spread across her cheeks.

Maybe tonight wouldn't be so awful, after all.

"Oh my," she said, comin' to stand near, lookin' me up and down with an appraisin' eye. "Don't you look just positively *dashing*."

The brilliance of her smile made me wonder if sufferin' these clothes was maybe worth it. "Uh..." I shifted stiffly in my shiny, uncomfortable shoes and cleared my throat, strugglin' to sort my tumblin' thoughts. "I mean, er, thank you kindly. And ... and you look ... very nice, yerself."

Good Lord, good thing I was gonna be a mute this evening.

Her blush deepened, and she glanced down at herself, brushin' at the front of her bodice. "Why thank you ever so much, Mr. Lynd. You are too kind." Then she hitched up the right side of her skirt high enough that a flare of alarm went through me, questionin' her intentions, and questionin' more my ability to stay focused with her showin' so much leg. But then I saw the row of little knives strapped around her thigh there, and a flare of somethin' else entirely went through me.

"I'll have these on me all night," she said. "In case we run into any trouble. They won't allow weapons on the premises. At least, not any they can see." She flashed me a grin and winked.

"Just be careful in there, boss," Bill said quietly. He'd dressed up a bit, himself, clad in his best suit fer the occasion, bein' as he was gonna be our coachman. It weren't much compared to the duds me and Sally wore, but apparently it were good enough, considerin' he'd be stayin' with the coach all night. As fer Professor Morton, he was gonna stay here, tied, guarded, and under lock and key until we could finish our business at the auction.

Bill looked to me then, and I could read the warnin' in his hard, dark eyes as easily as I could read those disapprovin' looks Holt liked to give me. *You better not get her killed.*

I had a good idea Sally would fare better than me inside that baron's residence if things went sideways, given her familiarity with the populace and those knives strapped to her thigh, but I dipped my chin in acknowledgement to him, anyway. Nothin' was gonna happen to her, or even to him, in this endeavor if I could help it. I had enough lives on my conscience already.

He switched his gaze back to Sally. "You ready?"

She took my arm, and I could smell her perfume again, subtle and sweet. "Shall we?"

I nodded. Mute already, it seemed.

And so we went, the three of us, and boarded Sally's coach. It weren't nothin' too fancy, but was passable, Sally said. I still didn't understand any of this. Why we had to wear these clothes, or why it mattered what type of coach we arrived in, or why the coachmen were expected to wait hours and hours fer us while we were inside.

Not that I particularly minded that last bit, though, really. Havin' a ride waitin' outside ready to go in case anythin' went wrong before our planned departure was some small reassurance. Especially since I couldn't have my guns on me. They were up top, with Bill, hidden away. Along with a rifle, and pistols fer Bill and Sally too, just in case.

Later in the night, closer to the time we'd be makin' a grab fer the lockbox, another of Sally's employees would bring us some horses up this way, and have 'em waitin' out back of the baron's house. One horse fer each of us was faster than a coach, and that way we could split up, and lessen the chance of any possible pursuit bein' able to follow. That same fella was also gonna be the one to cut the electricity, right after he dropped off the horses. That way Bill had time to set up those firecrackers, and could be waitin' to set 'em off soon as he saw the house go dark.

It seemed like a good enough plan.

Seemed like it could work.

Now, inside the coach, Sally and I sat across from each other on the cushioned benches. And these clothes were more awful to sit in than they were to stand in. And they were hot. Sally had a hand fan at least, but I didn't have nothin'. And the closer we got to Baron Haas' residence, the more I was sweatin'.

Not just because these clothes didn't breathe, or because I didn't have my guns, or because I was suddenly havin' all kinds of doubts about our plan ... but because I kept thinkin' about the last time I'd gone to one of these baron's residences.

And how horrifically everything had gone wrong.

"Are you all right?"

Sally's soft voice pulled me back from the nightmarish memories, but it took me another minute before I realized she was askin' at me.

"You're awfully pale. Are you feeling unwell?"

"No." I shook my head, then pulled at that damnable high collar around my neck again. It was damp with sweat. I shifted on the seat and tugged at the bottom of the jacket, too, tryin' to swallow. My mouth was too dry. "Just ... these damn clothes don't fit right. I tried to tell that woman of yers—"

"Ginger?"

"—I tried to tell her it was all too small..."

Sally smiled and reached over to pat my knee. "You look very debonair, Mr. Lynd. It all fits just as it should. You'll be all right." In the coach's swayin' lantern light, shadows slid back and forth across her face. "Now remember, as my manservant, your goal will be to remain as invisible as possible. Unless it's to perform one of those duties we discussed earlier, stay by my side at all times. Shouldn't be too many people speaking to you, but if anyone *should* start a conversation with you, just give them the sign for mute. You remember it?"

"Yeah." That part was easy enough, at least. A closed fist at the lips, essentially. It was all the other things that were gonna be more diffi-cult. And the *waitin'* was gonna be the hardest part of all.

"And please, don't fidget."

It was like she could read my thoughts.

"A restless servant will stand out something awful. Raise suspicion and make people wonder what kind of Lady I am and what kind of household I run."

I swallowed back the groan. "You sure we can't just shoot up the place and blow open the safe? Sounds like it might be easier..."

Sally lifted her eyebrows. "No. You'll be fine. You can do this." She leaned toward me, takin' my clenched fist in her gloved hand and pryin' open my fingers to give my palm a squeeze. "I have faith in you."

I opened my mouth to tell her that was a stupid thing to do, but the coach rolled to a stop in front of the Haas residence then, with its pristine wooden fence and bright blue and yellow banners. It was nearly dark now, and the glow from all its many windows lit up the night. Soft music drifted from the open front doors. Two men in tuxedos stood at the open fence gate, so motionless and expressionless they could have been statues.

Was that how I was supposed to act all night? Fuck me, this was gonna be the longest night of my life.

Sally jolted me from my musin's with a light smack to my knee and cleared her throat loudly. "The *door*."

"Shit, right." I stood from my seat and started to move past her to open the coach door for her, but she caught my arm.

"Don't be stumbling across my lap!"

"Oh, right. Sorry." I turned to disembark through the coach's left door and stepped down rather clumsily in all my stiff, tailored clothing. My hand went to smooth at the breast of my jacket, feelin' at the subtle outline of the strange glasses currently tucked into that inside pocket. Sally had given 'em to me to wear when all the lights went out. Said they'd help me see in the dark. I didn't really understand *how*, but I wanted to be sure they were still there, anyway, before I stepped into that big house.

They were, safe and sound, so I went around the back of the coach, tryin' to straighten my posture and adopt the same expressionless look as the two men in tuxedos as I came within sight of 'em. My heart pounded under that gold vest and starched shirt like I was goin' into a stand-off. I took in a deep, slow breath to calm it, and pulled the coach's right door open, then stepped back and offered up a hand.

Sally reached out to take it and smiled gratefully as she stepped down herself, a good deal more gracefully than I had done despite her corseted bodice and layers of bustle. Then she went on, and I shut the coach door and gave a salute to Bill, who nodded and clucked at the horses to move on to ... well, wherever the hell he was supposed to wait.

I turned to follow after Sally as another coach rolled to a stop behind us. I was sweatin' again, but the two men in tuxedos didn't even seem to notice me, and I quickened my pace to catch up with my *employer*.

It was a long walk, and as we neared the front porch I saw two more tuxedoed men, only these two were armed. They glanced over the two of us as we approached, and I sorely missed the weight of my pistols at my hips. But they only gave a nod to Sally and said nothin', made no move to stop us, as we stepped inside the place.

I squinted in the brightness of all the electric lights. The foyer was as big as most houses I'd seen, and a glitterin' electric chandelier in the top middle of it threw little rainbows down over everything below: walls, furniture, flowers, and people alike.

Another man in a tuxedo appeared in front of us so suddenly I startled. "No weapons allowed on the premises for tonight's event," he said. "If you have any on your person, I can take them now. They'll be returned to you upon your departure."

Sally gave him a gracious smile. "We have none, thank you."

"Very well. Any coats, hats, parasols, then?"

"Thank you, but no."

"Very well. The main auction is in the grand ballroom." He pointed the way with a white-gloved hand. "Other pieces are on display throughout the lower level, which you are free to peruse at your leisure." Now he made a grand, sweepin' gesture with the same hand. "The upper levels, however, are off limits. The baron requests that you respect his privacy. Anyone found wandering there will be asked to leave. I'm sure you understand."

"Most certainly," Sally said.

Asked to leave? That's it? Not thrown out? Or escorted out at gunpoint? Or tied to a chair and branded with the end of a hot prybar? This Baron Haas fellow sounded almost kinda reasonable.

Or maybe this was just how he treated those folk who had enough money to buy his trinkets.

Sally gave a delicate clearin' of her throat and stepped closer to the tuxedoed man. "And what about ... the *other* auction? The one taking place at precisely nine o'clock?"

The man's eyebrows lifted and his dull gaze sharpened a bit. He seemed to regard Sally now with a whole different kind of interest. "Ah.

Yes." He turned crisply on his heel to point down the wide hallway that stretched before us. "You will find the entrance to the cellar off the main kitchen. Straight through here, then your third right and first left."

"Thank you ever so much," Sally said.

Third right and first left. I repeated it to myself a few times and wondered if I'd actually remember it by the time nine o'clock rolled around. This whole place looked like a damn maze, with room after cavernous room all connected by wide, open doorways, and people movin' constantly through all of it.

"Do enjoy your time here this evening," this man in a tuxedo said. And then he was gone again, off to give the same speech to the next set of guests arrivin'.

"This way," Sally murmured to me over her shoulder. "Stay close." She made off toward the direction of the grand ballroom, and I made sure to follow close, all right. If I lost her in this sea of madness, I weren't sure I'd be able to find her again.

But it was hard to keep my focus on her, even with as radiant as she was lookin' this evening. There were a great many other ladies here in similar dress, and all the colors and feathers and jewels—and bosoms—were rather distractin'. The gentlemen in attendance, too, were all done up in suits and tuxedos and silk vests and more of those ridiculous neckerchiefs ... er, no ... cravats, they was called, or somethin' like that. Fancier than a neckerchief, they said.

But they sure just looked like neckerchiefs to me.

And in-between 'em all were the servants, or, if they were Baron Haas' people, more likely slaves, done up similar to me, but in varying colors, offerin' trays of drinks in tall, narrow glasses and little pieces of food no bigger than a bite. And those from the baron's household all easily identifiable from the same cut of their tuxedos ... sharp and well-tailored, but subtly more plain than those of the guests.

If all the people here weren't overwhelmin' enough, there were all those other *pieces* on display as we meandered through room after room. More Old World tech than I'd ever seen before by far. All so strange lookin', full of dials and gears and tubes. Enclosed in locked glass cases. And all under one roof.

I gawked at 'em as we passed and tried to ignore the uneasy feelin' they settled in my gut. Was my metal leg really like these tarnished, rusted things? Old World?

Like somethin' from those bedtime stories and fairy tales ... from a history so long gone no one could rightly remember it anymore?

I almost felt like I could hear my leg whirrin' suddenly beneath my pressed trousers, and thumpin' with each step in those shiny shoes. I was still limpin' ... always limpin', but at least it weren't so obvious anymore.

Weren't nothin' more than a mild lurch to my step these days, somethin' like an old injury not quite healed. Not enough to draw much notice.

I hoped.

We arrived at the grand ballroom at last, and I almost forgot this was the same house we'd entered into at the foyer. Seemed we'd walked fer miles, and I'd already lost my bearings.

There was a stage at the front, set with a table, and upon the table were lined up even more Old World pieces. Some of 'em no more than a random part. Some of 'em a great deal more complex. Some of 'em made me think of that gun Charlotte had lifted from Baron Whittaker, and I wondered how much somethin' like that might fetch at an auction like this.

Maybe I should consider sellin' it...

There were couches set up along the edges of the room, and ladies sat on some of 'em, attended by their servants. More tuxedoed men stood at the entrance, holdin' fistfuls of little paddles with numbers printed on them.

"Will you be bidding tonight, ma'am?" one asked as Sally paused in front of him.

"I will, indeed."

"Here you are, then." He handed her one of the numbered paddles.

Sally nodded her thanks and aimed straight fer one of the couches, and I trailed after her. I went back to tryin' to be expressionless, like those gents out front.

It was more difficult than I'd expected, given the nature of this room, its occupants, and the items up fer auction. I kept bein' inclined to stare, and my mouth kept droppin' open ... either from surprise at seein' somethin' so over-indulgent treated as if it were somethin' regular, or 'cause I was gonna say somethin' before rememberin' I was supposed to be a mute.

"Why, Ms. Wellman," came a man's voice, silky smooth in that false-pleasantries kinda way, "what a surprise to see you here."

I nearly ran into Sally's back as she halted abruptly, and only then did I realize the man was referrin' to *her*. To Sally.

And the man doin' the referrin' was Baron Haas, himself.

XX

BEST LAID PLANS

I recognized him from that photograph Nine-Fingered Nan had given me of him and his lady wife standin' next to that coach. And now that I saw him in person, up close, I realized it had been him I'd seen the afternoon before, givin' instructions to all those armed folk. He had his lady wife with him now, too, and she stood at his elbow in a shimmerin' green gown, drenched in pearls. She was smilin' toward Sally, but she also had that soft, pityin' look about her that I didn't much like.

"Didn't think you had the stomach for these old relics anymore," Baron Haas was sayin' now. "After the ... *accident*."

Sally's face had gone cool, carefully controlled like all the folk runnin' around here in those identical tuxedoes. She pulled a fan from her sleeve and snapped it open with a flick of her wrist, then managed a smile and a small curtsey as she lifted it to her face. "Baron Haas," she said by way of greetin'. "Lady Haas. What a pleasure to see you again."

Again? I remembered how she'd mentioned somethin' about it bein' past time to call upon Baron Haas, and my stomach tightened. I wished I'd have gone ahead and pressed her a little then, found out exactly what she were talkin' about. The way the baron and his lady wife were lookin' at her now was a bit too familiar fer my likin'. If they all had some kinda history, it woulda been nice to know more about it.

"My dear, it has been far too long," Lady Haas said. "You really should come and visit more often!"

Sally's smile thinned. "As your husband mentioned, Lady Haas ... I got out of the business, I'm afraid. But rumor has it you have some exceptional pieces up for sale this evening. I must admit, curiosity got the better of me. I could use a fresh relic or two for my establishment. You know the kind of draw they have to the ... baser population."

The baron smiled, too, then, but it looked genuine. He was tall and thin, not nearly the imposin' figure Baron Whittaker had made, and his hair was full gray and recedin'. He could have been the perfect picture of a kindly grandfather, if I hadn't known better.

"Indeed we do," he said. He seemed about to say more, but then paused and looked over to me.

I straightened as his gray eyes found mine, and realized I'd been starin' at him.

No, not starin'. *Glarin'.*

His gaze narrowed, and I remembered belatedly I weren't supposed to be makin' eye contact with any of the fancy folk. I dropped my own gaze quick to the floor, cursin' myself. My shoes were so shiny I could nearly see myself in 'em. And the floor as well, which I now noticed was highly polished pink marble.

"Your man have a problem, Ms. Wellman?" Baron Haas asked Sally, and his genial tone had gone as cool as Sally's expression.

Shit. If I'd screwed all this up just 'cause I'd forgotten where I was supposed to be lookin'...

"No, Baron, he does not," Sally said. "But I fear he is new to the position. He's a fast learner though, I'm certain of it. That, or he'll soon be looking elsewhere for employment."

She put an edge in her words that was real enough. Maybe I weren't really her manservant, or her employee, but it was a warnin' nonetheless. A warnin' to remember the instructions she'd given me before we'd come here, or we might be asked to leave, and then our whole plan was nothin' more than horseshit, and I'd be hard-pressed to get that lockbox.

"I see. Seems he could do to learn some manners."

I tensed at that, wishin' I could show him just what kinda manners I had, all right.

"I believe he was just leaving to fetch me a drink," Sally said, facin' me then. "Something with bubbles. Go on now."

I usually didn't take too kindly to people orderin' me around like that, but I had a disguise to maintain, so I kept my eyes downward and gave a crisp nod, hurryin' along to do her biddin'. It was a relief, anyway. I mighta strangled the baron with his ridiculous cravat if I'd stayed there much longer.

As it were, I was free now ... free to do some lookin' around on my journey to find Sally a bubbly drink. A big part of me wanted to go pokin' around the rest of the estate. Maybe find that safe. Maybe see if someone could open it fer me. But that was a stupid idea, and I discarded it as soon as I thought it.

I was dressed as a servant, and had not a single weapon. Weren't no one here who'd be convinced to do such a thing fer me. So all I did was hunt down that drink, which proved to be more of a challenge than it shoulda been.

Those waiters with the trays and the drinks kept movin' around, and they were clearly used to manueverin' around such large groups of people. Me, on the other hand, I weren't so used to it. And I had to be real careful not to bump into any of those fancy folk. Sally had warned me doin' that woulda been real, real offensive to 'em, apparently.

But, finally, I managed to wave a waiter down and grab up one of those tall, thin glasses. Didn't know what it was, but it had bubbles, just like she'd asked. Relieved, I turned to head back toward Sally ... and then froze.

I weren't in the grand ballroom no more. I was in some other room. Smaller, but richly furnished, heavily decorated, and lined with a great number of things worth stealin'.

Holt and I coulda lived a lifetime off only a few of the items in Baron Haas' collection. Forget robbin' banks. Robbin' barons looked to be a far more lucrative option. And maybe easier, too.

Maybe. We'd see about that.

But first ... first I had to figure out how in the hell to get back to Sally. Somehow, in my pursuit of this damned drink, I'd gotten myself all lost and turned around. *Goddamnit.* I wanted to say it out loud. Wanted to say a good number of things out loud right then.

But Sally had said swearin' was frowned upon here, too. And anyway, I was supposed to be a mute.

These fancy folk weren't no fun at all.

I bit back the urge to vehemently voice my frustrations and inhaled, instead. Then released it and willed myself to stay patient, stay calm. I started back in the direction I thought might be right, but as I went, the number of people I encountered dwindled, and I got the strong sense it weren't the right way at all.

And then, then I ended up in a kitchen. Waiters and cooks bustled about, readyin' all those drinks and all that bite-sized food.

Well shit. This surely weren't the right spot. I turned to head back the way I'd come and try a different route, but a low voice stopped me.

"Lost, are we?"

I looked over to see a man leanin' up against the kitchen wall, a lit cigar in one hand. He weren't no waiter or cook, surely. Not from the look of his black suit. His vest was silver, his cravat a snowy white. I remembered this time not to look him in the face, but he seemed vaguely familiar in my brief glimpse at him, anyway.

"Or maybe you were hoping to lift a thing or two off the premises?" He arched one black eyebrow at me, blue eyes accusatory. "Sneak away while no one was looking?"

My throat closed up, but I managed to shake my head so vigorously my starched collar chafed at my chin. He couldn't have known our plan to steal the lockbox, no way ... but it was entirely possible he might mistake me fer a servant wantin' to snatch somethin' else. Anythin' else. There was surely plenty to snatch around this place, if I'd wanted.

He grunted and straightened from the wall. "I've told Edward countless times these ridiculous events of his are just asking for trouble. But does he ever listen to me? Of course not. No one ever listens to me."

He weren't much older than me, and not much bigger ... maybe a little broader across the shoulders, is all, but there was somethin' ominous about his words. Somethin' about the way he purred them out, hardly more than a whisper. He stared at me with a hard, unblinkin' gaze that made my skin crawl. The intensity of it burned into my skin like that hot prybar Baron Whittaker had branded me with, and I stepped backward. I gave a hasty little bow and turned, hopin' fer a quick exit.

"Stop."

It was more than the word that made me go rigid. It was the way he said it. I'd heard that voice before. That cruel and commanding tone.

Baron Whittaker.

My skin went cold, and sweat slid down my temple to my throat to soak into that high collar.

"I didn't dismiss you, yet."

I just stood there, my back to him, stiff and motionless. I felt I should turn around to face him, but I couldn't get myself to move. My fingers gripped the stem of that glass so hard I thought I might snap it. That's why he looked familiar. He had his father's hair, and eyes, and nose. The new Baron Whittaker. He must have been.

"Just who do you belong to, anyway? I don't recognize you ... or your colors. Usually see the same people, over and over, till I'm just bored to tears. But here you are ... a fresh face ... and sneaking around. How curious."

I shook my head again, managed to take a half-step around to face him. Lifted the glass as if in explanation.

The activity of the kitchen went on around us, though none of its other occupants seemed concerned in the least with our conversation. I weren't sure what the protocol was here, or what I could expect. I suspected none of the other people in this kitchen would care much what happened to me, long as it didn't trouble them or their duties none.

The new Baron Whittaker tilted his head. "Well? I asked you a question. I could take your silence as insolence, you know. Doubt your master would be very pleased to hear about that."

I swallowed back my retort, heat stingin' my face at my inability to currently act against these bastards. I decided I liked this one just as much as I'd liked his father ... which was not at all. Least I'd be upsettin' their party here later, and stealin' that lockbox ... long as I suitably managed to get out of this current conversation, anyway.

I made myself give him another bow, deeper this time, suspectin' he liked bein' groveled at, and put my fist up to my lips to show him I was mute, instead of sendin' it right into his chin, which is where I woulda much rather have put it.

His flat, even stare didn't change at my signalin'. "Ah, I see. Isn't that a shame? But not uncommon, for those in your position. There are not many places for mutes in this life, are there?" A corner of his mouth quirked, and then he came to my side and threw an arm around my shoulders like we were old pals.

It was all I could do not to squirm out from under it.

He turned us toward the kitchen's exit, herded me through the doorway and back out into the wide hall.

I'd never tried so hard in all the time since I'd lost my natural leg to walk without a limp. If he noticed my uneven gait now, he didn't mention it.

"Well, it's no matter," he said. "No matter at all. I know how it feels to be set aside. Discarded. To be seen as ... *less*. At least you were able to find a place for yourself. At least people like you can find a role serving those better than themselves. Not a bad job, all in all. My place, on the other hand, was taken from me."

His fingers tightened on my shoulder, the hard press of 'em almost painful even through my velvet jacket.

"Ripped away from me, just as I nearly had it within my reach." He extended the arm he didn't have around my shoulders, and the hand that held the cigar, and made as if he were grabbin' a fistful of air. Then he heaved a sigh, and shook his head.

I had no idea what he was goin' on about. Wondered if he might be a ravin' lunatic, in truth.

"But! There is more than one way to skin a cat, so they say. I'll find my way again. Just as you managed to find your way, despite your ... disability. You managed to find safe and secure employment, didn't you? Indeed." He nodded to himself, not waitin' fer me to make any answer.

"Indeed you did. And so shall I. So shall I take my rightful place, soon enough. They'll see. Think they'll listen to me then, friend?"

He was mad. He had to be. He weren't talkin' any kinda sense.

Didn't matter though, as he didn't wait fer me to answer, again. He just kept on talkin'. "I always say, open and honest communication is one of the most important things to have in a household. To keep it running smoothly, you understand. To know who you can trust ... or not." He shrugged, his arm still wrapped tightly around my shoulders.

I searched frantically fer some escape, tried to think of some excuse to duck away, but we hadn't reached the rest of the guests yet, and without words, I was havin' a hard time thinkin' of how to do that.

"Many in my position would hire translators." He seemed oblivious to my discomfort. Or he was just ignorin' it. "If they needed to understand what their dumb servants were trying to say, I mean. To convert the language of signs into the language of words. But that seems ... an excess, doesn't it? Why not just learn the language of signs yourself? Why take the risk of any important details being lost to such a translation? How can you trust a person you can't speak with, directly?"

I didn't know what he was babblin' on about, nor did I care. I only cared that we didn't seem to be goin' in a direction that led back to the main event. He pulled me over into a side room, smaller than most I'd been in so far, but no less furnished or stuffed fulla valuables. There was a sword here, in this room, in a glass case on a table along the right wall, and I wondered if I could get to it, if I needed it.

And if I could get to it ... was it sharp enough to be of any use?

The baron released me, finally, and faced me, takin' a long draw on his cigar so that the end of it lit up bright and red. He blew the smoke out in a thick cloud, and smiled with his lips but not his eyes. "So, my dear lost soul," he said, "go on. You can tell me. Use your signs. I'm quite fluent in them. Tell me who you belong to. And why you were wandering around back here unsupervised?"

I only stared at him. Use my signs? What signs? The language of signs? I didn't know no language of signs ... Sally had insisted no one of any consequence would deign to hold a conversation with a servant such as myself this evening.

Seemed she had not considered this new Baron Whittaker. A dire miscalculation.

"Well?" he prompted after a moment. "Nothing?"

I ... tried somethin'. Wavin' my hands around, gesturin', movin' my fingers like I knew what I was doin'. Pointed back the way I thought the grand ballroom might be—though fer all I knew I was pointin' out back of the house—and to the drink in my hand.

His flat look grew increasingly incredulous.

He weren't buyin' it.

"My heavens," he said dryly, once my gesticulatin' had finished. "That is certainly no language of signs I've ever seen. Didn't your betters ever teach you the real thing? The standard? It's usually a requirement for your position ... and certainly a requirement for your type to join any baron's estate. You don't belong to a baron, do you?"

I shook my head, grittin' my teeth against his repeated use of that phrase: *belong to*.

"Mmm, of course you don't." His blue gaze narrowed, scrutinizin' me with a critical eye, and I tensed. Sally had also said no one of any consequence would take any notice of me in this servant's role, and yet here this man seemed very keen to learn everything there was to know about me. And if he really were the new Baron Whittaker ... he might have a personal interest in that circulatin' poster with my name on it. It was his father we'd murdered, after all.

How close would he have studied that sketch?

I waited, still as a statue, hardly darin' to breathe, wonderin' what I'd do if he recognized me.

"Well," he said at last, "let's just go on back to the grand ballroom, shall we? I'll escort you there, since you seem to be so lost. You can point out your master in the crowd, then we can have a talk with them about your many shortcomings." He held out a hand and gestured with his fingers, like I were some kinda small child who needed coaxin'. "Come on, now. This way."

It was all I could do to keep from scowlin' at him. Took all my willpower to keep my face smooth and expressionless as I stepped forward to obey. I only needed to make it till that private auction ...

only thirty more minutes. If I could just suffer this nonsense fer another thirty minutes, I'd have that lockbox.

And then I could get Ethelyn.

He could say whatever he wanted to me, say whatever he wanted to Sally, none of it mattered. Just so long as he didn't recognize me fer bein' the man who had murdered his father.

I drew up alongside him, and somethin' stung the back of my left hand. I yelped and jerked away from it, half the drink sloshin' out all over the nice embroidered cuff of my jacket. I did scowl then, not even tryin' to hide it, and glanced down to see a circle of reddened skin where it hurt.

"Well now," the baron said, "seems you've got a voice, after all."

I looked up to him sharply, startled by his statement. *Shit.*

He was grinnin' at me now, bitin' on his cigar. The glowin' end of it sure looked like that reddened circle on my hand...

My eyes narrowed as I realized what he must have done: touched that thing to me on purpose, just to see if I'd make any noise when I yelled. *Bastard.*

He took another long draw off it now, then exhaled the smoke at me in one long stream, makin' my eyes water. "And I know you can hear just fine. So why don't you answer me another question, friend. Why the ruse? Who are you, and why are you really here?"

I stared at him fer a minute, sortin' frantically through my options. And then I did the only thing that seemed reasonable at the moment.

I sent a left hook right into his jaw, hard as I could.

He surely weren't expectin' that, and it dropped him cold. His cigar rolled onto the carpet as he hit the floor and I crushed it out quickly with the toe of my shiny shoe. Then I shook out my fist, swearin' softly, and peeked into the hallway to see if anyone else were around.

They weren't. Wherever he'd taken me, seemed it were the unpopular part of the house.

But that served my purposes just fine, too.

I set Sally's drink down on the corner of the nearest finely carved, decorative table and hurried back to the unconscious baron. I was gonna have to work fast, and hope this part of the house would stay empty fer awhile longer.

And I was gonna need that sword.

By the time I managed to find my way back to Sally—after havin' retrieved her a fresh drink—I felt I'd been lost in this damn maze of a house fer hours. In the end, the string quartet had started up their soft music again, and I'd used that to eventually find my way back to the grand ballroom.

My heart was still racin' from my dealin's with that baron, lodged in my throat as I frantically searched the crowd fer Sally's familiar face. I was out of breath from draggin' the man's unconscious weight into a closet, and from wanderin' all over this damn place.

And I was sweatin' somethin' awful. We hadn't even gone after that lockbox yet...

I found Sally, finally, over by the couch where I'd left her—I glanced at the big pendulum clock at the front of the room—nearly forty minutes ago. Was that all it'd been? Well, she was still probably wonderin' where in the hell I'd run off to.

She looked as lovely as ever, speakin' with a trio of other ladies done up in ruffles and lace. They fanned themselves lazily, ignorin' the auction takin' place now on the stage, even though they all held those little paddles with numbers on 'em, too. Maybe they just weren't interested in this particular piece.

I drew up beside her, and she turned to me in surprise. I proffered the bubbly drink and gave her a nod, riskin' a look straight at her fer just a second, hopefully enough to convey the urgency roilin' around in me like those bubbles in her drink.

"*There* you are!" She smiled and took the drink, but to my dismay, made no attempt to dismiss herself from conversation with the other women. "I was beginning to wonder if you had gotten lost." She made it sound like a joke, and the other ladies giggled, but I heard the note of true concern in her voice. If only I could tell her the half of it...

"My *goodness*, Ms. Wellman," one of the women said, but she was lookin' at me. She was blond, with a great heap of curls piled atop her head, and dressed in layers of pink silk. She fanned herself vigorously as she spoke, her cheeks flushed nearly as pink as her dress. "But you certainly did find a looker, didn't you?"

I kept my eyes on the floor, but a flush started up my neck. I tried to ignore it. Tried to ignore the woman and the heat of her stare on me, too.

"That's right." Sally grinned herself and sipped her drink.

Goddamnit. Was she encouragin' this?

"Didn't take you as one to hire on servants," another of the women said. She had a rich umber complexion and wore a gown of deep blue. "Even if you did have the means."

I frowned and fidgeted, impatient, wonderin' if everyone in this place knew Sally already, wonderin' why she hadn't mentioned that durin' all our preparin', and wishin' they'd all just shut up and go away so I could tell Sally we might need to change up all those best laid plans...

Then I remembered I weren't supposed to fidget and quieted myself, though I felt I might break with the effort.

"Well," Sally said, "I make exceptions, from time to time. For certain purposes." She cleared her throat and lowered her voice. "You should see him *out* of his livery..."

I whipped my head up to stare at her, wide-eyed, and she winked at me.

The three women let out shocked gasps, then fell into fits of giggles behind their fans, and my bewildered stare turned into a glare.

Fuckin' hell. She *was* encouragin' this.

Sally hid her grin behind her fan, but her eyes shone above its lace-laden rim, laughin' all by themselves.

Glad she was havin' a good time at my expense, then. Meanwhile there was an unconscious baron locked in a closet somewhere rooms away, who was gonna be awful angry when he woke up. I tried to tell her as much in my expression, and gave the slightest of nods back toward where I'd come from while the other women were still distracted by thoughts of me unclothed, apparently.

Sally's brows twitched, and she sobered, and I hoped she'd finally gotten my unspoken message.

This whole bein' mute thing had turned out more complicated than I'd expected.

She cleared her throat again and dropped her fan. "Yes, well, thank you ever so much for the chat, ladies. But I fear it is nearly my time to bid, and I must turn my full attention to the task."

A chorus of understandin' pleasantries from the three women followed this statement, then a chorus of sickenly sweet goodbyes and promises to catch up another time, and then they all curtsied to each other, and I nearly forgot to bow to them myself, and they giggled and fanned themselves more, battin' eyelashes at me as they slid off with a rustle of silks.

Soon as they were out of earshot, I turned to Sally with my mouth already open, the urgency wantin' to explode outta me in a tumble of words.

But then I stopped myself.

Sally looked up at me expectantly, and all I could think was how she'd told me we had to be careful tonight. And her whole speech about her livelihood bein' here and all, and how she knew the folk of Blessing better than me, inside and out, and I swallowed all the things I was gonna tell her about hittin' Baron Whittaker and tyin' him up and stuffin' him in a closet.

I couldn't tell her any of that.

At best she might stab me with some of her knives, and at worst she might demand we high-tail it out of that baron's residence to make our escape before the other baron worked his way out of that closet.

And I couldn't afford either of those outcomes.

One of her eyebrows arched. "So? What is it?"

I shut my mouth. Shook my head. And tucked my left hand casually behind my back so she hopefully wouldn't notice the new, circular red burn on the top of it. "It's ... uh ... it's nothin'."

Her brown eyes narrowed. "You made me run those girls off for nothing? You sure? You seem awful agitated."

I shrugged and tried *not* to seem awful agitated. "Just ... had a time gettin' that drink of yers, is all." At least I weren't lyin'. That bit was true enough.

"I wondered. Started getting a little worried, truth be told. Why don't you just stay close the rest of the night? Don't want you getting lost. Not much longer till that private auction, anyway."

I nodded and glanced at the clock again. Only fifteen minutes till that private auction now, in fact. My eyes scanned the rest of the ballroom restlessly, searchin' fer the angry, disheveled face of the man I'd hit. But I didn't see him.

Not yet.

I prayed he'd stay locked in that closet till the lights went out, at least. Fifteen minutes ... that weren't so long, really. It was a big house. And I'd tied him good with the length of his own cravat. And gagged him, too. And pushed a chair up under the knob of the closet door. Surely that would buy us enough time to get out of sight, into that back hallway Rose had said would be the place to grab the lockbox ... and then there'd be no lights.

And we could get out in all the confusion.

It would be fine. We could still do this. I inhaled deeply through my nose and willed all the nerves jumpin' around in my gut to ease off. "Rose ain't signaled you yet?"

Sally shook her head incrementally. "Not yet."

The housekeeper was supposed to send a waiter to Sally with a tray of tiny lavender cakes and "warmest regards from a dear friend", and that meant Baron Haas was about to move the box. That meant we needed to head directly to the hallway behind the main kitchen.

Meanwhile, when the baron got close enough to that hallway himself, Rose would signal out the kitchen's back window ... out to the kid who was waitin' to cut the electricity. Somethin' to do with a candle and the curtains. And that would tell him it was time to turn out the lights.

Then ... then it'd be time to do our part.

"Uh oh," Sally said suddenly, and I jolted from my broodin'. "*That* could be a problem."

All those nerves flared up fresh and new again at her tone. She was lookin' to some point over my shoulder, and I hardly dared to ask. "What?"

"The new Baron Whittaker is here."

XXI

LIGHTS OUT

Shit.

How could he have gotten free of that closet so fast?

I turned stiffly, bracin' myself, but I didn't see him. "Where?"

Sally stepped closer to me, murmurin' behind her fan. "There. In the front, nearest to the auction table. Speaking with the lady in the cream dress. Red vest, silver cravat. See him?"

I saw the man she referred to now, sure enough, but it weren't the man I'd punched in the face. I frowned. "That ... *that's* the new Baron Whittaker?"

"Yes. I didn't think he'd be here ... the barons don't usually socialize with each other unless they have to..." She glanced up at me, then turned her attention back to him. "I don't think he'll recognize you dressed like that, but we should try to avoid him, anyway." She sighed. "This will complicate things."

I didn't understand. The man she referred to bore some resemblance to the late Baron Whittaker, sure ... his eyes, the jawline, the black hair swept back ... but if *he* were actually the new baron ... who in the hell had I just locked in a closet?

Things were gettin' complicated, all right.

"Come on," Sally said, jerkin' me out of my contemplatin'. "This way. We'll just wait near that hallway. Should be safe enough there; Baron Haas would never let that lockbox go to another baron if he ain't gonna keep it himself. Whittaker won't be going anywhere near that cellar. Nor anywhere where he might not be the focus of a great deal of attention."

I followed her as she made way fer the grand ballroom's exit, none too disappointed to put distance between us and Whittaker ... any Whittaker. And luckily fer me, Sally seemed to remember that butler's instructions on how to get there. In all the excitement since first arrivin', I'd plum forgot.

We reached the cellar soon enough, without incident, and it was easy to spot. Was a thick wooden door right off another kitchen—a different kitchen than the one I'd stumbled upon earlier. This one was, unbelievably, even larger and busier than the other one. A single armed man stood to the side of the big wooden door, lookin' bored.

We strolled right on by him, and he paid us no mind at all.

Just past the cellar entrance was the intersection with that back hallway. Sally paused there and fanned herself, glancin' down the hall in either direction. Bein' that this weren't anywhere near the main attraction, it was sparsely populated.

"*You!*"

The shout roared out over the general din of distant conversations, the light music of the string quartet, even the far away barkin' of the auctioneer in the grand ballroom, and startled everyone nearby. A ripple of gasps and shocked murmurs from the kitchen behind us followed it, and both Sally and I whipped around.

The hired man standin' outside the cellar slid his hand to his weapon.

I looked toward the source of the boomin' voice, and grimaced. It was *him*. Course he had to show up now. Course he couldn'ta waited even one more minute, just enough time fer us to get around that corner and out of sight.

He barreled toward me, and people cleared outta his way like he was some mad bull. He sure looked like some mad bull the way he was chargin', face twisted up in anger, eyes blazin', his once-neat hair now all mussed, his cravat missin', and a trickle of blood from the right corner of his mouth bright on his bruised chin.

Fer a heartbeat I was frozen, not knowin' how to react. The urge to draw and fire ran through me, old muscle memory by now, but I didn't have no guns on me. My hand twitched reflexively, but of course that did no good at all.

The hired man near the cellar stepped in front of us then, eclipsin' my view of the angry baron—or ... whoever he was. "Go on now," he told me over his shoulder. "Go on about your business. I'll take care of him. He's not supposed to be here."

He didn't have to tell me twice. I didn't understand it, but I'd take it. I weren't one to argue a rare stroke of good luck. So I turned and ushered Sally around the corner and into the hallway.

Just before I rounded the corner myself, I saw a woman dressed in regular range ridin' clothes intercept that man I'd punched, and she looked just as angry. But her anger was directed toward the man makin' a scene and scarin' all the guests. Her long brown braid was familiar, and I realized she must've been the woman I'd seen Baron Haas talkin' to with the rest of his security out front that day I'd been lurkin' around town.

"Mr. Miller!" she barked. "I've told you, in no uncertain terms, you are not welcome here!"

My mouth fell open just as someone grabbed my arm and yanked me around the corner. Sally. She fair near pushed me ahead of her, and we hurried down the length of the hall to where it ended, with the narrow back stair to our left and a closet to our right.

Sally gave a quick look around to be sure we were alone, then opened the closet door and stepped inside, draggin' me in after her and then pullin' the door shut behind us so only a tiny crack remained to see out of.

I sagged back against the shelves of fresh linens and waited fer my heart to stop tryin' to choke me.

Mr. Miller? As in Mr. Charles Miller? The man who'd put up that ludicrous bounty fer me? Fer Chrissakes, I'd been standin' right there with the man! Lookin' him right in the face, walkin' with him, talkin' with him ... or, bein' talked to by him. I supposed it was another stroke of good luck he hadn't recognized me at that point. I still didn't think he realized I were the one he wanted fer the murder of his pa ... but it sure seemed he wanted me now fer hittin' him in the face. Probably didn't appreciate bein' tied up and stuffed into a closet, neither.

Hell, if I'd of known he was Whittaker's bastard instead of the new Whittaker baron, I mighta just slit his throat with that old sword instead of only usin' it to cut up his cravat. Coulda saved myself a whole load of trouble and sleepless nights that way.

"Did she say Mr. Miller?" Sally hissed. "As in ... as in *Charles Miller*? The bastard?!"

"Don't rightly know," I whispered back, breathless. "Couldn't hear her too well myself." That was a lie. The woman's voice was nearly as loud as Miller's had been. But we were too close to gettin' that lockbox. I weren't about to let it all fall apart now.

Muffled shoutin' carried through the kitchen, the hall, and the cracked closet door, but I couldn't make out any words. I wondered if Mr. Miller would tell the woman or any other hired security what had happened, and if Haas' people would believe him if he did. Or if they'd care at all. I figured a servant layin' a hand on any of these uppity folk wouldn't be tolerated ... but if Baron Haas didn't want Miller here in the first place, and if Miller were a bastard child instead of a legiti-mate son ... well, maybe no one here would care what'd happened to him.

I could only hope.

"Was he looking for *you*?" Sally asked. "Did he recognize you? How is that possible? He's not even supposed to be here!"

"He didn't recognize me," I said, and I hoped it were the truth. At least in relation to the part about murderin' his father. Hittin' him in the face was another story, but I still didn't want to tell Sally about that part. "Don't think he was even talkin' to me just then. Musta been meanin' someone else."

I couldn't see Sally's expression in the dark of that closet, so I couldn't be sure if she believed me or not. But she said nothin' else fer a space, and we only stood there and waited, listened, and I held my breath, wishin' like hell I had a weapon.

The shoutin' moved off, grew fainter, and I dared to exhale, slow and quiet.

"Well," Sally whispered. "That was close."

"Yeah…" In the absence of a clear threat to my health, the ridiculous fact I was wedged into some wealthy baron's linen closet became suddenly apparent. "Ain't never stole nothin' before by hidin' in a closet," I muttered.

Sally gave a snort of dismissal. "Better than chance a confrontation at this juncture."

Well, she was probably right about that. I checked again for the outline of those slim glasses in my jacket pocket, but of course they hadn't gone nowhere since last I'd checked.

"You remember the plan?"

I scoffed. "Course I remember. You sure yer boys will come through? And Rose?"

She let out a little sigh, close enough in the tight confines of that closet that I could feel the puff of her breath against my cheek. "Of course. They've never let me down."

Must be nice to have people so reliable. "So Rose'll still signal when to cut the lights?" I pressed. "Even if she realizes you ain't where yer supposed to be to receive her warmest regards?"

Sally put a hand on my arm, maybe tryin' to reassure me. "Yes, Mr. Lynd. We made it clear. The lights go off no matter what. That way, even if we have to improvise, we'll get the cover of darkness to make our escape. Whatever happens. And whether or not we have the lockbox when we go."

"I ain't goin' nowhere without that lockbox," I growled.

She gave my arm a squeeze, but I supposed she knew better than to try and argue with me from my tone, 'cause she made no comment to that statement. Instead she only said, "Guess there's nothing else to do now but wait."

Sure, wait. Wait fer Baron Haas to come down those back stairs with the lockbox. Wait fer her man to cut the electricity. Wait fer Bill to set off those firecrackers.

I thought she was gonna move out into the hall again, then, but she stayed put. After a minute of her still not movin' fer the door, I ventured to ask. "You ... wanna wait here, in the ... in the closet?" I woulda much preferred waitin' out in the hall. The space in here weren't all that big to begin with, but the longer we stood in here, the smaller it seemed to get.

"Yes," she said, all matter-of-fact. "Safer that way. Won't due to be seen loitering around the area when there'd be no reason for guests to be doing so. Someone might remember seeing us milling about, and then tell Baron Haas about it later when he's trying to sort who stole from him. Not worth the risk. You understand."

"Er, sure." I swallowed. Reminded myself the baron would be comin' down those stairs any minute now. I considered puttin' those cat's eye glasses on now, but then figured seein' how close all the walls really were might make things worse. So I left 'em off, and focused instead on the pleasantness of Sally standin' so near.

But we didn't have to wait long, sure enough.

Several pairs of footsteps creaked down the stairs across the way from our closet, and I tensed. Sally reached out to grip my arm again, as if to dissuade me from leapin' out right then and there to grab the box ... which, admittedly, was a notion I'd been entertainin'. If I'd had any weapons on me, I mighta already done it.

But as it were, I stayed put. I stayed still and silent, and strained to see through the sliver of open door out into the hallway. Two armed men, more hired guns by the look of 'em, walked past, followed by Baron Haas himself, and a single armed man after him. It weren't any of them that made my heart jump, though, it was the square shape the baron carried.

The lockbox. Had to be.

I exhaled quietly at the sight of it. It was there ... *right there*. So close.

From what I could see of it through that little crack, it looked just like the sketch Nan had given me. Square-shaped, a row of five dials along the top of it. Made of some kind of metal that had gotten all rusted and greenish over so much time buried underground.

Didn't look so impressive, really.

All this trouble ... over *that*? And no one even knew how to open it, accordin' to Professor Morton. I wondered if he might be right about what could be inside it.

Doubtful.

I moved my hand to my breast pocket to grab fer those glasses, and that's when all the lights went out. The closet plunged into absolute darkness. Shocked gasps and confused mutterin's came from the folk outside, includin' from the men escortin' Baron Haas.

The distant music of the string quartet and barkin' of the auctioneer fell silent.

"Everyone stay calm!" Baron Haas called from where he'd frozen in the hallway. "No need to worry ... this happens frequently, I'm afraid. I'll have the lights back on in just a moment..."

I slipped the wire hooks of the glasses over my ears, folded out the lenses as Sally had instructed me back at her saloon, and then sucked in a breath as the closet brightened up fer me like someone had turned the electricity back on, just from what bare glimmer of light came in through the crack in the door. It was all in muted shades of color, and mostly shades of gray, but I could see everything ... the shelves of folded linens, the broom standin' in the corner, and Sally as she pushed the closet door open and stepped out into the hall...

Baron Haas dropped his voice, and to the men around him said, "Keep your eyes open. Get me to that cellar *now*. And then I want you finding out what happened to the lights. I don't like this..."

They answered him in the affirmative and moved off down the hall again, quicker than before, but Sally was already close on their heels. I followed her, and we caught up to 'em quick, our footsteps silenced by the thick carpet.

Sally hiked up her skirts then, and her blades were only a whisper of sound. The armed man bringin' up the rear was the first to fall, goin' down so fast and quiet none of the others even noticed. Then the two on either side of Baron Haas staggered, hands goin' to their necks in confused horror. The baron noticed that, finally, and clutched the lockbox to his chest as he watched 'em drop, spurtin' blood all over his nice carpet. His mouth fell open.

Of course, I weren't sure how much he could see, really, bein' that this hallway had no windows and no candles to offer him any light, but

I sprang forward anyway just as he was turnin' toward us and socked him in the jaw same as I'd done to Mr. Miller.

My fist caught him just as unawares as it had Mr. Miller, too. I yanked the box from his grip as he went sprawlin' to the floor, but he weren't unconscious yet. So I dropped to a knee next to him as he rolled, hands over a bloodied mouth, and clipped him again in the temple.

He went limp.

Satisfied, I straightened and shook out my fist, lookin' to Sally. "Sure we can't kill him?"

She rolled her eyes behind those multi-lensed glasses, but before she could make any kinda reply, Bill's firecrackers went off.

And they sounded like cannons, all right.

Seemed the high-brow folk had managed to remain mostly calm with the lights goin' out, 'specially with the main floor havin' some candles lit here and there and light comin' in from the big windows. But when those firecrackers started boomin' fit to nearly make my ears bleed, the main floor erupted into chaos.

Just like we'd wanted.

There were screams, shouts, and everyone started runnin' fer exits fast as they could manage.

"That's our cue," Sally said, and I couldn't agree more.

She retrieved her three knives, wiped 'em on the shirts of the dead, and tucked 'em away again under her skirts. Then we moved quick down that dark hallway and turned left to head past the cellar and the main kitchen, joinin' a flow of folk rushin' fer the back exit there.

But we hadn't got too far with that mob before I heard Baron Haas shoutin' behind us, out of breath and furious, "Stop! Everyone stop! No one leaves till I find out who stole from me!"

Shit. He hadn't stayed asleep very long. Shoulda gagged him and tied him, maybe, like I'd done to Mr. Miller. Kept him from soundin' the alarm till we were good and gone from this place.

Too late fer that now.

But he might as well have been talkin' to a herd of panicked cattle. Not a soul slowed their rush toward the door—any door.

Outside, those firecrackers boomed and crackled.

I dodged further inside the group of people makin' fer a hasty exit, holdin' that lockbox close, bounced and jostled between bodies. I glanced back once, saw Sally likewise swallowed up, not far behind me, and then I focused on findin' the actual exit.

There was one up ahead ... but a couple of the baron's hired security blocked it, guns drawn and lookin' ready fer a fight. They musta heard his shoutin', even over all the ruckus of panicked people and those firecrackers. The group of folks Sally and I were a part of drew up short in front of 'em and then milled around, talkin' excitedly amongst themselves like they weren't sure just what to do now.

I weren't sure just what to do now, neither.

XXII

ALL THAT IS OWED

"Quiet down, now," one of the men blockin' the door said. "Ain't nothin' to worry about. Just some firecrackers. Saw 'em myself out there ... real purty, they are."

"And you can see 'em for yourself after we search y'all," the other one said. "Make sure you ain't trying to take off with something you didn't pay for."

Many offended and aghast protests arose at that statement, and I bit back a swear of my own, glancin' to Sally again. She met my eyes, lookin' ridiculous in those multi-lensed glasses of hers, and nodded her head fractionally to our left. I looked that direction; saw a set of curvin' stairs leadin' to the second floor.

The floor we weren't supposed to be wanderin' around in.

But I figured I'd already stolen the baron's prized possession, surely violatin' his privacy couldn't be no worse. So I nodded back to her, then pushed through the people pressed close till I broke free of 'em, and headed fer the stairs.

Sally was right behind me.

It may have still been fairly dark in that big house, but the dim light shinin' through the big windows on either side of that back door was enough fer the two armed men to catch sight of us breakin' off from the herd.

"Hey!" one of 'em shouted. "Come back here! Don't be runnin' off!"

We only walked faster, till we broke into a jog and reached the stairway, then started up.

"Hey!" the man shouted behind us again, and I heard his bootsteps thump against the hardwood floors as he came after us. "You ain't supposed to go up there!"

Shit.

Sally drew up beside me and took my arm, pullin' me along. "Come on now," she hissed. "Time to move!"

I scowled at her. Easy enough fer her to say. She weren't constrained in unfamiliar clothes and hampered by a metal leg. In the absence of the initial surge of adrenaline, the damn thing had gone all heavy again, makin' my limp more pronounced. "If you woulda just let me bring my guns," I hissed back at her, "it wouldn't matter how fast we moved."

She gave a little *harrumph*. We'd nearly reached the second floor now, but that hired gun gained on us quick. He musta been leapin' up those damn stairs.

"Stop right now or I'm afraid I'll have to shoot ya!" He was only a little out of breath.

"Heaven forbid!" Sally said, even as we topped the stairs and ducked down the darkened hallway. Her skirts rustled, and she pressed somethin' into my chest as we hurried along, the plush carpet dampenin' our footsteps.

My free hand groped at it, and my eyebrows raised as I recognized its shape. A pistol. But not entirely familiar.

I frowned and glanced down at it. A pistol, all right, but like none I'd never seen before. More wood than metal, and with some kinda thin wires and tubes and little gears along the side. "What in the hell is this?"

"A gun," Sally said.

"Don't look like much of a gun to me," I muttered. "Where are the bullets? How you supposed to load it?"

She snorted. "The bullets are there. It's already loaded and primed."

"Primed?"

"Works like any other gun," she said. "You got twelve shots. Just pull the trigger. You'll see."

If we hadn't been in such a hurry, I'd have pulled her aside and demanded an explanation. As it were, we headed down a hall that seemed to have no end, passin' door after door, and more of those display cases and vases of flowers. And that hired gun still chased us. Outside, the noise from the firecrackers had ceased. I hoped that didn't bode ill fer Bill. I hoped our horses were out back, waitin'.

"And you've had this on you the whole time?" I asked. "All night? And you didn't think to give it to me till now?"

"Come on now, folks," the man behind us called out. "This is your last warnin'! I'm serious!"

I heard the click of his hammer even over the distance between us, and wondered how good his aim would be in such poor light.

Beside me, Sally shrugged. "You did well enough without it, didn't you? And anyway, I didn't fully trust you not to shoot Baron Haas, if you would have had it earlier."

I frowned, supposin' that was a fair enough point. My thumb fumbled at the top of the grip on the strange gun, but it had no hammer. *Just pull the trigger.* Sure. "What else you got under your skirts?" I mumbled.

"Ha!" Sally hooked a hand under my left bicep and yanked, pullin' me sideways just as the man chasin' us fired. She spun me around and pushed me back against one of the many doors, pressin' up close as he fired a second time, the bullet hissin' past to shatter one of the flower vases. "Wouldn't you like to know." She glanced to the pistol she'd given me. "You gonna use that thing or just hang onto it?"

My attention had gone abruptly to the feel of her pressin' up against me and her subtle floral scent, but I pulled it back with more difficulty than I'd have preferred, and put it on the man runnin' toward us and the smell of gunpowder, instead. I leveled the gun with no cylinder and no hammer at him, his figure bright enough through those cat's eye glasses fer steady aim. When I pulled the trigger, my weapon hardly made a sound. There was no muzzle flash. Only a soft *whuff* of air.

I woulda thought it had misfired or jammed, but I heard the bullet crack into the wall down the hall, and saw the man belatedly jerk away from it, lookin' as bewildered as I felt.

I'd missed. By a lot.

Sally was watchin'. "Haven't you ever fired a gun before, Mr. Lynd?"

I scowled and grumbled, and readjusted my aim to account fer the thing's minimal weight and lack of recoil. "It's too light."

"I'm sure."

My second shot landed in the man's right bicep and slowed him up some as he grimaced and swore, but then he was mad. He didn't bother with no more warnin's, and his aim was better, too, when he lifted his gun again, now that we'd stopped runnin'.

A click sounded from the door behind me and I nearly lost my balance altogether as it swung inward, the support against my back suddenly gone. I stumbled backward into the room and Sally came in after me, though it was clear from her lack of surprise or staggerin' that she'd been the one to open the door in the first place. She turned just as the hired man's third shot buried into the door frame and shut the door firmly, then locked it.

"What good is this gonna do us?" I demanded. "Now we're trapped!"

In answer, she only moved past me to the windows along the opposite wall, and opened one up. The night breeze stirred the curtains. I could hear people talkin' down below, and the clatter of coaches and drivers shoutin' to their horses.

My shoulders sagged as I realized her plan. "Oh you gotta be—"

The door rattled behind us as that man threw his shoulder into it, and we both jumped around toward it, me with that pistol ready, and Sally with a knife in-hand. The knob jostled, but held.

"This way, Mr. Lynd." Sally tucked her knife away and gathered up her skirts, then hiked a leg up and over the sill, duckin' through to climb out. She looked entirely ridiculous, doin' that in her fancy gown, the little top hat pinned to her hair.

The door rattled again.

I sent two shots into it; heard the man on the other side give a yell. Maybe I'd got him.

But then, in answer, he fired through the door too, and wood splintered into the room as his bullet chewed through with more force than mine had.

I swore and ducked away from it, hurryin' over to the window, where Sally had disappeared out of sight. Leanin' out, I saw her climbin' down a lattice-work fulla vines. I vaguely recalled that Bill had mentioned somethin' about climbin' vines all around the house when he'd come back from scoutin' the place, but at the time I hadn't thought nothin' of it. Had thought it a strange detail fer him to mention. Guess it had proven relevant, after all.

Guess there was nothin' fer it ... I was gonna have to follow her down.

Another shot punched into the wall next to me just as I swung my natural leg over the sill, and then one hit the window, shatterin' glass down all over me. "Fuckin' hell..." I tried to shake it off, grateful then fer that high collar keepin' the sharp shards outta my shirt. Somewhere in the back of my mind, I knew that hired man had to be out of bullets. He'd need to reload.

Sure enough, silence fell across the room as I guessed he did just that.

I didn't waste the chance; I swung my leg back over the sill into the room and marched across the floor, unlocked the splintered door, and yanked it open.

The man in the hall looked up at me in shock, the cylinder of his revolver open. His mouth fell open to match it as I raised that strange gun of Sally's and sent two rounds into his chest at point-blank range. He staggered backward with that look of shock still on his face, then dropped dead to the carpet.

I shoved that strange gun into the waist of my trousers and turned away from him, crossin' the room again back to the window. I scrambled through it a great deal less gracefully than Sally had, even in her corset and bustle and high-heeled boots, since I had to keep one arm around that lockbox, and my metal leg still liked to misbehave, but I managed to get myself through and onto that lattice.

I started down with my one free hand and one good leg, descendin' it like a ladder, cursin' and swearin' the whole way.

"Come on, Mr. Lynd," Sally called up, just loud enough to be heard above the general commotion goin' on around the house. "Hurry up, now."

I cursed some more. What the hell did she think I was doin'?

I tried to climb down faster, slipped, and fell the last several feet, hittin' the ground with a grunt. Sally rushed over to help haul me to my feet, and I thanked her breathlessly as we took off through the chaos, aimin' fer the back of Baron Haas' property where our horses shoulda been waitin'.

"Well," she huffed as we went, "that could have gone better."

"Coulda," I agreed, but I was too out of breath from hittin' the ground to offer anythin' more.

The firecrackers had gone silent, but there was still plenty of confusion around the place. Folk milled about bewildered and lost, others yelled fer their coaches, fixin' to make a hasty exit themselves, and those employed by Baron Haas were tryin' to round up those outside, tryin' to keep anyone from leavin'. Didn't seem they were havin' much luck, though.

Sally and me cut through it all, me holdin' that lockbox cradled tight to my chest.

We hurried away from the general commotion, out into the dark, but I could see well enough through those glasses. I wondered if she'd let me keep a pair ... they sure were provin' useful.

Baron Haas had a lot of property, and by the time we got close to the little copse of cottonwoods where our horses were tied, I was even more out of breath. But I saw 'em, waitin' there, and I didn't think I'd ever been so happy to see a horse. A feelin' came over me then, a kind of elation I'd never felt. Maybe this robbery coulda gone smoother, but I had the lockbox, and Sally's people had done just as they'd said, and we hadn't got shot.

I had what Nan wanted, and I was gonna get my sister.

We reached the horses. My awful little scruffy mount had been outfitted with the biggest saddlebag Bill could find, and I wedged the lockbox into it and buckled it up tight before mountin' up.

Sally hitched up her skirts again and started puttin' stuff into her own saddlebags—how exactly she'd stashed it under there, I had no idea—then finally mounted up herself and reined around to face me, catchin' me starin' at her. "What?"

"Er ... nothin'."

"I told you, I needed to claim back some things that were mine."

"All right..." I didn't bother to ask when or how she'd managed to grab 'em, or what or how Baron Haas had acquired things that were hers to begin with. Not that it mattered, anyway. That was her business. I had my own business to attend to.

"Will you be at the meeting spot?" she asked abruptly.

I blinked at her, realizin' then she'd seemed to read my thoughts before I'd had a chance to take stock of 'em myself. I *had* just been thinkin' then of ridin' straight to Bravebank with that lockbox. Straight to Nan. Straight to bargain fer my sister. All I had back at Sally's saloon were my pair of clothes, and my pair of pistols were still with Bill.

The clothes didn't much matter. But the pistols did. "Yeah," I said finally. "Yeah, I'll be there."

Her smile was clear as daylight through those glasses. "Good. Do be careful, Mr. Lynd."

"You be careful, yourself, hear?"

She gave a nod. "I'll see you there." And with that, she reined back around and spurred her horse, and galloped off into the night.

I turned my stolen mount in the opposite direction and urged it into a gallop as well, lettin' the wind wash over me like that elation at finally havin' my hands on that damn lockbox.

Didn't take long, though, before I heard hoofbeats comin' after me. A whole posse of 'em.

And I cursed again the fact I didn't have my pistols. All I had on me was that strange gun from Sally and six more bullets.

I urged my horse on faster, takin' him toward the edge of the valley Blessing was nestled into. At least I could see better than any man followin' me, and I tried to take advantage of that, hopin' the rough terrain would slow 'em up some.

Our meetin' spot was well outside of town, with the idea we'd clear out any potential pursuit before gettin' to it. But I couldn't go there now. Not with these fellas on my heels. I weren't sure how they'd seen me leave, or, even if they'd seen me, *why* they'd decided to chase me down, and especially in such numbers.

No one who'd bothered glancin' my way in the baron's yard had got a good look at what I'd taken, I was sure of it. But the how and the why didn't matter now … all that mattered was that I lost 'em. Somehow.

My poor horse was blowin' hard already. I was pushin' him too hard. And I couldn't afford to slow up, not yet. The posse followin' behind me had dropped back a bit, but not nearly enough.

Then a new sound rose up outta the night … a sound I'd never heard before. Somethin' like the roll of thunder combined with the snarl of some great beast, but it made the hairs on the back of my neck stand up, and my horse threw his head and pinned his ears, eyes showin' the whites.

It got louder, and louder, till I coulda sworn it shook the rocks around me. Till it vibrated in my skull and drowned out all the sounds of hooves.

My horse nearly came unhinged, and it was all I could do to keep control of him, keep him on-course. I didn't know what in this world could be causin' such a ruckus, but if I could make it into the next stretch of trees, maybe I could lose 'em—the posse *and* that horrendous noise…

Somethin' roared over the rise to my left and went airborne, a big, dark shape made of glintin' metal and that awful sound, and my horse leapt straight sideways in mid-gallop. I clung fer dear life to the saddle, jarred as his feet hit the ground again, then came loose as he pivoted and sprinted the opposite direction … right back toward that posse.

I landed in the dirt with an *oomfph*, all the air goin' outta me.

That horrible noise quieted into a low rumble and came up beside me, a strange-lookin' wheel made of metal plates rollin' in front of me through the little black spots dancin' in my vision. I was tryin' to breathe, but my lungs didn't seem to work right. My strained, shallow gasps rose little puffs of dust as I willed my body to get up. To grab that pistol currently jabbin' into my belly. To run.

It did none of those things.

Thunderin' hoofbeats arrived then ... the rest of that posse. They circled around me, and I heard their horses blowin' hard, and the chomp of bits, and ropes bein' slid from saddles and shook out. Lots of ropes.

"Go get his horse," a voice barked from over in the direction of that rumble, near that metal wheel. "It's got what you want on it."

No. No no no, not the lockbox...

"Maybe if you'd not insist on driving that *ridiculous* nightmare of a machine, his horse would not have spooked!" another man snapped back. But I heard a few of 'em peel off and go after my mount, anyway.

"And if I hadn't, you'd still be chasing him," the first man growled. "He had a good start on you, too. Would have reached those trees over there and then what? You'd have lost him."

My breathin' finally began to ease, and I focused on takin' in slow, deep gulps. My lungs stopped burnin'. That gun still pressed into my belly where it was smashed between me and the ground, and I inched my hand toward it, bit by bit.

"You underestimate my tracking abilities," the second man retorted.

The first gave a derisive snort. "And you severely overestimate them."

He sounded awful familiar...

"That's enough," came another voice, a woman's voice. "All of that is irrelevant. What matters is that we have him. So stop your bickering and secure him, would you?"

Several of the posse dismounted, then, and I watched their boots approach me. Least I'd recovered my air by now, but I hadn't managed to reach my gun, yet. I was out of time now, seemed like.

So I rolled, pulled the gun from the waistline of my pants, and fired quick at the bodies surroundin' me. There were five of 'em, and my six bullets hit 'em all in turn—three fell dead, two staggered back with shouts, still alive.

There was a lot of swearin', and then the two still livin' pulled their own guns, intent on murderin' me. But more shots rang out from the direction of the wheeled machine, and then those two fell to join the others in the dirt, no longer livin'.

Confused, I twisted around to see who had shot 'em ... and found Mr. Miller. He stood next to a two-wheeled metal contraption with a saddle in the middle of it, in his black suit with his missin' cravat, his hair even more mussed now, and that thin line of blood dried on his chin. He holstered his smokin' pistol on the side of his machine, and smiled at me.

Well fuck.

"Goddamnit, Miller!" the woman yelled. "How many times do I have to tell you to stop wasting good men?"

I turned back toward her only to find her nearly on top of me, and I didn't have no bullets left. I brought the gun at her, anyway, hopin' she'd maybe think I might, but she didn't slow. She whacked her own weapon into my wrist and sent Sally's gun flyin', then brought hers back and cracked it into my right temple.

Pain shocked through my skull and my vision flashed white as I went flat to my back, and those fancy glasses of Sally's flung off my face.

She grabbed my arm and hauled me back over onto my belly so I was face-down in the dirt again. Then she sat on me, and she was heavier than I'd expected.

Mr. Miller grunted. He leaned back against his growlin' machine, arms and ankles crossed, watchin' her try to truss me up, but he didn't lift a finger to help. "I think you and I have different opinions of what makes a good man," was all he said.

"I have no doubts about that," the woman muttered. She was tryin' to get ahold of my wrists, pull 'em back to her so she could tie 'em, but the pain in my head was only a fiery ache now, and I surely weren't gonna make the job easy on her.

I twisted and bucked and threw her off as neatly as my own horse had dumped me into this predicament, then rolled to sit on her chest and scrabbled fer her pistol.

She punched me in the jaw. A solid hit that snapped my teeth together and nearly knocked me off her. Then she wound that rope around my neck and yanked, simultaneously cuttin' off my air and pullin' me forward and downward, so that I lost my leverage.

She tossed me easy after that, and my fingers groped at the rope cuttin' into my throat as she staggered to her feet, pantin', makin' sure to keep it taut. "Thank you for your help, Miller," she commented breathlessly.

He shrugged. "Seems you have it handled."

I pushed onto my knees, then lurched at her, tryin' to put some slack in the rope so I could breathe even as black edged my vision. But she back-pedaled quick and pulled it tight again before I could get a full gulp of air.

I was gonna have to move faster...

Through the rushin' in my ears I heard more horses approach, then saw 'em. Three more men, and they were leadin' that scruffy mount of mine with its bulgin' saddlebag. He was unnerved and jumpy, eyes wide as he trailed reluctantly at the very end of his reins.

Fuck.

The new arrivals took in the scene at a glance, and Mr. Miller musta seen the looks on their faces same as I did.

"Easy there, boys," he called out. "We want him alive."

They hesitated, and in that moment I rushed the woman. Tackled her. Sucked in big breaths of air as the rope around my neck loosened. Fixed my hands around her own throat, nice and snug. Watched her eyes go wide.

The loop of a lasso settled around my shoulders then, and I'd only just released the woman's throat to try and free myself when it jerked me off her backwards so hard I lost all my air again. I was dragged several feet through the dirt, and by the time I stopped, the other two men were on me with more ropes.

I still didn't make it easy on 'em. It took both the men, and the woman, to finally get me tied, and by then we were all exhausted. I laid there gaspin' and glarin' up at all of 'em, covered in bruises and dust, while they all glared down at me. They'd got my wrists tied tight behind my back, my ankles tied, and left that loop tight around my shoulders, too. My head and my jaw both throbbed, and my heart raced fit to choke me.

This weren't turnin' out so good.

"Should beat the sense outta him for what he's done," one of the men growled.

"Should have shot him from the beginning," the woman said.

"Where's the fun in that?" Mr. Miller drawled, and the others turned to glare at him instead of me. Through all of this, he'd only stood there next to his strange machine and watched. Now, he dipped his chin in my direction. "Check his leg. The left one."

My racin' heart stuttered.

"You don't give the orders here, *Miller*," the woman hissed. "It's bad enough you dared show up tonight ... bad enough you caused a disgraceful, disgusting scene! You should be ashamed of yourself!"

That made him straighten, and anger flashed across his features. "If not for me, Edward Haas would have never known who'd stolen from him. You wouldn't have known where the thief went. And you wouldn't have him now."

A long, brown braid hung down the woman's back as she faced Mr. Miller and squared her shoulders. So it was her again. The one who'd intercepted him inside when he'd been comin' at me, who'd told him he wasn't welcome there. Why would he have helped her now? And how could he have known I'd taken anything?

"And let me assure you," she growled, "that is the *only* reason I'm tolerating your presence at this moment. Let me also assure you that while I will inform Baron Haas of your assistance here, it will surely *not* make up for the embarrassment you caused him earlier tonight."

Mr. Miller smiled again. "Whatever would make you think I wanted to somehow make apologies to such a pompous waste of space as Edward Haas? Absolutely not. I had a right to be there tonight same as anyone else."

The men accompanyin' the woman with the braid looked to each other and shifted on their feet, and I got the sense this was a long-runnin' point of contention. If they could just keep arguin' about it, though, maybe I could scoot off into the brush, get out of sight.

"We grow weary of your delusions, Miller," the woman said. "Now, run along. Your part is done. I'll be taking this thief back for proper justice."

"Not yet," Mr. Miller said. His tone called back memories of Baron Whittaker, and dread stirred in my gut. "This man murdered my father, I'm quite certain of it."

The others hadn't been expectin' that, and they suddenly looked uneasy. Even the woman's stiff stance softened, and she glanced down at me briefly before turnin' back to him. "How ... how can you be sure?"

He nodded toward me again. "I told you, check his leg. The left one."

The woman hesitated, then turned and nodded to her men. They came at me, one pullin' a knife from his belt.

I rolled and tried to slither away from their reachin' hands, but it was a futile endeavor. They grabbed me, hauled me back, and the third man dismounted and helped hold me down while the one with the knife cut the left leg of my expensive navy trousers and ripped it open.

He muttered curses as he saw the metal rods and stood up quick.

The hands holdin' my biceps and ankles twitched, but they were already clutchin' hard enough to bruise.

"Would you look at that," Mr. Miller said into the silence. "The demon himself. Just as I thought. Guess I'll be takin' him myself, in fact."

The woman seemed at a loss fer words.

Miller finally stirred from his spot beside his machine, joinin' the others to stand over me. I kept my eyes on the woman, my gaze borin' into the side of her face as she stared down at my leg, and willed with every ounce of me fer her to refuse to hand me over. I'd face her ... I'd face Baron Haas fer stealin' his lockbox ... but I'd heard too much about Mr. Charles Miller to think I'd have any hope of livin' if he took me.

She hissed a sigh and looked to my horse. "Fine. Fine, you take him. I suppose we have back what he took from us, anyway."

"No," I choked out. It was the first word I'd spoken since they'd run me down, and it made 'em all look at me like maybe they'd forgotten I was a man who could speak fer himself.

The Haas woman finally looked at me, even, and arched one eyebrow.

"Oh good," Mr. Miller said. "So you do speak. That will make things easier. We have so *very much* to talk about, after all."

"Let's go," the woman said. "I've had enough of this filth. Be sure you get his horse. We'll come back with the wagon for the bodies." She signaled to her men, and they released me, goin' back to their horses.

Mr. Miller cleared his throat loudly, theatrically, just as the others were mountin' up. "About that…" he began.

She paused as she was about to step into her stirrup and turned, clearly annoyed.

Miller's right hand moved, and the pop of a firearm echoed out into the night, makin' me and the horses jump.

Four shots, and the woman with the braid and her three remainin' men were dead, slumped on the ground. Two of 'em had weapons in-hand, but they'd been too slow, caught by surprise, shot in the back.

"Well now," Mr. Miller said. He slowly pushed the spring-loaded pistol back into his sleeve. "That's better, isn't it? I've been wanting to do that for a long time."

I only gaped up at him, my mouth still open.

He leaned down to pick the cat's eye glasses out of the dirt. They were a little bent now, and coated in a fine layer of dust. He studied them fer a minute, then carefully folded 'em and tucked 'em into the inside pocket of his jacket. "That's some interesting hardware you have there, friend."

I said nothin', all my muscles coiled and braced fer … somethin'. Anythin'. I didn't understand this man, didn't know him outside of what I'd heard about him up till now, but it was quickly becomin' apparent he was dangerously unbalanced.

He reached down again and took a full fistful of my velvet, gold-embroidered jacket, then hauled me to my feet. I wavered there unsteadily—it was hard to stand with my ankles tied so tight together—and he brushed the dirt off my shoulders.

"There we are." He'd adopted that strange purrin' tone again. "So good to finally meet you face-to-face. Now I can give back to you all that is owed, at last."

XXIII

THE BASTARD OF BLESSING

He started by payin' me back fer what I'd done to him at Baron Haas' residence.

His fist came flyin' outta the darkness and cracked into my jaw, and I hit the ground again hard, havin' no way to catch myself. I rolled, reelin', and tried to catch my breath. Waited fer the ringin' in my ears to go away.

Miller turned and went to his machine. He had saddlebags on it, like it was some kinda horse. Ugliest and loudest horse I'd ever seen, certainly. He rummaged around in one of those bags, then came back to me. I couldn't quite make out what was in his hand now that I didn't have those glasses on no more, despite the fact the moon hung over the horizon fat and full.

He came and sat down next to me; pulled my shoulders up into his lap like I were some kind of injured man in need of care. My head was poundin' somethin' awful now, sure, and the rest of me was bruised up good, too, but the last person I wanted any care from was him. I made to sit up and move away, but his left arm hooked around my neck tight, and his right hand pressed a cloth to my nose and mouth.

I knew the smell immediately. Same stuff the doc had used to put me to sleep when he'd found me already half-dead in the desert.

I struggled against Miller's hold, turnin' my head in attempts to dislodge that cloth, but his arm squeezed at my neck like a trap, and I couldn't get my wrists free of those ropes fer nothin'.

He weren't suffocatin' me; I could breathe well enough, pantin' into that cloth, but I was gettin' awful dizzy. Black washed in across my eyes, and I couldn't tell if that were from him squeezin' my neck or from that stuff.

My body got heavy, my struggles weakenin'. Just like when Dr. Balogh had done this to me, and I'd woken up later with a new metal leg. Only I had a good idea Mr. Charles Miller did not intend to be such a helpful soul as the good doctor had turned out to be ... if I woke up this time at all.

"Easy now," he said quietly. "It's just a little sleep. Just a little sleep and we'll be home real soon."

Terror shocked through me at those words, at the way he said 'em, and the jolt of adrenaline renewed my struggles. He almost lost his hold on me; my vision cleared fer just a second, but then he doubled-down. Clamped his arm like a noose on my throat and readjusted the cloth so a fresh wave of that sweet smell went full into my lungs.

The world spun circles, the darkness comin' on quick.

"Shhhh," he hissed. "Quiet down. You reap what you sow, friend, and it's time for the harvest. No need to be so upset about it."

I *was* upset about it. But I couldn't do nothin' about it, neither.

I fought as long as I could, long as I could hang on to a bare thread of consciousness, but eventually I couldn't hang on no more, and the sleep took me.

I had impressions of vibration and noise ... so much noise. And bein' carried, and I came to enough to drag my eyes open once, but all I saw were shiftin' patterns of light and shadow, and then there was that sweet smell again, and I went back under.

But I did wake up, eventually, risin' up out of a deep, murky darkness like surfacin' from the depths of a lake. Consciousness broke on me like a wave, and with it came an acute throbbin' in my head. And then nausea. I retched and tried to sit up, couldn't. I vomited anyway, turnin' my head just in time to keep it from goin' all over me. Most of it went over the edge of ... a table? Spattered against a hard floor below. I stared across now at a wall made of fitted stone, electric lanterns glowin' at intervals along it.

I frowned at it and spit, blinked hard, my mind sluggish and disoriented.

"Don't worry," said a voice, "it will pass."

I startled at the nearness of him, and my gaze shifted in his direction.

The bastard son of the late Baron Whittaker sat in a large leather armchair near a hearth set with a blazin' fire, one ankle crossed over the opposite knee, readin' a book. He'd cleaned up, too. Put his hair back in place, wiped that blood off his chin, donned a new suit, though one more casual than the one he'd worn to Baron Haas' auction.

Another armchair sat opposite him, empty. It looked fer all the world like he coulda been in the sittin' room of his own estate, enjoyin' a quiet evenin' ... if not fer everything else around him. And the more I saw, the more I wished to go back into that blissful dark of unknowin'.

A basket near the hearth held an inordinate number of brandin' irons, and just the sight of 'em had my right arm burnin' like it was on fire again already. A sideboard had been stocked with various bladed utensils and knives instead of various blends of whiskey. Ropes, cords, whips, and chains hung from hooks along one wall. A shelf behind his chair held books ... and the shelf beside that one held contraptions that were surely some kinda Old World tech, but their shapes were so unusual I couldn't even guess at their purposes. Sturdy wooden tables were set at intervals around the room, topped with sheets of pounded metal, and all fitted with thick leather restraints. There was a well in the far corner, a bucket of water next to it, and towels and rags stacked along its lip.

On one side of me was a small table laid out with items from a doctor's kit: stitchin' needle and thread, ointments, stethoscope, tourniquet, vials of medicine and syringes to inject them with. And on the other side of me was another small table with all my stuff lined up neat: the cat's eye glasses all clean, Sally's strange pistol ... the dialed lockbox. And my fancy clothes, folded crisply like they'd just come back from a wash.

My ... clothes?

I looked down at myself, and my heart quickened to see I was naked, all right, and strapped down tight to one of those tables. My metal leg gleamed dully in the light of the fire, fully exposed.

I groaned, closed my eyes, and thunked my head back to the table.

This weren't good. This weren't good at all.

A violent shiver racked my body and I retched again, addin' more vomit to the puddle.

Mr. Miller glanced up at me. Then he sighed, put the book's ribbon in his place, and closed it, settin' it aside on the arm of his chair. He shook his head and clucked his tongue as he stood. "Look at you. Making such a mess. And we haven't even started yet." He went to the well in the corner and brought over the bucket.

And dumped it directly on my face.

It was fuckin' *cold*. I gasped; inhaled some, coughed and spluttered and choked.

He turned and went back to the well, hooked the bucket on the pulley, dropped it down to refill it. "You know," he said conversationally as he worked, "you should consider yourself lucky. I don't invite just anyone here. Only our most privileged guests ever see this place." He cranked the bucket upward again and looked back to me over his shoulder.

I was shiverin' more now, worse than before. Pain gripped my temples in a vice, and that nausea threatened to come up again. I tried to swallow it back, unsure of his intentions fer that second bucket, but preferrin' he not dump it on my face again. I watched him warily as he took it from the pulley and walked to stand next to my table, smilin' down at me.

"Most troublesome folk I relegate to the cellar. It's an ... unpleasant place."

My eyes shifted involuntarily to the multitude of unpleasant devices surroundin' us now on every side, and I wondered how any place could be more unpleasant than this.

"Here, however..." He lifted one hand to gesture. "Here we can be much more comfortable."

I figured he must have meant that ironically.

He lifted the second bucket and I braced myself, but the icy water still took my breath away as he poured that one all down the length of me, soakin' most everything except my metal leg. "Fuck!" I spat. "Ain't you ever heard of heatin' a person's bath 'fore you go spongin' 'em down?!"

A broad smile split his face at my retort, and he answered without missin' a beat. "On the contrary, I find a cold bath much more invigorating. Makes the body feel *alive,* don't you think?"

I didn't think I felt any more alive now than I had before. Only colder, and the pain in my head sharper. And anyway, I was pretty sure I wouldn't want to be feelin' anythin' at all here soon enough.

His gaze went to my right bicep, where the shiny pink scars from his father's torture had not quite healed, and one of his hands came up to touch them, fingertips brushin' lightly across the bars of new skin.

I recoiled from his touch, or would have, if not fer the restraints keepin' me still. But I pulled at 'em, anyway, intensely dislikin' the way it felt. The way it stung, somehow, and sent gooseflesh racin' all across my body.

He lifted his hand, and his smile faded. His eyes, the cold, calculatin' eyes of his father, had gone hard. "We'll get you warmed up soon enough," he said softly.

He turned away and put the bucket back in its place, then wandered around the room gatherin' various things from various places into his arms. "You sure have a lot of fight in you, friend. But I prefer it that way. Makes for a much better experience, in my opinion. So much more *entertaining*." He paused in his gatherin' to glance at me. "I've got quite a special week planned for you. Of course, I will do my best to make you last longer than a week." He went back to his perusin' and collectin', and I pulled hard as I could against those restraints.

They didn't budge.

"But I must confess, the longest Father or I ever managed to keep a *guest* of ours alive has been six days. I have been refining my techniques of late, though, in anticipation of your arrival. So ... perhaps this time I could stretch your last days out to seven. Ten would be more satisfactory, of course, but I won't get greedy."

Ten days?! I tugged again at the leather straps at my wrists and ankles, but they were sturdy, the buckles thick. There weren't no windows in this place, and from the rock of the walls and floor, I got the sense we were underground. Of course. If this place were particularly constructed for this kind of grisly business ... there'd be no easy escape.

And no way fer anyone else outside to hear the screamin'.

My heart pounded wild in my chest as he came back to my tableside.

"My father was going to give me his name," he said abruptly. He pulled a hammer from his collection, laid it down on my damp chest. "Make me a legitimate Whittaker." Pliers came next, set down alongside the hammer. "He was going to give me the whole Whittaker estate, in fact. Give it to *me*, not my half-brother." He held up a jar, gave it a good shake, and put it beside the pliers. The inside of it *moved*. Writhed.

Fire ants.

Fuck me.

"Not to the fraud who is currently the head of the family ... to whom the estate was awarded upon my father's untimely death..." Now he put down a knife, a long, thin one made fer skinnin', and then two small pieces that looked almost like insects, only they were made outta metal. "Because he was *murdered* before he could make my induction into the family—my appointment as *heir*—legal and binding." The last thing he put down was a coil of rope with a noose in one end, and that one he laid on my belly.

I said nothin', my eyes locked on that jar of ants, but my breathin' gave away my opinion on all of this clear enough, anyway, especially with all that stuff lined up atop my chest. It all rose and fell, rapid and shallow, betrayin' my feelin's despite my silence.

"Now," Mr. Miller said, his hands grippin' my left forearm, "just how do you think I should repay the man who has taken so much from me? Who has, in fact, stolen away my very birthright?"

Still I said nothin'. I thought of Charlotte, then, and took solace in the fact she weren't here. He didn't have her. I'd already sent her that warnin'. She'd have had it days ago now. Even if he had people out lookin' fer her, she'd be ready fer 'em now, surely.

Maybe I wouldn't get to free Ethelyn, at this rate. Maybe I'd die here in this underground Hell ... but maybe I'd have at least saved Charlotte from sufferin' this same unpleasantness. If Mr. Charles Miller wanted to take his vengeance out on me, so be it. Long as he never got to her.

He was right, anyway. You reaped what you sowed, like Pa had told me so often growin' up, and I'd been sowin' a lotta violence these last eight years. Some mighta said I deserved whatever Miller wanted to do to me.

Hell, I mighta even agreed with 'em, on some level.

But that didn't mean I wouldn't have preferred a different end, if given the choice. Somethin' a lot quicker, at least.

Despite my best efforts to stay distracted, my attention went back to Miller as he plucked the pliers off my chest. He turned them from side to side in the light, and his hand on my left forearm slid down to the cuff of leather around my wrist.

Reflexively, I clenched that hand into a fist.

"So many choices," he muttered. "But then ... you *did* provide me the opportunity to end Baron Haas' bitch of a guard dog. She's been a thorn in my side for years. Head of his security, can you believe it? Been waiting for that chance a long time now ... and it has been *so hard* to be patient. Now she's dead, thanks to you." He replaced the pliers, turned, and walked casually over to the hearth. He pulled one of the brandin' irons from the basket, and my breathin' went all harsh and ragged.

I tried to slow it, to calm my racin' heart before he came back close.

He stuck the end of the iron into the fire and rested it there along the floor. Then clasped his hands behind his back and paced. "I'll tell Baron Haas it was you who murdered her, of course. And that it was you who murdered the rest of them, as well. Imagine his delight when I tell him I found you. He will most certainly want to come retrieve you for himself. And when he comes, well..." He stopped pacin' and faced me. Smiled again. "I'll murder him, too. Teach him what happens to those who throw me out of their house like nothing more than a common wretch."

I remembered the scene he'd caused at Baron Haas' auction. So he'd been thrown out after that, then. Good riddance. Except it seemed he hadn't left the premises soon enough to spare me this sufferin'. Somehow he musta seen me and Sally goin' out the back, or else seen the woman and her posse head out after me and followed.

"Though I suppose if not for that," he went on, and I wondered if he particularly enjoyed hearin' himself talk, "I might not have seen those fireworks. And if I had not gone to investigate just who was setting those off, perhaps I never would have seen you and your little friend sneaking off with something that didn't belong to you. And then perhaps I would not have had the rather clever idea to kill two birds with one stone: apprehend the man who helped kill my father, and get the Haas guard dog to do it for me ... thus luring her out to a place where I could, at last, eliminate her." He grinned down at me, and fear snaked through my belly at the thought of Bill and those fireworks. I hoped Miller hadn't recognized him. Hoped Miller hadn't abducted him, too, or killed him...

"But now that you are here," he said cheerily, "I can finally get answers to some of my *burning* questions. Questions like ... wherever did you get that metal leg of yours? And ... where is the woman Charlotte Harrison? And..." He went to the small side table that held my things—well, Sally's things, mostly—and placed his hands atop the lockbox. "And ... whatever would you want with *this*?"

I didn't mind him talkin' so much, long as he was talkin' instead of hurtin' me ... but I also didn't want to answer any of those questions. And I had a good idea that soon enough he was gonna stop talkin' and expect me to start answerin'.

"But let's not get ahead of ourselves." He took his hands from atop the lockbox and stepped away. "There will be plenty of time for conversation later. We have all week, after all. First we must decide exactly what kind of *motivation* your cooperation in our conversation might require." He stepped over to the shelf that held the Old Word contraptions again and browsed it as if it were his bookshelf. "I suspect you will be an exceptionally difficult man to wear down ... given that Father had no success during your time with him. And that is ... unusual, to say the least. Ah, here we are." He selected an object off the shelf, and it looked similar enough to a thing I was familiar with fer me to have a good guess at what it might do.

Miller brought it over to me: a short, thick metal rod with a trigger and a handle on one end and a circular pad on the other. He leaned his free hand on the edge of my table like it were a bartop and we were two old friends catchin' up. "You know," he said, "I can't decide if you are the bravest man I've ever met or the biggest fool I've ever met, coming right back into town so soon after what you did here. When I first saw you wandering lost in the Haas household, I didn't recognize you at all. The sketch is not quite accurate, is it? But it's close. It wasn't until we took a walk together, and I realized you had a limp, and that it was your left leg that was lame, that I wondered ... was it possible? Was it possible the man I'd been hunting all these weeks had shown up *here*? Had walked, literally, right into my arms?"

He held up the contraption, gave the trigger an experimental pull.

I flinched as electricity buzzed, snappin' across the circular pad at the end, despite the fact that's exactly what I'd been expectin' from it. I just kept thinkin', with my body damp from that water, and that sheet of metal underneath me, and one whole leg of mine made of metal, too ... I really didn't want him to touch me with that thing.

He released the trigger, and the electricity on the end of it went away.

I let out a slow breath.

"Still, if you had just kept playing your part ... perhaps I would have let it go. Perhaps I would not have been so eager to prove out my suspicions, passing it off as merely a coincidence. But you could never have done that, really, could you have? I could see it on your face the whole time we walked. How much servitude chafed at you." He smiled, and I was startin' to hate his smile more than Nine-Fingered Nan's, even. Least hers was born of true glee, however cruel. Mr. Miller's smile, on the other hand, was like somethin' dead. Somethin' painted on. Like somethin' he thought might be socially correct, but somethin' he didn't understand.

I looked away from him and fixed my eyes on the bookshelf: the least disturbin' thing about this room.

He pressed the circular end of the rod to my left shoulder and leaned in close. I balled my hands into fists, braced fer what I knew was comin'.

"I suppose I'm grateful for that. Otherwise I might never have discovered who you really were. I suppose it's even all right what you did to me there, as disgraceful as it was." His left hand rubbed absently at the bruise on his chin. "It's all right that you dared to strike me. That you ruined one of my favorite cravats. That you stuffed me into a closet. Just fine."

"Yeah?" I growled, and I turned my head back to glare at him. "Then why don't you unstrap me? Let's make it a fair fight. I'll put you down again no problem. Won't need none of that doctor's stuff to put you to sleep, neither."

The corner of his mouth twitched. And then he pulled the trigger on that rod and a sharp, white-hot agony seized me from head to toe. My muscles all clenched and I strained against those leather cuffs, woulda rolled around screamin' if I coulda, every place my skin touched metal searin' especially hot. But I couldn't writhe around and I couldn't scream, my voice stuck inside my throat, my teeth clamped so hard I thought they might break.

The cry only came out after it stopped, and all my muscles finally, mercifully, released, and I lay there pantin' and shudderin', my body steamin'. The tools still lined up across my chest burned like brands of their own where their metal touched my skin, and belatedly, I realized the two of 'em that looked like insects were *movin'* now.

The urge to flick 'em away, get 'em off me, was nearly overwhelmin' … but my wrists were trapped, and my body slow to respond to my mental wishes.

Mr. Miller ignored the two things crawlin' over me and brought the rod up to study it like he had those pliers earlier. "I must say," he mused, "the people of the Old World were truly ingenious. You should see some of the things we've pulled out of those ruins. Not everyone understands how to make them work, of course. But over the years ... I've become quite good at it. It does make you wonder, though ... what could have possibly caused the downfall of their civilization? People so clever, who invented such wonderful and terrifying things, who built such large cities all across this continent ... what happened to them? What brought about their end?"

He glanced down at me. "You ever stop and contemplate such things, friend?"

I hardly heard his question, too preoccupied by watchin' the little metal things explore the expanse of my chest. One looked somethin' like a centipede, a long, segmented body and all those tiny little legs, and it marched straight toward my face. I lost sight of it as it went beneath my chin, but I could feel it ... a light tickle movin' up my neck.

My muscles were startin' to regain feelin' now, and I squirmed, turnin' my head around every which way in a frantic attempt to dislodge the thing now movin' past my ear and up toward my temple. "What does it matter?" I gasped finally, hopin' maybe Miller would pull it off me if I started talkin'. "They're all dead and gone. Don't much matter how."

"Of course it matters," he countered. "Haven't you ever heard it said: Those who do not know their history are doomed to repeat it?"

The metal centipede crossed my temple, aimin' directly fer my left eye. I squeezed it shut. "Can't say I have."

Mr. Miller clucked his tongue. "My, my. Perhaps you *are* just a fool."

The centipede's multitude of legs crossed the corner of my shut eye, and then it *bit* my eyelid, the pain sharp and lancin'. I jerked and yelped, and renewed my efforts to try and shake it off.

It clung to my skin with all its legs, and bit me again.

"Ow, fuck, what the hell!"

"Ah." Mr. Miller leaned forward. "If you'll hold still..."

I quieted my efforts to dislodge the thing, and to my great relief, Miller plucked it off my eyelid. He held it between thumb and forefinger, and it writhed around lookin' fer all the world like a real insect.

My stomach turned at the look of it.

"Not yet, little one," Miller said to it. Then he looked back to me, and held it down in front of my nose.

I reared back from it as best I could, not wantin' it anywhere near me. My eyelid stung somethin' awful, and a little trickle of blood ran down off it to slip down over my temple like a tear.

Miller leaned his elbows on the edge of my table and put the electric rod, so similar to a hotshot but with a much bigger kick, down by my side. "Take this creature, for example," he said. "Fascinating piece of machinery. Found a whole lot of them down in the ruins. We didn't know what they were for, or what they did, for the longest time. But after some experimentation, we discovered they are quite adept at creating burrows. Specifically, they gravitate toward the eyes. Then they dig in there ... make a nice little tunnel. I hear it's excruciatingly painful. Or at least, it seems that way, judging by the sounds people make when I set these loose on them."

I tried not to think about how much that would hurt, or about how close that one had come to doin' just that on my own eye just now, or about how that was likely to still happen at some point in my severely shortened future.

Mr. Miller reached down and plucked the second metal insect up off my chest just as it had concluded its exploration. That one was less insect-shaped and more like a flat rectangle with eight, spider-like legs. But it wriggled around same as the first in Miller's fingers.

"And this one," he said, indicatin' the spider-ish one, "this one will peel the skin right off you. It's so small, though. It takes a *very* long time, as I'm sure you can imagine. I could do it much more efficiently, but," he shrugged, "I do want to keep you alive as long as possible. So, perhaps I shall let this one have a turn later. But not today. These two are more advanced than we'll get to today." He took 'em back to the shelf where he'd gotten 'em, droppin' 'em down into a jar and screwin' the lid on tight.

"But this..." he said as he came back toward my table, and he put a hand on the shin of my metal leg, patted it. "This is something I've never seen before. Never in all my years of studying Old World machines." He stooped over it and frowned, and never had I wished more to bring up that metal knee so I could smash it right into his nose.

The leg twitched and whirred, and to my great satisfaction, Mr. Charles Miller cringed back from it. He regained his arrogant confidence almost immediately, but it had been enough. Enough to know he was scared of it, at least on some level. Good.

He scowled, clearly unhappy with his brief loss of control, and went back to peerin' at it. His hands brushed over the rods and gears, and it was strange to know he was touchin' it, and yet feel nothin'. "It is not quite Old World, is it?"

"How should I know?" I said, and that was the truth. "I don't know, and I don't care. The thing's been nothin' but trouble since I got it. You want it? Take it fer all I care. And good riddance." That was the truth, too. The thing *had* been nothin' but trouble since I'd gotten it. And I could always get a new false leg. A different one that didn't make people want to cut it off me all the time. And maybe if I convinced him to take it from me, he'd unstrap that ankle. And then all I'd have to do was get the leg to do what I wanted it to do fer once, and maybe I could give Miller a broken nose or a broken jaw fer his trouble.

The thought made me happy, fer a little while. Till Miller turned his attention back to me instead of my leg, and I saw the look on his face. "Oh, I'll take the leg. Don't you worry about that. But not yet. Not yet. All in good time." He gave it another pat, then picked up the electrical rod again. "I have other work to do, first."

I opened my mouth to say somethin' else, to attempt to distract him further from inflictin' more pain, but he didn't seem interested in anythin' else I had to say. He lit up the end of that rod and pressed it into my shoulder again, and then all my words were gone, and all my thoughts collapsed into a world of hurt.

XXIV

ADVANTAGES

Fer days, he didn't ask me no questions.

I almost wished he would, just so I could have somethin' to focus on besides the pain. Least then I could occupy myself with thinkin' of creative ways to tell him to go fuck himself. Or concentrate on not speakin' at all.

But as it were, fer most of the first three days he only toyed with me. He'd threatened nearly every torture means I'd ever heard of, and several I hadn't ever heard of, but had only delivered on a few of those threats, stickin' to things that wouldn't leave no serious damage so long as they weren't applied too *generously*.

And he didn't apply 'em too generously. Yet. He measured it all out real careful-like, like he mighta been carvin' out some fine sculpture or puttin' together a rare delicacy of fine dinin' instead of just makin' a fella hurt. There'd been needles, and blades, and more of that freezin' water, and some of those fire ants, and he'd pulled off three fingernails from my left hand, one fer each day, and said he'd continue takin' one each day till the end, till I had none left. Ain't never felt a pain like that before; those had got the most yellin' and strugglin' outta me by far.

I'd almost—almost—pleaded with him not to take the third one ... but I had a good sense that was just what he wanted me to do, so I bit it all back, all the yellin' and the thrashin', much as I could manage. Though just thinkin' of him doin' that seven more times made me sweat. So I tried not to think about it. Nevermind the fact the fiery, pulsin' pain that still radiated from those fingers made it hard to forget.

And there'd been lots of that electrical rod. So much of that damned rod I'd blacked out a few times, lost most my sense several other times, and patches of red, angry skin lined my left arm and parts of my chest.

But worst were all the times in-between the pain. He'd sit in his chair and read while he waited fer me to recover myself. Sometimes he'd read aloud. Or he'd doctor me up some ... put ointment on the worst of the ant stings, stitch up the cut on my thigh that wouldn't stop bleedin', clean up my waste ... bring me food and whiskey.

I'd refused the food at first, no matter that it was better than most food I ate on a regular basis, and that the smell of it made my stomach twist in hunger. I weren't gonna accept such a thing from the likes of him. Weren't gonna make it easier on him to wring those ten days outta me. And he'd let me refuse it, at first. Didn't even make a fuss about it, fer which I was sorely disappointed. But I regretted it later, when he showed up with a funnel and a hose, shoved that hose down my throat, and poured some gruel down me.

Thought I was gonna die then, gaggin' and chokin'. That hose down my throat was worse than any of the rest of it, bringin' up a deep panic like I was bein' drowned. The next time he offered me real food, I took it. Let him spoon-feed it to me like I was some kind of invalid. And that's what terrified me most: the care he took in everything he did down here, his concern over seein' that I stayed alive, stayed coherent, fer as long as he wanted me that way. Like he enjoyed that part of it just as much as he enjoyed causin' the pain.

He was, by any measure, the most disturbed individual I had ever met.

I was sure now I'd die a horrific death at his hands, and yet ... there was still a part of me that struggled fer escape every time he left me alone. Still a part of me that kept thinkin' of ways I might get outta this, nevermind that I hadn't figured out how that might be yet.

It was the only thing keepin' me from losin' my mind entirely ... that, and remindin' myself over and over again it was better me here than Charlotte, or Sally. Least Charlotte was still safe. And Sally ... well, I was more concerned about her, bein' as Miller had mentioned he'd seen her leave with me that night. But she weren't here, at least. Maybe he hadn't recognized who she was. Maybe he didn't care. Maybe his glee at havin' me to torment was satisfyin' enough fer him at the moment. Or maybe he *had* recognized her, and he'd already told Baron Haas, and she'd already been dealt with accordin' to the law.

The thought gripped me with a horror stronger than any I'd felt facin' Mr. Miller's torture. But I had no way to know fer sure. And I dared not ask Miller himself. Didn't want him thinkin' I cared too awful much about her. In case he weren't concerned about her role in the robbery, or about the robbery itself—which I suspected he weren't, given he hadn't turned the lockbox back over to Haas yet—I surely didn't want to give him any reason at all to suddenly take an interest. And I feared he'd be all too eager to use such a thing against me if he knew I cared in the least.

Mr. Miller suddenly eclipsed my view of that dialed lockbox and I blinked. Hadn't even realized I'd been starin' at it. Dread stirred in my gut, so familiar now I hardly acknowledged it. Every bit of my bein' throbbed in constant, unendin' pain ... but each time he returned, he managed to find a new way to make it all so much worse.

He had a brandin' iron in hand tonight, and the end of it glowed white, havin' been in the fire all day. He put one in the fire every mornin', just to make me fret about it, I was sure, but he'd never used 'em. Not yet.

Now, I dragged my weary gaze up to his face, and through the heat shimmerin' off the hot end of that iron, I knew he meant to actually use it this time. The inside of me quailed, but I held my gaze steady, unblinkin'.

He turned from me, walked around to the right side of the table, and I watched him the whole way. When he stood by my shoulder, he held the iron down close to my face, until I had to turn my head away, and even then the heat felt blisterin' against my right cheek. My right hand balled into a fist—I didn't like to do that anymore with my left hand—and my body tensed. I clenched my teeth, wishin' suddenly he'd just get on with whatever he planned to do.

"They say my father had his eyes burned out," he said. The sear of heat left my face and traveled down the length of my body to stop over my groin, and my hands and feet jerked at the restraints, tryin' instinctively to cover myself.

But I couldn't, of course. I was strapped down tight and exposed and there weren't nothin' I could do about it. Nothin' at all.

"They say his genitals were badly burned, as well."

The heat got closer, hotter, and I gave a grunt of discomfort despite myself, fixin' my eyes on the ceilin'. Sweat beaded on my forehead, made the metal sheet against my back slick.

"I suppose it's only fair that I should repay you in kind."

I said nothin', rememberin' Baron Whittaker's shrill screams as Charlotte had shoved that glowin' crowbar into his face and into his goods. He'd deserved it, every bit of it ... his son deserved worse.

Then the heat drew away from my groin, and I dared to breathe.

"But maybe that wouldn't be entirely fair, after all," he mused. "I know you helped the woman free my father's slaves and burn down our estate. The redhead. Charlotte Harrison. But I also know it wasn't you who actually killed my father. That was her doing, so I heard. Her that burned out his eyes and his...." The iron shifted downward, the heat drawin' far too near my groin again, and I sucked in a breath, held it.

"Yes," he said quietly. "I know what she did. So perhaps I should save that particular indecency for her, yes? What do you think?"

The breath I'd been holdin' hissed out in a snarl. "You ain't gonna get her," I said. "So you might as well save yer threats."

He smiled. Looked amused, even. And withdrew the iron again, to my great relief. "On the contrary, friend. I received a telegram just today. My men in Pennsylvania have located her family home. They assure me they will collect her tonight, and they'll bring her back to the Territories by train. Back to where she *belongs*."

My body went cold at that news, the sweat chill on my skin.

"Yes! All the way in Pennsylvania. Quite a distance to travel. Makes her almost exotic, doesn't it? My father was enamored by her. Couldn't bring himself to just put her down, not even when she proved to be more trouble than she was worth. But I assure you, I will not have that problem."

My heart pulsed in my ears now, and a fear sharper than any I'd felt over these last three days set fire to my limbs. I fought against the restraints in a renewed effort to free myself. I'd sent a warnin' to Charlotte, sure ... but if they'd found her ... would she have prepared properly? Would she have taken my warnin' seriously? Had she even got it in the first place?

And how many men had Miller sent? What kind of protection did her family employ in the first place? There were too many things I didn't know ... I couldn't be certain of her safety from here, almost a whole country away, and I couldn't stand the thought of him gettin' to her.

"My, my," Mr. Miller purred, watchin' me fight those straps. "You don't much like that idea, do you? Interesting." He walked back to the left side of the table and pulled up one of the tall stools he sometimes used when his administerin' of pain was gonna take awhile. He took a seat now and peered down at me, and he still held that hot brandin' iron, though it seemed he'd forgotten about it fer the time bein'. "Tell me ... who is Charlotte Harrison to you? Is she more than just a passing acquaintance, perhaps?"

"No," I choked out, suddenly realizin' what he must be thinkin', and knowin' if he kept on down that line of thought, it'd only make things more terrible fer me and Charlotte both. Hell, I'd been so intent on keepin' his interest away from Sally, I'd let my worry over Charlotte slip too easy. "Hardly know her. Only used her to help me get to yer father." Well ... it was enough of the truth to sound convincin'.

"Hrmm." Miller turned the iron around in his hand absently, glanced upward toward the glowin' end of it. "Look at you. So talkative all of a sudden. What father did that night is starting to make a whole lot more sense now." He nodded thoughtfully. "I wondered why he'd sacrifice three perfectly healthy slaves. Now I understand." He kept on noddin', and then he stood from the stool and walked back to the fire, replacin' the iron.

I didn't understand what was happenin', why he'd suddenly decided against usin' it, but I was pretty sure it weren't because he was feelin' merciful.

"Father was always better at that than me," he admitted, comin' back to my table. "I learned quick how to make people hurt and how to make it last ... but he was always better at finding the weak spots. He could always find just the place to *press* to make people come undone." Miller put his hands on the edge of the table and leaned forward, loomin' over me. He chuckled, lost in the glee of his own personal revelation, whatever it was. He shook his head. "He'd always tell me: not all pain has to be physical! I think I finally see what he meant. So. Why don't you tell me more about this Charlotte Harrison?"

I glared up at him and kept my mouth shut. But I also stopped my strugglin' against the leather cuffs holdin' me to the table. I'd already given him too much with my first response. *Stupid.* Shoulda kept calm. Indifferent. Now he had somethin' to work with. Somethin' real.

"Maybe we should put your treatment on hold until she gets here, yes?" He retreated, goin' over to the next table to my left and trailin' a hand along its surface. "I'm thinking ... I could put her right here. Right next to you. And proper manners would demand I take care of her first. You wouldn't mind, would you?" He walked slowly around that table, and then back toward me, a malicious delight shinin' in his eyes.

I wanted to wipe that grin right off his face ... with a fist, a bullet, a brandin' iron ... I didn't much care, just anythin' that might change his twisted pleasure into the kind of fear he liked to bring about on other people. My own helplessness here was the most infuriatin' thing of all, bein' trapped and tied down and unable to do anythin' proper to put him in his place. The frustration, the rage, the hatred all roiled around inside with nowhere to go, gatherin' into a big ball of fire in my belly.

He perched atop the tall stool next to me again. "You wouldn't mind waiting while I exacted justice for my father's murder, would you? You could watch it all ... I have some truly extraordinary things planned for her, of course, being as she was the one to actually mutilate and murder him. Even better than what I have planned for you. Just you wait. It will be glorious…" His grin turned lecherous then, and he leaned toward me and dropped his voice, as if sharin' some kinda secret. "I always have *particular* fun with my women guests, anyway, and Ms. Harrison will certainly be no exception."

My tenuous control snapped. I surged against those restraints hard enough to make the table shudder, and Mr. Charles Miller started. There was a strange whirrin', clickin' sound, and then my metal leg *shifted—opened*—and came free of its cuff abruptly. I recognized the shapes of blades stickin' out from it in multiple places at nearly the same time I swung it toward Miller.

He'd jumped off his stool and whipped around at the noise, and the calf of my left leg struck him in the middle as he moved to catch hold of it, givin' him a gutful of knives.

He grunted as the blades sunk deep, at least three of 'em, but then I yanked my leg back and pulled 'em all free. Crimson bloomed across his white shirt and painted his hands as he clutched at his stomach. I aimed the metal foot at his face and gave him a good solid kick in the jaw, hearin' a satisfyin' crunch as he went flyin' back into his bookshelf.

It rocked as he crashed into it, a few of the books comin' loose to rain down over him. He slumped on the floor, dazed, but I didn't think he was out yet … or dead. Yet.

Adrenaline pounded fierce through my veins, makin' it hard to focus, hard to think. My other ankle and my two wrists were still secured to the table … I had to get those free too, somehow. I forced myself to look close at my metal leg now, no matter that doin' so in its current state brought up an unsettlin' uneasiness. Maybe I *were* some kinda demon…

It had never looked natural, of course, bein' all made of metal, but at least it had been generally in the shape of a leg. Now … now it looked like somethin' else entirely. There was still a foot at the bottom, but everything between that and where it attached to my thigh had damn near turned into an arsenal.

Thin, narrow knives stuck out of it like spikes from ankle to knee, and the side of my thigh had opened and extended, offerin' out a bigger, proper knife, and a ... a pistol. *What the fuck!?* How long had that thing been hidin' in there? I supposed it made sense Dr. Balogh hadn't told me about it while I'd been stayin' at his homestead ... but damn ... that thing woulda come in handy several times over by now if I'd known it was there.

Or if I'd known how to get to it.

I was surely gonna have to pay the good doctor another visit now. Have a little talk with him about anythin' else this leg might be hidin'. *If* I managed to get free of this damned table before Mr. Miller lurched up off that floor or called in reinforcements, anyway.

I heard him moanin' weakly down there, rollin' around.

I bent my left leg up, strainin' to reach fer the big knife holstered on my thigh with the sore, bloodied fingers of my left hand. I could only just barely touch the hilt. Grittin' my teeth, I pushed my wrist forward in its cuff until the leather bit hard into the already raw skin of my wrist. But I ignored it, finally gettin' my middle and index finger at the top of that knife hilt, hookin' it between 'em, and pullin' at it. It came free with little resistance and clattered to the table, and my heart came up in my throat as it nearly toppled over the edge.

My hand slammed down over the top of it just in time, stoppin' it. I gripped the hilt in my hand, turned it carefully so that the blade pointed backward and downward, and sawed awkwardly at that cuff.

The angle was bad, and the muscles in my hand and wrist burned with the effort of tryin' to keep it steady, tryin' to apply enough pressure to cut the leather, but not enough pressure to make it slip and cut my arm.

A blood-soaked hand rose up into my field of view and gripped the bottom left corner of my table, makin' me jump. I almost lost my hold on the knife. But then went back to cuttin' furiously, urgency cloggin' my throat.

The table creaked as Mr. Miller used it to haul himself up onto his knees. His face was good and bloodied now, and his jaw hung slack and a little crooked and I grimaced. He'd deserved that all right, but it sure didn't make a pretty sight.

He made some kinda noise, a furious growl that maybe he'd meant as a word, but I couldn't understand him. I kicked at his head again with my left foot, but he was out of reach. His left hand grabbed at my metal ankle below all the spikes, caught hold.

The cuff around my left wrist split, finally, and I pulled that wrist free with a cry of triumph, then wasted no time at all turnin' to unbuckle the one around my right wrist. With both wrists free, I sat up, then braced myself as the room swayed.

Mr. Miller struggled up to his feet, leanin' heavy on the end of the table and one hand around my metal ankle. His face was ashen gray, a sheen of sweat shinin' on his skin, but his eyes were clear ... and real, real angry.

I reached down to work at the buckle around my right ankle, the big knife still clutched in my left hand. My fingers trembled somethin' awful, and Miller used the opportunity to lunge at me, grabbin' at my left arm. The blood made his hands slick, and I managed to wrench away from him, then sank that big knife down into his shoulder.

He yelled, and his hands went to try and pull that fat blade from his flesh, but I yanked it out instead, keepin' hold of it, and then that last buckle around my ankle came loose, and I rolled off the table to the right.

I stumbled as my feet hit the floor and fell to my hands and knees with a grunt. Didn't matter that Miller hadn't been wantin' to leave permanent damage these last few days ... the torture had taken its toll, anyway. My body was stiff and weak, pain flarin' up fresh now that I was tryin' to get it to move.

Miller staggered around the table toward me and I scrambled up to my feet, reachin' fer that pistol holstered in my thigh with my right hand and prayin' the good doctor had put it in there loaded. I turned toward the Whittaker bastard and took aim at his chest, then pulled the trigger.

The hammer clicked on an empty chamber.

Fuck.

Miller limped forward and I went backward, riskin' a glance down to the gun. It was loaded ... the other chambers had bullets, I could see 'em right there ... I thumbed the hammer back again, watched the cylinder roll over to reveal the empty one, and gritted my teeth.

A safety measure, sure, which I supposed I appreciated given the fact the gun had been *inside my leg*, even if it were a metal leg, but I wanted all the bullets I could get right now, and I needed every shot to count.

Miller lurched at me and I opened fire, puttin' all five bullets into him. The gunfire reverberated off the stone walls and stone floor, deafenin', and the force of all those bullets knocked Miller stumblin' backward till he crashed to the floor, and he landed sittin' up against the lip of the well in the corner.

He sagged, his eyes not so angry anymore, but lookin' dazed and unfocused, starin' at the floor. His whole shirt front was soaked in red, and his breathin' rattled. Blood welled in his mouth, trickled out, and I took a few steps toward him slowly, the gun raised despite the fact I'd emptied it.

My ears rang and my heart thundered wild in my chest, my whole body achin', urgin' me to sit down and rest. But I couldn't. I half-expected him to get up again and come at me, like somethin' from one of those stories about the unnatural deeds of the worshipers of the dead.

But those were just stories, like I'd told Charlotte. And anyway, there weren't none of those necromancers here. Miller had taken three knives, five bullets and a good kick to the face ... he couldn't last. Not bleedin' out the way he was.

Didn't mean I was done with him, though. Not after what he'd done to me these last few days. Not after what he'd threatened to do to Charlotte.

So I holstered the pistol back in my ... leg ... put the big, proper knife back, too, and forced my feet to keep movin', careful not to cut myself on the blades that still stuck out of my left leg at all angles. I went to the hearth and grabbed up that brandin' iron he'd discarded only minutes ago, then hobbled back to him.

He didn't look at me as I stood glarin' down at him, didn't even try to turn his head. He only wheezed and gurgled, tryin' to breathe through all the blood in his mouth. The light in his eyes was fadin' fast.

"Go to Hell," I spat down at him. And then I pressed the glowin' end of that iron right *into* his face. He choked and flailed as his skin sizzled, maybe he tried to scream, but I figured his lungs were all fulla holes. I held it there despite his noises and struggles and weak attempts to dislodge it. Then I pulled it away, and echoin' what Charlotte had done to his father, jabbed it up between his legs fer good measure.

All his noises changed pitch, but then I threw the iron away, lettin' it clang against the stone floor, and went to the shelf that held all his Old World trinkets. I picked up the jar of metal insects and the jar of real insects—the fire ants—took a few steps back in his direction, and smashed 'em both to the floor by his side. The bugs—both real and manufactured—were more than happy to be free. They swarmed toward him, up his leg and over his arm, coverin' him quick as I backed away.

"See how you like it," I growled.

He twitched as they found his flesh, bitin', stingin', or burrowin' in, but he didn't have much life left in him now. Least what little he had left would be spent in misery, which was still better than he deserved.

I left him to the insects and kept backin' away, around to the small side table lined with all my things. I grabbed up my stack of folded fancy clothes, the multi-lensed glasses, and the lockbox with the dials, but didn't take the time to dress just yet. I wanted out of here first. Didn't want to spend one more minute in this Hell-hole. I searched frantically fer the exit.

The room was larger than I'd initially thought, but I found a stairway leadin' up in the far corner, and ascended it in earnest. I had to balance myself against the rough stone wall with my free hand, feelin' woozy now that the adrenaline had calmed a little. At the top of the stairs was a heavy wooden door. I turned the handle and pushed.

Nothin'.

Oh come on. Come on, please. Please. I closed my eyes briefly and took a breath, set my clothes and the lockbox down on the top stair, and tried the door handle again, leanin' my right shoulder into it. Nothin'. Locked.

I clenched my jaw against the swell of exhaustion, terror, desperation. Leaned my forehead against the wood and tried to think through the risin' panic.

Locked, sure. Maybe he'd lock it in case any of his *guests* managed to get off their table. Wouldn't want 'em to escape. But he was in here, too, tonight. There'd be a key somewhere. Maybe he carried the key with him. Or else there was another way out. Had to be.

I gathered myself, takin' in another few deep breaths, pushin' hard against the tightenin' in my chest, the flood of dread through my stomach as I turned around, and went back down the stairs. I went slow and careful, so as to not fall on my face, or slice myself with my knife-leg. My left hand grabbed up the huntin' knife from its leg holster again and gripped it, white-knuckled, as I crept around the corner at the bottom and searched out the body of Charles Miller.

He was still slumped against the wall of the well, his head drooped down on his chest now, and covered in his own blood and bugs both. Bitter satisfaction rose in me at the sight, though I wished I'd had the opportunity to inflict a lot more pain on him ... somethin' less rushed and more akin to what he'd done to me these last three days ... what he'd done to countless others before me.

Least now he was ended, one way or another. Least now he couldn't continue his twisted practices. Least now he couldn't hurt Charlotte.

Charlotte.

I needed to send her another warnin'. Needed to be sure his men didn't catch up to her ... somehow. And that meant I needed out of this godforsaken room.

My goddamn hands were shakin' again, but I kept the knife as ready as I could in my right hand as I approached him, wary of gettin' close to the ants. I leaned over him, keepin' as much distance as I could, and swatted several bugs off his blood-soaked suit jacket, then pulled back the sides of it to check its inside pockets. The first one was empty, but the second one ... the second one had somethin'. I slipped my hand down inside the bloodied silk linin' and closed my fingers around it. A key, all right. One of those big iron ones.

A few of those damn ants got too close, crawled up on my arm, and I yanked it back with the key in my fist and shook 'em off quick, before they could bite me again.

Then I turned away from the mess of a corpse that had once been the bastard Charles Miller and focused on those stairs, feelin' myself fadin'. By the time I got back to that wooden door, black spots wavered in my vision. I holstered the big knife; slipped the key into the lock and turned it, and the sound of it clickin' open was quite possibly the sweetest sound I'd ever heard.

I fell into the door more than pushed it, and it creaked open. The wash of fresh air startled me. Hadn't been expectin' that. I gathered up my clothes and the glasses and the lockbox again and stumbled through, then paused, strugglin' to orient myself.

It was dark, darker than Miller's dungeon had been, but my eyes slowly adjusted to the moonlight. A breeze ruffled my hair and brushed over my bare skin, raisin' gooseflesh. I took a deep breath of it, smellin' a town layered over the smell of a green valley, and lingerin' through that ... the smell of old fire. Ash. So it was night, then, and I was outside now. I squinted as my eyes adjusted, and eventually I recognized the loomin' dark shapes that surrounded me, and I realized where I was.

Standin' in the middle of the burned-out bulk of the Whittaker estate. The house. All around me were blackened walls, burned-up furniture, piles of ash. And the new, fresh beams of the repair effort. Some of the original house had survived, one of which was the wall and the door I'd just come out of. And Baron Whittaker's torture chamber, conveniently untouched given its underground nature.

Well I sure as hell weren't gonna stay here any longer than I had to.

I limped out of the house wreckage and into the open night and sat heavily in the grass. Stared down at my metal leg in the dim moonlight and fer the first time ... didn't exactly feel repulsed. Not even with all those things stickin' outta it.

If not fer that leg ... Miller surely would have killed me. And maybe Charlotte, too.

I swallowed hard, thinkin' all those things stickin' outta it were probably what Dr. Balogh had really meant when he'd mentioned it had *advantages*.

Advantages. Sure.

Now if only I could figure out how I'd gotten it to open like this in the first place, maybe those advantages would be worth somethin'. I scrubbed my hands over my face and took a deep breath, then went about tryin' to sort how to close up the damn thing. I couldn't very well get any pants on with it lookin' like this ... and I didn't much want to go wanderin' into town full naked and with my leg lookin' like this, neither.

But the more I looked at it, the more I didn't even know where to begin. I thought maybe the thigh holster was spring-loaded, and tried to push it inward, but it wouldn't budge. Seemed to have locked into place, or somethin'. And the blades all over my shin didn't seem to have any dull parts where I could safely take hold of 'em and try to fold 'em in, neither.

I sighed and finally gave up. I was much too tired and sore fer such nonsense, anyway.

Guess I was goin' into town full naked and with a leg fulla knives, after all.

Least it was good and dark out, and awful late. Maybe the streets would be empty, and I could stick to the back alleys. Not like I hadn't done that before.

I almost didn't make it up standin' again, and those black spots were gettin' bigger. I wavered fer a minute till I got my balance back, tried to ignore all the spots of pain pulsin' in my body, and picked up that lockbox and my clothes and those glasses again.

I trudged down the hill toward the lights of Blessing, limpin' heavy, focusin' on puttin' one foot in front of the other. It weren't that far. I could make it. There was one safe place I knew I could go there ... one safe place I could stay till I recovered my wits enough to go on to Bravebank with this damned lockbox.

Long as Miller or Baron Haas hadn't gotten to her. Long as they hadn't burned down her saloon.

Sally.

I just had to make it to Sally...

XXV

NIGHTMARES AND RUMORS

It was all I could do to stay outta that tunnel of black as I shambled down the hill and into town. Then I fought to keep my mind on-task, fought to keep myself oriented, fought fer every step in the right direction. My mind kept wantin' to wander, float off somewhere, and my body kept wantin' to just collapse into the dirt.

I staggered like an awful drunk; had to keep leanin' up against the sides of buildings to keep from fallin' over. Gettin' free of Mr. Miller had taken pretty much everything I'd had left, clearly.

The lockbox was still tucked under my right arm, its metal corners diggin' painfully into my skin from clutchin' it so hard. But I weren't about to loosen my grip on it. All of this was because of that damned thing, and I surely weren't gonna chance losin' it now.

Those fancy clothes I'd stacked on top of it, and I'd put the glasses on, hopin' they'd help brighten my darkenin' vision.

Vaguely, I recognized the alley I'd stumbled into. I was almost there. Almost to the Seven Knives. I pushed on.

Fortunately fer me, there weren't many people out and about at this hour, and most that were stayed out of the back streets. I came up on a few people here and there, hurtin' too much and too tired to care if they saw me, but they were all drunk or outright passed out, and they didn't seem to care about me lumberin' by, neither.

The one fella coherent enough to take real notice of me straightened up from where he'd been slouched against a wall, and his mouth fell open. He dropped the bottle of liquor he'd been swiggin'.

I only glared at him through the waves of black swimmin' over my eyes, not in the mood fer anythin' 'cept a bed at the moment.

"Holy Mother," he muttered. He scrubbed at his eyes, blinked hard, then stared at me again.

I kept glarin', and kept on hobblin' by.

He slid along the wall to the corner, then dodged around it and ran off into the darkness.

I supposed I probably did make a terrifyin' sight at the moment. Good. I weren't in any condition to handle any trouble. That, and the pistol holstered in my thigh was out of bullets. I'd have to talk to the good doctor about that, too. A gun weren't much good without bullets.

Finally, after what seemed like slow, agonizin' hours, I reached the back of the Seven Knives Saloon, and thank God it was still standin'. I lurched up to the door I'd snuck out of only ... what, days ago? Seemed like a good lot longer ago than that. The saloon's windows were all lit up, and I could hear the music and general merry-makin' even out here.

I pounded on the door with the flat of my left hand, then sagged against the door frame.

A minute or two passed, and I pounded on the door again, harder and more insistently this time.

It opened at last, and I saw Bill with a surly look on his face and a sawed-off shotgun pointed in my face before I realized I'd been puttin' more of my weight against the hand on the door than I'd reckoned, and I pitched forward over the threshold as he pulled the door open further.

Bill swore as he caught me in one arm. "What the fuck—what the hell happened to you?"

I murmured somethin' about bein' glad he was alive, and he dragged me inside the saloon's back hallway and kicked the door shut again with one foot. Surprised gasps and murmurs came from some-where nearby ... women. Some of Sally's girls musta been in the hall-way, too.

"Go get the boss," Bill snapped at 'em. "Quick! *Now!*"

Their light footsteps darted off along the worn wooden floor, and I wanted to say somethin' else to Bill as he attempted to get me propped up against a wall. My mouth opened, but no words came out. Couldn't remember what I was gonna say, anyway.

Least Sally was here. Least she hadn't got ratted out by Miller, or grabbed by any of Baron Haas' men. Least she was still safe.

I cradled the lockbox to my chest in both arms, hardly aware of Bill fussin' over me, and unable to understand what he was sayin', though it mostly just sounded like a lot of profanity.

I let go finally, and the blackness swallowed me.

I went right back to Mr. Miller's basement, strapped to that table, only now he had Charlotte, too. And Ethelyn, even. And Mama and Pa sat in the two armchairs over by the hearth, readin' their books. I yelled out at 'em, yelled that Miller had us all trapped down here, that they should run while they had the chance, but they didn't seem to hear me.

A voice came from my right and when I looked, there was that girl who I'd thought had been Ethelyn, who Taggert's men had murdered for no good reason at all, and the front of her dress was covered in blood. She walked toward me, her brown eyes full of tears. She reached fer me, opened her mouth, but only more blood came out.

I couldn't get away from her, and I couldn't help her. I couldn't move at all, held to that table.

Then Mama screamed, that horrific, wailin', hair-raisin' shriek she'd let loose when Pa had got shot, and my gaze whipped back to her only to see Pa slumped backward now, his face made a mess by buckshot and parts of his skull and brain drippin' all down the back of his armchair.

My own cry welled in my throat, mixin' with horror and nausea both, but then Mama's skirt caught fire. She didn't seem to notice, kneelin' next to Pa's chair and shakin' him like she could wake him up.

The fire crawled up her dress, over Pa's chair, across the floor to my table.

I couldn't move. Couldn't breathe. Couldn't scream.

The flames snaked over my own skin, and everything turned into fire and pain and my Mama's screams...

I jolted awake with a yell and found myself sittin' up in a bed, starin' out at a collection of people who all stared right back at me, their expressions rangin' from real concern to outright terror. I glanced 'em all over in turn as I struggled to bring myself back from the nightmare, my own terror still burnin' hot in my blood. Sweat soaked me, my heart raced, and I gulped air in big, ragged breaths, my body still tremblin'.

"Easy," Sally said softly as she stepped closer to the bedside. "It's all right." She pressed a palm to my damp forehead. "It was a dream. You're all right now."

A snort came from my right. "One helluva nightmare, more like."
Bill.

I turned toward him, found him holdin' on to my right arm with both hands. He released me and shrugged sheepishly. "Sorry. You were about to toss yerself from the bed."

The kid who had brought our horses the night we'd robbed Baron Haas was at the end of the bed, holdin' tight to my right leg under the sheets. He let go of me quick, too, and held up his hands as he backed away. "Boss's orders," he blurted.

I was about to look back to Sally when I recognized another of the people in the room.
Professor Morton.

He stood near my metal leg, which laid atop the sheets, and seemed frozen in place like a hare that might have sensed a predator lurkin' near. His eyes went so wide that monocle of his—this one unshattered—fell out of his eye to dangle against the breast of his vest.

"You," I growled. I made as if to jump off the bed and go after him, but several pairs of hands grabbed me and prevented me from doin' so at the same time as several voices raised in protest and told me to stay put.

"You don't need to be moving around just yet." Sally's voice cut out above the rest of 'em. "The doc ain't done with you yet. And anyway, the professor here is the one who managed to put that ... that leg of yours back together. He's done a fine job of it, considering."

I shifted my glare from the professor's pale face down to my leg. The knives and the thigh holster had disappeared, all right, tucked back in to the leg itself, somehow. It looked just like it had the day I'd first gotten it.

"Now look," an unfamiliar voice said, and I looked up again to see an older man with big, bushy mutton-chops and small round spectacles step forward. "You've suffered a lot of trauma..."

"You think?" I snarled.

"... you need to get some rest, try to stay calm. Your injuries aren't life-threatening, but if you try to do too much too fast, you could aggravate them and make them worse, make them take longer to heal."

"You the doctor then?"

He straightened and smoothed at his rumpled shirtfront. "That's right. Dr. Alton Abbot, at your service. Those burns were pretty bad." He nodded toward my left shoulder, and I realized there was a bandage wrapped around it now, goin' down nearly to my elbow, and wrapped around my chest, as well. All those places Miller had pressed that electrical rod to my skin. Another bandage wrapped mid-thigh around my left leg, around the seam where my natural flesh met the metal leg, and the three fingers with missin' fingernails had bandages around 'em, too. All the little cuts Miller had made all over me were freshly medicated, the deepest ones freshly stitched. And the ant bite blisters had ointment on 'em.

"Be careful not to pull out those stitches," the doc added. "And change the bandages on your fingers daily. If you notice excessive heat or redness there, or any discharge, you let me know right away. As for your ... er ... false leg ... well, I'm afraid that's outside my area of expertise. The professor here knows more about that nonsense than I do, so I leave it to him. I will return to check on you tomorrow."

"I'll be gone tomorrow." I said it reflexively, but even as the words left my mouth, I knew it weren't likely to happen. Not with the way I was currently feelin'. Might need a few more days, at this rate.

The doctor didn't believe it, neither. He gave a snort. "Most certainly not." He turned to Sally. "Under no circumstances allow him to leave these premises until I clear him to do so."

She nodded crisply. "Understood, Doctor."

"I'll leave when I damn well please," I muttered.

Sally glared at me and pursed her lips, and I effectively felt a little guilty fer my crassness.

I sighed heavily and rubbed at my eyes with the heels of my hands. "Fine. Fine. I'll ... I'll give it a few days. Maybe."

"Thank you, Doctor," she said to him, and he nodded and turned to go before drawin' up short and turnin' back toward my bed.

"Oh. Almost forgot." He drew a bottle from his bag and held it out fer me to see, then set it gently on the nightstand. "To ease your sleep. You need to rest. One swallow before bed each night, understand?"

"Sure."

"All right then. I'll be back tomorrow."

With that, he nodded a farewell to each individual still in the room and then took his leave. The only others remainin' I hadn't yet acknowledged were Nora and Nettie, both pressed in close behind Sally and huddled together, watchin' me with a mix of worry and curiosity. When I looked at 'em, they blushed and looked away, then started whisperin' to each other.

I released a long, slow breath and leaned back into the pillows, suddenly aware of how *good* they felt. Soft and yeildin', and nothin' like that terrible table Miller had put me on. I relaxed into 'em and closed my eyes. "How long was I out?"

"Not too awful long," Sally answered, and I felt her palm against my forehead again. "Few hours or so. I called the doc right away." Her hand withdrew, and I heard her turn and urge Nora and Nettie to skedaddle and get back to work. She dismissed the kid as well, the one who'd brought the horses.

I opened my eyes again to see that Bill had stayed, and so had Professor Morton.

"The girls told me of your metal leg," Sally said once the others had left and shut the door behind them, "but I admit, it is nothing like I expected."

"Yeah," I grumbled. "It ain't what I expected, neither."

"It's ... it's very unusual."

"I noticed."

"It's a wonder of engineering," Professor Morton put in softly.

He put a hand on the metal ankle, and I pulled the knee of that leg up to my chest to remove his hold, surprised when the leg actually did what I wanted.

Beside me, Sally pulled a bottle of whiskey and a glass from the nightstand and poured some, then offered it to me.

I accepted it with a grateful nod. Least it weren't that tea again.

"What happened?" she asked. The question was gentle, hesitant. "When you didn't show up at our meeting spot ... at first I feared the worst, but we heard the next morning you'd murdered a whole posse, including Ms. Fields—"

I nearly snorted the whiskey through my nose.

"—and I thought maybe ... maybe you'd decided to head on to where you needed to go right away, after all."

"No," I coughed, wincin' at the burn the whiskey had left in the wrong pipe. "No. I didn't murder that whole posse. I only murdered half of 'em. And it surely weren't me who murdered that woman, neither. It was Miller. Charles Miller."

Sally drew back, her eyes goin' wide as she pressed her hands to her sternum.

"Shit," Bill muttered from the other side of me. "I saw him get thrown out of the party, thought it awful amusin'. But then he didn't fully leave the premises. I thought he had, 'cept he showed up when I was settin' off those firecrackers and I had to get outta there quick 'fore he saw me. I wondered what he was doin' snoopin' around..."

"Apparently he was lookin' fer me," I said. "We had a ... a run-in with each other inside, before he was kicked out."

"What!?" Sally barked.

I only nodded, feelin' foolish now fer not tellin' her about that before. Maybe if I had ... maybe Miller wouldn'ta caught up to me outside. Maybe things woulda gone a lot different.

I told 'em all what had happened then, stickin' to the main points and sparin' most of the unpleasant details. But I mentioned Miller's two-wheeled machine and its horrific noise, how he'd murdered half that posse and the woman in charge of 'em, of the Hell that still existed beneath the ruined Whittaker manor, and that I'd only managed to escape because of my leg goin' haywire.

"It didn't go haywire," Professor Morton spoke up.

The rest of us looked at him.

"Huh?" I prompted. "The hell you talkin' about? Didn't you see the thing?"

"Of course I did. I studied it in great detail while the doctor was seeing to your injuries. I thoroughly investigated its structure and innards and I'm telling you, I saw nothing to indicate a malfunction."

"Meanin'?"

He blinked rapidly and shrugged. "Well ... well I don't know! I've never seen anything like this before ... but I'd say whatever it did was not a malfunction at all. More of ... of a purpose it was built for. You didn't trigger the release of those weapons?"

I shook my head again. "Naw. Had no idea they were there. Or that the leg could open at all."

He looked confused, but I had no intention of explainin' myself or the leg to him. In fact, his particular interest in the workin's of my leg made me remember the lockbox and how he'd wanted that, too, and I sat bolt upright again. "Where is it!?"

Sally startled, her gaze followin' mine as I frantically searched the room. "Where is what?"

"The lockbox! The one with the dials ... the one we took from Baron Haas! I had it—"

"We got it," Bill drawled. "We got it, don't get yer knickers all in a knot. It's locked up in Sally's office right now. Safe as can be."

"I want it." I glared at Professor Morton as I said it, and his face reddened, his hands ballin' into fists. "Here. With me. Now."

In the corner of my eye I saw Bill glance to Sally.

Belatedly, I realized I'd been awful crass again, and these people had been nothin' but kind to me since Sally had first kept that woman from bleedin' me out in those dark woods. I cleared my throat and added, "Please."

Sally sighed. "Bill, would you escort the professor back to his room and retrieve the lockbox, please? Bring it up?"

"Sure thing." Bill lumbered over to Professor Morton and waved him toward the door. "Come on, you. Time to go."

The professor shook his head. "If you still insist on depriving the scientific community of that lockbox—and potentially a key across the valley—then I'd least like to further study this leg—"

"No." Sally, Bill, and I all said it at the same time.

"My leg ain't one of yer artifacts," I said. "You stay away from it."

"I'm the one who put it back together for you!" he blustered.

"For which we are grateful," Sally offered.

"Even if you only did it under threat of bodily harm if you didn't," Bill added.

"But that's enough for tonight," Sally continued. "You should go back to your room, get some rest. You have a long journey ahead of you."

At that, the professor's face turned a darker shade of red, and it was clear he woulda liked to protest further. But Bill grabbed his arm in one hand and patted at the knife on his belt with the other hand, and Professor Morton relented. He turned and stalked off toward the door, and Bill followed close behind.

When they had gone, Sally poured me more whiskey. "Charles Miller is dead, then?" she asked, and cautious hope rang clear in her tone.

"Yes." I downed the second glass of liquor, wishin' again I coulda given him more of what he deserved. The smears of his blood had been wiped from my skin now, and if it weren't fer the points of pain all over me, the bandages and stitches and the stiff soreness of my muscles, I might've thought the last three days of torture had only been another nightmare.

Already it seemed foggy, far away, unbelievable.

"Good." She took my emptied glass and poured more whiskey, then downed that one, herself. "But you're going to have to leave town as soon as you're able, I'm afraid."

Well, that was fine by me. Didn't want to stay here any longer than I absolutely had to, anyway. Weren't nothin' about this town I liked, 'cept Sally and her saloon. "I got no quarrel with that arrangement," I admitted. "Though I was under the impression no one around here much liked Miller."

"Oh, they didn't. It won't be *his* murder you got to worry about. He never reported the fact he had you. Or the fact he had Baron Haas' lockbox all this time. So those posters up over your murder of Baron Whittaker are still around. Course, once Miller's body is found, that might change up who is offering the reward ... but Baron Whittaker the younger will still be out for blood, no doubts about that. And now you've got the murder of nine more people on you, too. That's ... that's a lot of murder. And Ms. Fields, especially. She was quite well-liked around these parts."

"I told you, I didn't—"

"That won't matter. There aren't any witnesses left alive to dispute the story Miller started, are there? No one around here liked Miller, no, but they'll still be more inclined to believe him over you, especially being that you're already wanted for the murder of a baron."

I sagged back into the pillows again. If not fer Sally havin' her livelihood here, I woulda been sorely tempted to act on the impulse I'd had that night in the woods when I'd first come back here: just burn the whole town to the ground. Wipe it all away.

If only...

"And our getaway from Baron Haas' residence was not as clean as I would have liked."

"I'd say," I grumbled.

"But it doesn't seem anyone identified us on the way out. So ... at least that part ended up in our favor."

"Sure."

"And since Miller never told anyone he had that lockbox, either ... I took the liberty of starting rumors that it was stolen by the Whittakers."

I lifted my brows, considerin'. The new Baron Whittaker *had* been there. So had a Whittaker bastard. "Does anyone believe it?"

Sally shrugged. "It's starting to gain some traction. The barons already hate each other, anyway. But these things take time. We'll just have to be patient."

There was a moment of silence between us, and I became acutely aware then of the fact I was still naked. Least the sheets covered me to the waist now, only my left leg layin' on top of 'em. I shifted the sheets and slid my metal foot down under 'em to cover it, too.

"I'm sorry," Sally said abruptly. "For what happened. I can't imagine what you've been through. If I would have known—"

I shook my head and waved away her apology. "You couldn't have."

"But if I would have," she repeated firmly, "I would have found a way to get you out of there."

I stared across at the opposite wall, notin' the way the glow of the electric lights didn't flicker. A small vanity sat against that wall, and my clothes and hat were set on top of it. My gunbelts were hung over the back of a chair in the corner. And it struck me as strange then that I believed her. I believed she woulda come after me.

I weren't sure I'd ever been certain of that fer anyone, not since my own parents had died, anyway. Most the time I couldn't even be certain of that with Holt. Most the time I weren't sure if he were gonna show up and help or leave me fer dead ... or shoot me himself.

"I know," I said quietly at last.

"And I'm sorry to have to insist that you take your leave so soon, especially after what you must have suffered from Miller. But I do think it's in your best interest."

"I would have to agree."

"Well—" Sally began, but then the door opened and Bill came in, the lockbox tucked under his arm.

"Here," he said, "here's your damn box. Would be safer locked in Sally's office, but if you insist, then fine. Here it is." He brought it over and thumped it down next to me on the mattress.

I put a hand over the top of it. "Thanks. Mind bringin' over my guns, too?"

He gave me a look. "You think that professor is gonna come up here and try to steal it from ya? We're keepin' him locked up so he don't cause no trouble. And we're escortin' him far up north later today. He won't be botherin' ya."

"I'd prefer to have 'em close by, anyway."

Bill studied me fer a minute, then glanced to Sally. She gave an almost imperceptible nod, and then Bill gave a very overdramatic sigh as he marched across the room to the chair. "In case you haven't noticed, I ain't the maid." He pulled my belts off the back of it. "And I ain't yer lackey, neither. You want anythin' else, you can get it yerself." He tossed 'em to me, and I winced as the weight of the pistols landed on my bruised, cut up, and ant-bit right leg.

But at least they were close, now. "Thanks," I said again.

"You should get some rest," Sally said. "If you can. We can talk more later." She handed me the bottle of medicine the doctor had left behind. "One swallow of this. Don't forget. And would you ... would you like someone to stay with you? I could send the girls back up. Nora and Nettie, I mean. Think they've taken a liking to you. They know plenty of stories, songs, verses ... might be nice to hear some familiar voices while you drift off?"

I stared down at the medicine in my hand, if only so she couldn't see the way her offer had affected me. I didn't understand how she could so often know my feelin's before I did, but she was right. To my surprise, bein' alone right now was about the last thing I wanted. So I nodded wordlessly, unable to speak around the sudden lump in my throat.

"All right. I'll send them up. And we'll speak more when you've rested. Good night, Mr. Lynd. Or ... good morning, I suppose."

Mornin'? I looked closer at the small clock on the vanity, realized it read almost five AM.

Mornin'!? Charlotte! Shit!

XXVI

COMIN' WITH THE STORM

A strangled noise came out of me and I threw back the sheets, fair near jumpin' out of the bed before Sally and Bill both grabbed hold of me.

"Whoa, whoa now there, Mister," Bill said, and he rather easily tossed me back down onto the mattress, where I promptly scrambled to get back up again. He pinned me with one big hand on my chest, much like he'd pinned me to the wall the night he'd followed me around town, and pointed a finger in my face like he was scoldin' a petulant child. "Doctor's orders, you stay in bed."

"What the heavens is the matter?" Sally asked, and her face had gone a shade paler.

"Charlotte," I gasped, tryin' to pry Bill's hand off of me. For fuck's sake, he was a big fella. "Telegram. Gotta send a telegram. Gotta warn her!"

Sally glanced to Bill, but he frowned and shook his head. "Who is Charlotte?" she asked.

"The girl," I spluttered. "The redhead! The slave I helped escape who came through your saloon weeks ago." I stopped fightin' Bill's hold, exhausted and pantin'. I just didn't have the strength fer it ... might not have had the strength fer it even had I not just spent three days stuck on a table bein' tortured. "Miller sent his men after her ... said they'd found her family home ... said they were gonna grab her tonight ... last night ... I need ... I need to warn her they're comin' ... may be too late already!"

"Dear God," Sally said.

Bill looked up at her. "Operator won't be there this early."

"Then where's he live?" I blurted. "I'll wake him the fuck up!"

"*You* won't be doing anything," Sally said, fixin' me with a stern glare. Then she turned to Bill.

He rolled his eyes. "Are you serious?"

She arched an eyebrow. "Use the telephone downstairs. It'll be faster."

"That operator may not be there this early, neither."

"Try it. If not, wake up Mr. Moeller. If he's reluctant to cooperate, you're the best one to manhandle him into compliance. But don't damage him. Bribe him, if you need to."

Bill gave another of his theatrical sighs and grumbled under his breath, but removed his hand from my chest and straightened. "Fine. Who do I call, and what do I say?"

Sally pulled out the nightstand drawer, removed a piece of paper and a pencil, and looked at me expectantly.

A telephone ... that *was* a better idea. Surely Charlotte's family had a telephone, if they had the kinda money she'd talked about. And surely the operators in the area would know of the family if they had that kinda money, too.

I closed my eyes, pressed the heels of my palms into 'em, tryin' to think. Tryin' to remember. The note she'd given me with her address on it was in my pack with all the rest of my stuff in Sonoita. But I'd looked at it plenty of times before then, before I'd had Sonoita's sheriff send her my first telegram, even. I'd looked at it enough times the paper was gettin' all worn and creased, while I worried over the fact I had nothin' to write her about.

Well, I had somethin' to write her about now. And I needed to do it quick.

Slowly, hesitantly, I recited the address back as it came to mind, then dropped my hands from my eyes and opened 'em to be sure Sally had it all down. "Her family name is Harrison," I added. "Tell her Baron Whittaker's bastard son sent some more men her way to collect her and bring her back here. Tell her to take all necessary precautions to prevent that from happenin'."

Sally scribbled it all down, then handed the paper to Bill.

"Hurry," I urged.

"What if there's no one on the other side to receive this message?" Bill asked.

"Then we'll keep trying until someone answers," Sally said. "Go on now, quick!"

Bill grumbled some more but increased his pace as he went fer the door, then stepped out and shut it behind him.

I pushed myself sittin' again, but Sally put a hand on my shoulder. "It's all right. He'll get through to someone."

"What if he don't?"

"He will. The bigger city exchanges usually have longer hours. There will be someone there."

"What if her family don't answer their phone? What if Miller's men already grabbed her?"

Sally gave me a gentle, patient look, though her lips pursed, and I didn't understand how she could be so calm. "Then there's nothing you can do from here about either of those things. We'll just have to wait and see. One thing at a time, Mr. Lynd."

Another jab of guilt hit my insides at her callin' me that name. After all of this she'd done fer me, I was still lyin' to her. I fidgeted in the bed, tired and hurtin' and warrin' over whether or not to tell Sally my real name, worried over Charlotte, waitin' fer Bill to come back, turnin' that medicine bottle over and over in my hands.

It seemed to take him hours, and the time ticked by as I sat there, hatin' my helplessness just as much now as I had when I'd been strapped to Miller's table. Sally watched me like a hawk, like she could tell I wanted to go down and check on Bill's progress despite the exhaustion and pain. She'd move around the room periodically, straightenin' the paintin' on the wall, fluffin' the pillows, peekin' through the window's curtain; the only clue she might be feelin' nearly as anxious as I.

At last Bill's heavy footsteps came stompin' down the hall, and both Sally and I looked toward the door expectantly as he entered, a little breathless, but lookin' pleased.

I hardly dared hope.

"Telephone worked," he said triumphantly. "Got through to Charlotte's father. He said she's there, safe and sound. They got the telegram you sent earlier, and he hired more protection for the whole family. Some ruffians did show up last night, but they were handled. All of 'em in pine boxes this mornin', he said."

My breath came out in a big rush of air and I collapsed back into the pillows.

Sally smiled down at me. "There, you see? Everything is taken care of."

Relief clogged my throat, and I didn't have no words.

"Now ... you get some rest while you can. I'll send Nora and Nettie up to keep you company. You let them know if you need anything else, understand?"

I nodded.

"All right, then." She turned to Bill and tipped her head in the direction of the door, and the both of 'em moved once more fer the exit.

Bill opened it fer her and waved her through, then followed her out, and the sound of the door closin' was loud in the resultin' silence.

I laid there starin' up at the ceilin', and I put one hand over the top of that lockbox, and the other hand over the top of my gunbelts. The bottle of medicine rested atop my chest, untouched fer the moment.

I closed my eyes against an unexpected swell of feelin's ... breathed through it, slow and deep. All that mattered now was that I had Nan's lockbox. And I was goin' back to Bravebank with it soon as I could manage to sit upright in a saddle and keep my senses well enough to ride in the right direction.

Shouldn't be long.

Not long now till I had Ethelyn back...

It was three full days till I felt strong enough to ride.

By then, Miller's death had been discovered and reported. The new Baron Whittaker had found him, the paper said, drawn to explorin' the ruins of his family estate when those workin' on its rebuild had found his half-brother's strange two-wheeled machine parked out back of it.

No one had liked him much, true enough, but murder was murder, and the town was already up in arms over the senior Whittaker's death weeks ago, the Haas posse's deaths more recently, and the robbery at the Haas residence. The paper didn't question the nature of the room Miller had been found in, nor did it seem to care much what Miller might have been doin' to the person who had murdered him. And accordin' to the newspaper's editor, the law didn't care too awful much, neither.

Least no bounties had been issued fer Miller's murderer ... yet. The article only begged that anyone havin' any knowledge of the incident come forward.

Fer questionin' only, they said.

They'd be waitin' a long time fer that one.

Still, Sally had me move to the cot in her office soon as I could, so as to make my presence as indiscernible from regular saloon business as possible. The cot weren't nearly as comfortable as her mattresses, but I'd slept on plenty worse, and I was grateful fer the refuge, anyway.

By dawn of the fourth day, she'd outfitted me with supplies enough to last me the ride to Bravebank, lent me a horse to replace the scruffy one we'd never found, and escorted me out of town and to the edge of the valley where the green started fadin' out into the reds and browns of the desert proper.

I'd said my goodbyes to Bill already three days ago, before he'd left to take Professor Morton up north. And I'd said my goodbyes to Nora and Nettie too, just the night before. All in all, I figured I owed Sally a whole helluva lot more than I could afford to repay right now.

The sun had just broke over the horizon, paintin' the sky a pale, pretty pink, when Sally reined up her horse, and I pulled my mount to a halt beside her.

"Well," she said. "This is as far as I go today. Guess this is goodbye, cowboy. Sure has been one hell of a ride."

"Yeah." I sat there fer a minute, searchin' fer words. I opened my mouth, closed it, and opened it again. "I ... I can't thank you enough fer everything you've done fer me here. Guess I owe you a lot more dish washin'."

That made her smile. She wore different clothes today than I'd ever seen her in: a regular ridin' outfit, with leather chaps and a bandana around her neck, and a hat that looked a lot like mine, only minus the bullet hole. The soft dawn light framed her in a blush of rose as she shook her head. "Like I told you when we first met, Mister, I'm in the business of rescuing people. It's all in a day's work. But don't you worry none, I'll keep your tab open. You can pay me back someday."

I glanced over my shoulder. Back toward Blessing. "Might be awhile. Don't think I should come around here again any time soon."

"No, I don't think you should," she agreed. Then she shrugged. "But you never know. Watch the papers. I might just have this place cleaned up sooner than you think."

The statement made a corner of my mouth quirk into almost a smile, and it felt strange. I couldn't remember the last time I'd smiled. "I believe you just might," I said.

"All right, then. Safe journeys to you, Mr. Lynd. I hope you get what you need." Her eyes dropped toward my saddlebag, where the lockbox had been stowed.

I sobered again and nodded. Swallowed. "Me too."

She started to turn her mare around to head back toward town.

"Sally..."

She reined the horse to face me, instead. "Yes?"

"Did you ... did you get what you needed from Baron Haas? That night we got the lockbox? Did you get what you were after?"

Her eyebrows lifted. "Why Mr. Lynd, how courteous of you to ask. I did, mostly. But I can be patient for the rest of it. I've waited this long ... I can wait awhile longer. The barons' days are numbered, mark my words."

"I would help more, if I could. If I didn't have ... other business that needed my immediate attention."

"I understand completely."

"And..." I rubbed a hand over my mouth, shiftin' in the saddle and questionin' the wisdom in what I was about to say. But the urge to come clean with her was nearly overwhelmin'. I couldn't ride away now, after everything she'd given me, without sayin' it. The lie had been chafin' at me fer days. "And ... and my name ain't Lynd. It's Delano. Van Delano."

To my shock, she didn't seem surprised at all.

She just nodded thoughtfully. "Well, that's all right. My name ain't Wellman, either. It's Clayton. Sally Clayton."

At my stupefied silence, she gave me a wink. Then turned her mare toward Blessing again. "See ya around, cowboy." She kicked her mare into a trot, leavin' only dust behind her in the brightenin' dawn.

I puzzled over Seven Knives Sally Clayton fer the first few hours of my ride back to Bravebank. I'd never suspected she might not be usin' her true name, neither. Not that she'd ever given me her surname directly. But Baron Haas and others at that auction had called her Wellman. And she'd had some kind of history there, that was certain. The fancy folk there had known her. And he'd had somethin' that belonged to her. More than one thing, it seemed.

If I ever did get back to Blessing, maybe I'd go ahead and ask her to tell that story. If she were goin' to trust me with her true name, maybe she'd actually tell it to me.

Maybe.

The horse she'd lent me was an old, skinny mare, but sturdy enough, and I kept a steady, brisk pace fer most the first day. Though truth be told ... I was wishin' I had Joe back. Guess I'd gotten more attached to that damned mule than I'd thought. He was still up in Sonoita, I reckoned. Maybe auctioned off by now. Maybe still waitin' unclaimed in its livery.

If I weren't in such a hurry to get back to Bravebank, I woulda gone back fer him. But time weren't on my side, here. I'd already been away too long, and I didn't know how long Nan would wait fer me to bring back her prize.

If not fer concern over pushin' my borrowed horse too hard, I woulda kept goin' right through the night. But as it were, I stopped to rest her and made camp, and as I sat starin' out at the stars on the horizon, my thoughts went back to Ethelyn.

How long had Nan had her, now? A few months, at least, musta been. I wondered how she was bein' treated. Wondered where she was bein' held. Wondered if Nan planned to ship her off on a boat by sea or a boat by air. Not that I'd ever seen an airboat myself, nor ever seen one pass over these parts, even, but I'd heard tales of 'em from drifters passin' through now and then.

There was a landin' field somewhere up north, somewhere in Utah, they said. If that were true, that was likely the nearest port. That was likely where Nan would take her. Maybe she was already there, waitin' on the next ship to come in. The thought made my heart wedge in my throat, and I had to fight down the urge to saddle up and ride on again.

She could just as well be somewhere else, somewhere Nan thought might be more secure fer safe-keepin'. All I really knew right now was that I needed to get this lockbox to Nan soon as I could, and that she'd better give me Ethelyn in return.

I laid back on my bedroll, starin' up at those stars, and didn't get much sleep.

I set out again just before dawn and pushed the horse as much as I dared all morning and into the afternoon. By then I was gettin' real close to Bravebank, and I also noticed the clouds startin' to knot together in the sky. They were buildin' up real tall, and the breeze had picked up into somethin' almost like a real wind, stirrin' dust and tumbleweeds.

A storm was comin', and comin' in fast.

I kicked the mare up into a trot, then into a canter. We rounded the base of a small rise, and the sprawl of Bravebank laid before me in the distance, dim through the haze. I kept the mare headin' straight fer it, kept nudgin' her to maintain her speed though she kept tryin' to slow up on me.

She was tired ... but we were almost there now. So close...

We'd nearly reached the edge of town when I saw the wall of dust comin' at us from the northwest. I swore and dropped the reins to pull my bandana up over my nose and mouth and shove my hat down tighter on my head.

Then I grabbed up the reins again and urged that poor tired mare into a gallop, hopin' to close the rest of the distance to town in a hurry.

It chased us all the way there, that storm, and swept over us just as we passed by the outermost buildings, the gust of wind strong enough to cause a stagger in the horse's stride and nearly buffet me from the saddle. Dust and grit stung the exposed parts of my skin and the sky darkened quick.

The folk left in the street ran fer cover, the horses tied at the hitchin' posts milled about and nickered nervously. The wind whipped down the alleys and made store signs creak, awnings flap, and loose shutters bang.

I heard the rain before it reached us, a sweepin', thunderous roar, and then it hit, all at once and like a sledgehammer. A solid curtain of water, slammin' into all the hard surfaces and beatin' everything into submission. I gasped as it instantly drenched me.

The mare slogged on through it, and I let her drop back into a slow, amblin' walk, mostly 'cause I couldn't hardly see where we was goin' anymore, anyway. Water ran in streams off my hat brim, and now that the dust had cleared, I tugged my bandana back down around my neck.

I went in the direction of the Stag Saloon ... I thought ... the streets all mud now and runnin' with water like little creeks.

So much fer tryin' to beat the storm.

Lightnin' speared the gloom ahead, and the crack of thunder afterward made me flinch despite myself. This weren't nothin' compared to the storms I'd seen as a kid in Kansas, but it'd been a long time since I'd been around one of those. And these desert storms were becomin' bad enough.

More lightnin' came, lots of it in quick succession, and more thunder rumblin' like some great beast. Then, finally, I saw the weak yellow glow of the Stag's front lights up ahead, strugglin' to pierce the rain's fury.

I pulled the mare up to the nearest hitchin' post and dismounted, tied her, and dug the lockbox out of the saddlebag it'd been crammed into. Most of me was wet now, soaked through, my whole shirtfront and my pants, and the mud slurped at my boots as I bowed my head against the onslaught of water and headed fer the front door. Least my oilskin duster and my hat kept a little of me dry.

I stepped up onto the boardwalk, ducked under the shelter of the front awning, and put the box up under my left arm so both hands were free. The Stag's door was usually left open durin' daylight hours, but they'd shut it tight now against the force of this squall. So I pushed my duster back behind my right holster, rested my hand lightly on that pistol's grip, and shouldered roughly through the door.

Lightnin' lit the sky again behind me and thunder cracked as I stepped inside the Stag Saloon. It faded just in time fer the bang of the door slammin' back against the wall to echo out just as loudly across the room.

All sober eyes turned in my direction, just like they had the time I'd come in holdin' that big, unwieldy cannon-gun. The place was packed, fuller than I'd ever seen it thanks to the ragin' storm outside, and the raucous murmur of conversation quieted at my arrival. The card shufflin' stilled, the folks on the way to or from the bar or goin' toward the stairs paused.

I stood there in the doorway, soppin' wet and drippin', a puddle of water spreadin' out around me on the floor, and my gaze raked across all the faces starin' at me ... and all those who weren't starin' at me, too.

Searchin' fer Nan, or either of those lieutenants she'd had with her last we'd talked.

I didn't see Nan. Didn't see those lieutenants, neither.

My glare landed finally on the barkeep. The same man who seemed to be here all the time. The same man who had spit in my coffee all those days ago.

But I'd surely been through far too much in my efforts to retrieve this lockbox to spend any more time waitin' around here fer Nan to show up whenever she damn well pleased. Or to suffer any more of that barkeep's disapproval.

So I narrowed my eyes, sent another murderous scowl out over all the gathered men of the Stag Saloon, and bellowed, "Where the fuck is Nine-Fingered Nan?!"

XXVII

PATIENCE IS A VIRTUE

No one answered.

Couple of the folk glanced to each other. Couple more folk suddenly found their cards or their food or their drink real, real interestin'. Couple of the saloon girls looked toward the barkeep.

I followed their gaze back to him, but he only met my stare in silence, his mouth firmly shut and turned down into a severe frown.

So I pulled my right pistol from my holster and stalked straight fer him.

People cleared outta my way in a hurry, some knockin' over their chairs or their drinks in their rush fer the door. Didn't seem to matter that the rain and lightnin' was still blowin' and howlin' outside, a good portion of the saloon's patrons fled out into it, seemingly more willin' to risk that kinda storm than whatever was gonna happen in here.

That suited me just fine.

The barkeep's eyes widened as I got closer to him, and his hands dropped below the bar.

But I had my gun up and aimed and hammer cocked before he

could do much else but lay hands on the weapon he kept stashed back there. "Hands up," I ordered. "Where I can see 'em. Nice and slow."

He went real still and his face went real pale, but he complied.

The sound of more chairs scootin' back and feet runnin' fer the door marked more of the patrons skedaddlin' out, wantin' no part of this trouble. 'Cept then I heard another sound, one not so friendly, the sound of sixguns clearin' leather and hammers clickin' back.

I stepped to my right at the same time I drew my left gun and spun, at the same time the guy behind me fired, and his bullets shattered bottles instead of my ribs.

The barkeep yelped and ducked behind his bar.

I fired my left pistol twice, caught the guy in the chest twice and he stumbled backward, starin' at me in surprise.

From the corner of my eye I saw the barkeep stand again, and now he had a sawed-off shotgun in his hand. I fired at him without lookin', got him in the gut, and he fell back against his shelves of alcohol lookin' even more surprised than the other guy.

The other guy finally gave up on livin' and dropped to his knees, then fell face-first to the floor.

More folk took that opportunity to get the hell out, and the saloon girls had all clustered together in the back corner, clutchin' at each other in terror.

I turned my attention back to the barkeep, but kept my left pistol leveled toward the saloon at large. "Hand it over," I said, noddin' at the shotgun gripped in his white-knuckled fist. "You might live through that shot. You won't live through another one."

His eyes burned with defiance, but he set his weapon slowly upon the bar top, slid it toward me. His other hand was pressed up against the bullet hole, and blood seeped between his fingers. Sweat beaded on his forehead. "Nan's gonna skin you for this," he spat.

"Let her try," I growled. "So long as she gets here quick." I holstered my left pistol and grabbed the sawed-off shotgun instead, albeit a bit clumsily with the lockbox still clamped to my side by my left elbow and bandages around three of those fingertips.

I turned toward the folk who remained in the saloon, then, most of 'em too drunk to know what was happenin', but some of 'em sober.

Those few watched me carefully, but none made a move fer their weapons. "Well?" I barked at 'em. "Anyone else got anythin' to say?"

Silence. Only the storm answered.

Outside, the sky was dark and angry, makin' the inside of the saloon seem brighter than usual. The door had been left open in all the hurry to get shut of this place, and the wind blew sheets of rain through to stir the muggy air, almost makin' my damp clothes feel chill. The force of the rain and wind against the building was nearly as loud as the thunder itself, vibratin' in my bones.

But still no one moved. No one said a word.

So I swung my glare back to the barkeep. "Where's Nan?" I demanded again.

When he hesitated, I shook my head and shook the pistol still aimed at him, too.

"She's ... she's conducting business," he finally ground out.

"Where? Here? Or somewhere else?"

"Here. In town. But I don't know where. I don't get involved in Nan's business."

"No?" I made a point of glancin' around the place we stood in. "But you run her saloon fer her, don't ya?"

His eyes narrowed. "She's in town somewhere. That's all I know."

"Then I guess you'd better go and find her."

He stared at me fer a minute, as if tryin' to figure if I were serious or not. But I was serious, all right, and I held his dubious gaze with a flat, even stare. He swallowed, his eyes droppin' down to the blood that stained his apron. "In case you hadn't noticed, you done shot me. And that storm out there—"

"Beats bein' dead," I said.

Another few heartbeats of silence passed, everyone else in that saloon holdin' stock still, like they was part of a photograph instead of livin', breathin' folk.

I thumbed back my hammer, and the motion roused the barkeep from where he slouched against his shelves. He straightened, grimaced in pain, and hobbled down the length of the bar toward the back door, glarin' somethin' fierce at me the whole way.

I glared right back at him, and tracked him with my pistol. "Tell her I got what she wanted. Meanwhile I'll have someone fetch the doc. He'll be waitin' fer you when you bring Nan back here. But I suggest you hurry. Don't want you bleedin' out on the way."

His only answer was another sour, hateful look over his shoulder, and then he pushed out through the door and stumbled into the storm.

Once the door had shut behind him I relaxed a bit, holstered my gun. I set the lockbox atop the bar and went around behind it myself, grabbin' up some whiskey and pourin' myself a healthy dose.

The doc. Fuck. Here in Bravebank, that would be Dr. Balogh. I needed to have a talk with him about my metal leg, sure ... eventually. But maybe not now. I didn't exactly want him here now, not when Nine-Fingered Nan would be arrivin' so soon. And I didn't exactly want him to see the man I'd just murdered, or the man I'd almost murdered. Didn't want him to realize his wife had been right about me from the beginnin'.

I muttered a few curses and threw back the whiskey. Then noticed those left in here were still starin' at me. "What?" I snapped. "Go on, go back to your business. Stay outta my way and I ain't got no quarrel with you."

But they did not go back to their business. The girls took the chance to dart up the stairs, maybe decidin' to hide up there. The men remainin' with their wits intact picked at their food or absently arranged and rearranged their cards, but they didn't seem too eager to fully believe my claim. One of 'em stood up real slow, his hands held out at his sides and well away from his gun, and walked over to shut the front door against the force of the monsoon. Then he turned and walked back to his chair, givin' me a little nod as he sat back down.

Well, it didn't matter if they believed me or not. Long as none of 'em tried to cause any trouble, I didn't care what else they did in here while waitin' out the storm.

And that's what we did. We waited.

I drank more whiskey and tried to settle my nerves. Tried not to think about what I was gonna do if this exchange didn't go down like it was supposed to. Tried not to think about Dr. Balogh findin' out I was a murderer, after all. Tried not to think about what Sheriff Jennings had said about not shootin' people.

Outside, the storm hurled rain and lightnin', and thunder shook the walls.

It couldn't have been that long, but it felt like forever before the back door opened again, and the barkeep staggered in. He was soaked through, his boots and pants caked in mud, the stain of red across his apron larger where he still clutched at it with one hand. His face had gone gray now, his lips pale. He hardly made it into the establishment before he tripped and fell to his hands and knees.

He was alone.

A flash of anger lit in me that turned my insides hot, feedin' off the warmth of the whiskey. "Where the fuck is Nan?" I bit off.

He shook his head, rain water streamin' off his hair. "She ... she's conducting business ... like I said. Says ... says ... she'll come by here later."

"*Later?*" The word came outta me in a rasp.

The barkeep lifted his head weakly. "Where's ... where's the doc?"

"*Where is she?*" I asked him again, ignorin' his question. "Where is Nan right now? Where's she conductin' this *business?*"

"She's ... she's with the sheriff. At the ... jailhouse. I need the doc ... please. Need him now..."

"He's on his way," I growled. I left his shotgun on the bar, but snatched up the lockbox again and made fer the front door, pointin' at the most timid-lookin' of the sober men at the tables as I passed. "You," I snapped. "Go get the doc."

Then I flung open the door and faced the storm once again. Surely it couldn't last much longer. These summer monsoons came in hard and wild, but their fury expended itself faster than the storms in the heartlands. I could wait it out ... could wait here fer Nan, too.

No. I'd waited on her long enough already. Waited on her three weeks to give me this damn fool errand in the first place. Waited on her to give me bad information so I could go out and get robbed, arrested, nearly hanged quick and almost killed slow.

No. I weren't gonna wait. Not fer this storm, and not fer Nan.

I bowed my head against the spittin' rain and turned down the boardwalk, toward the jailhouse. The sheriff was about the last person I wanted to see right now aside from Dr. Balogh, but even his threats weren't gonna stop me from makin' sure Nan kept her end of this deal.

So I stalked through the swirlin' gloom, holdin' that lockbox tight, grittin' my teeth in the gaps between the storefronts when the full force of the storm hit me. I almost couldn't see where I was goin' still, but I kept my head down and followed the line of buildings until the brick jailhouse finally loomed ahead, risin' from the tempest like a bulwark.

I marched straight fer it, went to the door, and barged inside with as much force as I had entered the Stag. A gust of wind came in with me, sprayin' water across the interior, makin' some of the men inside scowl and flinch away from the wet. I kicked the door shut behind me with a boot, my eyes locked on Nine-Fingered Nan.

She was there, all right. Sittin' in the sheriff's chair behind his desk. Her pale eyes lifted as the door slammed, and her men—four of 'em this time—turned to face me, hands slidin' toward their guns.

Sheriff Jennings stood to her right, and he looked awfully displeased, but he kept his arms crossed and made no move for a weapon himself.

I ignored him, ignored the four men clearly threatenin' to shoot me, and stomped directly toward Nan. Then took that lockbox and slammed it down onto the desk, right in front of her. Right on top of her spread of maps and papers. Water ran down off its nooks and crannies, trickled through its engravings, puddled underneath it. "There," I spat. "There's your damn lockbox. Now where is my sister?!"

Nine-Fingered Nan said nothin'. She only looked at me, her face unreadable. Then she leaned back in her chair and steepled her fingers, and her eyes dropped down to the strange metal box with its numbered dials.

Her four men closed in around me, standin' too close.

And some of the anger burnin' in me hot cooled off, dampened by an increasin' sense of apprehension.

Maybe I shouldn't have come here. Maybe I should have waited.

Nan nodded toward one of her goons and I tensed as he stepped forward, but he only picked up the lockbox himself. He turned it over and around, studyin' it. Then he untied his bandana from around his neck and used the cloth to pat the thing dry. That done, he offered it out to Nan.

She took it. Looked it over much the same as her man had.

I held my breath. But that had to be it. That had to be the one she'd wanted. It matched her sketch. It was important, Professor Morton had said so. Baron Haas had clearly known so as well, or else he wouldn't have gone through all that trouble to hold a private auction fer it.

Nan finished her inspection of it, and one of her eyebrows twitched. She set it carefully on the corner of the desk, out of the way of the maps and papers.

"That's right," I said, and I realized suddenly things had gone eerily silent outside. The storm musta finally calmed down, but now everything seemed too quiet. And my mouth was too dry as I tried to swallow. "I got it. Got your damn lockbox. And no thanks to your source up north. He musta fed you a wagon-load of horseshit. That coach weren't carryin' it. Lucky I found it at all."

She smiled a little at that, and finally spoke. "That so? Thought luck was yer pa's forte?"

I clenched my teeth against her sneerin' tone.

She stood from her chair, slow and unhurried. "But maybe he's passin' you some from beyond the grave, because I will admit, Delano … I did not expect you to come back here alive. And I most certainly did not expect you to come back here alive and with this box." She put a hand over it.

"But I did," I said. "So where's my sister?"

She cocked her head to one side. "Saw you shot my barkeep."

I managed to hold her stare and hide the inward grimace. "He tried to shoot me first."

"Heard you ran out a room stuffed fulla customers, too. Right out into that storm." She nodded toward the door, but kept her eyes on me.

Water dripped from my hat brim, and my wet clothes stuck heavy to my skin. Even still, the hair on my arms prickled. I kept my hands ready to draw, nevermind the fact I wouldn't win that one. "They did that of their own accord," I said flatly. "I didn't make no one leave."

"And yet they left because of you," Nan said. "A whole buncha men who could have been drinkin', gamblin', and whorin' durin' that storm ... all run off because you wanted to start trouble."

"I didn't want to start nothin'." I risked a glance at the sheriff, thinkin' this conversation sounded awful familiar. But his expression was entirely unsympathetic, and I looked quick back to Nan. "You told me to get that box and bring it back here, bring it back to the Stag, and that's what I did. I was lookin' fer you. I kept my end of our deal. Now it's yer turn."

She leaned back a little. Shifted her hands to rest on her matchin' pearl grips, and I noted the two of her men who'd been standin' behind me shuffled more to the sides.

My breath caught, even despite all the anger I'd stormed in here with. I fully expected her to shoot me just then. All this trouble, all this time, just to be shot down now. The tick of a clock from somewhere in the room was loud as the thunder had been just minutes ago. I hadn't even known the sheriff had had a clock before. Now it pulsed out a rhythm to match the rush of blood in my ears as I waited.

Waited fer her answer, whether in words or in lead.

"Well, Delano," she finally drawled, "turns out I got a telegram just today from that fella who wants yer sister."

Heat flooded my face, and all that anger came rushin' back. It was all I could do to stay still. To not draw. To not leap over the desk and throttle her.

"Ya see, I went ahead and told him there was another person interested in acquirin' the girl. As you can imagine, he was none too happy about that. He'd already sent his ship along this way, after all. Too late to call it back. Now, of course he does have other assets to retrieve once it arrives on this continent..." She shrugged. "But he's quite intent on collectin' yer sister along with the rest of 'em."

"That lockbox is worth more than she could ever be," I rasped.

"To some, maybe," she conceded. "But I ain't sellin' it, Delano. I'm usin' it. And as such, you've just been outbid."

I lunged halfway over the desk before her men caught me and hauled me backward, catchin' tight to my arms as I tried to go fer my guns next. One of 'em drove a fist hard into my gut, and I doubled over as all the air went outta me. Another of 'em kicked at the back of my knee and I went down, and I wrestled with 'em there fer a bit on the floor before they had me good, holdin' me on my knees with hands on my shoulders and both arms pinned behind my back.

"You sonuva motherless whore!" I tried to come up to my feet, to throw myself at her, wantin' nothin' more but to pummel her with my own two hands, but her men held me tight. "We had a deal!"

She had watched my attempt to tackle her and my struggle with her goons without so much as a flinch, without so much as lookin' like she might draw either of her guns. And even now she only looked down at me and smiled, seemin' more amused than anythin' else.

And that only made me angrier.

It swelled up in me so complete, so overwhelmin', I could hardly breathe.

"Sure we did," she said, her smile widenin'. "And now I've made a better deal with someone else. But I'm nothin' if not a businesswoman. So if yer willin' to make me a better offer, Delano, and, let's say, pay me back fer all the business you've cost me in the last month, well ... I'd be willin' to listen."

"I ... you ..." It was a struggle to get the words out past the rage stuck in my throat. "One person can't possibly be worth that much," I finally choked out.

Her eyebrows lifted, and she feigned a kind of disappointed sadness. "Tsk, tsk, Mr. Delano. Discountin' yer own sister like that. She'd be heartbroken to hear it."

"I ain't discountin' nothin'!"

"Then yer willin' to raise yer offer?"

Thought my heart might slam right outta my ribs as I glared up at her smug, self-satisfied smirk and tried to sort what else she could possibly want from me. She was playin' me ... usin' me fer sure ... just like Holt had said. But it didn't matter ... didn't matter till I had Ethelyn one way or another, either by gettin' her from Nan, or somehow trackin' her down and gettin' her free myself.

So I swallowed and gave a nod. "You know I am."

She grinned now. "Such a loyal brother. All right. I will write the buyer and let him know his offer has been met and raised. I will warn you though, he might just be willin' to go yet higher fer yer sister. She is ... well, she's got the most strikin' eyes, don't she? And it's rare to find a woman of her age with her virtue still intact. That alone makes her worth more than most."

I tried to surge up off the floor again, but her four men held me fast, wrestled me back down to my knees.

"Now, now," Nan scolded, "don't throw away this opportunity, Delano." She gathered up the papers spread out over the sheriff's desk and rolled the maps. Even the one I'd made slightly soggy by slammin' the wet lockbox on top of it. She stacked the papers up neat next to the old metal box and handed the rolled maps to the sheriff, who took them without a word. Then she picked up that lockbox I'd nearly died several times over for. "I want my money's worth outta you, sure. But I ain't got no qualms about puttin' down a dog that bites, neither." She leaned forward over the desk to meet my furious glare with a flat, cold stare of her own. "So you just be sure yer on yer best behavior around here, understand?"

I ground my teeth, silence bein' the best answer I could manage at the moment.

She straightened from the desk, ambled around to the front of it, and her men pulled me around roughly to face her square again. She reached into her shirt pocket with her free hand and pulled out a folded square of paper, held it up in two fingers. "Got this a few days ago. Thought if you did show up here again, alive, you might be interested." She stepped forward to slide the paper into my own damp shirt pocket. Then she stepped back again, and her pale gaze flicked over to the sheriff. "Lock him up fer awhile. A good, long while. He could stand to learn some patience. You and I will conclude our business later. Fer now, I'm hungry. I'm goin' fer some grub. And to maybe find myself a new barkeep."

I struggled against the hands that held me even as they dragged me backwards, toward one of the jail cells. "Enough of these goddamned games!" I blurted as she made fer the door. "Just tell me what you want!"

She paused. Turned halfway around toward me. In the absence of the ragin' storm, the quiet rang in my ears. One corner of her mouth quirked upwards. "I want you to wait, Mr. Delano. After all, patience is a virtue." She touched the brim of her hat and turned her back on me, steppin' out through the door into the late afternoon, the sky already clear again.

I scowled and swore, cursin' her name with every foul insult I could think of and fightin' her men until they hit me again; another to the gut and one to my face hard enough to make me see stars, and then they relieved me of my gun belts, dumped me on a cot in one of the cells, and slammed the barred door shut behind 'em.

I laid there curled around the pain in my stomach and gaspin', head throbbin', and heard 'em all move away to follow after Nine-Fingered Nan, sneerin' and mutterin' till they finally took their leave of the jail house.

Then it was just me and the sheriff.

I said nothin'. 'Couldn't have, anyway, not till I got my air back. I just stared at the back brick wall of that cell, shakin' and numb with all the frustration, anger ... rage. The skin all along my left shoulder and down the left side of my chest, the skin that had got all red and blistered from Miller's electrical rod, throbbed from so much manhandlin'. And I felt all those cuts and stings afresh, too, my three bandaged fingers raw and pulsin' from my struggles, my body sore and tired from the abuse at Miller's hands, the hard ridin' to get here, the blows from Nan's men.

All of that ... everything I'd been through and done to get that goddamned lockbox ... all of it fer nothin'.

Nan had what she wanted now. Would get more of what she wanted, too. And all I had was a debt that kept on growin'. A debt I was beginnin' to think could never be paid.

The rustle of papers drew my attention away from my self-loathin', and I heard the sheriff movin' around his jail house. Likely puttin' things back in order after Nan's visit. Then his footsteps came in my direction, but I didn't bother to acknowledge him.

Didn't move at all.

"Your sister, huh?" he asked, and his tone was gentler than I'd ever heard it.

Unexpected tears bit viciously into the backs of my eyes, so I closed 'em, squeezed 'em shut tight. "Yeah."

He grunted. Sounded thoughtful. But he said nothin' else, only moved off to putter around his jail house some more, and then he stepped out and left me alone.

Left me alone on that miserable cot in the near dark to wait. Wait on what, and wait how long, I couldn't imagine. And that was the worst part of it.

Eventually I remembered that paper Nan had stuck in my shirt pocket. I roused myself reluctantly, pushed up to sit against the bricks, and pulled it out. Unfolded it.

And as soon as I saw the ink scrawled across it, somethin' inside me broke.

My vision swam, the tears unstoppable now. I tried to blink them away, tried to read the words ... the handwriting bringin' back memories from long ago. It was recognizably *hers*, though far more refined and elegant than it had been as a child. Mama had always praised Ethelyn fer her penmanship ... it had always been a fair sight better than mine, despite the five extra years I had on her.

Van, dear brother,

They tell me you are still alive. They tell me they are bringing these letters to you. They tell me you are coming to get me. But it has been weeks now, and I am beginning to fear the worst. I fear they are lying, about all of it. I cannot fathom why they would tell such lies, except to torture me with the hope that it is all true ... and brother, it has been torture of the worst kind. Except for that, they have treated me fair decent enough, though I am told daily that is only because the man who wishes to buy me absolutely insists I am given to him unmarked, and that if they should ignore that condition, he will not pay for me, and then that Nine-Fingered Nan would flay them alive. But even that is miserable to endure, as I do not know how much longer I will be here, or how much longer such people can stand to obey orders, even if from someone they fear as much as they clearly fear Nine-Fingered Nan.

Brother, if you are still alive, I pray this letter finds you, and I pray you are able to come for me as they say you are. But please be careful. These people are vicious and cruel, and I could not bear to think of you murdered, too, for my sake.

May the Grace of God and the Holy Mother be with you.
With all of my hope and my heart,
Ethelyn.

The agony came outta me in great, shudderin' sobs as I read, and when I'd finished I sagged back against the wall and let all the rest of it out, too. When I'd spent it all, exhausted myself, wrung it all out, I just sat there, the letter held limply in my hands as I stared unseein' at the opposite wall.

Nan *did* have Ethelyn.

Now I knew that much at least fer certain.

Nan did have her. And I *would* find her.

Nan could hold me in her debt fer as long as she wanted, fer whatever she wanted, I weren't gonna let that merchant outbid me. His money could only go so far. But if Nan wanted more Old World artifacts, if she wanted more banks or stagecoaches robbed, hell, if she wanted to cross the Valley of Lightning itself, all that I could do. Or at least I'd try my damnedest.

She wanted me to be patient? Fine. I'd play this fuckin' game of hers, sure enough. She clearly didn't know how stubborn we Delanos could be. But she were about to find out.

Feelin' more resolved now, I straightened up off the wall and folded the letter carefully, then tucked it back into my shirt pocket. I scrubbed my hands over my face, then wiped it with my bandana. Pulled off my hat and tossed it to the end of the cot. Raked fingers through my damp hair.

Then stopped abruptly as I caught sight of the newspaper that had been discarded near the waste bucket. The front page had a large photograph of a mighty familiar man. I woulda recognized those bushy eyebrows, hooded eyes, and grumpy expression anywhere.

I lurched off the cot to grab up the paper, and fear stabbed into my belly as I folded it out so I could read the whole headline.

NOTORIOUS OUTLAW HOLT HAGGERTY TO DIE ON THE GALLOWS

The fear clamped hard, cuttin' off my breath. Frantically, I searched out the date on the paper. Three days ago. Then I skimmed the article, hardly seein' the words, the small print all blurrin' together as I looked fer the date they'd set fer him to hang.

Finally I found it ... fourteen days from the printin' of that article, they said. Wanted folk to have plenty of time to come from miles around to witness the spectacle, they said.

That gave him eleven more days. Eleven days from today.

In some town called Destry.

They were gonna hang him. They were gonna hang Holt.

And here I was, trapped in this cell fer who knew how long. I stood fast from the cot, crumpled the paper, and hurled it against the wall. *"Fuck!"*

EPILOGUE

A GILDED CAGE

She stood tall and proud, back straight, shoulders back, chin up, just like her mama had always taught her, and watched the airship lumber downward toward its designated landing field. She had always dreamed of seeing one, these airships, ever since she was a small child and had read about them in stories.

But there was no joy in her heart at seeing this one. No wonder. There was only a cold, bitter anger where her glee should have been. Where her heart should have been. She watched the airship land, alighting soft as a butterfly despite its bulk, and blinked away the tears.

They ran hot down her cheeks, overlaying old trails. She'd been crying for days. Quietly crying in the dark hours of the night and the early hours of the morning, knowing there was no one left to save her.

She had done well enough taking care of herself all these years. The Western Territories were no place for a young girl on her own, and yet she had survived. Not just survived, but *lived*. Had done all right for herself, considering. Until the day she'd let her guard slip, just enough, and Nine-Fingered Nan's web had caught her up.

And she'd been trapped ever since. Held close and secure,

auctioned off to the highest bidder. The agent of the man who had won her stood beside her now, as straight and tall and stoic as she was, but dressed in colorful silk instead of colorful cottons. He had a long black braid like hers, too, all the way down to the small of his back.

Japan, he said. That's where they were going.

That's where they were all going. So many of them. Most of them women, or small girls and boys, but some young men, as well. All meant to board this one man's airship.

She couldn't imagine how much money he must have had, to afford to buy all of these people. She knew how much he'd paid for her alone. If any of the rest of these people had prices even close to hers ... well, then this man from Japan was quite certainly richer than any person she'd ever heard of on the American continent.

The airship's boarding ramp descended, raising a cloud of dust as its bottom edge thumped into the barren ground of the airfield. This whole place was barren, she thought. Wide and empty, nothing but sandstone structures and dirt and an endless blue sky.

It might have been pretty, maybe, if it weren't the place her life would end.

A group of people descended the boarding ramp, their colorful silks looking as out of place against the drab landscape as the silks of the man who stood beside her. They hurried forward, toward her and the others. The others who had their hands bound like her, and manacles with a short chain around their ankles, and who were surrounded on all sides by mean-looking men and women with guns.

The man beside her, the agent, turned to her and swept out an arm toward the airship. As if inviting her to enter a party at a grand estate, instead of inviting her to board the contraption that would deliver her to a life of being some man's plaything.

She set her jaw. Blinked away more tears. And shuffled forward of her own accord, not waiting for Nine-Fingered Nan's brutal crew to coerce or push or shove her, like they'd been doing for the whole journey here.

She was met halfway to the boarding ramp by a cluster of women who had come off the airship, all Japanese, some gray-haired and some closer to her age, and they greeted her and the other terrified souls who followed her as if they were all long-lost family.

But the warm reception did not warm the coldness that had numbed her recently. Despite several efforts in the last few months, she had failed to save herself. And her brother was not coming for her. Perhaps he never had been.

They had told her he was. Told her he was going to buy her back from Nine-Fingered Nan. Soon as he got enough money, that's what they'd said he'd said.

She'd never been certain he was still alive to begin with ... but then two weeks ago, just before they'd started this trek north to the airfield, they had come to tell her he couldn't pay.

No. Not that he *couldn't*.

He *wouldn't*.

No one was worth that much, he'd said.

The band of outlaws had sure had fun at her expense with that. Taunting and jeering over the fact her own brother had given up on her. Making sure she knew they'd certainly have paid the price to have her, if they could afford it. If Nan wouldn't have skinned them alive for it.

That night was the first night she had shed tears in all her time of captivity.

Perhaps it was all a lie. Perhaps Van had never been coming for her. Perhaps he thought she was dead. Perhaps *he* was really dead.

It didn't matter now, in the end, anyway. He'd left her once, after that horrific night when their parents had been murdered. He'd left her with the smell of their burning homestead thick in the air, in the dark of those woods, and he'd never come back.

She supposed she was a fool for believing he'd come back now, even if he were alive.

So she stood tall and proud, shoulders back and chin up, and shuffled up that ramp in her shackles, and refused to look back.

The inside of the airship was a great deal larger than she'd expected. She was guided along by several more silk-clad crew, until finally being ushered into a plush, well-appointed room. It had all the comforts of an expensive, high-class inn, only there were multiple beds, and they were stacked and small. Eight of them total.

A middle-aged Japanese woman bustled in, her robe breath-taking in its number of exquisite embroidered roses. Combs set with real flowers and trails of pearls were tucked into her jet-black hair. "Sit," she instructed, patting at a cushioned bench. "Sit here."

Ethelyn Delano did as she was told, confusion prickling at her neck. None of this was what she had expected. She startled as the woman pulled a slender knife from her sash, then only grew more confused as the ropes around her wrists were cut, pulled off, and thrown away.

The knife disappeared back into the sash, and the woman gestured at Ethelyn's ankles. "Let me see?" In her other hand, she proffered a small key.

Ethelyn straightened her legs, and the manacle chain clinked. The heavy iron cuffs had chaffed at her skin, and it was raw and sore.

The woman dressed in roses shook her head and clucked her tongue at the sight, but unlocked the shackles and pulled them away, too. She straightened and turned as more young women were ushered into the room, all looking as bewildered as Ethelyn felt.

But the woman welcomed them in much the same way, instructing them all to sit, and removing their ropes and chains one by one. "Do not worry, *mina-san*," she said softly. "You are all safe now. All safe. You will have food and drink, and warmth and comfort. We will take care of you."

Ethelyn blinked, wondering if all of this was some sort of sick joke. Wondering if this was how this wealthy man eased his conscience, helped himself sleep at night after condemning so many people to a life of forced servitude.

A gilded cage was still a cage.

She glanced to the other women who had come in, but they all seemed as lost as she.

Their Japanese host turned to a cabinet and removed a whole porcelain tea set beset with pale blue flowers and gold accents. She went about preparing a pot, and out in the corridor a man in a plain black robe passed by, said something to the woman in a language Ethelyn couldn't understand, and then shut their door.

A low rumble started up from somewhere, the floor vibrating beneath Ethelyn's feet, the walls humming.

"Ah!" the woman of flowers said cheerily. "We depart! We have a long journey ahead, but you will be as comfortable as possible. Now ... who will have tea?"

Only silence answered her question as Ethelyn and the others looked among each other with many questions and no answers, and then Ethelyn gasped as the room shifted just slightly to one side.

They were lifting off, all right. Leaving the ground. Leaving the Western Territories and the American continent. Leaving the only place she'd ever known. She'd been kidnapped and sold, and yet this place and these people were already far different than she'd imagined.

If they were going to free her of her bonds, promise her warmth and comfort, and offer her tea ... maybe she had hope of freeing herself, after all. Eventually.

She'd done well enough over all these years.

And she'd done so by observing weaknesses and finding opportunity, no matter the circumstances.

Perhaps this journey ... this new life, even if in an unfamiliar land ... would be no different.

She cleared her throat, sat up straighter as she turned to face the woman, and raised a hand. She even managed a smile. The sugary sweet kind that had lured many a mark her way in the past. "I'll take some," she said. "I'll take some tea, please."

THE END

FREE BONUS ALERT!

PSST!! Want to find out what really happened during Van's night with Nora and Nettie?

If you are a fan of steamy scenes and lots of spice, then this free bonus scene is just for you!

But please note, this bonus is for MATURE AUDIENCES ONLY! By downloading this freebie, you're verifying you are 18+!

Not scared away yet? Then take a peek behind the curtain here....

https://jrfrontera.com/bathtimebonus/

BONES IN BLACKBIRD

THE LEGACY OF LUCKY LOGAN

J. R. FRONTERA

BONES IN BLACKBIRD

THE LEGACY OF LUCKY LOGAN
BOOK 3

WRITTEN BY
J.R. FRONTERA

PROCLAMATION from the WHITTAKER ESTATE OF BLESSING

WANTED!

for capture ALIVE

HAVE YOU

SEEN HIM

HAVE YOU

SEEN HIM

$50,000 REWARD

Name currently UNKNOWN, last seen fleeing Blessing. Wanted for ARSO
THEFT, AND MURDER. Has a LAME LEFT LEG MADE OF METAL and
walks with a noticeable LIMP. Considered EXTREMELY DANGEROUS.
MR. CHARLES MILLER has offered CASH REWARD PA
IN FULL UPON RETURN of this criminal ALIVE.

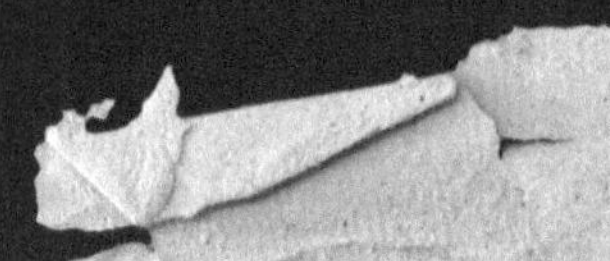

WESTERN UNION
TELEGRAM

The filing time shown in the date line on telegrams and day letters is STANDARD TIME at point of origin. Time of receipt is STANDARD TIME at point of destination.

DEAREST VAN

AM HOME SAFE. HOPE AND PRAY YOU AND SISTER ARE THE SAME. EVER SO GRATEFUL FOR YOUR AID. PLEASE CALL UPON MYSELF OR MY FAMILY IF YOU NEED ANYTHING. WILL SEND PROPER LETTER VERY SOON. PLEASE WRITE AS SOON AS YOU CAN.

THE COMPANY WILL APPRECIATE SUGGESTIONS FROM ITS PATRONS CONCERNING ITS SERVICE

Van, dear brother,

They tell me you are still alive. They tell me they are bringing these letters to you. They tell me you are coming to get me. But it has been weeks now, and I am beginning to fear the worst. I fear they are lying, about all of it. I cannot fathom why they would tell such lies, except to torture me with the hope that it is all true... and brother, it has been torture of the worst kind. Except for that, they have treated me fair decent enough, though I am told daily that is only because the man who wishes to buy me absolutely insists I am given to him unmarked, and that if they should ignore that condition, he will not pay for me, and then that Nine-Fingered Nan would flay them alive. But even that is miserable to endure, as I do not know how much longer I will be here, or how much longer such people can stand to obey orders, even if from someone they fear as much as they clearly fear Nine-Fingered Nan.

Brother, if you are still alive, I pray this letter finds you, and I pray you are able to come for me as they say you are. But please be careful. These people are vicious and cruel, and I could not bear to think of you murdered, too, for my sake.

May the Grace of God and the Holy Mother be with you.

With all of my hope and my heart,
Ethelyn.

THE DAILY NEWS

25c

NOTORIOUS OUTLAW HOLT HAGGERTY TO DIE ON THE GALLOWS

DESTRY, ARIZONA TERRITORY, AUGUST 30 – The dusty streets of our fair town are a-flutter with the thrilling news that the infamous outlaw Holt Haggerty has been sentenced to hang for his myriad of dastardly deeds. The gallows will be erected in the town square and the event is set for a fortnight from now, promising to draw spectators from miles around eager to witness justice served.

Haggerty, a name that strikes fear in the hearts of law-abiding citizens, stands accused of a veritable laundry list of crimes. His nefarious escapades include capital murder, assault, robbery, and arson, as well as more underhanded offenses such as theft, kidnapping, and forgery. Furthermore, the scoundrel has been known to impersonate officers of the law, sell stolen goods, rustle cattle, and steal horses with a callousness that leaves all sensible townsfolk shaking their heads in disbelief.

Captured just a week ago after a daring shootout on the outskirts of town – following Haggerty's failed attempt to rob Destry's bank – Haggerty has been the source of countless tales around campfires, each more exaggerated than the last. Local lawmen expressed relief at his capture, stating, "This ruffian thought himself invincible, but justice has a way of catching up with even the most slippery of snakes."

As the day of reckoning approaches, Sheriff Jacob "Buck" Bell is urging all citizens to come forth and witness the hanging. "It's a sight no decent person should miss," he remarked with grim determination. "Let it serve as a warning to any who dare cross the law. Even out here in the Territories, and especially in my town, there are consequences for outlawry."

Expectations run high as townsfolk prepare for this momentous occasion, eager not only to see Haggerty meet his end but to revel in the communal spirit of justice. The gallows, freshly built and looming, will stand as a stark reminder of the cost of a life lived in crime.

Mark your calendars, folks—September 13th shall be a day etched into the annals of Destry's history; a day when villainy shall be vanquished and the town—nay, the entirety of the Western Territories—will breathe easier knowing that one more outlaw has been sent to meet his Maker.

HANG 'EM HIGH

I couldn't see shit wearin' this bonnet.

Made me wonder how the women-folk put up with 'em.

I kept my eyes on the ground, mostly, bent over and holdin' a walkin' stick in my right hand. Partly to complete my disguise, and partly to help balance myself after standin' here fer hours. The crowd had arrived bit by bit over the course of the mornin', but I'd been one of the first ones here. Been here since dawn. Watched the sun come up over the town square ... over the gallows. Watched the shadows of those nooses stretch out long across the ground, and then slowly shorten as the day wore on.

The cotton dress I'd donned over my usual clothes was startin' to get awful hot, but there weren't nothin' I could do about that.

The hangin' was set fer noon. And noon was comin' up awful fast now.

The crowd had swelled, all right. Fillin' in around and behind me, men and women and children, and vendors sellin' cakes and rock candy and jerky, and tinctures and whiskey.

I ignored 'em, all of 'em, the spectators and the vendors both. Ran

over this plan of mine again and again in my mind, tryin' not to calculate too awful much the odds of gettin' killed in this venture.

I couldn't afford to get myself killed. Not when I still had to get
Ethelyn from Nan. But neither could I have stayed rottin' away in that
jail cell back in Bravebank while Holt got hanged. The man was an
insufferable, selfish bastard ... but damn it all, he'd saved my neck too
many times to count in the last eight years.

At least I owed him this. At least I owed him a try.

Sweat slipped down my face and I swiped at it with the back of my
left hand, then brushed that hand against my hip, feelin' at the outline
of my pistol beneath the skirt of the floral-patterned dress. I'd cut a
slit in the fabric there along both holsters, so they could be covered up
fer the most part, but still within easy reach fer when I needed 'em
quick.

I'd never pulled a job dressed like a woman before, but it'd seemed
the only way I was gonna have a chance of gettin' anywhere near this
place without bein' recognized or lookin' suspicious. And so far, it was
workin'.

Except fer this damned bonnet completely cuttin' off my peripheral
vision. It hid my face, sure enough, but the narrowed field of view
made me nervous, too.

I took a slow breath in and let it out just as slow. Glanced up to
look through the gallows scaffolding, across the square, to where I'd
tied my mule Joe and the skinny old mare Seven Knives Sally had
gifted me. I'd only barely managed to get Joe back from that livery in
Sonoita in time to make it here before the hangin', and as luck would
have it, I'd found Holt's horse in the Destry livery last night.

The hostler here was a downright drunk, so it'd been easy enough
to sneak the horse out, but I didn't exactly want him tied in the middle
of town considerin' the law had been notified of the missin' animal and
tack this mornin'.

So I'd left him outside town a ways, along our planned escape route.

If this plan of mine didn't end with both of us dead, I imagined
Holt would be mighty sore about havin' to ride that old mare outta
here, but then, she'd be carryin' him to freedom, so surely he'd get
over it.

I checked my line of sight to my distractions next, tryin' to only minimally turn my head so as to not reveal my very unladylike features to the folk pressin' in close on either side. Didn't want anyone realizin' I weren't no old lady till I was good and ready fer 'em to realize such a thing.

But they were still there, my distractions, three small bundles of dynamite I'd planted in the wee hours of the mornin', wedged up along the rooftops of some of the surroundin' buildings. One above a dentist, one above the bank, one above the post office. Two to my right and one to my left. Fairly easy shots from my vantage point here at the front of the crowd, but I'd have to be fast.

And not miss.

I took another slow breath in attempts to quiet my hummin' nerves.

Too much feelin' threw off yer aim, and I was feelin' an awful lot right now...

A commotion rose up among the crowd to my left, where the jailhouse sat along that side of the square, and I glanced that way to see the lawdogs leadin' Holt out.

My hand tightened around the top of the walkin' stick and I sucked in a breath.

He looked as grumpy as ever, hands bound together in front of him, a decent-sized gash along his left temple bruised and swollen. He was held by a deputy on either side, and had another man in front and behind him.

The crowd parted to allow 'em through to the gallows stairs, but booed and hissed as Holt passed, some shoutin' out that he was a murderer and a monster. A few flung pieces of rotten produce at him, fruit and vegetables that hit him in the chest with a wet smack, splattering a mess everywhere.

I shifted on my feet and clenched my jaw, eyein' my distractions again, memorizin' their locations. Then looked back to Holt to see him spittin' and yellin' insults at the townsfolk, which only earned him more rotten food and vehement invitations to go to Hell.

The sheriff and his deputies tried to settle the crowd some as they took Holt up the stairs, put him over the trap door, and settled the noose around his neck. And then they stepped back, positionin' themselves at the four corners of the stage. They didn't have their guns drawn, but they looked alert, all right.

It was generally known around these parts that Holt Haggerty didn't run with no gang, so they weren't likely expectin' a whole heap of trouble from any outsiders tryin' to save his neck. But it was also generally known that Holt Haggerty *did* often run with at least one other unsavory outlaw.

Me.

They were almost certainly expectin' me, and lookin' out fer me, too.

I tried to keep my head angled away from 'em, so all they'd see was a pretty floral bonnet and not my face while I ran more calculations in my head.

Four of 'em, the noose rope, my three distractions. I was gonna need both pistols. And every shot had to count.

Another man ascended the gallows stairs now. He was dressed in a rather nice suit and held a rolled up piece of paper in his hand. He motioned for the crowd to quiet, and to my surprise, they did. He stepped to the edge of the gallows platform and I dropped my gaze back quick to the dusty ground so he wouldn't notice my features as he scanned the masses spread out before him.

"Good people of Destry," he yelled out, "and all those gathered here from elsewhere in the Territories as witness! Today we will have, at last, the ending of a criminal outlaw who has terrorized our towns for far too long!"

The people cheered. Whooped and hollered.

He motioned them quiet again. "As Mayor of this fine town of Destry, I must commend our Sheriff Bell and his deputies, who apprehended this criminal before he could make off with much of our hard-earned money."

More cheerin' and shoutin' from the crowd.

Holt scowled and grumbled somethin', but it was lost beneath all the ruckus.

The mayor waited till the noise died down some, then continued,

"It will be my pleasure to oversee this execution, and I beg all of you here today to remember: crime does not pay."

It was my turn to scowl and grumble then, and I shifted again on my feet, my metal leg whirrin' softly beneath the skirts. Maybe crime didn't pay ... but it had kept me fed fer plenty of years now. Fed, and sometimes warm and comfortable, too.

"Now..." the mayor said. He unfurled the rolled paper. "Holt Haggerty, for the crimes of capital murder, assault, robbery, arson..."

That list was gettin' awful long. I wondered if my list were that long these days. Probably.

"... theft, kidnapping..."

Kidnapping? I didn't remember that one. But then, Holt had been an outlaw fer a long time. Certainly longer than just the eight years I'd been runnin' with him.

"... forgery, impersonating an officer of the law..."

All right, I *did* remember that one...

"... selling stolen goods, horse theft, and cattle rustling, I do hereby sentence you to hang by the neck until dead." The mayor gave a little nod of finality and curled up that paper, and another wave of murmurs and excited chatter circled through the gathered crowd.

The mayor squinted upward, to the stretch of blue above. Weren't a cloud in the sky. The merciless sun glared down at us full-bore, directly overhead.

High noon.

Time fer the hangin'. Time fer Holt Haggerty to die.

He looked back to Holt then, a rather smug look of satisfaction crossin' his pinched and sweaty features. "Well?" he asked. "Any last words?"

I risked a glance to Holt myself, lookin' up at him standin' on that gallows stage from beneath the shade of my bonnet, and I slipped my left hand through the cut in the skirt on my left hip to curl my fingers loose around my gun grip. The three middle fingers of that hand had bandages around their ends where Charles Miller had pulled off the fingernails not so long ago. And they were still sore, too. But I'd been practicin' drawin' and shootin' with those sore fingers since I'd escaped the Bravebank jail, till I was comfortable enough with 'em that I could rely on 'em today.

I eased my right hand downward now itself, along the length of the walkin' stick, closer to my right holster.

My heart beat in my throat. Sweat slid down my temples to run down my neck.

Holt glared out at the crowd pressed in on all sides and they hushed as he opened his mouth. "Yeah," he grunted. But then his clear blue gaze found mine, and he paused. Surprise went over his creased, grimy features, then a cautious hope, but he looked away again quick before any of those lawdogs could take an interest in what he might have seen. His face went hard and angry again, and he focused his glare on Destry's mayor. "Yeah," he said again, one corner of his mouth quirkin' into a smirk. "The best-laid schemes of mice and men often go awry, and leave us nothing but grief and pain, fer promised joy."

I rolled my eyes, cursin' him silently, hopin' his bein' cute wouldn't tip off those four armed men up there.

But the mayor only seemed perplexed, then shook his head. "Quoting literature will not gain you any sympathy here, Haggerty. Saying pretty words does not make you a civilized man."

Holt snorted in amusement. "You would know about that personally, wouldn'tcha, Mayor?"

The gathered masses booed at that comment, and shouts to get on with the hangin' already rang through the square.

The mayor agreed with 'em, 'cause he drew himself up straighter at Holt's insult and gestured to the sheriff. The sheriff nodded, pulled the black hood from where he'd had it tucked into his belt, and shook it out as he went to Holt's side.

"Goodbye, Haggerty," he said, and put the hood over Holt's head before Holt could snap anything in return. "And good riddance."

The mayor stepped over to the lever. All he had to do was pull it, and that trap door would swing open under Holt's feet, and he'd take a long drop on a short rope, his neck snappin' like a twig.

Unless I didn't miss.

I took in another slow, deep breath of the hot afternoon. Another trickle of sweat slipped down my face, but I didn't dare wipe it away. Not now. Not this close.

The mayor rested his hand atop the lever and affected a solemn expression. The masses around me went deathly quiet, their anticipation thick as mine, but fer entirely different reasons.

Someone across the square coughed, and a baby started cryin'.

A light breeze stirred, coolin' the sweat on my brow and shiftin' my floral skirts around my ankles.

"May God and the Holy Mother alike have mercy on your soul," the mayor said.

He pulled the lever.

ONE BULLET LEFT

I drew and fired twice before my walkin' stick hit the ground; one bullet fer the noose rope and one bullet fer the dynamite above the dentist's place. Holt grunted as he fell all the way through the trap door and hit the ground hard, and a split second later that dynamite blew a hole in the dentist's roof.

The crack of the explosion washed out over the crowd, many of whom screamed and ducked, many of whom turned tail and fled, pushin' and shovin' each other in their haste to vacate the premises. The mayor hit the floor of the scaffold, hands over his head, and those four armed lawdogs drew fast, too.

But I already had bullets ready fer 'em, firin' at two from my right pistol and two from my left pistol even as I lurched forward to duck beneath the gallows stage. All four of my shots hit home; I saw all four men stagger just before divin' into the shadows underneath 'em.

I went to Holt, who'd managed to push himself up sittin' and lifted his bound hands to yank the hood off his head. I shoved my right pistol back into its holster and grabbed him under one arm, haulin' him to his feet. "Come on," I hissed. "We gotta go."

"Nice dress," he muttered, followin' me out the other side of the scaffoldin' to run toward the horses. "And nice shootin'."

"We ain't out of this yet," I scowled back, and even as I twisted around to say it, I saw the sheriff up on the gallows put us in his sights.

I'd shot him, all right, but I hadn't killed him. I fired back at him with my left pistol and missed, but made him duck away, anyway. Then I switched my aim and planted a bullet in the dynamite above the bank.

It exploded with another crack, makin' Holt instinctively wince and duck, and keepin' that sheriff laid out flat, and promptin' a fresh wave of screams and shouts from the remainin' townsfolk. The rest of 'em fled fer cover now, terrified and confused, though a few brave souls seemed determined to hold their ground, hands hoverin' above their guns as they searched fer a target amid all the chaos.

We reached our mounts before they spotted us and I hiked up my skirts in a hurry, then fair near leapt up into my saddle, gatherin' the reins quick and tearin' that damned bonnet off my head so I could see proper.

Holt caught his saddle horn in both bound hands and swung up onto that skinny mare just as quick. "The hell is my horse?" he spat.

"Waitin' down the road," I ground out. "Let's just get the hell outta here, yeah?"

"With pleasure, kid."

We ducked as shots rang out behind us, and I pulled Joe around to put a bullet into the man who was shootin' at us.

It was the last in my left pistol's cylinder, so I holstered that one quick and switched hands, movin' the reins to my left and pullin' my right pistol just as that damned sheriff pushed to his feet again on the gallows.

I shot at him same time as he shot at me, and fire seared through my left bicep as his bullet tore through it. I yelled out and swore, but mine got him in the chest and he flung backwards, sprawlin' next to the mayor who was still all hunkered down.

I ground my teeth against the pain in my arm and fired my right pistol one last time, lightin' up my third distraction to punch a hole in the post office roof. Wood splinters rained down into the street, the few folk who were left in the square whippin' around to face the newest noise with a start.

Joe danced sideways under me, chewin' at his bit, but then I kicked him up into a gallop to get shut of this town quick, fer which he didn't need much convincin'. He didn't much like all the explosions and shootin', big ears swivelin' around all over the place and eyes rollin'. Well, he was probably gonna need to get used to that.

But fer now we high-tailed it outta there, and none too soon, neither.

I only had one bullet left. And it'd be mighty hard to reload with all my cartridges hidden under this damned dress.

Hard hoofbeats followed after me and Joe, and I glanced back once over my shoulder to make sure it was Holt.

It was. The noose still hung around his neck, the frayed end of it split by my bullet flappin' in the wind. He was bent low over his borrowed horse's neck, urgin' her on till we were runnin' side by side, flyin' down that road and fast puttin' distance between us and the town of Destry.

⚜

I'd kept Holt's gelding tied to a tree a ways off the road a few miles on, and we stopped there only long enough for him to switch mounts. Then we were off again, ponying the mare behind us despite Holt's protests she'd only slow us down, and we kept a hard pace northeast fer as long as the horses could manage.

It reminded me eerily of the time we'd fled Bravebank after murderin' three of Nan's men and makin' that deal with Taggert. The deal that had turned out to be no deal at all.

My fists tightened around my reins at the memory, but I shoved all of that away again soon enough. None of that mattered anymore. It was done. In the past. All I could do now was move forward ... and not repeat the same stupid mistakes.

No more makin' deals with anyone but Nine-Fingered Nan directly.

And no more givin' her what she wanted without seein' my sister in-person. In-person, and alive and well.

"Van!"

Holt's bark jolted me outta my stew of rage and I glanced over at him sharply.

"Horses need a rest," he said, noddin' toward his own, all lathered up and blowin' hard. "We should find a place to stop fer awhile."

"Oh. Right." Joe was all lathered, too, and that poor mare was draggin' at the end of her lead. We slowed 'em up and let 'em walk while we looked fer somewhere suitable to hole up, and eventually decided on wanderin' up onto a nearby mountain a ways where the bigger boulders would hide us and we'd have a good view out over the surroundin' land, so we could spot any pursuit comin' long before they reached us.

We dismounted there, and Holt held out his bound wrists. I fished under my skirts fer my knife and cut the thick coils of rope fer him.

He gave a hiss of relief as his hands were freed, then immediately reached up to pull the noose off his neck and toss it away. "That was closer than I ever wanted to be to dyin'," he muttered. Then he glanced up at me, clapped a hand on my shoulder. "Thanks, kid."

I shrugged. "You woulda done the same fer me."

I think.

Maybe the last time we'd seen each other we'd been throwin' fists, and he'd almost drowned me in that horse trough ... coulda drowned me in that horse trough easy enough ... but he hadn't. And anyway, he'd pulled me outta plenty of scrapes before that. Surely he woulda done the same again if I'd been facin' the noose, no matter our recent disagreements.

"Damn right," he said, and he sounded truthful enough.

But maybe he was just feelin' especially appreciative at the moment given his fresh brush with mortality.

"Only maybe not dressed like that."

I scoffed and shook my head, movin' away from his skeptical stare to start unsaddlin' Joe. "Only way I could get close enough to make the shot I did. Figured they'd be expectin' me to come and try to save yer neck. Figured you probably didn't want me to miss splittin' that rope."

He gave a grunt of agreement.

I made to pull the saddle off the mule, but the weight of it made that bullet hole in my left bicep flare somethin' awful, and I spat a curse as I lost my grip, the blanket and saddle both hittin' the ground in a heap.

Holt appeared at my side, hooded blue gaze takin' in the blood spread all down my left sleeve. It stained all the flowers on the dress there a deep, dark red. "You got shot," he stated flatly.

"Just a flesh wound," I managed. "I'll be alright." I hooked my right hand into the gullet of my saddle and pulled it over where I wanted it, then went back to get my blanket out of the dirt and shook it out, draped it over the saddle's cantle.

Holt eyed me the whole way, then went to his own saddle and started rummagin' in his bags fer supplies. "Why don't you let me take a look at it, anyway. Probably needs stitchin'."

"Probably," I conceded. "But we'd better see to our tracks first. And the horses."

Holt turned, frowned at me fer a minute, and then to my surprise, nodded instead of argued. He brought his handful of stuff over to me— whiskey, needle and stitchin' thread, a roll of bandages—and set it down atop a flat boulder to my right. "Fine. I'll see to our tracks. You get things settled here. And take off that godforsaken dress. When I get back I'll stitch you up."

I shrugged again. "All right."

He moved off down the path we'd come up on, grumblin' to himself.

"Holt."

He stopped and turned, quirkin' an eyebrow in question.

I pulled my left pistol, opened the cylinder, and dug out six bullets from under my dress. I loaded 'em, snapped the cylinder closed again, and tossed the gun to him. "You might need that."

He caught it neatly. Hefted it in his hand, then gave it a twirl and stuck it in his waistband. "Just might," he said. Then he went on down the path and disappeared from view, and I turned my attention to the horses.

And to gettin' out of that godforsaken dress.

III

ANY KIND OF FAMILY

It didn't take him long to return, but I was restless waitin', anyway. I paced back and forth along the little rise we'd stopped along, watchin' the stretch of land below until I finally saw him reappear.

He was alone. And no one followed him that I could see.

Satisfied, I went back to my saddlebags to get us a little somethin' to eat.

And so he wouldn't think I'd been too worried.

He rounded the bend just as I'd pulled out some bread and cheese and jerky. "Hungry?" I asked.

"Sure, some. But you ain't gettin' out of bein' stitched. So sit down and let me look at yer arm."

I sighed but did as he instructed, settlin' cross-legged on the ground and puttin' my back up against another big rock. In truth, it was nice to have a minute to rest. I'd been racin' against the clock ever since managin' to get outta that cell in Bravebank. Hardly had any decent sleep fer days. Now that I'd made it to Destry in time, and not only that, but managed to pull off my one-man rescue with both of us still alive ... well, that reality still seemed to be soakin' in. My body was finally startin' to relax a bit.

At least until Holt started pokin' and proddin' at that wound in my arm.

Then I ground my teeth against the fresh waves of pain.

He rolled up that shirt sleeve far as he could, then dumped some whiskey on the hole in my flesh.

I nearly came right up off the ground at that, swearin' as the bitin' sting went all the way through my arm. But Holt put his other hand against my chest and pushed me back down, holdin' me flat against the rock.

"Easy now," he said. "That's over. It's done. Just gotta stitch it now. Here." He pushed the whiskey bottle into my right hand. "Take a few swigs."

I glared murder at him, but took the bottle and did as he said fer that, too. Then I looked away and focused out on the far horizon, focused on breathin', focused on holdin' tight to that whiskey bottle, while he closed up the hole.

"Looks like it went all the way through," he said as he worked. "And missed the bone."

"Like I said," I ground out. "Just a flesh wound."

"Lucky it weren't worse," he muttered. "But I'll need to close it up on the exit side."

"Do whatever you need to do."

There was silence between us fer awhile, while Holt concentrated on his task and I concentrated on ignorin' the way the pain made me sweat. My left arm and shoulder were awful tender to the touch already, thanks to the treatment I'd suffered at the hands of Charles Miller ... thanks to that electrical rod of his. And now this. Another bullet. Another scar.

I switched my attention away from that unpleasant line of thought and instead tried to figure out just what to say to Holt. There were sure a lot of things I wanted to say to him right now. A lot of things I'd considered sayin' to him durin' all the days I'd been scramblin' to make it here in time to save him.

Things like remindin' him of how he'd almost killed me last time we'd seen each other.

Remindin' him *he'd* been the one to walk away from *me*. Things like tellin' him it'd been a stupid thing fer him to do, to attempt a bank robbery all by himself with me nowhere near by, nevermind the fact he mighta pulled off such a thing once ... he shoulda known better than to push his luck.

Weren't that what he was always tellin' me? And then he'd gone and done that himself, and look where it had landed him ... right into the noose.

I opened my mouth to say all those things, but then hesitated. And closed it again. All of a sudden I didn't have the energy fer it anymore.

Seemed Holt had somethin' to say himself, though, 'cause that's when he cleared his throat. "So," he started, still stitchin'. "Yer still alive."

"Fer now." I wanted to make the point that so was he, but only 'cause of me, but I swallowed it back. He was surely well enough aware of that. No need to rub it in. Gettin' his praise weren't why I'd rescued him, anyway.

"And ... any word from Nine-Fingered Nan?"

I swallowed back the bitter laugh, too. Instead all I said was, "Yeah."

Holt looked to me in surprise, then turned back to the stitchin'. "No shit? Well? What'd she say?"

I considered all the things he'd missed. Considered how all of it had ended. And decided he didn't need to know about most of it. I'd never hear the fuckin' end of it. So I only wet my lips and shook my head. "She said ... she said to keep waitin'."

Holt snorted.

"But she gave me this." I set the whiskey bottle aside and reached into my shirt pocket with my right hand, pullin' out the folded piece of paper I'd kept there since Nan had given it to me. "It's a letter. From Ethelyn."

Holt's hands stilled. He glanced to the paper in my fingers.

He didn't have to say nothin' fer me to see the skepticism written all over his grimy features. I gave him a hard glare in return. "Yes," I snapped. "It's her script. You can look at it yerself if you want."

"All right, all right," he relented. "Ease off. I ain't never seen the girl's writin'."

"Well I have. Lots. Mama was a schoolteacher, remember? Made us practice our letters all the damn time—"

"All right, I said." Holt tied off the thread he'd used to close up the exit wound at the back of my bicep and used his teeth to clip it. Then he sat back, exchangin' the thread and needle for the roll of bandages. He tore off a length, wrapped it over the holes a few times, and tied that off, too. "I ain't gonna fight you on that anymore, kid."

I'd kept on glarin' at him as he worked, but my expression softened at that admission of his. What exactly did that mean?

He sighed heavily and settled cross-legged next to me, then reached across my lap to snatch up the whiskey bottle fer himself. He took several heavy swigs before lowerin' it and swipin' the back of his hand across his mouth. "Look. When I was ... when I was sittin' in that cell fer all those days, waitin' to die ... I realized..." He stopped, shook his head, cleared his throat again. He looked away, squintin' out into the harsh daylight. "Well, I realized I had no one. I used to have the gang, ya know. Grew up with 'em. And they were all bad men, sure, but they was my family, through and through. We were at least loyal to each other, if not to nothin' else. And when all that started to fall apart, I had yer pa at least. We was like brothers, ya understand. Like brothers."

He took another swallow of whiskey, and I dropped my eyes to my hands in my lap and that letter still held between my fingers, rememberin' what part of this story I knew.

Growin' up on that ranch in Kansas, Pa had never said a word about Holt Haggerty. Never said a word about the gang he'd used to run with. Neither had Mama, though she must have known. She must have. Maybe she hadn't truly grasped the whole of Pa's sordid past—I still didn't think I did, even now—but she musta known somethin' about it, surely.

Holt shrugged. "But then that ended, too. And ... well, kid ... it's good to have family. Any kind of family. Bein' on yer own ain't all it's cracked up to be, especially out here. Most lone folk don't last long, and there's a reason fer that. So ... I guess what I'm tryin' to say is ... if ya really think yer sister might still be alive out there, and ya really think you might have a chance to get her, then a' course that's what you gotta do. And I'm ... I'm sorry fer always bein' such a bastard about it, I guess."

I lifted my eyes to him again in surprise—I didn't think I'd ever heard him apologize fer nothin'—but he was still lookin' out at the shimmerin' horizon. He kept starin' out there, rather resolutely, and swigged more whiskey.

A corner of my mouth quirked. "And if a damn fool uncle of yers really thinks he can get away with robbin' a bank a second time all on his lonesome and ends up gettin' himself arrested and put in the noose, well ... you refrain from tellin' him how stupid he is and save his ass, anyway."

Holt scoffed, lookin' at me sideways. "Save his neck, more like." He offered out the whiskey bottle and I took it, helpin' myself to more.

"Thanks fer comin' fer me, though, honestly," he said quietly. "Especially given the situation with Nan and yer sister. I thought fer sure I was a dead man."

I only shook my head. And covered my inability to find proper words by drinkin' yet more whiskey. Had I taken a risk leavin' Bravebank when Nan had instructed me to wait? Maybe. But she'd let me sit fer three weeks before, and I had a good idea she planned to let me sit fer even longer this time, if only 'cause she knew it made me hot under the collar.

But I weren't gonna let her manipulate me like that. Not anymore.

Just like I weren't gonna wait all that time coolin' my heels in a jail cell if I could instead save Holt's life.

Like he'd said, it was good to have family.

Any kind of family.

"Thanks fer stitchin' me up," I managed finally. Then I glanced to that gash on his temple and frowned. "Looks like maybe you shoulda had some stitchin' yerself."

He shrugged and shook his head. "Naw. That'll be fine." He

gestured to the bandaged three middle fingers of my left hand restin' in my lap. "What about that?"

"Uh." I lifted that hand, then winced as the motion lit pain in my bicep. "Nothin'. Ran into an old friend, that's all. It'll be fine."

He eyed me skeptically. "Uh huh." But to my relief, he didn't press further. "Welp," he said abruptly, pushin' to his feet. "We'd best move on. We can eat in the saddle. We'll need to take the long way 'round to Grave Gulch, make sure no one can follow our trail."

"Grave Gulch?" I repeated.

He looked down at me like I'd lost my mind. "Yeah. Where else you think we'd go? Those bastards took my guns *and* my hat ... I'm gonna need to get the ones I got stashed back at camp."

Well, that *did* make sense. But Grave Gulch was in the wrong direction fer where I needed to go. "I need to make another stop first."

His gaze narrowed. "Oh yeah? Where at?"

I got to my feet myself and handed him back his whiskey, though there weren't much left of it at this point, then tucked Ethelyn's letter back into my shirt pocket. "I need to pay a visit to the doc."

He frowned, lookin' me over. "I think I did a fine enough job on that—"

"No, not fer that." I lowered my left hand carefully, patted at my thigh. "Fer *this*."

Holt took a step backward. "The metal leg?"

I nodded.

"What, it been botherin' ya?"

"Naw, it's been fine, generally. But it ... it *did somethin'*, while you were away. And I don't know how it happened, or how to make it happen again ... or how to make it *not* happen again. I need some answers. And preferably sooner rather than later. Woulda gone to see him already, if I hadn't needed to come here fer you."

Holt took another step backward. "Whaddaya mean, it *did somethin'*?"

"I mean it ... it *did somethin'*." I tried to make an openin' gesture with my hands, then winced as my newly injured bicep twinged with pain again. "It ... it opened up. Had blades comin' outta it, and a pistol in there and everythin'."

Now his eyes went real wide. "A pistol? Inside? A pistol *inside* the leg?"

"Yeah. A pistol inside the leg."

He blinked rapidly and let out a long, low whistle. "Fer Chrissakes, boy, what you been smokin' while I was away?"

I scowled at him. "I ain't been smokin' nothin', damnit. I'm tellin' you, that's what happened. And I'm gonna go talk to the doc about it. Figure I'll pay him a house call. He's got a place just outside of Bravebank. So that's where I'm goin'. If ... if you wanna go on to Grave Gulch, you go ahead. I'll meet you there when I'm done with him."

Holt only looked at me fer a long minute more, then he turned away and went toward his saddlebags, chucklin' and shakin' his head. "Oh no, no no. I gotta hear this story. And what the doc has to say about it. See if he tosses you into the insane asylum."

I rolled my eyes and went toward my own stuff, grabbin' the blanket with one hand and walkin' over to Joe to throw it up over his back. "I ain't insane," I insisted. "I'm tellin' you, it happened."

Joe turned his big head toward me, prickin' up his big ears, and nickered softly. He snuffled at my pockets, but I pushed his nose away. That Sonoita hostler had soured him on sugar cubes, and now I was payin' the price. Don't even know why I'd taken the trouble to go all the way up there and get him, anyway. Surely weren't worth the effort.

He nudged me with his nose again.

"Lay off it, would you?" I snapped.

"Don't think the mule believes you, neither," Holt commented.

"Yeah, well, both of you shut it."

Holt only chuckled to himself again, and Joe only kept sniffin' at me fer sweets, but we managed to get saddled up anyway, and I ponied that mare behind me once more as we headed back down the mountain and angled toward Bravebank.

Toward Dr. Balogh's homestead.

HOUSE CALL

It took us another four days to get there, bein' as we took the long way 'round to throw off any pursuit, and paused sometimes to check fer a tail. But we stayed clear of anyone comin' after us, and by the time I spotted the Balogh windmill on the horizon the afternoon of the fourth day, we were fair certain we'd escaped the incident at Destry free and clear.

And by the time the Balogh house came into full view, I was fair certain somethin' was very, very wrong.

We approached from the south, givin' me a clear view of the little garden out back. Last I'd visited, the plants had been thrivin' and green. Now they were shriveled and dead. And the windmill weren't turnin'. The well bucket was overturned a distance from the well wall, and the barn doors were open.

Nothin' moved 'cept dust in the little breeze that cooled my skin.

I pulled Joe to a halt some distance out from the house, and my hand slid down to the iron on my hip.

"Don't look like anyone's home," Holt said.

My mouth went dry, my throat suddenly tight. *Goddamnit, Doc.*

What did you get yourself into? "Let's just be careful. Keep your eyes open." I drew my pistol, thumbed back the hammer, and nudged Joe onward.

We circled around toward the front of the house and found the door ajar; the window near it broken.

I tried to swallow, couldn't. My heart dropped into my stomach.

"This don't look promisin'," Holt muttered.

I ignored him, swingin' down from the saddle and headin' quick fer the door in a crouchin' run. I put my back up against the front frame of it and then peered around the corner, searchin' fer any movement inside.

There weren't none. Only shadows and sunlight, stillness and silence.

I put the barrel of my gun up against the door and pushed it open further, slow and careful, then winced as it creaked on stiff hinges.

I paused, waitin' fer anyone to reveal themselves at the noise, but there was nothin'.

Holt came up behind me, holdin' his borrowed pistol low and ready. "Anythin'?" he whispered.

I shook my head, then stepped inside. Into a disaster. The kitchen table and chairs had been overturned, floorboards ripped up, cupboards opened and their contents strewn all over the place. What few upholstered chairs sat in front of the fireplace had been torn up, and the ashes from the hearth itself scattered across the floor.

But there weren't no bodies. No blood. And no bullet holes.

"What the Devil happened here?" Holt breathed.

My heart pulsed in my throat as I moved toward the bedrooms, keepin' my pistol ready. I didn't understand what was goin' on here, but it surely weren't nothin' good. I kept thinkin' of that boy Radley helpin' me out, and of Fanni and Mrs. Balogh, who'd never fully trusted me. But they'd taken me into their home nonetheless. Fed me well and nursed me back to health. I'd always suspected their kindness might get 'em killed someday ... but I'd always hoped I'd be wrong, too.

"Goddamnit, Doc," I hissed. I knew he shouldn't have been flauntin' around that Old World tech ... I eased open the first bedroom door to find it ransacked same as the rest of the house. The bed was a mess, the bureau drawers yanked open, clothes all over the place. The other bedrooms were the same, too, includin' the guest bedroom I'd stayed in. Not even the lace curtains had survived the pillage; they'd been ripped down and tossed to the floor.

But there were no bodies and no blood, and I breathed a little easier as I rejoined Holt in the kitchen.

"Just who was this doctor, anyway?" he asked.

I shrugged. "Just a doctor. Bravebank's doctor." Just a doctor who could attach a metal leg to a person. A metal leg that could sometimes move on its own. A metal leg that could be its very own arsenal, if I could figure out how the hell to work it.

"Well," Holt mused, lookin' over the mess we stood in again, "someone wanted somethin' from him, clearly."

"Clearly."

"But no bodies," he said, echoin' my previous thoughts.

"But lots of their clothes are still here," I noted.

He nodded toward the aging produce strewn out across the wood stove and all over the floor. "And lots of food, too."

"Let's check the barn," I suggested.

We went out the back door nice and careful, past the wilted garden toward the open barn doors. It was dark in there beyond the rectangle of light comin' in through the front, and I paused at the entrance to squint into the blackness. I held my breath and listened, but everythin' was still quiet.

Too quiet.

Weren't no animal sounds comin' outta there. And the wagon was usually parked in the middle of it, in the space the rectangle of sun now illuminated. The space that was empty.

"Wagon's gone," I said quietly.

"And I don't hear no horses," Holt added.

"Mules," I corrected.

"Whatever."

A moan sounded out of the blackness, makin' me and Holt both jump and duck behind the barn walls, one of us on either side of the doorway, bringin' our guns up.

We waited there. Listened.

Another moan. Sounded like a man. Weak. Someone in pain.

"Fuck," I spat, and I dodged around the doorframe and moved into the darkness, strainin' to see after the dazzle of the afternoon sunlight.

"Van!" Holt hissed from behind me, but I paid him no mind, still searchin' fer the source of the voice.

"Hey," I said, feelin' at my belt for my coin pouch, which was also where I kept my matches. "Someone in here? Where are you?"

Another moan, close. To my right.

I could make out a dim shape there, just beyond the edge of the sunlight. Looked like a person sittin' down. In a chair, maybe. But all hunched over.

The fingers of my left hand finally found the matches amid my coin and pulled 'em out. I holstered my pistol to strike one, held it out toward the guy, and then winced. The flame revealed a man, all right, and he was sittin' in a chair, sure enough, but he'd been tied there. Wrists bound around the back of it and ankles tied to the legs, and he was all hunched over 'cause he seemed barely conscious. His face was a bruised, bloodied mess, both eyes swollen shut and blood runnin' from his mouth where it looked like he'd had several teeth knocked out.

I stepped back out of instinct, even as a flash of terror stabbed through me at thinking it mighta been Dr. Balogh. He was tall and thin like Dr. Balogh, but his face was so disfigured I weren't sure I could have been certain either way.

"Fuckin' hell," I whispered.

The match flame singed my fingertips and I hissed as I shook it out.

"That him?" Holt asked from the doorway. "That the doc?"

"I ... I can't tell," I admitted.

"I don't like this, Van. I think we oughta go."

"Yeah..." I murmured. "Yeah." But instead of turnin' to leave, I stepped forward again, pattin' gently at the man's knee. "Hey. Hey, you. You awake? Can you talk? What's yer name? Are ... are you..." I struggled to swallow. "You Dr. Balogh?"

"Van..." Holt started.

But he was interrupted by the sound of Joe's bastardized whinny.

I forgot about the bloodied man tied to the chair in front of me and whipped around, knowin' what the mule's overly social nature must be heraldin'. My frantic gaze met Holt's just as he realized the same thing, his eyes goin' wide.

But it was already too late.

Two silhouettes loomed up behind him just as he started to turn, and one cracked him over the head with a pistol. He went down to his hands and knees with a grunt, and my own gun was outta leather and takin' aim when a sharp voice cracked through the heat like a whip.

"Drop it or he dies, boy."

I registered the gun pointed at Holt's head at the same time I recognized the voice, and my finger stilled a hair's breadth from squeezin' down on my trigger. Instead I opened my hand, let the gun slip down and hang by its trigger guard, and I lifted my left hand too fer good measure, nevermind the fact it made my bicep twinge in protest.

The second shadow moved forward, her tall stature and wide-brimmed hat framed in the barn's doorway.

God-damned Nine-Fingered Nan. And she had one of her pistols trained on me.

"I said drop it."

Reluctantly, I did so.

"Well, well, well, *well*," she drawled then, and I noticed she did not holster her weapon. Nor did her lieutenant take his gun away from the back of Holt's head. "If it ain't Van Delano and the old man Haggerty himself. Imagine seein' you here."

THAT AIN'T A DEAL, THAT'S A GAMBLE

Nine-Fingered Nan walked toward me, her shadow stretchin' out in front of her as she approached, slow and unhurried like she always seemed to be.

Two more of her people appeared in the barn's doorway behind her, and one of 'em went to pick up Holt's pistol—my pistol—from where he'd dropped it in the dirt. They tucked it into their waistband, then stepped back to watch me and Nan, hands loose atop their own gun grips.

Looked like she had three men and one woman with her this time.

I wondered if she ever truly went anywhere alone.

Holt sat back on his heels, grumblin' and rubbin' at the back of his head. His fingers came away bloody.

But my focus went back to Nan as she neared, too close. I tensed, wantin' to step back, to move away, but instead I held my ground and met her cool, steady stare with a glare. I wondered how angry she'd be that I weren't where I was supposed to be right now.

Guess I was gonna find out.

She halted abruptly not three paces from me. "You," she said. "Yer an awful slippery little pup, ain't you? Guess that's probably how you've managed to live this long." She turned a half-step to look back at Holt. "And you. Ain't you supposed to be dead? Thought they was gonna hang you?"

Holt grunted. "Lotsa people was gonna hang me over the years. But I'm still livin', too."

"So I see." Nan turned back to me, pale blue eyes lookin' me over, calculatin'.

I resisted the urge to shift under her scrutiny; tried to figure if I could possibly snatch that pearl-gripped pistol from her hand and shoot her with it.

"That why you were so keen to get outta that cell I put you in?" Nan asked. "Had to go save the old man, eh? Huh. Well, ain't that touchin'? Just warms the heart." She smiled, holstered her pistol, and crossed into the barn's shadow to go to the man in the chair. "And now you're here. How ... *interestin'*."

I watched her warily from my own place in the shadow, but she only took a fistful of the beaten man's hair and pulled his head back to better expose the muddle of his face.

"No, Mr. Delano, this ain't Dr. Balogh," she said. "This is Dr. Wright. He replaced Dr. Balogh when Balogh apparently up and left a month ago. But turns out he's rather good friends with the Baloghs. They even told him where they took off to in such a hurry. Took some convincin' fer him to tell us about it, but ... well, he finally came to his senses." She shook her head and released his hair, and he slumped forward again. "Guess Bravebank's gonna need another new doctor."

My mind raced at this information, tryin' to put the pieces together. Had it been Nan's people who had trashed the house and beaten this Dr. Wright? And for what? Lookin' fer the doc and his family? Fer clues about where they mighta gone? But why?

I remembered Nan's interest in that old lockbox she'd had me steal from Baron Haas, remembered how Professor Morton—Head Curator of the Royal Museum, of all places—had said it was Old World, and my stomach twisted.

She *was* interested in Old World tech, and she musta found out Dr. Balogh knew somethin' about it. Again I got overly conscious of my left leg, possible Old World tech itself, and the seam where the metal rod went into my flesh pulsed.

Nan circled around the back of the man's chair, around behind me, to come up along my right side. She put a hand on my shoulder and leaned in close enough I could smell sweat and horse.

It was all I could do to not recoil. Somehow I managed to stay still, fists balled, starin' straight ahead at Holt, who watched me with the same tightly strung uncertainty I currently felt jumpin' around in my gut.

"I suppose the question now," Nan said slowly, "is what exactly are you doin' here, Delano? You just sprang Haggerty from the noose. Why come here, of all places?"

I swallowed, but said nothin'. My heart beat in my ears.

She leaned heavy on my shoulder, squeezin' with bony fingers. "Nothin' to say? Well, maybe you need some convincin', too." She gestured at her men, and the one behind Holt gave him another whack on the head. He fell forward, but two of 'em grabbed his arms and hauled him back up to his feet, where he staggered, sagged.

"No," I blurted. "No. No need fer convincin'."

"Better start talkin', then," Nan said.

I swallowed again, shook my head. "Weren't ... weren't nothin'. Nothin' important. Just payin' a house call on the way back to town, is all. Thought I'd check in on the family."

She smiled thinly. "Ain't that sweet. You friends with the Baloghs too, are ya?"

"No," I said quickly. "Not friends. More like ... more like acquaintances, maybe."

"I see. So you thought you'd pay a house call, check up on the family of your *acquaintance* Dr. Balogh, that it?"

I nodded.

"Uh huh. He gave you that leg, didn't he? The metal one."

A lance of alarm went through me at the question, but she didn't give me time to confirm or deny.

"I saw his workshop. It was quite impressive."

A frown flickered across my face despite myself. *Workshop? What workshop?*

"It's all makin' sense now, Delano," she said, and she mercifully released her grip on my shoulder, then gave it a hard clap and I grimaced. "Ya see, we've been watchin' this place fer weeks. Ever since my men first came here in search of the good doctor and found him gone. Watchin' and waitin'. All kinds of folk been showin' up here lately." She moved to stand sideways between me and Holt, who hung dazed between two of her men, and looked to each of us in turn. "We took the time to question each of 'em, a course, and I think the picture is finally startin' to become clear. Lucky fer you, Delano, 'cause that means I ain't gonna throw you right back into a cell. I had a deep, dark one in mind fer you, given your slippery nature, but now ... now I think you'll prove more useful here."

I resisted my first instinct, which was to tell her to go to Hell, and instead growled out, "How so?"

That was the point anyway, weren't it? Fer me to play this stupid game of hers. To give her what she wanted so she'd give me my sister. To prove I could make a bargain with me more worth her while than any deal she could make with a foreign merchant. To show her just how stubborn we Delanos could be.

Nine-Fingered Nan grinned at me. "I'm so glad you asked." She turned and went to the woman in the doorway, who handed over a folded newspaper without even bein' asked. Nan brought the newspaper to me, and I took it from her with a frown.

Unfolded it and stepped into the sunlight so I could read it proper.

The headline across the top of the front page said somethin' about thousands of birds fallin' out of the sky ... dead. My frown deepened. There weren't no thousands of birds in the desert ... but then I realized this hadn't happened here. It had happened near a town called Blackbird, all the way over in Akansa. And the paper was dated about two weeks ago.

I looked back to Nan and shrugged. "So? What's dead birds got to do with anythin'?"

Nan snatched the paper outta my hands. "It ain't about the dead birds, boy. It's about what killed 'em."

Oh. Well I hadn't read that part of it yet. "So what killed 'em, then?"

Now Nan shrugged, and she paced over to poor Dr. Wright again, gazin' down at him with her hands on her hips as she spoke. "Oh, lots of different people have lots of different theories about that. But the one I'm most interested in is the speculation there might be Old World ruins in the area."

Well there it was. Her own admission of her interest in Old World tech. Even still, there was lots that didn't seem to add up quite yet. "In Akansa?" I shook my head. "Never heard reports of any ruins there."

"Yet," Nan said.

Dr. Wright whimpered, and Nan turned on her heel to march back in my direction.

"And yet, accordin' to the doctor here, that's where the Balogh family headed off to in such a hurry. Curious, ain't it? Why would a doctor, a *good* doctor, mind you, suddenly up and leave his homestead and his work to drag his family cross-country in a wagon?"

I only stared at her, havin' no answers.

"It ain't the birds he cares about, I can tell you that," Nan supplied.

"Even if there were ruins there," I said, and I hoped there weren't, 'cause I didn't want nothin' to do with any Old World ruins, "how does that got anythin' to do with the birds?"

Nan arched an eyebrow at me. "Well now, you don't got to concern yerself with that part of it. What I want you to do is go to Blackbird and see if you can't find your *acquaintance* Dr. Balogh. Seems that's where he's gone off to, and I've got a good idea he went 'cause he's got a notion those ruins do exist, and he suspects he knows where. You go there and you find him. Sure he'll be glad to see a friendly face and all. You find him, you find those ruins, and then you send me a telegram back to Bravebank and you tell me exactly where they are, you understand?"

I didn't like the greedy gleam in her eye. Not at all. "What if ... what if he ain't there?"

Nan glanced back at the badly beaten Dr. Wright, then turned those pale eyes on me. "Oh, he's there."

"And if there ain't any ruins in Blackbird, after all?"

"Well then." She stepped closer. "Guess that means you ain't got nothin' left to bargain with." She turned away before I could protest, stridin' quick toward the barn door.

So I made my protests to her back. "That ain't fair! I ain't got no control over what may or may not be in that goddamned town! You can't put that on me!"

"Them's my terms, Mr. Delano," she said. "Take 'em or leave 'em."

I took a step after her, but three pistols moved quick to point at my chest and I drew up short. "That's horse shit!" I spat.

Nine-Fingered Nan reached the doorway, paused. "Oh, and one more thing." She spun back to face me, her black skirts flarin' out and then settlin' again around her booted ankles. "Time is of the essence here. I don't hear back from you in two weeks, I'm tellin' that man who wants yer sister he's won the bid, ya hear?"

I risked another step forward, and the three pistols lifted higher. Hammers clicked back. "*Goddamnit* ... look. I'll go to Blackbird. I'll find the doc. But you can't make the ruins a part of the deal ... that ain't no deal, that's a gamble."

Nan cocked her head to one side. "Then I guess it's a good thing luck runs in yer family, eh, Delano?" She chuckled. "Now you best get goin'. Time's a tickin'."

VI

REST IN PEACE

She left me standin' there, speechless and starin' after her in disbelief.

Her lieutenants followed her out, the two who held Holt dumpin' him to the dusty ground before doin' so.

And then they were gone, all of 'em, and soon enough I heard 'em ride off from the direction of the rear northern corner of the barn. A place Holt and I wouldn'ta been able to see 'em, or their horses, from where we'd come up from the south.

Watchin' and waitin', she'd said.

Fuck me.

Swearin', I reached down to grab my pistol outta the dirt and shoved it back where it belonged. Then I went to Holt, helped him sit.

He winced as he did so, a hand goin' to his head again. "Fuck," he growled.

"You okay?"

"No. Got one helluva fuckin' headache."

"Yeah..." I glanced over toward Dr. Wright. "Least yer still better off than the doctor here."

"Sure. Guess so."

I let him gather himself and stood, lookin' around fer my other pistol before I realized one of those lieutenants had made off with it. "Shit. They took my goddamned gun!"

Holt grunted. "Don't surprise me. No good sons-a-bitches, all of 'em." He struggled up to his feet and I reached out to steady him as he swayed a bit. "I'm fine. I'll be fine. But we better get on to Grave Gulch now that we're both out weapons."

I nodded.

Behind us, poor Dr. Wright let out another pitiful whimper.

I winced, looked back in his direction. "What should we do with *him?*"

Holt followed my gaze into the darkness, where the shadows mercifully masked the man's horrific injuries. "Put him out of his misery. That'd be the kind thing to do."

I sighed. Didn't much like the thought of it, but he was right.

So I drew my single remainin' iron and went to the man's chair. Now that I took the time to look closer as well as I could in the limited light, I realized the chair he'd been tied to had come from the house. It was one of the kitchen chairs. I hadn't even noticed one was missin' when we'd been inside earlier.

And Dr. Wright was in awful bad shape. Not just his face, but the rest of him, too. Looked like they'd broken both arms, and his legs, too. I hissed a breath through my teeth and shook my head. "Sorry, Mister. Real sorry. But it's gonna be over soon."

I took a step back, and in one shot ended the poor man's pain.

"May he rest in peace," Holt murmured.

After some deliberation, we decided to bury him.

Nevermind the fact we didn't really have time fer such a thing, nor were we in any shape to do it, considerin' the fact I still had that hole in my arm and Holt was still woozy from those knocks on the head.

But we decided to do it, anyway. Mostly 'cause it just seemed wrong to leave him sittin' there tied up when his end had been so miserable. And maybe there was a little part of me that felt obligated in some way, if he were really a friend of the Baloghs. They'd done plenty fer me when they didn't have to, and I feared that somehow, some way, Nan figurin' out what Dr. Balogh knew about Old World tech was maybe because of me. And if that were true, then what had happened to Dr. Wright was also maybe my fault.

I didn't exactly know how, but the notion kept naggin' at me, anyway. Maybe if I buried the man, I could bury that snakin' guilt along with him.

We cut his body free of the chair and dragged him out back of the barn, then some distance further.

And that's when we found those others Nan had mentioned durin' our little chat, and Holt spat a colorful string of profanity.

She'd made a pile of 'em, but certainly hadn't bothered to bury 'em. Looked to be at least four bodies, though it was hard to tell now as the scavengers had come to call; pulled 'em apart and eaten some of 'em. And the flies were nearly as thick as the stench.

"Fer fuck's sake!" Holt ended his tirade at last, but his face had gone awful pale.

I had nothin' to say, myself. I couldn't imagine who these people had been ... didn't want to imagine. Other friends? Family, even? Patients come to satisfy a curiosity about why the doc had suddenly vacated his office in town?

Or were they folk of a different nature? Treasure seekers or prospectors after the same ruins as Nan, who'd gotten wind about the doctor's particular hobby? Maybe even scholars like Professor Morton?

The possibilities were wide and varied, but likely none of 'em had deserved what had happened to 'em.

I swallowed back the bile in my throat and looked out across the stretch of desert beyond the pile of dead.

"We can't bury 'em all," Holt said.

"No. Just Dr. Wright." I nodded to the left, toward a big saguaro cactus. "Over there, how about? Seems as good a spot as any."

"Sure. Sure." Holt swiped at the sweat runnin' down his face with a sleeve. "Let's just get this over with and get the hell out of here."

It was near dusk by the time we finally got Dr. Wright properly laid to rest, retrieved our mounts, and left the Balogh homestead behind, both drenched in sweat and exhausted. But we kept our pace swift and rode in silence fer hours, travelin' well into the night before we drew up to make camp.

We made a small fire and ate a quick meal and listened to a band of coyotes yip and yowl in the distance.

I sat cross-legged on my bedroll, starin' hard into the flames and tryin' best I could to make sense of things. What could Nine-Fingered Nan possibly want with some Old World ruins in Akansa? She certainly didn't need any ancient trinkets fer status or money like the barons of Blessing seemed to like. And why had Dr. Balogh gone there, too? If he'd wanted ruins, why not go to those that had already been discovered, and weren't halfway across the continent?

I couldn't sort it. Couldn't make no sense of it at all, so eventually I gave up. Not like it mattered, anyway. I surely didn't care about any of that old stuff, nor what anyone else wanted to do with it. Didn't even care that Nan wanted some of it fer herself. She could have it all, far as I were concerned, long as she gave me Ethelyn.

Soft snorin' made me look up, across the fire. Holt laid there stretched out, already asleep.

I smiled despite myself and shook my head, then laid out atop my own blankets. Damn it all, but I'd kinda missed the old bastard. He was sure a lot easier to get along with when he weren't complainin' about every damn thing I did. He hadn't even asked me fer more about what Nan had been talkin' about back at the Balogh house. Hadn't said a word about her sayin' she was gonna throw me back in a cell, hadn't asked why I'd been locked up again in the first place, hadn't asked how I'd managed to get free, hadn't wanted to know about why there now seemed to be biddin' on my sister at play.

'Course, maybe all that was 'cause he'd been knocked nearly sense-less by that lieutenant.

Maybe he'd mostly missed that entire conversation.

Either way, I weren't gonna argue the outcome. I liked him keepin' quiet.

I dropped my hat onto my belly and then folded my hands under my head, starin' up at the stars and listenin' to those coyotes, and waited fer sleep.

I didn't sleep much, truth be told, my dreams fulla the sight of Dr. Wright's ruined face and that pile of bodies, and my bullet missin' Holt's hangin' rope, so that the last thing I saw before I jerked awake were his feet kickin' the air.

"Nightmare?" Holt asked quietly from somewhere to my right.

I sat up and scrubbed my hands over my face, notin' it was dawn now, the sun stainin' the sky above a deep pink. I took a deep breath of the cool mornin' air. "Yeah."

Holt grunted. His footsteps crunched over in my direction, and then there was a tin cup of coffee under my nose.

I took it gratefully with a nod of thanks. Well, he really *was* feelin' remorseful fer his past behavior, then. Maybe he needed to face the noose more often.

"Those still botherin' ya?" he asked.

"Always," I grumbled.

He'd made breakfast too, turned out: salted pork and beans and biscuits. We ate and saddled up and headed out again with little else said between us. I kept thinkin' about my dreams, and about how the hell I was supposed to find Dr. Balogh in Blackbird, and how I might somehow fulfill Nan's terms only *after* seein' Ethelyn myself if the old hag was expectin' a telegram. That was gonna make things a lot more complicated.

Well, guess I had time to figure it out, considerin' it was gonna be a long journey to get there in the first place.

We were finally comin' up on Grave Gulch three days later, nearin' the hills in which we'd made our semi-permanent camp, when I broached the subject with Holt. I'd been enjoyin' the quiet, sure, but now I wanted some answers.

"You gonna come with?" I asked. "To Blackbird, I mean?"

Holt glanced to me, his face reddened by the sun in the absence of a hat. "Ain't decided just yet."

"What else you figurin' on doin'?"

He shrugged. "Ain't decided that, neither."

I hoped he didn't plan to try and rob any more banks by himself. "Figure I'll supply up at camp. Then head on to the station over in Redemption, Lesser Texas. Given I don't got much time to do all this findin', I'll go by train far as I can, then ride the rest of the way."

Holt nodded. "You even know where Blackbird is?"

"No. Never heard of it. Figure I'll ask the locals once I hit the first station in Akansa."

Holt nodded again. "Good enough plan. You really think there's ruins there? Seems to me if there was, we'd of heard about it by now."

My stomach twisted at his statement, if only 'cause I agreed with him. But I didn't want to consider that possibility at the moment. So I only shrugged. "Guess we'll find out."

We passed the bleached bones of a human skeleton, tied up on sticks planted in the ground to make it look like it was still alive and standin'. The sentinels of Grave Gulch. Meant to warn away those who didn't follow the particular religion of the town's dominant cult.

But Holt and I hardly noticed 'em anymore. We rode on past, our mounts just as oblivious to the bones as we.

"What you gonna do if there ain't any ruins there?" Holt asked suddenly.

I gulped back the defensive swell of frustration, the urge to snap at him. It was a fair enough question, and one I'd possibly have to answer before the end of this errand. But I supposed I already knew the answer, anyway.

If there weren't no ruins, I'd have to figure out where Ethelyn was bein' held myself. And I'd have to figure that out before I broke the news about the ruins to Nan. Somehow. And then I'd have to confront Nan directly, and hope it went better than all the other times I'd tried to confront her. Hope I'd get the draw on her fer once. Hope I could end her before she ended me.

Then I'd have to go get Ethelyn.

I supposed the "*what* would I do" weren't so hard to figure out, after all.

It was the "*how* would I do it" that was the tricky part. And fer that, I had no answers yet.

I opened my mouth, closed it again, and blew out a heavy breath. "One thing at a time, old man."

Why did it seem I was always sayin' that?

We rounded a small rise up in the hills north of Grave Gulch to come upon the cave we'd made our home fer a good long while now.

And we both reined up sharply. My hand dropped down to the pistol at my hip.

A saddled horse was tethered to a bush just outside the cave entrance.

AN UNEXPECTED GUEST

"You expectin' guests?" Holt muttered under his breath.

"Naw. You?"

He shook his head. "You tell anyone about this place?"

This time I went ahead and glared at him. "'Course not. I ain't stupid. What about you?"

"'Course not."

Well, maybe they was just squatters. Happened upon the place accidentally and found it to their likin'. Least we'd found 'em now … hopefully before they'd had a chance to make off with any of our stuff inside. "Stay here," I instructed Holt. "You ain't got no guns. I'll go take a look."

"Be real careful," Holt said as I dismounted.

I didn't bother to reply. 'Course I'd be careful. I pulled my pistol and circled back around the rise we'd just come by, approachin' the cave mouth from the east side—the opposite side we'd originally approached from. I pressed my back up against the rock as I inched toward it, gun at the ready. The clearin' in front of it showed signs of a recent fire, smoke still risin' from the ashes. And there were fresh tracks in the dirt, too.

The horse itself was sturdy and well-built, a bay roan stallion with a shiny black mane and tail. It watched me draw nearer with only mild interest.

I paused at the edge of the cave's entrance and listened, but I didn't hear no one movin' around. Didn't hear no voices. I leaned forward, peeked around the curve of the rock.

Our crates were all still there, stacked just like we'd left 'em toward the back, right at the edge of the natural light. But one of the oil lamps had been lit and set atop 'em, illuminatin' the start of the cave's back chamber.

Still, I didn't see no one back there, and no movement, neither.

Frownin', I stepped inside, though I kept close to the wall and kept alert fer any shift of shadow.

"Stop right there," a woman ordered from somewhere the light didn't reach. And it was pitch black back there. "Don't get any funny ideas. I have you in my sights right this moment." A squealin' whine started up, one that sounded awful familiar. Almost sounded like that big cannon-gun did when it was warmin' up, about to spew a slew of bullets.

I stopped all right, and straightened, leanin' closer to the rock wall, strainin' to see into the blackness.

"Identify yourself," the woman ordered.

She sounded familiar, too. I went through the list of women I knew —women who mighta come here lookin' fer me—but the list was real, real short considerin' none of the possible candidates knew about this place. "Uh ... this is *my* place, lady," I ventured. "If anyone should be identifyin' themselves, it's you. You're the trespasser here. You wanna tell me what yer doin' squattin' at my camp?"

"Van?" The whinin' sound stopped abruptly. Someone shifted back there, and then bootsteps came across the rocky floor. She stepped outta the darkness finally, squintin' at me. And she was holdin' that big cannon-gun, sure enough.

The flash of long, wavy red hair in the lamp light spurred recognition and I lowered my own gun even as my mouth fell open. My mind struggled to comprehend. "Ch-Charlotte?"

Sayin' her name didn't make it make any more sense why she might be standin' in front of me right now. Why she had risked comin' back here after all she'd been through, after all *we'd* been through to get her back to Pennsylvania safely, after all I'd done to warn her about those men Charles Miller had sent after her.

She relaxed, her shoulders droppin' and that big gun tiltin' toward the ground. "Oh good, it *is* you. Hard to see your face properly with the daylight behind you like that. Sorry for ... for this." She hefted the gun. "But I had to be sure. Where in the world have you been, anyway? I've been waiting here for *days*."

I just kept starin' at her, my mouth still open.

She sighed, then turned to set the big gun on top of the nearest crate. She glanced to the dusty toes of her boots and cleared her throat, smoothin' at her skirts. "Well? Nothing to say?" Those dark blue eyes of hers lifted again to meet mine, and I managed at last to shut my mouth.

"Uh." There were too many questions. Too many things that didn't make no sense. I tried to sort through to the most important one. "What ... what are you doin' here?" I looked her over, looked around the cave, looked back over my shoulder toward her horse. "You all right? Everythin' okay? What's happened?"

She let out a little laugh. "Nothing's happened. I'm fine. I just ... well, truth be told, after everything that happened with Baron Whittaker and all, I found life back in Pennsylvania to be ... no longer satisfactory."

I frowned. What in the hell did that mean? Her family was rich, far as I could tell. And certainly goin' back to an actual home with carin' parents, real beds, and three guaranteed square meals a day was better than wanderin' around out here in the wilds.

"And ... and I was worried, too." Her smile faltered some. "You didn't say much in your telegram ... just that Charles Miller might be after me. And then I didn't hear from you again, and you never answered my other telegrams—or letters—and I feared that perhaps he had gotten ahold of *you*. I couldn't stand not knowing."

I blinked at her and tried to squash down the wrigglin' worm of guilt about not writin' her more. But I hadn't been back to Grave Gulch to check the post since before settin' off on the errand to get that lockbox. If she'd sent me other letters or telegrams, I hadn't even seen 'em yet. "So you ... so you came all the way back out here? Just fer that?" I hissed out a breath and shoved my gun back into the holster. "You shouldn'ta done that. It ain't safe."

She stood straighter, throwin' her shoulders back. "I went to Grave Gulch to check the papers when you didn't show up here. They said Charles Miller was murdered around a month or so ago, and the killer is still unknown and on the loose. I'd assumed that was your doing."

I winced at that statement. Not 'cause I regretted murderin' that bastard, I sure as hell didn't regret that one bit. But because if she'd heard that, she'd probably also heard the part where that whole posse had been murdered, and how they'd determined it musta been me who'd done it. Nevermind that *that* part of it weren't true. "Yeah," I admitted, decidin' not to bring up the posse, just in case she hadn't heard that bit yet. "But that don't mean it's safe around here. There's a new Baron Whittaker now, and he still wants my head fer killin' his pa, and maybe yers too."

"But your telegram said there weren't any bulletins of me up for that," she said, matter-of-factly.

I rolled my eyes. "Yeah, well ... we don't know what Miller mighta told the new Baron Whittaker about who killed their pa, do we? And anyway, just 'cause you don't got yer face on any posters don't mean it's safe around here. There are plenty of other folk who'd be plenty happy to rob you. Or kidnap you and sell you off. Again. Or worse." I stepped past her, checkin' over the cave's interior and notin' she'd made herself at home. Some of our crates were open, and she'd helped herself to some of the food stores. As well as re-organized 'em, looked like. And she had a little cook area set up, and a bed roll laid out. I reached down to start rollin' up the blankets of her pallet.

"Hey!"

I ignored her protests. "You need to get out of here. Go on back to Pennsylvania."

"I am most certainly *not* going back to Pennsylvania," she said with a huff, stalkin' over to me. "I came all the way back here to make sure *you* were safe. Since you couldn't bother to send a note and tell me so. And your sister. You never mentioned your sister. Did you get her?" She peered out toward the cave entrance. "Is she here?"

I paused in rollin' up her blankets, my fingers diggin' into the thick wool as my teeth clenched. "No," I growled out. "Not yet. Still workin' on that."

She sobered then, lookin' back to me. "Oh."

"What the blazes is goin' on in here?" Holt yelled, appearin' suddenly at the entrance astride his horse and leadin' Joe and the mare behind him.

Damn. I'd been so surprised to see Charlotte I'd completely forgotten to tell him the coast was clear.

"We got a visitor," I yelled back.

Holt dismounted and strode inside, then stopped short when he saw Charlotte.

I figured I musta looked just as surprised as he looked now when I'd first seen her, too.

Charlotte, fer her part, did not seem surprised to see him. She didn't look happy to see him, neither. "Ah," she said flatly. "It's you."

His clear blue eyes narrowed at her. "And it's you," he said.

"She was just leavin'," I said, and I handed Charlotte her rolled blankets. Then I went to her pack and started pickin' up her various other belongings and stowin' 'em inside.

"Well," she said, "it is certainly good to see you again as well."

Her affronted tone was hard to miss, and another twinge of guilt hit me. I straightened, one of her small iron skillets in-hand. "It ain't ... it ain't that I ain't glad to see you. It's just that it ain't safe, like I said. And if somethin' happened to you while you were here 'cause of me ... well, I got enough to deal with tryin' to get my sister back, understand? I don't want to have to worry about you too, is all."

Charlotte turned to face me, holdin' her roll of blankets to her chest. She wore one of her nice dresses again, like that purple one she'd bought in Peridot the day I'd seen her last, only this one was a pale blue that set off the red of her hair. "You don't have to worry about me," she said evenly. "I can take care of myself. Came all this way alone just fine, didn't I? And found your camp again, too. I had to make sure the Whittakers hadn't caught up to you. Or Charles Miller. And to see if you'd managed to free your sister."

I stuffed the skillet into her pack. "And just what did you figure you'd do if the Whittakers or Miller *had* gotten ahold of me?" I ventured, not botherin' to mention that they had, indeed, gotten ahold of me, and that I'd only barely escaped alive, but she'd missed that part. "You came here by yourself? What good would that have done?"

Her eyes narrowed. "My father is lobbying for a special organization back in the Republic as we speak. Ever since I was first kidnapped. And after I returned and told him everything that had happened, and after he received the telephone call about Miller sending men all the way back east after me, even though I'd escaped once already ... he nearly has Congress convinced to approve it."

Holt gave a rather loud snort of amusement. "Congress? Lady, ain't no one out here give a damn about what yer Congress says. Pardon the language, but it's the truth."

She spun a half-step to face him with a glare. "If Congress approves its formation, they'll move to work jointly with the Commune's Council, too. It won't just be the Republic's Congress involved. It'll be the Republic *and* the Commune, working together to clean up the Territories."

Holt and I both barked laughter at that idea.

But I swallowed mine back as she turned her blazin' blue glare on me. "Er ... okay," I relented. "All right. But I still don't see how an organization that don't exist yet would help you here and now, bein' that you came all by yerself."

She straightened her shoulders again and tilted her chin up defiantly. "My father has already started recruiting men himself. To form a private organization until the larger, federal one is approved. If needed, I could simply call upon them to help. He could have them here within days."

I lifted my brows. "That wouldn't do you no good if a person grabbed you again though, would it? You'd never get a chance to send word fer 'em. You shoulda brought 'em with you from the start."

Her defiant gaze softened, and her eyes dropped toward her boots again. "Well ... I didn't want them to know where I was going just yet. Didn't want father to know, either. He is insufferably controlling. He never would have allowed it."

I sent an alarmed look over her shoulder to Holt, who shook his head. Then I pulled my stare back to her. "Yer father don't even know yer here?"

She shook her head. "No. But my chambermaid knows. She and I are rather close. I left her a note with my whereabouts. Told her if I did not return within a certain time, she should give it to my father."

"Charlotte..." I found it hard to find the words without spittin' out a slew of profanities. "He's gonna be worried sick about you. Probably thinks you got snatched again. Probably organizin' those men to go out lookin' fer you right now!"

She pursed her lips, marchin' forward to grab her pack away from me. She threw the blankets down on top of it and started tyin' 'em on. "He won't. At least not yet. I told him I was leaving. I just didn't tell him where."

I only watched her, thinkin' about how worried her family must be, and she finished tyin' on the blankets and hefted the pack up and onto her shoulder.

"And anyway," she went on, "I'm a grown woman. I can make my own decisions about where I go, thank you very much."

Well, maybe that were true, but she *had* just admitted to not tellin' her father exactly where she'd headed off to, fer the express reason he wouldn'ta allowed her to go. Which sounded to me like maybe she couldn't act on her decisions as a grown woman as much as she might have liked.

But I decided not to mention any of that. Instead all I said was, "Well you can take the train back east from Redemption. Just so happens that's where we're headed, too. We'll take you there."

VIII

A FOOL'S ERRAND

"What about your sister?" Charlotte asked as I turned away from her to start gatherin' my own supplies outta crates. "Does Nan still have her? Did you find out where she is?"

Just as well I weren't facin' her no more, 'cause all her questions made me grimace. I focused on openin' one crate after the other, findin' myself another pistol—my last spare—and several more cases of bullets. "No," I said. "I mean ... yes, Nan still has her." I rolled open the cylinder of the new pistol and started loadin' it. "But no ... I ain't figured out where she is, yet. No one's been too keen to talk on that." I snapped the loaded cylinder closed, gave the new pistol a few experimental turns, then tucked it into my empty holster.

Across the way, Holt was rummagin' in some crates himself. He pulled out one of his other hats and shoved it onto his head, then withdrew another gunbelt, fittin' it around his hips.

And I scowled at what he pulled out of that crate next. A familiar bundle wrapped in oilcloth and tied with leather thongs. I preferred to keep that thing buried away, just like Pa had preferred it ... Holt preferred to try and pawn it off on me at least once a year, no matter that I kept tellin' him no.

He took the chance now, too, lookin' up at me with a raised brow at the same time as he lifted the package. I could read the expression on his face clear as day: *Might as well take this one now ... no use lettin' a perfectly good gun go to waste.*

But I narrowed my gaze and shook my head, makin' a point of pattin' the pistol I'd just settled into the holster at my hip.

He rolled his eyes and muttered somethin' I couldn't hear, but made no further arguments fer the time bein', to my relief. Instead, he just nestled the thing back into its place in the crate and resumed fishin' out his own replacement weapons.

Charlotte watched us both, one to the other.

I saw a frown pass over her face, but then turned back to my supplies as her gaze shifted in my direction.

"Then where are you going now?" she asked simply.

"To Redemption, like I said."

"All right, I mean *why?*"

I paused in pullin' out more stores of food and sighed heavily. I glanced over my shoulder to Holt, caught him watchin' me. But when my eyes met his, he only shrugged. He was gonna stay out of it, then. Had no opinion on if I should tell Charlotte about this newest errand or not. I didn't much want to tell her about it, myself.

Didn't want to chance her tellin' me it was a fool's errand.

I still expected Holt's good nature about the whole thing to end eventually, and I didn't need no one else tellin' me I was crazy fer doin' this. I already knew that well enough.

"Do you think she might be there?" Charlotte pressed at my silence. "Your sister?"

I resumed takin' stock of flour, cornmeal, lard, dried fruit, salted meat, and coffee. "I'm ... I'm makin' a trade," I said finally. "With Nine-Fingered Nan. I'm helpin' her find somethin', and then she's gonna give me my sister."

I waited fer Holt to say somethin', to go on about how Nan would never give me Ethelyn, or about how she was only fuckin' with me, but he said nothin'. Just kept his attention on readyin' his own spare pair of pistols.

Well, I was sure his grumblin' would return soon enough. And anyway, I was beginnin' to believe him. I'd do this one last errand fer Nan, sure ... but she weren't gettin' what she wanted outta me this time without me gettin' Ethelyn first. I'd make certain of that.

Somehow.

"Really?" Charlotte asked. She didn't sound convinced, neither. "And what she's looking for is in Redemption?"

"No. What she's looking for is in Blackbird, Akansa." I stuffed what food I'd chosen into another pack. "But we're gettin' on the train in Redemption, same as you. Well, *I'll* be gettin' on the train, anyway. Not sure about Holt."

He straightened from the crate he searched through, lookin' more himself now with his hat and two guns perched on his hips again. "I'll go," he said, then shrugged. "Might as well. Don't figure I got anywhere else I need to be."

A strange sorta relief filtered through me at his words. It was always nice to have another gun in the fight. I gave him a nod. "All right, then. Guess we're all gettin' on the train in Redemption." I looked back to Charlotte as I cinched up my pack. "You'd better be sure you got all your belongings. We're on a tight schedule; be leavin' this afternoon."

But she didn't move, only frowned. "*Blackbird*, Akansa?"

"Yeah..."

"The place where all the birds died?"

I blinked. "Er ... yeah. You know about that?"

"Everyone knows about that."

Holt and I glanced to each other. *We* hadn't known about that. Not till Nan had shoved that paper into my hands. But then, Holt had been locked in a jail cell awaitin' his own hangin' and I'd been pushin' hard to get there in time to save him. Neither of us had been payin' much attention to anythin' happenin' elsewhere.

"It's happened before, you know," Charlotte said.

"What's happened before?"

"This kind of die-off. Around Blackbird. There's some old texts that mention it. And tales the local tribes still tell about it."

I grunted, swingin' my pack up over my right shoulder. "Those texts and tales say anythin' about it bein' related to Old World stuff?"

Charlotte shrugged under the weight of her own pack. "Not particularly. They mostly attribute it to the actions of gods or goddesses. Or some beings called the Guardians."

"And how exactly do you know all this?" Holt demanded.

Charlotte fixed him with a witherin' look. "I like to read. You should try it sometime. Might find it enlightening."

He glowered at her, but I cleared my throat loudly before their bickerin' could escalate further. "We should best be goin'."

Alas, neither of 'em moved fer the exit. "What could Nine-Fingered Nan possibly want from Blackbird?" Charlotte mused.

"Maybe somethin' that ain't there," I admitted. "But she didn't give me a lot of time to search fer it, so we'd best be gettin' a move on, like I said." I reached out toward her with my left hand and gestured at her bag. "Here. Lemme take that fer you."

She arched an eyebrow, lookin' me over skeptically. Her gaze lingered on the bandages wrapped around my left bicep and the three middle fingers of my left hand. "You're hurt. Again."

I scoffed. "Yeah. That happens a lot. I'll be all right. Don't mean I can't carry yer pack out fer you."

She hesitated fer a moment more, then sighed and handed it over.

The weight of it made my arm protest somethin' awful, all right, but I bit back the grunt of pain and hefted it onto my left shoulder, then headed fer the horses.

❖

We loaded up, takin' all the extra canteens and usin' Sally's skinny mare like a pack horse, then headed out again, leavin' Grave Gulch behind as we followed the Gila River southeast. We'd keep to the river till afternoon tomorrow, then strike out across the desert fer another day before meetin' back up with it again. And after that it'd be another three days across the open before we reached Redemption. That leg of the ride concerned me most; especially now with Charlotte along.

There was a little minin' settlement in the middle of those three days we could stop over at, I supposed, but I'd heard tales it weren't the most civilized of places. Still, I didn't think we had any choice *but* to stop there, given it was the only guaranteed waterin' hole in that three-day stretch of desert.

And it weren't ever wise to pass up guaranteed water.

I tossed another glance to Charlotte as I brooded over such thoughts.

Turned out her skirts weren't skirts at all, but rather wide-legged pants so she could easily ride astride the saddle. Clever. She'd braided her long red hair, donned a straw hat, and buckled a gunbelt around her waist equipped with a sixgun.

It gave me some reassurance to see her with a weapon, and it made me think of her wieldin' that big cannon-gun the night we'd burned down the Whittaker estate. But we'd left that thing behind, too, put it back into the crate she'd dug it out of. I figured the pistol would be easier to manage, and easier to travel with. Least she hadn't come out here unprepared, seemed like. I wondered then how she'd crossed that desert from Redemption to get out here in the first place. Wondered if she'd done that ride all by her lonesome, or if maybe she'd hired a stagecoach. I hoped she'd hired a stagecoach; though if she hadn't, there was clearly a lot more I had to learn about Ms. Charlotte Harrison from Pennsylvania.

We rode mostly in silence through the afternoon into the evenin', though I had the naggin' feelin' both Charlotte and Holt had things to say. Hell, I had things to say, too, but I weren't exactly sure how to say any of 'em just yet. So I kept my silence, kept my focus on the trail ahead and Joe's big ears floppin' around in front of me.

We camped near the bank of the river just as the sun sank low behind the mountains in the distance. The water ran black as ink in the fadin' light, and Charlotte and I set about carin' fer the horses while Holt wandered a ways in search of more tinder fer the fire. He didn't have to go far; this area was littered with the dry, brittle skele-tons of dead cacti and brush.

Even still, soon as he was only a vague silhouette against the horizon, Charlotte dumped her saddle to the ground and turned to me. "He do that to you?"

Her sudden speakin' startled me, and I nearly dropped my own saddle. Somehow I managed to set it down semi-gracefully, then straightened with a frown. "Huh?"

"That." She waved toward my left bicep, where the bandage showed through the hole in my sleeve, then jerked her chin in Holt's direction. "He actually shoot you for hiding his money like you thought he might?"

It took me a long minute to process what she were sayin'. Then I remembered that the last time I'd seen her, Holt had nearly shot me fer wantin' to take the money he'd stolen from Blessing's bank to Nan. Only Charlotte had knocked him out before he could do so, and then I'd tied him up and taken the money, anyway. And at the time, I'd thought he might shoot me once he woke up and freed himself, sure.

But all of that seemed so long ago now. So much had happened since then. "Oh," I said finally. "No. No, not Holt. Someone else did that. He *was* awful put-out about it, but he didn't shoot me fer it." Punched me in the face, yeah. And nearly choked me out. But he hadn't shot me. He'd even come with me afterward to—we'd thought—confront Nine-Fingered Nan and get Ethelyn.

Instead it had only been Nan's man Taggert, double-crossin' her, and some poor nameless girl who'd somehow gotten caught up in all of it.

Memories of that dark-haired woman flashed through my mind again; memories of how she'd looked at me while she was dyin', blood gurglin' up between her lips. She'd died, and fer nothin'. Fer some cruel bastard's entertainment.

I swallowed hard and turned away from Charlotte before she could see any of the anger that welled up, hot and sudden. I focused instead on unpackin' Sally's mare, tryin' to breathe through it.

A light touch on my right arm a minute later made me jump and whirl around, nearly beltin' out a yell before I realized it was only Charlotte, come up close all silent-like.

She rocked backward as I whipped around quick to face her, eyes goin' real wide. "Oh, I'm sorry. I didn't ... didn't mean to startle you. I only wanted to say ... I brought your pistol back." She drew the gun on her hip and offered it out to me, and in the dusk's weak remainin' light, I saw it was indeed my gun.

The one I'd lent her when I'd sent her home to Pennsylvania.

I swallowed back my racin' heart, tryin' to cover up how much that touch of hers had alarmed me. Guess I weren't used to folk sneakin' up on me like that. At least, not any friendly folk. I pushed her hand and the gun back toward her. "No. You keep it. I don't need it."

"I brought my own gun," she said, shovin' it at me again. "It's yours. You should have it back. I don't need it, either."

She had it nearly pressed into my chest. I folded both my hands around it, around her hand that held it, and gently lowered it. "Charlotte..." But then I forgot what I was gonna say, distracted by the feel of her warm skin beneath my palms, a sharp contrast to the cool, smooth steel of the gun.

She only looked up at me, waitin' to hear what I was gonna say, and I realized abruptly how close she was standin', too. When had she got so close? She watched me, eyes searchin' my face, and made no move to pull either her hand or the gun from my grip.

"Charlotte," I tried again, and wet my lips. *Damn it all, Delano, focus.* I lifted my gaze away from her, cast it over to the bony horse that stood beside me. "Keep it. Please." There. That's what I'd been meanin' to say. I pushed it back at her again, and let go of it. Let go of her. Then turned resolutely to resume unloadin' the mare.

She stood there beside me fer another long minute, but I kept myself busy. Made my hands forget the feel of hers by rubbin' 'em across coarse blankets and scratchy twine and rough canvas.

"All right," she said finally, and then she sighed softly and settled my pistol back into her holster, steppin' away to go about readyin' the fire.

I drew a deep breath, exhaled slow and quiet.

Holt returned then with an armful of dead branches and withered cacti. He set the lot of it down next to where Charlotte crouched with the flint in-hand, and his hooded gaze swept over our makeshift campsite. "The hell you two been doin' this whole time? Get with it or we'll be eatin' dinner at midnight!"

I gave him a scowl, but picked up the pace, anyway.

The rest of our night passed quiet and uneventful, and the next day's ridin', too.

It weren't till the second night I spotted trouble.

IX

COPPERWELL CAMP

It was the silhouette of a rider against the horizon, fer just a second.

Or ... I *thought* it was.

We'd just settled ourselves into camp fer the night, and there was only the barest thread of light left in the sky. But we was in the flat of the desert now, with nothin' substantial around us fer miles and miles. The mountains were off to the north and east, and the river, too. A few scraggly plants and spiny cacti littered the flat, of course, but it weren't enough to hide a person.

I put a hand on Charlotte's arm as she pulled the tinder box from her pack. "Wait," I said quietly. "No fire."

"What is it?"

I shook my head, starin' hard into the distance where I swore I'd seen the person. But there was nothin' there now. I kept searchin' the horizon, strainin' to see any movement, any sign of another rider.

Holt stepped up beside me, gun already drawn, squintin' off in the same direction. "See somethin'?" he asked.

"Thought so." I cursed the fadin' light, cursed our lack of caution over the last day. We hadn't bothered to check our trail or cover our tracks, figurin' no one had tailed us to Grave Gulch, so we musta been free and clear when leavin' there.

But then, Holt and I both had our faces printed on plenty of posters around here. Someone coulda been after us for a whole multitude of reasons, not least of which was me recently rescuin' Holt from the noose.

"There hasn't been another soul out here all day," Charlotte whispered from the other side of me. She was also peerin' out into the dark now. "Or yesterday."

"Yeah..." And it was true. We'd been alone fer the whole of the journey so far. And in the daylight we could see mighty far across that flat stretch of desert.

Still, that didn't mean someone couldn't've ridden up durin' dusk, while we were preoccupied with our supplies and the horses. It also didn't mean the rider was hostile, if they *were* out there. But I didn't much want to take any chances.

Even if now there seemed to be no sign of 'em.

"Coulda been a deer," Holt ventured.

"No," I snapped. "It was a person. A rider. Hat 'n all."

Holt frowned. "Well, if they were out there, I don't see 'em now."

"Let's take watches," I said. "And no fire tonight. Just to be safe."

"You think ... they might mean us harm?" Charlotte asked.

After what she'd been through out here, I was surprised to hear her wonder such a thing.

Holt snorted in amusement. "Missus, we got all kindsa people after—"

I jabbed him in the side with my elbow.

He side-stepped away from me, rubbin' at his ribs and givin' me a look. But at least it seemed he'd caught my meanin'. "I mean, we got all kindsa bad people out here in the Territories. It's always better to assume they wanna rob and kill ya than to assume they're friendly."

Charlotte looked deeply concerned about that statement. Guess her talk of her father's organization cleanin' up the Territories had been mostly focused on Nine-Fingered Nan's operations and those barons of Blessing. Guess she hadn't figured the individuals out here could be just as dangerous sometimes.

"I'll take first watch," I said. "You two get some sleep."

"I'll take second watch," Holt said.

"And I'll take third," Charlotte offered.

"No," Holt and I said in unison.

"There's no need," I said as she opened her mouth to protest. "The two of us is more than enough to cover a night, and there's no use in you missin' out on sleep too if it ain't necessary."

She crossed her arms and tilted her head to one side, fixin' me with a challengin' glare I could only just barely see in the swiftly growin' dark. "Exactly. There's no need for you two to miss more sleep than you need when there are three of us here. We all take equal parts watch and we all get more sleep because of it."

Holt stepped up to put in his two cents. "We'll be alright on less sleep. We're used to it. Won't be no trouble fer us to take over while you get some quality rest—"

"Don't you go on putting up that selfless act on my account," Charlotte snapped, turnin' on him. "It doesn't become you, and I know better. You were ready to shoot Van over that money you stole— money he needed to free his sister!" She rounded on me before Holt could bluster out an objection to her assessment. "I didn't come out here to be coddled or treated like some fragile flower. I've had a whole lifetime of that, and I am quite through with it, thank you. I survived six months in the mines at Whittaker's ruins, remember? How much sleep do you think I got during that time? Huh? How much food or water? How many displays of human decency?" She shoved the tinder box rather violently back into her pack. "Not a lot. I will be just fine. And I will take third watch, or we'll be parting ways just as soon as the sun comes up. Understand?"

I considered her points, shiftin' on my feet. They were fair good ones, in truth. And I already knew she could shoot well enough. I glanced sideways at Holt, but he'd only got that grumpy look across his face again. So I nodded. Shrugged. "All right, fine. Fine. You take third watch."

"Thank you. That wasn't so hard now, was it?"

But she didn't give me time to answer that question. She only grabbed up her pack and marched off a ways to lay out her bedroll.

Holt muttered under his breath and holstered his pistol, then clapped me on the shoulder. "Keep yer eyes open, kid. And wake me if yer even the slightest bit suspicious." He dropped his voice so Charlotte couldn't hear. "I ain't got no plans to go back to that noose."

I nodded, and he went off to get settled fer sleep, too.

We didn't talk the rest of the evenin', and in fact Charlotte acted like me and Holt weren't even there. I tried my best to leave her be, to not spend overly long watchin' the dim shape of her huddled under her blankets after she fell asleep.

I tried to keep my eyes sweepin' the horizon instead, searchin' far as I could see in the silvery light of the full moon, lookin' fer distant fires and listenin' fer hoofbeats or voices.

But I saw nothin' out of the ordinary, and heard nothin', neither. And after awhile I began to wonder if maybe I'd just been seein' things.

Maybe I'd spent too many years an outlaw now, always on the run, suspicious of everyone, even Holt most times.

Maybe.

The night passed without incident, and even though I kept scannin' that horizon fer the whole of the next day, we never saw another rider. There was a stagecoach near midday goin' west, and we nodded greetings to the drivers and passengers and their armed escorts as we passed by each other, but those were the only other travelers we saw along the trail.

I was grateful neither Holt nor Charlotte bothered to bring up the fact that maybe I'd been mistaken about what I'd seen. And grateful too that both of 'em seemed still just as alert as me in watchin' fer anyone followin' us.

Maybe I'd been wrong ... maybe it'd just been a deer, after all. But an abundance of caution weren't never a bad thing, anyway, and we'd let our guard slip too much before. I didn't want it to happen again.

We came up on the mining camp of Copperwell in the late afternoon, the warped, agin' wood of its few buildings risin' up outta the shimmerin' desert flat like a mirage. Necessity had made it more than just a mining camp, I supposed, bein' as it was one of the only settlements out here in this wide open stretch of nothin', but it weren't quite a town, neither.

It had one hotel, two saloons, a corral for the horses, and water. And that was all we needed.

Big canvas tents were pitched all around the outskirts of the camp, encirclin' the hotel and the saloons. We rode through 'em, and I saw various other wares fer sale in some of the larger ones. We declined the invites of the vendors to peruse their goods, hot and weary and only wantin' some time to rest outta the saddle.

We dropped the horses off with the hostler first; paid fer 'em all to get some grain, and wandered over to the hotel to book our own rooms.

There was another disagreement there when Charlotte tried to pay fer all three, and then Holt and I tried to pay fer hers, and it escalated till I thought maybe the hotel proprietor might throw us all out. So we finally agreed to each pay fer our own, and Charlotte and I asked after baths, then looked expectantly to Holt, who was puttin' off a mighty powerful smell himself.

He grumbled about it, but begrudgingly slid over his coin fer the same.

The bathhouse was a separate building, and at least there was no argument about lettin' Charlotte go first. Bein' as she was a lady, and this camp was real scarce on women, I paced outside the door while she washed up to ensure none of the locals got any lewd ideas. When she'd finished, she emerged dressed in a fresh set of clothes, damp hair fallin' around her shoulders and smellin' of chamomile soap.

I walked her back to her room and saw her inside before I headed back down to wash up myself. It didn't take long. Copperwell's baths weren't so much *baths* as basins of tepid water you could scrub yerself with and dunk yer head into.

Still, it was somethin', and it felt good to rid myself of the crust of sweat and dust that had caked up after too many long days of ridin' hard. Made me think of Sally's baths, though ... made me *miss* Sally's baths. Hot water, good whiskey ... Nora and Nettie.

Shit.

I splashed more of Copperwell's water over my head, tryin' to bring myself back to the present. Back to the grimy little minin' camp instead of the boomin' river oasis of Blessing.

I toweled off, dressed again, and took advantage of the provided shavin' materials to purge myself of the lengthy stubble along my jaw. My hair was gettin' awful shaggy too; would need a cut soon. But that would have to wait. Copperwell didn't have no proper barber.

I stepped out into the early evenin' feelin' like a new man. Never-mind the fact this was a grimy little minin' camp. It beat the open desert any day.

Or at least, it beat the open desert long as it didn't harbor anyone tryin' to kill or collect me.

I wandered the streets a bit while I waited fer Holt to scrub up, and as the sun kept droppin' toward the west, the miners slowly started comin' back from their labors, and the tents and the places between the buildings gradually filled up.

The hotel had a restaurant, and some of the big tents offered food as well. And then, of course, there were the saloons. The place went from bein' all silent and still upon our arrival to gettin' awful loud and rowdy the closer it got to dusk.

Normally I wouldn'ta minded such a thing, woulda preferred it, in truth, since rowdy crowds were easy to get lost in. But tonight it made me a mite twitchy.

Maybe it was 'cause of that disappearin' rider I swore I'd seen the night before.

Or maybe it was just 'cause of Charlotte bein' here, too.

Either way, I kept my senses on high alert and my hands near my guns, and made my way back toward the hotel to collect the rest of my party fer supper.

CAN'T FIGHT YER NATURE

We ate at the hotel, bein' that it held the least number of locals and was therefore the quietest part of camp. Weren't much of a fare offered there, but I hadn't had much of a proper meal since I'd left the Bravebank jail, so I was more than happy fer somethin' other than hard biscuits and beans.

We sat at an old rickety table, the three of us, spoonin' up bowls of a cowboy stew made mostly of beef innards and topped with crumbled cornbread. Helped ourselves to some whiskey, too.

I sat in the chair facin' the front door of the establishment and lookin' out the big front windows, keepin' an eye out fer any trouble. Holt sat at the opposite side of the table, keepin' an eye on the back door.

And Charlotte sat next to me, mostly watchin' the other hotel guests—of which there was only two— as she downed her stew with as much gusto as any man.

The competin' piano music from the two saloons banged out across the main street—the only street—and filtered into our eatin' space, punctuated by hoots and hollers from men who'd already drank too much and the occasional angry yell from a man who'd just lost at cards or dice.

Charlotte finished her stew and pushed her empty bowl away.

I'd finished mine a little while ago; had sat back in my chair and crossed my arms, put a boot up onto the empty chair across from me, and been broodin' over all the noise outside while I waited fer her and Holt to finish.

"I want to go with you to Blackbird," she said abruptly.

I came up straight in my chair at that, my boot thumpin' back down to the floor as I twisted to face her. "What?"

Holt gave a little laugh into a heapin' spoonful of his third bowl. "Don't think so, Missus."

She glared across at him. "And why not?"

"'Cause we don't know exactly what we'll find in Blackbird," I answered fer him. "Or who. Could be dangerous."

"You don't say?" She turned sideways in her chair to face me and one eyebrow arched high. Despite the hat she'd been wearin' while ridin', the sun had pinkened her fair skin and darkened her freckles. She'd left her hair down since her bath to dry, and it framed her face now in wild waves as she stared me down. "I seem to recall being involved in dangerous situations before. Let me think ... how did that turn out?" She feigned concentration, bitin' her lip.

I opened my mouth to head her off, knowin' she musta been referrin' to the night we'd burned down the Whittaker estate, but she answered herself before I could get a word out.

"Oh that's right. I believe I was *not* the one to get knocked out and tied to a chair."

I shifted on the chair I sat on now, uncomfortable with that memory and with the volume of her voice. I glanced over at the other two older men takin' their supper here, but they didn't seem interested in our conversation. Still, I motioned fer her to keep it quiet. Didn't want to chance her yellin' out the Whittaker name when there was still that ridiculous bounty out fer me over that.

To my relief, she did drop her voice, but she didn't ease up on blastin' me. She leaned toward me, instead. "I seem to recall being the one to finish that job, and the one who saved you from a lot more suffering. Not to mention saved your life. So if you don't want me along, you'll need a better excuse than that."

Holt snorted another laugh into his stew. "She's got a point there, kid."

I turned away from her glare as unexpected heat rose into my face, focusin' instead on my empty stew bowl. I drummed my fingers against the table-top restlessly and tried to find the words that might express my reservations about her company without soundin' downright impolite. "If you would have stuck to our *plan*," I hissed, "and not been so hell-bent on revenge, that night mighta gone a lot differently."

Holt almost choked on his food. "Now where have I heard that said before?"

I glowered at him. It *did* sound an awful lot like what he was always sayin' to me ... but that didn't make it any less the truth.

"I had a chance to end that bastard," Charlotte growled through her teeth. "I couldn't just leave without trying. Or without freeing everyone I possibly could. Not after what I'd seen. You would have done the same. I know you would have."

"He sure woulda," Holt muttered.

I glared harder at him and shifted again in my seat, knowin' that was probably true, too. Still, he really weren't helpin' my case here. "Yeah, well ... well..." It weren't that I didn't *want* her along ... alright, no, it *were* that I didn't want her along ... but not fer the reasons she suspected, I reckoned.

"Yer family," I muttered finally. "They'll be worried sick. Might send those fellas yer pa hired out lookin' fer you."

She straightened in her chair. "My family will be worried about me just as much as they might worry about their prize stallion becoming injured and no longer able to breed."

Such an analogy was about the last thing I'd expected her to say, and I was caught not havin' the faintest idea how to reply.

Same as Holt, it seemed, as fer once he had nothin' to say, neither. But he dropped his spoon into his bowl, and his face twisted up like he was tryin' to make sense of her statement.

"Incidentally, their prize stallion is the horse I brought along for this journey." She sounded awful proud of herself. Fer a second, a half-smile pulled at her lips. But then her expression hardened again, and bein' as she'd struck me and Holt both speechless fer the moment, she elaborated. "Yes. That's right. I am the only daughter of six children, and the youngest. My parents have always seen me as a prize to shape and polish and offer out as a match to whoever might best serve *their* interests ... to whoever might extend the most advantageous arrangement in exchange for my hand in marriage. But now..." She dropped her eyes to the scuffed, sticky tabletop and her empty stew bowl. Huffed a sigh and slumped. "Now, after my six months in captivity, it seems I'm *damaged goods*. No longer suitable for any kind of match that might meet their previous hopes, or meet their highest standards." She gave a little shrug, studyin' her hands. "Only two places that might take me now, they say. Mr. Wellington—who is very, *very* much older than me, mind you—or the convent. So needless to say..." Her dark blue eyes flicked up to meet mine. "That is why I did not tell my father where I was going. And that is why I have no interest in going back to Pennsylvania. And why I wish to accompany you to Blackbird. Do you understand now?"

I sat there fer another long minute in silence, tryin' to digest this new information. I glanced to Holt, but he was only frownin' down into his food.

Damaged goods? How did they figure that, I wondered? And how could they say that about their own daughter? One who'd survived things plenty of others hadn't, and who'd managed to bring some good out of her harrowin' experience, too. Anger stirred in the pit of my stomach.

"And anyway," Charlotte said into the continued silence, "my parents are deeply grateful to you for your help in freeing me, you know. All of my family feels they owe you a debt they can never repay for getting me home safely, so that they might still have a chance to leverage me for some advantage or another. I'm sure it would put all their minds at ease to know I have you for a *chaperone*, no matter where we go."

I didn't like how she emphasized that word. I weren't fit to be anyone's chaperone, let alone hers. I had a hard enough time keepin' myself outta trouble—and alive—I surely didn't want to be responsible fer no one else.

Holt chuckled, apparently findin' that idea downright amusin'.

I supposed all those bulletins with my face on 'em hadn't found their way out to the East Republic yet. Maybe they never would. But if she or her family had any idea of even half the things I'd done in my life, they'd change their opinions of me right quick, I was sure of it.

"Charlotte..." I said again. "I just don't think it's a good idea fer you to—"

"Then let me put it a different way." She stood from her chair abruptly. "I am not going back to Pennsylvania. I've had enough of everyone else always deciding what I will or will not do, or where I can or cannot go. First my parents, then Nan's people, then the baron ... and when I returned home again I realized it might have certainly been more comfortable, but it wasn't all that different to being held by Baron Whittaker. And that..." She huffed a breath and shook her head. "I'm not living like that. Not anymore. So this is it, Mr. Delano. I'm going to do *something*, with or without you. I'll go to Blackbird to see what's there, because I've read about it and it's *interesting*," she shot a glare to Holt before bringin' that hard blue gaze back to me, "and maybe I'll even decide to live there, just because I feel like it. Or I'll go to Blackbird to help you look for whatever you need to find for Nan to get your sister back. You helped me get my revenge on Whittaker, I'd be more than happy to help you get your sister. But you just decide which you prefer."

I blinked up at her, tryin' to sort the implications of everythin' she'd just said.

"I suppose you have until Redemption to make up your mind. Now, if you'll excuse me, I think I'll retire for the night. The current company has exhausted me." She made to leave, then paused and turned back; grabbed the whiskey bottle off the table and took it with her.

"Hey now!" Holt protested, but she paid him no mind.

"Charlotte," I tried, but she didn't listen to me, neither.

She only marched on across the restaurant to the door that crossed into the hotel lobby and the stairway that led up to the rooms, went through, and disappeared.

I released a growl of frustration, turnin' back to my empty stew bowl.

Holt finally finished his third helpin' and pushed his own bowl away, swipin' the back of his hand across his mouth, and then his hand across his pants. "You sure know how to pick 'em," he muttered.

I pushed away my sudden disgust at his lack of table manners and growled at him, too. "I didn't pick no one." And I hadn't. Charlotte Harrison had burst into my room at the Seven Knives Saloon by chance. She'd been in trouble, needed help. So I'd helped her. It was just as simple as that.

Just as complicated as that.

"Y'know," Holt said, "it may not be so bad to have her along, now that I think about it."

I doubted that. "Oh yeah? How so?"

He shrugged, diggin' out a toothpick from his shirt pocket to pick at his teeth. "She seems pretty good in a fight."

"She knocked you over the head."

"Yeah, that's what I'm sayin'." One of his hands went up to touch gingerly at the spot she'd whacked him, even though that had been months ago. A spot I figured was still sore after Nan's lieutenants had more recently given him a good knock there, too. "And she did a fine job of it. Knocked me out cold. Seemed she did a fair enough job doctorin' ya up, too, after what that baron did to ya. And she said it herself, she *did* save yer life."

"Yeah," I admitted. "Sure." I wished she hadn't taken the whiskey with her. My glass was empty, and I coulda used more of it. "But just how was you plannin' to pay fer the train into Akansa, huh? I sure don't got enough left over to cover fer three of us plus our mounts. I barely had enough fer this meal. I gave all my money to Nan. And I got a notion you don't got that kinda money on you, neither."

As I'd expected, it seemed he'd already spent most of his share of that Blessing money. Least, I hadn't seen much of it left when we'd been gatherin' supplies at Grave Gulch.

And the way he chewed on that toothpick now, starin' down into his bowl, told me I'd guessed right. He only shrugged again. Then cast his eyes around the room before leanin' forward, over the table, and keepin' his voice low. "Figured we'd find some ... *generous* folk along the way who might be inclined to help us out."

"Uh huh." Of course that was his plan. But then, it had been my plan, too. Up until Charlotte had showed up at our camp. Up until she'd insisted on comin' with us to Blackbird. "That's a problem then, ain't it?"

Holt lifted his bushy brows, echoin' my question from earlier. "Eh? How so?"

I leaned forward over the table, too, and tilted my head in the direction Charlotte had disappeared. "You really want to do somethin' like that with her around?"

"Ha!"

His bark of laughter startled me, but he leaned back in his chair, tipped it back on its two rear legs briefly before lettin' it thump back to the floorboards. "Kid..." he paused, composed himself, and lowered his voice again. "You already got her involved in plenty of other things, remember? Bank robbery, arson, theft, *murder*."

I squirmed in my chair and gestured fer him to shut it, even though I was fair certain no one could hear anythin' he was sayin' above the ruckus comin' from outside.

"And I don't remember you bein' so concerned about her innocence at that juncture," Holt went on, ignorin' my discomfort. "She was perfectly happy to engage in those activities, weren't she? And it sure sounds to me like she all but stole away that horse she's been ridin'. So why not include her in our future engagements? Might be kinda nice to have a woman on board, ya know? Imagine the marks she could—"

"No," I snapped, and it came out harsher than I'd intended. "We ain't gettin' her involved, Holt."

He drew back a bit at my tone, those heavy brows of his drawin' down to hood his glare. "Well why the hell not?"

"Because," I hissed, "she only took part in those other *engagements* to get free of the baron. And to help me get Ethelyn back. She didn't come back here to lead a life of crime, Holt."

He grunted. "Sounded to me like she don't know what she came back here fer, really. She just said she's gonna do *somethin'*. How do you know a life of crime weren't on her list of possibilities?"

I narrowed my eyes at him. "Her father is tryin' to start a whole organization to come out here and clean up, fer fuck's sake. We can't ask her to get involved in any of our ... our *business* ... shouldn't even think it."

Holt crossed his arms and chewed harder on his toothpick. "Fine. What then? You gonna set her loose? Let her go off on her noble crusade all by her lonesome and probably end up right back in some baron's harem?"

I scowled; swiped up my whiskey glass. But it was still empty, so I scowled some more and slammed it back to the table, probably a little too hard. "No."

"Well then? I'm all ears, kid."

"I ... I dunno." I didn't want to cut her loose, no. And I didn't want her comin' with us to Blackbird, neither. I wanted her to get on the damn train and go home. To Pennsylvania. To the Republic. To her family with their gates and guards where I could at least be mostly certain she'd stay safe. "But we're gonna have to find a different way to afford that train, at least. I don't wanna have to take advantage of any *generous* folk while she's around."

"I see." Holt sat there starin' at me, passin' his toothpick from one side of his mouth to the other, arms still crossed.

I ignored his scrutiny and eyed my empty glass again. Decided I was gonna buy another bottle, my dwindlin' coin be damned. I'd just pushed my chair back from the table in order to go get it when Holt spoke again.

"It ain't really about her at all, is it?"

"The fuck is that supposed to mean?"

He leaned forward and squinted at me from under his hat, unfoldin' one arm to jab his index finger down on the table as he made his point. "It's about *you*."

"Huh?"

"You don't want her to see what kinda man you really are."

I pressed my palms flat against the table and pushed to my feet, glarin' down at him. "Yeah? And what kinda man is that?"

He mimicked my movements, puttin' his hands flat against the table to stand eye-to-eye with me. He leaned close, his clear blue gaze holdin' mine evenly. "Yer a fuckin' outlaw, Van," he whispered. "A criminal. A thief and a murderer. That's why you don't want her to come, ain't it? You don't want her to figure that out, 'cause apparently she ain't put it together yet?" He let out a low whistle and shook his head. "Good luck, kid. Ya can't fight yer nature."

"Oh it's my nature now, is it?" I bit off. "That ain't what you said back in Bravebank when you were wantin' me to pull another bank job with you. You were all afraid I was gonna go straight ... or did you forget that already?"

Holt snorted. "If ya ever manage to get yer sister, sure. Sure, I do think you'd give honest livin' a try, fer her sake if nothin' else ... *after* you find her. But before that..." He clucked his tongue and shook his head. "Before that ... well kid, I ain't sure there's anythin' you *wouldn't* do, if ya needed to."

"If I *needed to* bein' the key factor here, Holt."

"Like you *needed* to cut up Lloyd Renneker?"

I ground my teeth at the reminder of that deed. "He was reluctant to talk."

"Seems you mighta enjoyed it a little, though. Or maybe a lot."

"He deserved it," I growled.

"Everyone deserves somethin', kid. Includin' you and me. So like I said ... ya can't fight yer nature."

"It ain't my nature," I snapped. "Might be yers, but it ain't mine."

Holt straightened and lifted one bushy eyebrow. "Guess we'll see about that, won't we?"

"Guess we will."

He held my stare fer another minute, then finally blew out a breath and plucked that toothpick from between his teeth; flicked it off across the room. "All right. I'll leave you to yer self-righteous nonsense, then. I'm gonna go find me a game of cards. Maybe I can win us enough fer that train trip, eh?" He winked and gave my right arm a playful punch.

It landed just below the scars from Baron Whittaker and I clenched my teeth against the wince.

He turned and ambled away, unconcerned.

But I glared at his back until he stepped through the front door and left the establishment, and then I grumbled a good long string of profanity and went to get more whiskey.

Maybe I were an outlaw, but bein' such a thing had never been my first choice.

It weren't my nature.

Didn't matter that a whole stack of wanted posters might say otherwise. Didn't matter that my pa was once one of the worst to terrorize half the continent. Didn't matter what Holt said now.

It weren't.

And I was gonna drown the sharp edges of doubt needlin' at my mind in whiskey, so help me God.

XI

TIME TO GO

I drowned those doubts, all right.

And most my sense. Sat there and downed almost a whole bottle of whiskey all by my lonesome, watchin' the front door and the street outside through those windows as the sky grew darker and the lamps grew brighter.

The two older fellas who'd been havin' supper in the restaurant with us finished their meals and left, and over time a few other folk wandered in and ate and wandered out again.

I sat there till the hotel proprietor came along and told me he was closin' up and I had to go. He suggested one of the saloons, said they'd be open all night.

So I grabbed up that almost-empty bottle of whiskey and stumbled out the door and into the night. The cool air hit me and sobered me up a bit, and I eyed those two saloons. One was clearly a fancier establishment than the other: had two floors and a balcony where the other had only one floor and a canvas roof.

But neither seemed much to my taste this evenin'. I surely didn't wanna gamble, seein' as I was already awful low on money and was generally shit at it, anyway. And there was a part of me that suspected I shouldn't drink more than my current bottle, neither. At least, not if I wanted to make the ride tomorrow in any good time.

The piano music was bangin' away, the noise of general merry-makin' spillin' out into the street along with several drunk patrons. But I didn't hear Holt shoutin', and there hadn't yet been any shootin', so I figured he was farin' well enough at his cards.

That bein' the case, I pivoted in the street to go right back to the hotel. Lurched through the front doors and gave the man at the desk a nod as I started up the stairs. Had they always been so damned creaky?

I found the door to my room, but paused with my hand on the knob.

Charlotte had rented the next room over. And there was a flicker of light shinin' beneath the door.

It was awful late. What was she doin' still awake?

Curious, I stepped over to her door, instead. Hesitated. Took a breath. Took another swig of whiskey. And rapped my knuckles lightly on the wood.

There was a moment's pause before she answered. "Yes? Who is it?"

I started to lean my left shoulder against the wall, then grimaced as the bullet hole in my bicep made itself known and straightened again. "It's me. It's Van."

Another pause. Then, "What do you want?"

I grimaced again, this time from the coolness in her tone. "I ... I just wanted to, uh ... be sure you were all right in there?"

"I'm quite well, thank you."

"Do you ... need anythin'?"

"No. I'm fine, thank you."

I sighed and closed my eyes, leaned my forehead against the door so that my hat slid backwards and nearly fell off. "All right." A buncha other words clogged my throat. Words like, *Would you open the door? Can I come in? Can we talk about what I meant to say earlier...*

But none of those words came out, despite the fact my mouth opened.

"Are you drunk, Mr. Delano?"

The question surprised me, and I shut my mouth and pulled myself back from the door. Had I slurred that badly? "No," I said. But then I realized just how much this hallway seemed to sway. "Maybe."

Footsteps came across the floor and I stepped back as my heart jumped, my awareness sharpenin' when the door opened at last.

But it only opened a crack. And Charlotte stood there, lookin' up at me. Her hair was down, fallin' over her shoulders, and she wore the white blouse with the blue trim and blue skirt she'd been wearin' before, too. She looked me over, as if searchin' fer somethin', then brought her eyes back to my face. "You think it's wise to so heavily imbibe before a two-day ride across the desert?" she asked.

That weren't what I'd been expectin' her to say at all. But I shrugged. "I dunno. Try not to do much thinkin'. That's what this is fer." I brought up the whiskey bottle.

Her eyes widened at the sight of it. "Did you drink all of that by yourself?"

I squinted down at her, then squinted at the bottle. Was that a bad thing? "Maybe," I said.

She rolled her eyes and shook her head. "It's late, Mr. Delano. We have a long ride ahead of us tomorrow. Go to bed. Get some rest. And no more whiskey." She reached through the crack in the door and wrested the bottle from my grip. "You've clearly had enough."

"But—"

She shut the door in my face, nearly closin' my nose in it. "Good night, Mr. Delano," she called through it, and I heard the sound of her latchin' it. Then the sound of her footsteps movin' away.

I sighed again, saggin' against her door. But I still couldn't quite get myself to say those other words. I understood her sentiments, her desire to help and, given what she'd said about how her parents treated her, why she wouldn't be so eager to head back home. And I hadn't meant to upset her with my reluctance to have her company. But damn it all ... I was gonna get Ethelyn free, no matter what I had to do to do it.

And I weren't sure just what I was gonna have to do in Blackbird.

It could get ugly. Could get bad.

And if it did ... Holt was right. I didn't want Charlotte to see it.

Didn't want her to see what I might have to do.

Didn't want her to think I was that kinda man.

"G'night," I muttered into the door. It was all I could muster. Then I pushed myself away and straightened my hat; staggered down to my own room to get some rest like she'd said.

She was right, anyway. We had a long ride ahead of us still. And I was tired, sure enough. And lookin' forward to a real mattress. I locked my door behind me, threw myself down across the bed, and fell asleep wearin' my boots and my belts.

A gunshot jolted me awake.

Fer a second I thought it might have been a dream, but then there was shoutin' and sounds of a scuffle. Somewhere close.

Another gunshot split the night, and the second one finally got through the fog of sleep and whiskey. I scrambled off the bed, got my boots tangled in the sheets and fell hard. I swore, crawled free of 'em, and pushed up to my feet, gropin' fer my right pistol.

I remembered now. We were in Copperwell, in the hotel, and I'd drank too much whiskey. Again. I stumbled sideways as the room tilted, but then caught the wall to steady myself. Through the window I saw the moon, fat and full but duller now ... as the first brush of dawn lit the far horizon. The camp had fallen all quiet and still again.

Except fer whatever was goin' on outside now.

My first thought was that Holt had gotten into trouble. Maybe the cards hadn't gone his way, after all. Or maybe they *had* gone his way, a little too well fer someone else's likin'.

I ran to the window once I'd regained my balance and peered down at the street below. There were fellas fightin' there, all right. One looked dead, sprawled out in the dirt. But there were four more of 'em, and it looked like three against one. The fella gettin' beat on didn't look like Holt, though. His hat and duster were the wrong color, and his figure too tall and slim to be the old man.

Also, this guy looked like he knew how to fight.

Not that Holt couldn't hold his own in a scuffle, but this fella was doin' a decent job of fendin' off three other folk who clearly wanted him dead. I wondered why they didn't just try to shoot him, but then I noticed the pistols lyin' in the street. And the longer I watched, the more I realized every time a fella would try and grab fer his gun, the middle fella managed to thwart their efforts somehow.

Well, looked like he certainly had the situation handled. And anyway, if it weren't Holt, it weren't none of my business. I holstered my pistol and turned away from the window to head fer the door of my room, only weavin' a little as the world was still spinnin'.

This camp may not have had a sheriff, a jailhouse, or a gallows ... but any time folk got murdered in a place, Holt and I made sure to clear out. Murder made townsfolk start askin' a lot of questions, especially of outsiders. Made 'em jumpy. Suspicious. And prone to lynching.

Camps like Copperwell weren't no different.

I yanked open my door to find Holt already on the other side of it, about to knock.

"Time to go," he said.

"Yeah."

"Don't forget yer hat."

"Shit." I crossed back to the bed to retrieve it, shovin' it down on my head as Holt went to rap on Charlotte's door. I rejoined him just as she pulled it open a crack to peer through groggily.

"What's the matter? What's happening?"

"We gotta go," I said.

Worry replaced the vague sleepiness of her features. "What? Why? Did you..." She glanced to our guns, then over her shoulder toward the window behind her. "That wasn't *you* shooting, was it?"

"No," I assured her. "Not us."

"But someone did get murdered," Holt said. "And murder is a messy business. We don't wanna be around when the hammer drops over this little incident."

"Why?" she asked again. "We didn't have anything to do with it!"

"Just trust us." I stepped forward, put a hand against her door and pushed it open wider. "We've had experience with this a time or two. It's better if we leave now. Get yer things."

She looked like she might argue fer a space, but then she only sighed and nodded, scrubbin' her hands over her face. "All right. Give me a minute." She left the doorway to move into the room; started gatherin' up the stuff from the bedside table and the bureau, to include our first bottle of whiskey, which was still mostly full.

"Fast as you can," Holt prodded.

He was gettin' restless already, but so was I. The longer we stayed here, the greater the chance we'd get stuck here till the murder investigation concluded.

"Yes, yes," she hissed. "I understand the need for urgency. What about you two? No things to pack?"

"I didn't bring nothin'," Holt said.

"I left my things with my saddle," I said.

Charlotte sighed. "Of course you did." She tossed a brush into her pack and cinched it up, then threw it over her shoulder. "Ready. Let's go."

We went. Down the hall and down those creaky stairs, but then we turned to go out the back door of the restaurant, bein' as that fight was happenin' outside the hotel's front doors, and we surely didn't want to get involved.

The camp had roused a bit now, the gunfire havin' been a rather insistent wake-up call, and the continuin' sounds of the tussle drawin' an increasin' number of folk out of their tents to see just what the hell was goin' on.

Holt, Charlotte, and I ignored the flow of people headed fer the center of the camp and instead made our way to its outskirts, to the corral and our horses. We caught our four mounts, pulled our saddles outta the barn, and tacked up in record time. I double-checked all the canteens, makin' sure they were full.

They were.

We'd made sure to do that yesterday, shortly after arrivin'. Never knew when you might need to leave a place in a hurry, and this camp was the last chance fer guaranteed water till Redemption.

Satisfied on that account, I wedged my boot into the stirrup and was about to mount up when a voice spoke outta the pre-dawn gloom.

"Hold up there, Delano."

I froze. It was a man, but it weren't Holt who had said that.

"Ah ah," the voice said. "You too, Haggerty. Hands up where I can see 'em, both of you. *All* of you."

XII

LAWFUL BUSINESS

Somethin' hot lit in me at his mention of *all* of us.

He had no right to include Charlotte in this. Whatever *this* was.

"Hands *up*, Delano. *Now*."

I pulled my boot from my stirrup and hissed a breath through my teeth as I complied, holdin' my hands shoulder-high as I slowly turned around.

And I didn't like at all who I found there, standin' a few paces away with both guns drawn: one pointed at me and one pointed at Holt.

Least he didn't have nothin' aimed at Charlotte.

Duster. That fuckin' bounty hunter from Sonoita. His well-tailored clothes were streaked with dirt, his lip bloodied, and he had a cut on his left temple. That had been him in that tussle outside of the hotel, I was sure of it.

What I weren't sure of was how he'd managed to get free of those other three men and get over here without the camp residents noticin'.

I hadn't any idea how he'd managed to find me here, neither, though I certainly wondered then if it mighta been him I'd seen so briefly against the horizon the other night. But if it had been, why hadn't he made a move earlier? Why had he waited till we'd reached a camp, with plenty of other people around? Woulda been far easier on him to take me in the open desert.

"Who are you?" Charlotte demanded. She stood next to her horse, but they were both behind me and Joe, and I wondered if Duster could see the gunbelt she wore from his vantage point.

Didn't much matter either way though. I didn't think she was fast enough to get a good shot at him, especially not with me and Joe in the way. And I prayed she wouldn't try. I didn't want to get shot, neither by her nor Duster ... and I really didn't want *him* to shoot at her. I had a good feelin' he wouldn't miss.

"Howdy, ma'am," Duster said, and bein' that his two hands were currently occupied, he nodded in her direction in lieu of tippin' his hat. "Pleasure to make your acquaintance. The name is Dustin Barrett. But around here, most people just call me Duster."

His good manners raised my hackles and I gritted my teeth.

"Van, you know this fella?" Holt asked. He was off to my right, next to his gelding with his hands up same as me. I could see him calculatin' though, tryin' to figure if we had any chance if we drew against this man called Duster.

"More or less," I said. And I didn't think we had a chance, at least not with our hands up and guns still in leather, so I gave Holt an incremental shake of my head, warnin' him not to try it.

Duster smiled. "More or less," he agreed.

"And what business do you have with us, then, Mr. Barrett?" Charlotte asked pointedly. "Especially that would require you to point your weapons at my friends here?"

Duster's smile widened.

There was a commotion buildin' in the center of camp, and I wished he woulda picked better timin' fer this. If we didn't get outta this place soon, we might very well *all* end up lynched.

"Your friends?" he drawled. "I beg your pardon, ma'am, but you seem like much too sensible of a woman to call these two no-good outlaws your friends."

"I don't think you know much about me, Mr. Barrett," Charlotte answered coolly. "Or about these two men here. So I would appreciate it if you would lower those pistols. These men are escorting me cross country, and we have a long way to travel today. I'd like to get going."

"That's right, *Dustin*," I said. The commotion in camp was gettin' louder, and comin' our direction. "Seems you've caused quite a ruckus here. Probably best we be movin' on. Quick as possible. Maybe we can resume this business another time, yeah?" I took a step backward, toward Joe.

"We'll be gettin' out of here quick-like, all right," Duster agreed. "But you'll be comin' with me, Delano." He glanced toward Holt, then Charlotte. "And if you come quiet, I'll even let your friends go. Even as temptin' as it is to get two-for-one." He grinned toward Holt, who only scowled at him and spit into the dirt.

"Mr. Delano isn't going anywhere," Charlotte said evenly. "Am I correct in assuming you are a duly appointed warrant officer, Mr. Barrett?"

Duster's grin vanished, and his gaze sharpened as his eyes focused on Charlotte again. "That's correct, ma'am. Maybe you weren't aware, but these two men you've hired are worth quite a lot of money. This one especially." His right gun extended toward me. "Like I said, both no-good outlaws, wanted for various crimes across the Territories. It's my sworn duty to bring them to justice."

I wished he'd shut up already. I really didn't want him gettin' any more specific about my various crimes. And that crowd was comin' awful close now ... I wanted to be well away from here by the time they got here.

"Yes, yes," Charlotte said, seemingly as impatient as me. "And you're based out of where? The Commune? The Republic?"

Duster straightened, his pistols lowerin' just a bit. "The Commune. Council-appointed. Out of Abilene, Kansas, to be exact."

A jolt went through me at the mention of that town. I was familiar enough with that place. Had a lot of memories there ... a lot of memories I hadn't bothered to remember fer a lot of years.

"I see," Charlotte said. "Well then you've probably heard of my father, Senator John Henry Harrison out of Pennsylvania? And I can assure you, he will be *most* put out if you were to rob me of my escorts at this juncture."

I blinked; glanced again to Holt, but he looked as surprised as me. A senator? A fuckin' *senator* was her father?

Duster, too, seemed at a loss. His pistols lowered further, his brow creasin' with his frown.

"There he is!" came a shout, and I winced.

Well, they'd found us now.

"Hands up, Mister!" another man ordered, and I figured they musta been talkin' to Duster, since the rest of us already had our hands up. "Drop yer guns or we'll shoot!"

I shifted my gaze over Duster's shoulder, where the mob of miners were comin' down the main street at us, and most of 'em held weapons of some sort, everythin' from rifles and pistols to pickaxes and pitchforks.

Duster's shoulders sagged and he let out a long, heavy sigh.

"Shoulda just let us be on our way," I muttered.

He shot me a glare, but then he fixed a friendly, pleasant expression on his face and lifted his hands, letting his twin pistols hang off his index fingers. "Now, now, folks," he called out.

"Take it easy. I assure you, I'm on lawful business here."

"Murderin' a man don't seem too awful lawful to me!" someone shouted.

Duster looked straight at me when he answered. "What if that murdered man was a dangerous criminal, huh? You want that kind of person in your camp? I did you a favor."

"Yer gonna need to come with us, Mister," another miner spoke up, an elderly gentleman with rumpled white hair. "Surrender yer guns peacefully and come over to the saloon with us and we'll get everythin' sorted out."

The bounty hunter slowly turned around to face the crowd, who were pressin' up close now, fannin' out to gradually surround us, and our window of opportunity fer escape was fast closin' with that circle.

"Now look," Duster said, facin' down a good number of guns, and it was nice to have 'em not pointed at me fer once. "I can assure you, I was well within my rights to shoot that man. I didn't murder those other three, did I? Go on and check ... they're all still breathin'. Trust me, they didn't want the same for me. They were trying to murder *me*.

Now, if you'll excuse me, I have pressin' business to attend to. *Lawful* business, as I said. Just so happens I'm a duly appointed warrant officer, and these folks here are wanted by the law in several states and territories."

There was that title again. And the folk of Copperwell camp looked befuddled by it. But Duster nodded his head back toward me and Holt and Charlotte and I tensed as all those eyes shifted to us.

There was still a small openin' in the crowd to the north, and I looked to Holt to see if he were just as ready to spring as me.

He gave a barely perceptible nod.

"I've been after one of them for awhile now," Duster told that millin' mob. "So I'd appreciate it if you'd let me collect him, and then I'll be on my way. Outta your hair. And we can forget all of this unpleasantness."

I twisted to look back at Charlotte. She didn't seem as confident as she'd sounded just a minute ago, her face pale, eyes wide, and the reins of her horse gripped white-knuckled in one of her raised hands.

She met my questionin' gaze and lifted an eyebrow.

I tried to indicate our narrow escape path with only my eyes, but it were hard to tell if she understood what I was tryin' to say or not.

Well, guess she'd figure it out soon enough. I needed Duster to stop talkin'. With my luck, he'd convince these miners of his lawfulness, after all, and they'd *help* him round me up.

"Whaddaya mean?" someone shouted then from the back of the crowd. "You sayin' yer a ... a bounty hunter?"

"That's right," Duster said. "I am, indeed. Licensed and everything. Here, let me show you. Take it easy, now. I'm just gonna get my paperwork, understand?"

He bent down, slow and careful, and set his pistols on the ground. Then he straightened and, just as slow and careful, reached into his inside jacket pocket.

I didn't give a damn what he was gettin', whether it was his paperwork or another gun to put some of these miners outta their misery. It was the opportunity I'd been waitin' fer, so I spun around and flung myself up into my saddle ... then almost went off the other side as all that whiskey from the night before made the world tilt again.

I kicked my heels into Joe's sides even as I pulled myself back upright, twistin' my fingers into his stiff mane. He took off like a shot, nearly unseatin' me again, and galloped straight at the little space where the surroundin' folk were sparsest. But those few folk got out of his way quick, leapin' sideways with angry shouts as he barreled past.

Holt followed in a flash, and Charlotte after him, and we left Duster the bounty hunter swearin' and shoutin' in the middle of a mess of confused camp residents.

XIII

INTO REDEMPTION

We ran at a flat gallop as long as we dared to push the horses, moved in a zig-zag pattern and sometimes circled back around again to both confuse the tracks and check to see if we had anyone comin' after us.

But we finally had to slow our mad race across the desert, the horses lathered and winded and the sun now a fat, shimmerin' medallion of orange above the eastern horizon. So far, we hadn't seen no one else out here, no one followin', but that didn't mean they wouldn't be comin' eventually.

"Wh-what was all that?" Charlotte blurted breathlessly as soon as we'd slowed. Her eyes were bright from all the adrenaline and her straw hat had come loose, hangin' behind her from its tie. She dropped her reins to grab it with both hands and shove it back on her head, then attempted to smooth wavy red locks from her face.

"A hasty exit," Holt muttered. He was glarin' at me.

"No, not *that*," Charlotte spat. She waved wildly at the desert around us. "I mean all that weaving and circling! Are you still drunk? We could have made a lot more distance if you hadn't spent so much time wandering all over the place!"

"Helps make our tracks harder to follow," Holt said.

"And gives us a better look at anyone who might be wantin' to follow," I said.

Charlotte's eyes narrowed, and she looked from me to Holt and back again.

I prodded Joe onward a little faster, as much wantin' to put distance between us and Copperwell as wantin' to get out from under her suspicious stare. She was probably wonderin' why and how we knew so many tricks fer losin' people who might wanna come after us. And that, I had no inclination to explain.

"*Shit*!" Holt hissed suddenly, with enough vehemence that I reined up sharply to face him.

"What?"

"We left the goddamned mare!"

I looked over our little party with a start only to find he was right: in our rush to get outta that camp, we'd neglected to bring along Sally's skinny old mare, who had, consequently, been loaded up with nearly half our supplies. I opened my mouth to curse our idiocy ... then remembered Charlotte's company and closed it again, settlin' fer a frustrated growl instead.

"Well..." Charlotte said after a moment, "she probably would have just slowed us down, anyway."

"Yeah," Holt growled, "'cept she was holdin' about half our water. And we got two more days till we reach Redemption!"

I shook my head, grittin' my teeth. It weren't an ideal situation, not at all.

But bein' taken back to the new Baron Whittaker by the bounty hunter Duster woulda been *less* ideal, certainly.

"We'll have to be careful," I said. "Ration what we do got."

"Ya think?" Holt snapped.

I tossed him a glare. "What's crawled up yer hump now?"

"I'll tell ya what." He threw his reins down over his saddle horn. "Havin' a bounty hunter all over our ass, that's what. And a *licensed* one, at that!"

I shrugged. The licensed ones were the professionals, sure; the ones folk like me and Holt needed to watch out fer most ... but it weren't like we hadn't been hunted by plenty of fortune-seekers before. "He ain't after you. He's after *me*. And those miners'll keep him busy fer awhile sortin' out that murder, and we'll push on quick-like to Redemption and lose him on the train. He might know we're goin' there, but no way he'll guess our next stop. Too many possibilities out of Redemption. It'll take him months to check each one. Should be easy to stay ahead of him from there."

Holt sat still in his saddle and only looked at me, steady and unblinkin'. Like he didn't believe anythin' I'd just said. "I've lived a lot more years than you, kid. Got a lot longer list of deeds that might get those bounty hunters after me. And I just—" He paused and glanced to Charlotte, then looked back to me. "Well, we just had that incident in Destry, didn't we? So why don't ya tell me why this *licensed* bounty hunter is so keen to bring *you* in, but let *me* go? What'd I miss? What kinda bounty could that possibly be, and what in the hell did you do to deserve it?"

I hesitated. Nudged Joe onward again, and the other two followed me, keepin' pace to either side. I supposed at least Charlotte knew about this particular misdeed, so there weren't no real harm in tellin' Holt. He'd been a part of it, too, after all. In a way. So I let out a long, heavy sigh. "Remember good ol' Baron Whittaker?"

"Sure."

"Charlotte and I wrecked his estate, right? Freed all those slaves of his? And then ... well, and then Charlotte murdered him."

A frown creased Holt's grimy, sweaty features, and his clear blue gaze flicked over to the girl. "Charlotte?"

She nodded, but said nothin', her own gaze fixed straight ahead.

"How's that translate to that bounty hunter comin' after *you*, then?" Holt asked.

"The Whittaker family wanted to find those responsible ... they already knew who Charlotte was." I glanced to her from the corner of my eye, but she only kept starin' ahead. "But they didn't know who *I* was. They had a sketch made up of my face ... I dunno who coulda given 'em my description. I guess ... I guess one of the slaves who was there that night, is all I can figure. Maybe one was loyal to the Whittakers, or maybe one was convinced in some other horrible way to give me up. But somehow, they got pretty close to my face with that sketch, and noted my metal leg, and made the bounty fer me bein' delivered alive an amount that's made my life miserable ever since."

Holt grunted. "But there ain't no bounty fer the girl?"

I shook my head. "Far as I understand it, they were fairly confident they could track her down themselves, without help from other folk like bounty hunters." I remembered Miller's thugs havin' found Charlotte's home, remembered what he'd said he would do to her, and bile rose in my throat.

They'd gotten damn close to doin' just that, too.

Then I remembered what he'd done to me, and I swallowed and curled my left hand into a loose fist to hide those three fingers with missin' fingernails. I still kept 'em bandaged most times, but at least the nailbeds had hardened now, and they'd stopped bein' so sore and sticky.

We rode in stony silence fer a minute, till Holt said, "How much?"

"How much what?"

"How much is the bounty?"

"A lot."

"Van."

"What?" I turned my head to meet his glare and shrugged again. "What does it matter? You gonna collect it yerself?"

His glare turned into witherin' disgust. "Course not."

"Then it don't much matter, does it?"

"If I'm gonna be ridin' with ya, then I'd like to know what to expect fer the rest of our journey. So yeah, it matters. The lady here deserves to know, too. Maybe she'll change her mind about wantin' to come to Blackbird with us if it means she's gonna be chased outta every town we try to lay our heads in. How much we talkin' here, Van?"

I hesitated again. I glanced over to Charlotte once more only to find her lookin' at me now, an eyebrow quirked.

"He does raise a good point," she said. "I doubt it will deter me from going to Blackbird, but perhaps it will prevent future surprises, yes?"

"I doubt it," I grumbled. Not with the way my luck tended to run, anyway.

"Well at least ... maybe I could find a monetary way to dissuade these bounty hunters from their quest," Charlotte offered. "As I mentioned when we first met, my family *is* quite wealthy."

I tried to mask a wince, wishin' she hadn't announced that in front of Holt. Maybe he weren't eager to collect on *my* bounty, but I wouldn't put it past him to try and weasel some of Charlotte's money off her. "Nah," I said quick, before Holt could speak. He'd sat up straighter in his saddle already. "No need to get your family involved. Anyway, you already said you don't want nothin' to do with 'em anymore."

"I never said I would get my family involved."

"Then how did you plan to get that money?"

Charlotte looked away from me abruptly, fixin' her eyes on the flat of the desert that stretched before us. And I could swear it weren't just the sun and risin' heat that made her cheeks flush pink. "I ... I have some of my own, you know. Brought it with me."

I looked her over up and down again, and then over her pack, strapped to the back of her saddle, and her saddlebags. "And how would I know that if you never told me?"

She straightened her shoulders. "Well. Now you know."

"Guess I do."

"So," Holt said from the other side of me, "how much?"

I kept silent fer a spell, mullin' over if it might really be better to tell 'em or not. They'd probably find out themselves sooner or later, though. Or see the poster with their own eyes on some wall somewhere. So at last I heaved another sigh and had out with it. "Fifty thousand."

Holt yanked his gelding to a halt. "*Fifty thousand goddamned dollars?!*"

His voice echoed across the flat and I winced again, motionin' fer him to quiet down as I turned Joe around to face him.

"Van!" Charlotte gasped. She brought her stallion up alongside my mule, her face gone as pale as Holt's had gone red.

"You ain't never gonna get rid of that Mr. Barrett at that price," Holt hissed. "Nor anyone else in the whole expanse of the goddamned Territories!"

"Yeah," I muttered. "That's exactly what the Whittaker family hoped fer." That's what Charles Miller had planned on. And his plan had nearly worked several times over now. Nearly.

Holt spluttered, but it seemed he'd lost all his coherent words.

Charlotte reached over to put a hand on my arm. "Van, that's not fair. I ... I was the one who murdered the baron. They should be hunting me, not you."

"I still did plenty of damage to that estate," I offered.

She shook her head. "Not enough to warrant that kind of price." She looked back the way we'd come, back toward Copperwell camp, and worry furrowed her brow.

"If he gets free of that mob..." Holt looked back that way, too. Then he faced front again, and I could tell by the hardenin' of his expression he'd thought of a plan. "We could lead him into a trap," he said. "Ambush him. Get rid of him fer good."

Charlotte looked from one of us to the other. "You mean ... kill him?"

"Yeah," Holt said.

"I don't know..." Charlotte said, and she shifted uncomfortably in her saddle. "Murdering a licensed warrant officer is ... well, that might get the Council's attention. And not in a good way."

"More so than murderin' a metal baron?" Holt quipped.

The pink came back to Charlotte's cheeks as her mouth set into a firm line. "Yes. Much more so than that. And anyway, Baron Whittaker deserved what happened to him."

Both of Holt's bushy brows raised at that, and he looked pointedly at me with blue eyes gleamin'. "Ya don't say?" He was talkin' to Charlotte, but his look said somethin' else. Callin' to mind our argument from just the night before, and what I'd told him about Lloyd Renneker. He went on as I scowled and shook my head, shiftin' in my own saddle now, dislikin' many implications of this conversation. "Maybe this Mr. Barrett deserves it, too," Holt suggested. "After all, we don't really know him, do we?"

Despite Charlotte's misgivings, I considered the notion. Glanced out across the expanse of dust and cacti runnin' east to west and south far as the eye could see, and the distant mountains that cradled the river snakin' north of us. There was no place to hide out here. And little nearby rock to hide our tracks. The wind might cover 'em up eventually, or we could take the time to confuse 'em, but this particular stretch of desert weren't especially suited to ambushes.

"We'd have to go north to find a suitable place," I said. "To the mountains and the river."

Now it were Holt who shrugged. "We'd have shelter, at least. And water. And the water would attract game, too. Probably eat and drink better than we have in days."

I wet my cracked lips, or tried to, already thirsty. And the world felt all wobbly on account of that whiskey, my head achin' now, too. Havin' a camp by the river fer a few days didn't sound too awful bad right now, in truth, and neither did gettin' that bloodhound of a bounty hunter off my back fer good...

But Nan had only given me two weeks to find those damned ruins, if they even existed ... I surely didn't have time to be hidin' out fer days hopin' that Duster fella would walk into our trap. The journey to Blackbird alone would take half that time, and that was *if* we didn't have no more setbacks or delays.

So instead of agreein' with the old man, I shook my head. "We can't. Don't got that kinda time. Nan expects to hear from me in two weeks, remember? And it's already been six days."

His mouth pressed into a thin line of disapproval.

In answer, I only prodded Joe back into motion and kept goin' southeast, acutely aware of Charlotte's hand slidin' off my arm as I did so. "We'll make it," I said, forcin' all the confidence I could muster into my tone, though it was more fer Charlotte's benefit than Holt's. "We got a head start. We'll keep up the pace, push on hard, sleep in shifts and forego any fires. Only gotta stay clear of him fer two more days."

Charlotte trailed after me, sayin' nothin' about my plan, which I hoped meant she found it credible enough.

Holt followed after us eventually, too, although he kept mutterin' under his breath. He clearly did not find my plan credible enough, but there weren't nothin' fer it except to keep on toward Redemption.

We'd need to quicken our pace, though, and stay alert.

And if I did happen to see that bounty hunter again between now and Redemption, I was gonna put a bullet in him.

The next two days were a hot, miserable drag. We baked under the sun, movin' as fast as we dared, but still not fast enough for my likin'. I kept watch fer another silhouette on the horizon, day and night, but we never saw one.

The horses had little to forage out here and less grain, thanks to the loss of our pack horse, and we sacrificed a good portion of our water to 'em, preferrin' they stay in good condition in order to deliver us to relief in Redemption more quickly.

We had little to eat ourselves, bein' as we'd abandoned the notion of nighttime fires ... or at least, we had little to eat that was very palatable. But we made do. The second afternoon we happened upon a rattlesnake, so we made a quick, small fire in the daylight to cook it up fer some real meat.

But then we moved on again.

Through it all, we hardly spoke, wantin' to conserve our energy—and our spit.

And through it all, Charlotte never complained once.

Not sure why I kept expectin' her to. Like she'd been keen to remind me and Holt, she'd endured far worse durin' her six months at the Whittaker estate. Surely she could handle this desert ride, even with fewer supplies than we mighta preferred. But I guess the fact she'd been raised an easterner and come from a wealthy family—with a Senator fer a father, of all things—had stuck in my mind, and my expectations of her kept tryin' to align with all my previous experiences with such people.

We plodded into the bustlin' town of Redemption, Lesser Texas at dusk on the second day and went straight to the nearest water trough. We were plum spent and so were the horses, all of us covered again in layers of sweat and dust. Our canteens were dry, our food supplies nearly gone, but we'd stayed ahead of that bounty hunter and survived the ride, and that was all that mattered. We let the horses drink while I took stock of the shops that lined this particular street.

The sun was fallin' quick into the west, brushin' that horizon in shades of purple, pink and orange. Yellow squares of light shone out all down the lane as the shops lit their inside lanterns, and the music from numerous saloons spilled out into the evenin', minglin' with the smells of horse manure, fire smoke, sawdust and smeltin' iron, and whatever happened to be cookin' at all the various establishments.

My stomach growled. But there were several things needin' to be done before I could see to that, and some of 'em needed to be done before the stores closed fer the night.

Too bad we were runnin' so low on money.

I glanced to Charlotte. She was slumped in her saddle, lookin' as exhausted as I felt. She'd braided her hair as usual, but long strands of it had come loose throughout the day and fallen across her face and down her neck, curly and damp with sweat.

And a surge of anger welled in me at seein' her in such a state. Anger at Duster fer havin' accosted us at Copperwell, forcin' us to push harder than I woulda liked over the last two days. Anger at Charlotte herself fer leavin' the safety and comfort of her own home to come out here. Anger at myself fer not bein' more insistent that she go on back home ... fer bein' the reason that bounty hunter was after us ... fer ever gettin' her involved with my predicament in the first place.

She shouldn't have to endure this. Any of this.

I pulled my gaze away from her as she started to turn her head and silently cursed myself fer all of it. "I'll get us rooms fer the night," I croaked, then cleared my throat. Days in the heat with little water had withered my voice.

"I'll go with you," Charlotte said immediately, pullin' her stallion from the trough.

"No," I snapped, then checked my tone when her eyes widened. "No," I repeated, gentle this time. "You and Holt should go by the general store. Replenish our food stores before it closes up fer the night. We'll want to be on the first train outta here in the mornin'. Won't give us much time fer shoppin' then. We should do it now."

She studied me fer a minute, like she might be weighin' my points to determine their true value.

I didn't miss the displeased glare Holt sent me, neither. He saw through my reasonin', anyway, even if Charlotte hadn't quite worked it out yet.

I wanted him gettin' those supplies honestly this time, and if he had Charlotte along, he'd be forced to do it that way. No matter that it'd probably cost him the rest of his coin. We'd figure out how to fix that later.

"All right," she said at last. "Fine."

"Think you can handle that?" I asked Holt.

He straightened indignantly in his saddle and pulled his gelding away from the trough, too. "Sure. I can handle that."

"Good. Then I'll secure stalls fer the horses and rooms fer us. Meet me back at..." I scanned the multitude of signs that spanned the length of the street in the swiftly fadin' daylight till I found one that seemed suitable. "Meet me back at the Ownby Boarding House."

"Sure," Holt said, and then he nodded at Charlotte, and the two of 'em headed off.

I headed off myself, toward the boardin' house. Looked like an okay establishment; well-built and well cared fer, but lackin' the kinda finesse to it that would suggest we couldn't afford it. So I hitched Joe up in front of it and went inside. Got us three rooms and ordered us food and whiskey, and then *I* was outta coin.

Weren't sure exactly how we'd get on that train tomorrow ... guess we'd have to figure that out later, too.

Night had come full-on and I was just startin' to get worried when Holt and Charlotte finally appeared, and I let out a breath of relief as they made their way over to my table.

"Everythin' go all right?" I waved at the place's proprietor, and he nodded, then gestured fer a young lady I guessed were his daughter from their vague resemblance, and she slipped into the back to grab our food.

"Sure," Holt said. He pulled out a chair fer Charlotte, then one fer himself.

I raised my brows at the old man. Hadn't known he possessed any manners.

"Yes," Charlotte said, droppin' down into the seat with a thankful sigh. "Fine. We should have enough to last us several more days in the saddle."

"Bein' as we don't exactly know how far the train can take us toward Blackbird, yet," Holt added.

"Good. Good."

The young lady emerged from the back, balancin' three heapin' plates, and set 'em down one in front of each of us. Beef and onions, carrots and potatoes, cornbread. She swiped her hands on her apron and smiled at us. "I'll be right back with your whiskey."

She disappeared again.

The three of us fell to eatin' without much talkin', tired and hungry as we were, and when the young woman returned with our bottle of whiskey and three glasses, we helped ourselves to that, too. When we'd finished our meal, I volunteered to take the horses to the livery. Urged Holt and Charlotte to go ahead and retire fer the night, since we'd need an early start the next day.

To my surprise, neither of 'em argued. Not even Holt. The heat and dehydration musta drained him more than I'd suspected.

We all said our good nights, and I made sure the both of 'em had retired to their rooms, and Charlotte had locked hers, before I headed back out to get the horses. I'd take 'em to the livery, sure.

But then I was gonna look around Redemption some more, see if I couldn't find us some ... *charitable donations*.

XIV

GOOD SAMARITAN

Robbin' folk in the middle of a town was always tricky.

Drunks made the easiest targets, of course, but they also tended to carry little coin, considerin' they'd already spent most of it on their drink, or sometimes other vices.

The best time to rob a person in the middle of a town was in the evenin', when they'd finished their daily work and had gathered up what money they had before headin' out to the saloon or the brothel fer the night. If you could catch 'em before they spent it, you could get awful lucky sometimes.

But I'd already missed that opportunity. All of Redemption's folks were already wherever they wanted to be fer the night. In their homes, in the saloons, in the brothels. Already spendin' that money.

Fer awhile I just walked the streets, observin' people, considerin' my options. Redemption was a fair-sized town, and it had its share of the wealthier population. Robbin' rich folk had a better pay-off, but it was also riskier. Rich folk tended to get real mad about bein' robbed. And they had the money and the influence to convince the law to do somethin' about it. And sometimes they held long-standin' grudges.

And sometimes they posted a fifty-thousand dollar bounty fer you and made yer life miserable.

I sighed and pulled up the collar of my duster against possibly bein' recognized fer want of that particular sum of money.

I angled toward an electric sign that proclaimed the presence of a stage theater and movie house. Wealthier folk liked to go to those places, I knew. Liked to think it gave 'em culture, or somethin'. Whatever that meant. Least, that's what Mama had always told me.

Not that we hadn't gone to such shows a time or two as a family, ourselves.

I lingered around the establishment until whatever show that had been playin' ended, and folks started pourin' outta the place. They were all talkin' excitedly and looked in awful high spirits. Well, someone's night was about to have a bad turn.

But they'd get over it. Coulda been worse. They coulda had a sister bein' held by Nine-Fingered Nan. Coulda had to have their leg sawed off. Coulda had a whole buncha shady individuals wantin' to take off the metal replacement, too. Coulda had a licensed bounty hunter after 'em.

I scanned quick over the departin' crowd, tryin' to decide on the best target, until a mighty familiar figure over at the other corner of the building caught my eye.

And it was right about that time he recognized me, too.

I straightened from where I'd leaned against the front wall of the establishment. "*Holt?!*"

"*Van?!*" he hissed back. "The hell are you doin' here? Thought you went to put up the horses!"

"I did!" I crossed over to him, excusin' my way through the rest of the people exitin' the theater to plant myself right in front of him, crossin' my arms. "And I thought *you* said you were gonna get some sleep?"

"Ha! Fat chance of that. Came to take some air."

I squinted at him. "We're an awful long way from that boardin' house."

He squinted back at me. "And an awful long way from the livery, too."

I blew out a breath and uncrossed my arms, puttin' my hands instead on the tops of my guns. That was a fair point, but I weren't sure I should tell him my real purpose here. I glanced back toward the dispersin' crowd. If I didn't go quick, decide on someone to follow, I was gonna miss my chance...

"Unbelievable," Holt muttered, bringin' my focus back to him.

"What's unbelievable?"

"Yer out here lookin' fer donations, ain't you?"

"I just—"

"After all that nonsense you spouted off the other day about it not bein' yer nature—"

"It ain't," I snapped. "It ain't my nature, it's *necessary*." I jabbed a finger into his chest with the last word.

He knocked my hand away.

"We gotta get on that train tomorrow," I hissed, mindful of the people who still meandered by occasionally. "And we're outta money."

"Yeah," Holt said, also keepin' his voice low now, "that's what I been sayin'. But you had to go and get up on yer High Horse, didn't ya? You said we had to do it honest."

"Yeah, well..." I shifted on my feet, lookin' again to the stragglers that were left now, wanderin' away into the dark. "Turns out we don't got time fer that."

"Ya don't say?"

I didn't much appreciate his scathin' tone and shot him a glare.

"So?" he prompted. "We gonna do this or not? You pick a target yet?"

"Naw," I grumbled. "Saw yer ugly mug and stopped lookin'."

He scoffed. "Good thing I'm here, then. I got someone in mind."

Again, I turned to look about the front of the place, which had now almost entirely emptied. "And where, exactly, would this person be?"

Holt smiled beneath his scraggly gray beard and slapped a hand to my shoulder. "Just follow me, kid." He stepped around me and headed off with a rather confident stride, so I followed, all right.

It became clear just who he'd selected soon enough. We caught up to 'em as they walked leisurely arm-in-arm, a young couple, finely dressed. Probably married only a few weeks, judgin' by the blush that graced the woman's cheeks and the stupid grin plastered across the man's face.

They turned a corner to head toward the numerous residences built just outside the town proper, and I saw the glint of a pocket watch at his breast, and a fat ring on her left hand. Not to mention the pearls around her neck, and her earrings. And whatever money they happened to have on 'em, of course.

They were a good pick. A real good pick.

I moved to Holt's side, gave him a nudge. "Good Samaritan?" I whispered.

He looked to me in surprise, then grinned and nodded. He darted off down the next alley to our left to get ahead of our couple and pick a good spot in another alley, and I kept followin' 'em. It was a ploy we'd engaged in many times over our years together.

Holt played the victim; a poor, hapless old man, and I played the bad guy, preyin' on the weak. Acted like I was robbin' him just as our real target passed by. It only worked on a certain type of people, of course, but that certain type would *always* intervene, sure enough.

They'd rush right into the alley to save the poor old man, and then we'd rob 'em blind.

This young couple ... well, they sure looked like just the type of folk who'd rush to Holt's aid, all right.

And as it turned out, they were.

We got back to Ownby's Boarding House before midnight with more than enough cash to cover our three seats and three stalls on the train, plus a fair amount of jewelry to sell, too, fer more cash or maybe fer trade ... once we found a proper place to sell or trade 'em.

That couple had been awful put-out, a course, but mostly they'd just seemed genuinely shocked and horrified that their noble effort to prevent an injustice had backfired so spectacularly as to leave 'em without all of their hard-earned cash, one of their wedding gifts, and two of their family heirlooms.

Well, they were awful young still. They'd figure it out eventually.

We'd tied 'em real good and gagged 'em and left 'em in a spot no one would find 'em fer a good long while. Long enough fer us to get outta town. But not long enough to cause 'em any real bodily harm.

And so, Holt and I went to bed that night feelin' awful proud of ourselves. We hadn't had a robbery go so quiet and smooth fer a good long while.

I shut myself in my room almost whistlin'. Hung up my hat and my gunbelts, set my boots by the end of the bed, and crawled under the covers. Couldn't remember the last time I'd laid down fer sleep feelin' so content.

Oh wait. That's right. There was that night at the Seven Knives Saloon, after Nora and Nettie had given me their very particular attentions fer hours on end and taken everythin' outta me.

But aside from that night, it'd been a long, long while, certainly.

I slipped just as easily into sleep this night ... only sleep didn't treat me so gentle.

The nightmares came again strong as ever.

I snapped awake with the echo of my own yell still in my ears, adrenaline tinglin' in my limbs. Took me a minute to come out of it, realize where I was, and the soft light of dawn comin' through the crack in the curtain was a welcome relief.

Meant I didn't have to go back there. Back to those damned nightmares.

Couldn't even remember which one this had been. Mama and Pa's murder? My frantic search fer Ethelyn? Findin' her dead? That poor nameless girl lookin' up at me while she died in my arms? Or maybe it had been Charles Miller again with his pliers and knives and brandin' irons.

I shuddered, exhaled, and sagged back onto the mattress, skin damp with sweat.

Well, none of that mattered now. I was awake again, and with no time to entertain any of those horrors. I fumbled at the night table beside me till my fingers found the stolen pocket watch. I grabbed it, flipped it open, checked the time.

Oh good. Train station should be open by now. And we had plenty of time fer breakfast, gettin' the horses, and gettin' to the platform to buy our tickets before the train itself arrived.

I scrubbed a hand over my face and clambered out of bed. Put myself back together slowly, feelin' more tired than I woulda liked thanks to those awful dreams. I stopped in front of the small mirror above the vanity to tidy myself up a bit, but there weren't too much I could do without another bath and a shave and maybe a laundry service. Maybe I shoulda took advantage of those things while we were here.

Funny how the regular presence of a woman seemed to constantly remind me of how rough I looked.

Scowlin' and shakin' my head, I gave up.

I went to Charlotte's room first, hopin' to have at least a few minutes with her before Holt brought down the mood, as he was invariably known to do.

I rapped on her door, then swore and belatedly tucked in my wayward shirt-tail.

But she didn't answer.

I knocked again, waited.

Still no answer.

I shifted on my feet, glanced both ways down the empty hall. Maybe she was just especially exhausted from our two-day ride. So I knocked again, hard and forceful this time, loud enough to wake her, but hopefully not loud enough to wake anyone else in the nearby rooms. "Charlotte? You awake in there?"

Silence. No murmured voices in reply. No footsteps across the floor. Nothin'.

Concern tightened in my belly. I knocked one more time, rattlin' the door in its frame. "Charlotte? You all right?"

The door to my left yanked open and a thin, disheveled man dressed only in his union suit stepped out, glarin' at me through heavy lidded, waterin' eyes. "Hey!" he slurred. "The hell is goin' on out here? Folk tryin' ta sleep!"

The door behind me opened then, too. Holt's room.

I didn't even turn around as I heard him step out into the hall. "What is it?" he asked, and I could tell by the strain in his voice he was ready fer trouble. Probably already had his guns on and his hand ready, too.

But I didn't answer him, or the man to my left. Instead I dropped my own hand down to rest lightly on the grip of my right pistol, set my left shoulder against Charlotte's door with a wince, and tried the knob.

To my surprise, the door swung open freely, and I nearly pitched face-first onto the floor as I stumbled through it. I'd expected it to be locked.

It had not been locked.

I righted myself and took in the room at a glance, the concern in my belly hardenin' into dread. Not only had the door not been locked...

Charlotte was gone.

XV

GONE MISSIN'

Fer a good long minute I just stood there starin' at the empty bed, my breath stuck in my throat as my mind raced through all the terrible possibilities of where she mighta gone or what mighta happened to her.

I hardly heard Holt step in behind me, hardly saw him come up beside me, hard gaze sweepin' the room.

"Huh," he said. "She's gone."

The bed was neatly made, sheets tucked into crisp corners and everythin'. Weren't a trace of any of her stuff anywhere. The window was closed, the curtains opened to let in the soft mornin' light.

Sure didn't look like someone had grabbed her, anyway. No signs of a struggle, none of her belongings left behind.

"Well. That'll sure make our train trip cheaper," Holt stated. Then he turned and ambled back out into the hall, apologizin' to the man next door and lettin' him know there weren't no trouble. There was more murmured conversation, and then the sound of the neighborin' door shuttin' again.

But I still just stood there, strugglin' to understand.

Had she ... had she just left? On her own? Of her own free will?

Why? And ... and where would she go? Was it 'cause of me? Was it 'cause I'd snapped at her last night? 'Cause I hadn't let her come with me to the livery? 'Cause we'd made such a fuss when she'd first said she wanted to come with us to Blackbird? Would she have gone there by herself, then? Without us?

"Van?"

I startled and turned around to see Holt in the doorway.

He arched an eyebrow and jerked his chin in the direction of the stairs at the end of the hall. "You comin'? I want some decent grub before we get stuck inside a train fer days."

I blinked. Frowned. Looked back over my shoulder to peer at the empty room one last time. But there was just nothin'. Nothin' out of the ordinary. Nothin' that might tell me where she'd gone, or why. Not even a note. I sighed and pulled off my hat to run my fingers through my hair, then resettled it back on my head. "Sure. Yeah. I'm comin'."

Holt gave a snort as I left the room and pulled the door shut again behind me. "Are you ... are you *sulkin'*?"

"What? No."

"Uh huh. That why you look like a god-damned kicked puppy?"

I growled as I pushed my hat a little lower on my head, a little forward to shade my face a bit more as we headed fer the stairs. "Don't know what yer talkin' about," I muttered. "Don't like the thought of her out there on her own, is all. You should know that."

"Oh I think I know that, all right."

I glared at him, and we started down the stairs. "She's already been nabbed once. And that was all the way over in Pennsylvania! You'd think she'd know better than to go wandering off all by her lonesome, especially around here."

"You'd think," Holt agreed, but I got the sense he was patronizin' me. He went on again before I could make a rebuke. "Just look at it this way, kid. Now we don't gotta worry about how we do things, right? Remember how you were all worked up about hidin' our business? Now we don't gotta fret about it. Good riddance, I say."

"You were the one who said she might be good in a fight," I pointed out.

We reached the main floor and the common room, set with multiple tables and already startin' to fill with people takin' breakfast. And yet it lacked the presence of any red-haired women as much as the room upstairs had. Another wave of concern twisted at my gut. If only she had at least said *where* she might be goin'...

Holt waved at the man behind the desk across the way, and he gave a nod in acknowledgement. Then the old man turned to me. "Yeah, sure. I did say she might be good in a fight. But you made it clear you wouldn't be lettin' her do any fightin'." He dropped his voice. "Or any robbin' or murderin'." He raised his voice again. "So what's the use, then? And if she can't be useful, then her takin' off is good riddance. That's all I'm sayin'."

I only grumbled at him, havin' no good argument to the contrary. He was right. Right about all of it. Charlotte bein' gone *would* make things a whole lot easier, especially once we got to Blackbird.

Too bad all his good reasonin' weren't makin' me feel no better about it.

He picked a table, and we sat, and the same young lady as the night before brought us coffee, heapin' bowls of porridge, boiled eggs and a plate of dried fruit. Holt dug into his, but I found myself without much of an appetite. So I mostly just picked at mine, managed a few bites, and then a familiar figure stepped through the boarding house front door.

I shot to my feet so fast I bumped the table, and Holt swore as his coffee sloshed out into his porridge.

"Charlotte!" I barked.

She looked my direction in surprise, then smiled as she recognized us and made her way to our table. "Oh good, you're awake. I was about to come up and rouse you."

She wore an outfit I hadn't yet seen on this trip, and I wondered where she'd been stashin' it. It was cream-colored and clean, all except the rim of her flared ridin' pants, anyway, which were caked in dirt same as her boots. The top was a fitted jacket, and a purple silk neckerchief—scarf—was bunched at her neck. She looked like she'd had a wash herself, all shiny and clean, and she'd wrapped her long hair into a coiled bun, donned her straw hat again, and wore that gunbelt with my old pistol smart around her hips.

I stared at her. "I ... you, uh ... you..."

"You left," Holt said flatly. "Gave us quite a fright, young lady."

I managed to pull my gaze away from Charlotte long enough to squint down dubiously at him. He kept eatin', not payin' any attention to either me or Charlotte and surely not lookin' concerned in the least about her brief disappearance.

She, too, eyed him skeptically. "Oh my, really?"

"Well, ya sure gave *one* of us a fright," he grumbled into his porridge.

I cleared my throat as Charlotte looked back to me with a frown. "I was just, uh ... concerned," I managed. "You know ... you might still have people out there lookin' fer you, Miller's men, maybe ... or someone else, even, and I thought ... I mean I didn't want ... I think it's better if none of us wander off alone." I spit the last of it out all at once, frustrated by the sudden difficulty of findin' the right words.

She lifted her eyebrows. "Oh? *None* of us should wander off alone?" She gave me a pointed look, then shifted it to Holt, but he was focused on his food.

Warmth rose into my cheeks as I realized she was probably seein' right through to my real meanin', but I stuck by my claim. "None of us. Not after what happened at Copperwell."

"Ah." Her dark blue eyes came back to me. "I see." Whether or not she believed me now, she let it go, to my relief. "Well, as you can plainly see, I am perfectly fine. The morning has been productive, but uneventful. I only went to freshen up and purchase our train tickets—"

"*What?*" I blurted the word in unison with Holt.

She had his full attention now. He dropped his spoon into his bowl and sat back in his chair, starin' up wide-eyed at her.

Charlotte looked at the both of us like maybe we'd gone crazy. "Whatever is the matter with that? Aren't we taking the train to Blackbird? Wasn't that the plan?"

"You shouldn't have paid our passage," I said, and I grabbed immediately for the little pouch on my belt that held all my coin. And that stolen pocket watch. And that stolen ring. "Here. I'll pay you back fer mine."

"No," Charlotte said. "Absolutely not. It's a long trip, and not cheap, especially with our mounts. Do you think I came out here without funds for supplies or travel? Or for anything else I might need? I've got plenty to cover it, just let me do you this kindness."

"No," Holt and I both said in unison again.

Charlotte seemed awful put-out, then. An expression came over her face that reminded me somewhat of the way she'd looked the night she'd ended Baron Whittaker, her glare bright and fierce as she raked it across me and Holt both. "This is precisely why I left early this morning," she hissed. "So I needn't have this argument yet again. I will not take your money, either of you. If you put it on that table, that's where it will stay. Now, I'm going to have some breakfast. I suggest you finish yours. The train leaves promptly at eight twenty-two."

With that, she spun sharply on her heel and left us—again— choosin' an entirely different table to sit at.

I watched after her with my hand still searchin' in my belt pouch ... but I gave up shortly after with a sigh. Least she weren't wanderin' around the Territories somewhere by herself. Least she hadn't left us entirely. And that bein' the case, I didn't need her any more upset with me than she was already.

"Ain't right," Holt muttered, sittin' forward in his seat to resume his meal. "Her spendin' all that money on the likes of us. That woman is almost as stubborn as you."

I snorted. "Maybe." I took my seat back and picked up my spoon again. I watched Charlotte from the corner of my eye as she received her food and coffee, half of me wantin' to go over there to try and make amends. But maybe I'd wait till she didn't look quite so angry.

She *had* burned out Baron Whittaker's eyes, after all. And burned up his genitals. And then shot him point-blank. And she'd knocked Holt out cold, as well, when she'd thought the old man was gonna shoot me.

Yeah, I'd just wait. Few more minutes wouldn't hurt nothin'....

"Hey," Holt said suddenly. "How much money you think she's got on her, anyway?"

I switched my gaze back to him quick and fixed him with the most serious look I could muster. "No," I said, and it came out dead serious. "Absolutely not."

He lifted his hands, porridge drippin' off his spoon to spatter the table. "All right, all right. Don't get yer dander up. Was just curious, is all. But how much you think her family is really worth?"

"Holt. You lift even one coin off her and I swear to the Holy Mother you'll regret me savin' yer neck."

He grinned, then chuckled and shook his head. "Careful, boy. That kinda talk can get ya into trouble."

I shrugged. "I don't mind trouble. Me and trouble get along just fine."

That got a bark of laughter outta him. "Do ya now?"

"Sure."

"Uh huh." He chuckled again and let out a low whistle. "Sure, kid. Sure. Like I said, just curious, is all. Just curious." He went back to his porridge, scrapin' out what was left of it, actin' like our conversation hadn't happened at all.

I glared at him fer a good long while more, till I was certain he'd got the notion of robbin' Charlotte or her family outta his head. Then, finally, I relaxed and tucked into my own food at last.

Too bad it was cold now.

XVI

BETTER SAFE THAN DEAD

Eight twenty-two came sooner than I'd expected.

We passed the rest of breakfast, the journey to the livery, the fetchin' of our horses, and the ride to the station in a stiff silence that itched at me good as a swarm of sand flies. But I weren't sure exactly how to fix it, so I just stayed silent, hunched in my saddle and broodin' over how we'd even ended up in this state.

We got to the train platform just as the thing itself pulled up, hissin' and steamin' and blowin' its whistle fit to make all the horses nervous. But we coaxed 'em up to it, showed the conductor our honest-bought tickets, and he pointed us in the direction of the livestock car. So we moseyed on down that way, dismounted, showed our tickets again, and handed our mounts off to the handlers.

Charlotte spoke to them at length, insistin' our animals be treated with utmost care, makin' sure that was clearly understood, and handin' over some extra money to ensure complete comprehension.

Holt and I stuck close by in the meantime, both watchin' the bustle of the platform with wary interest. We didn't travel much by train, neither of us. Didn't have much use fer it, most times. And truth be told, I didn't much like it.

Didn't much like all these people runnin' about here, neither. Good place fer pick-pockets. Hard to keep track of all the faces to try and note which ones might be familiar or not.

Or friendly or not.

My scannin' gaze stuck suddenly on the hulkin' shadow of a man standin' at one corner of the station building. He leaned his shoulder casually against the wall, and his ankles were crossed and his chin dipped low like he didn't have a care in the world, but there was somethin' about him I didn't like.

Maybe it were the fact I couldn't see his face beneath the lowered brim of his hat. Maybe it were the way he was all tucked into the shadows of the building and the awning that covered all the benches fer waitin' passengers. Maybe it were the fact he weren't sittin', but nor was he involved in any other business like all the rest of the people on the platform currently.

He was only standin' there. Loose and still—too still, thumbs tucked into his gunbelt.

A crawlin' sensation rippled up my arms, like he was somehow watchin' me without watchin', and my right hand went down to my gun. I brushed the grip fer reassurance, kept my palm there restin' lightly.

Better safe than dead.

I glanced to Holt, but he was lookin' out in the other direction.

So I squinted back at the shadowed man, and entertained the idea of goin' over to confront him. If he were just a fella mindin' his own business, no harm would come of it. But if he were a man after me fer that fifty thousand dollars—or any multitude of other reasons—it'd be better to put a bullet in him now.

Except ... except there were an awful lot of witnesses here, if it did happen to come to that.

"Shit," I muttered.

A commotion at the train car behind me made me tense and turn, only to find it was Charlotte's stallion causin' the ruckus. Holt's gelding and my mule had boarded easily enough, but the roan was none too happy about this situation. He pinned his ears and danced away from the handler, eyes goin' wide as the man tried to lead him up the ramp.

The handler held tight to the reins as the stallion reared up a little, and I swore more under my breath. This was just what we needed. A damn horse causin' a scene, drawin' all kinds of attention...

"Hey," Charlotte said sharply, and I thought she was talkin' to the man tryin' to lead her horse before I realized her glare was fixed on her mount, instead. She stalked over to him and took the reins back from the pale-faced handler, then turned to the horse and pointed a finger at him like he were a child instead of a thousand-pound animal. "You stop that," she scolded. "This is no time for that nonsense. Behave yourself!"

The roan blew at her loudly, still dancin' and throwin' his head. But his ears had come up now instead of bein' pinned flat-back, and swiveled around as if he were tryin' to take in the whole platform at once.

Charlotte turned to the man still waitin' beside the ramp. "Why don't you show me what stall you want him in? I'll take him."

The man nodded wordlessly. He looked relieved. I didn't blame him.

An angry stallion weren't nothin' you wanted to mess with.

They all disappeared inside the train car, the roan followin' Charlotte up into the dim interior with hardly a hesitation.

I took that chance to turn back and check on that shadowy man I didn't much like. But he was still just standin' there. He hadn't moved at all. Hadn't looked up at the commotion.

Maybe he weren't here fer me. Maybe he weren't a threat at all.

Maybe he were just a real tired fella who'd fallen asleep standin' up.

Maybe I was startin' to get just as jumpy as Holt.

I shook my head and followed up the ramp after Charlotte and her horse just to keep an eye on things, but paused in the doorway to stay out of the way as they got the roan settled.

Charlotte untacked him, urged him into the little stall, and patted his neck as he snorted again. "There, there, now, Sugar. You'll be all right." She pulled another handful of dollars from her belt pouch for the man who stood watchin' her, bewildered. "For the trouble," she told him. "He can be a little bull-headed, but he's not mean-spirited. Now, like I said, I want exceptional care for him and the others in my party, you understand? I trust you can see to that?"

The man took the money in one grubby hand and nodded. "Sure thing, ma'am."

I watched him close through narrowed eyes, but he seemed honest enough. Didn't seem to have the twitchy nature common to most unsavory types.

And so, our mounts all taken care of, Charlotte and I descended the ramp and rejoined with Holt to make our way back to the passenger cars and get our own selves similarly settled fer the journey.

I kept my hand light on my pistol grip, once again tossin' a glance to that sleepy shadowed man as we passed him by, separated by at least twenty yards and plenty of busy folk. Still, he didn't stir. Didn't so much as twitch.

Some of the tension in my knotted shoulders relaxed. I caught up to Charlotte's side just as Holt was askin', "You really name that beast of yers Sugar, or is that just yer chosen term of endearment?"

She scoffed. "That's his name. And he's hardly a beast."

"Coulda fooled me," I commented.

"What kinda name is *Sugar* for a *stallion*, anyway?" Holt said.

Charlotte's eyes narrowed as she turned to glare at him. "It's a mighty fine name, thank you very much. For a mighty fine steed. He really is sweet as sugar most the time. The train has him upset, that's all."

Holt grunted. "The train has me upset, too. Never much liked bein' stuck fer hours in a little tin can."

Charlotte and I both ignored his grumblin', as we'd reached the conductor once more. We flashed those tickets a third time, and he ushered us pleasantly on board.

I let Charlotte and Holt climb the stairs first and went up last myself. A prickle at the back of my neck made me turn just as I topped 'em; a naggin' feelin' to take one last look across the platform. Just to be sure.

A habit honed by years of livin' as an outlaw now, and sharpened by the outstandin' presence of that fifty thousand dollar bounty on my head.

My eyes went first toward that shadowed man leanin' against the wall. Another habit.

Only he weren't there no more.

He was gone.

My fingers tightened around the railin' that encircled the back of the train car, my heart jumpin'. I searched the millin' crowd below me frantically, but saw no one there that resembled him.

He'd vanished.

I hardly noticed our walk through the various cars toward our seats, preoccupied by thoughts of that suspicious, shadowed fella, and by checkin' every face we passed to see if they looked familiar.

But I didn't see anyone recognizable on the train; didn't even see anyone who resembled the fella from outside. Fer some reason that didn't make me feel no better, and I was still distracted by the time we reached our berths.

"Here we are," Charlotte said. She'd stopped outside a pair of wooden slidin' doors. "I'll take this one. You two have the next two down the way, next door." She nodded her head to the right, further toward the front of the train.

Holt let out a low whistle, lookin' over the doors we stood in front of and then over at the next two sets of doors. "Three? You got us each our own space?"

Charlotte shrugged. "Sure. Seemed the most comfortable option." She slid open one of her doors to reveal the chamber on the other side, and the sight of it finally made me forget my frettin'.

I'd never seen a train space like it, that was fer certain.

Of course, on the rare occasions I happened to travel by train, I always picked the cheap seats. The hard wooden benches in the back. Never could afford anythin' better than that. Certainly never anythin' like this.

It was spectacular.

Plushly furnished, the walls wood-paneled, with an upholstered chair and a small table tucked in underneath a luxurious-looking bunk draped with thick bedsheets, and a window framed in floral-patterned curtains. It even had electric lights.

Charlotte cleared her throat and I blinked, comin' outta my stupor to look to her in question.

"You boys want to get settled?" she prompted. "The train will be pulling out soon and they'll want everyone seated."

"Oh," I said. "Right."

As if emphasizin' her point, the steam engine gave a long, loud blow of its whistle.

I moved to take the compartment next to hers, and Holt took the one next to mine, mutterin' under his breath. A pair of finely dressed folk squeezed past us in the corridor as we reached our respective doors, and I couldn't help but notice the way they wrinkled their noses as they passed.

Well. We probably coulda used another wash, sure.

And I bet we stood out like sore thumbs here, too, and not just because of our smell. Our clothes were sweat-stained, covered in dust, and clearly not new. A stark contrast to their own sparklin' clean tweed suits.

They probably wondered how in the hell we'd managed to find our way up here.

Suddenly self-conscious, I stepped quickly into my compartment and slid the doors shut behind me. At least these fancy berths offered a lot of privacy. We'd be safe enough from pryin' eyes and contemptuous looks enclosed in these here spaces. And the doors even locked, too.

I locked mine now and heaved a sigh of relief, sinkin' down into the chair and finally allowin' myself to relax.

The hard part of this journey was over with, now. This train would speed us along across the country and get us to Akansa in no time. Then I just had to find Blackbird, find Dr. Balogh, find those ruins, and then figure out what exactly I was gonna do with that information.

What exactly I was gonna do with Nine-Fingered Nan.

I leaned back in that soft chair and tipped my hat down over my face. Well, I had two whole days stuck in this damned tin can, like Holt had said.

Surely I could think of somethin' by then.

XVII

HUNTED

Turned out it only took one day trapped in that little tin can to make me restless as a caged circus tiger. I walked through the cars a bit, tryin' to settle myself, till the other passengers started givin' me suspicious side-eye and one of the train employees told me I really needed to sit down as I was makin' folk nervous.

Guess I probably did look more like someone who might rob 'em rather than just another traveler. So then I occupied myself by takin' little walks each time we stopped at a station. And in-between stops, sometimes I found a game of cards or dice in the lounge car. We took lunch and then dinner in the fancy kitchen car set aside fer the wealthy folk with the private berths.

Wealthy folk like we was pretendin' to be at the moment.

I had to admit, it was better than the jerky and bread I usually brought with me.

After dinner, Charlotte gave me one of her books and told me to read to soothe my mind, but I couldn't seem to focus on the words. There was too much botherin' me still. Too much left unknown and uncertain.

So I gave up. Shut the book and set it aside and went back to that kitchen car. They had a bar there. A bar that served up plenty of whiskey.

If there was anythin' that could soothe my mind of its many concerns, it'd be whiskey.

The rhythmic noise of the train coastin' along the tracks, the slight sway of the car, the dim nighttime scenery blurrin' by outside the windows ... it was all kinda mesmerizin'. I sat there on one cushioned bench fer who knew how long, just watchin' the land outside slide gradually from brown and barren into one more green and fulla trees, swayin' along with the motion of the car, helped along somewhat by the three-fourths bottle of whiskey I'd drank by then.

To my surprise, Holt hadn't wandered in here yet. But he'd been deep into a game of poker last I'd seen him, and he was a hard man to get away from his cards even on his bad days.

And Charlotte ... well of course Charlotte weren't in here drinkin' herself stupid. She was still shut up in her little private room, probably readin' like a proper lady would. Or maybe doin' somethin' else they liked to do. Somethin' productive.

That left me here on my bench, all by my lonesome.

Just me and my whiskey.

Well, I supposed there were a few other fellas here, sure, leanin' on the bar and makin' small talk with each other. But none of 'em paid me any mind except fer tossin' me one of those contemptuous looks now and then.

I ignored 'em. Weren't nothin' I weren't used to.

It was real, real late by the time I roused myself from that mesmerizin' view to finally head back to my little room. Figured I should probably sleep some tonight. And I was far enough along into the bottle now I thought that might be possible.

And so I staggered outta the kitchen car and down the narrow corridors of those sleeper cars till my weary, blurred vision found my own little hidey hole. I slid the door open, but then paused in confusion.

It was dark in there. The only light came from what shone through the doorway from the corridor I stood in. My shadow stretched out long in the middle of the rectangle of light, and I stood there frownin', sure I'd left the lamp on.

Maybe the damn thing had burnt out while I'd been gone.

Grumblin', I crossed the small space to the opposite wall where the light had been screwed into place next to the window. My fingers fumbled fer the chain, except then I noticed those floral curtains had been pulled shut.

I might not have been sure about the light, but I was damn sure about the curtains, even in my inebriated state. I'd left 'em open.

I straightened; pulled the chain fer the light even as I set the mostly empty whiskey bottle down onto the table and swept my hand back fer my right pistol.

The light didn't come on. My foggy mind had barely registered that fact when a brush of sound came from behind me and I whirled, pullin' my piece, just as the door to my room shut.

Plunged into abrupt darkness, I didn't see the fist that came down onto my right wrist and jarred my pistol outta my grip. Then there was another fist that drove into my gut. I doubled over with a grunt only to get a crack in the chin that sent me staggerin' back into that table seein' stars.

The whiskey bottle rolled off onto the carpeted floor and I followed soon after it, strugglin' to regather my wits. I groped fer my left pistol, but hands on the back of my duster hauled me up to my feet, and I got slammed face-first up against the back wall, up against that curtained window, and my right arm got twisted brutally behind my back till a cry wrenched outta me. Felt like my shoulder was about to come outta the socket.

"All right, all right, take it easy," I ground through my teeth. "What the fuck do you want?"

The man holdin' me to the wall and nearly pullin' off my arm grunted. His free hand went to my left hip and relieved me of my second pistol. I heard it thump to the carpet, too. "Just you, Delano," he said. "You're worth enough all on your own."

I ground my teeth. Goddamned bounty hunters.

"You're an awful popular fella these days, ain't you?" he said, and I realized he sounded awful familiar. "Keep havin' to wade through a line of folk just to get at you, seems like. So here's what's gonna happen. You're gonna come with me, nice and quiet." I heard the clink of manacles as he pulled 'em from his belt. "We're gonna go have a seat in the mail car, and we're gonna get off at the next stop." He cuffed my right wrist, grabbed my left arm and wrenched it behind my back too. "And you ain't gonna cause any trouble at all, now, are ya?"

I opened my mouth to tell him there wasn't a chance of that in Hell, braced myself to push back off the wall into him, but before I could either speak or act, the door to my little room slid open force-fully, jarrin' on its hinges, and another shadow loomed in the resultin' splash of light.

The click of a hammer pulled back punctuated the sharp order, "Don't you move or I'll blow a hole right through you."

The bounty hunter and I both froze.

Charlotte. But my relief was short-lived, realizin' if she blew a hole through him, she'd blow a hole right through me, too. Surely she knew that.

Surely the bounty hunter also knew that.

Nevertheless, her intrusion gave him pause. I felt his weight shift from leanin' on me, presumably to look back at her and judge the true nature of what threat she might pose, but both his hands had been preoccupied with cuffin' me. He didn't have a weapon ready to point back at her.

He cleared his throat. "Good evenin', ma'am. Apologies if I woke you. But I think you'd rather not get involved in this. Like I told you before, it's all lawful business, and discharging a firearm, especially toward a warrant officer while he's trying to conduct that lawful busi-ness, on a train full of innocent folk no less, won't be taken well by local law, I can tell you that."

Warrant office—fuckin' hell. No wonder he sounded familiar.

It was that goddamned bloodhound of a bounty hunter Duster. Dustin Barrett.

Fuck me.

How in the hell he'd managed to squirrel away from Copperwell so quick after committin' murder, or track us across all that open desert without bein' spotted, or get on board this train along with us unnoticed was beyond me.

But none of that mattered now. All that mattered was how I was gonna manage to get away from him this time, trapped on a movin' train cuttin' through the middle of nowhere. A train fulla innocent folk, just like he'd said.

There were lots of witnesses here. Lots of people who could turn on us quick.

Fuck.

"And like I told *you* before, Mr. Barrett," Charlotte said coolly, "I have hired these men on business. For the time being, at least, they are under my protection ... and that of my father."

Duster gave a little laugh. "Ma'am, that's not exactly how this works. I don't think you understand what this man stands accused of—"

I planted a boot against the wall in front of me and shoved myself backwards, crashin' into him hard and knockin' him off balance. We both went down to the floor, me landin' on top of him, and I heard the air go out of him with an *oof*. His grip on my arms loosened; I yanked out of his hold and rolled off him, jumped to my feet—stumbled a bit thanks to the whiskey and that crack on my chin—and searched frantically fer a gun.

The nearest one was the pistol held outstretched in Charlotte's hands. My pistol. The one I'd given her. She still held it toward the bounty hunter, who was scramblin' to his feet now himself, but her eyes were on me. Her mouth opened like she were about to tell me somethin', and I realized abruptly she was still in her nightgown.

I'd never seen her in a night dress before.

Duster lurched up standin' behind me and the motion in my peripheral view pulled me from my momentary distraction. I snatched the gun from Charlotte's hands and darted past her out into the narrow hall.

"Van!" she blurted.

But I paid her no mind, chargin' away from her and headin' fer the car's back door.

Duster came after me, as I'd known he would; I heard Charlotte's alarmed gasp as he musta shoved past her.

"Mr. Barrett, I demand you stop this pursuit immediately!" she yelled out after us, but the bounty hunter didn't pay her any more mind than I had. He did not stop his pursuit, didn't even slow it. His runnin' boots thumped quick on the carpet behind me, gainin' fast.

He was taller than me, and had a longer stride.

Not to mention hadn't downed a whole bottle of whiskey just recently.

I couldn't outrun him fer long.

I shouldered through the car's back door, jumped the gap to the next car, and shoved the pistol into my holster so I could climb up on the railin' and then jump to grab hold of the edge of the roof. My left bicep strongly protested as I hauled myself up, and I hoped I hadn't just pulled out all of Holt's stitches. The pain pulsed from the bullet hole now, sharp and angry. I gritted my teeth and tried to ignore it.

Duster burst through the door behind me, but I weren't quite quick enough in my climb, and he saw my boots disappear up top.

So he started up after me.

"*Shit*." I shoved back to my feet and staggered again, this time not just 'cause of the whiskey, but 'cause of the swayin' train and the fierce wind that came with such a vehicle hurtlin' unhindered down a track in the middle of nowhere.

I suddenly questioned the wisdom of my decision to come up here. There were fewer obstacles in my path and fewer witnesses, sure ... but that also meant there were fewer obstacles fer Duster, and fewer witnesses to anythin' *he* might do, too.

'Cept then I remembered I had the high ground here.

So I braced my feet against the push of the wind and leveled my pistol at his head just as it appeared over his scrabblin' hands at the lip of the roof.

The manacles he hadn't quite managed to get on me dangled from my right wrist, and even though the rest of the world was all a bit wobbly, my hand was steady.

I glared down at him as he paused his climb. "Think real careful about how you want this to go down, bounty hunter."

He glared back up at me. "I could say the same to you, Delano."

"'Cept I ain't the one with a gun pointed at my face."

He smiled, gave a tilt of his chin in acknowledgement. "No. But like I told the lady, shootin' a licensed warrant officer won't reflect well on you with the local law. With any law anywhere, matter of fact."

I scoffed. Had to shout to be heard above the rushin' wind. "You seen all my posters, Mister. You think me shootin' another peace officer is gonna make any difference to the opinion of any law about me? I hardly think so. Shot a sheriff down in Destry just about two weeks back, even. I surely won't blink over shootin' you just the same." I thumbed my hammer back to make my point more clear.

Truth be told, most days I woulda shot him already. Woulda ended him without even thinkin' about it, and thrown his body off the train.

Why didn't I just shoot him now? My finger twitched on the trigger, but didn't pull.

All I kept thinkin' was how he'd been willin' to let that Sonoita sheriff give me a trial. I'd been locked up, easy pickin's fer a bounty hunter to make off with, and worth fifty thousand dollars ... and Duster had been willin' to chance sacrificin' that kinda money. Fer what? Respect fer his friend? Respect fer what Sheriff Longley was tryin' to do out here in the Territories? Respect fer the law?

Charlotte burst through the back door of the car we'd just come out of, still in her night dress, red hair whippin' wild around her face, and jolted me abruptly from my contemplations. She had another pistol, one of those I'd dropped back in my room.

I was about to yell out at her to go back inside, to stay outta this, not wantin' to chance her gettin' a poster of her own, but Duster took advantage of my eyes comin' off him and hooked a hand around my left ankle.

That was my metal ankle, so I didn't feel his hand grab me, but I sure felt it when he yanked my leg out from under me. I crashed to the roof, my pistol firin' as it jarred, but the bullet went wide. I landed on my back with a grunt, and then that bastard of a bounty hunter leveraged himself up onto the roof quick as a cat and pounced on me just as I was tryin' to roll back to my feet.

Charlotte shouted somethin', but I couldn't understand her.

I was too preoccupied with wrestlin' the man sittin' on top of me. I twisted under him and brought my gun hard across his face.

He sagged sideways, givin' me space to press the barrel of my pistol right up to his heart.

I didn't have time to fire; his left fist smashed into my right wrist hard enough to make my hand go numb. The gun went flyin'. It skittered away across the roof, disappeared over the edge.

"Fuckin' hell," I spat.

"God damnit, Delano," he growled, takin' two fistfuls of the front of my duster, "you are *really* starting to piss me off."

I grinned up at him. "That's what I'm good fer."

He cocked a fist back, presumably meant to knock me unconscious and shut me up fer awhile, but a shot rang out instead and the bounty hunter yelled as a spray of blood painted the left shoulder of his jacket.

The hand that woulda landed in my face went instead to cover the wound. Just a graze, looked like, but I'm sure it still hurt like hell.

I didn't waste time feelin' sorry fer him. I hit him good in the chin like he'd done to me earlier and shoved him off while he was reelin'. Then I jumped to my feet and whirled toward Charlotte, who'd climbed up here herself now, damnit. "Go back inside!" I snapped at her. "You don't want this on you."

I didn't wait fer her to reply or to argue, but took off again across the roof, aimin' fer the back of the train. Weren't entirely sure what my plan was ... didn't exactly have a plan at all, I supposed, I only knew I didn't want Charlotte involved in any of it.

Thumpin' bootsteps came after me again soon enough, too heavy to be hers with her bare feet and her night dress.

So Duster was up again and on the chase.

Fine. Long as he weren't payin' no attention to Charlotte fer nickin' him in the shoulder. Long as she didn't follow after us, too.

I came up quick on the end of this car; made the leap over the gap onto the roof of the next car.

And stumbled as the train made a curve around a rock bluff.

I hit my knees closer to the roof's edge than I woulda liked; got a dizzyin' view of the ground blurrin' by below, but then I was up and runnin' again.

And Duster right behind me.

Someone fired.

I ducked, but I couldn't tell if it was the bounty hunter or Charlotte shootin'.

Out here, the train's wheels clatterin' along the tracks was especially loud, and the damn wind whistlin' past didn't help things none, neither.

But I didn't slow, just kept on runnin', jumpin' from car to car.

Two more shots barked from behind, but I weren't too worried about 'em aimin' at me. At least, not aimin' fer a mortal wound.

Charlotte wouldn't be the one shootin' at me, clearly, and if Mr. Dustin Barret wanted that fifty thousand dollars, he was gonna have to get me to the Whittakers alive. At least that poster had been very explicit about that condition.

Else he probably woulda shot me back in my room when he'd got the jump on me, and I'd already be dead.

But if he thought I was gonna make takin' me alive easy on him, well, he was sorely mistaken.

I made another jump onto the next car, but only barely made it across. That whiskey was takin' its toll, and all this runnin' and jumpin'. My lungs and legs burned, muscles weakenin' as they tired out.

Goddamn, I didn't remember this train bein' so long.

But I was almost to the end of it now. Then I was gonna throw that Duster bastard over the side of it and be done with him. Quick and clean. And none of those innocent folk below would ever have to know anything about it...

"Delano!" Duster roared. "I swear to God, the more you make me chase you, the more hurt I'm gonna lay on you once I get ahold of you!"

"Too bad you need me alive fer that money," I called over my shoulder.

"Don't mean I can't shoot you plenty of places that won't kill you," he snarled back.

A bullet pinged off the train roof to my left, makin' me swear and jerk sideways, then stumble again.

Almost fell off the train my own damn self before I regained my balance and continued my run. If only I had any guns left to shoot back at him...

The memory of the one tucked away inside my metal leg came to me then, and I shuddered at all the other memories that came along with it. If only I could figure out how I'd managed to make the leg open ... I tried to will it open, now, runnin' along that train roof, tried to picture myself murderin' Duster just like I'd intended to murder Charles Miller at the time my leg had weaponized.

But nothin' happened. It stayed just as it always was, a regular collection of rods and gears, and I scowled.

Just as well, I supposed. Weren't sure how I'd get to all those weapons anyway, bein' as I was actually wearin' pants at the moment. And it surely weren't worth shuckin' those right now to try and figure it out.

I jumped yet another gap between cars—but in my current weary state I didn't quite make the distance. My boots missed the next roof and I flailed as I fell, only barely catchin' hold of the edge.

But my left arm was havin' none of this, and the bullet hole in my bicep spiked agony all the way up into my shoulder as I struggled to pull myself up. I hissed a curse as my grip slipped and I hit the deck below, anyway.

I was too slow to get up, breathin' hard and the world still rockin' from the train and the whiskey.

Duster dropped down next to me.

"All right," I panted, usin' the rail to haul myself back to my feet. "All right. Maybe we can talk about this—"

He decked me hard in the face.

I went backwards into the train car's door with the force of it, stumbled through it, right into the aisle between the rows of hard wooden benches.

The cheap seats.

The folk sittin' in 'em gasped at my rather forceful entrance into their space, some of 'em startled from their uncomfortable slumber.

But I used the momentum to turn and keep on goin', staggerin' down the aisle and noddin' pleasantly to people as I passed 'em, despite my now-throbbin' head and the fact I tasted blood. "Howdy, folks."

They stared at me wide-eyed and murmurs circled in my wake, around Duster, who stalked after me.

But he was movin' a lot slower now, too. I suspected he didn't want to cause a scene, neither. Maybe he'd managed to get outta Copperwell awful fast after his murder there, but it had cost him his prize that mornin', anyway.

Surely he didn't want that to happen again here.

So we both only walked quick down that aisle, stayin' as quiet and non-threatenin' as we could manage, and I made it to the back door and went through it, but stepped to the side and pulled my knife instead of tryin' to make the roof again or go through the next car.

We'd almost reached the caboose now, the mail car, and everyone knew the mail car carried a few armed gents nearby or inside to guard the enclosed valuables. I didn't want to get anywhere near those gents. Not fer this business.

I moved soon as Duster stepped through that doorway himself, aimin' a stab at his heart.

He was quick as a goddamned snake, blockin' the downward arc of my knife with his left forearm and drivin' his right fist into my gut again. I doubled over his arm as all the air went outta me, but even as I choked, tryin' to breathe again, I saw the glint of his right pistol's grip.

So close.

I snatched it fast with my left hand and straightened, spinnin' it on my index finger to land it properly in my palm, but he'd felt me pull it and was already movin' sideways as I fired.

The bullet that shoulda gone through his face instead splintered a chunk outta the back corner of the car we'd just come out of. Some of the folk inside screamed.

I ignored 'em, adjustin' my aim in an instant; saw the bounty hunter draw his second pistol at the same time he stepped toward me, and I didn't wait to see if maybe he'd go ahead and shoot me, and all that money be damned.

I fired again.

It weren't my best shot, not by far, but it tore through his chest high on the right side and made him stagger back with a cry. I braced my own self against the deck's railin' with my right hand and gave him a good solid kick in the chest with my metal foot.

He careened backward, hit the rail on the other side and then went over it, and disappeared into that blurrin' landscape.

I slumped, tryin' to get my air back, my grip on the railin' the only thing holdin' me up. I looked down to the gun in my left hand. It was a nice one. Well, he'd owed me a pistol anyway. I holstered it and limped to the opposite side of the narrow deck to lean over the rail and look back along the tracks.

We'd already left him far behind, the train movin' at such a speed that even if the fall hadn't killed him, he'd of never been able to catch onto it by the time it was already gone. A horse couldn'ta even caught up to this train at this speed. But he didn't have no horse, neither.

Injured the way he was, stuck in the middle of nowhere with no horse and no supplies ... well, I didn't put his odds of survival at too awful good.

And that was just fine with me.

I pushed away from the rail to turn back to the car fulla folk in the cheap seats. And realized they were all starin' horrified at me. That back door stood wide open, givin' 'em all a good, clear view of what I'd done to Mr. Dustin Barrett.

I straightened with a wince and cleared my throat. Tucked my right hand casually behind my back so maybe they wouldn't notice the manacles hangin' off that wrist. Tried to look unconcerned as I jerked my chin back in the direction of where the bounty hunter had disappeared along the tracks. And said the first thing that came to mind. "No ticket."

Their eyes grew wider. They looked from one to the other in a moment of shocked silence, and then all frantically scrambled to produce their own tickets, which they held up and waved about fer my benefit.

I blinked. Hadn't expected that to work.

But since it had, I made a show of glancin' over all of 'em as I ambled slowly back through the car, down the aisle between the seats. Now that the rush of the chase and the fight was over, all the hurt settled in and made itself at home. My left arm throbbed somethin' awful around that bullet wound, my chin and my middle were sore, and he'd split my lip with that last punch.

I swiped at the blood on my chin with a sleeve, nearly at the opposite door when Charlotte came through it and stopped me up short.

She halted abruptly herself, wild eyes lookin' me over before searchin' around the rest of the car. She gripped one of my pistols in her right hand, still wore her night dress and had no shoes, and her long hair was loose and wind-whipped, tangled and fallin' every which way, makin' her look more like a degenerate than a lady.

The people behind us gasped and murmured again at her appearance and I grimaced, takin' her shoulder to gently turn her around and usher her out of their view. I shut the door behind us and shrugged carefully outta my duster.

"Where is he?" she asked. "Where's Mr. Barrett?"

I swallowed. Shook my head as I settled my duster over her own shoulders and tugged it tight around her. "He's, uh ... he won't bother us anymore."

She stepped back from me with a start. "Did you kill him?!"

"No," I blurted before thinkin'. But then as she fixed me with a certainly skeptical look, I doubled down. "No. Only convinced him that maybe chasin' me weren't the wisest of decisions." Well, it weren't exactly a lie. I *hadn't* killed him. Directly.

Guess that was probably the real reason why I hadn't blown a hole through his skull when I'd had the chance up on the roof: Charlotte.

She was sure complicatin' things, all right. If not fer her, I coulda taken care of Mr. Barrett with a whole lot less effort. And a whole lot fewer bruises.

Her dark blue gaze narrowed up at me now, but I only reached out and lightly pried the pistol from her grip, slippin' it back into my other holster. Then I put an arm around her again and ushered her onward, back toward our berths.

"Do I need to speak to him further myself?" she asked.

"No. No, I think he got the message clear enough." I resisted the urge to look back over my shoulder, over the rail. That bounty hunter would be miles back by now. I opened the next door fer Charlotte, waved her through.

In truth I woulda rather not had both of us paradin' down the center aisle between curious and suspicious folk in our current state, but there was nothin' much to be done fer it. I weren't gonna take Charlotte back the whole way on the roof, and anyway, I didn't think I had the energy to climb up there again myself.

She held my duster close around herself as we went, and we made the rest of the walk to our rooms in silence.

"However did you end up like this?" Charlotte asked suddenly, softly.

I jolted from broodin' over my tussle with Mr. Dustin Barrett—over the fact I'd let him get the jump on me so good—to look at her with a start.

We sat in her room now, with its workin' electrical lamp, and I'd shucked my shirt so she could look at that hole in my bicep. I'd pulled out Holt's stitches in all the excitement, all right. But it'd been long enough now they looked about ready to come out anyway, so she was pullin' the rest of 'em free fer me and cleanin' it all up, and I had a fresh bottle of whiskey clutched in my right hand to dull the angry fire of the process.

We'd already picked the lock on those manacles and set 'em aside, so I'd been starin' into the steady shine of that lamp and tryin' to distract myself from the uncomfortableness of the scrubbin'.

And from the fact Charlotte was leanin' so close.

But her question surprised me enough to make me forget all that. I frowned at her. "I had a run-in with a particularly determined bounty hunter who is particularly good at huntin' people. And also particularly good at throwin' punches." I ran my tongue gingerly over the fresh split in my bottom lip and then winced. My head was achin', too.

She glanced up from her work on my arm, then pursed her lips and shook her head. Her red hair was still an awful mess, but she'd shed my well-worn duster now for a velvet house robe instead. Another garment I hadn't yet seen on our trip. And she'd pulled all these medical supplies from her pack, too. Made me wonder what else she might have hidden away in there.

"No," she chided. "I mean how did you end up like *this*." Her eyes flicked downward toward the mostly healed wound in my bicep. "Living like this. Getting shot at so much. Having men like Mr. Barrett after you. Having to be on the run so often. Always looking over your shoulder ... barely having a thing to call your own." She raised her eyes to mine again, and then her gaze wandered over my face, also bruised and bloodied thanks to Mr. Barrett, and to the scars over the rest of me.

Scars from Baron Whittaker's crowbar. Scars from Mr. Miller's electrical rod. A few others here and there from various jobs, scuffles, and barfights. And that weren't countin' the stripes on my back, neither. Those from Mr. Fisher when I'd been accused of stealin' his wife's fine silver.

I shifted on the plush armchair at that memory, at the familiar stab of bitter anger that always came with it, and shrugged. "Just do what I gotta do to survive," I muttered, and I weren't entirely sure then if I was really talkin' to her or myself. "Till I find Ethelyn."

Charlotte sat quiet fer a minute, seemingly contemplatin', but then she went back to those stitches. "That man you travel with—"

"Holt?"

"Yes. Holt. He's not your father."

I gave a snort and shook my head. "No. No he is not."

"So how did you end up with a man like him? You don't seem very much alike. I know he didn't really want to help me back in Blessing. And he would have kept all that money for himself. And I certainly know if he had been the one tied to that chair being tortured at Baron Whittaker's place, he would have let the baron kill all those slaves if it meant less pain for himself."

I tightened my grip on that whiskey bottle, knowin' it was probably true.

"He would have given me up right away, too. And probably told Whittaker where to find the doctor who made that leg."

Also probably true, unfortunately, so I said nothin'.

"But *you* didn't," Charlotte said, and she paused in her work again to sit back on her stool. "All along the way across the country, after those bandits kidnapped me, sometimes I was able to yell for help. And yet ... no one lifted a finger to aid me. You were the first person who seemed to care at all in a long time ... and then you even seemed to care about those strangers you didn't even know. So how in the world did you end up traveling with a man like Holt, living a life like ... like *this?*" She gestured at my sorry state.

I almost wanted to laugh. But it weren't funny, really. And the laugh stuck in my throat and then choked into somethin' that felt more like a sob, anyway, so I only ended up drinkin' more whiskey. "Dunno," I said finally. "Just bad luck, I guess."

Or good luck, dependin' on which way you looked at it. If not fer Holt findin' me, and carin' enough about the son of his once-best-friend to spring me, I woulda hanged at sixteen. Though whether or not the last eight years had been better than bein' dead ... well, sometimes I couldn't be sure.

Charlotte was quiet fer another long moment, long enough that the silence started to make me itchy. But then she asked, "Do you ever ... do you ever get tired of it? Of living like this?"

The question drew a long, quiet breath outta me that I made sure she couldn't hear over the sound of the train coastin' down the tracks, and I shrugged again. "Don't think about it much, I suppose."

And I didn't. Least, not anymore. No use lamentin' a fact I couldn't change.

"What about ... *after* you free your sister? What will you do then?"

My frown came back.

Charlotte just sat there on her stool in her velvet house robe, watchin' me like she'd just asked the most innocent question in the world.

So I gulped more whiskey and turned to stare out the window at the darkened scenery streakin' by. Truth be told, I'd never much entertained the idea of a life after findin' Ethelyn. Weren't ever sure I'd even live long enough to find her in the first place.

And now that I knew Nine-Fingered Nan had her, I was even less certain of that. And even more certain of the fact that if I did live long enough to find her, and free her, I'd die doin' it.

"Don't know," was all I said. It came out rough, so I cleared my throat. "Guess we'll see."

Charlotte did not seem especially pleased with my lack of specificity regardin' my future. She sighed, then resumed her attentions on my arm. She gave one final tug on the last piece of thread, and then I was free of those stitches. She wrapped a fresh bandage around her fine work before packin' up all her supplies. "I suppose at least you have a purpose in life," she said at last. "A drive. A function. As for myself ... admittedly, I'm feeling rather lost. I don't ... I don't have anything for myself, like you have with trying to free your sister. When I realized I didn't want any of what my parents had planned for my future ... that I'd had quite enough of being controlled by others ... well, I had hoped that maybe I could at least help you, if you still needed it. I thought maybe I could help you like you had helped me."

I looked back at her at this confession.

"This is ... this is all rather overwhelming," her gaze wandered to the bullet hole in my arm again, "but at least it's a choice. At least it's a choice I can make for myself. Although I'm not entirely sure how helpful I've managed to be up to this point."

I looked around at her plush accommodations ... accommodations Holt and I would have never sprung fer ourselves, and then glanced pointedly at my freshly bandaged arm. Maybe she *was* complicatin' things, sure, but she'd also been useful a time or two. "You do a fine job of doctorin', I can tell you that. Better'n Holt. And ... and you're pretty good in a fight, too."

A faint trace of a smile pulled at her lips. "Only thanks to my eldest brother. He taught me many things he was not supposed to. Things not becoming of a lady." She sobered suddenly, and her gaze shifted away.

On impulse, I reached my left hand out to cover the top of hers. I understood that feelin' of bein' lost well enough. Had felt it myself fer years, back when I'd thought Ethelyn had perished along with my cousin in Colorado.

And I wished then that I could help Charlotte somehow ... give her her own purpose. And preferably one that didn't involve Nine-Fingered Nan, or any kinda personal vendetta that would likely get her killed.

Maybe ... maybe after. After Ethelyn was free and Nan was dealt with, if I happened to still be livin', maybe then it might be somethin' I could entertain...

Charlotte cleared her throat and stood abruptly, pullin' her hand out from under mine. "Sometimes it seems like you might be trying to die on purpose, you know," she murmured.

I blinked at her abrupt change in subject, her abrupt movement, tried to pull myself back from darin' to think about a future. And scoffed. "Not hardly. If that's what I was tryin' to do, well ... I'd be dead already. Woulda let our friend Duster take me just now, if that were the case. Nah." I drank more whiskey, straight from the bottle. "Dyin's easy out here. It's stayin' alive that's the hard part."

"Hmmph. Well." She moved across the small space to stuff the medical supplies back into her pack. Then she straightened, smoothed at her velvet robe, and plucked my shirt from where I'd tossed it over the top of the small table. She handed it out to me, and I took it in my left hand with only a little wince. "After we get your sister, if you should want a different sort of life—one quite a bit less hazardous to your health—I'm certain my family could use a man of your caliber on their estate."

I almost spit the whiskey I'd just swigged.

"I may not have particularly enjoyed my life there, but just because I will not be returning doesn't mean *you* couldn't find gainful employment there. Or ... or once I find a place to finally settle myself, I would be more than happy to welcome you there, also. I could use the help, I'm sure. You and your sister both," she finished, ignorin' my wheezin' and coughin'.

I glanced up at her through waterin' eyes and tried to recover my air around the whiskey I'd sucked down the wrong pipe. "Charlotte," I croaked, but then I stopped myself. I'd been about to tell her that her family would be far more inclined to see me hanged than offer me room and board at their estate, once they realized I weren't exactly the caliber of man they'd expected.

Maybe my deeds hadn't circulated to the Republic yet. But they would, in time. After long enough of me runnin' free, escapin' the law, escapin' justice ... it'd all catch up to me eventually. It always did.

Pa had always told me that. Course at the time I'd thought he'd meant it more in a figurative sense, warnin' me away from potentially wanderin' down a bad path. Didn't realize he was referrin' to his own personal sins till long after, after he and Mama were dead. After Holt had found me and filled me in on what parts of Pa's past I'd never known about.

Until then, I'd never suspected.

I wondered if Charlotte suspected anythin' of me now. My stomach twisted at the thought, though I couldn't be sure if I hoped she was entirely innocent of suspicion, or if I hoped she had some inklin' so as not to be entirely disappointed later.

I shook my head and swallowed back the bitterness that rose in my throat. "Charlotte ... I ... I couldn't do that."

She tilted her head to one side. "Why not? Wouldn't it be better? For you and her both. You could have a roof over your head, a real bed, three square meals a day, a paycheck." She paused. "And more than one shirt."

I grunted, wet my lips. "I have more than one shirt." I had two, to be exact.

"Oh. Well ... maybe you should put on another one for now, then. We'll have that one laundered." She nodded to the one still in my hands.

I dropped my eyes down to it as well and then winced at its condition. That woulda been a good idea, sure. Except... "Er. My other one is still with all my other stuff. With the mule. In the livestock car."

"Oh." She sighed. "No matter then. But would you at least consider my offer? Please?"

I gave a sigh myself. Let the whiskey bottle sit on the table so I could scrub that hand over the unbruised part of my face and rake it through my shaggy hair. It was long enough now it was startin' to curl. Had those waves to it, like Mama's hair. Reluctantly, I nodded. "Sure. Fine."

She seemed to relax a little at that, even smiled. "Thank you. That's all I'm asking. Just consider it."

"Yeah. All right." But I wouldn't. I couldn't. I couldn't do that to her. Or to her family. Or to myself. Even just her mention of all those things, all those things I couldn't have—not now, and probably not ever—had dredged up a wash of that old, sour anger.

That kinda life had been taken from me the night Mama and Pa were killed.

And I'd gone and destroyed my chances fer it in the future by runnin' with Holt fer so long. By agreein' to aid him in so many nefarious exploits. By bein' so hell-bent on findin' my sister I'd gone and done some truly terrible things.

"Well." I shook myself outta that dark place and pushed stiffly to my feet. "We'd best turn in. Get some sleep. Thank you fer ... patchin' me up. Again. And fer comin' over to see what all the ruckus was about in the first place. Might not have got out of that scuffle otherwise."

She gave a nod, grabbed the whiskey bottle from the table and took a long swig herself.

I lifted a brow, wonderin' if my influence was startin' to rub off on her, then wonderin' if I found that upsettin' or amusin'. I couldn't quite decide.

She offered the bottle back to me. "Let's just hope that's the last time I patch you up for a good long while, yes?"

I took my hat from where I'd set it on the arm of the chair and settled it back on my head, then took the whiskey. "Yeah. Let's hope."

But I didn't even have time to drink to that sentiment before a commotion erupted in the hall outside. And it sounded like … singin'.

Charlotte and I looked to each other in confusion, and I set the whiskey bottle down again to rest my hand light on that fancy pistol of Duster's as I went to Charlotte's door, my shirt still clutched in my other hand.

I hooked one finger in the door handle and slid it open a crack to peer out, even as the singin' got closer, and louder, and I was fair sure I recognized the voice.

Sure enough, bout that time, Holt came into view in the corridor. He weaved back and forth in the narrow space, and if it weren't fer the walls on either side of him, I weren't sure he'd have been able to stay standin'. But he seemed in real high spirits, grinnin' ear to ear, face flushed with alcohol, and beltin' out snatches of every song I'd ever heard him sing in no sensical order whatsoever.

Damn fool old man was drunk as a skunk.

And he was too loud. Much too loud.

Especially considerin' my recent encounter with Mr. Barrett. Now was the time fer us to be layin' low, unheard and unseen 'til we could get far away from all the people on this train, especially those folk back in that car of cheap seats who'd seen me knock a man over the rail.

"*Holt*!" I hissed. "The hell are you doin'? You wanna get everyone on this train angry at us? Keep it down, would ya?"

He stopped singin', paused in the hall leanin' against the outside wall, and looked up at me in surprise, like he'd just realized I was there, standin' halfway out of Charlotte's room. He blinked at me. "Eh? Van? Van! There ya are! I've been tryin' ta find ya ... gotta tell ya ... I jus' *owned* these fancy boys at poker, I did!" Thought his grin would split his face in half, and his blue eyes twinkled with more merriment than I figured I'd ever seen outta him. He wheezed a laugh. "Ya won't *believe* the winnin's I took in—we're gonna be livin' high on the hog, we are!"

I motioned frantically fer him to lower his voice. "Holt! Come on now, keep it down. Folk tryin' to sleep around here."

Charlotte stepped up next to me at the door to observe the spectacle herself. The arm of her velvet robe brushed against the bare skin of my left elbow. Absently, I noted it really *was* as soft as it looked.

"Pffft. Sleep. Who needs it?" Holt waved a hand dismissively and stumbled toward us. "I gotta tell you about this game! I had a streak goin', let me tell ya. Those boys ain't seen nothin' like it—"

He stopped abruptly again when he realized Charlotte was there. He stared at her fer a minute like he'd forgotten who she was, and then he looked back to me and seemed to really see me fer the first time, too. He squinted, his boisterous story forgotten. "Hey. What happened to yer face?"

I sighed, but before I could tell him we'd talk about that later, his eyes went rapidly over the rest of me, then between me and Charlotte. His expression changed from confusion to comprehension, and his bushy eyebrows rose high. "Ahhhhh. *Sleep.* Hah! Sure, sure, I see how it is. You two got some *business* to take care of, do ya?"

"What?"

"No need to be coy about it, I seen the way you two look at each other. I understand. I been there too, ya know. A long time ago, sure, but I know how it goes—"

My face flamed as I suddenly realized what he was goin' on about and instinctively I stepped away from Charlotte, out into the hall.

"That ain't what this is about," I snapped, frantically hopin' to shut him up before he went on and said somethin' even more embarrassin'. "I pulled out those stitches and she was fixin' 'em."

He lurched off the wall and held up his hands, swayin' in place. "All right, sure, whatever you say."

I shook out my shirt with a snap and shrugged into it. "I was just leavin'. To go to bed. Which is just what you should do, damn fool. 'Fore you bring a whole train-load of angry people down on us." To illustrate my point, I stalked over to him and caught a fistful of his coat, pullin' him over toward his own door.

He stumbled along beside me, chucklin' under his breath despite my less-than-hospitable treatment. "All right, yeah. Let's go to bed. I'll tell you about my game tomorrow. And you can tell me what happened to yer face." He dropped his voice down into a harsh whisper as I pulled his door open. "And about how things went with the lady." He winked, but I only grumbled at him and shoved him into his room like it mighta been a jail cell.

I wished it was. I wished I could lock him in there now so I could be sure he wouldn't cause no more trouble ... or say no more stupid things.

"Good night, you old bastard," I growled, and then I shut the door on him. But I could still hear him laughin' to himself on the other side. Scowlin', I turned to head to my own room and caught sight of Charlotte still standin' in the doorway to hers.

She had her hands clasped together tight, and a visible flush pinked her cheeks even in the soft hallway lights. She looked mortified.

Well, so was I. Could still feel my ears burnin'. So all I managed was a nod in her direction as I fumbled at openin' my door. "Night," I muttered.

She nodded in return, her gaze droppin' from mine quick. "Good night," she whispered, and then she slipped from sight and shut her door, and I heard the click as she locked it.

That's when I realized that other bottle of whiskey was still in there.

I swore as I stepped into my darkened berth. Well, I weren't goin' back fer it now. Not after bein' humiliated like that.

Damnable nosy old man. He'd ruined everythin'.

The next day's journey passed blessedly uneventfully.

Holt slept off his drink most the day, which was certainly fine by me. Charlotte and I took breakfast together, both of us refusin' to acknowledge Holt's comments from the night before, and to my relief, the awkward stiffness of our conversation gradually eased.

I didn't pace the train between meals this time, and I only stepped off briefly at our first stop in Akansa to ask after the location of Blackbird and its nearest station, at which point I was told we'd want to get off at Arkopolis and ride north into Blackbird from there.

The rest of the time we stayed shut up in our rooms, not wantin' to risk any chance encounters, or remind anyone of what they mighta seen in the middle of the night last night.

When Holt finally did rouse from his slumber I cornered him while he was in the dinin' car, filled him in on my encounter with Mr. Barrett, but left out the details I didn't want him blurtin' to Charlotte durin' his next drunken episode. Even still, his eyes went wide at my story and he set down his mug of coffee, his plate of half-eaten eggs forgotten.

"Damn, kid. All that happen while I was playin' cards?"

I nodded.

He squinted at me, then glanced around the car where we sat. He leaned forward over the little table. "You *sure* you didn't kill him? The lady ain't here; you can tell me if you did."

"I didn't."

He grunted and sat back in his chair. "Just find it hard to believe a man like him would give up on such a bounty so easily."

I scoffed and shook my head. "I never said it was easy."

"Guess not." He picked up his coffee mug again and watched me over the rim of it. "Can't help but notice that shiny new pistol on yer hip, though. That one of his? He just *give* it to you, then? A token of yer new-found friendship, was it?"

He sipped innocently at his coffee while I growled at him. "He owed me one."

Holt snorted and shook his head. Set his mug down again to return to his eggs with a shrug. "All right. If you say you got him taken care of then I believe ya. Just as long as I don't gotta worry about him showin' up outta nowhere and pointin' a pistol in my face no more."

"You don't."

"Good. Good fer you, kid. Now ... let me tell you about that game of cards!"

He did, in great detail, but since I had nothin' else to do I let him go on at length. To my surprise he'd played the whole thing honest; a true rarity when it came to Holt Haggerty's poker playin'. Maybe it'd only been 'cause he'd been so drunk he hadn't trusted himself to cheat in a way that wouldn't get him noticed. Or maybe it was only 'cause we were stuck on this damned train fer a whole nother day, makin' it far more difficult to effect a quick exit should any suspicions be aroused.

But the long and short of it was that Holt had gained us quite a bit more coin. And that was never a bad thing.

By the time we disembarked fer good at the town of Arkopolis, I was both feelin' better and worse about the rest of this errand. Better in that Holt and I now had a fair bit of cash saved up between the two of us so we wouldn't have to rely on Charlotte no more in that regard. Useful fer any more supplies we might need ... or fer makin' bribes, which I suspected we might also need.

And worse in that we'd already spent more than one whole week of the two Nan had given me to find Dr. Balogh and those possibly non-existant ruins just travelin'. And we wouldn't get to Blackbird until tomorrow.

Day nine. Day nine, and I hadn't even set foot in Blackbird yet. Not only that, but I still didn't know how I was gonna manage to not send that telegram without seein' Ethelyn first. Didn't even have any ideas.

My fingers brushed Ethelyn's folded letter, tucked into the breast pocket of my shirt, as we waited fer our mounts. Then, once we had 'em and got tacked up—and Charlotte finished her thorough investigation of Sugar's health and well-bein'—we mounted up and headed straight outta town, wastin' no time on pleasantries.

I'd never been to Arkopolis. Never been to Akansa, in fact, despite havin' grown up in the Commune myself. Maybe, if we hadn't been in such a damned hurry, I woulda taken a few days to familiarize myself with the place.

But we didn't have the time. So I settled myself with sight-seein' from the saddle as we went at a steady pace down cobbled streets toward the single bridge that spanned a wide, sluggish river.

And despite the fact we were clearly on the outskirts of the town proper ... I could tell without doubt Arkopolis was the biggest town I'd yet set foot into. Could almost be called a city, even. Most of its buildings were stone and brick, and sat in fat clusters toward the town center. But things were busy even out here.

The train station itself was near the riverbank, and there was a big wharf on the bank, too, not far from the station. Several boats were moored there; looked like maybe some smaller fishin' vessels, and some bigger ones probably fulla furs or ores or precious metals. And there was one big flat one fulla logs. Warehouses stretched far into the distance, big wagons pulled by draft horses hauled goods back and forth, and it all reeked of fish.

Charlotte and I were preoccupied by all the activity, but Holt rode on through it as if he'd seen it all countless times before.

He probably had. He'd told me the gang he and Pa had rode with once had taken its origin in the south. Then they'd gradually moved north and west, pillagin' from place to place to avoid the law. Surely they'd been through here at some point.

A chill crept over me at that thought, as our horse's hooves thumped across the thick wooden planks of the bridge, and the slow, muddy water of the river churned beneath us, and we left the sprawl of Arkopolis behind.

Had Pa himself crossed this bridge once? Ridin' alongside Holt just like I was now? Only with a lot of other bad men alongside him, too, I suspected, accordin' to Holt's stories. And the worst of them in the lead: Paul Johnson. A man eventually known as Kill 'Em All Paul.

Holt didn't often share details of the jobs he and Pa had helped orchestrate under the leadership of Paul Johnson, but I often wondered just how bad they got. A man didn't get a name like *Kill 'Em All Paul* fer nothin'.

In all his years before havin' a family and that ranch in Kansas ... what had Pa *really* done?

What had Holt done?

"Ya can't fight yer nature."

Holt's words from a few nights ago floated back to me, along with the memories of some of the worst things I'd done myself in years past. Robberies gone wrong, innocent people killed. Lawmen along the way, tryin' to protect those innocents, gunned down like I'd done to that sheriff in Destry. Plenty of honorable men, too, men like Mr. Dustin Barrett, laid in the ground now 'cause of me. Then there was Nan's man Lloyd Renneker, who I'd cut on till he was near unrecognizable and then bled out like a swine.

Well, he hadn't been innocent, nor honorable, and certainly no decent kinda man ... but maybe he hadn't deserved such an end, anyway. Maybe.

Suddenly I didn't like this bridge much. Or the lazy expanse of dark river stretchin' out below. Or the busy bustle of Arkopolis behind us.

I pressed my heels to Joe's sides and he picked up his pace. "Come on," I snapped to Holt and Charlotte as he passed 'em by, "we're wastin' time."

GUARDIAN ANGELS

The town of Blackbird was chaos.

So much chaos the town itself couldn't contain it all. It started miles out along the road, where we joined a slow throng of folk movin' toward the settlement, and passed wagon after wagon and camp after camp of more folk who'd established themselves alongside the rutted path.

All kinds of folk.

Prospectors, miners, traders, loggers, and tradesmen of all sorts. Several groups of Natives. Sometimes a clergyman here and there, some with a cluster of followers around 'em and some alone. There were families, too ... lots of families. Even a handful of travelin' actors, their wagon painted in bright colors.

And, as we drew closer to the town itself, a few certain ... *unsettled* individuals made themselves known. Yellin' out to those of us who passed to beware the temptations of the machines, fer they were the work of the Devil, and that path led straight to Hell. Or that the Old World itself weren't even real and had never existed at all, and we'd all been sold on one big lie. Or that the Great Awakening was comin', whatever that was, and we should all cleanse ourselves in preparation fer the return of the Guardians.

One fella had even dressed himself up like a crow. Or some kinda black bird, anyway. Put black feathers all over himself and everythin', and he ran up to us screechin' and hollerin' and carryin' on about how his eyes had been opened to the Truth so relentlessly and enthusiastically that I had to pull back my duster and put a hand on my gun to finally scare him off.

Then he went on down the road to bother the next people in line.

"Afraid there's no more room in town," another man said as we ambled by his tent.

When I glanced down to him, I noted his black garb—thankfully devoid of feathers—and the stiff white collar. Another clergyman, then. He spread his hands as my eyes met his, indicatin' his bubblin' stew pot and full tent. Looked like he'd already collected plenty of lost sheep, wearily and warily huddled around the food or sprawled out on blankets.

"You are welcome to join us, if you wish," he said.

I shook my head. "No thanks."

"Are you certain? Room and board in Blackbird is booked up for months."

"Good thing we ain't lookin' fer room or board, then," I muttered, and I kicked Joe into a trot to squeeze past the folks trudgin' along in front of us.

Charlotte and Holt followed after me, and I heard Charlotte thank the man politely fer his offer as she went by.

We may not have needed room and board, no, as we had plenty of our own supplies, but hearin' such news put me on edge, anyway. And seein' the state of the town itself as we finally reached it only darkened my mood further.

I'd never seen so many people wedged into one place in my life. Blackbird weren't a big town to begin with, maybe not even the size of Bravebank, but its streets were less streets now and more rivers of people.

And the noise ... so much talkin' and shoutin' all at once, mixed with all the regular sounds of a bustlin' town, which Blackbird had apparently become abruptly and unexpectedly. I guessed it musta had somethin' to do with all those birds dyin'. Although why so many people might be so interested in such a thing, I couldn't fathom.

They were sure makin' my life awful miserable right now, though, and I didn't much appreciate that given my urgent business. I stuck close to Charlotte as we waded through the crowds, aware that she painted the picture of an easy mark even if she weren't, and looked a good one at that with the well-made cut of that cream-colored outfit and the way she carried herself in the saddle.

Least her stallion seemed just as put out by the masses as me; more than once he pinned his ears and bared his teeth at a person who ventured too close, sendin' 'em shyin' away quick. My mule and Holt's gelding, on the other hand, could have cared less about the press of bodies. They shouldered on through like the people weren't nothin' more than long grass.

"How in the hell we supposed to find that doctor of yers in this mess?" Holt called back to me, twistin' in his saddle. He was currently leadin' the way through this nightmarish fray.

I shrugged, scowlin' heavily. "How in the fuck should I know?" Then I winced, rememberin' Charlotte was right beside me. Mama woulda slapped me good fer swearin' like that in front of a lady. But I guess she weren't around no more. And I guess Sally had been right about me. Sometimes—most times—it was all too easy to forget my manners, given the company I most often kept these days.

I raked my gaze across the building fronts along Main Street. We'd about reached the center of town now, and it was near noon. Periodic clouds scudded across the sun, sendin' periodic shadows over all of us below, but they did little to relieve the muggy heat of midday.

It weren't nearly as hot as the desert, but I'd forgot how swampy the air got around here. Like it was tryin' to drown you just by breathin'. My shirt stuck against my skin, and sweat pooled beneath my hat rim and dripped down my temples.

My eyes stopped on the nearest saloon. I weren't sure if Dr. Balogh was the kinda man to frequent a saloon, but then, there weren't many types of men who didn't, and anyway, the saloons were always the best place to get information no matter where you went.

Whiskey loosened lips, and barkeeps tended to hear a whole lot, whether they were meant to or not.

"Start with a saloon," I yelled back at Holt.

He swiveled in his saddle, takin' in the street like I had just done. "Which one?"

"Just pick one!"

"All right." He shrugged and pulled his gelding left, aimin' fer the closest establishment, a place called Ace in the Hole.

I hoped it'd be my Ace in the Hole, all right.

It was as packed as any other place along Main Street, with all its hitchin' rails in front full up. We milled about there fer a space, tryin' to find a place to fit our mounts, and shoutin' from out front of the store next door drew my attention.

There was a lot of shoutin' goin' on up and down the street, of course, and most of it had blended into just noise. But this particular shoutin' was different. First off, it sounded awful distressed. And secondly, it included a woman's voice.

I pulled Joe to a halt and switched my gaze from lookin' fer a hitchin' rail to lookin' at the little knot of people who seemed to be havin' a disagreement. There were three men, all rough-lookin' and obviously drunk, and they surrounded a small family. The husband had his hands up, tryin' to dissuade the other three gentlemen from violence, but his lip was already bloodied. The wife clutched two small children to her; one in her arms and one clingin' to her skirts.

Passersby had given them some space, wary of the situation, yet scurryin' on by with hardly a second glance. No one wanted to get involved.

I didn't blame 'em. That was usually my rule, too.

Usually.

I swung down off Joe and went straight in their direction.

"Van..." Holt started from behind me, but he didn't try too awful hard. His protests turned into swearin', and then in my peripheral vision I saw him dismount and head after me.

In all my years of ridin' with Holt, I'd had one rule. We never bothered families.

Couldn't very well abide others botherin' families, neither.

So I walked right up to those rough-lookin' men and flicked back my duster to rest my hands light and casual on my gun grips. The worn, familiar one of my own on my left and the worn, strange one of Duster's on my right. "Afternoon, gentlemen," I announced loudly. When they all turned to face me in surprise, I tipped my hat to the woman. "Ma'am." Then I switched my gaze to the nearest ruffian. "There some kinda problem here?"

He sneered at me, and I couldn't help but notice his two friends step closer.

I also noticed, to my great dismay, that Charlotte had followed Holt in followin' me. She came to stand to my left, and the glare she fixed on those three men made me think of the night she'd burned off Baron Whittaker's balls.

Almost without thinkin' I raised my left arm, as if holdin' her off, like she might whip out that sixgun on her hip and gun down all three of 'em right then.

Well. I had no doubt she was at least entertainin' that idea. I was entertainin' that idea myself. But we couldn't very well do such a thing in the middle of the busy thoroughfare in broad daylight. And I preferred not to do such a thing in front of kids, neither.

"Damn right there's a problem!" the man nearest us snarled. "But I don't see how it's any of yer business ... so why don't you just move on along?"

I shook my head. "'Fraid I can't do that."

He straightened, though he swayed in place, and squinted at me through watery eyes. "Oh no? You *sure* you wanna get involved in another man's *private* business?" He twitched back his coat, too.

"Now look fellas," the husband spoke up, glancin' between all of us. "There's no need for this. Please. Come on, now."

"He's right," I said to the man starin' me down. "There ain't no need fer this."

"You don't even know what this is about," he snapped back.

"No need. I see you and yer friends harassin' a family—a family with young kids to boot—and I see the lady cryin'," I nodded toward the wife, who had tears streaked down her cheeks, "and I don't got the best manners myself, I admit ... but I know that ain't right, no matter what quarrel you mighta got here. So." I shrugged. "You got yer friends and I got mine. But I ain't gonna let you bother this family no more, nor lay another hand on any of 'em. We ain't goin' nowhere. You just decide how you wanna continue this."

A silence stretched between us, and the man I watched glanced from me to Holt to Charlotte, and then to his two friends, then back to the family they'd been hasslin'.

"We're all just trying to make a living here, fellas." The husband tried talkin' sense again, though I guessed that's also what he'd been tryin' to do when he'd got hit in the face. Some men just didn't respond to talkin' sense. "I bought that jackhammer fair and square, Mister. Now Robbie's gone off to get the sheriff ... so I figure you got two choices. You can leave it be, go on about your day, and I'm sure more equipment will be arriving in due time and you can get what you need then. Or you can stay, and we'll talk out this grievance with the sheriff, and you can see which of us the law agrees with. We can see what the sheriff thinks of you and your friends assaulting me and my family for nothing more than being in front of you in line!"

Over to my right, Holt shifted on his feet; shot me a look.

I didn't particularly want to come face-to-face with a strange town's sheriff, neither, nevermind that we hadn't done nothin' wrong here yet.

The nearest drunk's lip twitched at the husband's claim. "You think yer boy'll find the sheriff in any good time in this mess?" He forgot his guns, lifted his arms dramatically as he looked around at all the people flowin' past. Then he threw back his head and guffawed, and his two friends chuckled, too. "Fat chance of that! Whooeee!" He finally stopped laughin' and slapped his knee. "Boy probably got his own self lost by now! By the time he finds his way back here, sheriff or not, we'll have got what we want from you and be long gone, that's fer sure."

"Somebody call for the sheriff?"

We all startled at the nearness of the dusky voice, turned in surprise to see a woman with golden brown skin sittin' astride a tall black horse, and I let my duster fall back quick over my guns at the sight of the star on her chest.

A boy of about twelve or so sat behind her, arms wrapped around her waist.

Must have been Robbie. So he'd found the sheriff in this mess, after all. He reminded me a little of Radley, and my stomach turned at the thought of the Balogh family bein' a part of this mess, too. And at the thought of Dr. Balogh's propensity fer foolish kindness.

Given the current state of this town, the doc and his family had probably already been fleeced fer everythin' they owned.

"Yeah," I said, shakin' off my worries fer the Baloghs and figurin' it best to make it clear real fast I weren't one of the aggressors here. "Seems these gentlemen have some kind of disagreement. And certain parties," I glared at the nearest drunkard, "seemed like they were near to violence."

"They attacked my pa," the boy said sullenly from behind the sheriff.

"That so?" She fixed a deadly glare on the three men surroundin' that family. She was alone, didn't have no deputies with her as back-up, but there was a mean-looking sawed-off strapped to her thigh and she had the look about her of someone who was far past tired of folk causin' trouble.

Their bravado deflated beneath her glower, but their leader tried to splutter one last excuse. "This greedy little dirt-grubbin' maggot bought the last jackhammer! And we *need* that equipment fer our prospectin' venture!"

"I told you," the husband snapped, "it's first-come, first served! That's how a queue works! Ain't you ever bought anything honest from a store before? Good God, man!"

The drunk straightened his shoulders and growled. "You callin' me a thief ya no good—"

"Enough!" the sheriff barked. She pulled her sawed-off free of its holster and reined her horse right into the middle of our little group, so that we all had to step back some. But to my relief, her ire was still focused on those other three gentlemen, instead of on me and mine. "Look here, fellas. I am sick and tired of this petty bickering. And my jail is full-up. So in the interest of efficiency and my well of patience currently running bone-dry, I'll give you till the count of three to get out of my sight or I'm gonna put all three of you in the ground. No jail-time, no trial, no noose, just dead. You understand?"

"But—"

"One."

The fella's two friends skedaddled like quail startled from a bush, disappearin' into the passin' crowd without even a backward glance fer their stalwart leader.

"But he's the one who—"

"Two." She pulled back her twin hammers.

The man spat curses and back-pedaled quick. Never seen a man move so fast, in fact. "Yer just lucky I respect the law, Mister!" he yelled back over his shoulder, glarin' at the husband. Then he cast his mean eyes toward me. "And you! Keep meddlin' in other people's business and just see where you end up!"

"Three," the sheriff said. She leveled her gun at him, though he must have known same as me she weren't gonna take a shot with him so near to so many other folk now.

Still, it had the desired effect. He made a little squeak of alarm and dodged into the general public after his friends, disappearin' quick from sight, all right. The rest of us watched after him fer a good long minute anyway ... to be sure he weren't gonna change his mind and come back shootin'.

When that didn't happen, the sheriff hissed a sigh and holstered her weapon. Then she turned in her saddle to help the boy Robbie slide down off her horse.

"You done good, son," the man said, touslin' the boy's hair. He looked up to the sheriff. "Thank you for coming. I know you must be busy," he glanced around at the swarmin' streets, "but we wouldn't have asked after you if I hadn't truly feared for the safety of my family."

"Mmmhmm." She adjusted her hat atop a thick mane of glossy black spirals. "You got a permit for that equipment, then?"

The man shifted on his feet, glanced to his wife. "Well ... we were going that way to obtain one when we were confronted by those lowlifes."

The sheriff nodded. "Uh-huh. See that you get one before you operate that jackhammer. This ain't a free-for-all, despite what it looks like."

"Yes, ma'am. Of course, ma'am."

I started to back away from 'em, myself. Now that the threat had passed, we had no more business here. And I woulda preferred not to draw the notice of—

"And you."

I froze, goin' rigid. Blackbird's sheriff stared down at me from atop her horse. Holt sent me a cuttin' glare; Charlotte seemed completely at ease. But of course she did. She didn't have wanted posters of her face up all over the Territories. And she hadn't been facin' the noose just near on two weeks ago, neither. I swallowed, but tipped my hat to the lawwoman. "Sheriff."

She passed a hard gaze between all of us. "Fancy yourselves some kinda guardian angels, do you?"

Well, that was better than her accusin' us of bein' murderers and thieves. But I shifted on my feet regardless under her scrutiny and shrugged. "Just don't like seein' small men pickin' on families, is all."

"We didn't mean to over-step, Sheriff," Charlotte offered. "But I'm sure your resources are stretched thin. We couldn't just walk on by and let that family get robbed."

The sheriff arched one eyebrow and looked out over Main Street. "And yet hundreds of other folk could have," she commented. She heaved another sigh and then swung down off her horse, wavin' a farewell to the family as they went on about their business before turnin' back to us and askin' abruptly, "How would you three feel about being deputized?"

"Er..."

It was absolutely the last thing I thought I'd ever be asked, and I hadn't the faintest idea how to answer. I looked to Holt, but he only stood slack-jawed and wide-eyed, gapin' at the woman. Charlotte, too, seemed surprised, but she held her composure a lot better than Holt. When my eyes met hers, she shrugged.

"I..." I tried to think of somethin' to say. Acceptin' might put us in this sheriff's good graces. Might offer us some kind of protection from other law around these parts. But it also might put us in greater contact with other law around these parts, and I weren't keen fer greater contact with any law in any context, as a rule. Not to mention we hadn't come here to help keep law and order ... we'd come here to find Dr. Balogh and maybe some Old World ruins. "We, uh ... well we..."

"Congratulations, then," the sheriff said, slappin' me on the shoulder right above that bullet wound so I grimaced. She extended her hand and I took it, still feelin' numb as she shook mine heartily enough to jar my teeth together. "Sheriff Madeleine Reeves. Welcome to Blackbird. Pleased to meet you. Don't got any stars for you, I'm afraid. Fresh outta those. But I'll have some paperwork drawn up for you to keep on your person. For proof, should anyone doubt your claims."

"Uh..." She let go my hand and shook Charlotte's next, just as enthusiastically, and then Holt's, too. The old man looked like he'd got gut-shot, still speechless.

"Anyway. Let me buy you a drink. Come on now." She caught up her horse's reins and led him toward the Ace in the Hole saloon.

Charlotte, Holt and I gathered up our wayward mounts just the same and followed after her wordlessly, and she led us around the back of the joint where things were mildly less crowded. We found a stack of lumber there suitable fer keepin' horses put, looped reins over boards, and headed fer the saloon's rear door.

I glanced back at Charlotte's stallion as we went. "You sure he'll behave himself out here alone?"

She rolled her eyes. "Of course he will."

"You sure this is such a great idea?" Holt muttered at my other side, and he sent an almost imperceptible nod toward Sheriff Madeleine Reeves.

I shook my head, keepin' my voice low. "No. No I am not. But maybe she can answer some of our questions."

And hopefully she won't be askin' too many of her own...

XXI

BONES IN BLACKBIRD

We found ourselves crowded at the end of a crowded oaken bar, in the midst of a crowded Ace in the Hole saloon. It was rowdy and loud, and there were three men behind the bar servin' up drinks, but they could still hardly keep up.

One of 'em glanced at us four as we wedged ourselves into a space, a space that grew bigger as some of the fellas at the bar saw the sheriff's star and made room ... or just plain took their leave. The barkeep who had spotted us did a double-take at the star, himself, then came our way.

He was a small, slight fella with greased hair and a thin moustache, and he looked as haggard and weary as the sheriff herself. He shook his head. "Sorry, Sheriff. Well's about run dry around here."

She shrugged. "Just give us a round of whatever you've got left."

He pursed his lips. "You sure? All I got is the ... er, well ... the 'shine, but not the good stuff. Afraid it's better for lightin' fires than drinkin'. Can't promise it won't make you blind."

"Don't much care at this point, Eaton."

"All right, then." He slid us four shot glasses and pulled a grimy stoneware shoulder jug from beneath the bar. He uncorked it, then sloshed some into each glass, nowhere near as graceful about it as Sally had been with that high quality whiskey of hers.

"Just leave the jug," Sheriff Reeves said.

The barkeep hesitated, but then shrugged himself and stuck the cork back in the top of it. He set the whole jug at the sheriff's elbow. "Suit yourself."

"We're celebrating, Eaton," she said, and picked up her glass.

Charlotte, Holt, and I echoed her motion. The smell of the stuff made my eyes water. *God damn.* Weren't exactly lookin' forward to drinkin' it, but I knew better than to refuse it, too.

Eaton leaned on the bartop. "Oh? That so? Watchu celebratin'?"

"More deputies!" Reeves lifted her glass. "These three. Newly appointed." She gestured at us with her drink-free hand. "Deputy ... er..." Her dark brown eyes fixed on me. "Deputy...?"

"Lynd," I blurted. "Van DerLynd."

She dipped her chin in acknowledgement and raised her glass even higher. "Deputy DerLynd ... Deputy...?"

Now she was lookin' at Holt, and he straightened from his slouch on the bar and cleared his throat. "Henry Jones," he said.

I really hoped Charlotte understood what we were doin' here.

When the sheriff looked her way, Charlotte offered a smile and gave her real name ... though at least she said nothin' about Holt and mine's bein' fake.

"Good," Sheriff Reeves said. "All right, then." She turned back to the barkeep Eaton. "Meet Deputy DerLynd, Deputy Jones, and Deputy Harrison. They'll have paperwork by the end of today, but go on and spread the word best you can, would ya?"

"Sure thing, Sheriff."

She turned back to us, holdin' forth her glass. "To your new appointments!" Then she tossed the stuff back.

The three of us raised our glasses, too, and I took a breath and sucked it down myself.

It lit things on fire, all right. All my insides, all at once, burnin' down my throat and up my nose. I coughed despite myself, blinkin' back tears.

Charlotte and Holt didn't fare no better than me, but the sheriff herself hardly seemed fazed. She poured us all another round.

"Congratulations, folks," Eaton said. He was smilin' now under his little moustache. Probably amused by the effects of that swill on us outsiders. But he sobered up soon enough. "It's a noble thing you're doin'. Sheriff needs all the help she can get." He nodded out toward the rowdy floor of his saloon. "As you can probably tell by the current state of this place."

"Is all of this—" Charlotte started, but then she paused to cough and clear her throat, likely still feelin' the effects of that 'shine down her gullet. I know I still was. She took a breath and tried again. "Is all of this because of those birds dying?"

"Something like that," Sheriff Reeves said.

"Mostly," Eaton agreed. "Folk wanna come see it for themselves. Or they think it's some kind of Divine Providence. Or a sign from the Devil. Or they think it's got somethin' to do with the Old World and they've come to seek their fortunes. Or to try and study it."

That made me think of Professor Morton and Her Royal Majesty the Queen of Canada, who'd also been keen on acquirin' that lockbox I'd given over to Nan. I wondered if they'd heard news of this happenstance in Blackbird that far north, and if they had, if the Queen would send another emissary. I hoped not. The professor had left me to die ... either from the desert or by the noose ... and I didn't want to meet any other folk like him, certainly.

"Had half a mind to throw our newspaper editor in jail," Sheriff Reeves muttered. "That blasted article he wrote—and sent to every other goddamned town on the continent, too, seems like—got everyone all riled up. Brought the whole country to our doorstep, seems like." She threw back her second shot.

I only stared down into mine.

"We can't keep up," Eaton admitted. "I'm fair near outta drink, and food, too. Everywhere else all over town is the same. General store is plum cleaned out, all our equipment's been bought up..."

The sheriff grunted as she poured herself a third shot.

Brave woman.

"I've sent some riders out to Jefferson, to request aid from the

Council," she said. "Hoping they can send in the army, maybe, and some wagon-loads of supplies."

"And let's hope we get an answer quick," Eaton added. "Otherwise I don't know what we're gonna do. There ain't enough game left around here to keep feedin' all these people, especially not after the die-off. Folk are already gettin' mean enough with what shortages we got now. Hate to see it get worse."

Charlotte frowned, leanin' over the bar on her elbows.

I kept my eye on the host of other men in this place, some of whom were leerin' at her from across the room in ways I didn't much like. I turned to stand sideways, facin' Charlotte and the sheriff and Holt, and let my duster fall back again to show that fancy gun on my hip. As much as I woulda liked puttin' 'em in their place right off, we didn't really have time fer all of that. So I hoped us standin' here with the sheriff herself and the reminder of my weapon might be enough to discourage any ideas of untoward behavior.

"Wait," Charlotte was sayin', "what do you mean there's not enough game? Because of over-hunting with all these people in the area? Or ... or do you mean other animals died too, besides the birds?"

The barkeep shook his head. "It weren't just the birds, ma'am. Deputy. It was everythin'."

My wanderin' glare snapped back to him at that answer, alarm grippin' my gut.

"*Everything?*" Charlotte repeated.

Eaton nodded gravely. "Everythin'. Birds, deer, rabbits, foxes ... even people. Plants and trees fared all right, I suppose, but anythin' else livin' within that place seems to have just dropped dead where they stood. Or flew, as it happened."

Holt whispered somethin' I couldn't hear and sucked down his second shot of 'shine.

Myself, I tried to wet my lips with somethin' other than 'shine and swallowed. "That place? What place, exactly?"

"You didn't read that bastard editor's article, then?" Sheriff Reeves chuckled and grinned at me. "I think you might be the only one on this whole continent!"

I shifted on my feet and shrugged. "Didn't manage to read all of it, no..."

"Well..." Eaton began, and then he leaned an elbow on the bar, too, like he was tellin' us a secret. Though by the sound of it, the location of this strange occurrence weren't secret at all. "The start of it is about an hour's ride out west of town. Far as we can tell, folk and animals all dropped dead in about a three-mile radius, but that's the closest it got to us. Praise be to God and the Mother that's as far as it went."

"And no one knows what caused it?" Charlotte asked. She managed to look deeply disturbed and intensely curious at the same time. I could fair near see her tryin' to work out the puzzle herself, even now, sortin' through information and tryin' to figure where all the pieces fit together. I supposed those books she'd read about this kind of incident hadn't mentioned such details.

And I supposed I only cared about those pieces fittin' together if they led me to some Old World ruins. Or to Dr. Balogh and his family.

"No one knows." The sheriff shook her head. "We thought at first it might be some kind of plague."

"But plagues don't usually stay within an area only a few miles wide," Eaton said.

"And no one else has died since," Sheriff Reeves added. Then she paused, shrugged. "Well. No one's died of *mysterious causes* since."

"What about that area now?" I asked. "People and animals still droppin' dead there?" Much as I loathed the idea ... I had a good sense we were gonna need to go there and have a poke around ourselves. And that was gonna prove difficult if somethin' unexplained was still killin' things.

But the barkeep and the sheriff shook their heads in unison.

"Oh no." It was Sheriff Reeves who answered this time. "If only. But no. Place is safe as can be now, it seems. It's been swarmed with all kinds of folk over the last three weeks or so, like Eaton said. Religious pilgrims, those that fancy themselves removers of evil, prospectors, miners, fortune-seekers, academic types of many interests ... you name it, those folk have been there. And aside from them sometimes murdering each other in fits of jealous rage or some kinda disagreement or another ... they've all managed to stay alive."

I frowned heavily at this news and stared back down into my little glass of 'shine. All of this sounded like one big goddamned nightmare. A nightmare I didn't want no part of.

The sheriff heaved a sigh and fixed her gaze on the three of us once more. One corner of her mouth quirked into a wry smile. "So. It seems you've picked a very fine time to visit my very fine town, don't it? Tell me then, if you didn't even read that whole article about the birds ... what business brings *you* here? Come to see the circus in general? Or are you maybe some of those treasure hunters?"

Holt didn't even hear her question, I don't think. He stared past the barkeep's shoulder to the empty shelves behind, lookin' downright pale and unsettled, like maybe he'd seen a ghost. Charlotte furrowed her brow and chewed at her lip and turned her own glass of 'shine around in circles.

Guess that left me to answer, then. I decided to start with the part of our journey here that would seem the most regular and friendly, and not with the part where I planned to find some Old World ruins for a notorious outlaw. "We're, uh ... we're actually just lookin' fer someone. A friend who came up here 'bout a month or so back. Thought we'd join up with him, see how he was gettin' on."

Charlotte looked up to me sharply at that, frownin'.

And a jolt of alarm went through me at realizin' I'd never told her about Dr. Balogh and his family, neither. Here we were usin' fake names and talkin' about a fella she'd never heard mentioned before ... and it was too late to clue her in.

I hoped she wouldn't ask no questions that might make Sheriff Reeves suspicious. Hoped she'd keep on playin' along as best she could.

To my relief, the sheriff missed Charlotte's brief puzzled look, too busy quirkin' an eyebrow at me. "Oh yeah? Well good luck finding him in this mess." She tossed a glance over the full interior of the saloon.

"Yeah," I grumbled. "Was gonna start here, actually. In the saloons, I mean. Ask around. He's a doctor ... a medical doctor, and a foreigner. Got a thick accent. Name's Balogh."

The sheriff straightened from the bar, and the barkeep Eaton, who'd been driftin' off to see to other customers down the way, stepped back our way quick. "Balogh?" he repeated.

"Yeah. He woulda had a family with him, too. Wife, daughter, son—"

"You friends with that nutter?" Eaton squawked.

I turned to face the bar square at his reaction, forgettin' all the men I'd been keepin' eyes on fer makin' lewd looks at Charlotte, hope and relief both shootin' through me. "You've seen him?"

Eaton scoffed. "Seen him? Yeah. I'd say. He came through town before all this nonsense began, tryin' to get us all to pick up and move. The whole town! He wanted the whole town abandoned! Ravin' lunatic, is what he is."

"Eaton," the sheriff chided.

"Well it's the truth," the barkeep muttered.

"B-before?" I asked, strugglin' to make sense of this. "He came through *before* the birds all died?"

"Yeah." Eaton pulled the towel off his shoulder and grabbed up a glass from under his bar, wipin' at it furiously like he needed an outlet fer his sudden frustration. "Maybe two weeks before. Came through and told us all to leave. Said it weren't safe."

"Well," Sheriff Reeves put in, "it almost wasn't. That circle of death is sure closer than I'd like, I'll tell you that. Blackbird coulda been nothing more than just a lot of bones, like the rest of the woods..."

Eaton scoffed again, scrubbin' harder at the glass.

"He knew that was going to happen?" Charlotte asked before I could venture the question myself. "Is that why he was telling everyone to leave?"

The sheriff shrugged. "Who knows. He was never very specific about why it wasn't safe here. Which is why no one believed him. I, uh ... well. I locked him up for a night for disturbing the peace. He still didn't settle down, so I told him he and his family needed to leave town by the end of that day or they'd be getting an armed escort to the nearest train station."

I bit back the swell of frustration and the string of curses that came with it and exhaled a long breath, instead. "So he's ... he's gone then?"

The lawwoman nodded. "He is. I'm sorry. He all but got ran out of town."

"And good riddance," Eaton muttered.

"I'm sorry," Sheriff Reeves said again. "But your friend wasn't very popular around here."

"Uh huh." Well. I supposed a part of me was relieved that Dr. Balogh and his family had managed to avoid all the unpleasantness and danger of the current overcrowded nature of Blackbird. But his absence sure did make things more difficult, too. I drummed my fingers against the bartop, tryin' to figure exactly what to do now.

"Did he mention where he might be going?" Charlotte spoke up. She seemed to be playin' along just fine, all right. "When he left town? Or did he talk about any other places he might be interested in, or that were also unsafe?"

"Not that I know of," the sheriff said. "He just seemed awful concerned about this area. Of course, after the ... the *incident* ... myself and some others went out looking for him. I wanted to ask him some very specific questions at that point, you understand. To see what he'd really known, if anything, about the occurrence before it'd happened. See if maybe he'd even caused it, somehow. But we couldn't find him. Not a trace."

My stomach twisted at this news and I swallowed.

"Heard him and some of our local nutters whisperin' together a time or two," Eaton offered. "Talkin' about the Oracle and those strange Seers."

"The ... Oracle?" Charlotte asked. Her gaze suddenly sharpened. "The Natives of this area have old legends that mention such a person ... are they ... are they real?"

Holt muttered somethin' else and reached fer the jug of 'shine, pourin' himself some more.

I watched him through narrowed eyes, but he wouldn't look at me. Only threw back his third shot and then turned away from the bar, amblin' over toward the poker tables. I wanted to yell out after him to get back here, that this weren't no time fer cards, that I didn't like the sound of this no more than he did, but the barkeep Eaton answered Charlotte's question before I could open my mouth and drew my attention back to the conversation at hand.

"Yeah," he was sayin'. "Not sure what those legends might say about an Oracle, but the one we got around here is real enough. Far as flesh and blood goes, anyway. Crazy old coot lives out in the woods. With some other strange folk, too. They ain't exactly a cult ... ain't exactly a religion ... but they ain't exactly normal, either. They don't usually bother no one, though. We leave each other alone for the most part."

"For the most part," Sheriff Reeves agreed. "'Cept for recently. They don't much like all these strangers wrecking their woods. I've tried to keep the prospecting and mining operations under control, but ... well." She waved her hand around at the crowded saloon once more. "Like I said, I don't have the resources to keep up. That's why I've been hiring more deputies wherever I can. Why I just hired you three." She flashed Charlotte and I a brilliant smile, looking happy enough with our appointments that I felt guilty we wouldn't actually be of any help to her.

"Er, right," I muttered. "So Dr. Balogh ... he seemed interested in these strange folk livin' out in the woods?"

Eaton shrugged. "Ain't exactly sure how *interested* he mighta been in them ... but he was talkin' about them a time or two with some other locals, certainly. I do know that. I figured with his nonsensical ravin' he was goin' on about, he'd get along with those crazies just fine."

"But if they all live in the woods," Charlotte said then, "were they killed by the ... the *incident?*"

For that answer the barkeep deferred to the sheriff, lookin' to her with his eyebrows raised in question.

She shook her head again. "Not all of them. Some of them, sure. But most of them, no."

"But if something killed everything in that three-mile radius," Charlotte mused, "then how did they...?"

Sheriff Reeves turned to face Charlotte square, leanin' one elbow on the bar. "Not all of them live within that specific area. And those that do that survived ... well ... they don't much like to talk to outsiders. And frankly, we don't much like to talk to them, neither. I did track a few of them down, sure, after the incident, for questioning, like I wanted to do for your friend. What few I could manage to catch weren't keen on talking. Mostly they just babbled nonsense." She sighed and dropped her gaze down to her glass, contemplating it, seemed like.

I contemplated mine, too, my mind all tangled up with too many things that didn't make no sense.

"Look," the sheriff said, turnin' back toward me, "I don't know what happened to your friend. I do know he left town and took his wagon out into those woods, along the road to the west. Right toward that circle of death. Now, like I said ... I didn't find no trace of him or his wagon out there. Never found his body or any of his family's ... it's possible he rode on through the area before the incident occurred."

"Or not," Eaton murmured.

The sheriff and I both glared at him and he took a step back, holdin' up his hands.

"There's a lot of ground to cover out there, is all I'm sayin'," he protested.

"Those Seers out there might have seen him pass through," the sheriff continued. "Or the Oracle—" she paused, pursed her lips, sighed, "—*Ms. Dorcas Higgins*—might know something, since the rest of them kinda look to her as their unofficial leader. But if I were you ... I'd just let it be. Between those unpredictable woods folk, these greedy new arrivals and maybe even some of Nine-Fingered Nan's men lurking around—"

Charlotte and I looked to each other in alarm at precisely the same time.

"Wait, what?" I blurted.

"Nine-Fingered Nan," Eaton said, driftin' back our way again. "You heard of her, ain't you?"

"Yeah," I managed to strangle out. "Course I've heard of her."

The sheriff gave a nod. "I got word a few weeks ago from a friend down in Bravebank—that's where she's got her base of operations set up for the time being, seems like—and he said he'd heard some of her crew talking about coming up here. Warned me to be ready for trouble. Guess the old outlaw herself saw that blasted article in the papers and took some kind of interest."

My whole body felt numb again. "Yeah," I muttered.

"Course I've had my hands full of trouble anyway ever since the incident itself," Sheriff Reeves went on. "If any of Nan's people *are* here, they haven't announced themselves yet. Or they've just blended in with the rest of the trouble-makers."

"And let's hope it stays that way," Eaton added. "Last thing we need around here is havin' to deal with Nine-Fingered Nan and her outfit."

"Yeah..." I muttered again.

Sheriff Reeves shook her head and picked up her little glass of 'shine, raisin' it in the slow, somber way you did when toastin' to someone's farewell. "Like I said. I'm sorry. But I think your friend and his family are goners."

I watched her down yet another shot of that 'shine and tried to ignore the sick churnin' in my gut at the finality in her words. At the news from her friend, which I was pretty sure meant I might not have been the only one here in Blackbird on Nan's business right now. Tried to ignore the restless urgency crawlin' all over my nerves and makin' it nearly impossible to stand still.

I didn't have time fer this nonsense. Didn't have time to save Dr. Balogh from himself, if he weren't dead already. But then, Nan had only really wanted the location of those ruins, if there were any. And if some folk thought Old World ruins might have caused such an incident of death like Nan had said—nevermind the fact that seemed quite impossible to me—then if there *were* any ruins, they'd probably be somewhere within that circle of death.

We were gonna have to go there, all right. Go and search around those woods and see if any of those eager academics or treasure hunters had found anything yet.

And maybe ask questions of those Seers and that Oracle woman, too. If we could find 'em. And if we could get 'em to talk.

God damnit.

Finally, at long last, I picked up my own second shot of 'shine and tossed it back. I coughed again as it flared down my throat, spread warmth slow through my insides. "Well," I said when I'd recovered myself. "Guess you'd better tell me where I can find this Oracle."

XXII

A CRUMB TO FOLLOW

We headed out immediately, as we had no time to spare.

Especially not if we were gonna have to go on some wild goose chase.

I pulled Holt away from his broody observation of, not a poker game as I'd expected, but a woman sittin' at a back table readin' cards fer one fella after another. From the snatches of their conversations I could hear, sounded like they were all wantin' her to tell 'em how fortunate they might be in their recent quest fer treasure.

Fer a second—just a second—I entertained the notion of sittin' down there myself. Maybe the cards could point me in the direction of Dr. Balogh and his family. Or toward some Old World ruins like Nan wanted. Or maybe give me some inklin' of how I was supposed to deal with Nan and free Ethelyn without endin' up dead.

But the line was long. And we didn't have time to wait. And anyway, I weren't even sure if I believed in all that stuff. So instead I only tugged Holt away from his watchin', sent solid glares around to all the men still showin' far too much interest in Charlotte as I ushered her out, and we left Sheriff Reeves to her drink and Eaton the barkeep to his rowdy saloon.

We headed outta town to the west, along the rutted path the sheriff had assured us would lead right into the heart of the area affected by *the incident*. She'd been less sure of the location of any so-called Seers or that so-called Oracle woman, but she'd recounted all the rumors fer us anyway in the hopes they might guide us in the right direction.

My mood had considerably soured in the wake of our discussion with Blackbird's sheriff, bein' as I was becomin' increasingly certain I weren't gonna find what Nan wanted. And if I didn't ... well. I needed to get my hands on one of Nan's crew who might know where she was keepin' Ethelyn. I wondered if Sheriff Jennings back in Bravebank might know, even.

He'd refused to discuss Nan's business with me before, sure. And he sure didn't much like me. But after I'd brought Nan that lockbox, and he'd found out she was holdin' my sister, and she'd ordered him to lock me up fer a good long while ... well, he'd softened up toward me a bit after that.

And he mighta even been the one to help orchestrate my escape from his jailhouse, too.

Couldn't prove it, necessarily, no. But the circumstances didn't quite add up, otherwise.

Which meant I'd only gotten out with enough time to save Holt because of him.

And if that were the case, I owed him one. Holt and I both did, in fact. If he were now inclined to share with me specifics of Nan's business, I'd be certain to repay him in kind.

If he were still reluctant, though...

I shifted in my saddle, watchin' Joe's long ears swivel in front of me as we moved at a brisk walk beneath the dappled shade of so many trees.

Well, I was runnin' outta time quick, in more ways than one. And I'd done worse to better men than Sheriff Jennings. I was gonna have to make him talk, one way or another.

Charlotte rode up beside me and cleared her throat, startlin' me from my broodin'. "So. This man we supposedly came up here to find, Dr. Balogh ... I thought at first he was just a ruse you made up to avoid telling Sheriff Reeves our true purpose here, but it seems he's real enough. Does he have something to do with what Nan wants from you, then?"

I sighed. But there weren't no use in not tellin' her about the doc now, I supposed. "In a manner of speakin'. She's got some kinda interest in him, I think. He's the one who ... who, ah, who gave me the metal leg."

Charlotte's eyebrows lifted clear into her hat brim. "And now he's here? In Blackbird? And he came *before* the incident and was telling everyone to leave before anything ever happened? That can't be a coincidence..."

I shrugged. "I mean, it *could* be..." But I doubted it. Not with the way Nine-Fingered Nan was actin' back at his homestead.

Charlotte shook her head. "If he has the knowledge to make a leg like yours, integrate it with a living body ... then he comes up here..." She looked to me suddenly with eyes bright and blazin'. "Maybe these die-offs really *do* have something to do with the Old World..."

I didn't much like that thought, even if it meant I was more likely to find what Nan wanted. Neither did I like the thought of the metal currently fused with my bones bein' somethin' Old World, itself...

"We oughta ride on through here, Van," Holt muttered abruptly from behind us. "This place is cursed. Don't like the feel of it."

I rolled my eyes. First Charlotte leapin' into disturbin' theories and now Holt with his incessant suspicion. But in truth, it were high past time fer him to start complainin' about somethin', so I supposed I shoulda expected it. Couldn't believe we'd got this far without his grumblin', really. "We'll ride wherever those ruins might be, Holt," I said. "If we ride on through, then we ride on through. If we don't ... well then we don't."

He scowled somethin' under his breath. Probably callin' me names. Things like *bull-headed idiot* and *stubborn sonuvabitch*. But not like he hadn't called me those things plenty of times before. "We oughta go back to Grave Gulch," he finally said loud enough fer me to hear.

I shook my head. "I ain't goin' all the way back to Grave Gulch after we just got here. And not without seein' what's what around here." I turned in my saddle to look back at him. "And anyway, you knew why I was comin' here and you seemed fine with it, then. Why you suddenly so spooked?"

He looked at me steadily from beneath the shade of his hat. Then shrugged. "Birds dyin' off is one thing. *Everything* dyin' off is an entirely different thing. And I never agreed to go lookin' fer that Oracle woman or any of the rest of her flock. Those people ain't right in the head, Van. Don't want nothin' to do with 'em."

"I'm sure there's a perfectly reasonable explanation for what happened here," Charlotte offered.

While I appreciated her calm, given the circumstances, I weren't sure myself if that were true. I couldn't fathom a *perfectly reasonable* reason for every livin' thing within a three-mile radius to suddenly drop dead. But I didn't say that aloud. Didn't want to give Holt any more reason to be suspicious.

And anyway, I was still stuck on the phrasin' of the last thing he'd said. I reined Joe to a halt in the middle of the narrow road and turned him around to face Holt. "Wait. You had dealin's with those Seer folk before?"

He pulled his gelding to a stop, too, but his flat stare at me didn't waver. It was a long time till he answered, though. Long enough I opened my mouth to repeat my question when he finally spoke. "Yeah." It came out hesitant, reluctant. "Long time ago. With yer pa."

I straightened in my saddle. Well that was somethin'. Curiosity and unease both pricked at my insides. I cleared my throat. "And Paul?"

Holt shook his head once. "Nope. Just me and yer pa."

Charlotte brought her stallion around to stand beside my mule again, lookin' between us. She didn't know about my pa. Or that he'd once ridden with Kill 'Em All Paul Johnson. Growin' up in the Republic, she might not have even ever heard of Kill 'Em All Paul.

And I was gonna try to keep it that way fer as long as I could manage.

"Think you can remember where you found 'em?" I asked.

Holt grunted. "Doubt it. Like I said, it was a long time ago. But even if I did, I wouldn't go there. I'm tellin' you, Van. Those people ain't right."

Frustration at his reluctance welled and I stepped Joe a little closer to his gelding, preparin' to tell him just how I felt about his superstitious nonsense. But I'd only just opened my mouth when a horrific mechanical ruckus erupted from the woods off to my left, and all our horses started, and what birds had come back to this area after escaping death took flight.

"Blazin' Hell!" Holt spat, wrestlin' his gelding back under control. "What is that?!"

Charlotte kept her restless stallion prancin' in circles as he pinned his ears and chomped at his bit, but only shook her head and yelled out, "Sounds like mining equipment."

Minin'.... Good. Maybe they'd found somethin'. Maybe they'd have some answers.

I turned Joe toward the noise, though he was none too happy about it, and spurred him off the road and into the woods.

Holt and Charlotte followed me, though I got the sense the old man, at least, shared the same opinion about this venture as my mule.

We waded through the underbrush fer a ways, climbed a rise littered with large boulders, and then I could see the source of the noise itself.

It was a machine, all right. A big monster of one, lookin' almost like a livin' creature as it squatted over the ground. It had four big legs for support, jointed at intervals to make it adjustable in height, I reckoned, and in the middle of those legs was a round, bulky body. A big drill poked out from the bottom of that body, raisin' steam as it chewed into the rocky ground below it, and a man standin' next to it dumped buckets of water down into the ever-widenin' hole.

He had a wagon fitted with a big water tank, looked kinda like a fire wagon, and harnessed to four horses, and he filled bucket after bucket from the tank to dump down that hole he was drillin'.

It made an awful ruckus, that drill grindin' through all that rock, but I urged Joe up close to the machine anyway until the man realized he had visitors and startled, droppin' the bucket he'd just picked up and dartin' fer the shotgun he had propped up against the wagon wheel.

His machine was so goddamned loud he didn't hear me draw, and he was so intent on reachin' fer his own weapon he didn't *see* me draw, neither. Couldn't even hardly hear the report of Duster's pistol as I fired, but the man saw the bullet splinter a sideboard of his wagon clear enough, and then another pinged into his shotgun and knocked it into the carpet of old leaves coverin' the ground, and he jerked backward with his hands raised.

He turned toward us, eyes frantic, and yelled somethin'.

But I couldn't hear him over all the racket of the drill.

"What?" I belted out myself. I kept the pistol trained on him, but I gestured with my other hand toward my ear, then shook my head and pointed at his machine. "Turn that thing off!"

He nodded. Lifted his hands higher and scrambled over to the thing, then, givin' me one more cautious look, grabbed hold of a lever on the side of it and cranked it downward.

Gradually the drill wound down until it finally stopped, and we were all plunged into a blissful quiet.

I breathed a sigh of relief.

The man by the machine raised his hands again. He was awful thin, his shirt tied around his waist and his dirt-smeared skin slick with sweat. His hair was all matted to his forehead and he looked real, real worried. "What ... what do you want?" he blurted. "I ain't worth your time. I ain't got nothing left, understand?"

I glanced to his machine, then to the wagon and its four sturdy horses. "Looks to me like you got a whole lot."

He shook his head. "It ain't mine. None of it. I only operate it. For Mr. Jenkins of the South Pacific Railroad."

I frowned, my gun arm lowerin' some.

"You steal any of his equipment and you'll have to answer to him," the man warned.

"I ain't gonna steal yer stuff. *His* stuff." I holstered my pistol—Duster's pistol—and swung down off Joe. "You runnin' all this yerself?"

He lowered his hands slowly, uncertainly, eyein' me warily as I approached. "Yeah. For now. There were more of us, but..." He shrugged. "We got robbed awhile back. Two of the others got kilt in the tussle. Then three of the others tried to steal from Mr. Jenkins themselves. I stopped one of 'em ... the other two ran off. Ain't seen 'em since."

I grunted. Stepped close to the machine and leaned over the lip of the hole to peer down into it. Then glanced back to him. "You a loyal company man then, Mister?"

He shrugged again. "I dunno. I just know it ain't smart to double-cross Mr. Jenkins. And I'd like to stay alive and get paid. That's all."

"Understandable."

"What do you want?" he repeated. "Look, I'm sorry, but I ain't got nothing to spare. So if you ain't gonna rob me ... well then I got work to do. No offense, Mister."

He added that last part hastily, eyes twitchin' down to my guns.

I sighed. "I just got a few questions, is all. You answer 'em fer me right quick and we'll be on our way, no fuss."

His eyes narrowed. "You've already been askin' questions, Mister. You got more questions?"

"Seems I do."

"Yeah? What kinda questions?"

I glanced toward the hole he'd made in the rock again. "You find somethin' down there?"

His narrowed gaze turned hard. "I don't know. Maybe."

"You drillin' through rock fer the fun of it, then?"

He scoffed, shifted impatiently on his feet, sparin' a look over my shoulder at Holt and Charlotte before lookin' back to me. "That's why I'm drilling, Mister. To see if there *might* be something down there. But I ain't sure yet. When I get deeper, then I might be sure."

"But you *suspect* there's somethin' down there? In this particular spot, yeah? That's why yer drillin' here instead of anywhere else?"

He shifted around again restlessly, clearly unhappy with my questions. "Sure. I guess. Look, all I know is Mr. Jenkin's fancy metal detector found something around here somewhere. Could be ore. Could be Old World remnants. Could just be some old rusted parts from a broken down wagon that's rotted away. All I know is I gotta investigate every damn beep of that thing, so that's what I'm doing. All right?"

"But you ain't found anythin' here fer sure?"

"No. Ain't found nothing nowhere yet. Least not anything Mr. Jenkins would want."

"Nothin' Old World?"

He shook his head.

I stared him down fer a good long while, frustration wellin' fresh again at bein' confronted with another dead end. He fidgeted under my glare, so I stepped forward quick, shoved him up against one of the legs of his machine, and drew that fancy pistol to press into his ribs.

He squawked in alarm, hands flyin' up, and I heard Charlotte bark my name from behind me.

Fer a second my anger faltered, but then I remembered what else was at stake here. And it was a lot more than just Charlotte's opinion of what kinda man I was. So I kept my gun jabbed into that man's side and my left hand pushed into his chest, holdin' him up against the machine, and I ignored Holt and Charlotte both. "You wanna stay alive and get paid?" I growled at him.

He swallowed, nodded vigorously.

"Then you better not be lyin' to me. You *sure* you ain't found nothin' Old World around here? Anywhere?"

This time he shook his head vigorously. "No, I ain't found nothin'. I swear!"

"I realize you might think I'd take it from you, if you had somethin', especially given the fact I'm standin' here right now with a gun in yer ribs," I stuck it in a little harder and he winced, "but that ain't what I'm here fer. I'm just tryin' to gather some information, understand?"

"Sure," he blurted. "Sure."

"And I need to be sure you ain't tellin' me no lies. I find the near prospect of dyin' often tends to refresh a person's memory. So?" I pulled my hammer back. "Is it workin'? Anythin' comin' back to you that you mighta previously forgot to mention?"

"No! No, I swear, Mister. I been out here weeks and ain't seen so much as a scrap from the Old World I swear it!"

"Van..." Charlotte tried again.

"How about anyone else?" I asked the man. "You heard of anyone else findin' anything around here?"

He seemed relieved to get the focus off of himself. "T-there was one, I think. Name of Billy Thorn. Heard he found a few trinkets buried and rusted-out ... the usual kinda stuff."

My heart leapt. It was a start, anyway. "Where? Where'd he find these things?"

The man shrugged bony shoulders. "Maybe a mile or so further west. B-But Billy ... but Billy disappeared. No one knows where he went. You ask me, I think the Seers got him. They've been sabotaging my equipment every chance they get. And his was the only claim I know of that came up with anything remotely valuable. He wouldn't just up and leave it."

I scowled. I surely didn't want no more mysteries added to this whole circumstance, but Mr. Thorn's claim was still the best lead I'd had yet, so I pressed on. "All right, then, Mister. You just give me yer best directions to this Billy Thorn's spot and we'll be on our way."

"You—you sure you wanna go there, Mister? Lotsa people been tryin' to move in on his claim, I heard, but strange stuff keeps happenin' there. Keeps scarin' people off. People keep sayin' that place is haunted. Maybe by Billy himself, if he's dead. Or it's just cursed."

"What kinda strange stuff?" Holt asked abruptly.

The man glanced over at him. "Things going missing. Stuff moving that shouldn't be moving. Fires not burning, whispers in the trees. That kinda thing."

"Uh huh," Holt said. "See, Van, what'd I tell ya?"

I gritted my teeth and leaned a little more weight against the hand I had splayed across the skinny man's chest. "Just tell me where it is, would you?"

He swallowed again. "All—all right, take it easy. You wanna go there, that's your business. I won't stop you."

"*I* ain't goin' there," Holt grumbled.

"Could you also tell us if you've seen a man and his family pass through here?" Charlotte asked. "Would have been a few weeks back. There're foreigners, and they would have had a wagon and two children, a boy and a girl."

Now the man looked toward her, and he frowned. "Missus, I seen a lot of families pass through here, and several of 'em foreigners. You're gonna have to be more specific."

"Name's Balogh," I said, and my heart picked up pace as I waited fer his answer. I hadn't even been thinkin' of the doc and his family, truth be told, too intent on findin' what Nan wanted now that I maybe had a little crumb to follow, and I didn't much like the snake of guilt and shame and self-loathin' that slithered through my gut at that realization. "He's tall and thin, mustached, wears spectacles. His wife's got long brown hair, looks a hard-workin' woman. And his daughter is about my age. His son is maybe ten or twelve. Ring any bells?"

The man frowned. "Not particularly. But like I said, a lot of people come through here. And I don't always see 'em all, you know."

"Sure," I growled. "Well if you do happen to see someone like that come through, tell 'em an old friend is lookin' fer 'em, and to come find me at Billy Thorn's claim."

He blinked. "You planning on staying there awhile?"

"I dunno. Maybe. But that's where he can start, if you see him."

"All right..."

"Now, you were gonna tell me exactly where that claim was, yeah?"

He wet his lips and cleared his throat. "Don't know that I got much of a choice."

"Not if you wanna stay alive in order to keep gettin' paid," I agreed.

He sighed, his chest risin' and fallin' under my hand. "Just remember what I told ya 'bout the curse and all. One of you—all of you—ends up dead, or missing, and I ain't gonna be responsible, you understand?"

My patience was wearin' real, real thin and my next words came out through gritted teeth. "You don't tell me where that place is right now and *you'll* be the one endin' up dead, Mister."

"Okay, *okay*! Fer Chrissakes, I was getting to that..."

He gave us directions, and I warned him if they proved to be faulty I'd be comin' right back to pay him another visit, but he insisted he was tellin' the truth. So I let him go, went back to Joe and mounted up, though I kept my pistol bared and ready, just in case he decided to try and teach me a lesson with his shotgun fer pushin' him around.

But he didn't.

He only stood there next to his machine and glared at all of us.

I gave him a smile and touched the brim of my hat. "Much obliged, Mister. Good luck to you."

He only scowled in answer, so I urged Joe off to the west and scowled myself when the mule nickered to the wagon horses as we passed. But we kept on goin', past the wagon with the water tank, past the big machine with its big drill, and made our way deeper into the woods.

Deeper into that circle of death.

Despite Holt's claim he weren't gonna go to the place Billy Thorn had disappeared, he trailed along behind me. And Charlotte, too.

Over the noise of all our horses steppin' through underbrush and years' worth of fallen leaves, I could hear him grumblin'.

But Charlotte said nothin'.

I chanced a glance back over my shoulder at the two of 'em and found 'em both glarin' at me, though I suspected each fer very different reasons.

My own scowl deepened as I turned quick again to the front and set my jaw, then urged Joe onward a little faster. We went at a trot through all those trees, and I did my best to ignore the twin glares of disapproval borin' into my back.

We found the spot easily enough, as it was obviously marked by the dark mouth of a cave in one particularly steep hillside. The cave itself was shaded by a large rock shelf juttin' outward from the hill, and the space beneath that shelter had been cleared out pretty good, leavin' a nice, flat, open area.

There were signs of people comin' through all around the clearin', all right: underbrush trampled and broken, mats of half-rotted leaves overturned by the tread of many hooves. Looked like Billy Thorn had left a lot of his things behind, too. He'd fashioned a table out of some rough-cut branches and a chair to go along with it. There were tools strewn out along the top of the table, includin' a magnifyin' glass, but whatever he'd been lookin' at seemed to have disappeared along with him.

His bedroll was set back under the overhang of rock, and the remains of a campfire were there, too. Despite the other fella's claim that fires wouldn't burn here, the logs piled up were blackened. So they'd burned at some point, it seemed.

Charlotte and I walked the horses around the perimeter, takin' in the scene. Holt had stopped a ways back, decidin' that was close enough fer him, and there hadn't been nothin' I could say to convince him to come any closer. So I'd given up.

Let him stay there, then, with his irrational fears. Weren't no matter to me.

But as Charlotte and I slowly circled around that clearin', I noticed the things hangin' in the trees that surrounded it.

Skulls.

Looked like cats, maybe. Bobcats. And foxes or coyotes. Maybe some opossums. And birds ... lots of little birds, and some bigger birds, too—hawks and the like. They'd been tied together in groups of two to six with strips of rawhide or dried sinew and hung from the lower branches, and some were decorated with ribbons or beads or feathers.

I wondered who had put them there. The strange forest people called the Seers? Or maybe it had been Billy Thorn himself? Maybe he'd thought doin' such a thing would scare off anyone lookin' to steal from him. Or maybe he'd just gone plum crazy and run off to join those forest people himself, and nothin' ill had befallen him at all.

Well. So many empty eye-sockets starin' down at me from those trees weren't exactly the most pleasant sensation, but the colorful beads and ribbons that adorned 'em didn't exactly lend the most ominous air to 'em, neither. And anyway, havin' had our camp in Grave Gulch fer so long now, I was mighty used to bein' stared at by the long dead.

Weren't so sure about how Charlotte might feel about all these bones, though.

I glanced to her, but she weren't payin' any attention to 'em. Instead, she maneuvered her stallion toward a younger tree and dismounted, then looped her reins around the trunk.

I weren't sure if she'd even seen the skulls yet. I decided not to mention 'em, fer now.

I followed her motions; dismounted and tied Joe to a tree. Then I trudged over to the clearin' where Charlotte was already pokin' around.

"You didn't have to threaten that poor man," she commented as I joined her.

I scowled and kicked at the campfire's logs, stirrin' up a little cloud of ash. But it had gone cold long ago. "I don't got time to be diplomatic," I growled. "I'm runnin' outta time. Nan don't hear from me soon, she's gonna sell my sister. I need answers ... and I need 'em quick."

She was lookin' at me now instead of at Billy Thorn's abandoned claim, but I didn't want to face her just then. Didn't want to see her disapproval ... or her pity. So I turned away from her and paced over to the entrance of the cave, searchin' fer any other clues maybe left there.

"What happened?" Charlotte asked. "After I left from Peridot? You'd said you were going to go meet Nine-Fingered Nan with all that money and buy your sister back..."

"Yeah." Anger swelled hot and strong enough to choke off the rest of my words. I paused at the mouth of the cave and stared hard into its pitch blackness, as if it had any answers. As if it could tell me why I'd been such a fuckin' fool.

"But ... that didn't happen?"

"No," I spat.

"Something ... went wrong?"

She asked it gently, delicately, as if fully aware of how much such a simple question could sting. But sting it did. Still. I scrubbed a hand over my face. "Yeah." Little over a full week now of travelin' together and I'd managed to avoid explainin' this. But I supposed I couldn't avoid it forever. Not if she was gonna insist on accompanyin' us fer the rest of this venture, especially. "Nan and I were both double-crossed by a traitor in her gang," I managed, though I kept my gaze locked on the impenetrable blackness of the cave. "The deal I'd made before for Ethelyn had never been a deal with Nine-Fingered Nan. Once I figured that out ... I did go back to Nan. With all that money. And offered it to her for my sister."

Charlotte's boots sounded on the rock as she stepped closer. "And?"

"And..." I ran a hand over my mouth, careful of the tender spot on my bottom lip where Duster's fist had split it. Felt sharp stubble along my jaw and sighed heavily. "And ... Nan upped the price fer my sister. Considerably."

There was a moment of silence. Then Charlotte ventured, "But she didn't murder you."

A snort of a laugh escaped despite myself. "No. No she didn't."

"And she didn't decide to sell *you* off, either."

"Not exactly." Though near enough. She *had* threatened to turn me over to the Whittakers if I failed to bring her that lockbox. I swallowed, curled my left fingers with their bandaged tips loosely into a fist.

Seemed she just kept sendin' me off on errands she was sure would get me killed, instead.

The memory of the old hag's maddenin' smirk as she'd departed the Bravebank jailhouse after orderin' me locked up still haunted my sleep. I'd never wanted to put a bullet into someone as badly as I wanted to put a bullet into Nine-Fingered Nan. And I had a good sense she knew that. Had a good sense she would have liked to see me try. Again.

I wondered if she'd put me down if I did. Or if she'd only keep toyin' with me. Shoot me in the other leg, maybe. Or in the arm. Or perhaps she'd try to take off my trigger finger, too. "She enjoys pullin' my strings too much to kill me, I reckon," I muttered. "Or to sell me off. At least fer now."

"So she sent you here to find something she wants. And then she'll trade you that for your sister?"

"So she says."

"You don't believe her?"

"Not anymore." I moved a little further into the cave, restless with the anger this conversation had stirred up inside. The cooler underground air was a welcome relief from the still, muggy heat of the woods.

"If you don't think she's going to make the trade for your sister, then why try so hard to find the thing she wants?"

I turned to face her with a glare, but mostly only 'cause it was a question I'd been askin' myself since we'd headed out from Grave Gulch. "I need to stall her. Delay her sellin' off Ethelyn. If I can find what she wants, maybe I can bait a trap with it. Somehow." It was the best plan I had so far, despite not bein' much of one.

"And what if you don't find it?"

"Well then..." I weren't sure I should tell Charlotte that part of it. But she was lookin' at me now with such a worried, concerned expression I couldn't bring myself to give her the same answer I'd given Holt. I cleared my throat. "Then I'm gonna lie and tell her I *did* find it. And then hope to God I can find Ethelyn myself before she realizes I played her."

I left out the part where I was gonna bleed Bravebank dry to find Ethelyn if I had to.

"And what about Dr. Balogh?"

I let out a breath and turned away from her again, hooked my thumbs into my belts, and shook my head. "Things would be easier if I could find him, I think. Nan thinks he came up here fer the same thing she wants. She thinks he knows where it is. And maybe he does. Or maybe he did. But maybe he's dead now. In any event, he's gone, one way or another. So I guess he ain't gonna be of any help."

A thread of worry weaseled into my gut at the thought of the doc and his family and what could have possibly happened to 'em, but I refused to dwell on it. I had my own problems to deal with here. Plenty of my own goddamned problems.

"What is it exactly she wants, then?" Charlotte asked, followin' me into the cave.

She studied the walls like I was doin' ... but I was only doin' it to look busy. To keep myself from pacin' a hole in the floor, or from goin' back to that fella with the drill to beat more answers out of him.

"She wants ruins," I said. "Old World ruins. She thinks there's some out here, and she wants me to find 'em fer her."

Charlotte laughed abruptly, and the sound bounced back into the cave and then echoed out again.

I turned to face her, surprised at her reaction, and more surprised by the fact her laughin' didn't seem to prick at my simmerin' anger like I woulda expected it to. Instead, it was almost a welcome relief. I'd never heard her laugh like that; full and unrestrained. Never seen her throw back her head and smile like she was doin' now, but it seemed to somehow bring a light into all the darkness I'd been feelin' lately, bright and fleetin', and I wished I could hear her laugh more often.

Preferably about somethin' genuinely funny.

She finally wrestled her amusement under control and shook her head, spreadin' her arms out to the sides. "And just how exactly does she think that's possible? Sometimes it takes teams of professional archeologists a *lifetime* to successfully locate any ruins, or else they're found by regular folk purely by chance!"

I shrugged, nodded. "I suspect she don't think it's possible. At least, not in the timeframe she's given me. Unless I could find the doc. If he really does know where some ruins might be around here like she thinks he does, and I could find him ... then maybe it'd be possible. But otherwise..." I trailed off, shiftin' to look down into the depths of the cave's darkness again.

Otherwise, Charlotte was right. The chances of me findin' any ruins that hadn't already been accounted fer weren't good. Weren't good at all.

Charlotte followed my gaze. "Well," she said, steppin' closer, "if that Billy Thorn found anything Old World around here, he almost certainly found it in there."

"Almost certainly," I agreed. Too bad whatever he'd found had vanished along with him. I wondered if he might actually still be down in that cave. Lost, maybe. Or trapped. My stomach turned. Truth be told, I didn't really feel so much inclined to head in there after him. Even if it were the best lead I had on the existence of any ruins, and the best chance I had at findin' anythin' else Old World to entice Nan with into a place where I might have a chance to murder her.

Charlotte took another step closer and put a hand on my arm, then sighed heavily. "Guess we'd better take a look."

"Yeah. Guess we'd better."

Charlotte pulled a bulky, square-shaped box from one of her packs, and it weren't until she flipped a switch on the side of it and a beam of light flared out one end of it that I realized it was some kind of battery powered spotlight.

It was bigger and heavier than I would have ideally liked to have taken explorin' through an unknown underground space, but I surely liked the idea of havin' it to see by a lot more than just my puny matches or a candle.

I hadn't thought to bring a lantern with me. And there weren't none of those left here at Billy's camp, neither.

I pulled a roll of twine I kept in my pack fer tyin' various things and knotted the end of it around the tree closest to the edge of the clearin'. When Charlotte looked to me in question, I explained to her there weren't no way in Hell I was goin' into that cave without a guide-rope to get us back out.

"We don't even know how deep it is," she said.

I shrugged. "It was deep enough fer Billy to find somethin' in, weren't it?"

She thought on that fer a minute, but conceded the point.

Then I made sure I had all my matches in my belt pouch, and all of Charlotte's matches, too, just in case that battery light of hers burned out. And then with me unrollin' the twine behind us, and Charlotte blazin' the way ahead with her spotlight, we made our way carefully into the depths.

The cave was deep, all right.

And we weren't the only ones who'd been along this way recently.

There were boot-prints in the soft silt that had gathered in some of the rock depressions. And moccasin prints. And the prints of unshod people, and plenty of paw-prints, too. Now and then we found a circle of ash where someone had made a fire, the nearby cave walls blackened with soot.

"Stay close," I whispered to Charlotte, and I switched the twine to my left hand so my right could be ready to draw. It was only just occurrin' to me that some of the people who'd come after Billy Thorn's treasure might still be in here.

In answer, Charlotte moved close enough to bump elbows. I noted she was keepin' her right hand free, too. Part of me wanted to draw her even closer than that, put an arm around her shoulders or waist, maybe, but that weren't very practical in the close confines of a cave, and with both of us maybe needin' to pull iron at some point, so I resisted the urge.

We moved onward, explorin' every bit of the cave we could get to as best we could. The main mouth of it was fairly wide, but it quickly narrowed and split, then opened again into a few smaller chambers linked by small tunnels. When we hit a dead-end we doubled back again, and we found more signs of people and animals prowlin' about even in the deepest parts ... but we didn't find Billy Thorn.

Or anyone else still lurkin' about.

Or any Old World trinkets.

Water dripped slowly off stalactites and the walls glistened in Charlotte's light, and we found some places where it looked like Billy had been excavatin' ... him or someone else, anyway. It was a whole lot more organized than that other fella's blunt drillin', but nothin' of interest had been left behind.

We'd been in here hours, seemed like, and I was almost cold now from my sweat dryin' in the chill air. Frustration tightened my chest and clogged my throat at findin' nothin', *again*, and the rock walls that engulfed us only seemed to pull in closer and closer with every minute that passed.

Felt like I couldn't breathe; my attempts to gulp air sent clouds of vapor curlin' around my head, and I gripped at what remained of my ball of twine in my left hand hard enough to send little flares of pain shockin' up from my bandaged fingers.

I turned on my heel, away from the wall I'd been starin' at—from yet another dead end—from yet more nothin'—and started windin' up the line of twine as I followed it back toward the cave entrance. "Come on," I spat at Charlotte. "There ain't nothin' here."

Her light swayed as she hurried to catch up, but I kept my pace brisk enough she nearly had to jog to stay next to me. I wanted out of this goddamned place. I'd had enough of its oppressive darkness, its deafenin' silence, its suffocatin' closeness.

"Well..." Charlotte asked from beside me, "what now?"

I shook my head. Stepped around a cluster of stalagmites. "Now I guess I got more questions fer our friend with the drill."

She said nothin' fer a time, and I expected her to suggest I do somethin' else, instead. But after a while she only said, "Maybe you can be more diplomatic this time."

"Maybe." But I had no intention of bein' more diplomatic this time. In fact I had every intention of puttin' the fear of God into the man. Whatever would get him to tell me everything he knew about everyone in these woods, that's what I was gonna do. If I had to interrogate every single person diggin' around in this area to get what I needed, I'd do it.

Maybe I could even use my new status as a deputy to make all my questionin' *official*.

"Maybe you can just tell Nan the ruins are here," Charlotte suggested suddenly. "It seems a reasonable enough place."

"Maybe." I turned sideways to slide through an especially narrow passage, the rock scrapin' at my chest and back fer several feet, and my feelin' of bein' squeezed and suffocated only intensified. I hardly waited fer Charlotte to come through after me with the light before settin' off again, windin' the twine fast as I could, more anxious than ever to get back to daylight.

I wondered if Nan would believe me, if I told her such a thing. She'd told me once I shoulda known better than to lie to her, when I'd claimed to know nothin' about the bank robbery in Blessing, but I couldn't see how she'd know if I was lyin' or not in this instance.

Wouldn't be no wanted posters out fer me because I'd looked around a cave or asked a few questions of folk. And she was several states and half a Territory away. If I sent her a telegram and told her the ruins were here, would she ask fer some kinda proof? And what kinda proof could she possibly want? What kinda proof could I possibly send her, bein' as we were currently so far removed from each other?

She hadn't mentioned anything about that—about needin' any kinda proof fer anything I found. She'd only said to find the doc, and follow him to the ruins, and then send her that location.

But the doc weren't here no more, and there didn't seem to be no ruins, neither.

Would she expect me to send her a lie? Would she have planned fer that?

Tryin' to account fer all these uncertainties was makin' my head hurt. And tryin' to guess at what Nan might be expectin' or not expectin' from me was near impossible. Any time I'd ever thought I'd had her figured out before, I'd been wrong. And the first time my misjudgment had nearly got me killed.

My left thigh twinged where the metal rod buried into the flesh, like the false leg could tell I was once more lamentin' the loss of my natural one.

I was so involved in my ruminations on what to do about Nine-Fingered Nan and her impossible request of me that I hardly noticed the air gradually warmin', gradually buildin' in humidity. It weren't till Charlotte's light spilled out into the clearin' and splashed against the trunks of so many trees that I realized we'd finally reached the surface again, and we'd been in the cave so long that the sun had already set.

I paused there to close my eyes and draw in a few deep breaths of the open air.

Joe nickered at us.

The night sounds here were nearly overwhelmin'; cicadas and crickets and even the familiar song of some tree frogs singin' a thunderous chorus I hadn't heard since I'd left the plains and trees of the Commune fer the desert of the Territories years ago. Fer a minute I went back to all those summer nights at our ranch in Kansas, when we'd been a family together, worried only about gettin' through the next winter.

Before any of this nightmare had started.

"Van!" Charlotte cried.

My eyes snapped open as she grabbed my arm and I was already pullin', the alarm in her voice sparkin' the instinct without me even havin' to think.

I found a target illuminated by her spotlight, directly in front of us at the edge of the clearin'. But my finger stilled on the trigger as my mind finally registered the multitude of nocked arrows already pointed at us ... as Charlotte swept the light around in a panic, and I realized we were entirely surrounded.

XXIV

THE DEEPER YOU GO

I lowered my gun slowly at the same time I lifted my other hand, hopin' to show these folks I didn't intend to harm 'em so long as they didn't try to harm us.

Charlotte's light stopped on the figure directly in front of us again, the only one who didn't have a visible weapon, and who was clearly the leader of this outfit. She was an old woman, thick and weathered, her gray hair plaited into two long braids that hung over her shoulders. She had a necklace of bird skulls and wore a cloak of black fur with a standin' collar of black feathers that framed her head.

Despite the fact Charlotte had the spotlight trained square on her, she didn't squint. Her eyes were milky white.

Blind, then.

Except she seemed to be starin' right at us.

"Hey ... hey, now," I croaked, and I slid my pistol back down nice and slow into its holster. A quick glance at the rest of those who surrounded us showed mostly clothes made outta rough-sewn shirts and trousers of cotton or canvas, with some furs and skins here and there. Nearly all their weapons were bows, spears, or knives, but there were more than a few guns, too.

There were several tribes of Natives in this area, sure, and yet these people didn't seem to quite match up with what I knew of those tribes. These musta been some of those forest people Sheriff Reeves had mentioned.

The Seers.

I remembered what the man with the drill had said about 'em sabotagin' his equipment every chance they got and swallowed. Charlotte's hand still gripped at my arm, clutchin' hard enough to almost hurt. But at least she hadn't gone fer her own weapon.

Didn't want these folk to fill us fulla arrows unnecessarily.

"Easy," I urged, and I turned my gaze back to the blind woman. "Easy there. We ain't no fortune-seekers, all right? Ain't miners or prospectors ... we're just lookin' fer a friend." I didn't think it wise at the moment to tell 'em we were essentially just like everyone else out here tearin' up their woods: ultimately, I wanted those Old World ruins, too.

Just fer different reasons than most.

The woman said nothin'. None of 'em did. They hardly even moved. Just stood there and stared at us.

My heart crawled into my throat as the silence stretched, until finally I tried again. "Look ... like I said ... we're just lookin' fer a friend. If you'll kindly let us pass, let us get to our mounts ... we'll just be on our way. Get out of your hair. You'll never even know we were here. How does that sound?"

As if to convince her—as if she could see me—I tossed the ball of twine to the ground. My right hand lifted away from my gun grip. "All right?" I prodded.

Her lips pursed, the first motion she'd made since we'd emerged from the cave only to find her waitin', and I braced myself to maybe have to draw again and go down in a storm of arrows.

But all she said was, "You have a poisoned soul, young man."

I blinked, frowned, and looked around the clearin' like maybe she was talkin' to someone else.

Charlotte's grip on my arm loosened a bit, and she shifted on her feet, tossin' me a confused look.

But I surely didn't have no answers, so I only shrugged.

"Though not as dark as your father's," the woman said, and I snapped my attention back to her quick. "He has paid his price now, I see. It is just as I foretold."

Murmurs of agreement circled through her followers at her statement, but I was still strugglin' to sort out just what exactly she was goin' on about. Her mention of my father had made me think of Pa, of course, and how he'd met his end. My heart pulsed in my ears now as I recalled what Holt had said just earlier today about him and Pa havin' dealings with these Seers before.

She could have known my father, sure, but how could she have known who I was now? Without bein' able to see my face, and without me havin' introduced myself?

That ... that was impossible.

Surely she was only spoutin' nonsense, like Sheriff Reeves had said these people were inclined to do. Makin' generalizations that could possibly apply to a wide variety of folk...

But even still, those milky white eyes were fixed on me like she could see just fine, and I didn't like at all the cold unease that crept across my skin at bein' held under that unwaverin' gaze.

"Your price is still to be determined," she said. "The deeper you go, the steeper the price. Surely your father told you that?"

You reap what you sow, and it's time for the harvest...

So Charles Miller had said ... I suddenly felt like I couldn't breathe again.

"Van," Charlotte hissed, "what is she talking about?"

I shook my head, but I couldn't get any words out. She couldn't know who I was ... she couldn't even *see*...

"You have a great darkness ahead of you," the old woman said, "and a poisoned soul may not survive it. You should look to yourself before you lose yourself. If that darkness swallows you..." She shook her head slowly, gravely. "You will not return from it."

"What does that mean?" Charlotte finally demanded, steppin' forward.

It was my turn to grab her arm now, as the rows of bows on either side of us lifted, the arrows drawn back a little further.

The old woman turned her clouded gaze to Charlotte. "It is only a warning," she said simply. "A favor to a loving father who realized he had lost his way too late."

My throat and the backs of my eyes burned with an unexpected rage toward this strange and cryptic woman ... or maybe ... maybe the rage was fer my pa, who hadn't seen fit to tell his family of his former life ... who hadn't bothered to warn us what his past might bring down on all the rest of us ... who'd seemed to willingly welcome death that night, who had maybe even given himself over without a fight to a fate prescribed long before by a blind woman who liked to babble nonsense.

"Enough," I rasped, and it was all I could do to keep that rage in check. I struggled to even out my tone, but I did nothin' to hide the glare I bored into the side of that old woman's face. "Enough of this. I don't know what yer goin' on about, but all we want is to be movin' on, understand? If you'll just let us retrieve our mounts—"

"I know what you seek, Van Delano," she said sharply, and her use of my name sent me rockin' back a step.

I swallowed all the rest of what I was gonna say, the rage abruptly doused by a shock of alarm. *How?* How could she have possibly—

"I have seen your role in the Great Awakening, and I know you walk with one of the Old Ones, else I would rid our woods of your poison right now. You have not come here seeking atonement or forgiveness as your father once did ... you have come here only seeking to destroy, and that is something we cannot abide."

"I—I didn't come to destroy nothin'," I protested. So at least she weren't right about *everything*. "I told you, we only came to find—"

"You cannot lie to me, Van Delano. As I said, I know what you seek here. And you will not find it without first being Judged."

"Sounds like yer doin' plenty of judgin' already," I growled. I'd been about to say we were only lookin' fer Dr. Balogh. Which weren't exactly the whole truth, but it *was* partially the truth. And anyway, the fact I hadn't come here to destroy nothin' was the full truth, no matter what this crazy old woman thought.

"I do not Judge," she said. "Only the Guardians Judge." She lifted her hands abruptly, palms upward, and flames blazed to life at the remains of Billy's campfire.

Charlotte yelped in surprise and I spat a curse as I pulled her around behind me, and we both staggered backward away from the heat and the brightness now radiatin' from the center of the clearin'.

The old woman stepped forward, closer to the fire. The orange glow of it lit up her heavily wrinkled features, glowed against the whites of her eyes, shone against her collar of black feathers.

I searched frantically around the circle of her followers, tryin' to see if there was a place we could barrel through, tryin' to calculate if we could shoot our way out of this without also goin' down ourselves, but they were clustered in tight and all watchin' us real, real close.

The old woman stepped closer, and Charlotte and I stepped backward again.

"Van..." Charlotte whispered. She was lookin' over her shoulder.

I could hardly hear her over the rushin' in my ears, the poundin' of my own heart against my ribs, but I followed her terrified gaze and found more of those Seers had moved in around behind us to cut off access to the cave, so that our backs were already almost up against the points of their arrows.

Charlotte's spotlight flickered, then went dark.

The fire in the middle roared high, high enough to illuminate some of the trees around us, and those skulls hangin' from the branches caught my eye again. I swear they'd been facin' the other way when we'd rode in ... I swear they had ... but now they were all facin' toward us, starin' down at us with those empty eye sockets.

Fuckin' hell. We should have listened to Holt.

We never should have come here.

I wondered if he had any idea what was happenin' over here, or if he was sound asleep already. I wondered if he *did* have some inklin' that we were in trouble, if he'd bother to help us out, considerin' the situation.

I wondered if there was really anything he could do to aid us, anyway, as one man against all these armed folk.

As one man against ... against whatever this woman was.

I cursed myself fer not listenin' to him, fer so easily passin' off his worries, and then I forced myself to step forward again, toward the fire. It was nearly the size of a full-on bonfire now, unnaturally large fer the few logs that fed it ... but the heat it gave off felt natural enough, searin' my skin as I faced off across from the old woman.

"Van?" Charlotte hissed from behind me. "What are you doing?"

My instincts screamed at me to run, but we had nowhere to run to. The only thing left to do here was face her, so I held my ground despite the fear that pulsed through my blood, despite my heart tryin' to choke me as I spoke. "All right," I said, slow and even. "Fine. You wanna judge me, you go ahead and judge me. But why don't you just let her go?" I pointed back at Charlotte. "She ain't got nothin' to do with this. She only came along to help outta the goodness of her heart ... you say I'm the one with a poisoned soul, huh? Well then she's the opposite of that. She don't need any judgin' ... why don't you just let her go on her way?"

Charlotte stepped up next to me quick. "You want to judge him, you can judge me, too."

Goddamnit. I turned a glare on her. "Charlotte—"

"We've all got poisoned souls, lady," Charlotte said, completely ignorin' my protests. "Maybe some worse than others, sure, but we've all got something we don't like inside ourselves, things we've done we'd rather forget ... even you, I'm willing to bet. So why don't you drop this pretentious façade and let's all just go our separate ways, no hard feelings."

The blind old woman turned her sightless eyes to Charlotte. "You are lost, girl. Decide what you want and find your own path. Following does not become you."

Before Charlotte or I could make any sense of that, one of the woman's gnarled hands tucked into a fold of her buckskin tunic and emerged clutchin' somethin'. "I do not Judge," she said again. "Only the Guardians Judge." She threw whatever she was holdin' into the fire and a great column of smoke billowed up and outward almost immediately, obscurin' her from my view.

I reeled backward as it clouded around me and coughed. It was potent, whatever it was; it stung my eyes and my throat and I tried not to breathe it in, pullin' my bandana up over my nose and mouth. I turned to Charlotte to make sure she'd done the same thing, but I could hardly see her through the dark, swirlin' haze. She'd dropped her bulky spotlight, now useless, and her hands were up by her mouth.

I thought I could make out her scarf pressed up over her nose; tried to move closer to see better, but I couldn't seem to walk a straight line. The ground felt like it was rockin'. Swayin' like I mighta been aboard a boat instead of on solid land. I stumbled, tripped, and hit my knees.

My eyes watered, vision blurrin'.

I heard the old woman dronin' on, her voice washin' over me warped and muffled. Sounded like I was underwater. Felt like I was underwater. Felt like I was swimmin' through a thick, soupy murk.

"Only the Enlightened may enter the Temple," she said.

Or, I thought that's what she said. It was hard to be sure. Hard to understand her, and even harder to make sense outta her ramblin'.

"If the Guardians judge you worthy, if you are Cleansed, you may gain what you seek. If the Guardians deem you unfit, as they did Mr. Thorn before you ... you shall be cast into Exile, and wander lost in the In-Between until you perish."

The ... the what? I was gettin' real tired of her nonsense. I lurched to my feet and stumbled toward her. My vision had gone all wobbly and bright, all the colors somehow more vivid and pulsin' in time with my heart. A chant had started from somewhere, surroundin' me and strangely soothin' ... like some kinda lullaby.

I couldn't see all those people with their arrows anymore.

All I saw now was the fire and the little sparks of its embers, floatin' around me like fireflies. And the woman. The old blind woman who must of have been the Oracle. She stood facin' me and spread her wings.

Wings?

I stopped my advance toward her. Swayed in place, hardly able to keep my feet, and stared at her.

She had wings, all right. Great big black ones instead of arms, and now she had the head of a crow, too. She looked right at me with her beady crow eyes, no longer blind.

"You stink of death, Van Delano," the crow hissed. *"You smell of murder."*

The big black wings stretched, folded toward me, and I yelled out as they engulfed me, plunging me into darkness. I tried to fight my way out of them, tried to push 'em off, claw 'em away, but my hands found nothin' to grab onto.

I groped fer my gun—Duster's gun—pulled it. I could hardly lift it. It felt like a stone ... heavy and unwieldy, clumsy in my grip. It was wet. Confused, I glanced down and found it covered in blood.

I dropped it quick, but the blood was already all over my hand ... both hands. And as I gawked down at 'em, tryin' to figure where all that blood had come from, a little circle of red appeared on my shirt, right over my heart. I watched with detached fascination as the circle grew gradually bigger, until the blood soaked my shirtfront. I touched it gingerly, but there was no pain.

At first.

The darkness that enveloped me flashed into a brilliant light, so bright and hot I cried out and threw my arm up over my face, staggerin' away from it.

It ... it was our house. In Kansas. Burnin'. Burnin' like it had that night those men had come fer Pa, and Mama had begged me to take Ethelyn and run. Hide. And I had, I'd done it fer her, and they'd murdered her, too. By the time I'd got back, it was too late.

The pain hit then, comin' with the wave of grief like a sledgehammer to my chest. I choked, gasped, hit my hands and knees in the dirt. Clutched at my blood-soaked shirt.

A shape darted in front of me. A shadow across the intense light of the blazin' fire.

Through my swimmin' vision, I saw it make a beeline fer the small stretch of trees clustered at the back of our family's acreage.

Ethelyn. I knew it was her. Knew it in my bones.

I had to follow her ... had to go after her. Had to find her *now*. If I let her go now, I'd lose her forever.

So I shoved back to my feet, grittin' my teeth against the hooks of agony that pulled at my ribs with every breath, and followed her. The pain got worse with every step, but somehow I kept goin'. By the time I stumbled beneath the branches of those trees, a vice squeezed at my chest so tight I could hardly draw breath. Black edged my vision, and yet I pushed on.

"Ethelyn," I whispered. "Ethelyn ... I'm here. I'm here..."

And then, suddenly and without a sound, she stood in front of me. My ten-year-old sister, with her dark hair disheveled and her jade-colored eyes fulla tears. She glared up at me, lookin' furious.

"Ethelyn..."

I don't know where she'd got the gun, but she pointed it at me now, and it was much too big fer her. She had to hold it with both hands, and it trembled as she tried to hold it steady.

"Ethelyn—"

She shot me.

Fresh pain exploded through my chest. At such close range the force of the bullet punchin' into me sent me sprawlin'. And then I stared up into the branches of cottonwood trees. And I watched spots of black and the sparks of embers float by. And I tasted blood.

Ethelyn came to stand over me. Mama and Pa joined her, and they all stared down at me like I was some stranger.

I opened my mouth, but only blood came out. I couldn't speak. Couldn't breathe. Couldn't even writhe around with the pain shockin' all through me now. My body was heavy and numb.

"What have you done?" Mama whispered.

I couldn't tell if she was talkin' to me fer ... well, all the things I'd done since this night, or Ethelyn, fer shootin' her own brother.

"The deeper you go, the steeper the price," Pa said.

I glared at him, twitchin' in my efforts to get up. My fists clenched handfuls of old, wet leaves. I wished I could get the words out. I wished I could tell him I knew the kinda person he'd been now. I knew what he'd done, I knew how deep he'd gone, and he'd gone deeper than any of the rest of us. He had no right to be here now talkin' down at me.

All of this was 'cause of him. He'd started this. He'd started all of this...

"*One so stained cannot be Cleansed without consequence.*"

That was a different voice. It reverberated in my head. I couldn't tell where it was comin' from.

Mama, Pa, and Ethelyn vanished into plumes of black smoke all at once, and my heart jumped at their sudden absence, at havin' 'em yanked away from me yet again. I scrabbled at their last remainin' smoky wisps, but they dissolved away even as I clutched at 'em.

Another voice cried out then. Somewhere far away. Not mine, but one I recognized.

She sounded in trouble.

I rolled onto my side, gaspin' and spittin' blood. Clutched more fistfuls of leaves as I tried to haul myself toward her. "Char—Charlotte?" I'd tried to yell it, but it came out almost soundless. I just didn't have the breath to speak.

Everything had gone dark again. I laid in a vast void of nothin', though I could feel a solid ground beneath me, still smell the sharp, sweet scent of rottin' vegetation. The slow rockin' of the world turned into a sickenin' spinnin', and then I was holdin' onto all those leaves tryin' to anchor myself. Tryin' to make it stop.

But it didn't stop.

It just kept spinnin' and spinnin', faster and faster, pinnin' me flat, until finally, at last, that blackness swept over my mind, too, and I fell into a blissful unawareness.

XXV

THE ORACLE

I woke to a chill, a splittin' headache and a sick feelin' in my gut. The nausea lurched up my throat and I rolled quick onto my side to vomit into leaves. Then I groaned and rolled the other way, away from my mess, and tried to blink my blurry vision clear.

There were leaves ... a lotta leaves. A whole carpet of 'em. And trees ... a lotta trees. With underbrush fillin' up most the space beneath 'em, and the dim light of dawn givin' me just enough light to see by. Birds chirped cheerily, a few flittin' above me from branch to branch.

Birds.

Then I remembered, and I came full awake with a gasp and sat up quick, hands goin' to my chest. It was whole. Unbloodied.

And shirtless.

With a start, I realized I had no clothes on at all. Well, that explained the chill. The days mighta still been warm enough around here, but the nights were quick to cool off. I'd been passed out in the middle of nowhere in this forest buck-naked, and there were strange white markings painted all over my body. And the bandages around the bullet wound in my left bicep and those around my three left fingers were fresh and new. Swearin', I scrubbed at the lines of paint over my left forearm. If I tried hard enough, I could smear it. It weren't permanent, at least, but it was gonna take a good long bath to get rid of it, looked like.

I gave up on the markings and rubbed my hands over my face, tryin' to get my bearings. I didn't recognize where I was. Certainly I weren't near Billy Thorn's claim anymore. A quick look around showed no signs of our horses, or any of my things, or Charlotte. Or Holt.

Shit.

I scrambled up to my feet fer a better vantage point to survey the area and swayed a little. I felt woozy. Weak and stiff. And strange to be standin' there naked with my metal leg in full view again. Maybe there weren't no one here at the moment to see it … but those Seer folk musta discovered it at some point.

I hadn't drawn these markings myself.

Or … I didn't think I had. I didn't remember doin' it, anyway. Of course, I didn't remember *them* doin' it, neither. It unnerved me to think they mighta stripped me and painted me and I'd not the faintest idea they'd been doin' it.

I shuddered at the thought. But at least they hadn't strapped me to a table to torture me. And they hadn't sawed off my metal leg fer themselves. They'd only dumped me naked in the middle of nowhere, it seemed. Still not a scenario I was particularly happy with … but this one I had a chance of rectifyin'. And gettin' outta it shouldn't require the weaponization of my false leg, neither.

I hoped. Especially since I hadn't figured out how I'd done that in the first place.

There was a small creek that snaked through the trees to my right, flowin' around a few more of those big, lichen-covered rocks and fallin' off a little shelf to make a miniature waterfall. Ferns grew in abundance around here, and if it weren't fer my current predicament and the urgency of the errand that had brought me out here in the first place, it mighta been a pretty, peaceful spot.

To my left was another of those steep hills so common in this area, with several rock shelves layered within it draped with grapevines and tangles of wild rose.

The sound of shiftin' leaves and brush to my right jerked my attention that way again and I crouched instinctively, suddenly severely lamentin' my lack of weapons. Or clothes.

I didn't see nothin' there, though. Or no one. Just that creek and those big rocks and all those ferns.

The sound came again, and then around the curve of one of the rocks I caught a glimpse of wavy red hair. My heart jumped. "Charlotte!"

There was a brief pause, and then her head peeked out over the top of the boulder. Leaves clung to her disheveled hair, and she squinted at me. "Van?"

Belatedly, I remembered my naked state and dropped a hand down to cover myself, duckin' a bit lower behind the cluster of bushes I currently crouched behind. From what I could see of her, she'd been painted with the strange white markings, too, drawn in patterns over her face.

I suspected my face probably looked the same then. "Are you all right?"

She frowned, looked around at the woods same as I had done. "I ... I think so. Got a bad headache."

"Yeah. Me too."

"Where are our things?"

"I got no idea."

"Where are we?"

"Don't know that neither."

She sucked in a deep breath and let it out slow, then closed her eyes and rubbed at her temples.

"You sure you're all right?" My right hand absently drifted back to my chest, feelin' at the place Ethelyn's bullet had slammed into me. But the skin was unbroken. And I could breathe just fine now, no pain.

Hallucinations. Damn strong ones, too. So vivid.

Charlotte had had her own, I was sure of it. I'd heard her yellin' just before I'd passed out.

"Yes." She opened her eyes and dropped her hands. "Just a

headache. The rest of me seems fine. But I would much prefer to be properly dressed right now, of course. And to have the rest of our things."

Dressed. Sure. That woulda been nice.

I couldn't see any of her except her head above that rock, but I supposed she musta been naked, too, then. I shifted my eyes away from her. Didn't want her to think I was the kinda man who might take advantage of such a situation. "You stay here," I instructed. "I'll go see if I can figure out where we are ... see if I can find our things."

"Naked?"

I gave a grunt and shrugged. "Well ... what else are we gonna do? We won't get nowhere just waitin' here."

She didn't seem to like this idea none, but she knew I was right. There was nothin' else to be done fer it. We couldn't just sit around and hope our stuff would re-appear. "All ... all right," she relented at last. "Just ... be careful."

"Yeah. I'll do my best." I supposed at least anyone I might happen to come across wouldn't have nothin' to steal off me. I stood from my crouch and kept my back to Charlotte, aimin' fer some semblance of modesty as propriety might demand, or at least fer as much modesty as could be managed in this situation, and tried to ignore the flush of heat in my neck.

If I were gonna be naked with Charlotte, I woulda preferred it be under much different circumstances. Our ridiculous situation now was just all kinds of awkward and unfortunate.

I faced that steep hill with its rocks and its rose bushes, but I certainly weren't goin' up that with nothin' to protect my skin from those thorns. So I decided to go around, instead.

The dawn had brightened now, makin' directions more clear.

And revealin' more of those skulls hung in the low branches. All starin' down at me in uniform.

I muttered curses and turned my back to 'em, tryin' to focus on a plan instead of on how their sightless gaze made my skin crawl now.

Over the rise was east, and the creek went that way, too. I'd try that way first.

Only I didn't even get to start out before people appeared at the top of the hill, and lined up all down the sides of it. Seers, by the looks of their mis-matched clothes, and front and center of 'em, starin' down at me with her unseeing eyes, was that old woman.

I stepped backward with a growl, coverin' myself with my hands again. "So this is what you do to people? Drug 'em and steal everything they've got?"

She ignored my questions and my scathin' tone. "Give thanks, Van Delano. For you have awoken, and with your mind intact. The Guardians have passed their Judgement. You have been given another chance. Both of you."

Three of her followers stepped forward then, two men and one woman. They came carefully down the rise. The woman carried a stack of clothing, with my hat set on top. One of the men had my boots in one hand and Charlotte's in the other hand. And the second man carried a wooden tray set with food. As he got closer, I saw it was baked fish, eggs, peaches, and carved wooden cups fulla drink.

The woman with our clothes stopped next to me first, but I kept my eyes on the old one at the top of the hill. Only after her younger follower had set some folded garments—and my hat—at my feet and moved on toward Charlotte did I glance down at what she'd left.

I snatched up my hat, stuck it back on my head, and noticed the clothes beneath it were not my clothes. They were the rough-sewn, patchwork type like some of the other Seers wore. I scowled, grabbed the shirt, and shook it at the old woman as if she could see me. "These ain't my clothes. Where did you put *my* clothes?"

"My dear child, you have been Cleansed," she stated flatly. "And your clothes as well. They were burned."

Charlotte's noise of dismay from behind me echoed the twistin' in my own chest. "*B-burned!?* You can't just—you can't just go around burnin' people's things!"

The man with our boots set mine down next to me, then caught my arm as I made to move forward up the hill. I swung around without even thinkin' and cracked a fist into his jaw, sendin' him staggerin' back.

"Van!" Charlotte blurted.

There were arrows and guns out again and aimed at us in a flash, but the old woman held up a hand and kept 'em from firin' even as I realized maybe that hadn't been the wisest thing to do.

But I held my ground unwaverin', fists clenched as I glared up at her and growled, "Tell yer people to keep their hands off me."

Her lips pressed into a hard line. "Only those clothes you wore during your Judgement were burned. The rest of your possessions are quite safe. They will be here for you when you return."

"Return?" I had so many other questions, so many issues with the things she was sayin', it was hard to decide which to bring up first. I was mostly stuck on the fact I'd had Ethelyn's letter folded up in my shirt's pocket. If that shirt had been burned, then the letter had gone with it. I spluttered fer a minute, angry at the gall of these people and at a loss fer what to do about it.

Angry that they'd subjected Charlotte and I both to their nightmarish so-called Judgement, then stripped us naked and marked us and dumped us out here, wherever this was, and now had burned things that belonged to *us*. *Important* things.

"Nothing important was lost to you," the Oracle said abruptly, once again effectively dampenin' my mountin' anger with her disturbin' ability to read my thoughts. "Items of true value were preserved and placed with the rest of your things. You have lost nothing ... but you have gained everything. You have seen what future awaits you upon your current path ... and you have been given the chance to choose a different one. A chance sought by many, but offered to very few. Do not waste this opportunity."

The man I'd punched in the face was rubbin' at his jaw with his free hand and glared at me as he made his way toward Charlotte to hand off her shoes. Then he made a wide circle around me on his way back to the others.

I glanced down to the shirt in my hand. The letter ... did she mean they'd rescued the letter?

"Now," the old woman continued, as if all of this was perfectly normal, "you will have breakfast. And then, if you wish, you may enter the Temple."

What *Temple*? What the hell was she on about? Grumblin', I shrugged into the provided shirt, buttoned it, and then reached down fer the trousers. Well, they weren't mine, but they were better than goin' around naked. "I don't know nothin' about any temple," I snapped at her. "Like I told you, we were only lookin' fer a friend."

The man with the tray of food reached me just as I'd finished makin' myself decent, and he handed me a plate and a cup.

I had half a mind to throw it right back in his face, and yet there were things about these people—or the old woman, at least—I still didn't quite understand. And there was a part of me that didn't want to risk makin' her too awful angry. Not to mention all those weapons now currently aimed at us.

I weren't entirely sure of what she might be capable of, and I didn't exactly want to find out. So I took the plate and only glared at the man as he scurried off toward Charlotte's rock.

"You were *not* only looking for a friend," the Oracle stated dryly from atop her hill. "You were seeking the Temple. But as it happens, your friend already resides within."

That made me turn back around toward her quick. "What?"

"What temple?" Charlotte asked.

"The Temple of the Old Ones," the woman said. She spread her arms. "It is beneath us even now. Your friend has been chosen as the Messenger. The one who will bring the Great Awakening. He resides within the Temple now, conducting his work."

I twisted to look over my shoulder at Charlotte, to see if maybe she was makin' any sense outta any of this. The heavy frown on her face told me all I needed to know. She'd finished donnin' a pair of borrowed clothes as well now, rough and drab compared to the cream-colored number she'd been wearin' before. She set her plate down on the rock she'd been hidin' behind.

"You will find him there," the Oracle went on. "Perhaps. The Guardians have given you passage for now, but they will be watching. See that you do not squander their trust."

She was makin' my headache worse. "All right, lady, look." I bent to put my plate and cup on the ground, then straightened. "How about you just point us in the direction of our things? And tell us which way it is we started from, so we can get back to our other friend, too. And then we'll just be movin' on, leave you folk to your business."

To my surprise, she smiled.

The three followers of hers who had brought us our things clambered halfway up the rise to one of the rock outcroppings all overgrown and grabbed at the tangle of grapevines and thorn bushes. They hauled the plants to one side to reveal a small, dark hole.

Almost looked like a burrow of some kind.

"Here is what you seek, Van Delano," the Oracle said. "Enter or do not enter, but this will be your only chance. If you turn away now, we will not bring you here again."

What in the fuck did that mean? I stared at the small round hole in the hillside, hardly big enough for me to squeeze through, I reckoned. My chest tightened at just the thought of attemptin' it and I swallowed.

Footsteps through the leaves behind me heralded Charlotte's approach, and she came to stand next to me. "You called it the Temple of the Old Ones. Do you mean *that*," she pointed at the burrow, "leads to an Old World find?"

The woman called the Oracle dropped her arms back to her sides, and her smile broadened. But all she said was, "It leads to what you want, my dear girl."

An Old World find... My breathin' quickened at the thought of maybe actually findin' Old World ruins. Findin' ruins none of those other treasure-hunters had discovered yet. That maybe no one had discovered yet. Except fer these strange forest people, anyway, and I didn't think they had any real good idea of what they'd found.

If that's what this really was.

I had no way to know fer sure. And I still weren't convinced that blind old woman even actually knew what it was I was lookin' fer in the first place, or that she was referrin' to Dr. Balogh specifically when mentionin' my "friend". This could have been some kinda trap. Or another delusion from unstable people ... a possibly deadly delusion. They'd get me to wedge myself through that hole and I'd get trapped in some cave till I died a slow death of starvation. Or they'd seal me in that little place under the hill, buried alive, and I'd suffocate.

My mouth went dry, though I tried to wet my lips, anyway.

Charlotte stepped closer, touched her hand to my arm. "That could be it," she whispered. "Old World remnants, under this hill."

"Yeah," I murmured back. "Or our graves."

"Well we have to at least look!" She stepped forward before I could make any argument to the contrary and once again addressed the Oracle. "Seeing as you took our things ... would you happen to have any matches on you? Or a torch of some kind? So we may ... see our way ... to the Temple?"

The old woman gave a nod. "We will provide you with light."

"And my guns," I blurted.

All eyes turned toward me and I shifted on bare feet. Hadn't put my boots back on yet. But I took a step forward then, too. "If I'm gonna go crawlin' around in a dark hole, I'd prefer to have my weapons back. You *do* have 'em, don't you?"

She took a stretch of time to answer, just long enough fer an edge of panic to start creepin' into my thoughts. But then she said, "Yes. Your guns are safe."

"Well good. That's good then." I stuck my hands on my hips ... my empty hips ... tapped my fingers there restlessly. These borrowed clothes were itchy and a little too big. I wanted my own stuff back. All of it. "I'd like 'em back, then," I repeated, when no one made a move to possibly go and retrieve 'em. "My guns. I'd like 'em back. Before we go into the ... er, Temple, and all. Please."

The old woman tilted her chin up and looked down her nose at me. I swear it was like she weren't blind at all. "You may have light. You might have need of that. But you will have no need of weapons in the Temple."

I glared up at her, anger warmin' in my blood again. "I'd like 'em back, anyhow."

"You may have your pistols back ... or you may enter the Temple. Not both."

I tensed, glancin' over her row of followers. There were quite a lot of 'em, and they were quite well-armed, themselves. I didn't have much chance of gettin' my way here.

"I'm sure it will be all right," Charlotte said to me. Then she turned to the old woman. "You said you'll return our things to us afterward, yes?"

"Yes," the old woman agreed. "If you return, your possessions will be waiting for you."

"*If?*" I repeated, and I sent Charlotte a pointed look.

She ignored me. I hoped her ignorin' my concerns wouldn't turn out as disastrous as me ignorin' Holt's concerns had.

"Let's just go have a quick look, then." She went toward the hole in the hill.

"Wait, Charlotte..." I started after her, remembered I didn't have any shoes, and went back to pull on my boots real fast. Then went after her again. "We don't know what's in there."

She stopped to turn toward me, and I was struck by the enthusiasm in her expression, the brightness of her deep blue gaze. "Only one way to find out, isn't there?"

"What if it ain't safe?"

"Then I will inform you of such a thing when I get inside."

I blinked at her.

"You stay here," she elaborated. "I'll go have a quick look, then let you know if it's safe or not." She started to turn away again, but I caught her elbow and pulled her back around.

"I ain't lettin' you go in there first!"

She squared her shoulders. "Why ever not?"

"Because..." Because if I let her go in there first, and somethin' happened to her, I'd have yet another face to haunt my nightmares. And those were gettin' awful crowded these days. *Goddamnit.* I looked back to that little hole and my stomach turned. This was not what I'd wanted. Not at all. There had better be Old World *somethin'* through there ... or this Oracle woman and her band of lunatics were gonna regret all of this when I got back out.

If I got back out.

"Because that ain't right, that's why," I finally spat. "I'll ... I'll go." I gave Charlotte's arm a squeeze. "Then you can follow me, if it's safe."

Charlotte pursed her lips, but the Oracle spoke before she could.

"As I said, the Temple is safe enough. You will have no need of weapons."

I scoffed. "Yeah, well, you'll excuse me if I don't exactly take yer word fer it, given what you've put us through so far. You said you had some kinda light?"

"Indeed." The woman gestured with one hand, and two of her people came forward, each holding a thick stick bound with strips of green and dry bark and dried grasses on one end.

Wonderful. So we'd be crawlin' through a hole with only a crude torch fer light, then. And no way to find our way back out of whatever we were goin' into. Just wonderful.

"But first," the Oracle said, and she pointed to our abandoned plates. "You will eat."

XXVI

ONLY NIGHTMARES

I surely didn't wanna eat. I didn't wanna take anything from that old woman or any of her people. Weren't sure what it would do to me, fer one thing. Didn't trust that they wouldn't try to drug me again. And I didn't wanna waste any more time, fer another thing.

Nevermind that my stomach was growlin' somethin' awful at the moment, and doubly so when one of those men went and got my plate and my cup and brought it right to me again.

Charlotte didn't seem keen on takin' the time fer a meal, neither, but as had been the case since we'd first run into this band of forest folk ... it didn't seem we had much choice in the matter.

So we both took our food and settled down on whatever seat we could find—myself on a rock and Charlotte on a fallen tree—and we ate quick as we could manage, watchin' each other the whole time.

Not sure what we were watchin' for. Signs of a poison, maybe, or bein' drugged again. Or maybe I was just tryin' to be sure Charlotte didn't finish first and make a beeline fer that hole before I could stop her.

I also didn't like how the Oracle woman and all her followers just stood there and watched us eat. They didn't say a word, hardly even moved, just stood there and watched us.

Made me feel like some kinda exotic animal on display at one of those travelin' circus shows, and it only made me try and eat faster. The food itself weren't too awful, though, and the queasiness in my stomach and weakness in my muscles seemed to fade as I ate. To my surprise, the drink was honey wine instead of water. And that made me think of Holt.

"We got another friend, you know," I said, settin' aside my cup to wipe my hands on my borrowed pants. "Traveled here with him. An older fella. Gray hair and a gray beard. Left him a ways back from that cave you first found us at. You happen to see him anywhere around here?"

The Oracle gave another smile, but this one was tight-lipped. "Yes. We know of your friend."

"Oh good. You might want to ... bring him here. I think he would have an interest in this Temple as well."

The old woman shook her head. "I am afraid not. He has not undergone the Judgement, or the Cleansing."

I regarded her silently fer a minute. "What, you didn't throw stuff into his fire, too?"

She folded her hands into her sleeves. "He does not search for what you search for, Van Delano. He refused to be Judged. And refused to be Cleansed. Therefore, he may not enter the Temple."

I frowned at her, wonderin' how exactly a person could refuse to be judged when that *judgement* entailed her throwin' stuff into a fire unannounced. But all I asked was, "Well where is he then?"

"He is where you left him."

"Does he know you abducted us? Does he know where we are now?"

"He has been made aware you are on your own journey, for now."

That made my frown deepen. I remembered how unsettled he had seemed when we'd first been discussin' these Seers. If he knew they'd gotten ahold of me and Charlotte now ... would he even stick around to see what became of us? Or would he give us up fer lost and head outta here ... back to Grave Gulch, maybe? Would he bother tryin' to track us down? To save us from these people, should things go sideways once we crawled into that hole?

Of all those scenarios, I figured the first was probably most likely.

But then ... I *had* just saved his neck from the noose, quite literally. Maybe he'd feel he owed me more than usual. Maybe that would lend him enough resolve to stand up to these folks. If he caught 'em by surprise, he might have a chance at downin' most of 'em before they could return fire.

But of course, that would depend on him findin' us here in the first place. And bein' that I hadn't the faintest idea of where exactly we were ... I weren't sure how possible that might be.

"It's all right," Charlotte said from across the way, and I jolted outta my contemplations. "It will be easier without him, anyway. And faster with just the two of us."

I narrowed my eyes at her. I'd always suspected she didn't have a great likin' fer Holt Haggerty, but I didn't much like her passin' him off so easily, neither.

She set her nearly empty plate aside and stood, and I was quick to follow her actions. I held out a hand and gestured fer one of the torches before she could. "All right. Fine. We'll go in, then. But if we don't come out ... if *I* don't come out ... and he's still around, would you just tell him..." I stopped, hesitated. Took the torch that was offered and let the guy light it with a match. Well, I couldn't tell these people what I really wanted to say to Holt in that case. So I only sighed. "Just tell him I said thanks. Fer comin' all this way with me."

The Oracle gave a nod.

And then, as I saw Charlotte take the second torch, I moved quick toward that damned hole. The vegetation was pulled back again so I could get to it. But everything in me balked at the notion of goin' in there.

I didn't much like tight places.

And this was the smallest place I'd ever considered crawlin' into, fer sure. I stood there and stared at it while my goddamned heart went all flighty, and my breath came hard and fast, and I kept clenchin' and unclenchin' my free hand.

Charlotte came to stand behind me, and the expectation rollin' off her was nearly a physical thing. Clearly *she* had no qualms about tight places, it seemed.

"Wait here," I told her, though it came out as a croak. I cleared my throat and tried again. "Wait here. And I'll let you know if it's safe once I get through."

"I'll just come after you," she said.

"Then we might both be stuck in there. Just wait fer a space first, all right?"

She rolled her eyes. "All right. Fine. Are you going to go then or not?"

"Yeah," I growled. "Yeah, I'm gonna go." *Goddamnit.* I faced the hole again, inhaled deeply, and lowered down to crawl into it. The smell of earth was nearly overwhelmin', and that fear of bein' buried alive rose up sharp and powerful as I slid my head and shoulders through, holdin' the torch out in front.

I had to belly-crawl, the space was so small. The walls on either side nearly touched my shoulders, the ceilin' scraped against the top of my hat, and I had the thought then that if I *had* had my guns on me, the grips mighta got caught and I might not have been able to fit through here at all.

I kept my eyes on the torch, on the flame itself, used it as a focus point to keep my mind off the tightness in my chest, off the nearly crushin' grip of panic as I slithered deeper and deeper into darkness.

Deeper and deeper underground.

What little light filtered in around me from the openin' I'd left behind suddenly darkened, and for a second I froze, the panic clutchin' like a vice and cuttin' off my air.

But then I heard the sounds of another person shufflin' along the packed dirt, heard Charlotte's periodic grunts as she pulled herself through the cramped space after me, and my breath came out in an explosive exhale. Followed by a string of muttered curses.

"Goddamnit, I told you to wait fer a space!" I hissed. But there weren't nothin' I could do about it now. I couldn't even turn back to look at her.

"I did."

"You did not! I only just started in! Did you even wait till my boots were out of sight?"

"There's no way I'm letting you get out of sight, Mister. No way I'm letting you go into this alone. Now go on." I felt her hand tap the side of my boot. "Why'd you stop?"

"Go on back out." I knew she wouldn't do it, but I had to try anyway. "I don't want us both trapped in here."

"We're not going to get trapped."

"You don't know that."

"And you don't know that we *will* get trapped, either. Now will you just get a move on, already?" She tapped my boot again.

I ground my teeth, already feelin' plenty trapped. Trapped now between her and the rest of this tunnel, wherever it went. The air was thick and soupy, or at least it felt that way to me, and sweat beaded on my forehead and upper lip. Damp earth pressed into my forearms and my belly. The torch guttered.

I swallowed hard and concentrated all my bein' on movin' forward. Crawled, bit by bit, squashin' the well of terror by allowin' myself to hope this would eventually lead us to some real Old World ruins.

To hope the crazy old Oracle and her followers weren't talkin' complete nonsense, despite what other horrors they'd delivered upon us beforehand.

To hope that it might be exactly what Nine-Fingered Nan wanted, and that it would be the last thing I'd need to free my sister.

The flame at the end of my stick lit only a short way ahead, and all it kept illuminatin' was more tunnel. The dirt eventually gave way to damp rock, the light from the entrance we'd started from gradually fadin'. Until at last there was only darkness around us, and only my flame to lead us.

We were movin' at a downhill slant, though, and just when I thought the mountin' panic in me might shatter my tenuous hold on it, I realized my hat didn't scrape the ceilin' no more. And the walls were a little further away from my shoulders.

The tunnel was gettin' a little wider. Finally. And slantin' downward at a steeper angle.

I inhaled a slow, deep breath. Maybe this really would turn out all right, after all.

Except then my arms and my chest fell away into nothin', and in my flailin' around tryin' to catch myself, I dropped the torch. It fell, spinnin', before clatterin' to hard ground some distance below.

My hands scrabbled at smooth rock, but there weren't nothin' good to hang onto, and my weight had already shifted too far forward to stop myself.

Guess I was goin' in after it.

My stomach lurched as I plummeted, and I tried to tuck and roll mid-air so at least I wouldn't land on my head. It sorta worked.

"Van!"

Charlotte's cry echoed out from above just before I landed hard on my back with a grunt, and everything went black.

The smell of damp earth and stone coupled with the faint aroma of an unfamiliar soap drifted into my consciousness, followed by the sensation of a hand pattin' at my cheek. And somethin' soft under my back, and somethin' ticklin' my forehead. And there was whisperin', too, though I couldn't make out the words.

I mumbled, shifted, lifted my left hand to swipe at the thing ticklin' me.

The whispers turned into words. "You're awake! Oh thank the Mother! Are you all right? Is anything broken?"

That was a good question. I took a minute to think about it. To take note of how the rest of me felt. I moved each limb carefully, experimentally, but all seemed in good workin' order. Even the metal one. My shoulders were a little sore, and my headache was worse again ... but aside from that, I seemed more or less whole. "All ... all good," I croaked. I'd been winded by the fall; only just now fully regainin' my air.

I pulled my eyes open and stared directly up into Charlotte's face.

She was real close, leanin' over me. The torch's weak glow threw patterns of light and shadow across her features, and the ends of her hair still tickled at my forehead. I realized she'd pulled me halfway up into her lap in her efforts to rouse me. She had one arm around under my head, almost cradlin' me, and her other hand had been the one pattin' my cheek.

"Good," she whispered, smilin' down at me. "Good. You gave me quite a scare there, Mister." She stroked my cheek absently, and I lifted my hand again to sweep aside the curtain of red hair ticklin' my forehead. It was silky in my fist.

I figured I should probably say somethin' then, or maybe make attempts to get up and resume our search for Old World ruins ... but I rather liked my current position, in truth.

Alas, the moment came to an abrupt end when Charlotte pushed me off her lap and stood.

Confused and displeased by her sudden departure, I laid there on the cold, hard ground fer another long minute and stared up into blackness.

She went to retrieve my discarded torch and paced a distance to my left.

Well, at least this place was a good deal larger than that tunnel had been, then. Maybe this was where we'd be trapped to die a slow death. I watched her maneuver carefully over uneven ground to study the leftmost wall in her torch-light and sighed. Supposed it was some small mercy I wouldn't have to die alone.

She went a few steps to her right and lifted the torch to reveal the rungs of a wooden ladder.

Oh. Well. Maybe we wouldn't have to die down here, after all.

I groaned and rolled over onto my side at last, then pushed myself up sittin'. I scrubbed at my face and groped around fer my hat, which I finally found and put back where it belonged.

"After you discovered this ... hole," Charlotte said, "I realized there was a ladder leading down here. It wasn't easy to get onto, of course, given the tight space of that tunnel. But it made for a much more graceful decent than the one you managed."

"Yeah. Imagine that's so." I struggled up to my feet with a wince, sore and with my head still poundin'. "You got that other torch somewhere?"

"Yes. Should be right there next to you. Although I thought it probably best to conserve the fuel. We're not sure how long we'll be down here, after all."

"Right." Smart thinkin'. But I bent down and felt around fer the second torch, anyway. Just so I could have it in-hand as soon as we might need it. I picked it up just as Charlotte made her way back over to me.

"If you're feeling up for it, we should explore this chamber. See if there's anything here, or if there's more to this cavern."

I nodded, then swept out an arm. "Sure. After you. Unless you'd rather I lead?"

She paused to regard me fer a second, eyes sweepin' me over and lips pursed. "Maybe not after that fall you just took. Don't want you dropping down any more holes."

I grumbled as she resumed her walk past the ladder, fell in to step close behind her. "Don't want you droppin' down no holes, neither."

"Trust me, I'm watching for them."

"See that you do."

We followed the perimeter of the chamber we were in, but found only regular rock formations you might find in any cave ... and some peculiar piles of rubble. Mostly more rock, but broken up into pieces. A few shaped stones were tossed in here and there, and some heavily rusted iron-work.

Charlotte bent to study the iron pieces, but I didn't bother. They didn't look Old World, and my patience was startin' to wear thin again. How long were we supposed to wander around down here in the dark?

"This don't look like no Temple to me," I growled as Charlotte finally satisfied her curiosity and stood. "Looks like just another cave. Same as all the rest."

She shrugged. "Maybe. But these piles of rock had to come from somewhere." She lifted our single torch high, peerin' at the walls closest to us, clearly tryin' to illuminate the ceilin', too. But it was too high. "This chamber might not be natural."

"Still don't look like no Temple."

"Well ... the Oracle's people might have a different definition than you about what constitutes a Temple."

"Think they might have a different definition than me about a lot of things," I muttered. But then, as Charlotte kept movin' on, I followed once again and said more loudly, "So you agree that blind old woman must be the Oracle?"

I watched the back of Charlotte's head nod, her red hair highlighted by the flickerin' torch light. "Yes. She must be. She fits the sheriff's description of the Oracle well enough."

"Sure. 'Cept the sheriff never said nothin' about the Oracle bein' blind."

"True. But everything else seems to fit. Including her little band of followers."

I snorted. "I wouldn't exactly call it a *little* band of followers..."

"Do you think what she says is true?" Charlotte asked abruptly. She stopped and turned to face me, and I'd been followin' so close I nearly ran into her. I drew up short, looked down into her upturned face with its white-painted designs. "About you?" She put her free hand on my chest. "And me?"

"No." I answered immediately, without hesitation. "I think she's a sick individual who enjoys playin' a part. I think she enjoys scarin' people and prescribin' futures to gullible souls."

Gullible souls like my pa, it seemed.

Charlotte's gaze drifted away from mine, and her fingers on my chest tightened, catchin' a fistful of my borrowed shirt.

The action, simple as it was, stirred thoughts in me I had no business thinkin' right now. I swallowed. Standin' here like this just the two of us, surrounded by darkness and silence, was really not helpin' quiet those sudden thoughts, neither.

"Did you see things last night?" Charlotte asked quietly. "After ... after she made that smoke?"

Her eyes came back to my face and I tried to banish all my wanderin' thoughts at once, as if she could see 'em all somehow by lookin' at me. "Yeah," I managed. "I did. You too?"

She nodded. "Bad things," she whispered.

My own nightmares from last night came back to me. So vivid and clear. That bullet goin' into me, right at the place where Charlotte's hand was now. Ethelyn and Mama and Pa, all starin' down at me. Judgin' me.

I cleared my throat and closed a hand around Charlotte's. "Yeah. Me too. But it ain't real, Charlotte." I squeezed her palm. "All of that were only nightmares. Just that old woman tryin' to amplify our fears. Usin' 'em against us to complete the role she likes to play. That's all."

Charlotte was quiet fer another minute, chewin' at her bottom lip. But at last she nodded again, and squeezed my hand in return. "You're right. Of course you're right."

It was nice to hear someone say that now and then.

She released my hand and pulled away, takin' in a deep breath and then lettin' it out in a heavy sigh. "Well. Let's not let her do that to us anymore."

"Oh, I don't plan to." In truth, I was still entertainin' the idea of shootin' the old woman soon as I got my guns back.

"Good. All right. Guess we'd better get back to looking around, huh? Before this torch goes out."

"Probably a good idea."

"Right." She turned around smartly and headed off, and I trailed after her again.

I hoped we'd find somethin' soon. I really needed somethin' to distract me from thinkin' of how much I'd liked wakin' up in her lap earlier, or of how much I already missed the feel of her palm pressed against my chest.

"There's got to be another chamber around here somewhere," Charlotte said. Her words echoed softly back to us from the darkness. "This may not look like your version of a temple ... but it also doesn't seem to fit with even a very primitive definition of a temple, either. And it doesn't really look like any of the ruins I saw in—"

She yelped and jumped backwards, crashin' into me.

Instinctively I groped fer guns that weren't there, then scowled and in their absence, brandished my unlit torch like a club.

Charlotte leaned into me, but she held her flame out forward far enough I could just barely make out what had startled her.

My heart wedged into my throat.

People.

Faceless people. Or ... some semblance of people. Two of 'em, standin' at stiff attention to either side of a yawnin' black entrance to another cavern. They were tall, sleek, motionless ... and completely made outta metal.

XXVII

TRESPASSIN'

Fer a good long minute Charlotte and I just stood there starin' at those things.

Then Charlotte moved into a defensive stance, holdin' her torch same as me, ready to swing it at any attackers. And the both of us stood there side-by-side, ready to fight ... only nothin' happened.

Those faceless metal people didn't move.

...maybe they were just statues.

Feelin' foolish now, I lowered my torch and tried to slow my racin' heart. Stepped cautiously closer to 'em. Looked 'em over good.

I'd never seen anything like 'em before. Not even in Blessing.

Charlotte approached slowly as well, and held her torch out close to one, sweepin' the light over its unnatural body. They were made of metal plates that had been shaped and polished to resemble the form of a human, and fitted tightly together at the joints. Except where a human face would be, these statues had only another smooth metal plate, oval-shaped.

Both held swords, the tips buried into the ground at their toes and the grips wrapped in their exquisitely crafted metal hands.

Unlike the other iron pieces we'd found earlier ... these statues weren't rusted at all. All their metal was still new-lookin', like they'd been oiled and polished on the regular.

I frowned, and my gaze stuck on the nearest one's leg. It looked kinda like my own metal leg. It looked real, real similar, in fact.

I took a step backward, my leg suddenly feelin' awful heavy and sluggish. And it ached, down in the half-bone of my thigh, and the place where metal met flesh ached, too.

"Incredible," Charlotte murmured. She was leanin' real close to one of the metal monuments, her nose almost touchin' it as she squinted at an elbow joint. "The engineering here is incredible. I've never seen anything like it."

"Me neither." I glanced into the utter blackness of the openin' beyond these two metal soldiers and wondered what they might be guardin'. My heart quickened again. I hardly dared hope what I wanted might be through the next stretch of dark.

But then I realized what Charlotte had just said, and I pulled my gaze back to her. "Wait. You ain't seen nothin' like this before? Not even at Whittaker's place? Down in his ruins, I mean?"

She shook her head. "No. They've been mining those Blessing ruins for years ... those families don't want anyone to know, but they're about all cleaned out. Not much left there anymore. And certainly nothing even close to this. Certainly nothing in such good condition. I mean look at them! They look newly built, don't they?" She ran her free hand over one smooth, shiny arm.

"Yeah ... maybe don't touch them."

Charlotte tossed me a look that was both skeptical and disapprovin' at the same time. "Oh come on, now. Touching them won't hurt anything. Do you *know* how much Old World stuff I've touched? Even smuggled out a few tiny pieces from Whittaker, when I could manage. It can look scary sometimes ... but in the end, it's all just a heap of old metal."

A sick feelin' squirmed in my gut, memories of those little metal bugs down in Charles Miller's dungeon flashin' through my mind. And that electrical rod of his that bit so much worse than any hotshot. And ... and my leg ... transformed into so many blades...

I cleared my throat. "Uh huh." I figured she didn't know about any of that stuff. Baron Whittaker surely wouldn't have shared the truth about such discoveries with his slaves. I stepped forward quick and grabbed her wrist, pullin' her hand away from the thing.

She whipped a glare at me, but I held tight even as she tried to yank away from my grip.

"Please, Charlotte. Trust me on this."

Somethin' in my voice musta convinced her, 'cause she stopped tryin' to twist her arm free. But her glare remained hard and bright.

"I've had … experiences," I told her. "Where they weren't just heaps of old metal, after all. Some of those scars you saw earlier … they weren't made by bullets."

Her glare softened at that, but her eyes narrowed, too. I could fair near *see* all the questions crowdin' her features.

So I let go of her wrist before she could ask any of 'em and turned to study the sword in the hands of the right-most statue.

"All right," she said softly. "Fine. No touching. I'd just like to know when and where you had your *experiences* … I didn't think you were very familiar with Old World artifacts?"

"I ain't," I admitted. "Only had a few run-ins with the stuff. But none of those run-ins have been particularly pleasant. Let's just leave it at that fer now."

She made a noise like that answer weren't satisfactory at all, but I occupied myself with tryin' to work the grip of that sword from delicately jointed metal fingers.

The arrival of more light over my shoulder preceded Charlotte's sharp scoldin'. "Hey. I thought you *just said* we shouldn't be touching these things!"

"I ain't touchin' it." But I was. Though just a little. Just enough to pry the fingers off the sword grip. They moved easier than I'd thought they would. "Just tryin' to get us some kind of real weapon, is all."

"That's still touching it."

"As little as possible," I insisted. "And just to get this sword. I ain't goin' around strokin' the thing like it's a prize thoroughbred!"

Charlotte scoffed. "I was not *stroking* it—"

The sword came free at last. Satisfied, I hefted it in my right hand, keepin' our extra torch in my left. It was quite a bit heavier than I'd anticipated. Difficult to wield in one hand. And probably not all that sharp, given its age and the fact it'd been made fer decoration rather than combat.

Still, it'd be better than a stick, if we ran into any trouble.

"Happy now?" Charlotte asked.

I looked to her, found her glarin' at me again with her torch in one hand and the other hand fisted on her hip. I nodded. "Yeah."

She sighed. "Good. Let's go, then. See what's through here." She nodded to the near darkness. "And no more *touching*, right?"

"Right."

And so we went, steppin' through the yawnin' mouth of another passageway, this one blessedly wide and open. Charlotte led with her torch held high, and I followed close behind her with the sword at the ready.

We didn't go far before runnin' across more statues, only these seemed more sophisticated than their metal counterparts. They wore clothes, fer one thing. Elaborate costumes the likes of which I'd never seen ... not even in travelin' troupes or circuses. Some looked kinda familiar though. Almost resembled those religious sisters I'd seen a time or two. Even had heavy golden crosses danglin' against their breasts. But these had been outfitted with a kind of crown, also made of gold, that framed their head with thin spikes. Almost looked like a sun risin' behind 'em as we passed, or a halo, maybe, Charlotte's torch-light makin' 'em glimmer.

Their heads were bowed, their black-gloved hands folded in some-thin' like prayer.

Maybe this really *was* some kind of religious temple...

After those were some dressed in red gowns, embroidered with gold thread and with high, stiff collars. The sisters had had only black cloth beneath their hoods ... but these dressed in red were somehow more disturbin'. They still had no faces, only bulbous heads painted in the same red and gold patterns as the rest of 'em. They wore gold gloves, and the ends of their fingers were tipped with golden claws.

And then there were some that I thought at first were more like regular statues, bein' mostly naked men and women in dramatic poses, carved outta smooth white marble. But as we got closer to 'em, I realized they weren't marble, after all. They were porcelain, instead. And they weren't one solid piece like regular statues, neither. Like all the rest we'd passed up till now, they had joints in all the right places. Except the joints of these shone with gold.

And these ... these had faces.

Beautiful faces.

Except the last one. Well, no ... she was still beautiful, in truth, but also terrifyin' in a way that made the hairs on the back of my neck stand up, and I stepped even closer to Charlotte. Three small human skulls had been shaped atop her brow, and two curvin' horns made of more gold rose from her temples. Half of her shinin' porcelain face was missin', revealin' a golden skeleton beneath, and one empty eye socket.

There was sure a lot of gold down here...

I gaped at that last statue as we hurried past, the bright reflection of the torch off porcelain and gold fadin' as we moved away, and the half-demon woman gradually sinkin' back into blackness, until she was entirely lost again from sight.

Then there were no more statues ... just a deep and endless darkness, all around us.

I bumped into Charlotte as she slowed.

"What ... what is this place?" My voice echoed softly into nothingness. I hadn't really meant to ask that question out loud.

Charlotte shook her head. "Seems like some kind of collection." She whispered it, though we were the only ones in this place, and I was pretty sure the statues didn't care about our conversation. She swept her torch out to either side as far as she could reach, but the only thing we could see in its little circle of light was the rocky floor. "I think we're in another big chamber," she added. "Maybe it's best to proceed forward first? See what's directly ahead? And if it's only a dead end, we'll follow the walls until we make a full exploration of this particular cavern. Agreed?"

"Sure..." I thought I heard somethin' behind us. I turned quick, heart leapin', brandishin' my sword. The sound came again, outta the dark.

Clink. Clink. Clink.

"Charlotte," I breathed. "You hear that?"

She turned to face it, too, stepped up beside me and held the torch forward. "Yes."

Fer a second there was nothin', and I only held my breath and waited. The sword was makin' my arm burn and tremble with the effort of keepin' it aloft, so I dropped our extra torch with a clatter to the ground and gripped it two-handed.

Much better.

Nevermind I hadn't the faintest idea how to use a sword. Except to try and stick the enemy with the pointy end.

Clink. Clink. Clink.

Charlotte and I both sucked in a breath. It was closer now.

There was movement, just at the edge of the torchlight, and Charlotte let out a squeak of alarm.

Myself, I let out a streak of profanity, not carin' a whit whose company I was in.

'Cause the thing makin' that noise, the thing currently walkin' right at us, was that demon-woman statue. She was *movin'*, and she moved as fluid and natural as any flesh-and-blood person, and the profanity kept on comin' outta my mouth even as Charlotte and I hastily backed away from her.

But she kept on comin' at us. Delicate porcelain feet with toes all jointed in gold makin' that *clink, clink, clink* sound against the cave's rock floor as she walked.

"Ch-Charlotte." I finally managed to form a regular word. "You ever seen one of these before?"

She only shook her head stiffly. Struck dumb, I guess. I felt near the same. Thought my heart might burst right on out through my mouth, and the rushin' in my ears now almost drowned the sound of those porcelain feet. I didn't understand what this thing was, or how it was movin' like that, or what it might want from us, or what its purpose here could possibly be.

"*Non intrabis.*"

It ... it *spoke*. The mouth didn't move, but the words had come from it, unmistakably.

Its tone was female, smooth and lyrical, as it repeated the phrase again. "*Non intrabis.*"

The exposed golden half of the statue's skull and those long, curvin' horns shone brighter and brighter in our torchlight as she advanced, faster now, until Charlotte and I could hardly retreat quick enough without trippin' over ourselves or this uneven ground.

"You ... you shall not enter," Charlotte blurted suddenly.

I could hardly spare a glance at her as we scrambled backwards. "Huh?"

"That's what it's saying. *Non intrabis.* 'You shall not enter.' It doesn't want us here."

I snorted incredulously. "Oh great. Well it's a little late for that. And anyway ... it's blockin' the exit! Maybe you can tell it that?"

"Tibi malevo—"

We did trip, then, both of us, over stuff strewn all over the ground, interruptin' Charlotte's attempts to talk to the thing, and we fell back into a heap of ... somethin'.

Parts. It was a heap of parts. Metal plates and springs and rods and gears of all sorts, but I only barely got a look at it before pushin' myself up standin' again and heftin' that sword, readyin' fer a good strong swing.

"Tibi malevolentiam non habemus!" Charlotte shouted, just as the demon-woman statue had pulled back an arm and spread long, golden claws, presumably aimin' a strike at me, herself.

But she paused at Charlotte's words.

Fer a heartbeat there was silence, stillness.

And then I brought that sword down hard, choppin' into the place where the statue's porcelain neck met her porcelain shoulder. The fragile ceramic shattered, pieces flyin', cracks splinterin' all down her chest and shoulder from where the blade had buried.

Sparks lit the gloom, and her horned head fell sideways.

I'd severed half her neck, exposin' a tangle of wires.

"Van!" Charlotte sprang up off the heap of scraps herself. "What are you *doing*!?"

"Savin' us," I grumbled. And that Oracle woman had said we wouldn't need our weapons here. Yeah, sure. I yanked the sword out.

"I just told her we meant her no harm!"

Oh. I let the sword fall so the tip of it rested against the ground. "Well how was I supposed to know that! I don't even know what language that is—and I certainly can't understand it! I thought you were tellin' her to get outta the way!"

"First I was going to tell her we weren't here to cause any trouble—and then you go and do that!" She gestured at the almost-severed head.

"It was gonna attack me," I insisted. And it was. Why else would it have spread its claws like that?

More sparks shot from the wires I'd chopped through, and then the statue lurched forward, causin' Charlotte and I to jump back.

I landed in the pile of metal scraps and fell again, goddamnit. There were too many loose pieces, and they all just kept rollin' out from underneath me even as I attempted once more to get to my feet.

Charlotte had been more self-aware this time and smartly avoided the scrap-heap, but it seemed the demon-woman statue was more intent on me, anyway. She came right at me, her danglin' head not seemin' to slow her down none.

Well shit.

"*Periculum deprehenet!*" she said, loud enough this time that her words echoed off the rocky walls around us. Her smooth and lyrical voice weren't quite right now, thanks to the blow from my sword, I imagined. It was rougher and a little deeper. "*Periculum deprehenet!*" she repeated. "*Periculum deprehenet!*"

"Now what's she sayin'?" I shouted over at Charlotte as the statue closed in on me, and I was still tryin' to untangle myself from junk.

I caught the sword grip in both hands and raised the blade just in time to block the swing from those long, golden claws.

The porcelain along its forearm cracked where it hit steel.

"She says you're a threat," Charlotte offered. "Probably because you tried to chop her head off."

"She was gonna attack me first!" I blocked another swing from its other arm, and that porcelain cracked, too. Well, if it kept this up long enough, there wouldn't be nothin' of it left.

"*Periculum deprehenet!*" it shouted again.

Charlotte picked her way over toward us, careful not to fall herself.

I was still pinned against all that scrap and doin' my best to ward off those claws. At such close range I couldn't do much with such a giant sword except block 'em.

"Hey!" Charlotte shouted. She waved the torch around, tryin' to get the statue's attention. "Prohibere! State! Disiungere!"

"*Now* what are you tellin' it?" The next blow jarred my arm as I blocked it. Either the livin' statue was tryin' harder now, or I was tirin' out. Or maybe both. Most of the ceramic along its arms had fallen off now, and I decided I'd liked it more with it on. Beneath the porcelain was a thin metal frame in the shape of a human limb, and that frame was all fulla wires and gears and pistons.

Like my leg.

"I'm telling her to stop," Charlotte said.

"I don't think she's getting the point," I grunted. The tips of her claws came awful close to my face with the next swing, and this time, instead of just drawin' back and swipin' again, her long fingers gripped my blade.

Uh oh.

Without real flesh and blood, the sharp edges of the steel weren't no consequence at all.

She yanked, and the sword came outta my grip with shockin' ease. She tossed it away.

Fuck.

I rolled, only barely missin' a good rake of her claws.

Pieces of discarded scrap sprayed out over me as she struck the pile of junk instead of me. And then I was up on my feet again, and I dodged around behind her to make fer the sword she'd thrown away.

Except the light from our single torch didn't reach that far, so I only had a vague notion of where the weapon mighta landed. I dropped to my hands and knees, gropin' blindly along the ground.

"Van—" Charlotte started, but her warnin' was drowned by the statue lettin' out a long, mechanical hiss.

It spun, and lunged at me.

XXVIII

OUR END

"Charlotte!" I barked, just before throwin' myself sideways. Golden claws sparked off empty rock. "I need light!"

I didn't have much time to register what Charlotte was doin' over there with our only torch ... all I knew was that fer some reason she weren't bringin' it any closer, and I sorely needed it right about now.

The statue kept lungin' at me, and I kept barely dodgin' it, but it was also drivin' me back deeper and deeper into darkness, and I was pretty sure now I was movin' further and further away from that sword, too.

"Charlotte!" I tried again.

"Van," she finally answered. "We ... we have a serious problem here."

"That so?" I growled. "I hadn't noticed." But even despite the obviousness of her statement, the dread in her tone made my stomach clench. I ducked another swing from the demon-woman statue and risked a sprint through the black, back in Charlotte's direction, back toward our second discarded torch, back toward the sword.

"No," Charlotte snapped, voice echoin' out over the noise of the statue skitterin' after me. "*Look.*"

I chanced a glance even as I ran, and my steps slowed as I realized the true depths of her declaration.

There were other statues movin' now, too, emergin' slowly from the gloom and closin' in all around us. Others made of porcelain and gold like the one now so intent on murderin' me. And some of those in the red dresses, some of those religious sisters, and even, it seemed, the two metal soldiers we'd first passed, one still holdin' its sword and lookin' like it was ready to use it. And there were some we hadn't seen before, too, and animals, even. Birds, butterflies and some kinda other flyin' insect that moved too fast to see clearly.

Terror prickled over my scalp, wedged my heart into my throat. *Holy fu—*

Somethin' slammed into my right shoulder and knocked me clean off my feet. I hit the rocky ground hard and rolled till I came up against the base of a big stalagmite, and then I just laid there gaspin' and starin' up into blackness, takin' account of all the new bruises pulsin' along my body.

Except then, dim through the darkness, the remains of that demon-woman lurched into view. Much of her porcelain was gone now along her limbs, leavin' only her smooth torso and danglin' head intact. But still she came at me. She just weren't givin' up.

I wondered if she'd been the one to knock me sprawlin'. If so, there was an awful lot of strength in those dainty metal limbs.

"Van!"

Charlotte sounded far off now. I roused myself with a groan, forcin' myself to roll over even as my faithful statuesque pursuer closed the distance between us.

But I was too slow this time.

Her cold fingers caught me around the throat just as I stood, and they certainly didn't seem so delicate now. They clutched in an iron grip, hard and unyieldin', and then my feet were kickin' air.

She slammed me back into one of the cave's rough walls, metal grip squeezin' till I thought she might sever my head off my shoulders like I almost did to her.

My hands clawed at her arm and fingers, my boots kicked her in the chest and face; desperate, instinctive measures, but I knew it was all useless.

The black closed in quick this time, but there was one last thing I had to do. I struggled hard to suck down a thread of air. "Charlotte," I strangled out, and I hoped to God she could hear me from wherever she was now. "Get ... get out. *Run.* No ... no weapons."

Then I gagged as those metal fingers tightened, and my struggles weakened.

Maybe that Oracle had been right. Maybe I shouldn't have taken that sword.

Maybe that's why this statue had come after me and not Charlotte.

Maybe those others had only been after me, too. Maybe she could still get out...

A sharp crunch and crack sounded from somewhere near, and a sizzlin' noise, and then the pressure around my throat abruptly let go, and I crumpled in a heap to the cave floor.

Fer a minute all I could do was gag and wretch and drink air in great, heavin' gulps, tryin' to remember how to breathe. A circle of pain pulsed around my neck where hard metal had dug into my flesh, but the black in my vision finally cleared, and I blinked as I realized the light of Charlotte's torch was nearer now.

I pushed myself up to sit against the wall ... and saw Charlotte and the demon statue right in front of me, circlin' each other. The torch was on the ground between 'em, and Charlotte had the sword in both hands. The statue had a big hole in the ceramic of its torso now, right through its chest, and more sparks lit inside as it moved. Golden claws glinted in the flickerin' torchlight as it made multiple grabs for the sword blade, but each time Charlotte danced back outta reach.

Damn it all. I'd told her to *run.* I'd told her *no weapons*! Now she was just as much a target as me. And the rest of those mechanical monstrosities were still comin' our way, the big one with the sword out front and leadin' the way.

"Charlotte," I rasped, then coughed. It hurt to talk. "Charlotte ... we gotta get outta here."

She dodged in fast at the statue's next grab and swung the sword at the thing's left knee. The lower half of that leg snapped clean off, and the statue crashed to the ground.

She hacked its head off with another strong swing, finally finishin' the job I'd started. And then, fer good measure I figured, she stabbed the sword point down into its chest one final time, right into the place its heart woulda been, had it been made of flesh.

Its metal body jerked and twitched, then went still.

But all those others were comin', so much closer now. Already the fast flyin' insects had found us, buzzin' around our heads like bees as Charlotte ran over to me, planted the sword tip onto the ground, and held out her free hand.

I scowled up at her and swatted one of the bees away. "I said ... I said *no* weapons."

She shrugged and shook her head. "And I told *you* I wasn't going to let you get out of my sight, didn't I? Good thing, too."

I growled but took her hand, and she helped haul me to my feet. I wavered there fer a minute as the room spun and my head pounded. Then I nodded toward the sword. "You..." I winced. My voice sounded like I'd been chewin' gravel and every word made my throat ache fresh. "You know how to use that thing?"

She glanced down to the massive blade. "Well enough, I guess. I suppose this is quite different than a saber, in truth, but the fundamentals are generally the same."

"Fundamentals? The fundamentals of what?"

"Sword combat. My brother and I ... we used to fence together."

I'd never heard of fencin' combat before, but I also didn't have no more time to be askin' more questions. All those other statues were gettin' far too close fer comfort. I went to grab up the torch, gutterin' lower than I'd like now, then caught Charlotte's arm with my other hand and pulled her after me. "Come on, let's go. Quick! 'Fore those other things catch up to us."

She came after me, but slower than I'd like. "What about finding your ruins?"

I laughed, then winced again and put a hand to my bruised throat. "In case you hadn't noticed, those things want to kill us. You think we can fight through all of 'em and live?"

The answer was no, no way in Hell, not with just the two of us and one old sword, but Charlotte took the time to pause and take account of the metal beasts clamberin' our way like maybe we might have a chance at it, if she could do the math right.

I stopped, went back to her and took her arm again, pullin' her onward. "*No*, the answer is no," I hissed. "Whatever these things are, they're good enough. If we can get outta here alive, I'll give 'em all to Nan. There's enough gold and machinery in here to make anyone happy. And maybe they'll murder that old hag fer me, too, once she gets here."

"All right. Good plan."

Charlotte matched my pace then, to my relief, but we didn't get far before slowin' again. I swept the fadin' torch out in front of us, but all the rock looked all the same. In the dark and havin' been preoccupied with not bein' murdered, I'd completely lost my bearings. Panic welled, sharp and urgent. I tried to swallow it back. "I ... I don't remember which way is out."

"Me neither," Charlotte whispered. She turned to stand back-to-back with me, liftin' that ridiculous sword like she was gonna take on the whole metal army all by herself. "Find a wall and follow it," she suggested. "We'll find the exit eventually."

But not fast enough. And then we'd corner ourselves nice and neat for those guardians, too. I swatted away another of the buzzin' bees and turned to face the same direction as she. We couldn't see most of the things comin' fer us now, only hear 'em. A constant din of metal against rock, rusty gears turnin' fer the first time in a long time, the whir of mechanical wings, and voices. Voices murmurin' that same phrase over and over again: "*Periculum deprehenet!*"

Through the black, they sounded like people. Flesh and blood people.

Gooseflesh crawled up my arms and made the hairs on the back of my neck prickle. They'd already surrounded us.

There was no way out.

The other sword came outta the dark first, followed by the gleamin' outline of one of those metal soldiers. Charlotte lifted her sword to meet it and the blades sparked as they crashed together with teeth-jarrin' force.

I ducked instinctively, and Charlotte staggered under the power of the soldier's blow. I dropped the torch, straightenin' to put both hands around Charlotte's on the sword's hilt. We strained to push the abomination back, but even together could only make incremental progress.

"Van ... get back!" Charlotte ground through her teeth. "Get out of the way!"

"You can't hold it by yourself!" It was almost too strong fer both of us.

"If you would get out of the way I could maneuver correctly!"

"If I let go it's gonna cut you in half!"

"I told you I know how to use this thing ... so let me use it!"

"It's too strong fer you! Let me have the sword and I'll hold it off long enough fer you to make a run fer it!"

"Why do you keep trying so hard to get yourself killed? I thought you wanted to save your sister!"

Before I could explain to her there weren't no way in Hell I was gonna let her die down here, the sword we pushed against abruptly withdrew. I nearly fell on my face, and Charlotte staggered forward a few steps.

The next strike came almost immediately, skimmin' over my head close enough to knock off my hat, but again Charlotte met it blade fer blade, sparks lightin' the dark once more.

The bees swarmed around us, and every time one brushed against my skin I cringed away like it stung even though it hadn't. The memory of those metal insects Charles Miller had kept in jars in his dungeon—and what they were capable of—was still much too fresh in mind.

I swatted one off my arm and crushed it under my boot when it hit the ground.

Charlotte danced with the metal soldier ... it looked all the world like dancin' ... not like they were tryin' to hack each other into pieces, and I was left absolutely fuckin' helpless. I had no weapons. Not a goddamned thing.

The second metal soldier stepped into view and I grabbed up the only thing I had—our torch. This soldier didn't have a sword, at least, but I only registered what it *did* have in-hand when it leveled it at me.

A pistol.

Fer a heartbeat I froze.

It weren't the weapon itself that had caught me so off-guard, it was the leg holster that stuck outta the thing's right thigh.

It looked ... it looked just like the holster in *my* metal thigh.

Nausea hit me like a fist in the gut, a cold sweat racin' over my skin as I stared down the barrel of that gun.

And then it fired.

I woulda been dead. Shoulda been. The bullet shoulda hit me right between the eyes, but fer once, time was on my side. Time had corroded whatever ancient bullets had been in that chamber, and when the pin hit the primer, the whole thing exploded.

I flinched away from the mini-fireball and turned toward Charlotte.

The metal man she'd been fightin' had momentarily paused, distracted by the noise and light of its companion's misfortune.

Charlotte brought her blade down hard across its elbows, and its own sword clattered to the ground.

I dropped the torch quick and dove fer it, grabbed it up and rolled to my feet, only vaguely notin' the way my left bicep throbbed. If I'd re-injured that damn thing again...

But there was no time to worry about that. I swung at the nearest metal soldier's neck, the one whose sword I'd just stolen, and took its head off.

Seemed these swords were made fer combat, after all.

To my dismay, that didn't stop it. But it did slow it down some, and its arms didn't seem to be workin' right no more, neither. Charlotte and I both moved fer the second one now, who seemed awful confused by its weapon malfunction.

Its right hand was missin' now, and in the absence of a blade or a firearm, and with Charlotte and I both descendin' on it with a vengeance, it adopted the same strategy as the demon-woman.

It swung its remainin' fist hard, right at Charlotte's head.

She parried it with her sword, and I drove the point of mine through a thin gap in the metal plates of its side.

It jerked, straightened, and went rigid. Like it went from somethin' livin' back into a lifeless statue. And then it fell over, topplin' like some great tree to land with a crash.

Well. Maybe this might actually be—

A flash of red and gold surged into my peripheral vision and I spun quick, barely blockin' a blow from one of those statues with the domed faces and the elaborate red gowns. She took another swipe with her other hand and I yelled out as her claws raked across my right forearm. I shifted my weight to my right foot and gave her a good solid kick with my left foot, much like I'd done to Duster the bounty hunter, and like him, this thing went reelin' backward.

A cry from Charlotte made me whip around toward her just in time to see her go to her knees. Four bloody gashes had been ripped in the back of her shirt, and one of the red and gold things stepped up behind her, wrappin' a golden-gloved hand around her throat like that demon had done to me earlier.

I lunged forward, swingin' my blade in a flat arc with all the strength I could muster. I caught the thing good in the back of the head and its neck bent forward all unnatural-like, its face now pressed against its own breast. It let go of Charlotte, twisted toward me. And I drove my sword right through its elaborate gown and into its metal torso hard as I could.

But I didn't hit a gap in its plates this time like I had fer the other one.

The hilt jarred in my hands as the blade bounced right off. Least the force of my stab knocked it back a few steps, though it righted itself quickly enough and came at me again.

To my left, from the corner of my eye, I saw Charlotte on her feet again, sword back in-hand and tryin' her damnedest to hold off more of the metal bastards.

God damn. There were just too many of 'em. And we couldn't even tell which way was out anymore...

My attention went abruptly back to the thing in the red gown and golden gloves. I tried to do like I'd seen Charlotte do, dartin' in quick fer a stab or a swing and then leapin' back again, only barely keepin' its claws away from me. And on my left, Charlotte did the same, and fer what seemed like eternity we hacked at those things, reducin' some of 'em to scrap, but not enough.

My arms and shoulders ached, sweat ran into my eyes, and those goddamned bees swarmed everywhere, fillin' my ears with their endless dronin', constantly tryin' to land on me and do who knew what. I kept havin' to shake 'em off in-between all the fightin'.

Our torch had nearly gone out now ... it was gettin' harder and harder to see where the things were comin' from. Soon, it'd go out entirely.

And that would be our end. These metal abominations would rip us apart.

Part of me wished I'd just give up already. There weren't no way outta here alive. Why did I keep fightin'?

Why couldn't I just put down this sword and let 'em take me?

And yet, despite such thoughts ... I just kept on tryin', battlin' fer every last minute I had left, I guess. Musta been that Delano stubbornness.

It just wouldn't let me quit. Even when I shoulda.

Charlotte and I stood back-to-back now, pressed close by the crowd of things intent on killin' us. Her fight hadn't waned in all this time, neither. No matter she musta been plum exhausted same as me. No matter those gashes across her back musta hurt like hell, just as much and more as those I had across my right forearm, and that bullet-hole in my left bicep.

And yet she'd never slowed, never wavered.

Her steady presence against my back hardened my resolve.

If I was gonna die down here today ... at least I weren't gonna die alone.

Except then ... well ... all those things tryin' to kill us just *stopped*.

The metal statues all froze, wherever they happened to be, right in the middle of whatever they happened to be doin'. The birds, butterflies, and bees dropped like rocks to the cave floor, as abruptly unanimated as they had become animated. Some of 'em broke as they landed, and their pieces scattered.

Charlotte and I stood there in the middle of 'em all, and the only sound in the sudden ringin' silence was our harsh breathin'. We kept our swords raised and ready in what dim, sputterin' light of the torch was left, but nothin' moved.

Then another, different kinda sound filled the gloom. A deep, electrical kinda buzzin' noise. And one by one, all around us, lightbulbs flared to life. They were bare and threw out only weak yellow light, strung along on wire nailed high on the walls, but they illuminated the place well enough. Certainly better than our one torch had.

I blinked as they revealed the chamber we stood in, and all the carnage we had caused.

This particular cavern was a big one, all right. Wide and roughly circular, with a high, arched ceilin'. We'd been closer to the exit tunnel than I'd thought—it was over to my left only maybe twenty yards or so. To my right, over against the far back wall, was that heap of scrap parts Charlotte and I had stumbled into. Another tunnel, also strung with lightbulbs, opened up next to it. We were surrounded now by several more of the statues that had come alive ... but there were plenty more of 'em still standin' lined up in various places. And some other animals, too. All metal, like their human-ish counterparts. A few dogs, looked like. And a cat and a horse.

We stood ready fer another long minute, but when things remained quiet and still, I let out a long breath and lowered my sword. My arms burned with the effort of wieldin' it fer so long, the muscles tremblin'. I weren't in the habit of thankin' Divine Providence ... but I mighta muttered some words of gratitude just then.

"Van..." Charlotte whispered.

"I think we're in the clear."

"No. I can't ... something's ... something's wrong..."

I turned to face her in time to see her sword drop, the steel clangin' against rock. Her eyes had gone all glassy. She swooned.

I abandoned my own sword to catch her as she fell, then lowered her gently to the ground. She stared up past me at the cavern's ceilin', unfocused and unblinkin'. Fear shoved up my throat. "Charlotte? Charlotte!" I shook her shoulders. Smoothed messy waves of red hair away from her face and patted her cheek. Gently at first, then harder.

She didn't respond. Didn't so much as blink. She was limp and lifeless. Far too much like that poor nameless girl I'd watched die up in the Bone Spur Mountains.

"Charlotte! Can you hear me? What's wrong? Tell me what's wrong!"

But she didn't. My own heart beat too hard, too fast, as I felt fer a pulse. Her chest weren't risin' and fallin' ... there weren't no warm puffs of air comin' from her nose or mouth. She weren't breathin' at all.

She looked dead already.

I hissed curses between my teeth and tried to get my hands to stop shakin', tried to focus on seperatin' the throb of my own heart pulsin' through me from the beat of Charlotte's I was frantically tryin' to find.

And all the while my mind was racin'. Tryin' to sort how I might get her outta here, tryin' to figure if there was any chance in Hell I could get her medical attention in a timely manner, or if it was already too late.

Then I felt somethin' beneath my fingers. A pulse, all right.

I choked on the swell of relief, but it was short-lived. She may have had a pulse fer now ... but she still weren't breathin'. *Why ain't she breathin'?*

If she didn't start breathin' soon, she was gonna suffocate. Suffocate fer no good goddamned reason at all....

"Mr. Delano!"

The voice, out of nowhere and suddenly so close, made me spring up to my feet and startle so badly I tripped, fallin' back into one of the frozen metal statues. It and myself both went down to the floor in a tangle, but I rolled free of it quick, grabbed one of the swords and came up to my feet again ready to use it.

The other statues around us still didn't move, but there was another person here now, an actual flesh and blood human bein', though I couldn't see much of him under all the equipment he was wearin'. He had a tall, thin build, and a leather apron covered him from chest to knees. The apron itself had a multitude of pockets and loops sewn onto its front, and every one of the pockets and loops had somethin' stuck into it: tools, vials, flasks, rolled-up papers...

His left arm had leather on it too, a cuff around his bicep and one on his forearm, and both were just as fulla stuff as his apron. Pipes and vials and even a—a lightbulb? And on his wrist was somethin' that looked like a clock or a gauge of some sort, and somethin' like a little leather-bound book he had opened, but instead of pages, it had a row of little buttons inside it.

I could only gape at him, takin' in his ridiculous appearance and half-believin' he weren't even real.

"Well I certainly did not expect to see *you* here!" Half his face was covered by an enormous eyepatch equipped with telescopin' lenses similar to those cat's eye glasses of Sally's.

But even so, I recognized the voice, the heavy accent. The wiry build and the finely groomed mustache.

"Doc—Doctor—Doctor Balogh?" I finally spluttered.

Vaguely, I remembered that blind old woman had mentioned "my friend" was already down here. I'd thought her crazy, of course. She couldn't have known who I was lookin' fer ... I'd never told her outright.

And yet ... here he was. Dr. Balogh. The man I'd been searchin' fer all along.

Before I could blurt out what had happened to Charlotte—or any of the many, *many* questions I had fer him—he spotted her, sprawled out there on the ground beside me, and his one visible eye widened.

"Goodness gracious!" He rushed forward, duckin' beneath the outstretched arms of statues, and knelt at her side, immediately feelin' fer a pulse like I had just done. "What's wrong with her? Is she hurt?"

A swell of anger clogged my throat at such an absurd question. "Well she ain't just takin' a nap," I snapped.

"I *mean* did you see what happened to her to put her in this state?" The doc pulled a thing from his apron and clicked a button on it, and a little beam of light came out one end of it, which he proceeded to shine in Charlotte's eyes, one after the other.

I stepped closer to watch what he was doin', lettin' the sword lower again. That little thing he had ... it was like Charlotte's big spotlight, only so small. I'd never seen one that small before. "No," I said. "I didn't see nothin'. She got scratched by one of the red things, but so did I." I glanced to my right forearm, where blood had crusted at the edges of the tears in my shirt sleeve.

"There is still a pulse, that is good," he murmured. "But no pupillary constriction in response to light stimulus."

"Err. She ain't breathin'," I offered, havin' no idea the implications of what he'd just said.

"Was she hit by any of the flying creatures? A bee, bird, or butterfly, by chance?"

"I ... I dunno. She never said nothin' if she was. The bees kept landin' all over me but I kept swattin' 'em off. I didn't have much time to be watchin' her too, ya know. These things were tryin' to kill us." I gestured at 'em all, still circled around us and reachin' with claws outstretched.

"They were reacting to your weapons." He managed to sound

rather accusatory as he replaced the tiny spotlight into its appropriate apron loop and then removed a small vial and a syringe from other loops.

I scoffed. "Well I ain't gonna walk into the pitch-black depths of some strange cave without any kinda weapon! Who knows what coulda been in here ... and it was a good thing I grabbed somethin', too. Else these things woulda ended us quick."

The doc let out a long hiss of a breath. "If you would have left the swords where they belonged, none of these would have activated. You would not have been attacked at all." He jabbed the needle into the top of his selected vial and drew some of the liquid up into the syringe.

I shifted on my feet. "Yeah, well ... what if there'd been a bear in here? Or some deranged flesh-and-blood person?"

"There isn't," Dr. Balogh said crisply. He took Charlotte's left arm and pushed the needle into the crook of her elbow.

I glanced away as it pierced her skin, stomach rollin'. My mind flashed back to Miller's dungeon yet again, and the needles he'd used on me there, and bile rose in the back of my throat. I fought against the sudden rush of memories, the waves of ghostly pain that rippled along my body with 'em, and swallowed hard, turnin' away from Charlotte and the doc entirely.

But then I was lookin' at those terrifyin' metal statues, made all the more terrifyin' by the fact I could see 'em so much more clearly now. So I raised my eyes upward, focused on one of the bare lightbulbs hangin' on the wall, and tried to distract myself. "What ... what're you doin'?"

"Administering an antidote."

I spun back toward him. "Antidote? She was poisoned?!"

"Seems that way, yes. Her symptoms indicate she was likely stung by one of the bees. They carry a paralytic mixture the ancients often used for hunting in certain locales, and then in later centuries, it was often used for covert assassinations. If left untreated, the victim will die by suffocation."

Bile soured in my mouth again, this time fer a whole different reason. "But ... but she ain't gonna die, right? You gave her the antidote, so she ain't gonna die. Right?"

He turned to look over his shoulder at me, lips pressed into a hard line. He pulled his absurd telescope eyepatch down to hang around his neck so he could fix both eyes on me square, and he glared in a way he'd never done when I'd been stayin' at his homestead, not even when I'd been so angry about my missin' leg and lashed out. "The antidote will work against the paralysis, allow her to breathe again. Eventually she will have full muscle control again, probably within a few minutes. But her full recovery depends on how long she was in a paralyzed state. How long was she like this before I arrived?"

"Not ... not long. Maybe a minute or so."

He gave a nod. "Then I think she will suffer no permanent effects." He turned back toward her and pressed his fingers to the side of her neck again. "But I will need to perform resuscitation procedures to mimic breathing until she regains control. Come. Quick." He stood and gestured at me. "Leave that sword and carry her. Follow me. We need to get her back to my laboratory so I can keep a proper eye on her recovery."

Laboratory? But he was already duckin' underneath the statues' arms again and headin' out across the cavern, so I hurried to do as he said. I laid the sword down, grabbed up my hat from where it'd fallen durin' the fight and shoved it back onto my head, and went to Charlotte to scoop her up. It weren't as easy as it shoulda been, given my arms were already exhausted from all the fightin' with a blade, and I had both my wounds and Charlotte's to be careful of.

But I managed to get one arm under her shoulders and one in the crook of her knees and lifted her with only a grimace. That old bullet wound in my left arm didn't like this much, but I pushed on, followin' the doc across the big open space to the lighted tunnel near the scrap pile.

And I couldn't help but notice as we walked that there were human bones in here, too. Few and far between, but unmistakable nonetheless. And Charlotte and I had nearly joined 'em.

We passed through the mouth of the lighted tunnel, where some old rails started along the floor, bolted into the rock. A handcar waited at the near end of 'em, and they stretched on through the tunnel far as I could see. And so did those lights.

By the time we reached the rail car, after our brisk walk across the cavern's expanse and my limp more pronounced under an extra person to carry, I was winded again. That fight with those metal abominations had taken more outta me than I'd realized.

Doctor Balogh motioned toward the cart. "Set her there. Gently now."

I gave him a look. What did he think I was gonna do? Throw her down like a sack of grain? "What is this place, anyway?" I got Charlotte situated comfortable as I could, stretched out flat on her back along the hard wooden platform.

The doc hopped up onto the hand car. "A cache."

I grunted and climbed up after him. "A cache? Of what? Murderous statues?"

He grunted and took a knee next to Charlotte again. "Of some of the finest examples of engineering the Old World ever had to offer. Of course, you managed to destroy some of the most exquisite pieces in your rampage. Hundreds of years they rested here, safe, only to be reduced to ruin within a matter of minutes after your arrival."

A multitude of thoughts shot through my mind at his accusation, at his tone. My neck still ached where the one of those "exquisite pieces" had nearly squeezed my head right off my body. "Well I weren't gonna let 'em just murder me."

"Now I understand the reason for these caches in the first place," Balogh murmured, dismissin' my protest. Then, louder, he said, "You know how to work one of these things?"

"Course I do."

"Good. Get going then. Fast as you can manage. I've set the junctions already; this track will take us straight to my lab. Meantime, I'll work on keeping oxygen flowing to the young lady's brain."

"All right." I swallowed, not likin' the mention of oxygen and brains too awful much, and stepped around to the side of the car that would allow me to both see down the track in the direction we were headed and keep an eye on the doc and Charlotte both.

Then I grabbed the handle and set about pumpin' it, fast as I could manage, just as he'd said. It was slow buildin' momentum at first, but once I got us goin' along those rails, we picked up speed right quick.

The wheels on this car and even the track itself were awful well-oiled. I wondered if they'd been around down here as long as those statues, or if they were a newer addition.

Beside me, Doctor Balogh went about his medical business with Charlotte, alternatin' pushin' on her chest with the flat of his palms and usin' a little bellows pulled from his apron to shove air into her mouth.

It was all I could do to let him do it. It sure didn't look like he was tryin' to save her. It looked like he was tryin' to kill her. A minute stretched by of him workin', and me keepin' our car movin', the string of lightbulbs flashin' by along the wall to my right. Occasionally I caught glimpses of more scrap piled into dead-end alcoves, or bizarre-lookin' machinery built into the rock itself, or other railway off-shoots that looked to have collapsed in on themselves with so much time neglected.

The rattle of our car slidin' down the tracks filled the silence, till I couldn't take it no more. "You *sure* that's meant to keep her alive?"

"Oh, absolutely."

"All right. But ... yer sure? Positively certain?"

He paused his work and sat back on his heels, twistin' to face me. "Son, I've been a doctor for almost longer than you've been alive. I know what I'm doing."

I scowled at his use of that term "son" again and focused back on the track ahead of us. "Yeah. Fine."

"If you were really so concerned for her safety," he muttered, barely audible over the dull rumble of our cart sailin' down those rails, "you should have left those swords alone."

"I told you," I snapped back at him, "I ain't wanderin' into an unknown place unarmed. And anyway, how was I supposed to know takin' one of those swords would wake up all those monsters?"

He shook his head and turned his attention back to Charlotte. "For you to have found your way in here at all means the Oracle must have granted you passage. You've got her markings all over you, too. That's what happened, isn't it? You went through her Judgement?"

I growled, givin' my handle another few good, strong pumps, wishin' I could get my hands around that old woman's throat. "We got attacked and drugged, that's what. And robbed. That woman ain't no Oracle. She's a thief who hides behind magic tricks. And maybe she's a would-be murderer, too."

"But she told you that you would not need your weapons in here, did she not?"

I dropped my glare back down to him, found him starin' steadily at me. "She failed to mention bringing a weapon would anger the murderin' statues," I hissed.

"But she told you no weapons?"

"Sure. She mentioned it. I just ain't inclined to listen to a woman who's just drugged and robbed me, is all."

Doctor Balogh sighed and turned away from me. "She did not rob you. She will return your things to you upon your exit."

"How do you know that?"

"Because I have been out myself. Several times. And each time she is there waiting for me ... *with* my belongings."

I peered at his back, lookin' over all the strange things stashed in his arm cuffs again. Remembered that the old woman had also said somethin' about "my friend" doin' a particular kind of work down here, and all those questions I'd had upon first seein' him show up out in that cavern of statues came back to me. "What are you doin' down here anyway, Doc?"

"I could ask you the same thing."

"Yeah, well, I asked you first."

Charlotte gasped and choked, and Dr. Balogh sat back at the same time I stepped forward to get a better look at her, relief springin' through me. Color had returned to her face, and she blinked slowly, heavily. Her fingers twitched. But she was breathin' now. Breathin' on her own.

"There we are," Dr. Balogh said. He tucked his little bellows into its appropriate apron pocket, then picked up one of her hands and massaged it. "Take it easy. Take it slow. Feeling will return to normal for you soon. You are lucky I found you when I did."

Then he turned to me, and his gentle, soothin' tone went sharp. "What are you doing? Man the controls, would you? We've almost reached the lab now, be ready to brake. Unless you want to wreck the cart, too?"

"No," I grumbled, but heat stung my face despite myself. I stepped quick back to the pump handle; located the brake lever and got ready to ease it back.

Up ahead not too far now our tunnel opened out into another chamber, and the tracks terminated there in a big wooden board painted with fat black and yellow diagonal stripes. The paint looked new.

Perplexed, I pulled the brake nonetheless as we approached, and our hand car eased to a halt before the big painted board with only some mild screechin'.

Dr. Balogh dismounted the platform and waved at me to follow. "Come now. Bring her. Follow me."

I climbed down myself, went around to gently lift Charlotte again, though at least this time she weren't entirely limp. She was awake and aware now, and I muttered apologies when I saw her wince as my arm passed under her back. But I managed to lift her, and she leaned her head against my shoulder, one hand loosely clutchin' a fistful of my shirt.

I followed the doc into another big chamber ... even bigger than the one we'd just left, and this one more brightly lit and outfitted with a great deal more machinery. The dull thunder of rushin' water echoed from somewhere, but my gawkin' gaze came to a full stop as it fell upon a familiar figure.

Someone I'd hoped I wouldn't have to face again. Someone I'd planned to actively avoid, preferably fer the rest of my life.

But there was no avoidin' her now. She stood there starin' right at me—and lookin' more sour at the sight than probably any other person who had ever laid eyes on me.

Mrs. Hannah Balogh.

XXX

EVERYONE DIES

I looked away from her quick as her mouth opened; practically ran after the doc as he headed fer the left side of the chamber.

To my great relief, his wife did not follow. Nor did she yell out whatever it was she mighta been intent on first sayin' at the sight of me. I didn't think I could put off that conversation fer as long as I would have liked ... but I'd surely try my best to put it off as long as I could possibly manage.

There was a circle of bed rolls over in this area, and an old wooden table set with four stools. Dr. Balogh reached down to pull a blanket from one of the beds and spread it out over the table, then motioned fer me to put Charlotte there.

I set her on the edge of it, and with proppin' one hand against my shoulder, she was able to sit on her own, though she still seemed awful woozy.

"My heavens!" the doc spat as he noted the slashes along her back. His bright gaze lifted to glare at me again over her shoulder. "Why did you not tell me about these?!"

I glared right back. "I was a little more concerned over the fact she weren't breathin'! And then if I recall correctly, you were orderin' me around and tellin' me to act all quick-like. Didn't have much of a chance to mention 'em, did I?"

He shook his head and muttered somethin' I couldn't make out, then proceeded to fuss over Charlotte fer a minute while I helped to steady her, askin' her to blink and turn her head and move her arms and legs. She was able to comply with all his requests, so he shined that little light into her eyes again, and then nodded and moved around to look at the gashes on her back.

She sucked in a breath as he tried to pluck her shirt away from the torn edges of skin.

I winced myself. Hers were worse than the ones I'd gotten on my arm.

Dr. Balogh clucked his tongue as he studied 'em. "Well, young lady, you seem to be recovering from the poison well enough. But these are going to need to be cleaned and stitched, I'm afraid."

"Charlotte," she mumbled. She lifted a hand to rub it over her face. "My name is Charlotte."

The doc straightened and came around the table to stand in front of her. He held out a hand. "And I am Doctor Henri Balogh. Pleased to make your acquaintance, Charlotte."

She shook his proffered hand. "Likewise, Doctor."

"If you'll just lie down on the table on your stomach, I can take a better look at your back. Get those wounds fixed up. My wife Hannah will have a fresh blouse you can borrow."

Charlotte nodded wearily, shiftin' carefully to lie down.

I tried to help her best I could. "You all right? You scared the daylights outta me. Thought you were dead."

"Oh, sure. I'm fine." But she sounded tired, as exhausted as I felt myself. "Just thought I'd give you a little taste of your own medicine."

I frowned. "A taste of my own—"

"Yes. You're always giving me a fright, trying to get yourself killed. Making me worry. Now you know what it's like."

I didn't exactly know what to say to that, except I didn't like that worryin'. Not at all. Before I could manage to reply, Dr. Balogh caught my attention, ordered me to bring over some old pipes stacked against the wall. So we could form a make-shift partition, he said, to give Charlotte some privacy while he stitched her up.

While I worked on that, he called his wife over, tellin' her they needed to prepare a suitable "medical environment". She went off to fetch other things, but I kept my focus solely on those pipes and didn't dare even glance at her.

Soon enough I'd tied some tall pipes to the legs on one long-side of the table at the doc's instruction, and tied another pipe across the top of those, and then we draped some blankets over it to create a kind of blind.

Mrs. Balogh had brought over a whole kit of medical supplies, and then the doc shooed me away.

"Go on now," he said. "I must get to work. She will be just fine. My daughter Fanni will see to your arm. She's quite good at doctoring herself, you know."

"Fanni?"

"That's right. Go on. I'll let you know when I'm done here."

"I'll be all right," Charlotte murmured. She reached out fer my hand and squeezed it.

I hesitated, though not 'cause of any worry over Charlotte. I had no fear Dr. Balogh would chop off any of her limbs to replace 'em with machine parts. And aside from that affinity fer Old World tech, I had no doubts he were a good doctor. More it were the fact I'd forgotten the doc had brought his children with him, and I was as reluctant to face them as I was to face Mrs. Balogh.

But it was her glare that finally moved me. I could feel it burnin' holes in me, and when I finally glanced up to confirm it, she was givin' me a hard stare, all right.

So I nodded and gave Charlotte's hand a quick squeeze in return before hastily movin' off, around the makeshift wall of blankets and back toward the center of the chamber, where a small portable stove had been set up with a stew pot atop it.

I wondered how they'd gotten all this stuff down here. Surely that pot hadn't been left in here all this time ... or if it had, they wouldn't be eatin' out of it. Surely it woulda been rusted through by now. They had to have brought it with 'em, or purchased it in town, along with a whole lot of other stuff I noted spread around this chamber now.

But they couldn't have taken all that through that little tunnel Charlotte and I had crawled through. No way. There musta been some other entrance somewhere...

I slowed as I spotted the children, both of 'em, and both starin' at me just about as hard as their mother had been. They stood near a big workbench littered with tools and ... machine parts.

I recalled Nan had said she'd found Dr. Balogh's workshop, back at his homestead near Bravebank. Maybe he'd just come here to continue whatever work he'd started there. My left leg twinged and I scowled, then made my way over toward the stove.

Maybe the doc thought his daughter could fix up my arm, but I weren't gonna impose on her. Not after what I'd done to their family last time ... and not with the way the girl was lookin' at me now.

So I just went and took a seat in the middle of the place, starin' at the cold stove and tryin' to decipher what murmurin' was goin' on behind those blankets.

Didn't take long fer the kids to come to me, though.

I had a strong urge to get up and leave as they approached, but it woulda been a futile endeavor, in the end. Where was I gonna go? I didn't know my way around this place, whatever it was. And I surely didn't want to get trapped in another dark chamber with more murderous statues. Nor could I have left Charlotte here, anyway.

So I stayed put, cross-legged on the cool, flat rock of the chamber floor, and stared into nothin' with enough determination you mighta thought I was contemplatin' the mysteries of the universe instead of just how much I didn't wanna face the kind-hearted family I'd once stole from.

The boy Radley sat cross-legged beside me to my left, while Fanni moved a different direction, and then I heard her rustlin' around some-where behind me, and the sound of water bein' poured.

There was silence between me and the boy fer a space, and then he said, simply and without preamble, "Your leg seems a lot better now."

I only nodded. There was a lot I wanted to say to him. A lot I wanted to apologize fer, even, but none of the things I could think to say just then seemed right. None of 'em seemed like enough.

Then Fanni reappeared to my right, holdin' a bowl of water, a roll of bandages, and a small jar of what suspiciously looked like some of Blackbird's moonshine. A clean rag was draped over her arm. She settled herself on my other side, and again I was overcome with the urge to get up and leave.

To escape the situation all together.

"Let me see your arm," she ordered.

It was the first thing she'd said to me since I'd first laid eyes on her upon wakin' up in her house months ago. All that time I'd spent with her family, and she hadn't said a word to me. Now, I swallowed at her cool tone. "I can clean it up myself. No need fer you to do it." I reached fer the water bowl, but she pulled it away from me, eyes flashin'.

"You want it to get infected? Want father to chop off your arm, too?"

"No..."

"Then I will do it."

"Ya know, I've done plenty of doctorin' myself, Missus. And I ain't died yet."

Her gaze narrowed. "But you would have. Before, when my father pulled you out of the desert. You would have died right then if not for him. And it was your kind of doctoring that gave you that infection in the first place—that killed the flesh of your leg so there was no other choice but to amputate it."

I looked away from her and back to the stove at that, knowin' damn well it were true, but not willin' to admit it out loud.

"And just now, too, if father had not ordered off the attack, you would have been killed for certain."

Ordered off the attack? Wait, did that mean Dr. Balogh could ... could *control* those things?

"She's right," Radley put in from my other side.

I scowled, not needin' his input here.

"So give me your arm," Fanni said again, but she didn't wait fer me to comply. She grabbed my right wrist and yanked it toward her, and then I winced as she pushed my sleeve up to my elbow, bein' none too gentle about it. "And I'll make sure it is all done *properly*."

So maybe that's why she really wanted to do it herself. Maybe this was her way of makin' me pay fer betrayin' her family's trust, in whatever small way she could. She'd fix me up, sure. But not without makin' it hurt some.

I inhaled sharply and clenched my teeth against spittin' out a curse as she slapped the rag—now soaked in water—onto my forearm and started scrubbin' at the crusted blood and torn skin.

Reflexively, I attempted to jerk my wrist outta her grip, but she held onto me with fingers nearly as strong as that statue's, I swear. "Not sure such vigorous scrubbin' is really necessary," I managed to grit out. "Those cuts ain't that deep."

"Oh, I see," she replied smoothly. But she did not ease up on her scrubbin'. "Then you've dealt with these automatons before?"

"These ... these what?"

"Automatons." She dunked the bloodied rag into the water bowl, rinsed it, squeezed it out, and scrubbed some more. "Those things that attacked you?"

It was all I could do to sit still under her rough administrations. "No ... nope. Can't say I have."

"Well then. Why don't you just leave the doctoring to me, being as you don't know anything about them, or what kind of wounds they can inflict."

I nodded, hopin' if maybe I agreed with her, she'd gentle up some. "Yeah, all right. All right, sure."

She finally stopped scrubbin' and tossed the rag back into the bowl. My arm throbbed a whole lot worse now than it had when she'd started. She didn't let go of my wrist, but reached fer the little jar of moonshine next. She propped it between her knees and twisted off the top, and I tried to yank my arm away from her again, anticipatin' her dumpin' it over those cuts.

She flashed me a glare, pullin' my arm back into her lap, and instead offered the jar out to me.

Oh. I took it from her with my left hand with a little sheepish nod and downed a good third of it, this time welcomin' that searin' burn all down my gullet.

"Which kind was it?" she asked.

I blinked back the eye-waterin' fire of the 'shine to squint at her and coughed. "What kind was what?"

"The automaton that scratched you," Radley said. "What'd it look like?"

"Oh. It was red and gold. Had a fancy dress and a domed face." I took another swig of the 'shine.

"A Siren then," Fanni said, and she snatched the moonshine jar away from me and dumped the rest of it over my arm.

My yell echoed out across the chamber, and I managed to wrench my arm full away from her this time, bringin' it across my body to cradle it protectively. Though there weren't nothin' I could do now about that alcohol seepin' down into those cuts. Just had to grit my teeth and wait fer the white-hot burnin' to fade.

"Everything all right out there?" Dr. Balogh called from behind his wall of blankets.

"Just fine," Fanni answered, fixin' me with a hard look. "Our *guest* is being a baby, that's all." She threw the roll of bandages at me and scooped up the bowl of dirty water and the rag, then stood. "Wrap it up," she spat. "You'll be fine."

Then she turned and marched back over to that workbench, tossin' the bowl to grab up some parts, goin' back to whatever she was doin' before I arrived, I supposed.

"You'll be fine, Mr. Delano," Dr. Balogh's disembodied voice said. "You're very lucky it wasn't much worse."

"Fer fuck's sake," I hissed. "I think it was better before." The 'shine's fire still ate into the flesh of my arm, though it was finally startin' to ease off. I picked up the roll of bandages with my left hand and started to unwind a length of it.

"I'll get you something to cut it with," Radley said quietly, and he stood and wandered off, then returned shortly with a small knife and handed it over.

"Thanks," I muttered. Well, *he* didn't seem to have too many hard feelin's toward me, at least. If he was bein' so helpful, maybe his mama had never found out he'd been the one to aid me in my escape that night. Or the one to bring me my guns.

Maybe he'd never got whooped fer it.

I hoped he hadn't. I cut what I needed off the gauze roll and started to wrap it around the freshly oozin' slashes across my forearm, though awful clumsily given I only had one hand to work with.

Radley sighed and knelt in front of me. "Here, let me help."

I did. He was far gentler than his sister, windin' the length of bandage at just the right snugness from my wrist to my elbow, then tyin' it off.

"Yer ... yer pa get the money I left fer him?" I croaked. "Fer the mule and the saddle I took?"

"Yeah." He sat back, admirin' his work.

"Yer ma and yer sister know about that?" I glanced up to Fanni's back, but she ignored me now. I'd done this family wrong, sure, but I'd tried to make it right later, too.

"Yeah." Radley followed my gaze toward his sister, then looked toward the wall of blankets his parents worked behind. "Otherwise I think Mama might have shot you on sight when you walked in here. Or turned you over to Sheriff Reeves for being a horse thief."

Sheriff Reeves. What would she have thought of that, I wondered? Her newly appointed deputy, turned out to be a horse thief.

A horse thief and a whole lot more worse than that.

I grunted and gave a nod, suddenly wishin' fer more of that 'shine. It would have numbed things up right quick. And not just the lingerin' pain in my arm.

"Why didn't you come back?" Radley asked suddenly, quietly, so the rest of his family wouldn't hear. He settled himself cross-legged again, right in front of me, and looked at me with that plainly open, innocently curious look only children could manage. "You said you were gonna come back. Bring back our mule and all, and then you didn't. You *promised*, Mister."

I dropped my gaze away from that look, studied my hands in my lap and those strange painted designs scrawled all over the backs of 'em, and wet my lips. Nodded again. "I ... I, uh ... ran into some trouble. Didn't want to lead it back to you and yer family. I'm sorry."

That weren't entirely untrue.

The boy frowned, and his eyes flicked over my person. "We heard there was a shoot-out in town the day after you left. Three men killed. Was that you?"

At last, I didn't have to lie. I shook my head. "No. No that wasn't me."

He seemed to relax a little at that, and I decided not to mention the fact the man who *had* killed those gents was my long-time partner, and he was waitin' fer me somewhere out in the forest above us even now.

"What about your guns?" Radley gestured at my empty hips, where my weapons shoulda been. "Thought you didn't like to go nowhere without them?"

"Yeah. I don't." I sighed and rubbed my left hand over my face, exhaustion hittin' me full force again. "Didn't have a choice this time. Crazy old lady took 'em from me. Wouldn't give 'em back."

"The Oracle?"

"So she calls herself."

"Well why were you attacked then? The machines are only supposed to attack anyone coming in with weapons."

I lowered my hand and peered at him. "Only *supposed* to attack...? Now what the hell does that mean?"

Radley winced and looked over his shoulder again, toward the wall of blankets. "Shhh," he hissed. "Mind your language, Mister. Mama's already mighty sore at you. I wouldn't give her any more reason to dislike you."

I snorted. "Kid, I think your mama is gonna dislike me no matter what I do."

"Well don't let her hear you talking like that. She'll send you right back to those machines to finish you off."

I rolled my eyes, rememberin' those rules she'd listed out to me the night I'd woken to find her sittin' next to my bed with a big ol' knife in her hand. "Yeah. I'll try my best. So those machines. You say they're only supposed to attack people bringin' in weapons?"

He nodded. "That's right."

"How many people find their way down here, exactly?" I couldn't imagine it was very many, given that little burrow we'd had to crawl through to find this place. But then again, it was possible others had found a different way in. A larger, more obvious entrance, maybe; the same entrance the Balogh's musta brought all this stuff in through.

Radley shrugged. "Not many. Most don't pass the Oracle's Judgement, I guess. And if they don't pass, she doesn't let them in. And if they *do* get in, they always bring weapons, seems like. The machines end up killing them. Except for us. We listened to the Oracle. Pa didn't bring a single weapon when he came in here." The boy spread his hands and smiled. "Now we've been living here for weeks, safe as can be."

I thought of all the people crowdin' into Blackbird right now, and all the people frantically searchin' up at surface level fer just this kinda place, and shook my head. "I think it's likely that someday, and probably someday soon, that Oracle is gonna find someone who won't take no fer an answer. She's gonna get herself killed. Her and all her followers, too."

Radley gave me a strange look. "She can't be killed, Mister. She's the Oracle."

I let out another laugh. "Oh, anyone can be killed, kid. Sorry to break the news to you ... but everyone dies."

His lips pursed, brows lowerin' over his eyes. "Not her. Her magic protects her."

"Oh fer the love of..." I sighed heavily and scrubbed at my eyes. "She tell you that?"

"Uh huh."

"'Course she did. All right. So she can't be killed. Fine. Yer tellin' me no one has found their way in here without her showin' 'em the way?"

"Not yet. That's why she's there, you know. Her and her followers, they're the protectors of this place. Pa told me they've been here for generations, guarding it."

All of this nonsense was worsenin' my headache. "And what about you? You face that so-called Oracle's Judgement, too?"

He nodded stoically.

I hoped he hadn't seen the kinda things I'd seen. Hoped he'd had far more pleasant visions. I shifted some on that hard rock ground and cleared my throat. "So if you don't got any weapons on your person, those statues ... what? Just stand there?"

He nodded again. "They only activate in response to a threat."

I frowned. Well. I guess me stealin' one of their swords and almost hackin' off that horned statue's head *would* count as a threat. To them, anyway. Those strange words they'd been chantin' made sense now, in that respect. "They ... are they ... are they Old World?"

I almost couldn't get myself to ask. Memories of the metal soldier's all-too-familiar leg holster flashed through my mind, and that sick feelin' churned in my stomach afresh.

But Radley brightened at the question, eyes agleam with sudden enthusiasm. "Oh yes! All of them. Father says it's the most impressive collection of whole, operational Old World relics he's ever seen. You should have seen him when we first arrived ... I thought he might burst he was so excited."

"Uh huh." Just what I needed. Yet another person seemingly obsessed with a civilization dead and gone a long, long time ago. "Thought your pa was a doctor," I commented. "What's he want with a bunch of old machines?"

The boy gave a snort. "Machines are the future, Mister. Don't you know that?"

"No." All the old stories started comin' back to me. The ones Mama had used to tell me and Ethelyn before bed. The ones Ethelyn had loved so very much, she'd daydreamed about 'em far more often than Mama had cared fer. "Ain't that what they say caused the Great Fall in the first place? Machines? Sounds to me like they're the past, not the future."

Radley's expression darkened. "Father says those are just stories."

"Ah. Well. What does he say caused the Great Fall, then?"

"People. People like you and me. Same as every other disaster in history."

I chuckled. He had a point there. But was most certainly only parrotin' what he'd heard his pa say before. I wondered if he had any real good understandin' of what that really meant. "Suppose that's true enough," I admitted. "So ... yer pa ... he can control those things?"

Radley sat up a little straighter, almost puffed out his chest, even. "Sure he can. Worked on it for weeks. Ever since we got here, really."

"Huh." I rubbed absently at my bruised throat. That changed things, certainly. Machines that could murder—or not—upon command. Had Nan suspected somethin' of the sort was down here? Was that why she'd been so intent on findin' ruins in this area?

The thugs in her employ were bad enough.

But *these* kind of things in the hands of Nine-Fingered Nan would be ... truly terrifyin'. Deadly. Unstoppable.

And handin' her such weapons just might be the price fer Ethelyn's freedom.

I swallowed, winced as my throat ached, and sighed again. "So the other people who pass the Oracle's Judgement, who come on in here ... where are they now?"

The boy sobered quick. But before he could make a reply, a woman's voice answered from behind me.

"They are all dead."

XXXI

NO TIME FOR TOMORROWS

I startled, twisted around to see Mrs. Balogh standin' there. I hadn't heard her approach. I wondered how long she'd been there; how much of our conversation she'd heard.

"They are all dead," she said again. "Just as you should be. All bringing weapons when they should not, just as you did. And they paid the price."

Reflexively, I scrambled to my feet and pulled off my hat to clutch it to my chest; long-dormant memories of manners springin' to the front of mind again suddenly. Probably 'cause of that look she was givin' me now.

"If your companion had not spoken the language of the Engineers and caught my husband's attention, and had my husband not been so keen to preserve the rare Mortiferum Wraith you were single-handedly destroying, he might not have stopped the machines in time to save you, either."

I'd always found the re-discovery of impeccable manners to smooth my own mama's ire ... maybe it'd work on Radley's mama, too. I cleared my throat again and offered her a nod. "Ma'am. Mrs. Balogh. Hannah."

She crossed her arms. "Mrs. Balogh."

"Mrs. Balogh. I don't exactly know what a Mortifer ... uh, Mortifera-whatsit Wraith is—"

"It is the automaton you ruined. The one with golden horns. *Very* rare. We have never found one intact, in fact, let alone one that could still operate. But I suppose you put an end to that, didn't you?"

Damn. She really didn't like me much. I resisted the urge to put a hand back up to my bruised throat. Rare or not, that thing had most definitely tried to kill me. And rare or not, I weren't just gonna let it end me without some kinda fight. "Er, well ... I didn't realize ... I guess I didn't take much time to consider its value, bein' as it was surely intent on killin' us. But if it was somehow important to you and your family ... then I'm sorry fer it bein' destroyed. I do appreciate your husband sparin' us, though. Even if at the cost of that ... that Wraith. And thank you kindly fer your hospitality." I shifted awkwardly on my feet. "Uh, again."

Her eyes narrowed. "You planning to steal from us again?"

I shook my head vigorously. "No, no ma'am. Course not. And, uh, well ... well I didn't exactly *steal* ... I paid fer the mule, didn't I? And the saddle, too."

"A week later," she stated flatly. "That is a week we had to go without our wagon. And I had already sold off some of our furniture, some of my husband's equipment, to have enough to afford another mule before we received your payment."

I winced. Turned my hat round and round in my hands. "I'm ... I'm very sorry, ma'am. To have put you and your family at such an inconvenience. I had urgent business that could not wait. And then ... as I told your son here ... I ran into some trouble. *Not* the shootin' in town," I put in quick, as I saw the question formin' on her face. "That weren't me." I surely weren't gonna tell her that was still the trouble I'd had, even if I hadn't been the one doin' the actual shootin'. "But I had trouble nonetheless. And I ... I didn't want to bring it back on you or your children. That's all."

That weren't all. Not even close. But that was all I was ever gonna tell her, and I'd insist that was all of it till my dyin' day if I had to, hand on the Good Book, itself.

Her rigid stance softened a bit. "Perhaps you have gained some wisdom since last I saw you."

I scoffed. "I, uh, I don't know about that, ma'am." More like I'd just gained more guilt. Guilt over flat-out stealin' from the first people to show me real kindness in years. Well, I'd done what I could in the end to make it right ... I only had to hope it'd be enough. Fer me and them both.

"Well then, what are you doing down here? Come seeking to be rich like all the other fools?"

The question took me off-guard, and I realized I weren't exactly sure how I should answer that.

Beside me, Radley got to his feet as well, lookin' up at me just as expectantly as his ma. "Yeah, Mister. What're you doing here, anyway?"

"We were looking for you," came a weak, unsteady voice, and I looked toward my left to see Charlotte walkin' stiffly in our direction. She grimaced with the movement and wore an unfamiliar light-blue blouse with her borrowed rough-spun trousers, but at least she was movin' around on her own now.

Dr. Balogh followed her, lookin' none too pleased. "Miss Charlotte, you really should try to rest. At least until I can be sure that poison has fully cleared your system!"

She shook her head. "I'm fine, Doctor. Feeling much better now, thank you."

But I went to her anyway, puttin' my hat back on before I took her arm and helped her to sit on a stool on the other side of the stove.

Dr. Balogh frowned, shinin' that little light into her eyes again. "Fine. You just take it easy, young lady. I'm going to keep an eye on you for the next few hours though, understand?"

Charlotte nodded.

"Looking for us?" Radley repeated. He grabbed another nearby stool and dragged it over next to Charlotte, perchin' atop it eagerly to face her. "Really? How come?"

"Because, er..." I paused again, glanced from his bright gaze over to the highly suspicious stare of his ma. I didn't exactly want to mention Nine-Fingered Nan's involvement in any of this, so I decided to stick with the original reason I'd been seekin' out the good doctor. "Because my leg ... the false one ... it did somethin' strange a few weeks back."

That caught Dr. Balogh's attention. He stopped fussin' over Charlotte and turned to face me, eyebrows archin'. He'd put that telescopin' eyepatch back over his right eye and looked just as ridiculous now as he had upon first appearin' in the cavern. "Oh? Something strange, you say?"

"Yeah."

Charlotte gave me a puzzled look, and I realized all at once I'd never mentioned to her anythin' about that leg doin' strange things, or that I'd like to ask the doc about it if I did ever manage to find him.

I hoped she wouldn't bring up any of the other reasons we'd been lookin' fer this family...

The doc shooed his son off the stool next to Charlotte and then patted the top of it. "Well come here, then. Have a seat. Let's take a look at it."

I did as he instructed.

"Take off your shoe and lift your pants' leg, please."

I did that, too, rollin' the leg of my trousers so that my left knee and everythin' below it was exposed.

Radley crept in at his father's elbow, starin' at the metal, and the doctor bent down to peer at the thing through his eyepatch contraption.

"Hrmm," he murmured. "Everything appears normal here. What did it do, exactly?"

"It *opened*," I said flatly. "It opened, and there were blades all over it." I waved at the shin of it. "Blades all along here, from ankle to knee. And here," I pointed to the half of my thigh that was metal, currently still covered by my pants, "there was a holster that came out. Carried a pistol and a knife."

Dr. Balogh straightened, then sighed. He pulled the eyepatch down to hang around his neck again. "Son, that is nothing strange at all. That is what it is *supposed* to do."

I glared at him. "You never thought to maybe tell me I was carryin' around an arsenal *inside my damned leg*?!"

Radley gasped at the same time I caught the sharp look from Mrs. Balogh from the corner of my eye.

"Sorry," I muttered. "But you gotta understand what a shock that was, to find out all that stuff had been in there this whole time. And then it all came out ... and I didn't know how I'd activated it, or how to use it ... or how to close it all back up."

The doc pursed his lips. "Mmmhmm. I had planned to send you with a schematic for the leg, remember? And to teach you how to deploy those weapons, and how to sheath them again. But you left ... prematurely." He crossed his arms. "Didn't you?"

I growled, droppin' my glare back to the ground.

"Remember I told you this false leg has advantages?"

"Yeah, I remember."

"Well, *those* are your advantages."

"Yeah. I figured as much. But they don't do me much good if I don't know they exist, do they? Or if I don't know how to work 'em."

"I suppose it is a good thing you came back to me, then." The doc leaned forward and slid his fingers along the side of my left thigh, makin' me yelp in surprise and jump sideways. But then his fingers reached the metal part, so I didn't feel 'em no more, and suddenly all those blades popped outta my shin again.

I gave another yelp of alarm and sprang off the chair.

Radley, Mrs. Balogh, and Charlotte gasped in unison, and even Fanni over at the workbench was watchin' me now, her eyes real wide.

"There, you see?" Dr. Balogh offered. "Easy enough to deploy, yes? And," he reached down to grip the flat of one blade between thumb and forefinger, "if you press inward on any blade, it comes free." He demonstrated with the blade currently in his fingers, and held it up triumphantly. "Therefore, each knife has multiple uses." He whipped around abruptly and hurled the knife toward the wooden table Charlotte had been stitched on. The blade sank deep into one of the thick wooden legs.

I stared at it, then turned to stare at the doc, and I realized my mouth was hangin' open.

I shut it with a click. Glanced to Charlotte. She looked as bewildered as I felt.

I was beginnin' to think Dr. Balogh might be a lot more than just a doctor.

He grinned at me, then reached fer my left thigh again, but I side-stepped outta his reach.

"Now, now, hold still. You want to learn how to deploy that holster or not?"

"I—I don't even know how you managed to deploy the knives..."

"Right here," he said. He stepped closer, took my left hand and guided it to the metal side of my thigh. "There are buttons. High one for the knives. Low one for the holster. Go on. Give the holster a try."

My mouth was too dry, my heart pulsin' in my throat fer reasons I weren't entirely sure of. All I knew was that seein' this leg open up like this, and seein' all those knives again, reminded me too much of the night I'd planted three of 'em into Charles Miller's gut.

I tried to breathe through it, focusin' on the feel of the metal leg's little irregularities through the trouser fabric. I rolled them up further to reveal the place that holster had extended, and then I pushed on the place Dr. Balogh had indicated.

A compartment slid open with a soft whir and the holster folded outta it, offerin' up its pistol and the fat blade of the huntin' knife.

"Oh my goodness," Charlotte breathed. She leaned so far forward on her stool I thought she might just fall right off of it. But her dark blue eyes shone bright with curiosity, and I didn't think her face had ever lit up the way it was now. "I've ... I've never seen anything like that before..."

"I have," I growled. "On one of those metal soldiers. Just now. When we were fightin' 'em. One of 'em was gonna shoot me. This leg..." I had to stop fer a second, an unexpected surge of that sick feelin' pushin' up my throat again. "This leg looks an awful lot like one of theirs. Doc." I looked him square in the face. "Did you attach the leg of one of those *things* to me?"

Mrs. Balogh went quickly to her husband's side at my question, catchin' hold of his arm. "*Henri!* You said you were not performing those surgeries anymore. Not with the Old World relics! The programming—"

"It's all right, Hannah, it's all right." He cut her off, turnin' to face her and takin' her hands in his, givin' 'em a squeeze.

I watched 'em both warily, not likin' the implications of her reaction.

But the doctor himself seemed wholly unconcerned. He granted her a soft, patient smile. "It is not Old World, my dear. It is my own design."

His wife didn't seem all that much more pleased with that news, but it eased the tightness in my own belly somewhat. He turned to me.

"No, son. That leg of yours is not from one of the Paladins—the metal soldiers, as you called them. I constructed it myself." He squared his shoulders and lifted his chin a little, like such a thing were quite an accomplishment. Which I supposed it were. "I *did* model it off the Paladin construction, yes, I admit. And perhaps a few of the internal pieces were borrowed from defunct Paladin models ... but this is cutting-edge medicine and science we are dealing with here ... I had to have *some* sort of reference to start with!"

"*Henri!*" Hannah hissed again toward his ear. And then she switched to their native language, and whatever else she said to him was lost on me.

He said somethin' back to her, soundin' defensive. And then he looked to me again. "I thought a man found shot, bleeding, and near death in the desert might have need of such further advantages some-day. But of course you would not use such weapons against me or my family."

It weren't a question, and he looked me hard in the eyes as he said it.

I shook my head immediately. And not just 'cause Charlotte was sittin' right there. "No. No I wouldn't, you got my word. You've saved my life twice over now, Doc. I, uh ... well to be honest, I figure I still owe you."

I owed a lot of people a lot of things right now, seemed like.

Hannah grunted and crossed her arms again. "Indeed you do."

"Well then," Dr. Balogh said, and his momentary severity vanished quick as it had come. "We have that settled. Now, as for how you put the weapons away ... simply press each button again."

I frowned. Were it really that easy? Had I really wandered naked all the way into Blessing when I coulda done somethin' as simple as push a few buttons? Grumblin', I did as he said. And then I grumbled some more as the blades folded quick back outta sight, sure enough, and the holster folded and slid inward, too, and the compartment closed.

Fuckin' hell. It *was* that easy.

I let my pants leg drop, rollin' it back down to my ankle and then steppin' back into my left boot. "Good to know," I muttered.

Only I hadn't used those buttons down in Miller's dungeon, when the leg had opened the first time. Was that *supposed* to happen?

Suddenly I didn't wanna know the answer to that question. After the doc's mention of how he'd taken *inspiration* fer my leg from those metal monsters, it was somethin' I couldn't bring myself to ask. Didn't wanna think of it doin' things on its own ... even if those things had ended up savin' my life.

It hadn't opened on its own since then, anyway. Was probably just a malfunction.

"That's incredible!" Charlotte blurted. She looked to Dr. Balogh. "You said you constructed that yourself?"

"Indeed I did, young lady."

"Would you ... would you mind showing me how?"

Dr. Balogh chuckled at the question, but Radley sprang forward before his father could make an answer, practically jumpin' up and down in excitement. "Oh yes! He can show you! He's teaching me, too, and Fanni! I built a rabbit all by myself—it even hops! You wanna see it?"

"Radley," Mrs. Balogh began.

"I'd love to," Charlotte said.

"Yes," Dr. Balogh said, "I can show you if you'd like, Miss Charlotte, but it is not a simple matter. It will take some time. And is a bit too much for so soon after your recent exertions, I think. Why don't we eat something first, and then you can rest, and tomorrow I can give you a tour of the workshop?"

Workshop. Nan had mentioned a workshop back at their Bravebank home, too.

But I didn't have time fer no workshop tours, or fer waitin' on any more tomorrows.

I cleared my throat loudly, breakin' up their disturbin' enthusiasm over machines.

They all fell quiet, and all eyes turned to me. Includin' Fanni's again from across the cavern. And then I didn't know what I was gonna say to 'em, what possible excuse I could make fer why Charlotte and I might need to leave so quick, and why they needed to leave their so-called treasure trove of automatons so quick, too.

But I was gonna tell Nan about this place ... and I didn't want the Balogh family here when she came fer it.

"Yes?" Dr. Balogh prompted when I only stood there starin' back at 'em. "Something to add, son?"

I *really* wished he'd stop callin' me that.

"Oh," Charlotte said softly. "I'm afraid we can't stay long, Doctor."

Relief unknotted in my chest, and I exhaled quietly. Good ol' Charlotte with her proper politeness. She'd think of some good reason to offer for our quick departure, and fer why the family should leave as well, surely.

"No?" Confusion creased the doctor's forehead. "Why ever not? We have plenty of space here, plenty of food."

"You have a very nice set-up here," Charlotte agreed. "Your family is very resourceful, I can see that clearly enough. And we thank you very kindly for your offer, and for your medical aid. But ... Van helped me out of a very bad situation once, and now he's trying to help his sister out of a very bad situation, too, and I've offered to help him. And we don't have much time left to make sure she stays safe."

"My heavens," Dr. Balogh murmured.

Over at the workbench, Fanni stopped what she was workin' on and turned to face us.

Mrs. Balogh's expression morphed from one of stern suspicion to horrified pity, and Radley went to her side and took her hand.

I shifted on my feet, uncomfortable with the honesty, wishin' she hadn't exactly told 'em so much. Here I was, always tryin' to keep other people outta my business, and it seemed they just kept gettin' dragged in, anyway.

"And to make sure she stays safe," Charlotte continued, "Nine-Fingered Nan wants this place for herself. So, Doctor, you and your family should grab what you can and leave, as soon as you can. Go on and head back to your home."

Stricken silence followed her words.

I grimaced. Well. That was certainly *not* how I'd hoped that would go.

XXXII

TALES OF FLYIN' PIGS

"Absolutely not," Dr. Balogh said finally, breakin' the stretchin' silence. Then, louder and more forcefully, he repeated, "Absolutely not! Nine-Fingered Nan and her type must never find this place, nor any of those metal barons! This place has been preserved, guarded, for generations! Only very few ever find their way in here and live to see its wonders, and even fewer ever get back out ... and there is a good reason why those few have not shared such a great discovery with the rest of the world. Because if they do, it will be torn apart by the greedy. You know that as well as I do."

"Maybe," I conceded. "But Nan knows there's somethin' here. 'Cause of all those birds dyin', I guess. She saw it in the papers. And she's got a strong suspicion already that you know somethin' about it, too, Doc. She..." I hesitated. Sighed and wet my lips, lookin' around to the children and wonderin' how much exactly to tell 'em all. In truth I didn't want to tell 'em any of it, but Charlotte had already opened that can of worms, so there weren't no point in beatin' around the bush now. "She ... she was stakin' out yer home, Doc. She was there when I first went there, lookin' fer you about my leg actin' up. She's the one who told me you'd lit outta town weeks before and came up this way. She was waitin' around fer anyone who came to call on you ... planned to interrogate 'em as to yer whereabouts and why you mighta left so suddenly. Which is how she discovered you went to Blackbird, I suppose."

The good doctor's already pale complexion whitened further at this news. He glanced to his wife in alarm.

I cleared my throat again. "I'm sorry, but she got to yer friend Dr. Wright. I'm afraid he's..." Again, I glanced to the kids. But surely they already knew what I was about to say, anyway. "He's dead. Buried him myself."

Mrs. Balogh muttered somethin' in their native tongue.

Dr. Balogh swallowed visibly. "So you did not just come all this way looking for me about your leg."

I shook my head. "No, sir. I came lookin' fer you in the hopes you'd lead me to this place. But it turned out I found this place myself, and then found you."

Mrs. Balogh straightened at her husband's side, and her eyes glittered as she glared at me. "So you *are* like all the others, then. We should have let the machines take you."

Charlotte stood from her stool, wincin' as she did so. "Now, now, we aren't like those others at all. Those others up there digging around on the surface are just looking for treasure. Trinkets to sell in the hopes of striking it rich. We're here looking to save a young woman's life. I'd say that's nothing alike at all."

Mrs. Balogh took a step forward. "And what do you think Nine-Fingered Nan is after, eh? Do you think she cares about saving anyone's life? What do you think she might do with a place like this, with machines like this, if she were to find it?"

Charlotte held the woman's hard stare evenly, but I saw the uncertainty flicker across her face. She frowned, and then at last she broke eye contact with the older woman to glance at me.

But it were true. I already knew exactly what someone like Nine-Fingered Nan might do with a place like this, with an army of machines like the ones that had attacked us.

But that weren't my problem.

"Look," I said, "if I don't give Nan some Old World ruins ... she's gonna sell my sister. Already got a buyer lined up, one willin' to pay more money than I could ever afford in a lifetime, someone overseas. If I don't give Nan somethin', and soon, I'll lose my sister. You understand?"

More silence.

Over by the workbench, Fanni chewed at her lip and turned a wrench round and round in her hands, glancin' from me to her parents and back again. Radley huddled at his mother's side, but it seemed the elder Baloghs were at a loss fer words fer a spell.

Until finally Dr. Balogh stirred, and he shook his head and marched forward. "I don't think you fully understand what this place is, young man." He waved at me to follow him, and then turned smartly toward the right of this large, central atrium, where another smaller tunnel led off into the distance. "Come. Follow me, and I'll show you."

I trailed after him, curious despite myself, and Charlotte followed after me.

And behind her came the rest of the family: Mrs. Balogh and Radley and even Fanni, bringin' up the rear.

We ducked into this other tunnel, which was also strung with lights, but this one weren't so open. It was narrow, with many twists and turns and crowded with damp, shiny cave formations in all shapes. Columns, ribbons, curtains, and delicate little tubes hangin' off the ceilin' were everywhere.

We dodged 'em best we could, and as we went, the sound of that rushin' water got louder and louder. Until we emerged into another room, this one clearly altered by man, and I stopped abruptly at its entrance and stared, mouth agape.

On the other side of this cavern was a massive water wheel, fed by a crashin' waterfall comin' down outta the ceilin', and churnin' just above a thick stream that meandered along the floor to eventually disappear beneath the left-hand wall. But this water wheel weren't attached to no mill ... instead it were attached to a whole 'nother wall of machinery.

I couldn't make sense outta that wall. It was like nothin' I'd ever seen before. So I only stared at it, speechless, till Charlotte came up on my right and caught my arm, pressin' into my side.

Slowly, I stumbled forward so that she'd have room to pass. But she didn't. She only stayed there with me, holdin' onto my arm and leanin' into me.

The rest of the Balogh family squeezed around us, goin' to join the doctor.

He went to the wall of machinery and then turned on his heel to face the rest of us, like he were maybe a schoolteacher about to give a lesson. "Son, this entire system of caverns and chambers is not only the greatest cache of preserved Old World machinery in existence—as far as I know—but it is one of the most revolutionary discoveries in science."

I scowled and rolled my eyes. Not just because he kept calling me *son*, but also 'cause he was startin' to sound an awful lot like Professor Morton.

"Growing up on this continent, you've surely heard the stories of the ancient walking cities?"

My heart stuttered a little at his mention of those, my mind flashin' back to what the professor had said about that dialed lockbox maybe holdin' a key inside to cross the Valley of Lightning. The legends that surrounded the Valley's origin and the tales of old moving cities were nearly inseparable. Course I'd heard those stories. Along with all the rest.

"Sure," I muttered. "So? I've heard plenty of tales of flyin' pigs, too. Don't mean nothin'."

Dr. Balogh shrugged. "Perhaps you are right. But I've been studying this place for nearly a month now, and as far as I can determine, this," he pointed at the water wheel, "and this," he pointed at the wall of machines, "are the basis of a very large power station."

"A power station?" I repeated.

"Like ... a generator of some kind?" Charlotte ventured.

Dr. Balogh nodded. "Similar to that in a way, yes. Or perhaps more like a battery. It seems this wheel generates power, which these devices then store."

"For what purpose?" Charlotte asked. She let go of my arm to wander into the room herself, going to the bank of machines and squintin' at 'em.

"Electricity," Mrs. Balogh supplied, pointin' at the weak bulbs which illuminated this particular space.

"And much more than that," Dr. Balogh said. "Although admittedly, I do not fully understand this operation or precisely how it works yet. It seems to utilize more than simple electricity—perhaps it even incorporates caerium—but I have been unable to prove that thus far."

"Caerium?" Charlotte asked. "I thought that was all gone?"

Dr. Balogh gave her a nod, but I had no idea what either of 'em were talkin' about. I'd never even heard that word before, though it sounded much too similar to the words those murderous statues had been sayin' fer my comfort.

"As did I," the doc said. "But perhaps that is not true, after all. Further study remains to be done, certainly."

"It runs the cities!" Radley blurted, startlin' me.

"What ... what cities?" I couldn't help askin', nevermind that I already knew the answer. I just couldn't believe it.

"The moving ones," Fanni said dryly, fixin' me with a level stare. She walked in front of the various control banks with their numerous levers and gears and buttons and ran her fingers over 'em lightly. "It would take a lot of power to move a whole city. There were once stations like this one, built across the continent, to generate and store power, ready for the next city that needed a recharge to come along."

"The relays that would have transferred the power from these battery banks to the cities' engines would have been at surface level," Dr. Balogh said. "And it appears they have all been destroyed, or buried, perhaps, either by natural or man-made means. But this station still operates as it was designed to, even centuries later, generating and storing electricity."

"Until it overloads," Mrs. Balogh finished flatly. "When it can store no more."

The doctor nodded. "As you know ... there is no longer anything for this station to charge. Over so much time, its storage capacity was overtaxed, and it suffered a catastrophic overload."

"But father fixed it!" Radley shouted again.

I could only stand there starin' at all of 'em, and I felt like maybe I might be losin' my mind.

"Not entirely," Dr. Balogh said. "But I did manage to weaken the battery's discharge, at least. I tried to warn the citizens of Blackbird they were in danger ... of course they did not listen."

Charlotte glanced back to me, and I knew she must be thinkin' of what that barkeep had said about the good doctor bein' a ravin' lunatic.

"At that point, I knew the only way to save the town would be to try and negate the effects of an overload."

I held up my hand fer a pause while I struggled to sort all this nonsense he was spoutin'. "Hold up. Wait. Yer sayin' you knew about this place and that an overload might happen ... *before* you went into Blackbird?"

"Oh yes. I've known about this place for quite some time, Mr. Delano. I have been studying the Engineers of old since before I studied medicine. And it all begins to become clear if you know where and how to look."

He grinned at me, but I didn't like that answer any more than I woulda liked it if he'd told me he dreamed all this up in some nightmare. If he'd managed to find this place, despite the Oracle and the so-called Guardians, surely that meant that other such interested and learned parties wouldn't be far behind.

And I had a good feelin' none of 'em would be inclined to share.

"So," Charlotte mused, "the birds and other animals that died ... was that because these batteries here discharged?"

Now the doc nodded. "That is correct, yes. Unfortunately, the pulse of voltage sent out from this place electrocuted many living things in the area. But it would have been a quick death. Nearly instantaneous. However, if I had not managed to dampen the discharge..." He shook his head. "It would have been much worse. Much, much worse. All of Blackbird would likely be dead. And the forest might have caught on fire and who knows how far that would have spread."

Charlotte's eyes widened. "Does that mean it will happen again, sometime in the future?"

"Yes," Fanni answered. "But we've been working on the system, trying to see if we can rechannel the power somehow to prevent that."

Dr. Balogh shrugged. "It would not happen now for some time. A few generations more, at least. But if I am able to do it, then I will do it."

I couldn't think of a single word to say in response to any of this madness.

As if he could sense my state of mind, Dr. Balogh crossed the room and put a hand on my shoulder. "I am sorry, son. But from what I have seen here ... those walking cities of old are quite a bit more real than your flying pigs."

I shrugged off his hand. "Unless yer wrong," I growled. "This kinda place coulda been built fer any number of reasons."

He didn't seem angered by my claim. Only adopted a kind of resigned acceptance and sighed. "Perhaps. But why don't I pour you a drink and tell you a little more, and then you can see what you think."

I didn't want to hear no more about battery banks or movin' cities or things bein' electrocuted by that point, but I *did* mightily want that drink, so I followed the doctor back through that twistin', turnin' tunnel to the main chamber, and then I found myself sittin' at the big wooden table Charlotte had been stitched up on, which had now been reverted back to a table meant just fer eatin'.

Mr. and Mrs. Balogh sat too, and Charlotte, but Fanni was charged with takin' Radley off somewhere else, outta sight and outta earshot, and he protested that notion a great deal ... at least until his mama got real cross with him and gave him a strong talkin' to in their native language.

Then he sulked off with his older sister at last, though his face was still all pinched up in a petulant scowl.

But it was better this way. He didn't need to hear some of what I might be havin' to tell his parents.

Dr. Balogh had a big jug of that Blackbird 'shine, and as much as the stuff had seemed undesirable in town, it was now lookin' better and better. I poured myself a generous helpin' ... then remembered my manners and offered it to Charlotte first.

She declined.

The elder Baloghs each had themselves a much more conservative pour, and then the doc launched into a story about some fella named Francesco Garavoglia, an Italian sculptor and Engineer who was, accordin' to what few records remained of the time before the Great Fall, quite renowned fer his skill at makin' automatons of the type that had attacked me and Charlotte. And accordin' to this man's journals—which Dr. Balogh brought out fer show and tell right then and there even, two thick leather-bound tomes written in a language I couldn't read—he was still livin' durin' the collapse of everythin'.

In an effort to preserve himself and his creations, he hid away in caverns like the one we sat in now, eventually settlin' into this very one, in fact. And over years, he built a collection. The *cache*, as Dr. Balogh had called it. Until conditions on the surface got too dire, and he gave up on hopin' things might improve durin' his dwindlin' lifetime.

So he blocked off the entrances to this particular power station, programmed all his creations—and those from other builders he'd collected—to "guard and protect" this space, and killed himself.

Charlotte was engrossed in flippin' through the yellowed journal pages scrawled with faded ink at the end of that story, but I only stared down into my tin cup.

Somehow, it'd got empty.

Dr. Balogh went on to tell us where Francesco's remains could be found—in the deepest cavern, apparently—and how the man's detailed journals had enabled the doc to eventually figure out how the power storage here worked well enough to dampen the overload discharge.

And they had also been what had enabled him to control the automatons well enough to stop 'em before me and Charlotte had been murdered. He held up his left forearm with its leather cuff and beamed. Pointed to the pad embedded into it with all the little buttons.

That's how he did it, he said.

Charlotte looked like she mighta just found a whole heap-load of real treasure, all right. She babbled excitedly to the doc and his missus about the incredibility of findin' a first-hand account of the Great Fall, and how valuable that could be in and of itself, and on and on about this Francesco fella.

As fer me, all their talk muddled together so as to be nonsensical, and my head was spinnin'. Though I didn't think it was 'cause of the 'shine this time.

I stood abruptly, too fast, knockin' my stool over.

The others looked up to me in alarm, but then I just stood there, not knowin' exactly what my plan had been in the first place.

Charlotte reached out to take my hand. "Are you all right?"

Was I? I weren't. But I couldn't explain it, not in the least. "I ... I need some air," I said finally. No matter that this atrium we now sat in was bigger than most buildings I'd ever been in. It was startin' to feel too small, and the air too thick. "There another way outta this place, or do I need to go back through all those killer statues?"

The three of 'em all stared at me blankly.

Then Dr. Balogh blinked. "You ... you want to leave?"

What about my question had been unclear, I wondered? Course I wanted to leave. If I had my way, I'd never set foot in this blasted place again. But I managed to keep my frustration, my disgust, in check and only said, "Yeah. Just need some air. Some real air. Sunshine. Trees. That's ... what all you said just now ... that's a lot to take in, you understand?"

The doc sat back on his stool, nodded thoughtfully. "Yes. I under-stand. Of course. I will ... I will show you the way out."

Mrs. Balogh spat something quickly in their own language, and Dr. Balogh answered her in kind, and I really wished I could understand what the hell they were sayin', especially as I was quite certain they were talkin' about me.

But whatever they had discussed, the doc also stood and moved around the table. He held out an arm toward the back of the chamber. "This way. There is a larger exit toward the back."

I nodded. 'Course there was a larger exit toward the back. 'Course they'd made me crawl through a goddamned burrow to get in here when there was a perfectly good, human-sized entrance somewhere else. I scowled as I followed after him, and we made our way through more of this massive cave without a word. The ground sloped steeply upward, until by the time we slowed again I was fair near outta breath and my hair was damp beneath my hat brim.

I tensed as we passed several more of those statues lined up along the walls, but these didn't move. There were four of the metal soldiers with swords this time, and two of those with red and gold gowns and golden claws.

The endless string of lightbulbs ended, but not too far ahead I saw sunlight filterin' through a thick wall of brush and vines.

It looked impassable, but there were tracks of wagon wheels in the mud here. Must've been somethin' that could be moved aside easy enough. I frowned, a sudden thought occurin' to me. "Doc?"

"Yes?"

"Where's yer wagon now? And yer mules? I didn't seem 'em inside."

He smiled faintly. "Of course not. Underground is no place for animals. We have left what belongings we did not want beneath the surface in the capable hands of the Oracle, Ms. Higgins."

I snorted. "And you trust her to take care of 'em fer you?"

"Yes, of course."

"You don't think she'd steal 'em, or sell 'em off fer cash?"

He gave me a puzzled look. "She has not done so as of yet. Unlike my present company, mind you."

I winced. Well, point taken. I gave a little cough. "I'll just, uh ... take a little walk..."

But Dr. Balogh caught my arm as I moved to step forward, and I drew up short to look at him only to see he'd turned gravely serious again. "Mr. Delano. If you have a mind to return here with Nine-Fingered Nan, or any other unsavory types who might look to take advantage of this place for their own power or gain..." He glanced over his shoulder to the human-like machines all lined up behind us, currently as still as the statues they fully appeared to be. "I will not stop these from destroying you or anyone else you might bring with you. Do I make myself clear?"

Fer a heartbeat I considered goin' back on my word ... considered usin' the weapons nestled inside my false leg right now to force him to give me that little leather cuff he used to control those things. Then I considered the fact I probably wouldn't even need to use a weapon ... I coulda probably just overpowered him without one to take the thing ... but all those thoughts left again just as soon as they came.

Guess I didn't really wanna have to do that. So I only gave a nod myself. "Just wanna take a walk, Doc."

"Very well, then. The Oracle will show you the way back if you become lost."

I laughed and shook my head, certain there must be somethin' in these woods makin' everyone around here crazy. "All right, sure. Sure." And then I shoved my way through all those plants without waitin' fer him to say anythin' else, never so relieved to feel sunshine on my face as I came out the other side.

The sound of a nicker startled me, and I whipped around to find Joe standin' there, tied to a nearby tree. He was saddled and everythin', and my duster was draped over his saddle and my gunbelts looped over the saddle horn.

Fer a good long minute I only stared at him, certain I must be goin' as crazy as everyone else. But then he nickered again, big ears perked straight up, and stomped a hoof.

So ... I weren't seein' things.

I glanced around at the woods, but I didn't see that old woman or any of her followers. Musta been past midday now, the sun shinin' bright through all the leaves and bakin' things good and hard beneath its glare, but a soft breeze stirred the muggy air and the branches overhead, makin' the shadows around me shift.

Birds called out to each other here and there, but there was no other noise. No other sign of any other people close by.

A mountin' sense of unease crawled up my neck as I went to the mule and pulled my gunbelts off him first. I kept all my senses on high alert as I strapped 'em round my hips again, checked to be sure both pistols were loaded proper.

If the so-called Oracle had been kind enough to return my things to me ... why weren't Charlotte's stallion and all her things here, too? And how long had Joe been tied out here, just waitin' fer me?

Scowlin', but feelin' much better now with my guns back, I grabbed up my duster and shook it out, shrugged into it, checked the inside pocket, and let out a long breath of relief as my fingers found both Ethelyn's folded letter and her necklace I'd taken back from Taggert.

I closed my eyes, just fer a heartbeat, and remembered what the Oracle had said about nothin' of value bein' lost. Maybe she hadn't been lyin'.

But I still didn't trust her none.

I untied Joe and swung up into the saddle, urgin' him off immediately, though I weren't exactly sure where I was goin'. I knew where I *wanted* to go, sure. Right into Blackbird.

Right to the telegram operator.

'Course, I had no idea whereabouts I was currently, so that would have to wait till I got my bearings back.

I noted the landmarks around me, what the curtain of plants looked like that led into that network of caves underground, committin' 'em to memory so I could get back here without the help of that crazy old woman. And then I headed first toward the sound of water, and when I reached the creek, I dismounted again and stripped, and did my best to scrub off all those damned painted marks all over my skin. Though of course I avoided the areas of my most recent injuries: the place that bullet had got me in the left bicep, and the place that statue had got me on my right forearm.

When I'd done my best and my skin was all red and raw from all my scrubbin', I dressed again quickly and mounted back up to follow the creek, suspectin' it would eventually lead me to somewhere I recognized.

It didn't, but eventually it did lead me to another prospector, and I asked him fer directions toward town, which he helpfully provided.

And so it was that as the sun sank low to the west, Joe and I moseyed once more into the town of Blackbird.

It was no less crowded and chaotic than I had left it just the day before, but Joe and I waded through it just the same. I went right fer the post office, all right, bein' as that's where the telegram operator was housed.

I went right fer it ... and then I kept Joe walkin' right on by it.

And I cursed myself fer my hesitation. Fer the feelings that lumped in my throat right now and fired anger hot through my limbs. So instead I pointed Joe toward the Ace in the Hole saloon. Goin' back to somethin' at least a little familiar in this mess of a town.

Goin' back to the one thing I knew I could always count on to numb all those feelings ... at least fer a time.

I squeezed Joe in-between two tired-lookin' mares at the hitchin' rail; nearly had to climb over the top of 'em to dismount, but I managed. Then I looped his reins and headed inside and went straight fer the bar.

Eaton was there and lookin' even more haggard than he had before. He lifted his brows and came over to me as I wedged myself into a narrow space between elbows. "Deputy DerLynd. Good to see you again."

His use of that title gained me a little more space from the men to either side of me, fer which I was mighty grateful.

"'Fraid I got even less now than I did before," he said.

I slapped several coins to the bartop and shrugged. "Don't care. Just give me somethin'."

"All right." The coins were replaced with a glass, into which he poured a clear liquid.

Guess it was to be more 'shine then.

"Where's your lady friend?" He slid me the glass.

"She's got better places to be than here." I took it, downed it, and signaled fer another.

His brows went up again as he poured a second, and his gaze flicked briefly to the bloody tears in my right shirt sleeve. "No luck findin' your friend, then?"

"Naw." It was better to lie about that than to get into all the specifics, I reckoned. And anyway, I didn't want no one else 'cept Nan knowin' about that particular place.

And Nan only 'cause I had no other choice in the matter.

I threw back the second glass, then slapped down more coin. "Just leave the jug."

Eaton hesitated. "I'm afraid I've had to impose a drink consumption maximum per person, Deputy. Else I'd already be dry—"

"I'll get you more."

That proclamation made the heads on either side of me turn, too.

"You ... you got a way to do that?" Eaton asked.

"I'll drive the damn wagon out myself to hunt some down. Just give me the damn jug, would ya?" I pushed my coin toward him.

He hesitated a minute more, glancin' to the men on either side of me before finally givin' a nod, and settin' the whole jug of 'shine down in front of me. "Well, all right. But you just remember what you said about gettin' me more, you understand?"

"Sure thing. I'll ride out first thing in the mornin'." I was gettin' good at makin' promises I had no intention of keepin'.

I threw back a third and a fourth glass of 'shine while Eaton stood there starin' at me and ignorin' his other customers, until he finally said, as I was pourin' the fifth glass, "You all right there, Deputy?"

"Sure," I coughed. "Just fine."

He looked about to say more, but a touch on my elbow then made me start and jump around, only to look straight into the face of Holt.

I squinted at him, sure we'd left him behind yesterday in those woods when we'd gone to investigate Billy Thorn's abandoned claim, grumblin' somethin' about curses.

"The girl all right?" he asked.

I blinked back the blur in my eyes left by the sting of that 'shine, but he was still standin' there afterward, real as Joe had been, it seemed. "Charlotte? Yeah, sure, she's fine."

He nodded, then tilted his chin back toward the main floor of the saloon. "C'mon. I got a table."

A table? He'd been here awhile, then. I glared at his back as he turned away and ambled off through the crowd, wonderin' if he hadn't waited fer us at all after we'd left him in those woods. Wonderin' if he'd come straight back here, instead. Wonderin' if he'd been here drinkin' and gamblin' the whole time Charlotte and I had been dealin' with that old Oracle and fightin' fer our lives underground against killer tin cans.

But I turned to snatch up my glass and my half-emptied jug of 'shine and followed after him anyway, still preferrin' his company to that of a nosy barkeep who looked about to be askin' more questions I didn't wanna answer.

Holt had a small table in the back of the joint, hardly big enough fer two, and there was a tin plate of half-eaten food in front of him.

I took the chair opposite. "How long you been here, then?"

"Awhile. Long enough to see you storm in just now. I waved. You didn't see me?"

"No."

He sighed. "Fer Chrissakes, kid, it's like you got blinders on, sometimes. You gotta learn to look around more."

I only scowled at him and muttered somethin' about lookin' around plenty.

"You want any grub?" He indicated his plate.

I hardly had to look at the stuff to know I didn't. Blackbird musta been runnin' low on supplies, all right. Saloons were servin' up some kinda gruel now, it seemed, thick and pasty and burned in places. My stomach growled anyway, as I hadn't eaten since breakfast, but I fed it more 'shine instead. "Naw," I said.

Besides, the 'shine would work faster without it. And it was already startin' to work.

I could feel it warmin' my insides, loosenin' the tension in my shoulders, dullin' the sharp edges of the anger and disgust roilin' around in my belly. And the Ace in the Hole saloon was startin' to sway a little, too.

Holt pushed his plate aside and folded his arms on the table, then leaned forward. "What did ya see?"

I paused before throwin' back more 'shine and eyed him. "Whaddaya mean, what did I see?"

"The Oracle," he said, almost whisperin' it like it was some kinda secret. "What did she show ya? I know you found her; her people came and told me they had you. So? What did ya see?"

My gaze narrowed at the question, at his confession that he'd known those Seers had grabbed me and Charlotte, but he'd only come back to town and not bothered to try and rescue us. "What makes you think I saw anything?" I growled.

He pointed one grimy finger toward my glass. "You've been suckin' down that 'shine like water, fer one thing, when before you could hardly stomach the stuff. And fer another thing ... yer pa had that same look on his face after he saw her, too."

The mention of my pa stopped me again, this time with the glass halfway to my mouth.

"That's what she does, kid," Holt said. "That's why they call her the Oracle. She shows you yer future. Why you think I'm so keen to avoid the old witch?" He straightened in his chair and shook his head. "I know my own future well enough. Don't need to see it prematurely."

I set my glass back down hard enough to slosh some 'shine onto the table. The anger bubbled up again, but I kept it bottled this time. I'd just saved the old bastard from the noose, after all, and as frustratin' as I found him sometimes, me actin' out against him hadn't ended so well fer me recently.

So I only hissed out an impatient breath. "And why didn't you mention yer run-in with the Oracle before, exactly?"

"I *did*. I told you me and yer pa had had dealin's with those Seer folk, didn't I? And I woulda told you more, but you wouldn't listen. You stormed off into those woods hell-bent on findin' Old World remnants, then you marched right into that cursed place, and you found the Oracle, didn't ya? And somethin' happened. Just like with yer pa. He came out with that same look in his eyes you got now. Like you saw somethin' you didn't wanna see."

I growled some more and gulped down the 'shine, fixin' my eyes somewhere else, anywhere else but on the old man, so maybe he wouldn't talk no more about how I looked like my pa.

The thought of it made my stomach turn. The thought of my pa maybe sittin' here like I was sittin' now, across from Holt—a much younger Holt—maybe hatin' himself and drinkin' himself stupid, too.

The Oracle had mentioned him, somehow. Somehow, she'd known who I was, known who my pa was...

A favor to a loving father who realized he had lost his way too late...

My jaw clenched reflexively at the memory of the Oracle's words. A lovin' father ... a lovin' father who had preached to his son about consequences without, it seemed, takin' into account the consequences of all his own previous sins. And now the rest of us had had to pay the price fer 'em, too.

I wiped a hand across my mouth. "Yeah, well ... he ever tell you what he saw?"

Holt shook his head. "Not a word about it. But he weren't never the same, if ya ask me. And after that..." Holt sat back in his chair, liftin' his hands in surrender. "After that he went back to his ranch, back to his wife and his kids, and he ... well he told me not to come around no more. Told me if he ever saw me on his doorstep again, he'd shoot me dead."

The 'shine mighta made the silence seem longer than it was, but this was a part of the story I hadn't ever heard before. I eased back in my own chair, thinkin' over all the other things Holt had told me over the years, all the other stories about the things he and pa had done together, all the time they'd spent ridin' together, about how he'd come to think of my pa as a brother, and that was a big part of why he'd come searchin' fer me and my sister in the first place after hearin' our parents had been murdered.

A sudden bitterness rose in my throat.

Holt crossed his arms and shrugged. "So? What'd ya see? You gonna tell me to go get lost now, too?"

I swallowed. Shook my head. And my answer came out as a croak. "Naw. No. No I ain't, Holt."

Another silence stretched out between us, until I poured a sixth full glass of 'shine and then slid it across the table, offerin' it to him, instead.

His brows lifted, but he accepted it without a word. Lifted it as if in toast, and sucked it down with nearly as much gusto as I had been downin' the stuff myself.

I lifted the jug, ready to pour him another, but he shook his head as he pushed the glass back at me. "No thanks, kid. Think you need it more than me."

Well, he was probably right about that. So I helped myself to more.

And then I asked the question that wanted to be asked, nevermind the fact I had a feelin' I didn't really wanna know the answer. "Holt ... what was Pa doin' here, anyway? When you say he found the Oracle? If he already had the ranch in Kansas and was married and all, why was he all the way down here? And with you?"

The hint of a smile pulled at one corner of the old man's mouth. He shrugged. "He was lookin' fer somethin'. Always seemed to be lookin' fer somethin', long as I rode with him. Yer ma settled him down mostly, far as I could tell fer the time I was allowed to visit, but every now and then he'd get restless again. Always called on me to ride with him, and we went all over the place. Went to see a lot of priests and other religious folk. Anyone yer pa thought could talk to any kinda god, seemed like."

I frowned. None of that seemed to match up to the other stories I'd been told about him, or to how he'd ever acted when I'd known him growin' up. "Why?"

Holt chuckled and pulled off his hat to scratch at his head. "Yer pa ... he was an interestin' fella. To be honest, kid, at the time I was convinced he was lookin' fer forgiveness from the Almighty and mercy from the Mother. Maybe some kinda Salvation fer his soul. Somethin' like that."

"Did he ever find it?"

The old man snorted and shoved his hat back on his head. "I dunno. Guess I hope so. All I know is that this place was our last stop. He'd heard tales of that Oracle somewhere, and I guess he wanted to meet her fer himself. Maybe he thought she'd have some kinda answers no one else had given him yet. 'Course I thought it was all nonsense. But when we got here ... when he found her ... then he came back with that look in his eyes..." He trailed off, blowin' out a long breath. "Kid, I ain't never seen yer pa look scared before that day. Never forget it long as I live."

I grunted, drank more 'shine. My jug was runnin' low now, and I wondered if I might be able to convince good ol' Eaton to spare me another. "Well, I ain't scared," I muttered. And I weren't.

I was angry.

"But you saw her, didn't ya?" Holt pressed, leanin' forward again.

"We found someone who *thinks* she's somethin'. You ask me, she's nothin' more than a thief and a liar."

"So she didn't show you nothin'? You didn't see nothin'?"

The saloon had grown a fair deal more unsteady now, even with me seated. I wrapped both hands around my glass, as if I could anchor myself with it, and flashes of that wakin' nightmare pulsed across my eyes like maybe I was relivin' it right now. I blinked hard to try and clear it, to ignore the feel of my own hands wet with blood, and some of it mine, pourin' from that bullet hole over my heart. "I most certainly didn't see my future."

Holt seemed disappointed. He frowned, leaned back in his chair, then pulled his plate of half-eaten food over to start pokin' at it with his fork. "Well, maybe yer pa didn't see his, neither. But he saw somethin', all right. Somethin' he didn't like at all, I reckon. Like I said, I didn't see him no more after we left here, so I can't say fer certain."

I tossed an agitated glance around the saloon, around at all the bodies pressed close, and the slant of the settin' sun comin' in through the front windows. If I was gonna go send that telegram today, I was runnin' outta daylight to do it in.

"You find anythin' at that fella's abandoned claim besides the Seer folk then?" Holt asked. His gaze went pointedly toward the bloody tears in my shirt sleeve, and his eyebrow quirked. "Seems you were gone a long time."

I turned my glare back to him, the irritation at myself fer my blasted indecision risin' hot again and comin' out as irritation toward him. "How would you know? Did you even wait till we were outta sight before you turned tail and headed back here to yer drink and yer cards?"

He stood fast at my accusation and I pushed my chair back just as fast, leavin' enough room between us that I could draw unhindered.

But he only glowered down at me. "What'd you expect me to do? Wait there till I rotted away? Those Seer people told me you were alive and that they were gonna take you to what ya wanted, so I figured that was good enough. I knew you'd wander back into town eventually, and so you did, didn't ya?"

"I'm certainly glad you were there to back us up if things had gone sideways," I commented flatly.

He scoffed. "I'll back you up in a fight with a fair chance of survival, Van. But not in a fight against creatures like that Oracle. I ain't stupid. I'd think you wouldn't be neither, after all yer past experiences."

I scowled at him. "She ain't no creature, Holt. It's one blind old lady and her band of misguided followers. Most of 'em didn't even have proper clothes to wear, and there was hardly a gun among 'em."

"Yeah?" Holt planted his palms against the table and leaned down toward me. "Well then how'd she manage to get to yer pa, huh? Fastest gun in the Territories—maybe on the whole continent—meanest sonuvabitch since Paul Johnson ... and she got to him good, kid. Like I said, I ain't never seen him scared of nothin' till he met her."

I pursed my lips in disapproval, thinkin' he shoulda known that answer already. "He weren't that man anymore when he found her, Holt. You know that."

Some of the hardness went out of his face at that, and he drew back a bit. "Maybe not. But you think the man you knew as yer pa growin' up woulda been scared of some blind old lady? Huh?"

I looked back down to my empty glass, realized my hands were on my gun grips. I drummed my fingers against 'em. He wouldn't have been.

The realization made my skin prickle.

What *had* he seen? Maybe it hadn't been a vision at all that had spooked him.

Maybe he'd gone down into the ruins themselves, like I had. Maybe he'd seen the metal statues move ... and maybe they'd attacked him, too. Maybe he knew that was all wrong and shouldn't exist in the first place.

"See?" Holt prodded at my silence. "You know as well as I do he wouldn'ta got spooked like that if she was just some blind old lady out in the woods with a band of misguided followers. That's why I didn't go with ya, Van. Why I didn't stick around. If somethin's gonna spook Lucky Logan Delano like that ... well you can bet I ain't goin' anywhere near it. And I tried to tell you not to go, neither, but, well..." He shook his head and sighed, then resumed his seat. "Yer about as bull-headed as your pa, ain't never listened to me, anyway. So. What could I do? Just gotta let you go and make yer own damn fool mistakes. Hope to God you don't end up dead."

I swallowed, still starin' at my empty glass. Maybe he had a point.

My quarrel weren't with him, anyway. Not this time. Slowly, I let myself relax, then pulled my chair back up to the table. "Almost *did* end up dead," I muttered.

Holt hissed through his teeth. "Figures."

"But we found … we found a lot."

He arched an eyebrow. "Oh yeah?"

"Yeah. You don't wanna know. But it should be good enough fer the old hag Nan. More than enough."

"Fer yer sister, you mean?"

I nodded.

"Anythin' we could skim off the top to make a profit on?"

Despite myself, I smiled down into my glass and seriously contemplated pourin' myself another. It'd be my last one. But the drink had nearly done its job. Nearly. I'd just about drowned all that anger and self-loathin', and I'd figured out just what I was gonna tell Nine-Fingered Nan. "Nothin' you'd want," I said. "Trust me."

Holt Haggerty woulda up and plain pissed himself if he woulda seen any of those statues move like I had.

He *harumphed* like he didn't entirely believe me, but I didn't mind if he believed me or not. I went ahead and poured my last glass of 'shine, swallowed it back, and stood, then stumbled before catchin' myself on the back of my chair.

"You got somewhere to be?" Holt asked.

"Yeah. I do. Don't wait up fer me. Though I guess I ain't gotta worry so much about you doin' that, eh?"

His lips pressed into a thin line, but I didn't wait fer him to make a reply. I turned away from him and my empty moonshine jug and my empty glass and shoved through all the millin' bodies toward the saloon's door.

Time was runnin' out, and I had a message to send.

I didn't bother retrievin' Joe, bein' as the streets were so crowded I figured I could make faster time on my own two feet along the slightly less-crowded boardwalks. And so that's what I did, dartin' and weavin' around all the folk still wrappin' up their daily business, tryin' to make it to the post office before it closed up shop fer the night.

Dusk had come by the time I reached it, but its front lanterns were still lit, so I stepped quick through the door and shut it behind me.

The mail clerk was there behind his counter, and he looked up and gave me a smile as I crossed the creaky wooden planks of his floor. "Howdy there, Mister. What can I do fer you this fine evening?"

"Just need to send a telegram, is all."

"Ah. That would be Mr. Brown over there."

I followed the direction of his gesture to see a hunch-backed old man with wispy white hair sittin' at a desk in the far corner. He turned at the sound of his name and offered a gap-toothed smile, the thick lenses of his spectacles magnifyin' his eyes. He waved me over. "This way, young man. I can get you fixed up."

"Much obliged. Unless ... you don't happen to have a telephone, do ya?"

"'Fraid not. The lines haven't come out this far from Arkopolis yet."

I waved away his apology. "It's all right. Telegram will do just fine."

"Very good, then." He pulled off one of his telegram note sheets, grabbed up his pencil in gnarled fingers, licked the tip of it, and poised to write. "To whom is this message addressed, and where's it going?"

I hesitated. Shifted on my feet and wet my lips. I certainly couldn't tell him this was fer Nine-Fingered Nan. Surely that mail clerk had a weapon behind his counter, and if they thought I ran with her gang, he'd be apt to shoot me dead on the spot. I cleared my throat. "It's going to Bravebank, Arizona Territory. To, uh ... address it to Sheriff Jennings."

A flicker of surprise creased the old man's face, but he wrote out the necessary instructions dutifully. "Very well. And what's the message, then?"

"The message ... the message is..." It was hard to figure how to phrase it proper under the influence of so much 'shine. All the things I wanted to say were far too forward. These gents here woulda caught on quick, and Nan, if she read such things, would cart my sister off overseas in a heartbeat.

I had to be clever about this. Had to think.

And now I was regrettin' drownin' all my sense in liquor.

God damn, why do I always do that?

"Mister?" the old telegram operator asked. "You got a message you want to send, or...? We're closing up soon, and if you want this received on the other end—"

"Yeah, yeah. Yeah, I got a message." I took off my hat and swiped my fingers through damp, wavy locks before shovin' the hat back on again. "Tell Sheriff Jennings ... I found what his employer was askin' about."

"All right." He started to write.

Behind us, the bell rang as the front door opened again, and bootsteps crossed the creaky floorboards. And then another set of boots. And another.

I looked up to see what kinda party could want business at the post so late in the day, even as I dropped my hands a bit lower, toward my mis-matched grips, and turned to face 'em.

Four men sidled in, shut the door behind 'em, and lined up along the front wall blockin' the exit like they were waitin' fer somethin'.

I glanced quick to the mail clerk, but the concern clearly written all over his face now meant he weren't privy to whatever this was. Mr. Brown had also stopped writin' my message, starin' at the newcomers with eyes made all the larger by his spectacles.

I stepped in front of the old man and kept my stance wide, my guns visible. In my experience, men were a lot like dogs: when they traveled in packs, they got dangerous. And the larger the group, the more trouble they liked to stir up. But I kept my tone amicable enough. "Fellas. If you'd like some privacy to conduct yer business, I was just finishin' mine."

The one in front of the door was the broadest of the group, with a black mustache that ran into thick black muttonchops. He crossed his arms as he cracked a smile. "Well now. Just so happens it's *your* business we're interested in."

My heart picked up pace at that statement ... the space was too small and there were too many of 'em at close range to be happy with this arrangement if there was gonna be a fight ... but then, he could have meant a lot of different things by sayin' that. I was currently involved in several "business" ventures, after all, and currently wanted in several different states, or maybe they'd just overheard any number of things. Or been under false impressions entirely. Or had the wrong man entirely.

So I kept my voice calm despite my hummin' nerves. "I see. 'Fraid I don't recognize you gentlemen. Refresh my memory, would you? What business of mine do you hold interest in, exactly?"

The man by the door jutted his chin out toward me, his gray eyes flickin' over my shoulder toward Mr. Brown. "Yer message. Who ya sendin' a message to, huh? Better be to Nine-Fingered Nan, 'cause yer time's just about up, boy."

I gritted my teeth against their use of Nan's name. So much fer my attempt at clever secrecy. Then the implications of his words finally got through the muddle of all the 'shine, and my focus sharpened. I looked 'em all over again, payin' more attention. I was pretty sure the man with the muttonchops had been there at Dr. Balogh's house. The rest of 'em I weren't so certain.

I swallowed, wonderin' what it meant that he was here. That there were others here.

Sheriff Reeves had said she'd heard some of Nan's crew was about in Blackbird ... but that was different than some of that crew knowin' I was here, too, and knowin' that I'd been instructed to send Nan a telegram...

"Yeah..." I answered slowly. "Yeah. I got a message to send her."

"You found it?" The squawked question came from the skinniest one near the mail counter. He weren't young, but the stubble across his chin was all patchy. He stepped forward, brown eyes agleam. "Where is it?"

I scoffed at him, and looked over the rest of the group, too. "You think I'm stupid enough to tell you? After Taggert and whoever it was that told Nan that lockbox was in the wrong coach? Don't think so, fellas. I'll give Nan the location, and no one else."

And I weren't even really gonna give it to Nan, but these thugs didn't need to know that. Least, not yet.

The mail clerk edged back from his counter, puttin' distance between himself and the boys by the door.

The one with muttonchops laughed. "You think yer gettin' some kinda choice in this? That's cute. And yer a fool if you thought Nan didn't know the lockbox weren't in that coach. She knew. She just wanted to watch you jump when she said jump." His laugh got louder, and the other three chuckled along with him. "And, well, I guess you killin' all those men inside fer her was what she really wanted."

My hands balled into fists.

His laughin' finally subsided. "She sent other people after that lockbox, people she trusted more than you. That business at the Haas residence ... that was all you then, I reckon, eh?" He shook his head when I didn't answer. "Well I'll give you credit where credit is due, boy. Sure made things difficult fer us there. And took that thing right out from under us. Oh well. Guess Nan still got what she wanted, didn't she?"

That hummin' in my nerves ... I was hearin' it in my ears now, too. And this little room had suddenly got too cramped and too hot.

"And she's gonna get what she wants now, too," he said, and he took a long step forward.

I had no room to step back; Mr. Brown and his desk were right behind me.

"You think she'd trust you and you alone fer somethin' this big? You think she don't know you might try and tell her a lie? Try and double-cross her, even? That's why we're here, see? Make sure that don't happen. We've been followin' you all the way from Balogh's place, hopin' you'd lead us right to it."

"Lost you in those woods, though," the skinny one said, "and that bounty hunter shadow of yers was a big pain-in-the-ass, too."

The big guy shot him a glare, then turned back to me.

"But here we are. All together again. Figured you'd have to come by here sometime in the next three days, so we kept our eyes on the place. Even if you were gonna lie, you'd want to tell Nan somethin' before the deadline, wouldn't ya? Make sure yer sister stayed *safe*?"

He leered when he said that last part, and I pulled Duster's shiny gold and ivory pistol smooth from my holster and fired from the hip. Didn't need to aim so much at such close range, but the bullet went right where I wanted it, and that was right up through that man's chin and out the top of his head.

Brains splattered, his fellows gave yells of alarm and jumped away from the gore, and I had time to fire twice more into the man to my right and drop him before the other two recovered their wits and grabbed fer their own weapons.

The two bodies hit the floor at the same time I did, landin' back behind Mr. Brown's desk and pullin' the old man down with me, then kickin' his desk over to use fer cover.

"Hey!" he protested, but I only shoved him back into the corner and motioned fer him to stay put.

A shotgun roared from across the room and I winced as more gore splattered the front window. An answerin' pistol shot punctuated a cry of pain, and I peeked up over the top of the desk to see the skinny man with the patch-work stubble had shot the mail clerk, who staggered back, clutchin' the shotgun, and there was only half of the third thug left, sprawled out across the floor now along with the other two dead.

Nan's last remainin' man was takin' aim again at the mail clerk, but I shot him in the leg. Caught him right in the meat of the back of his right thigh, and he went down to one knee with a yell, grabbin' at it.

I stood from my cover quick and pulled my second pistol too as I advanced on him. "Drop it," I ordered, pointin' my left iron straight at his head. Then I pointed the gold-plated one at the mail clerk. "You too."

He'd been hit in the chest and I weren't sure he was gonna live, but he gripped that shotgun in both white-knuckled hands, and I couldn't take no chances of endin' up like that half of a fella on the floor.

I kept most my attention on Nan's man though, bein' as he was the bigger threat, and from the corner of my eye I saw the mail clerk stumble back into his wall of mail cubbies and then slide slowly to the floor. Well, he mighta still been breathin', but I supposed I didn't have to worry too much about him, after all. So I glared down at Nan's last man, instead.

He hadn't let go his piece, but neither had he tried to shoot me with it.

I aimed both my guns at his head. "Go on, drop it. 'Less you wanna end up like yer friends here."

He grinned up at me. "Go on, then. Whatchu waitin' fer? Think I'm scared of dyin'?" He scoffed and spit, and the wad of phlegm landed on my shirt front. "At this rate I'll see you in Hell real soon, son."

I pistol-whipped him across the face good and hard, and while he was reelin' I holstered my left pistol and pulled his outta his grip, shovin' it into my waistband.

A shotgun cocked to my left and I dove fer the floor just as buck-shot peppered the air where I'd just been standin'. If Nan's man had been sittin' up, it woulda taken his head right off. Instead it all buried into the opposite wall, shreddin' a few stacks of waitin' mail.

Swearin', I rolled toward the old telegram operator's overturned desk. "Mr. Brown!" I yelled. "I'd really prefer not to kill you! I just want to send my message, all right? I ain't affiliated with these boys, understand?"

My answer was another cock of the shotgun. "Sounds to me like you are."

I scrambled to my feet and vaulted the edge of the desk just as he fired through it, sendin' splinters flyin'.

He hadn't expected me to come right at him, and I was on top of him before he could swing the shotgun back around toward me. I caught the barrel of it in my left hand as he attempted to do so and gave him a good shove with my right foot in the chest, just enough to yank the gun from his hands and send him sprawlin'.

Hopefully not enough to injure him.

"Well I ain't," I hissed, but I holstered Duster's pistol and leveled the shotgun at him anyway, just to make my point clear. "If I were, I wouldn't be shootin' 'em up now, would I?"

He struggled up off the floor to sit and glared at me.

"And I wouldn't be standin' here talkin' at you ... I woulda already killed you. And yer sheriff wouldn'ta made me a deputy neither, now, would she have?"

A flicker of doubt broke through his glower.

I risked a glance toward Nan's man. He looked awful dazed from that blow I'd given him, but he was tryin' to regain his feet, staggerin' and stumblin'.

The mail clerk hadn't yet reappeared from behind his counter, and I feared he mighta already expired.

I turned quick back to Mr. Brown. We'd made a lot of noise here, and there were still bits of guts painted across the front window, and I most likely didn't have a lot of time before someone of the lawful variety showed up to take stock of the situation. "That's right," I told Mr. Brown. "Sheriff Reeves deputized me. Just yesterday. So look ... I'm gonna ask this man here some questions. Then I'm gonna need to send that message. Why don't you go and fetch the doc fer yer friend over there? And tell the law you had some of Nan's crew come in here, but Deputy DerLynd dispatched 'em fer you."

The anger and disgust on his face smoothed away some at that. "D-Deputy DerLynd?"

I gave a nod, glanced again over to Nan's man. He was upright now, and hobblin' over toward the mail counter. Likely goin' fer that other shotgun. I had to make this fast.

I pointed my own shotgun toward the ceiling, stepped forward and held down a hand to help the old man to his feet. "That's right. Deputy DerLynd. That's me. You trust Sheriff Reeves, don't ya? Ask her when you see her, she'll have my paperwork. Think she'd deputize me if I was really workin' fer Nine-Fingered Nan?"

He accepted my hand up, but didn't quite look entirely convinced.

"Would I ask you to fetch the law, if that were the case?"

He frowned. "Er ... guess probably not."

"All right. So you go and get the doc and tell folk not to worry about the ruckus we caused here, and I'll take care of this last fella."

He considered, and I went ahead and went after the last man, steppin' around the bodies and the gore on the floor.

"Well ... all right," Mr. Brown said finally. "But if you still want a message sent, you might have ruined my machine when you kicked over my desk."

I winced and muttered curses. "We'll have to address that later." I caught Nan's man just as he was reachin' down fer that other shotgun, all right. I grabbed him by the suspenders and yanked him backwards.

He came around swingin', caught me in the left side of the face and sent me stumblin' into the mail counter. He swiped my left pistol as I went off-balance, then shoved the barrel into my gut.

But I had that shotgun held vertical, so I swept its butt hard left and into his wrist, jarrin' the gun outta his hand before he could fire. And then I brought it up and gave him another good crack across the face.

He went backwards with the force of this one, tripped over the slumped form of the mail clerk and fell, then scrambled away from me as I advanced on him, till he was trapped in the corner. Penned in by two walls and the counter.

I smiled down at him, but from the corner of my eye I saw Mr. Brown still standin' there, starin' at me. "Mr. Brown," I said, "you'd better go and get the doc quick-like. Yer friend don't look like he's doin' too good back here. Don't worry 'bout me. I got this under control."

The old man hesitated, but finally shuffled toward the door. "You ... you sure?"

"Sure. I'll be just fine."

Mr. Brown nodded. "All ... all right ... I'll be back soon as I can."

"Sure." I hoped he wouldn't be back *too* soon.

He changed the sign at the door to read CLOSED, then stepped out quick and shut the door behind him.

I gave Nan's man sittin' at my feet my full attention again. "Ah, alone at last."

He returned my smile, though his was all bloodied from me crackin' my gun into his face. He was missin' a tooth now, too, I noticed. "You really are as dumb as she thinks you are," he rasped. "You know what she'll do to you once she finds out what you did here? You won't be gettin' yer sister back, I can tell you that. Not ever."

The urge to make his head disappear with this shotgun swelled hot as all that 'shine swimmin' through my blood, but I managed to resist doin' it. He was right. Nan couldn't know I'd just murdered more of her men, especially if they didn't happen to be traitors like Taggert. The three severed fingers from that poor nameless girl still haunted my sleep ... and maybe Nan wouldn't disfigure Ethelyn like that, not if that merchant so keenly wanted her ... but I had no doubts Nan would be apt to gleefully increase the debt I owed to her at the very least. And who knew what else, besides.

But I kept all that thinkin' to myself, and only fixed the man below me with a cool, hard stare. "Well now, why do you think I left you alive? Think I couldn't have murdered you by now if I'd wanted to? Naw, I got other plans fer you."

His eyes narrowed, and his grin grew wider. "Oh yeah? That so? *Deputy* DerLynd gonna turn me over to the law? Join the crowd of smug, self-satisfied law-abidin' folks to watch me hang so it's all *official?*"

I grunted. Shook my head. Leaned one elbow on the counter next to me. "Naw. Nothin' like that. I was thinkin' more along the lines of ... well ... you ever hear about what I did to Lloyd Renneker?"

Some of the malicious mockery went outta his expression at that, and his grin faltered.

"Only now, see, I had the pleasure of bein' a *guest* of Mr. Charles Miller's in Blessing about a month back, and maybe you don't know about the particular kinda *hospitality* he provides, but lemme tell you, it's one-of-a-kind. Maybe you also heard about what happened to him?"

His grin turned into a frown now, and he looked me over like maybe he was rethinkin' his previous opinion of me. "That was ... you?"

"Sure it was. But I gotta admit, I learned a lot durin' my three days with Mr. Miller. Before I killed him, I mean. I bet, if I had Lloyd Renneker here again, to do all that over again, I bet I could do a much better job of it. I bet I could get him to last at least three times as long."

I paused, acted like I'd just got a good idea, and leaned forward a little, like I was gonna tell Nan's man a secret. "Guess it's a good thing I got you now, huh? How about we go test that notion?"

He came up off the floor at me but I dodged him this time, givin' him a good shove as I ducked so that he crashed right back down to the floor. Then I jumped on him, tossin' the shotgun onto the counter so I could put a knee into him and wrestle his arms behind his back. I grabbed the closest thing to me that could work to restrain him, and that was a roll of twine on one of the low shelves. It was awful thin, but I wrapped it thick and tight around his wrists before tyin' it off. He flopped around like a damned fish, cursin' me and makin' all kinds of threats, but I managed to stay on top of him long enough to tie him and shove his bandana in his mouth to shut him up. Then I dumped out a bag of mail next to the mail clerk while mutterin' apologies—though I was pretty sure he was dead—and put the emptied sack over Nan's man's head.

"There. That's better. Come on, now." I retrieved my left pistol from the floor and put it back where it belonged, set the one I'd grabbed from him and stuck in my waistband next to the shotgun, then hauled him up to his feet. "We've got a *lot* to talk about."

XXXV

BROKEN PROMISES

I took him out the back door, guidin' him with a hand around his bicep as he limped along, and tried to avoid the thicker knot of folk that had gathered in front of the post office. I kept to the back streets, and anyone we passed who seemed concerned by the sight of me haulin' around a bound man with a sack over his head, I introduced myself to as Deputy DerLynd and told 'em I was on the sheriff's business.

Most folk seemed otherwise too preoccupied with their own troubles, or else didn't care enough to question me further, and we reached the back of the Ace in the Hole saloon soon enough.

I kicked the back of his good knee, sendin' him down into the dirt. He rolled, growlin' somethin' I couldn't understand around his bandana, and then I pulled him up sittin'. "You just stay here a minute, yeah? I'm gonna go grab our ride."

I didn't expect him to stay put, of course, but he couldn't go far with a bullet in his leg and without bein' able to see nothin', so I went quick to the front of the saloon to fetch Joe.

Holt was waitin' there already, leaned up against one of the support posts fer the awning, and I drew up short at the sight of him, scowled, then continued my march to my mount. "Can't talk," I said, twitchin' my reins from the hitchin' rail. "Got business."

He appeared unbothered by my brusque declaration. "You hear all that ruckus down by the post office?"

"Sure did."

"You suddenly seem in an awful hurry."

"Sure am." I mounted up, backed Joe out of the tight space.

"You have somethin' to do with that ruckus there?"

"Might have. But fer now, like I said, I got business to tend to." I touched the brim of my hat. "Good luck with yer cards." I turned Joe away just as Holt's face twisted into an awful glower and kicked the mule up into a trot to go around the side of the building into the back.

My catch was tryin' to make a run fer it, all right, but he hadn't got too far at all, havin' run blind right smack into that pile of lumber. I rounded the corner of the saloon just in time to see him stumble over a piece of it and hit the dirt again.

I rode Joe up beside him and reached back to pull my lasso loose from my pack. Didn't need to use it too often ... but fer situations like these, it sure came in handy. "Tsk, tsk, Mister. I told you to stay put. I was gonna let you have a ride ... but now I think yer gonna have to walk."

He struggled back to his feet, turned away from my voice, and tried to run off again.

I sighed and shook out my rope. Now he was just makin' it easier on me. My loop sailed true, settled neatly around his neck, and I gave it a good yank.

He jerked to a stop with a strangled yelp and hit the ground hard on his back in a cloud of dust.

Holt rounded the saloon's corner atop his black gelding just as I was closin' the distance between myself and my quarry, coilin' up the rope slack as I went to keep it semi-taut. He reined up on the other side of the unfortunate man groanin' in the dirt and let out a low whistle. "Well, well. Got yerself a prize now, did ya?"

"One of Nan's crew," I said. I wrapped what was left of the rope around my horn and pulled, usin' the leverage to drag the skinny man standin' by his neck. He finally got his feet under him well enough to put weight on his own legs—or at least his one good one—and then he stood there wheezin' and gaggin' through his bandana and that sack fer a spell, leanin' against Joe's shoulder. I let him recover his air.

Didn't want him dyin' on me yet.

"Says they've been followin' us since we left Balogh's place," I told Holt. "Says Nan never cared about me sendin' her anything, or tellin' her about anything. She just wanted him and the others to follow me, see if I found what she wanted, and if I did, to tell her about it themselves. She didn't trust me not to lie or double-cross her, apparently."

Holt's face darkened, his bushy brows drawin' down low. "So ... yer sister?"

The man at Joe's shoulder coughed a laugh through his gag, so I pulled that rope around his neck tight again till he had to stand up on his tiptoes to get any air at all, and then I left him like that while I answered Holt's question. "That's what I'm gonna find out from this fella here. As well as a whole lot more."

"And the others?"

"He's the only one left."

"So he's the business you got to tend to?"

"Sure enough."

Holt sat quiet in his saddle fer a long moment, and the dark of night deepened around us even as the bustle of Blackbird continued on unbroken, and the gaspin' rasps of the man at the end of my rope filled the space between us.

"This the road you wanna go down?" Holt asked at last. "Well and truly? Yer playin' with fire, ya know, kid. Pokin' the bear. You keep this up and one of these days Nan is gonna come fer you full-force. And that'll be it. Fer you and yer sister."

"Not if I get to her first," I growled. "You don't gotta be part of this, Holt. Like I said, it's my business. You just go on back to yer cards." I nudged Joe onward, only lettin' that rope out a little so that Nan's man had to stagger along beside me or risk bein' dragged by his neck. And I went directly fer the woods that edged the outermost perimeter of Blackbird.

The woods outside the circle of the *incident*. The woods no one seemed bothered with, currently.

Didn't want any accidental witnesses fer what I was gonna do next.

"Fuck you, Van," Holt muttered from behind me, and he rode up next to me on his gelding. "You even know how to conduct a proper interrogation?"

"Sure I do. Done it plenty of times now."

"Not sure I'd call what you did to Renneker an *interrogation*."

"It got me what I wanted."

"Guess so. But there's an art to doin' it proper, ya know."

My gaze dropped down to my left hand on the reins, where even in the growin' dark the white tips of the bandages around my three middle fingers was visible. Those nails hadn't grown back yet. And all the old pains Miller had inflicted on me durin' those three days came back now, ripplin' ghostly across my skin, and I drew in a deep, quiet breath. "Yeah. I know."

His name was Silas Lowery, the skinny man with the patchy stubble.

And he weren't afraid of dyin', no, but like most men, he didn't prefer to be in a great deal of pain. Holt and I took him far out into those woods, and we laid the hurt on him good.

Took most the night, but I stayed patient. Just like Charles Miller.

We made Silas Lowery hurt, then we doctored him up a bit, let him feel better fer a time before we hurt him again. I didn't have all the tools Miller had had, though admittedly I wished I did just then. And I never woulda thought I'd have ever wished such things on another person. But findin' out Nan had purposefully misled me regardin' that lockbox, and had never intended to let me use my discovery in Blackbird to bargain with, had put me in one hell of a murderous mood.

And if I couldn't take out my frustrations on Nan herself, then her man Silas was gonna have to suffer, instead.

So I made do with what I *did* have: my knife, and rope, and a fire. And I promised Silas I'd kill him quick if he just told me what I wanted to know.

It took some convincin', but eventually he realized that between myself and Holt, we were gonna make his end real, real unpleasant and real, real lengthy unless he cooperated.

And so he did. Finally. Near dawn, I'd squeezed outta him everythin' I was gonna get, it seemed.

I paced under the thick canopy of trees, at the very edge of our little fire's light, and contemplated my new knowledge. I'd hoped fer more ... but at least it was somethin'. More than I'd had before.

Silas Lowery didn't know where Nan was keepin' Ethelyn. He'd said only her top lieutenants were trusted with that kinda information. But he *did* know she'd be shipped off via airship, if she was sold, and that they'd leave from that airfield in southern Utah. The one I'd heard about but never seen.

He also didn't exactly know what Nan had been hopin' to find here in Blackbird. Didn't know what she was specifically lookin' fer, but he suspected it had somethin' to do with her plan to cross the Valley of Lightning. She was buildin' a whole special vehicle fer the crossin', even, he'd said, out in the wilds west of Bravebank, and I wondered if that's what Sheriff Jennings had been referrin' to when he'd mentioned her *industry expansion*.

Holt and I had both laughed at this notion, but Mr. Silas Lowery was adamant Nine-Fingered Nan had a good lead on how she might cross that expanse of a death trap. We pressed him fer how exactly she planned on doin' it, but he didn't know the details on that, neither. Claimed that was also information reserved only fer her closest lieutenants.

And when we'd asked why a person like Nan might be interested in the other side of the Valley, Silas had said somethin' about her wantin' Califia fer herself.

Holt and I had another good laugh at that. Califia was somethin' else from all those old stories. The thing Ethelyn had been most enamored with as a child, in fact: a big, gleamin' city. The last one left from the world that had existed before the Great Fall, the stories said. A utopia of humanity, fulla inventions the likes of which we folk on this side of the Valley couldn't even imagine.

It was, of course, all horse shit. More fairy tales.

There'd never been any proof Califia existed, or had ever existed.

No one had ever managed to cross the Valley of Lightning ... no one had ever come to our side from the other side, neither. It was a generally accepted fact that the old minefield extended all the way to the western coast. And after hundreds of years of failed attempts to explore it or cross it, it was also a generally accepted fact that the Valley was just there, immutable, impenetrable, and would be there till the end of time, and that was that.

If Nine-Fingered Nan had bought in to the legend of Califia and whatever treasures it might hold, that was all fine by me. If she thought she could manage to get across the Valley in some kinda custom-built vehicle, that was also fine by me. *More* than fine, in fact.

I *wanted* her to try it, even. Wanted her to get fried tryin'. Woulda liked to have been there myself to see it, too. Woulda loved to have seen Nine-Fingered Nan, outlaw queen of the Western Territories, scourge of the Americas, reduced to nothin' more than a blackened, smokin' skeleton.

But first ... first I had to find Ethelyn. Make sure she weren't shipped off.

"I could go to the airfield," I murmured aloud, haltin' my pacin'. "Plant myself and stay awhile. Check the manifests. See if anyone shows up with Ethelyn."

Holt leaned back against a tree trunk, crossed his arms and shook his head. "All the way in Utah? It'd take you weeks to cover that distance. Yer sister could be shipped off while yer still en route and you'd never know. Nan ain't stupid. She'd do all that with fewest witnesses possible. Probably wouldn't be anyone not on her payroll around at the time, and you can be sure there'd be no traceable manifests, neither."

I went back to pacin'. He was right. The airfield was too far. Gettin' there would take too long, and the results of such a journey were too uncertain to risk it.

Silas had said somethin' about Nan givin' him and the rest of the group she'd sent after me a codeword to use in their communications back to her, to let her know it was really her crew sendin' word ... *Eldorado*, he'd said it was.

Fittin', I supposed, bein' that name had somethin' to do with lost cities of gold, but also amusin', since it'd long been known that Eldorado didn't exist. And neither did this other city Nan was apparently so keen on findin'.

But I could send somethin' back to her myself now, use that codeword, tell her they'd found the motherload and to come on out to collect. Could even give her a false location, and she'd believe it, 'cause she'd think it was her own people givin' her that information.

But if she thought she was comin' to collect ... if she thought there was really somethin' here she wanted ... would she come in force?

Maybe. And she certainly wouldn't come with Ethelyn to trade, in that case.

I stopped pacin' again abruptly and went to crouch in front of the slumped and bleedin' Silas Lowery. He flinched away from me, but I didn't plan on hurtin' him no more fer the moment. Instead all I asked was, "How bad does Nan hope there's ruins here?"

He shrugged weakly. "I ... I dunno. A lot, I guess. She's ... she's been after others ... but they don't got what she wants. Been ... been watchin' this place ... long time. But can't ... the Oracle..."

I frowned. Leaned a little closer to hear him better. "What about the Oracle?"

He gave a little shake of his head, then winced. Spit blood into the carpet of leaves beneath him. "She ... she can't get past. Damn Oracle. None of us ... none of us can. Been sendin' ... people up this way fer months now. They never come back. That's why ... why she sent you. Otherwise..." He choked out a short, painful laugh. "Otherwise she wouldn'ta ... wouldn'ta bothered with you."

My frown deepened. Well now. *That* was somethin'.

Somethin' I could use. I stood, turned, and grabbed up my saddle, startlin' Joe out of his doze.

Holt straightened up off his tree. "Where ya goin' now?"

"Back into town. Gonna send Nan a message."

"Please don't tell me yer thinkin' of marchin' off to try and shoot her again? I know you and yer pa have got to be some of the luckiest goddamned bastards I've ever met in my life ... but you've said it yerself: yer pa's luck didn't serve him so well in the end, did it? You keep pushin' it, yers is gonna run dry, too."

I threw the saddle up onto Joe's back and pulled my cinch tight, then reached for my bridle, hooked on the nub of a nearby tree. "You didn't seem to have so much of a problem with me doin' that when you came along with yer rifle."

"I think that certainly helped even the odds, yeah," Holt admitted. "You gonna let me do that again? And hope we get the old coot herself this time instead of one of her lackeys?"

I shrugged. "Maybe. Not entirely sure yet." I slipped the bit into Joe's mouth, wrangled the headpiece over his big ears, and then went to retrieve my pack and my bedroll to strap 'em back to my saddle. I hadn't even bothered unpackin' 'em when we'd made camp here, fully expectin' I wouldn't be doin' nothin' but gettin' answers outta Mr. Lowery.

Holt cleared his throat. "So you ain't got a plan at all, then?"

Still preachin' at me about plans, even after all these years. I paused in coilin' up my rope, took in a deep breath and exhaled slowly. "Yeah. I got a plan."

Sorta.

"Let's hear it, then."

I rolled my eyes and stuffed my rope into my pack. "I'm gonna give Nan that codeword our friend Silas there mentioned ... tell her Blackbird has what she wants."

"Yer gonna pretend to be him?" Holt jerked his chin in Silas' direction.

"That's right. And I'm gonna tell her Delano can get past the Oracle ... and he'll tell her how just as soon as he has his sister. So if she wants her ruins, she'd better come and get 'em, and bring the girl."

Holt grunted, one hand pullin' at his scraggly beard as he apparently mulled over this plan of mine.

I swung up into my saddle and gathered my reins, heart beatin' too hard, anger rushin' hot in my blood, but Holt snatched the side of Joe's bridle just as I was about to spur him into motion. I glared down at him with a look viler than I'd probably ever given him.

But he held my gaze unflinchin'. "You wanna bring Nine-Fingered Nan into a whole town fulla folk?"

I hesitated, rememberin' tales of how she'd burned whole towns to the ground sometimes, if they didn't comply with her wishes. I swallowed. "I'll ... I'll tell her the ruins are somewhere else. Outside of town."

Holt didn't let go of Joe's bridle. "Somewhere we can have high ground. Like last time."

I nodded, knowin' he meant the time we'd murdered Taggert and his band of traitors. He didn't know about the most recent time I'd confronted Nan, when I'd stormed into her viper's nest blind with rage like a goddamned idiot. The thought sobered me a bit, dulled some of the anger that again churned up my insides. He was right. Again.

If I was gonna do this ... I had to do it right. No more fuckin' around. No more games. No more expectin' Nan to keep her end of the deal.

I just needed her to bring me Ethelyn. Then I'd grab my sister and get the fuck out, and none of the rest of it mattered.

"Yeah," I muttered. "Somewhere like that."

"All right." Holt stepped up to Joe's shoulder. "There's an old lumber mill, abandoned, fallin' apart, not too far southwest of Blackbird. Paul used to use it sometimes as a base when we were runnin' jobs up here. You tell her that's where you'll meet her. Plenty of spots there fer us to set up with rifles, and it's on the bank of the river and cleared out some. Be better visibility."

I nodded. Swallowed again. My mouth suddenly felt like cotton. "So ... if she does come ... you'll help me even out the odds?"

Holt sighed heavily and shook his head, finally lettin' go of Joe's bridle to pat the mule on the neck. "Kid, to be honest, I still think it's suicide. But I woulda told you yer hare-brained scheme to free me from the noose was suicide, too. Woulda told you it never woulda worked. Especially with you in that ridiculous dress. But here I am, alive and kickin'. Didn't get my neck stretched after all. So, hell." He shrugged. "Maybe this plan of yers will work, too, and we'll finally be free of Nine-Fingered Nan." He grunted. "Wouldn't that be somethin'?"

"Yeah," I muttered. "Sure would be."

"Long as," he said, and he held up a finger, "you stay smart about it.

And that luck of yers holds out. And I'm there with my long rifle. Then maybe ... *maybe* you got a chance."

"Guess I'll have to take that chance."

"If this is really the hill you wanna die on..."

I glanced down to him at that, found him lookin' up at me again. Joe nosed at his pockets, but he ignored the mule. And I said nothin'.

He sighed again, nodded as if in resignation, and stepped away from my mount. "Right. Sure, then. Sure. Guess this is the best chance yer probably gonna get, all right."

"Then I'm gonna go set the bait."

Holt pulled his right pistol. "Fine. I'll take care of our friend here, if yer done with him."

"No."

Holt stopped short on his way toward Silas Lowery and turned back toward me with a frown. "You ain't done with him?"

That old familiar anger came back, seeped deep through my bones as I glared toward what was left of Nan's man. "No, I'm done with him. But leave him. Let the wolves take care of him."

Holt straightened, blinked. Pulled off his hat and scratched at his head with his thumb before puttin' it back on. "Van. He gave us what we wanted. We got what we needed outta him. Let's just put him outta his misery—"

"No, Holt."

"Van—"

"*No.*" I walked Joe closer, closer to Holt and closer to Silas. "You leave him to die slow, understand? To rot. Fer the wolves and the crows to eat on ... hopefully while he's still alive to feel it."

Silas made a choked noise from where he knelt, tied to a tree with plenty of bones broken and things peeled off him. "But ... but you promised..."

"Yeah," I snarled at him, "I did. And yer boss promised she'd give me my sister if I brought her that lockbox. Well I took her that goddamned lockbox, and do you see my sister?" I didn't wait fer an answer. "You didn't seem to have a problem with broken promises before, when it was *me* gettin' played, did ya? I seem to recall you findin' it awful amusin', in fact. Guess it ain't so funny anymore, is it?"

I didn't wait fer him to answer, but switched my glare to Holt, instead. "Let him know what it feels like to have the terms of the deal changed after he already delivered his end of it."

Holt shook his head. "Fer Chrissakes, Van. You don't gotta be like her."

"Don't I? Thought you said bein' a thief and a murderer was in my nature?"

"Not this. This is low, even fer the likes of us. And especially fer you."

I stepped Joe a little closer to him, slidin' my right hand over toward Duster's smooth ivory grip. "After everythin' Nan has done to me ... what she's taken from me ... this is what she gets. What anyone workin' fer her gets. Leave him, Holt."

The old man stared up at me fer another long minute, then blew out a long breath through his teeth and holstered his pistol. "All right. All right, fine. But this is on you, understand?"

"Sure. Don't bother me none."

Holt muttered somethin' as he went fer his own saddle. "I'm goin' to town then, too. Gonna find a stiff drink and a heavy whore. Ain't stayin' around here fer this."

"You do that. I'll find you after I send the message."

"Sure."

Silas whimpered and twitched. "C'mon, please. Please, you promised..."

I reined Joe away from him, not even givin' him a backward glance. His end wouldn't be no fun, certainly. We'd done things to him that surely hurt, but wouldn't kill him quick. And there was a lot of blood. Predators would be here sniffin' around before too long, happy to pull him apart bit by bit, to finish the job we'd started.

The thought brought me great satisfaction as I kicked Joe into a trot and left Holt saddlin' up behind me, and soon enough even the desperate, broken pleas of Silas Lowery were lost to the fresh peacefulness of a new dawn.

XXXVI

A SPECIFIC KIND OF LOST

I reached the Blackbird post office before it opened fer the day and waited uneasily in the back, tryin' to stay as out-of-sight from anyone and everyone as possible, till I saw Mr. Brown headin' down the board-walk at last.

I waited a bit to give him time to unlock the place and get settled in, but then I risked goin' around to the front, tied Joe, and strode on in.

He startled at the sound of the bell and turned in his chair, hands already on his shotgun. He'd left it atop his desk now; no longer hidden away. But he let go of it as he recognized me and slowly stood.

His desk had been righted again, and his telegraph machine was all set up again, but there was a big hole in the desktop next to it. And there was still a sizable bloodstain on the floor, too.

I stepped around it as I crossed the room toward him.

His hands lifted. "Now look, Deputy, I don't want no more trouble in here today, all right? Don't think anyone will be in here for weeks after yesterday. You scared 'em all off!"

"I don't plan on any more trouble here, Mr. Brown."

He eyed me dubiously but resumed his seat. "Well that's good. Because Sheriff Reeves wants to talk to you. Said if I happened to see you again, to tell you to go check in at her office."

Check in? I weren't certain whether that might mean she wanted to question me about the specifics of yesterday's murders or put me behind bars for 'em. Either way, it didn't matter. I had no intention of checkin' in at her office. But I nodded to Mr. Brown. "Sure. Soon as I get that message sent. Afraid it's rather urgent."

"All right. The machine seems to still be in working order, at least. Hey, what happened to that other fella?"

I frowned. "What other fella?"

"The one you said you were going take in for questioning. Sheriff Reeves said you never showed up with him at the jailhouse."

"Uh, yeah." I shifted on my feet, restlessness prickin' at my nerves. "Ran into some ... complications. He tried to escape. Had to put him down."

"Ah." Mr. Brown nodded thoughtfully, then swiveled his chair around back to his desk, to my relief. "Well, good riddance. The more of that filth gone from this world the better, if you ask me."

"I wholeheartedly agree, Mr. Brown."

"Okay then, Deputy." I gritted my teeth at his use of that title again. He took up one of his sheets of paper and his pencil. "What's that message of yours?"

I went up to his desk and laid a hand over the top of his shotgun. "Now look, Mr. Brown. I'm gonna tell you this message, and you might find it rather alarmin'. But you should know ... I'm workin' with the ... with the marshal service from the Republic in attempts to end Nine-Fingered Nan's reign of terror out here." Boy, my lies were sure gettin' elaborate these days. But then, Charlotte *had* said her Senator father was lobbyin' fer some kinda big lawful force to send out here, so maybe it weren't as far from the truth as it sounded.

Mr. Brown turned his chair around to look at me, skepticism and concern written all over his wrinkled and deeply tanned face. His gaze flicked down to the hand I had over his shotgun. "That a fact?"

"That's right, sir. So if you don't want Nan herself to come up here with her whole outfit and raze this town to the ground, I suggest you send out exactly what I tell you to send out, and don't ask no questions." I picked up the shotgun. "And I'm gonna hang onto this fer you, too, till my message is sent."

His eyes narrowed behind his spectacles. His expression hardened, but after another long, silent minute of glarin' at me, he only swiveled back to face his machine and lifted his pencil again. "Well then. Let's hear it."

"All right. Address it to Nine-Fingered Nan herself. Goin' to Bravebank, Arizona Territory."

He looked sideways at me, and I could tell he weren't very confident in the tale I'd just spun. But it didn't matter whether he believed me or not. All that mattered was that he sent my message.

So I instructed him to tell her that Blackbird had what she wanted, out in a place several miles southwest of town by an old, abandoned lumber mill, and that Delano had managed to find a way past the Oracle, even—I'd seen it with my own eyes—and that he was more than willin' to share this secret once he had his sister physically in-hand.

Told her we were keepin' Delano safe fer her, that we'd all be waitin' at that mill fer her arrival, and she should get here just as soon as she could so we could proceed.

Then I included the word *Eldorado*, and signed it *Silas*.

Mr. Brown seemed continually more perplexed as I recounted these things, but recorded all of it dutifully, and then he tapped it all out on his machine. When that was done, he tore up his little note paper and tossed it into the trash. "There we are. All set. I suppose ... you don't plan to pay?"

I snorted. "On the contrary, Mr. Brown." I fished out some coin with the hand that weren't holdin' his shotgun and set it on the corner of his desk. Gave him a little extra, too. "I appreciate yer services very much. And anyway, what kinda law-abidin' deputy would I be if I went around not payin' folk?"

He took the money, but squinted up at me with high suspicion. "Appreciate it. You can come by later and I'll have any response I receive in the meantime ready for you."

I settled myself back against one edge of his desk and cradled that shotgun. "I'll wait."

He blinked at me from behind his thick spectacles. "Er ... but that could take hours. Maybe even days. Depends on the person receiving the message, you know. When they receive it and when they feel like replying—"

"I know how it works, Mr. Brown."

"And you just figure you'll wait around here all that time?"

I shrugged. "Sure. All that I just told you is sensitive information, Mr. Brown. Wouldn't want you goin' off to share it around."

He pursed his lips. Clearly that's exactly what he'd been hopin' to do. Probably hopin' he could go straight to the sheriff so she could come sort out which parts of my story were true or not. "Why don't you at least go see Sheriff Reeves?" he suggested. "She seemed real keen to talk to you."

I bet she is. "After I get a reply, Mr. Brown. Like I said, this is urgent business. I need to hear the response just as soon as it comes in."

He looked none too happy about this, but in the end couldn't seem to muster a way to dissuade me, so he gave up, grumblin'. "So you aim to bring her *here*, huh? Nine-Fingered Nan, right to our town?"

"Not to town directly."

"Close enough," he growled. "I don't know what you're really on about, Mister, but I sure as hell hope you know what you're doing." He went on about his daily business after a few more mumbled complaints, and I stayed there leanin' against his desk and holdin' on to that shotgun, ruminatin' on the chances of this plan workin'.

The hours passed, and the day slipped into late mornin'. But things inside the post office stayed quiet. I took to helpin' Mr. Brown sort mail, bein' as I had nothin' else to do and he'd said his mail clerk friend was still at the doc's and weren't expected to live. Though I still made sure to keep that shotgun well outta his reach.

And he still weren't happy with me, or happy in general, so I tried to console him by remindin' him those who had shot his friend had already got the justice they deserved, at least. And that it had mostly been me who'd given it to 'em.

He only nodded silently, and we went back to sortin' mail.

My stomach growled, wantin' food, and the churnin' restlessness jumpin' around in the rest of my insides wanted some drink to calm it, but I resisted both.

I suspected it would be Nine-Fingered Nan herself who would answer me, and if that were the case, I couldn't risk Mr. Brown interpretin' that when I weren't around. He'd take it straight to Sheriff Reeves, I imagined.

Finally, near midday, his machine started whirrin', and I jumped up from my piles of mail and grabbed up the shotgun, too.

Mr. Brown eyed me, but crossed to it slow. He took his chair, picked up the end of the tape, and started writin' down what it said.

I came to stand next to him and peered over his shoulder, readin' his scrawl as he put it down. It was addressed back to Silas, all right.

From *her*.

My hands tightened around the shotgun till my fingers ached, and my breathin' turned all harsh and ragged.

TELL DELANO I'LL BRING THE GIRL. HOLD HIM. GET HAGGERTY TOO. WILL ARRIVE IN TEN DAYS. KEEP THEM COHERENT.

And that was all.

She signed it *Eldorado* herself, but no name.

Didn't matter, though. I knew who it was from.

She was comin'.

I snatched up the telegram tape and the paper Mr. Brown had written the message on and shoved them both into my pocket. But I couldn't risk the old man tellin' anyone else about this meetin' of mine or gettin' any kind of law involved. Ten days was too long to chance him keepin' quiet about any of this.

Too long...

I gritted my teeth. *Shit.*

I laid the shotgun down across his desk and put my other hand on his shoulder. "Thank you fer yer help, Mr. Brown." Then I put a bullet through his forehead quick, before he could register anythin' was wrong.

He jerked and sagged in his chair, head lollin' back, and I slipped my pistol back into its holster still smokin' and made fer the door.

There was another mess splattered all over the inside of this post office now, and I had no stomach fer it.

I stepped out onto the boardwalk in front and kept my hat brim lowered, not even checkin' to see if anyone outside had taken notice of the gunfire this time. Surely they would eventually, given yesterday's events here; I needed to be gone—long gone—quick as I could manage.

So I mounted up in a hurry and pointed Joe off in search of Holt.

Checked a few of the brothels first, then checked the Ace in the Hole saloon and tried to avoid the notice of Eaton, bein' as I didn't have the fresh stock of liquor I'd promised him.

I found Holt there though, sure enough, at one end of the bar, and pulled my hat down even lower as I approached.

He saw me anyway, turned toward me casually and lifted those bushy brows of his. "Well?"

"Time to go," I said.

"Again?"

"That's right. You get what you needed?"

Disappointment clouded his features. "Sorta. Could use more drink, though."

"Yeah. Me too."

"Hey Deputy!"

I flinched at Eaton's call. *Shit.* So he'd seen me after all. I hooked a hand around Holt's arm and pulled him away from the bar. "Come on, we gotta go."

He growled at me, but threw back what little drink he had left and then flipped a few coins to the bartop before pullin' his arm free to follow me.

We made fast fer the door.

"Deputy!" Eaton called out again behind us. "Hey now, don't you forget your promise!"

Shit. I lifted a hand in a little wave and tossed him a backward glance. "Sure thing, friend, workin' on it now."

That seemed to satisfy him somewhat. He nodded, then opened his mouth again just as I reached the door to his establishment.

"Oh yeah, and Sheriff Reeves wants to talk to ya! Stop by her office on your way out, would you?"

I winced again. "Yeah, sure, will do." I shouldered through the door before he could add anything else and wasted no time in climbin' aboard Joe.

Holt followed suite and swung up onto his gelding. "What's all that about?"

"Nothin' important. Deputy business."

Holt snorted a laugh but I ignored him, my eyes already focused down the street on another crowd gatherin' in front of the post office. So my latest deed had been discovered, then. Well, that's the way we needed to go, but we could go around. Outside town. Through all the trees to stay out of sight.

I reined Joe in the opposite direction, pushed on through the throngs of folk that flowed down Main Street.

Holt caught sight of that growin' crowd now, too, and his amusement turned into a scowl. He hissed a curse as he followed after me. "God damnit, Van, what did you do now?"

"Didn't have a choice," I said.

"Anyone see you?"

"Maybe."

He muttered more curses. "And the message? You send it?"

"Yeah, I sent it." I slowed Joe up a bit to let Holt catch up with me, and my heart still beat too hard as I tried to tell him about Nan's answer. "She's comin'," I finally strangled out. "She's gonna come. With Ethelyn. To the mill."

Surprise smoothed the discontent on the old man's face. "No shit? When?"

"Ten days from now."

He grunted, looked over his shoulder to the commotion growin' at the post office. "Seems you've stirred up this place an awful lot fer us havin' to stay here another ten days."

"We ain't gonna stay here," I said, and I kicked Joe up into a trot as we neared the end of Main Street and the mobs of folk thinned out a bit.

Holt matched my pace. "Oh no?"

"Naw. I've got a place we can lay low fer awhile, should be safe enough. Just follow me."

I intended to take him back to the cave where I'd left Charlotte and the Balogh family. Back to that rear entrance where we wouldn't have to crawl through a blasted burrow or get past so many of those murderous statues.

He mighta taken issue with just those few bodies made outta metal anyway, but as long as the doc kept 'em all quiet, surely Holt would find their company more pleasant than bein' chased outta Blackbird by an angry mob or bein' strung up by Blackbird's sheriff.

So we went around the town through the woods and eventually ambled west along the same path we'd taken only days before, till we reached the place I'd rejoined that road from the north after leavin' the cave myself.

I led us off the road at that point, goin' by memory and followin' the landmarks I'd taken note of on my way back into town. Except ... except it seemed we kept goin' in circles.

I reined Joe up in front of the old dead oak with a split trunk we'd passed at least twice now, and a ripple of dread fluttered in my gut.

Holt reined up beside me. "Yer lost, ain't ya?"

I swore under my breath, lookin' around at all the trees that surrounded us. The afternoon was growin' late, the shadows stretchin' long. Things seemed too quiet; the call of two near crows yellin' at each other too loud. I swallowed. "I ain't lost..."

I'd come by this tree before, I was sure of it. It even had the clusters of small animal skulls hangin' from its low branches, just like the one I'd passed before. I'd been goin' south at the time, which meant we needed to go north now. And that's where we'd headed, just an hour or so ago. We'd gone north. I could still see where our mounts had disturbed the underbrush and mats of old leaves.

And yet somehow we'd ended up back here again.

Holt sighed, droppin' both hands to his saddle horn. "We're goin' in circles, Van."

"That ... that don't make no sense..."

"Sure it does. Happens sometimes when you get lost."

"I ain't lost," I snapped. "I came this way before. We should go north from here."

"All right, so let's go north then."

"We did. Before. And now we're back here again."

"Well that don't make no sense."

I glared at him. "That's what I just said."

He shrugged. "We musta got turned around at some point. These woods are tricky like that. Everythin' looks so similar. So many trees you can't orient yerself proper."

"I ain't a child no more, Holt. I know how to check my direction and check landmarks. I'm tellin' you, I've been followin' the landmarks all this time."

He sat quiet fer a time, then nodded. "All right. Well. Let's try again. Talk me through 'em as we go."

It was the same thing he'd used to tell me when he'd first been helpin' me hone my directional skills, and it raised my hackles that he was talkin' at me like that again now. But I clenched my teeth against snappin' at him fer it.

Either we *were* really lost ... or I was losin' my mind. Maybe he could help me figure out which.

I prodded Joe into motion again, headin' north. "North from this tree," I muttered.

And so we went. Again.

And some time later ... we were right back at that goddamned tree, split trunk and hangin' skulls and all.

Holt twisted in his saddle to squint out at all the woods that surrounded us. "What in the hell..."

The dread that had stirred in my gut before now sharpened into a real kinda fear. We shouldn't be lost. Not both of us. Not like this. And we both couldn't be losin' our minds ... could we? "I told you," I whispered. "Told you I was followin' the landmarks..."

The sound of rustlin' leaves and underbrush nearby had both of us with guns in-hand and ready, watchin' the trees. Eventually, people emerged. Came toward us on all sides, slow and unhurried. They had weapons, but didn't seem intent on usin' 'em.

My heart sank as I recognized their patch-work clothes. It was those goddamned Seers again. I sighed and holstered my pistols.

"Van…" Holt prompted.

I shook my head, not havin' the energy to explain it all, and remembered then what Dr. Balogh had said about the Oracle showin' me the way back if I got lost. He'd failed to mention it might be a very *specific* kind of lost.

I heard Holt's hammers click back and looked to him sharply, only to realize the Oracle had appeared right in front of us, and I hadn't even noticed. I reached over to push his arms down, forcin' his guns to lower.

"Stop," I hissed. "She's gonna show us the way out." I straightened and looked to the old woman. "Ain't you? Yer gonna take us back to the Temple?"

She folded her hands in front of her. "You, yes."

"What Temple?" Holt asked.

I swept my hands back to my own grips again. "I ain't goin' nowhere without him. Yer gonna have to take us both."

"You will follow us," was all she said in reply, and then she turned and made her way off through the trees, and her band of disciples closed in around Holt and me, and the old man glared at me with a look that broadcast his displeasure and suspicion loud and clear.

But so long as she was gonna escort the both of us without argument, I weren't gonna begrudge the guidance. Even if havin' all her people surround us like this made me real uneasy. And even if the implications of 'em all meldin' outta nowhere after Holt and I had been wanderin' in circles fer hours made the hairs on the back of my neck stand up.

Long as we made it back to that cave, I could sort out the rest of it later.

XXXVII

DEVIL ON THE DOORSTEP

The sun had sunk low to the western horizon again by the time we reached the place. We'd followed all the same landmarks Holt and I had followed before ... only this time, somehow, we didn't go in circles.

That uneasy feelin' jumped around in my gut now somethin' awful, but at least we'd finally gotten where I'd been tryin' to go all day.

The Oracle's loyal band loosened their knot around me and Holt and moved off into the trees. The old blind woman herself turned to face us again, and Holt looked about as unhappy as I'd ever seen him.

"Here we are," the Oracle said. "You may re-enter," she nodded toward me. Then she looked to Holt as if she could see. "If you will submit to Judgement, and should you pass, you may enter as well."

"And like I told you before," Holt snarled, "you can go fuck yerself."

"Holt."

He turned his burnin' glare toward me. "I ain't doin' it, Van. I seen what she does to enough people ... heard enough stories ... I ain't doin' it."

I sighed, my shoulders saggin'. Maybe I could have shot down the old woman and many of her followers and gotten inside with Holt, but with their numbers, they could have easily overtaken us soon as I had to reload. Not to mention I didn't want the Baloghs findin' out later that I'd done somethin' like that.

And I didn't think I believed what Radley had said about the Oracle havin' magic, exactly ... but there was surely somethin' about these Seer folks that didn't quite add up. And frankly, I was too tired to bother testin' any of that tonight.

So I only rubbed at my eyes and shrugged. "Fine. Fine, sure. Have it yer way." My hand dropped back to my saddle horn. "In that case, look, there's a big ol' cave underground here. Bigger than any I've ever seen before. And it's Old World, all right, through and through."

Holt's anger faltered. He looked around the woods again, like he might be able to see such a thing up here on the surface somehow.

I filled him in on only the most important aspects of what was below: the fact it used to be a power station, could still function as a power station even after all this time, and that it had overloaded, and the discharge had been what had killed so many animals in the area. Then I told him about the doc and his family bein' holed up in there fer awhile now, studyin' the thing, and that I'd left Charlotte there fer safe keepin' while I saw to other business in town.

I didn't mention the movin', murderin' statues. Or Francesco Whats-His-Name.

And then I was kinda glad he kept refusin' to face that so-called *Judgement*.

Was probably better he never knew about those things, anyway.

By the time I was done with my story, Holt stared at me like I'd gone stark ravin' mad.

Well, I wouldn'ta believed any of it myself if I hadn't seen it with my own two eyes.

"Should be safe enough here," I said as I dismounted, ignorin' his look. "If you wanna make camp nearby." Then I stopped with reins in-hand. "You ain't gonna leave again, are ya? If I go inside that cave fer awhile ... I ain't gonna come back out later and find you gone?"

That seemed to knock him outta his stupor somewhat, 'cause he scowled down at me. "Where would I go now, huh? You've got Black-bird all in a fuss thanks to that business at the post office. And Sheriff

Reeves knows I ride with you. If she finds me in town, she'd surely ask me as to yer whereabouts. And I don't feel much inclined to be talkin' to no sheriff on yer behalf, I can tell you that."

"So you'll stay, then?"

A mighty frown crossed his face, and he glanced toward the Oracle. Then muttered curses. But he gave a nod. "I told ya I'd help with this damn fool plan," he snapped. "And so I will. Though if I'd known you were gonna lead me to a place fulla these folk," he jerked his chin out toward the blind woman, "I woulda elected to camp somewhere else."

I tossed a glance to the Oracle myself, then stepped up close to Holt and dropped my voice. "Look, these people are strange, I'll give you that—"

"More than strange," he growled.

"—and I'm not sure they're entirely right in the head—"

"Most certainly ain't."

"—but they *did* lead us back here. This is the right location. The cave entrance is there." I nodded in the direction of the tangle of vines and brush. "They coulda ambushed us back there. Killed us easy and left us to rot. But they didn't. I think ... I think if we just keep playin' by their rules, at least fer now, things'll be all right."

Holt tore his accusatory glare away from the Oracle to plant it on me, instead, then leaned over in his saddle to murmur, "Thought you said she was a liar and a thief?"

Well. I shifted on my feet. I *had* said that. I still thought that.

Maybe. Mostly.

But she *had* given my things back. And she *had* brought me back here. I shrugged. "Yeah, well. So are we."

He straightened in his saddle at that.

"It's only fer a few days, Holt. While we get ready fer Nan's arrival. Right?"

"Yeah," he grumbled. "Right. Guess I don't got anywhere else I can go now, anyway. But don't you be in there too long. We got to go over the plan."

I sighed and tied Joe's reins to the nearest tree. "Sure. Won't be long. Never liked those deep caves much, anyway."

Holt snorted. "Right."

I unbuckled my gunbelts and looped them over my saddle horn like they'd been when I'd first come outta the cave, and Holt nudged his gelding up beside me.

"What the hell are ya doin'?"

"No weapons inside. Long story."

"Longer than the one you just told me about everythin' else?"

"Much longer."

He squinted at me. "You sure that's such a wise idea?"

I scoffed and gave a nod. "Yeah. Yeah I'm sure."

He surely thought I must be mad now, but he made no other comment as I headed toward the cave's back entrance, the bigger, roomier entrance, to my relief. If I had my way, I'd never shimmy through another hole as tight as the one we'd first entered from in my life. I watched the Oracle warily as I went, half-expectin' her to stop me, or to claim I needed a second Judgement, or some other such nonsense.

But she only stood there quietly, hands folded, and the twilight sounds of the forest filled the space.

Honestly, her silence was almost more unnervin' than her babblin'.

But at last, just as I was searchin' fer a suitable place to pull aside all those plants, she spoke. Guess she didn't want to disappoint.

"It is not too late for you, Van Delano."

I paused with my left hand wrapped around a particularly thick stalk of grapevine and turned back toward her. "What the hell is that supposed to mean?"

She regarded me calmly. "It is as I said before. You face a great darkness. Already you court its arrival ... welcome it, even. But that is how your father lost his way. The deeper you go, the steeper the price. He would not want you to make the same mistakes as he."

I ground my teeth as fresh anger surged. I *really* didn't like her talkin' about Pa. "Maybe you don't know nothin' about my father."

"Just remember," she said. "It was too late for him. It is too late for your friend, here." She looked to Holt. "That is why he resists Judgement so strongly. He knows it."

A flicker of alarm lanced into me as I looked to Holt, too, even if I didn't prescribe to all this preachin' of hers.

But Holt only shook his head and reined his gelding around. "I'll make camp over yonder," he spat. "I've had enough of this. You come find me when yer done in there, got it, kid?"

"Yeah. I will."

He rode off, and I shot a final glare toward the Oracle before turnin' my attention back to the wall of plants.

"Just remember," she said again, but I weren't gonna entertain her notions no more, so I ignored her and shoved my way through the tangle of leaves and stems till I stumbled free on the other side.

They'd left the lights on fer me.

Or at least the lights along a certain path were still lit, so I followed those, and sure enough I ended up back at that main atrium.

Just in time fer dinner, it seemed.

Everyone looked up from their food as I entered, and Charlotte's eyebrows lifted at the sight of me. "Ah," she said matter-of-factly. "You're back. Must have been some walk."

"Yeah..." I muttered, ignorin' the twinge of guilt. "Sorry. Went to find Holt." I wandered toward the table as the smell of cooked meat made my stomach twist somethin' awful, and I realized I was much missin' bein' able to have a proper hot meal.

The doc and his wife stood as I approached, and he went off to retrieve another stool while his wife went about puttin' together another plate.

And suddenly I felt like an intruder here, interruptin' the family dinner, marchin' in unannounced after a lengthy absence. Reflexively, I took off my hat again, despite the fact this weren't no real house. "Oh, uh, you don't have to trouble yerself fer me," I said. "Didn't mean to disturb yer dinner ... you go on ahead and finish up."

But Fanni and Radley had already moved to one side of the table, and Dr. Balogh had put the extra stool in beside Charlotte on the other side, and Mrs. Balogh had a plateful of food set there.

"Nonsense," Hannah said. "It is no trouble to fix you a plate of food compared to what other trouble you have already caused us. Now sit and eat."

I swallowed, nodded. "All ... all right. Thank you." And so I did, takin' the stool and settin' my hat in my lap so I could dig into roasted bird, potatoes and carrots with much enthusiasm—until I noted the looks the Baloghs were all givin' me and paused.

Charlotte cleared her throat.

I had the distinct impression she was tryin' to tell me somethin', but I couldn't figure out what.

The doc and his wife took their seats again, one at each head of the table, and then Mrs. Balogh leaned forward, clearly addressin' me. "It is customary to say Grace before partaking of a meal at this table, Mr. Delano. Have you forgotten this already?"

I currently had a mouth full of food, so I gulped it down and sat back on my stool. Hell. I *had* forgotten. "Uh, right. Sorry. Uh..."

Shit. There'd been plenty of awkward, silent dinners durin' those three weeks I'd been laid up at their homestead, and I did remember now that there'd always been a prayer beforehand, but I'd never had to say one myself. I'd just bowed my head and gone along with whatever she had happened to say.

Now, they were all lookin' at me. Waitin'.

I folded my hands and bowed my head, mind racin' back to all the things I'd heard her say before those dinners, back to the prayers my own family had used to say durin' those quiet evenings that almost seemed more like dreams now than somethin' that had once been real. "Uh..." I closed my eyes to block out their starin' and cleared my throat. "Heavenly Father, bless this food and the hands that made it ... and, er, bring prosperity to this kind family for their sharin' of it. Thanks be also to the Holy Mother for providin' such sustenance, and may She keep us all safe. Amen."

The family echoed my *amen* and I tried to hide the grimace as I shifted on the stool. Well, that was surely another thing I hoped I'd never have to do again.

But Mrs. Balogh seemed satisfied with my effort, and they all went back to eatin' again, so I deemed it safe to resume eatin', myself.

Maybe it would have been better to not have come back here at all.

Now that I took the time to think about it ... I weren't really sure why I *had* come back here. I'd wanted a safe place to wait fer Nan's arrival, sure ... but I coulda done that out in the woods on the surface, makin' camp with Holt...

"So," Dr. Balogh began, pullin' me away from my ruminations. "Did you manage to find your friend? Holt, is it? Miss Charlotte told us he has been your traveling companion for quite some time."

"Uh, yeah. Yeah, I found him." I glanced to Charlotte, worried then about what else she might have been tellin' this family in my absence.

But she only nodded, then focused her attention back on her meal. Her hair was a mess and she still had those white painted markings all over her ... and I suddenly wondered how she'd been while I was gone. How were those wounds across her back? Had she been comfortable down here? Had the Baloghs been tendin' to her needs adequately? And then I felt an awful guilt fer leavin' her so abruptly with no explanation, and fer stayin' gone as long as I had.

I didn't owe her an explanation, I supposed, didn't owe her nothin', really. I'd never wanted her to come along on this journey, after all, even if she had certainly saved my life when that demon statue had been tryin' to strangle me. I'd repaid her fer that already anyway, keepin' another of those statues from doin' the same to her. But that guilt settled nice and heavy across my shoulders, regardless, and I wished I knew exactly why.

"Would he also like some supper?" Dr. Balogh was askin'.

"Uh ... what?"

"Your friend, Holt," Dr. Balogh repeated. "Would he like some supper as well? We could take some out to him if he is nearby."

I blinked, finally movin' my attention back to the doc, a less pleasant sight than watchin' Charlotte, though at least he'd shed that strange leather apron now. He wore that leather cuff around his left forearm, though. "Oh. Right. Sure, he's nearby. Camped up top. Don't like these deep caves much. I'm sure he'd appreciate a bite though ... if you've got enough to spare. Otherwise I'm sure he'll manage. He's a resourceful ol' bast—errr." At least I'd caught myself that time. I tried again, studiously avoidin' Mrs. Balogh's stare. "He's ... very resourceful.

I'm sure he'll be just fine without. Wouldn't want to deplete yer stores. I know huntin' is scarce around these parts."

"That's certainly true," Dr. Balogh agreed. "But the blackbirds are numerous enough. There are so many of them here. They may be small, but ... snare enough of them and you can make a decent meal. I'm sure we can spare another plate or two. When we are finished here, I will gather some dinner for your friend as well."

That'd probably make Holt's night, I figured. Didn't think he'd had nothin' to eat except that half-burned gruel since we'd reached Blackbird. "Well ... thank you. That's ... that's mighty kind of you."

"Our pleasure, Mr. Delano," Dr. Balogh said, and he resumed his meal lookin' quite pleased with himself, indeed.

That awkward silence fell again, and I shoveled food into my mouth quick as I could so I could shortly be done with it.

But Mrs. Balogh spoke again before I could quite make my escape. "You may take the west chamber for the night, if you like. It is a bit damp, but it will suffice."

The offer took me by surprise. "Oh, uh, I ain't stayin', ma'am."

Everyone stopped eatin', Radley with his mouth fulla food.

"No?" Mrs. Balogh asked.

"No." I could feel Charlotte lookin' at me then, but I resisted meetin' her gaze like I'd avoided Mrs. Balogh's just before. And I realized at that moment I couldn't tell her—or the Baloghs—about my plan to meet Nan at that abandoned mill. They'd all insist it was suicide, just as Holt was inclined to do, or worse, attempt to come along and get themselves killed. But all eyes were on me now again, expectant, relieved, suspicious, offended ... a whole mix of things, and I shifted on my stool. "I mean, I do plan on stayin' around the area fer awhile, and thank you fer the offer and all, but like my friend, I don't much like livin' underground. I'll just camp up on the surface fer the night. It's what I'm used to, anyway."

"Are you certain?" Dr. Balogh pressed. "There is plenty of room here if you'd prefer a roof ... even if it is a damp roof."

I shook my head. "No thanks. But I do appreciate the offer."

"Very well, then. But if you should change your mind, the offer is still there, understand? You and Miss Charlotte—and your friend Holt —are all welcome to stay here as long as you need."

"Sure."

Mrs. Balogh sat back in her chair. "So, Mr. Delano." She wiped at her mouth with a napkin. "Have you brought back with you any unsavory individuals wishing to take this cave for themselves? Are they outside now, waiting?"

Again, everyone paused their eatin' and watched me, and the rushin' of that distant waterfall sounded like thunder in the quiet.

I swallowed my food and met her even stare square this time. "No ma'am, I did not. And the only one waitin' outside is Holt."

Her eyes narrowed. "Is that so?"

"Yes," I hissed, frustration wellin' despite my best efforts to restrain it.

Dr. Balogh cleared his throat loudly, probably in attempts to head off the argument he sensed brewin' between me and his wife. "Miss Charlotte has told us a little about your sister's terrible predicament. If you are willing to tell us more ... perhaps we can help you retrieve her. Without putting such a valuable asset as this power station into the hands of a terrorist."

I dropped my eyes back down to my nearly empty plate, and suddenly had no more appetite. An offer to help my sister from people who didn't even know her. Who'd already saved my life ... twice. Who'd kept me well-fed and comfortably sheltered all the time I'd spent in their company. And even despite all I'd taken from 'em last time.

That's why I'd come back here. Seekin' all those comforts again, like a goddamned moth to a flame. Same reason I'd lamented havin' to leave Sally's place so much, too.

But nothin' good ever came outta gettin' too comfortable. "Yeah. Maybe," I managed to choke out, and there was a sour taste in my mouth.

Dr. Wright came to mind, tied to that chair and beaten to a pulp, and then there was bile in the back of my throat.

Nine-Fingered Nan and her crew would destroy this family. Just like she'd destroyed so many others. Here they were, gathered around a dinin' table in the middle of the greatest Old World find I figured there'd ever been, actin' like all of this were normal. Actin' like this was their own house. Actin' like they had not a care in the world, like there weren't no other greater dangers out there.

And I was sittin' right there among 'em, actin' like I belonged.

A thief and a liar and a murderer—fresh from the murder of an innocent, no less, killed by my own hand this time—who'd just invited Nine-Fingered Nan herself to bring her crew up here from the west. I was bringin' the Devil right to their doorstep.

I pushed my stool back, feelin' ill. I couldn't let Nan get anywhere near this cave. Anywhere near this family. And the longer I stayed here, the greater the chance they'd get pulled into my maelstrom, too. I caught up my hat, then stood and cleared my throat. "If you'll excuse me, I'd best be goin'. I'd like to set up camp before it gets full-on dark. But thank you ... thank you very much fer the meal."

Dr. Balogh stood again. "Let me get a plate for your friend."

I pushed my hat back on and waited restlessly while he did so, well aware of all the eyes still watchin' me, Charlotte's most of all. There were a lot of questions on her face, and I didn't wanna have to answer any of 'em. I didn't wanna have to lie to her. So as soon as the doc had handed me that plate fer Holt, I tipped my hat to the family, thanked 'em again fer the food, bid 'em all good night, and tried to leave in a hurry.

"Oh, Mr. Delano?"

I gritted my teeth and tried to keep my frustration in check as I drew up short and turned to face the table again. "Yeah, Doc?"

"Come on by again in the morning, would you? I have further instructions you might find useful for that leg of yours."

Further instructions? Beyond how to deploy a whole damned arsenal from the thing? What more could he possibly have to tell me? But I nodded. "Sure thing, Doc."

"Very good. Good night, Mr. Delano."

"Good night." I all but fled the cave.

XXXVIII

TROUBLIN' THOUGHTS

I grabbed up Joe's reins once I was in daylight again and followed the thin trail of smoke in the distance to where Holt had made his camp. It was near dark by then, and Holt was mighty happy indeed to receive that plate of real food.

"From the Baloghs," I said as I handed it over.

"Well I'll be damned." His eyes got nearly as big as saucers as he accepted it. "I see why you were so keen to return here now, Oracle or not. Real cookin', huh?"

"Yeah. Real cookin'." I pulled my pack from Joe and started layin' out my things, then unsaddled him, gave him a quick brush, and put him on the picket line with Holt's horse fer the night.

By the time I was done with that, Holt had cleaned his plate. He set it aside and wiped greasy hands on his pants. "That family ain't sore about the stuff you stole from 'em?"

I shrugged. "I paid 'em back fer all that, remember? With some of the money we—you—got from that bank."

"Oh right. More of my share you took without askin'."

I ignored his jab. "Otherwise, yeah, think they would have been awful sore about it." I didn't bother to mention what Radley had said about their mama otherwise turnin' me in to Sheriff Reeves fer bein' a horse thief. I sat down cross-legged on my bedroll, starin' into Holt's small fire. "Think they're still a little put out by it, though."

"But not put out enough not to feed you."

"Seems that way."

Holt grunted. "So they think we're ... what? Just drifters, then? Mostly honest and law-abidin', but down on our luck?"

"That's right."

"Uh-huh." There was silence fer a minute as he joined me in starin' into the fire. Then he glanced up at me over the flames. "You tell 'em about Nan?"

I shook my head. "No. Hell no. They've already offered to help without knowin' the full nature of things, and that's bad enough. I don't want 'em involved. Not any of 'em."

"And Charlotte?"

"Especially not her."

"So you didn't tell her, neither."

"No."

Another stretch of silence passed between us, and Holt picked up a nearby stick and poked at the fire's logs with it. Then he gave a heavy sigh and shook his head. "Ya know, kid, that old blind woman was right. It's too late fer me."

I glanced up at him sharply, but he kept his gaze on the burnin' logs he poked at.

"This family, the Baloghs, I mean, and Charlotte ... they could be yer chance to start over again, ya know. You ever think about that? Startin' over? Settlin' down, tryin' to live proper, like yer pa did?"

My jaw clenched as his eyes came up at last, but then it was me who looked away, shiftin' my sights to my mule, who lazily snuffled around the dead leaves underfoot. I pulled at a few random tufts of grass stickin' out from under my bedroll myself, then tore 'em up into little pieces as I moved my glare back to Holt again. "No," I lied. "I started that way, Holt. Would still be livin' that life if no one had come along and taken it from me. But now, no." I shook my head, tossed the pieces of grass into the fire. "No. It'd all be a lie, anyway. Just like what Pa was livin'."

Holt frowned at me, and the flames made shadows dance across his face. "You think yer pa was livin' a lie?"

"On the ranch? With me and Ethelyn and Mama? Yeah." My voice cracked. I'd never said these things aloud before. But now, as I said 'em, the truth of it solidified. And all of it one big brick of bitterness wedged in my throat. "Yeah. Or it wouldn't have ended the way it did, would it have?"

Holt's frown deepened, and I could tell he'd never considered it that way before.

It didn't matter. Like most things that plagued my sleep these days, it was all in the past. Nothin' to be done fer it now except to regret it all. And keep movin' forward, toward the hope of givin' Ethelyn a future she wouldn't someday regret.

"So," I prompted when Holt remained in contemplative quiet. "You got some kinda plan fer how to deal with Nan or what?"

He hissed a breath through his teeth and threw his stick into the fire. "Sure. Hell with it. Life was gettin' borin', anyway."

By the time Holt had laid out his ideas, and I had added a few of my own, night had descended over the forest we sat in, and the wanin' crescent moon shone high in the sky. And I was feelin' pretty confident about our chances by then, too.

We didn't know how many Nan would be bringin' with her, but we'd planned fer a lot, just in case. If she happened to bring fewer along, well, that would just make our job easier.

Even still, fer a long time after Holt had fallen asleep and lay there across the fire softly snorin', I laid on my own pallet and just stared up into those trees. It'd been a long time since I'd been around trees of this size and number. The canopy of leaves above me fluttered, shivered in the gentle night breeze, highlighted dim orange on the underside from our dwindlin' fire and flashin' pale silver on their topsides from the moonlight.

All around me, the forest hummed with insect life. Seemed they had been spared from the power station's discharge, unfortunately. I had to swat off mosquitos more than once. Well, I hadn't missed them none, fer certain. In the distance I heard coyotes, and that made me think of Silas Lowery.

I hoped he was gettin' devoured right about now.

Only then I thought of Mr. Brown, and that made me sit up and rub my hands over my face. I hadn't wanted to have to kill that old man, damnit.

I gave up on sleep with a heavy sigh and stood, grabbin' up my gunbelts to put 'em back on. Just in case. Then I grabbed up my hat and put it back on, too. Just a habit.

Joe perked his ears at my standin' and nickered.

I scowled at him. "Shush, you."

He nickered again and I whispered curses, but Holt didn't so much as twitch. Rollin' my eyes and shakin' my head, I left Joe and Holt and our little camp and wandered toward the stream I'd scrubbed myself in earlier. I could hear it, just barely beneath the chorus of insects, and I went carefully in that direction, followin' faint, dappled moonlight and tryin' not to make too much noise as I pushed through all that underbrush. Though truth be told, it was hard to hear much over the deafenin' cacophony of insects out here.

I was just passin' by the entrance to the cave on my way to the creek when a rustle of somethin' and flicker of movement in that direction made me whip around with both guns drawn.

Only to face the shadow of another person, and the glint of their own outstretched pistol.

"Van?" she hissed.

I let out an explosive breath. "Charlotte? What the hell! Yer gonna get shot sneakin' around the woods like that."

She holstered her gun and waded her way through the brush toward me, pullin' at her skirts as they were continually snagged. "I could say the same for you, you know. Thought you might have been a bear. Didn't expect you to be up and roaming about."

I grunted and shoved my own guns back into their holsters. "I didn't expect you to be up and roaming about, neither. What's wrong? You okay?"

"I'm just fine. Couldn't sleep, is all."

I growled and crossed my arms as she finally reached me. "So you think it's smart to come out here and wander around the woods in the middle of the night? All by yourself?"

She crossed her arms to mirror me, cockin' her head. "Why not? That's what *you're* doing. And anyway, I'm armed. I was coming to look for you, matter of fact. Where's Holt?" She pulled her gaze away from me to look around at the darkened forest.

I nodded back in the direction I'd come from. "Over there a ways. Sleepin'."

She turned back to me. "Where are you going, then?"

I shrugged. "I couldn't sleep, neither. Was goin' to the creek to sit fer a spell. Maybe splash some cold water on my face. Not used to this humidity no more."

"I'll come with you, then."

I peered down at her in the dark, all kinds of mixed feelin's risin' up in me at that statement. "You sure yer all right? The Baloghs treatin' you okay and all?"

She nodded. "Oh yes. Yes, they are a very pleasant family, aren't they? Very generous."

"Yeah. Very generous." And lucky. Lucky their kindnesses thus far hadn't got 'em murdered.

"And quite intelligent, too. All of them. Even the children. Makes me think ... makes me wonder ... how different my life might have been if I'd have been born to parents more like Mr. and Mrs. Balogh."

I lifted my brows. "Instead of to parents like your senator father? I dunno, you keep throwin' his name around out here, and it's at least made that bounty hunter Duster hesitate a time or two. He mighta been able to take me in if not fer that."

She sighed, and her crossed arms looked more like she was huggin' herself. "It didn't do any good at all. It's never done any good at all ... only made life more miserable." She stared off into the distance as she said it, and again I got the sense that maybe there was somethin' botherin' her she weren't tellin' me about. I cleared my throat. "Charlotte. What's wrong?"

She hesitated fer a long minute, but then spat it out. "You're planning something. You're planning something, and you want to leave me out of it."

I was glad of the dark then, so she couldn't see me wince at that accusation. Goddamnit. I should have known there weren't no way in Hell I could come back here without havin' to answer her questions at some point.

But she didn't wait fer me to confirm or deny her statement. "Are you going to tell Nan about this place? Because if you are, we need to make sure the Baloghs are out of there, even if we have to hogtie them and carry them out ourselves."

The thought of doin' such a thing made me snort in amusement. "You'd ... you'd help me do somethin' like that?"

"If we had to. I know they don't want Nan to have this place ... but they don't understand. They don't understand what it's like to be kidnapped and held captive and sold off. And I'm not..." Her voice broke and she paused, took a breath. "I'm not going to let that happen to your sister if I can help it. Even if it means letting Nan take this place." Another pause. "I'd make sure to take the most valuable things out first, though. Like those journals. And Dr. Balogh's controls for the automatons. And anyway, I think those things would take care of Nan and her crew, don't you? There's so many of them ... if Nan and her gang went in there with all their weapons ... they'd get destroyed by those things. Don't you think?"

I nodded. "Probably. If the Oracle let them through."

"The Oracle? You think she'd stand up to Nine-Fingered Nan, even?"

"Something tells me she would." I wasn't goin' to mention what Radley had said about that crazy old woman havin' magic, nor what Silas Lowry had said about her holdin' off Nan's people so far.

"She'd be killed," Charlotte whispered. "And all her followers too, probably."

"Most likely."

A stretch of silence passed between us then, as we stood awkwardly beneath all those trees, and I gritted my teeth as the urge welled in me to go ahead and tell her my plan. To save her the frettin' over the Baloghs and a crazy old witch woman and her misguided disciples. "I'm ... I'm not gonna tell Nan about the cave," I blurted finally.

Charlotte looked to me sharply. "But ... your sister..."

"Just so happens another opportunity came up," I said reluctantly, tryin' to stay as vague as I could about just *how* that opportunity had come up. "I'm settin' a trap, instead. A trap fer Nan."

"A trap? And Holt knows about this?"

"Yes."

She straightened, her hands droppin' back to her sides. "But you didn't see fit to tell *me*."

I shifted, able to feel her glare even if I couldn't see it. "Charlotte ... we don't know how many Nan might bring with her."

"Which is why you should have *more* people on your side, not fewer."

I sighed and scrubbed my hands over my face. "You've been through enough, all right? I'm not gonna ask you to take part in somethin' like that—"

"You don't have to ask. I'm *telling* you, that's why I'm here. That's why I went all the way back to Grave Gulch in the first place. I want to help, Van. What else am I going to do?"

"Stay in that cave with the Baloghs," I muttered. "Stay safe."

"And yet you don't seem concerned for your partner Holt's safety," she shot back.

I snorted. "Holt? He's a mean old bastard who's been livin' on the run almost since he was born. No, guess I ain't that worried fer his safety." Though even as I said it, I recalled that Nan had specifically mentioned him in her telegram. She'd instructed her men to bring Haggerty to the mill, as well. And I suddenly wondered why.

"You were happy enough to bring me along when we went to Baron Whittaker's place," Charlotte hissed, pullin' my attention back to her. "You sure didn't seem so concerned for my safety then. Did you even really care about my situation at all? Did you actually want to *help* me ... or were you just using me to get what *you* wanted?"

I winced again. "Charlotte..."

"Now that I'm no longer *useful*, it's better to hide me away I suppose, is it? I suppose I have no real value to you unless I can directly get you something you want, huh?"

"That's not what I—"

"Baron Whittaker would have killed you if not for me. And that thing in there," she pointed back toward the cave, "it would have killed you, too, if not for me. Maybe you don't think I'm all that useful anymore ... but it seems like you *need* my help a great deal, Van Delano."

I hooked my thumbs into my belts and wet my lips, shiftin' my gaze out into the stretchin' darkness. Heat stung my face, her angry claim about me usin' her at the Whittakers' place hittin' a little too close to home. But it weren't like that ... not *all* like that ... I mighta used her to an extent, sure. But I had also wanted to help her ... I really had...

The sounds of all the insects thundered in my skull as I pondered her points. They were so goddamned loud out here. But all I could think of was her bein' stung by that mechanical bee, and droppin' limp in my arms, and starin' up at the cavern roof with a glassy, unfocused gaze, and I swallowed hard. "Charlotte," I finally said. "I weren't ... I weren't just usin' you. Before. And I ain't discountin' what you've done, or that you've saved my life—"

"More than once."

"More than once. But this ... this is Nine-Fingered Nan. She's already got my sister, and she's been usin' that against me fer months. Just fuckin' with me. Just fer fun, I think. And this might finally be my chance to get Ethelyn back, sure, but I also can't risk Nan gettin' ahold of anyone else—" I stopped before I could say it.

Anyone else I care about.

I swallowed again, cleared my throat. "Anyone else she could use against me. Or kill just to spite me. Understand?"

"You don't think I could hold my own against Nan?"

"You know you can't."

"But you can?"

I laughed despite myself. "Naw. Naw, Charlotte, I sure can't. She's the reason I have this metal leg in the first place. That's why we're settin' a trap. So we don't have to face her directly, 'cause none of us would live through that."

Charlotte crossed her arms again and lifted her chin. "Then it sounds like you have nothing to worry about if I come along, doesn't it?"

Now she was just makin' me angry. I stepped toward her and pulled my thumbs from my belts so I could point a finger in her face. "*No*. You ain't comin', Charlotte. All right? And neither are the Baloghs. I don't need yer help, and I don't need their help. Yer gonna stay here, stay in that cave, stay with the Baloghs, and yer all gonna stay out of the way, got it?"

She glared at me somethin' fierce. I was close enough now I could see her face clear enough, and her eyes blazed like they had when she'd shot down the baron from the back of one of his own horses. Her fists clenched and her breath came harsh and fast through gritted teeth.

Fer a second I thought she was gonna slap me ... or maybe worse.

Maybe I shoulda disarmed her first.

"I thought you were different," she spat at last. "Thought you were different from all those arrogant, useless men of the Republic, from the cruel, self-absorbed barons of the Territories ... all they ever saw me as was something to possess, something pretty to put on a shelf, to collect, to *keep safe* ... but I guess you aren't so different from them after all, are you?"

I opened my mouth, affronted by such a comparison, but she didn't give me a chance to speak.

"Fine. If that's the way you want it ... goodbye then, Mr. Delano." She spun on her heel and marched back toward the cave, and I watched her go with the protest still stuck in my throat.

But I swallowed it all back. I wanted to argue her point, sure. *She* probably wanted me to argue her point, too. She probably wanted me to come after her, to take back what I'd said and invite her to come along on this damn fool venture of mine, after all.

But part of what she'd said had been right enough ... this *was* the way I wanted it.

Well, maybe not *entirely* the way I wanted it. I didn't want her mad at me. And I didn't want her thinkin' I was anythin' like the barons of

Blessing. But mostly I didn't want her tryin' to come along with me and Holt when we went to take on Nan. So if her bein' mad at me was the only way to achieve that ... then I'd let her be mad at me.

I'd let her think I was somethin' like those barons of Blessing, I guess.

Long as she stayed safe.

I watched her stalk up to the overgrowth that covered the cave entrance and angrily shove some of it aside to disappear inside, and then I let out a breath and growled, turnin' away to resume my walk toward the creek.

When I reached it, I knelt on the bank and splashed the water over my face and the back of my neck. I took off my hat and ran some through my sweat-damp hair, too. It was cool against the muggy night. Felt good.

And I tried to focus on that, the simple pleasure of the cool water runnin' over my skin, instead of on all the troublesome thoughts tumblin' over and over in my mind.

Instead of on the sudden realization that Nan had surely asked fer Holt to be brought to the mill too because she knew I cared.

She knew I cared, and she planned to kill him once she got there. Or worse.

And I was no longer certain at all she'd bring my sister along with her.

But even if she didn't ... I couldn't take Holt there. I couldn't take Charlotte, and I couldn't bring Holt.

Both of 'em would only be liabilities. Tools fer Nan to use.

I was gonna have to go alone.

XXXIX

FAREWELLS

The next day brought an overcast sky and rain, but Holt and I went about readyin' our plan despite the weather. All but the dynamite, anyway. That would have to wait till things dried up again.

We gathered all the guns and ammo we had on us, and we rode down to the abandoned mill to scope things out. We took stock of what else we'd need, and then Holt grumbled a great deal about havin' to go back into town to purchase yet more weapons and ammunition.

But I certainly couldn't go. Not after what I'd done at the post office, and with the sheriff already on the look-out fer me. So he left to go acquire those things while I set up what we already had.

And I didn't say a word to him about the fact I weren't gonna let him help me on the day Nan finally arrived. I knew better. I'd have to just leave without him when the time came, and figure out some way to keep him from followin' once he realized I'd gone.

But fer now, I only focused on settin' up. Plantin' trip lines, mappin' out the interior of the rottin' building, already half-collapsed. I checked the sturdiness of its upper floor, noted the places that would still hold my weight ... and the places that wouldn't.

I leaned my rifle in one corner near an upper window, stacked a few boxes of bullets next to it. Left a few boxes of pistol rounds in other strategic places, put the dynamite in a place it'd stay dry till the rain stopped.

Holt returned in the early evenin' with two more rifles, one more pistol, another bundle of rope, and less ammo than I would have liked. And even grumpier than he'd been before, claimin' Blackbird's over-populated status was havin' a toll on their supply of weapons same as the supply of everything else.

But it was somethin', at least, and it'd have to do.

We camped at the mill fer the night, not wantin' to ride back in these woods in the dark, and finished our set-up of what we had the next day. I wanted more dynamite, but Holt said Blackbird was all out, on account of so many people suddenly becomin' prospectors around these parts.

So I told him I'd just steal it. And so all that next day, I took Joe around the woods that surrounded Blackbird, searchin' fer treasure-seekers, and when I found a few that looked suitable to rob, I robbed 'em. Took their dynamite and their shovels and pickaxes and knives, and the two pistols they had and all their bullets, even their whiskey, and loaded it all up on Joe. Then left 'em bound and gagged at their dig site and headed back to Holt.

The third day was spent mostly diggin'. Plantin' the dynamite and makin' pits. The sun had come out again by then, but the rain had at least taken some of the humidity away with it, and it weren't quite so stifflin' warm anymore.

By the fourth day, we'd done all we could. We double-checked our work, strategized our positions, worked out the order of which perch and gun we'd use and when.

And all the while I wondered if this was really gonna work. And if I should let Holt come, after all. And if I didn't, how was I gonna get him to stay behind?

And then, in the absence of anythin' else to prepare, thoughts of Charlotte came back unbidden, and the weight of that look she'd given me settled heavy on my shoulders. Angry.

No, *furious*.

Betrayed.

That's what it was. She'd looked at me like maybe I really *were* one of those barons.

Disgusted.

I *really* didn't like her lookin' at me like that.

And I hardly slept at all on that fourth night.

On the fifth day we headed back toward the underground power station, though most everything in me was fully against doin' so. Weren't no reason fer me to go back, really, except to show the Baloghs —and maybe Charlotte—that I weren't as bad a man as Mrs. Balogh feared I was.

I wanted to tell 'em I weren't gonna lead Nan to their discovery. And then I was gonna tell 'em I was leavin' the area. So they wouldn't question me further on how I planned to get my sister back, and hopefully wouldn't mention again their offer to help me do so. And I was gonna give 'em some money, too, although Holt didn't know about that part yet.

Seemed the least I could do fer 'em, given all they'd done fer me of late, and fer Charlotte.

This time I weren't surprised at all when the Oracle stepped out from behind a big oak to block our way. Holt didn't say nothin' this time, neither. Only sat there in his saddle glowerin' at her, a hand on his pistol grip.

I didn't bother reachin' fer my weapons. Just stared her down, and she stared back at me with her sightless eyes. Then she turned without a word, and we followed her back to the cave again.

She merged back into the forest once we reached it with no partin' wisdom fer once, seemingly meltin' clean away, and Holt whispered a curse as I dismounted and started to unbuckle my gunbelts.

"I really don't like her," he muttered. "Somethin' ain't right about her. About any of this." He gestured toward the cave.

"Yeah." It was hard to disagree with him on that count. Every time I saw that old woman, my skin prickled. But there was nothin' fer it. Magic or not, she seemed to be the only way anyone could find this damned place. Good thing she favored the Baloghs ... and seemed to favor us. At least fer the time bein'. "But we're leavin' soon, remember? And then we ain't never comin' back here."

Holt grunted. "I think that's about the smartest thing I've heard you say in years."

I scowled at him and tossed my belts over my saddle horn. "I'll be back soon. Don't go nowhere."

"Yeah, yeah. Sure."

I reached the main atrium to find it empty. Curious and slightly concerned, I decided to check that chamber the Baloghs had shown me as the main battery room next. The one with the big water wheel.

Sure enough, Dr. Balogh was in there fussin' about by the wall of machinery. He had that telescopin' eyepatch on again, and when I cleared my throat loudly, he startled and whipped around.

"My goodness! You mustn't sneak up on people like that." He pulled the eyepatch down to look at me square. "Nice of you to decide to drop by again ... did you forget I'd asked you to come by so I could talk to you more about that leg of yours? Thought perhaps you had run off for good this time."

"Oh." I glanced down reflexively to my left leg, my fingers brushin' against the metal part of my thigh. "Sorry. Yes, uh ... I did forget. I've had ... other things on my mind lately."

The doctor frowned at me. "I see. Well, would you like to know how to operate that leg properly or not?"

"I ... er, didn't you show me before? With the knives and the gun and all that?" Mentionin' that hidden pistol reminded me to make sure it was loaded. And ideally, I needed a way to be sure it was easily accessible, too. Couldn't always be rollin' up my pants—or takin' 'em off entirely—to get at that thing if I wanted it.

Dr. Balogh barked a little laugh at my question. "Goodness, no. There is a great deal more to it than that, son. Come here, I'll show you." He waved me to the right side of the chamber, the side opposite the big wheel and the underground stream. There was a small table and stool set up there; looked new. The wood still fresh. But the surface of the table was already covered with tools and gadgets, some of 'em modern and some of 'em Old World.

The doc patted the top of the stool. "Go on. Have a seat."

I did so reluctantly, unsure of whether or not I really wanted to learn anything else about this leg of mine. I leaned an elbow against the edge of the table, sweepin' my gaze across all the trinkets strewn there. Then I pulled my arm away again in a hurry as I spotted some of those little metal centipedes like Mr. Miller had used.

These weren't movin', but I weren't gonna take any chances.

I stood, pulled the stool further away from the table, and then sat once more as Dr. Balogh found what he'd been lookin' fer in those pockets of his apron and held it up triumphantly. "Ah ha. Here we are."

It was a little turnscrew.

Frownin' now, I watched as he pulled that ridiculous eyepatch back up onto his eye and leaned over me. "Well? Let's see it."

I sighed and rolled up that trouser leg, far as I could.

"There we are. Now, you've been keeping it clean, yes?"

"Uhhh..."

There was a rubber cuff at the top of the metal part of my leg, the part nearest what was left of my actual thigh. It cupped around the natural end of my leg, so that the margin' of flesh and metal looked more natural. That part could be removed, I knew; I'd seen the doc do it several times while I'd been stayin' with him the first time, and when he'd shown me how to wash it up good and proper.

But I didn't like to take that part off much myself. Removin' it exposed the metal rod underneath, showin' it clear as day stickin' directly outta my flesh, like a metal bone with all the meat carved off. And then there was that scar plainly visible, too. A big, dark one, runnin' down both sides of my thigh toward the place where my skin puckered around the rod, and lookin' at it too much made my stomach turn.

So I didn't look at it. And I didn't usually take that rubber part off. Not anymore. Not since leavin' his homestead, mostly. Mostly I just tried to forget that leg was metal entirely. If I never looked at it, these days I could almost forget, sometimes.

Except fer the part that the feelin' there was all numb. And it didn't always work quite right.

But Dr. Balogh pressed the release on the rubber cuff now, makin' it loosen from around my thigh, and I opened my mouth to protest as he pulled the edges of it downward.

Only he reeled backwards before I could say anythin'. "Goodness gracious, man! Don't you ever bathe?"

"Sure I do," I growled. "It's just that I—"

"I told you to keep it clean, did I not?" He marched over to grab a wooden bucket from near the chamber's entrance and then filled it with water from the stream.

"Well sure, but I—"

"Told you that if you did not clean it properly, you might get another infection?"

I glared at him as he marched back in my direction, pullin' a handkerchief from one front pocket of his apron. Truth be told I didn't really remember him sayin' that, but I hadn't much listened to anythin' he'd told me durin' those three weeks. I'd been preoccupied by the general horror of havin' a missin' leg, and the nearly overwhelmin' urgency to get to Bravebank to make the deal fer my sister.

He put the bucket down at my feet and tossed the handkerchief into it. "Here. Please clean that up. The cuff as well. It's a wonder you don't have an infection already. The place where that rod exits your flesh never entirely heals, you know. If you do not clean it properly, it is a direct route for sickness to invade your body."

I grumbled as I soaked the handkerchief and then started wipin' carefully around the end of my stump of a thigh, suckin' a breath through my teeth as the cold water hit my skin. That seemed like a pretty important detail he maybe should have made more clear durin' my first stay at his place. But then, maybe he *had* made it clear, and I just hadn't wanted to hear it. "I didn't ask you to put this leg on me, Doc. I never wanted it in the first place."

He was back over at the table, rummagin' through all those various devices, but he turned back to face me at my statement and raised his eyebrows. "Oh no? I suppose that's true. Would you like me to take it back, then? Since it seems clear you are incapable of taking care of it properly in the first place…"

He stepped toward me with that turnscrew in one hand and several very small pouches of some kind of liquid in his other hand, but I lifted my own hands as he approached.

"No. No, no need fer that. I'm just sayin' … I'm just sayin' I don't understand all of it, is all."

"That is why you are here now, is it not? I'll explain it to you, so you can understand, and then take care of it, yes?"

That weren't at all why I'd come here, or what I'd planned to be doin' right now, but I supposed it *would* be good to understand the thing better if I was gonna be stuck with it. "Sure," I muttered.

"Good." He knelt down in front of my stool and started messin' about with the rubber cuff as I finished washin' it up. There were little pockets along the inside of it, turned out, and he removed some empty pouches from those pockets and then slipped the full pouches down into them, instead. "Medicine," he explained as he caught my confused look. "I see the original store I supplied you with was used. Not surprising, considering you were out and about walking and riding much earlier than you should have been."

I remembered clear enough how rough those first weeks away from his homestead had been, how much the place where my leg had been cut off hurt. The fevers and chills, and the feel of little needles prickin' my skin. Damn. So all of that had been true, as well. The leg *had* had medicines in it to help me heal.

If it hadn't, maybe I woulda come down with another infection, just like he'd said.

I finished cleanin' up the grimy, sweat-crusted skin that had been beneath that cuff and dropped the handkerchief back into the bucket.

Dr. Balogh finished his work refillin' those medicines. "Those should last you awhile." He glanced up at me. "Perhaps. If you are smart about it. Should only deploy if absolutely necessary. But if it should deploy, there are very few doctors in this country who could supply you with more."

"Why don't that surprise me?"

"So I suppose if you should need more, go east. Or come see me again, yes?"

"You mean if your obsession with puttin' metal limbs on people don't get you killed before then? Sure."

He gave me a flat stare, clearly not appreciatin' my quip. "And if your habit for not listening to people wiser than yourself does not get *you* killed before then. Yes."

"Fine. Where you gonna be by then, though? Plannin' to stay here fer a spell? After what happened to yer friend Dr. Wright ... I don't think you should go back to Bravebank. Not unless you hear Nine-Fingered Nan and her nest of vipers has been burned out, anyway. And you'd better be damn sure it's actually true, and not just a rumor. I think she's gunnin' fer you, Doc."

"That could be true," he admitted. "But no, I do not think we will return to Bravebank any time soon. The work to be done here is too important. We will likely stay here 'for a spell,' yes."

"All right then." But I had no plans to come back here. Just like I'd told Holt. I'd done without the doc's strange kind of medicine fer plenty of years before now. If it ran out, so be it. I weren't gonna face that Oracle no more, nor risk runnin' into Blackbird's sheriff again.

"Now this," he said, and he held up the turnscrew, "this is for you. It is very important, so do not lose it, understand?"

I took it from him with a frown and turned it around in my hand. It looked almost like a regular turnscrew, worn wooden handle and all, 'cept the head of it looked kinda like a star. "Oh yeah? What's so important about it?"

"That is how you take the leg off, should you ever want to."

I blinked at the tool in my hand, then looked back down to my leg. "Take ... take the leg *off*? Why would I ever want to do that?"

Dr. Balogh shrugged, then moved back toward his table. "There may be times in which you want to detach it for various reasons. Or, like you just said, you never wanted that leg in the first place. Now you have a way to be free of it, I suppose."

I peered at his back as he rummaged some more, gettin' the distinct impression he found my dislike of this leg somehow akin to a personal insult. I sighed. "Doc..."

"It is all right," he said as he turned from the table and made his way back to me. "I understand. As I said before, losing a limb is difficult. For anyone. It is understandable you would be upset. I had hoped you would grow accustomed to that one over time, however."

"I have," I admitted. "Mostly. And havin' some kinda leg is surely better than havin' no leg at all."

"My thoughts exactly."

"But it's caused quite a fuss, too, you know," I told him as he stopped in front of my stool again. "In certain circles. Got people thinkin' I'm a demon and all kinds of crazy things. And some people ... some people wantin' to cut it off me and all."

He arched an eyebrow above his eyepatch. "Really?"

"Yes."

"Oh dear. Seems the Territories are even more uncivilized than I had guessed. Perhaps Hannah was right, and we never should have settled there in the first place."

I squinted up at him. "I believe I told you that the first day I woke up in your house."

He pursed his lips. "I suppose you did, didn't you? Well, I am dreadfully sorry for any trouble that leg has caused you to that effect. I did not think the general public here would be quite so prejudiced against the mechanical limbs."

"Ain't exactly all fer 'em myself," I muttered, and then, as the doctor opened his mouth, elaborated. "But I'm grateful fer yer help, anyway. Then and recently. You saved my life, Doc ... twice. And Charlotte's, too. And I do appreciate that. Even if ... even if I still ain't too sure about this leg."

He closed his mouth, then nodded. "Of course. Of course, son. You are most welcome. I hope you are able to make good use of the rest of your life ... now that it has been rescued twice."

I grunted, sure he was tryin' to imply somethin'. Maybe that I should quit my drifter ways and settle down. Stop carryin' around two guns while lookin' fer trouble. But in truth my life had been rescued more than twice. There were plenty of other people who'd been good enough to step in when I'd most needed 'em lately. The thought sobered me, and I dropped my gaze toward the doctor's cluttered table. Maybe, if anythin', those people had granted me another chance to free Ethelyn. Or at the very least, a chance to rid the Territories of Nine-Fingered Nan.

I could only hope.

Hope. That soul killer.

"Here," Dr. Balogh said suddenly, startlin' me outta my ruminations.

I looked up to see him holdin' out another turnscrew. "Another one?"

He nodded. "I told you, it is very important. Now you have two. Surely you will not misplace both of them."

I rolled my eyes, but it probably *was* better to have two. I reached out fer the second one, but he pulled it away and then knelt in front of my stool again.

"Let me show you how it works. You paying attention?"

"Yeah," I growled.

"Very good. Now, you must use this type of turnscrew, understand? There are screws here," he touched a finger to the left side of my metal knee, "and here." He touched the right side. "And here and here." He tapped both the bottom and top of it, too. "All four must be loosened, and then this part will come free." He indicated the leg from the knee downward. "To put it back on, then, you will simply realign the leg with here," he tapped the end of the rod that stuck out from my flesh, "and the screw-holes, and replace all four screws again. Understand?"

"Seems easy enough."

"It is." Dr. Balogh placed the head of the turnscrew into one of the screws and gave it a few turns to demonstrate how it loosened, then tightened it back up again. "Although it will take some time to loosen or tighten all four screws, so do keep that in mind. Also." He put a hand on my metal knee and then looked up to lock eyes with me, his face gravely serious. "If you do take it off, be certain you fully tighten all four screws before you go walking around on it again, understand? Or else the lower leg will not be secure, and you might risk it becoming detached mid-stride."

"Uh, sure. Got it, Doc." That didn't sound particularly pleasant. I didn't think I was gonna bother takin' it off much, though. But maybe

... maybe it might be nice to have it off for a good long bath now and then...

"*And*," he kept on, "if you remove the lower half, *do not lose the screws*! Be sure you put them someplace special for safekeeping. They are another thing you will not easily find just anywhere."

"Right." Not bein' able to attach the thing again didn't sound particularly pleasant, neither. Guess if I was gonna take those good long baths, I was gonna have to be real careful about it.

"So, here you are." He handed me the second turnscrew and then stood, liftin' his hands triumphantly. "And there you have it. All the basics of your leg. I also have a schematic for it, should you wish to have that ... let me see where I put it..." He turned once more and went to a basket set near one leg of his table. It was stuffed with long rolled papers that looked somethin' like maps, and he pulled several out one after the other, unrollin' 'em to glance at their contents before tossin' 'em to the tabletop.

While he was doin' that, I fished a folded stack of currency outta my shirt pocket and tucked both turnscrews into it, instead.

"Ah! Yes, here it is." He brought one of the rolled tubes of paper over to me and unfurled it to reveal a pencil-sketched mechanical map of some kind. "This. This is your leg. Is it not beautiful?"

I squinted at that drawin', but couldn't make heads nor tails of it. It made no sense to me at all. "Uh ... sure. Whatever you say, Doc."

"Would you like to take this, also?" He rolled it back up and offered it to me.

"Er, you know ... I don't think I've got much use fer somethin' like that, Doc. Wouldn't be able to make sense outta it if I tried. You should probably go ahead and keep it."

"Are you certain?"

"Yeah. Yeah I'm certain. You keep it. Fer ... reference fer yer future work, or somethin'."

"Well, all right." He shrugged. "I suppose I could use it to model another such leg off of..."

"Yeah. You do that." Then maybe I wouldn't be the only demon wanderin' the Territories...

"I have also left room in the leg for the addition of more ... *advantages*, should you want them."

"*More?*"

"Certainly." He tapped the end of the rolled schematic against the open palm of his opposite hand as he grinned down at me. "That is the most exciting thing about the merging of flesh and metal, Mr. Delano. The possibilities! Endless possibilities!"

"I ... I think what I've got is good enough fer now, Doc. Already havin' a hard enough time keepin' up with all of this, you understand."

"Oh." His enthusiasm dampened considerably. "Yes, of course. Of course I understand. But if you should change your mind later, you can always come back. Same as for the refilling of those medicines."

"Sure. Sure thing, Doc." I couldn't imagine what else he might want to put in this leg. It seemed full enough as it was. "And, uh ... I have this. Fer you." I held out the stack of cash. It was a good part of what Holt and I had stolen from that young couple in Redemption, and just about all we had left now after our supply shoppin' in Blackbird.

He stared at it fer a good full minute, felt like. Then he pulled down his eyepatch and looked from it to me and back again. "For me?"

"Fer you and yer family, yeah." I waggled the money in front of him. "Go on. Take it, would ya?"

He did so, but slowly. "My goodness. Whatever is this for?"

I snorted a laugh. "You serious? Fer all the things we was just talkin' about, Doc. Fer savin' my life—twice. Fer savin' Charlotte. Fer givin' me a leg, even if it is a lot of trouble. And fer takin' us in here, me and Charlotte. And fer the food, too. And ... and to help make things right from before. When I stole—er, *borrowed* yer mule and all."

"That is ... very generous of you, son."

I ground my teeth. "Can you *please* stop callin' me that?"

"You did not have to do this, however. We require no payment for our aid."

"I know. But take it anyway. Would make me feel better."

He stared down at it fer another minute, then nodded and tucked it away into another apron pocket as he said, "So you are leaving now."

I blinked at the statement, then sighed and went about pullin' that rubber cuff back up over my stump of a thigh. "Yeah. I'm leavin' now."

"And you are certain you do not want our help in your attempts to retrieve your sister?"

I grimaced and braced myself fer an argument. "No. Most certainly not. Nan is already lookin' fer you, Doc. And it ain't gonna be pretty if she finds you. You don't want to risk that. Don't want to risk yer family, neither. I'll handle gettin' my sister back. You all just look out fer yerselves, ya hear?"

To my surprise, he *didn't* argue. Only watched thoughtfully as I smoothed that rubber up along my stump and then rolled down my pants leg. "Very well then," he said at last. "That's where you are going now? To get your sister?"

"That's right."

"And you will not bring Nan to this place?"

I shook my head. "No. I ain't doin' that no more."

He smiled a little at that, and I'm sure he thought me not bringin' Nan here was a demonstration of my good nature, some kinda proof against what his wife thought of me.

And I was happy to let him go on believin' that.

"Good then. You are a very resourceful man, Mr. Delano. I was convinced you were as good as dead when you prematurely left our homestead those months ago. And yet here you are. Alive, in this place, and having passed the Oracle's Judgement, as well."

Even the mention of that old woman made me squirmy, and I stood from the stool.

Dr. Balogh held out a hand. "Good luck to you, s——" He caught himself this time, smiled. "Good luck to you, sir. I have no doubt you will find a way to free your sister."

Felt like a whole knot of things came loose in my chest hearin' him say that.

I didn't think anyone had ever said that to me since I'd first started off on my journey to find her. Swallowin' against a sudden well of emotion, I could only nod as I gripped his hand and shook it. I took a breath, cleared my throat. "Thank you. Thank you, Doctor. Could you possibly do one other thing fer me?"

"If I am able, certainly."

"Could you be sure Charlotte stays here, with you? She has a mind to accompany me, but I'd prefer she stay outta danger, too. And I know she enjoys the company of yer family."

Dr. Balogh considered my request, puttin' the schematic of my leg back in its basket. "I could try to keep her preoccupied, yes. But I will not hold anyone here against their will."

"Of course not, no. I understand. I would never ask you to." Even if that *would* make things easier, fer certain. "But sure, if you could ... keep her preoccupied, I'd be much obliged."

The doc leaned back against the edge of the table and nodded. "I will try my best. She seems to have taken a liking to the engineering side of things. It is quite complicated. Could occupy her for years if she fully applied herself."

"Sure. That would be awful helpful."

"Will you send her down then, on your way out?"

I paused in my walk toward the chamber's exit and turned back to face him. "Huh?"

"Will you send her down on your way out?"

"I ... I thought she was already down here? Somewhere."

Dr. Balogh frowned and straightened up off the table. "She is not. I have not seen her for a few days now ... I assumed she had rejoined you on the surface. Did she not?"

Panic lit through my limbs, mind racin' with all manner of things that could have happened to her, thinkin' of where she could have possibly gone and why, and my whole body went hot with it. Anger came next, anger and frustration and exasperation. Why couldn't she just *stay put*? Why couldn't she *understand*? And why did she have to do this to me *now*?

"No," I managed to snarl out. "She did not."

XL

THE STORIES ARE ALMOST NEVER TRUE

I stormed from the cave in a fury, startlin' both my mule and Holt's gelding and even the old man himself, who'd been checkin' the cylinder of one of his pistols till I came burstin' through that curtain of vines. Then he spat a curse and had that gun up and aimed at me in the blink of an eye.

Only he lowered it again as he realized who it was comin' outta there. "What's the matter?" he asked as I reached him.

I shook my head, grabbin' down my belts from my saddle to put 'em back on. "Charlotte is gone."

His shoulders relaxed as he released a breath. "That's all? By the way you stormed outta there, I thought somethin' was real, real wrong."

"Somethin' *is* real, real wrong, Holt," I snapped.

"But I thought you didn't want her goin' with us, anyway?"

"I don't."

Holt rolled his eyes and shoved his gun into his holster. "Well then why the hell are you so worked up? Ain't it better this way? Now you don't gotta fight with her about stayin' put."

"I already fought with her," I grumbled as I gathered Joe's reins and swung up onto him.

"Huh?"

"The other night … we had a … disagreement. I think that's why she left."

Holt shrugged. "All right. I fail to see why that's such a bad thing. Makes our job easier, don't it?"

"It's the same as before, Holt." I reined Joe around to face him. "She shouldn't be out here at all, much less out here wanderin' around alone. Who knows where she went, or what mighta happened to her now, goddamnit."

Holt put his hands atop his saddle horn and leaned forward a little. "Seems to me she's a grown woman and can take care of herself, kid. Don't you remember what she yelled at us fer on our way to Redemption? She said herself—she ain't no fragile flower. And she's got a point. Six months in the Whittaker mines … I reckon most women from her kinda background couldn't have lasted a week in those conditions, much less six months."

"But she still got grabbed the first time, didn't she? I'm gonna go look fer her."

"Look fer—kid, we ain't got time fer that! Nan's gonna be here in five days, maybe less!"

"Then that gives me at least three days to try and track her down." I prodded Joe into motion, headin' out into the woods.

Holt rode up beside me quick and reached out to grab my reins, pullin' Joe to a stop.

I whipped a glare at him, but he spoke before I could demand he let go.

"And just how do you propose to find her, anyway, huh? She could be anywhere by now. Take a minute and *think*, would ya? You ain't responsible fer her, Van. She's made her own choices. She chose to come back out here despite what happened to her last time. She chose to ride with us to Blackbird. And then she chose to leave again. She's a free woman … she can do what she wants. Even if her choices ain't smart ones. Hell, when has that ever stopped *you*, eh? You know how many times I've had to let you ride off into doin' somethin' stupid?"

"And yet who was the one with their neck in the noose just a few weeks back?" I growled.

"I ain't sayin' I'm much smarter," Holt admitted, "but you know of the two of us, I'm the one better at stoppin' to think first, and that's what you need to do now. Somehow you've got me talked into this other damn fool plan of yers to ambush Nine-Fingered Nan herself, and if we're gonna do that I need you focused. And we need to be ready long before she's scheduled to arrive, too, and you know that."

I kept on glarin' at him, but he was right, damn it all.

"Long as I've known you, all you've wanted was to find yer sister," he said quietly. "Despite me tellin' you most those years she must be dead. You kept on tryin', anyway, only givin' it a pause when weather stopped you, or when you thought that avalanche had got her. More stubborn and bull-headed than yer pa even, you are, and trust me, he's a hard man to beat. But I guess you were right ... all this time, and you were right about her still livin'. You want to chance fuckin' up this opportunity, everythin' we've been workin' on the last few days—everythin' you've been through up till now—just to try and find another woman who likely don't need yer help anyway?"

I ground my teeth, fingers clenched around my reins.

Holt let go of 'em, sittin' back in his own saddle. "I know yer infatuated with that girl—"

"I ain't *infatuated*—"

"—but if you ain't got a notion to stop tryin' to get yerself killed and settle down with her, well ... well, Van, then frankly, she deserves someone better. Guess you gotta make yer own choices too, kid. But tell me now what yer gonna do, cuz if yer goin' off on another wild goose chase, I'm just gonna head on back toward Grave Gulch. I sure as hell ain't goin' up against Nan without you."

I sat fer another long minute in silence, glarin' out at the woods around us, watchin' the leaves rustle softly in the breeze, listenin' to the birds and the insects. Joe snorted and shook his head, chewin' the bit like he was waitin' to hear my answer, too.

I weren't infatuated with Charlotte...

But I remembered how nice it had felt bein' cradled on her lap, the silky feel of her hair in my fist, the things that had stirred inside me when she'd clutched at my shirt, and that terrible, chokin' terror when she'd swooned in the cave, and I'd thought fer sure she was dead.

I swallowed hard. Fuckin' hell. I *was* infatuated with Charlotte.

But she *did* deserve someone better. Even had I not been plannin' to head into a maelstrom of a gunfight in the next few days, even had I wanted to settle down with her, as Holt had suggested ... she deserved someone better. Someone far better than me.

"Fine," I spat finally. "Fine. Yer right. Yer right ... we can't abandon our plan. Can't risk Nan beatin' us to the mill. Charlotte ... Charlotte will be fine. She can take care of herself, sure."

I almost believed it. I wanted to believe it. She'd done well enough against those murderous metal statues. Well enough ... until one had nearly strangled her. Until one had poisoned her.

Please let her be all right. Let her be safe...

I didn't even know who I was talkin' to. God wouldn't be doin' me no favors after what I'd done with my life. The Holy Mother, neither. But maybe they'd take mercy on Charlotte fer her own sake.

Swearin' under my breath, I reined Joe back around toward the same campsite Holt and I had made in the area days ago. "But let's camp here awhile, anyway. See if she comes back."

"Van..."

"We can plan well enough from here, too. We'll leave enough time to get back to mill early."

The old man let out an exaggerated sigh and several mumbled complaints about not wantin' to settle so close to the Oracle's territory again, but followed after me on his gelding anyway.

The Oracle. Had she had Charlotte's stallion ready and waitin' fer her when she'd come out of the cave wantin' to leave, like Joe had been ready fer me? Or had Charlotte simply left on foot, with no supplies? Surely not. She was too smart fer that. She must've taken her mount, and all her gear.

Fer some reason that thought only made me angrier.

The Oracle. Somehow, I was gonna have to find her again, and ask her just what she happened to know about Charlotte Harrison's recent disappearance.

We set up camp again, nearish to the cave, and tried to work out what other strategy we could fer our ambush, but my thoughts kept driftin' now and then to Charlotte, and then that anger and anxiety would rise again, and I'd struggle to redirect it.

If Holt noted my continued distracted state, he didn't mention it.

But he was right. I had to let it go. I had to let Charlotte go. I couldn't afford this kind of fractured concentration. Not if I was gonna face Nan again.

I waited till after dark, till Holt was asleep, to mess with that pistol tucked away inside my leg. Kept the fire goin' strong so I'd have enough light to find that button and do my work, and then I pressed it, and jumped despite myself when the holster extended. I pulled that sixgun free and loaded it quick, replaced it, pressed the button again and watched with a strange fascination as it all folded back inside. Then I pulled my pack close, grabbed up my knife, and went about fashionin' a way to get at it easy, just in case.

I cut a flap in the left thigh of my pants, over the place where that holster would come out. Then picked out a needle and thread—the kind meant fer mendin' clothes instead of flesh—and two of the spare buttons I kept around fer repairin' shirts, and sewed 'em to the two bottom corners of the flap. When that was done, I improvised some buttonholes and tested it a few times to make sure I could open it all right and get to that release trigger quick.

It still weren't ideal, but it were a great deal more convenient than shuckin' my pants entirely, or havin' to pause to roll up the leg. A few seconds now was all I needed to get to that gun easy enough.

Satisfied with that fer the time bein', I put all my supplies away and then sighed, starin' into the fire and lettin' it die down a little. Well, this was gonna be another night I didn't sleep, seemed like, so I didn't bother. I stood again and paced, and Joe watched me sleepily from his picket line at the edge of the fire's glow.

I glared at him. "Why'd she leave, huh?"

His big head lifted at the sound of my voice, long ears swivelin'.

"Don't she know that's a stupid idea? She's smarter than that…"

He nickered softly.

"Damnit." I walked to my pack, dug out an apple, and went to offer it to him, pattin' his neck absently as he bit it in half, smearin' my hand with drool. Only then I caught Holt's gelding starin' at me and sighed. Joe took the rest of the apple from my palm, so I retrieved my last apple and gave it to Holt's horse, givin' him a pat too, then wiped my slimy hand on my shirt.

"I'm gonna take a walk," I told the horses. And I shook my head as I started off into the dark. Talkin' to the horses. Maybe I really *was* just losin' my mind entirely...

I looked fer the Oracle that night. And over the next few days and nights, too, but she never appeared. Didn't sleep much those last few nights, neither, though I managed a few hours of naps throughout most days when the exhaustion finally caught up to me.

Holt and I ate sparingly, considerin' there weren't much game about still, and little to nothin' available in Blackbird, and I didn't wanna impose on the Baloghs no more. We shifted our camp further away from the cave, so that if the family happened to come out fer supplies or a try at huntin', they wouldn't catch sight of us and start askin' questions.

And I kept my eye out fer Charlotte's return, but she never showed, neither.

I'd asked Dr. Balogh to watch fer her while he continued his business here, for however long he stayed here, and he'd agreed, of course. He'd also agreed to take care of her, shelter her, if she did happen to come back. But I really woulda felt better about it if she'd come back while I was still around. Sooner rather than later. I really woulda liked to have made my peace with her, if I could have, before ridin' off to whatever was gonna come next.

But I guess it weren't meant to be.

By the night before we were set to leave fer the mill, to really put our plan into motion, Holt and I were both wound real tight. We could hardly sit still, neither of us, continually makin' rounds through our meager camp to check that everything was in order, to make sure we hadn't forgotten nothin'. Which, we hadn't. 'Cause we'd already checked and rechecked it all at least fifteen times before.

When at last we were weary of repeatin' the same tasks over and over again, dusk had fallen once more. At dawn, we'd make our way southwest to the road that passed closest to that old mill, and we'd wait fer Nan. And then lead her right into our trap.

Or, *I* would.

I was gonna leave Holt here. And not give Nan the chance to murder him.

But fer now, we both retrieved our last remainin' bottles of whiskey —some I'd stolen off those unfortunate prospectors in the area days ago—and we set about drinkin' and reminiscin'. Hopin' the alcohol would soothe our nerves, let us eventually fall asleep so we could then wake up and finally get this done with.

Holt was gettin' real drunk, and so was I, though I tried to keep my wits about me better than he, if only 'cause I was gonna need to sneak off here in a little while after he passed out.

He pulled a sixshooter from his pack all of a sudden and held it up in the firelight, and my stomach turned as I recognized it. He shouldn't have had that here. And most certainly should not have had that here *unwrapped*.

It was bright and shiny, even in the dark, reflectin' the dancin' flames along its cylinder and barrel almost perfect as a mirror. Pa might've kept it hidden away at the ranch, but he'd clearly still taken care of it. And then so had Holt.

And now here it was, in the open again. Unburied. Unwrapped. In the hand of a killer again. Its silver platin' etched in elegant scrollwork and crude tally marks.

So many tally marks.

I hissed a breath through my teeth. "Goddamnit, Holt. I thought I told you to put that thing back where it belonged?"

He shrugged. "Well, I did. But then I changed my mind. I still think you oughta take it, especially now." He turned it around to offer me the well-worn ivory grip.

I shook my head. "And my answer is still no."

"If you wanna end Nine-Fingered Nan, you should do it with this. Only right."

I snorted. "You don't even know that it was Pa who shot off her finger. Or that he did it with that gun."

Holt gave a slow nod. "True. But that's the way the story goes. And I'm almost sure it's mostly true."

"You know as well as I do the stories are almost never true."

"'Cept those about Lucky Logan," he countered. "Or me. Or Kill 'Em All Paul."

I sighed, leaned back against my saddle to regard him across the fire. "I ain't takin' a strange gun into a fight as important as this one, Holt. And it's a long barrel; it'll add time to my draw. Time I can't afford. I ain't gonna chance it. You wanna use it, you go on ahead. I'm perfectly happy with what I got here." I patted at my own two pistols.

Nevermind that one of 'em had been a strange gun itself not too long ago. Duster's pistol sat tucked nice and neat into my right holster. I was gettin' used to it just fine by now.

"It ain't mine to use," Holt said.

"Well it ain't mine, neither."

Holt dropped his arm, pullin' the offered pistol back into his lap. "More yours than mine," he muttered.

I straightened up off my saddle, sat cross-legged and leaned forward toward him. "Holt. Pa thought of you like a brother. And you thought the same of him. You've told me this more times than I can count, old man. And you came lookin' fer me and Ethelyn when you heard he and Mama had been killed, took care of me best you could ... Pa woulda wanted you to have it. It's as much yers as it is mine, understand?"

He stared down at the sixgun's shiny surface fer another long minute. "I dunno, kid..."

"Well I ain't takin' it. So you have it. And that's that."

And that *was* that. We didn't talk about it no more the rest of the evenin', and eventually Holt did pass out, snorin' somethin' awful and still in his boots, his hat knocked askew from where he'd fallen sideways sittin' up.

I fell asleep sittin' up myself fer awhile, chin drooped against my chest, till I jolted awake again sometime in the middle of the night swearin', and then scrambled to gather all my things to leave before Holt woke up again.

I stumbled around in the dark, our fire now burnin' low and only a young moon in the sky, but I managed to get my pack together and Joe saddled up without too much trouble. The world was gently swayin' as I grabbed Holt's horse from the picket line, too.

If I lived through facin' down Nan again, Holt might very well kill me himself fer what I was about to do. Fer real this time. But I'd take that chance. Long as he stayed safe.

Like Charlotte. I really hoped Charlotte was still safe.

I left him most his things, includin' his pistols and Pa's old gun, but took both his huntin' rifle and his long rifle, and then I saddled up his gelding and ponied him behind me as I headed off into the night.

The trees shrouded the sky from sight, made it hard to navigate. Made it especially hard to see, given the bare sliver of a moon hardly lit anything in the first place. But I went slow and let Joe find his own way, and when I reached the occasional clearin', I'd stop to check the stars and orient myself, and I kept headin' in generally the right direction.

By dawn, I was well on my way toward that mill, and the effects of all the whiskey were startin' to wear off. I kept a look-out for the Oracle or any of her people the whole way, and yet they remained out of sight. Didn't even see any of their strange, decorated skulls hung up in the trees this time.

I hoped me takin' Holt's horse and saddle would delay him long enough fer me to take care of Nan and her crew before he could manage to find another way there ... which I had no doubt he *would* find another way there, eventually.

And he'd be spittin' mad by then, too, probably.

But one problem at a time.

By mid-mornin', I reached the road that ran north past the mill, and I checked the rutted path fer fresh tracks. My heart picked up pace at the state of it. There were an awful lot of new tracks, looked like. Of course, there'd been an awful lot of people headin' this way from all over of late, on account of the *incident* at Blackbird and rumors of Old World association with it.

These could have been left by Nan's crew ... or someone else entirely.

Surely Nan couldn't have got here quite that fast. I didn't think.

Even still, as I prodded Joe on down the overgrown lane that branched off from that road, the lane that would lead directly to the mill, I kept my hand light on the grip of my right pistol, and my eyes and ears on full alert.

My apprehension eased somewhat as I went; the brush and old leaves that now choked the lane looked to be mostly undisturbed. Whoever had gone by on the main road hadn't turned off here. Meanin' my surprises fer Nan and her crew shoulda been safe.

I guided Joe and Holt's gelding around our traps to the main grounds of the mill itself, then dismounted and tied Joe to a nearby sapling so I could check over the place, just to be sure. But everythin' was in place and the old building still empty.

Only then did I let myself relax, exhalin' slow and even. I took the horses off a ways to the west of the mill, deep into the woods where they'd hopefully stay outta the way of bullets, and got 'em settled to wait there awhile. I ate the last of my food, forcin' it down, and drank the last of my whiskey.

Then I took Holt's two rifles and walked back to the mill to place 'em somewhere good, and once that was done, I walked back up the lane to the main road. There was a hedge tree there at the side of it, a big, old one with gnarled bark and twisted, tangled branches, some of which came all the way to the ground.

I climbed my way up into the thing, swearin' as some of its thorns caught on my clothes, and settled myself in the crook of its main fork, pullin' Duster's pistol to be ready. I could see glimpses of the road below through the canopy of leaves. I'd be able to see anyone comin' up this way long before they ever saw me.

And I had a decent enough shot at the two bundles of dynamite we'd planted along the sides of the road from here, too.

Now all I had to do was wait.

XLI

AMBUSH

I woke to the sound of voices with a start and almost dropped the pistol that had been in my lap, then almost fell out of the damn tree. I caught myself just in time, bracin' a hand and a boot against the branches and grittin' my teeth against the burn where the rough bark had chafed at my skin.

Slowly, carefully, I wedged myself back into my seat at the fork, then took a breath and scooped up the loose gun. I scrubbed my left hand vigorously over my face and blinked away the grogginess to peer down at the road below. It was late in the day now, the sun anglin' sharply west and all the trees throwin' out long shadows, but through the dappled light I saw two riders come into view, amblin' at an easy walk.

But they were kitted up real good, armed to the teeth, and I sat up straighter in my treeside perch, strainin' to get a good look at 'em between all the leaves.

They were awful grimy, their faces shinin' with sweat and shirts nearly soaked through. Their horses were damp, too, and tired. One man had shoulder-length, dirty blond hair and a short blonde beard, and the other short brown hair and a goatee streaked with gray. They both wore hats, old beat-up ones stained with sweat around their hat brims.

They were talkin' amongst themselves, and as they got closer I could finally make out what they were sayin'.

"—this is all a waste of time," the blond one said. "Don't know why she keeps playin' with this fool. Don't understand why she hasn't strung him up or flayed him alive by now." He spit off to one side of his horse.

The other man, clearly the elder of the two, only shook his head. "And why does a cat fuck around with a mouse before bitin' its head off?" He shrugged. "It's entertainment, that's all. When she's bored of 'em, she'll kill 'em."

"Well ain't none of this entertainin' to me," the blond one scowled. "All this way, fer what? So she can bat him around some more?"

"Naw," the one with the goatee drawled. "Think this might be it. Especially if Lowery really got that information out of him."

I tensed at the mention of Lowery, my heart jumpin'. They were right below me now, and they reined to a halt. I held perfectly still up in my perch, though my heart was thunderin' blood in my ears somethin' fierce so I could hardly hear 'em.

These were Nine-Fingered Nan's men.

The blond one gave a snort. "You know Lowery. Wouldn't surprise me at all if he didn't even have Delano when he sent that wire."

My throat closed up at the mention of my name. These were *definitely* Nan's men...

The elder one grunted. "Then he'd better have him by now. Else *he'll* be the one the boss flays alive instead of Delano."

Well, they didn't have to worry about that. I'd already flayed Lowery good enough. He'd be long dead by now.

The man below me fished in his shirt pocket, then held up a compass and peered at it fer a second before lookin' around at the woods.

I held my breath.

"Looks like this is it. I think."

The blond one made a show of lookin' around, too. "*What* is it? We're in the middle of nowhere."

"Yeah. That's the point. Should be a road goin' west, boss said. Think this is it, see there?" He pointed to the overgrown lane that led to the mill, and my hand tightened around my pistol grip. "See some fresh tracks goin' that way, too. That's gotta be it."

The blond one shrugged. "If you say so."

"I say so. C'mon, let's go give it a look. Tell Lowery to lay out the red carpet. Tell him he better damn well have what he said he had."

"Yeah, all right."

They ambled down the lane toward the mill in no more hurry than they'd been amblin' down the road, and I only watched after 'em with my mind all in a jumble.

Why were there only two of 'em? Where the hell was Nan?

Where the hell was Ethelyn?

I looked off down the road to the south from my vantage point, far as I could see with all the other trees blockin' my view, but I didn't see no other riders comin' this way, nor no cloud of dust risin' in the distance to signal the approach of any.

She couldn't have sent just two of her lackeys. No way. Not fer somethin' this big, surely.

I looked back after the two men who'd gone on down the lane. I could hear their horses pushin' through the underbrush. If they set off any of those traps Holt and I had worked so hard on settin' up ... if they found any of my stashed weapons...

Damn it all to Hell ... I couldn't decide if I should follow after 'em to make sure they didn't do neither of those things or stay in my tree in case more of 'em showed up.

My first urge was to drop down and go after 'em, end both of 'em before they had a chance to do either.

But somethin' made me hesitate. Pause and think fer a second. Holt woulda been proud. Maybe all those years of his naggin' was finally payin' off.

Lay out the red carpet, the older one had said. Which meant someone important must be comin'.

Nan. It's gotta be Nan. She musta been comin' after all. Perhaps these two were just her scouts, her recon men, sent ahead to clear the road of trouble and flush out any attempted ambushes. If they did find any of my traps or my stashed weapons, I'd have to make sure they didn't get the word back to her.

Of course, then I wondered... would she be expectin' 'em to come back with word of what lay ahead? When would she expect 'em to report? If they didn't come back with news by a certain time, would she arrive expectin' a fight? Or maybe she wouldn't come at all...

My heart quickened again and I ground my teeth against the war of frantic thoughts, the twist of conflictin' emotions roilin' in my gut, the agony of indecision.

But in the end, I stayed put. I stayed hidden in the branches of that tree, and I listened for yells or shouts or the snap of small branches bein' broken, but no unusual sounds broke the late afternoon hush of the forest. The air had grown uncomfortably still, everything around me seemin' to hold its breath just as much as I was doin'.

Finally, I forced myself to breathe out. Wished fer a breeze of some kind. My shirt had started stickin' to me and sweat made trails down my temples and the back of my neck. It was unusually warm fer this time of year, seemed like. Summer shoulda started fadin' by now in this part of the country, givin' way to the cooler days of autumn. Alas, such was not my luck.

I held my breath again as the sound of horses reached my ears, comin' back this way from the mill. How much time had it been? A half hour or so, at least. It was the two gents who'd gone down the lane before. They hadn't set off any of our traps, then. I couldn't be sure if they'd found my other weapons or not, but it looked like they hadn't acquired any new ones on their persons. If they had, they'd apparently decided to let 'em be.

But they both wore studious frowns now, their brows furrowed. They rode beneath me without a word to each other, and then turned back the way they'd come and trotted off out of sight.

I sat there frownin' after 'em, wonderin' if I'd just made a big mistake.

But surely an empty mill, even in the event of Lowery's absence, and even if they'd seen the left ammunitions, surely that wouldn't be nearly enough to frighten off Nine-Fingered Nan. Stashed weapons without no one around to fire 'em were just more loot fer her and her crew to steal.

So I resisted the nearly overwhelmin' urge to follow after 'em and instead stayed still in my tree once again. I'd wait a little longer. See who else might come on up the road. Nan had to be comin'.

She had to be....

It was another two hours at least and my legs had all but gone numb and a cramp had started to smart in my back before the sounds of more riders comin' from the south jolted me back into high alert. There was a dust trail this time, a brown haze hangin' low over the tops of the trees in the distance, and I cursed myself fer not notin' it earlier.

This was a big group. A real big group.

The sound of a whole lotta hooves grew closer, and the creak of a whole lotta leather. Low murmured voices, and the soft rumble and groan of a loaded wagon or two.

The sun had dipped into early evenin', the shadows deepenin', the heat of the afternoon finally easin'. But the air was still and breathless, thick and heavy like a storm might be comin' soon.

The first riders of the group trotted into view and I gulped at that soupy air, tryin' to still nerves that felt suddenly electric.

They were an awful rough-lookin' bunch. A rag-tag spread of individuals rangin' in age from probably fifteen up to mid-sixties or so, mostly men with a handful of women, though the two sexes were nearly indistinguishable from each other in this particular outfit. They wore mostly dirt-encrusted and threadbare clothin', with a few here and there sportin' fancier fare, and the occasional expensive and high-fashion item that stood out clear as day as not belongin' in a group like theirs. Stolen, most-like.

There were two wagons, loaded up with supplies. One covered over with canvas, and the other a chuck wagon. They moseyed on along in the middle of the road, and all the riders surrounded 'em, front, back, and sides.

I shifted in my hard, awkward seat and squinted, leanin' forward some to try and get a better view. Of all those people comin' up the road, there were only two familiar faces I cared about findin': Nine-Fingered Nan's ... and Ethelyn's.

My sweepin', searchin' gaze finally stuck on a figure dressed all in black with a wide-brimmed hat. Silver-white hair fell down around her shoulders, and a bandolier crossed one shoulder. She rode her tall bay horse a few lengths in front of the first wagon, surrounded on all sides by plenty of her gang.

Nine-Fingered Nan.

The two men on either side of her looked familiar. They were the two who had been there flankin' Nan when I'd brought back Taggert's gutted body. Their sharp gazes raked the woods around 'em almost constantly, their hands on their grips already.

Those would be two of her top lieutenants then. Men who would know about Nan's plans to expand west or make a try fer Califia. Men who would know where Ethelyn might be bein' held, or where she was supposed to be shipped off from...

Ethelyn.

I steadied myself in the fork of the hedge and lifted my free left hand to shield my eyes, despite the fact the later hour meant there was no overhead sun to glare down at me. And I started at the beginnin' of the horde of riders and I checked every face, lookin' frantically fer a pale young woman with long, dark hair and jade-colored eyes.

I found the two men who had come by earlier to scout the place ... but no Ethelyn.

The first of the gang rode beneath me now, paused fer only a second, and then turned left to go down the brush-choked lane toward the mill.

The blood rushed in my ears loud as thunder, and the knuckles of the hand that clenched my revolver matched its ivory grip. I could feel myself shakin', heat floodin' my insides.

Nan herself had nearly reached me now. She looked straight ahead. Didn't bother scannin' the woods fer threats. Maybe she trusted her men that much. Or maybe she thought herself indestructible. Her pearl grips gleamed in the dappled orange light that speared through the trees.

Ethelyn coulda been hidden away in that canvas-covered wagon.

She coulda been.

Or she coulda been somewhere else. Still held captive. Or already sold.

All the hooves and the weight of the wagons rollin' over that hard-packed dirt road masked the sound of my hammer clickin' back.

I took aim at her horse between the edges of my motionless canopy of leaves, and fired.

The gunshot cracked across the stagnant air, shatterin' the stillness, and I saw Nan go down in a tangle even as I rolled quick from my position to drop from the tree and land with a grunt in the brush below.

Her gang was fast; even faster than I'd suspected they'd be. A hail of bullets shredded the leaves above me, sprayed chunks of bark down over me, and buried into the hedge's thick branches where I'd been sittin' hardly a second ago.

I wasted no time. I sprinted.

Tore through the underbrush along the side of the lane, toward the mill, right past those of her crew who'd already started in that direction, and I left their surprised shouts behind as I dodged around a few of the pits Holt and I had dug.

More bullets followed me, but fewer now that I had all the woods fer cover and kept zig-zaggin' between all those trunks, and most of 'em couldn't see me now, or couldn't fire at me without risk of hittin' one of their own instead. Those closest to me gave chase with more shoutin', their horses plungin' through the brush as recklessly as me.

I led 'em straight fer our traps ... and sure enough, I heard two of 'em go down into those pits with an awful yell of curses and the shriekin' of horses.

But I didn't bother lookin' back. More of 'em were comin' still, the noise of the first pursuers who'd gone down soon replaced by fresh ones. I ran across the lane and freed the rough-hewn stick lever that would release our trip line, then dodged behind another sprawlin' hedge just as more bullets hissed over my right shoulder.

The sound of bodies crashin' into the brush erupted behind me, and more horses squealin'. So I'd downed a few more, then. I ignored the clenchin' in my chest, the burnin' in my lungs, and pushed on, runnin' fast as I could manage.

The remainin' few who chased me now fell back a bit, likely wary of what else I might spring on 'em, not wantin' to end up like their companions. It was just what I needed; some space to work with.

I ducked behind a big oak and then whipped around the other side of it, sightin' back at 'em. Three squeezes of my trigger and I shot two off their horses and caught the third in the shoulder, almost unseatin' him. He righted himself at the last second and spurred his horse straight at me. His pistol leveled, too, and I shot him again. Red bloomed across his chest.

He sagged in the saddle as his horse charged past me and I ran after it till it slowed in confusion, ears flickin' around in all directions and eyes wide at all the commotion. Then I caught the dead rider's sleeve and yanked him off, planted a foot into a stirrup and hauled myself up into the abandoned seat.

I'd hardly settled myself before I spurred the horse back into motion, and we once again tore through the brush toward the mill, the sounds of pursuit growin' louder again. But I was almost there...

I passed one of our planted bundles of dynamite, waited till I figured I was far enough away from it, and then reined my horse around sharply. I fired at the explosives once, twice, and my cylinder clicked empty. Swearin', I jerked my left pistol free of its holster and finally hit the dynamite with the third shot, and the blast shook the trees and took out three more of Nan's crew just as they'd been takin' aim.

My borrowed horse reared and pinned its ears. Pieces of flesh— both human and animal—spattered down into the loam. And as soon as my horse hit all four feet again, I turned him back toward the mill and urged him onward. He ran on in a near panic, barely controllable. We almost went right over another of the pits ourselves, but I managed to yank him to the right at the last second.

My ears were ringin' now, but I could hear what was left of Nan's gang shoutin' at each other in attempts to make a plan, to figure out who the fuck I was, and they were still pushin' through the woods after me, but spreadin' out more now.

I stayed low over my horse's neck to avoid all the sweepin'

branches, kept him weavin' through all those trees, heard another rider behind me go into the pit I'd almost fell in myself.

Then I broke out into the open of the riverbank, with the flat of the water on my right and the loomin', overgrown mill building on my left, and I tried to slow my horse's wild dash. He threw up his head and sat back on his haunches, then reared again, sprayin' spittle as he shrieked his displeasure at this whole situation.

I held on till he came down again, but then I slid off quick and gave his rear a slap. He didn't need no other encouragement from me, though. He was off like a shot again in the next second, barely missin' more bullets that came at us outta the trees behind.

I ran fer the building.

A bullet pinged into the calf of my metal leg and I stumbled, then practically fell through the gapin' doorway into the dark interior of the mill's main cuttin' floor. More bullets chewed into the wood of the walls and the door frame.

I scrambled to my feet and went to the bulwark of logs Holt and I had nailed together. It was heavier and harder to move by myself; I had to lean my shoulder into it and push with all my strength to move it ... but finally it shifted, leaned ... and then fell across the open doorway just as it was supposed to. There were other ways in, of course, but Holt and I had boarded all those up. It would keep 'em out fer at least long enough fer me to get into a good shootin' position...

And that's what I did. I went to the front window, also boarded up, but with cracks left large enough to put a gun barrel through. And I reloaded Duster's pistol, and filled the empty chamber from my left gun so they'd be ready when I needed 'em. Then I grabbed up the fully loaded rifle waitin' fer me and took a knee, took aim through one of those cracks.

Nan's crew was just arrivin', pourin' into the flat open of the riverbank on lathered, blown horses and lookin' real, real angry. Some fired into the front of the building just fer spite, their bullets punchin' little holes into the rotten wood fer spears of dim daylight to filter through into the dark.

Splinters rained down over me, but they were aimin' too high. I didn't bother duckin', didn't flinch away. I counted 'em quick; there were only twelve on horses now. Seemed I'd managed to cut their numbers in half durin' my mad race through the woods, though by my measure I only knew fer sure that six of the missin' were dead.

But I'd take what I could get. I put the closest of the twelve in my rifle sights as the apparent leader of those remainin' barked at the rest of 'em to stop shootin'. My heart jumped as I realized he was one of Nan's lieutenants. One of those who'd been ridin' at her side.

I didn't see Nan herself in this group, but that weren't surprisin'. I'd taken out her horse, after all. It was a long walk to the mill without a horse.

I gritted my teeth at the thought of the outlaw boss, hoped maybe she'd fall into our last remainin' pit on her way, and then pulled my focus back to these men and women at hand. Ten men. Two women.

The lieutenant was instructin' the rest to fan out, surround the building. Cover the exits and watch the windows. And wait. Fer Nan.

He told one of the men to go back fer her, in fact. Give her a ride so she might reach us in a more timely fashion.

I shook my head. That weren't gonna work fer me at all. So I switched my aim to the man who'd turned his horse back toward the road, breathed out, and fired.

He went clean off his horse in a spray of blood.

That made seven dead fer sure.

The others yelled, and I flattened myself to the floor quick as they opened fire on the building again. The boards across my window cracked and split under their assault. I kept hold of my rifle and crawled to the next window, then cautiously raised onto my knees again to take a peek out from there.

Seemed the lieutenant had lost his tenuous control of the others. They weren't listenin' to his shouted orders now. Some rode fer cover in the trees beyond the mill, others were circlin' on the bank as they emptied their cylinders and then reloaded in turn. And one of the women had fished out a bottle of whiskey from her saddlebag.

Fer a minute I watched her, confused as to what purpose whiskey could currently serve her. Till I saw her soakin' a rag with it, and then stuffin' the end of the rag into the bottle.

Well. Two could play that game. Holt and I had stashed bundles of dynamite all over this place. I took aim at the one closest to the woman and fired again.

This time I only needed one shot.

The explosion blew apart one man and stunned his horse, and knocked both the woman and her horse to the ground. Her animal was quick to roll back to its feet and take off riderless into the woods, but the woman didn't move. Unconscious or dead, least she wouldn't be lightin' anythin' on fire no more.

The others fought to keep their horses from boltin', and I took advantage of their distraction. Four more were dead soon enough.

That left only five.

The lieutenant turned tail and ran, gallopin' away toward the road.

I swore, trackin' him with my rifle, but he was into the trees again before I could get off a good shot, and I had to flatten to the floor again as the four he left behind regained their wits enough to return fire at last.

Their hoofbeats pounded up close, and then a fist punched through the boards across the window just above my head.

I swore some more and jumped to my feet, abandonin' that rifle to make fer the rickety stairs in the back corner of this main room.

Bullets followed after me, and the sound of more splinterin' wood as they cleared out the rest of that window. I jumped up and onto the big log carriage, the contraption that had once fed felled tree trunks to the saws, and yelled as a shot grazed the top of my right shoulder. It stung, spread fire all down my arm, but I ignored it. Jumped down from the carriage and ran behind the saws, duckin' instinctively as more bullets sparked off the blades.

Finally I made the stairs and went up 'em two at a time.

The wood groaned under my boots, but Holt and I had tested 'em several times while settin' up. They'd hold. At least fer long enough.

Bootsteps pounded across the floor beneath me, clomped up the stairs behind me, and I dove fer the floor just as a gunshot cracked close-range. It made my ears ring again, but it also told me just where that fella was. I rolled soon as I hit the worn old floorboards and pulled both pistols, firin' multiple times into ... one of the women, turned out.

Her face went slack with shock. Blood trickled from her mouth. Then she staggered backwards and toppled down the stairs, tumblin' right into the two men tryin' to come up.

I holstered my irons and rolled back to my stomach to crawl quick to the second rifle we'd stashed. Picked it up as I pushed my back up against the wall and swung it around toward the stairs in time for the two men to shove the dead woman over the rail. She fell with a sickenin' thump to the lower floor. They looked up just as I fired.

I caught the guy in front right between the eyes. He fell back into the arms of the guy behind. I cocked the rifle again, but the angle was no good. The stair's railin' and the body of the first guy blocked any potentially fatal shot.

I hissed a curse under my breath.

And then I heard a different kind of noise from down below. The shatterin' of glass, and the whoosh of flame. Then the crackle and pop of somethin' far too familiar.

Burnin' wood.

XLII

ONE LAST PROBLEM

I clambered up onto my knees and risked a glance through one of the upper windows, which Holt and I had also haphazardly boarded up, although not as solidly as the bottom panes. Though these windows up here were small, there was plenty of space between the planks fer me to look down below to the riverbank and the front of the mill.

Two of Nan's crew stood out there, starin' at the building and their most recent handy work with self-satisfied expressions. Smoke started tricklin' out around that fortress of logs I'd pushed down across the door. One of 'em standin' down there was the woman I'd tried to blow up with dynamite.

Guess she'd only been knocked out, then. Shame.

A grunt and the creak of more old wood brought my attention back to the man left on the stairs behind me quick, and I turned toward him again just in time to see him shove the dead man's body out of his way.

We fired at each other in unison, but I was divin' sideways as I did so.

His bullet punched a hole through an empty wall, and mine went wide over his right shoulder.

Then he was chargin' at me across the floor.

I sprang to my feet, dropped the rifle and went fer my right gun and my next shot caught him in the left side. But it didn't slow him up at all. He was on me in the next instant, one hand around my right wrist to shove my gun outta his face just as I fired again, and that bullet buried harmlessly into the ceiling.

The barrel of his pistol shoved into my ribs hard enough to bruise, but my left hand swept across my body and knocked off his aim, so his next bullet only barely missed hittin' me in the right hip instead of goin' through my heart. The gunfire was deafenin' at such close-range, the gunsmoke acrid and sharp in my nose, the heat of the discharge warm against my belly.

Too close.

I gave him a good head-butt, makin' him stagger back a few steps, and as he did so I wrenched my wrist outta his grip. Unexpectedly, he twisted away from me even as he stumbled, then turned right back around and cracked a left hook into the side of my face.

Stars burst across my vision and I went reelin' into the wooden railin' that separated this half of a second floor from a long drop to the first floor. I lost my grip on my pistol as I frantically scrabbled fer a hold on the railin' to keep myself from pitchin' head-first over it, then scowled more curses as I watched my weapon fall. It clanged against the edge of one of the rusted saws below and bounced away into smoke and darkness.

I whirled off the rail to face the man, but he'd hurt himself, too, throwin' that punch so hard. He winced and sucked in a breath, one hand goin' to that bullet hole I'd made in his side. His shirt was soaked red there, and the rest of it damp with sweat and grime, and he had the smell of a lot of days in the saddle on him.

Even still, his face split into a grin as he lurched at me.

I went fer my left pistol; he brought his own gun down into my hand as I lifted it and I cried out as the metal smashed into all those little bones. My second gun hit the floorboards, and then he had both hands wrapped around my throat and squeezed till I thought my eyes would bulge from my skull.

"Big mistake, boy," he growled, the words hardly more than a rumble beneath the rushin' and ringin' in my ears. "What, you thought you could bring down Nine-Fingered Nan and her gang ... all by yerself?" He guffawed, squeezed tighter, leaned me hard into the railin' so I was as much hangin' onto his arms to keep from fallin' as I was tryin' to loosen his fingers from my throat.

"Think ... think ... I did a pretty ... pretty fair job," I managed to gasp.

He pushed me backwards a little more, so I was damn near halfway over the rail already. The edge of the top board cut painfully into the small of my back. I abandoned my efforts to loosen his grip and instead clutched at his shirt sleeve. If I was goin' over, he was comin' with me.

"Hardly," he scoffed. "This ain't all of us. And anyway, yer little tricks out there just pissed off more of us than you killed." He smiled again, but even through my darkenin' vision I could see the strain in his features, the sweat that slid down his dirt-streaked face. He was hurtin' same as me. I mighta even killed him with that bullet I'd got in him.

He loosened his death grip around my throat a bit and I sucked air greedily. Some of the black haze that had curtained across my eyes cleared.

He squinted at me. "You that Delano kid the boss came here fer? Shit, you ain't as good as they say you are, are ya? Well, I think she'll be awful happy to see yer still alive after all that business out there in the woods. Guess there's somethin' you got she wants real bad, eh? Maybe I'll take you out to her myself, then. Or ... *or*..." He gave me a shove and a strangled noise came outta me as my boots momentarily left the floor. If not fer his hold on my throat and my desperate grab at his arms, I'd have been tumblin' down to break across those saws. "Or maybe I'll just toss ya over now," he said. "Claim you were already dead when I found ya. Would save us all a whole lotta trouble, I think. She'd never know, would she?"

I kept my right hand clamped firmly around his forearm, but slid my left hand down to that flap I'd made in the thigh of my pants and groped at it till I managed to unbutton it. "Guess ... guess not," I rasped. I fumbled fer that little button on the side of my metal leg till I felt it, and pressed.

The compartment there whirred open; the holster extendin' with a hiss.

The man contemplatin' murderin' me frowned. Confusion flickered across his face as he glanced down toward the noise.

I pulled that sixgun free and shot him four times in the chest, just fer good measure.

His hold on my throat slackened and I gulped full breaths at last till my lungs stopped burnin'. But he didn't seem to understand what was happenin'. He just kept starin' down at my smokin' pistol, and then his arms dropped limp to his sides, and his eyes lifted to find my face.

He coughed, blood bubblin' in his mouth.

"What?" I prompted huskily, my voice all rough from bein' strangled. "No one mentioned my demon metal leg?"

He blinked once. And then collapsed forward, right at me.

I barely side-stepped his body, slidin' left along the rail just in time. But his dead weight proved too much fer the old, rotten wood, especially after we'd been pushin' against it fer so long. The boards snapped, and he crashed right through 'em to plummet down to the first floor.

Just enough of my own weight had been leanin' against that railin' fer it to unbalance me as it gave way, and I flailed as I felt myself fallin' too.

I twisted and caught the edge of the second-story floor with my left hand as I dropped, then grabbed on quick with my right hand. I dug my fingers into the cracks between the floorboards; struggled to haul myself back up. The old bullet hole in my left bicep and the new graze in my right shoulder screamed in protest, but it was either that or let go and get cut in half like a log.

My boots kicked empty air, tryin' fer leverage, till I finally hooked my elbows up over the floor above and then pulled the rest of me onto it after. I rolled onto my back gaspin', heart throbbin' wild in my chest, starin' up at a dilapidated ceiling.

I didn't have time to be restin', but fer a space I just laid there anyway. My temples pulsed in pain, and my forehead where I'd cracked it into that other man's skull, and my right cheek where he'd decked me, and my throat where he'd nearly squeezed the life outta me, and all my other old and new injuries alike had lit with fresh agony.

A tendril of black smoke drifted across my vision, and I became vaguely aware of a roarin' fire now down below.

The fire. Right.

The smoke thickened, fillin' all the mill's open space and crawlin' toward what little cracks Holt and I had left available in the building. The smell of burnin' wood and heated iron reached me, and I had no more time to be layin' around.

With a groan I forced myself to roll over again and then pushed to my hands and knees. I gathered up my two dropped pistols—the left one and the one from my leg—and I loaded both cylinders full again before puttin' 'em both into belt holsters. There was no gettin' back that nice pistol of Duster's now, and I couldn't afford the added time of gettin' the other one outta my leg if I needed it again. So fer now, I put the more familiar gun in my right holster and tucked the smaller sixgun from my leg into the left. Then I folded in the leg holster, closed its compartment, and buttoned the flap over it.

That done, I got painfully to my feet and went to the little window again, scoopin' up the rifle on the way. I sagged against the wall, pantin'. The smoke had made its way up here now, and it was gettin' harder to breathe. I wouldn't be able to stay in this fortress of mine much longer.

The two left of Nan's crew were still down on the riverbank, pacin' back and forth like caged big cats. The woman I'd almost blown up was limpin'. Only now I saw others too, comin' outta the woods and onto the bank. Most walkin' but a few ridin', and some nursin' injuries. A few broken legs and arms, looked like. And some with cuts across their faces or stainin' their shirts and pants red in places.

Musta been the others I'd felled before with our traps. They were finally catchin' up.

"Come on out here you cowardly dog!"

My gaze went back to the limpin' woman at her yell. I brought the rifle up to my shoulder and sighted down the barrel.

"We've got you surrounded!" Her voice echoed out across the water, into the trees.

Sure enough, the seven newcomers, even with as haggard as they looked, drifted off toward each side of the mill.

"That whole building is goin' up in flames, dog!" she shouted. "You gonna burn up hidin' away like a scared little child or you gonna come out here and fight us like a man?!"

I gave a snort. Nine against one weren't fair odds by any count. And anyway, pride didn't serve a dead man none at all, as Holt liked to say.

"Hoss?" the man in front with her yelled out now. "Murray? Hollingsworth? You all still in there?"

I lifted a brow. Those must have been the three who'd come after me.

He got no answer of course, and that made him growl curses and pace again. One of the men who'd come from the woods cradlin' his right arm spoke up. "Maybe they killed him, too. Maybe they're all dead in there."

I stifled a cough and swung the rifle around to my right, to sight at the fella who was about to go around the mill's far corner. If they did surround the place, I wouldn't be able to pick 'em off one by one anymore. And that wouldn't do.

I squeezed the trigger, and then it was eight against one.

I worked the lever action quick as I could and took down two more before the rest scrambled into places out of my view and I swore.

The woman was shoutin' again, orderin' the others to stay off the bank. Tellin' 'em to cover the doors and windows and wait me out. I'd burn up soon, she said. Or suffocate. Or they'd get me when I tried to come out.

Well, all of that were true enough.

I let myself cough at last and shouldered the rifle. Pulled my bandana up over my nose and mouth and blinked waterin' eyes. The smoke was gettin' real thick up here, and the heat had become almost unbearable. The air shimmered with it as I left my window perch and made fer the office in the corner of this second story. The door had been left open and hung half off its hinges. I moved past the old desk with its stacks of curled, yellowed documents and past the mildewed chair to the side window. We'd boarded this one up pretty good given there was an awning below it, figurin' that might give others on the outside a good opportunity to climb up in here.

Only now I was hopin' to use it to get down from here.

Cursin' our thoroughness, I grabbed at each board and yanked, tearin' 'em free. Sharp, stabbin' pains shot through my bruised left hand and bloodied right shoulder at the effort and as soon as I'd made a hole big enough to crawl through I shook out my hand with a wince.

The crash of some kinda equipment fallin' from the first floor reached me even inside the office, and the walls around me groaned. The floor shifted under my boots.

Shit.

I leapt fer the window, threw myself outta it and landed hard on the awning beyond on my left shoulder. I cried out as the impact jarred my sore arm, but then I was rollin' down the angle of its roof straight fer the ground.

A resonant *whump* I could feel in my bones sounded from behind me, and the roof I was rollin' down suddenly dropped away from under me, and I was fallin'.

The awning hit the ground first, and then I hit the awning on my stomach with a grunt and rolled off into the brush.

"He's here!" a man shouted. "He's here, I got him!"

Shit. I tried to move and fell into a coughin' fit. Blinked more tears outta my eyes. They felt all gritty, and my throat stung somethin' awful. I'd lost my hat somewhere, but at least I still had all my guns on me.

I managed to push up onto my knees, and someone yanked the rifle off my shoulder.

All right, well at least I still had my pistols on me.

I looked up into the barrel of another sixgun and lifted my hands slowly.

The other five left of Nan's gang were runnin' our way.

But this man's hand was shakin'. He was awful roughed up.

A series of explosions soundin' like gunfire popped from behind me and instinctively I dropped back to my belly, coverin' my head with my hands. The man holdin' a pistol at me jumped, liftin' his gun to point at the mill.

Then I remembered all that ammunition Holt and I had left stashed inside there.

Another series of pops came from the other side of the mill, and the fella in front of me jumped again. Those other five whirled to face it, too.

I surged to my knees and pulled my own guns, emptyin' both in a matter of seconds, shootin' down all six remainin' of Nan's crew.

And then it was just me. Kneelin' there in the dirt, my whole body achin', and the old lumber mill hardly more now than a monstrous blaze belchin' black smoke up into the darkenin' sky.

I took a minute to breathe ... to let the fact I was still alive sink in.

More bullets caught in the flames exploded, but I didn't even flinch this time. Instead I dragged myself standin' and retrieved my rifle once more. Slung it over my shoulder. And went about reloadin' my two pistols yet again almost without thinkin'. The actions automatic and mechanical.

There was just one last problem.

Nine-Fingered Nan weren't here.

I hadn't seen that lieutenant of hers since he'd run off up toward the road, neither.

Were they still there even now, waitin'? Maybe waitin' to see how the rest of the gang fared? Waitin' fer news that it was all clear, that the way was safe, that the threat had been taken care of?

Or maybe they hadn't waited at all. Maybe they'd kept on movin' in search of a suitable hideout. Maybe they were settin' up camp somewhere else. Or maybe ... maybe they'd gone straight into the town of Blackbird to take whatever they could take and burn the rest of it down.

My gaze flicked upward in the direction of the town, toward the tree line. Lookin' fer smoke.

But there weren't none I could see on the horizon except what the mill was currently puttin' out.

My stomach turned at such thoughts, and I shoved the pistol I'd finished reloadin' back into its holster with more force than necessary. I'd thought Nan woulda followed her crew. Woulda chased me down same as them fer shootin' her horse out from under her.

If she was back on the road, or had moved on to hide somewhere else in these woods, or had gone into Blackbird...

I clenched my jaw and shook my head, then moved away from the swelterin' heat of the burnin' mill. I spotted my hat a little distance away and swiped it up, shovin' it back down onto my head with a satisfied grunt.

I came out from around the side of the mill and went toward the river next, plannin' to dunk my head into it. Tugged my bandana off my face and took a few good gulps of smoke-free air.

Well, least Nan wouldn't have so many guns around her now. I'd just have to go get Joe and head back to the road myself, see if I could track her down, no matter where she'd gone.

"Mr. Delano."

The voice echoed out from beneath the trees, over the roarin' and cracklin' of the mill fire.

I froze.

The forest shadows had got so deep now I could hardly make out her figure.

But there she was. Across the stretch of open gravel riverbank, standin' beneath the trees and starin' right at me. She stepped forward as my eyes finally found her, into the dusky light of evenin', and the glow of the burnin' mill turned her belt buckle and pearl grips orange.

That lieutenant of hers was a step behind her and to her right, holdin' his rifle leveled at me.

Fuckin' hell.

"I wondered if all this might be your doing." She walked toward me, slow and easy. "That was quite a show, I'll give you that."

I turned nice and slow myself to face her square, and I kept my hands outward at my sides ... away from my guns, but not too far.

She stopped nearly twenty paces from me. Just far enough fer a draw.

I stayed ready, every muscle on alert, and tried to remember to breathe. Tried not to let her see the way my nerves were hummin'. But my heart was runnin' wild again, and I hardly dared blink. The light of day was fadin' quick, and the darker it got, the harder it was to see if she might go fer her guns.

"I suppose you killed Mr. Lowery?" she asked.

I gave a nod. "As slow as I could."

She smiled, but her lieutenant cocked his rifle with a snarl and I tensed.

She lifted a hand to stay his shot, but never took her eyes off me. Instead, she took hold of the man's rifle without lookin' and pushed it downward. He glanced at her in clear disappointment, openin' his mouth to protest, but in the end he said not a word. He only switched his gaze to me and glared somethin' fierce.

"And the rest of 'em, too," I added, fer his benefit. "The others with Lowery. Shot 'em all down like dogs. Like all these fellas." I lifted my hands a little higher to indicate the dead bodies that littered the place.

Nine-Fingered Nan tilted her chin up as she eyed me. "Ya know, yer pa murdered a lot of folk ... but he weren't much into torture. He was more of a quick-and-clean-kill kinda man. You, on the other hand, you got no issue with makin' a person hurt to get what you want, do ya? You might be just as slippery and hard to kill as yer pa, just as much a murderer and a thief, but you got a cruel streak in ya he sure didn't have." Her grin widened. "Just my style."

I only glared back at her, but the words brought bile to my throat anyway.

In the heartbeat of resultin' silence I heard a strange, unfamiliar sound, faint and far-off. A steady thrummin' sort of noise, and it seemed to be comin' from the sky. But I couldn't look up; couldn't glance in that direction. If I so much as shifted my eyes away from Nan, she might shoot me.

Her lieutenant heard it, too, though. From the corner of my eye I saw him tense and turn, searchin' fer the source.

But Nan herself ignored it entirely. Keepin' her stare locked on me, unblinkin'. "Just the kinda man I could use in my outfit, if you were so inclined," she said. "Which is lucky fer you, 'cause it means I'll give you one more chance to tell me what you found out here. You see, Mr. Delano, I've just come a real long way. A real long way in search of somethin' real important to me. And you just kilt my horse. A damn good horse. And then you shot up all my men." She waved a hand around at the dead. "Another five of our horses had to be put down back there, too, thanks to those snares of yers. That's an awful lot you owe me now, Mr. Delano. A whole awful lot. So you can start by tellin' me how exactly I get past the Oracle. And you can tell me if you ever managed to find that doctor friend of yers, and if you happened to find any Old World items of any consequence in these parts. We'll start with that. And once you tell me all of that, I'll decide whether or not I'm gonna tan yer hide."

Now it was my turn to smile. I thought it felt natural enough, nevermind the fact my ears were ringin' again, and my heart throbbed so hard in my throat I thought I might choke on it. "Well," I managed to drawl, "see now that's the thing. Turns out I already paid my dues. All this," I spread my hands, "this is what I owed you. Fer all the things you've done to me lately. Fer all yer ... *entertainment*. See this, this was all real entertainin' to *me*. But I'm done fuckin' around now, Nan. All I want is my sister. Tell me where you've got her or I swear ... I swear I'll finish what I started here ... I'll destroy everythin' you've got."

She laughed.

Her man lifted his rifle quick, but just as quick Nan caught the barrel of it and shoved it downward again, her laughter cut short. She motioned fer him to stay put, and then she took a few more steps forward, movin' closer to me.

That thrummin' noise was gettin' louder.

I stood my ground despite a nearly overwhelmin' urge to move away from her. But she stopped again at only ten paces, and she fixed me with a flat, even stare. "Yer pa already did that a long time ago, boy." She scoffed and shook her head. "Ya know, I used to be like you. Passionate and full of rage. The desire for revenge colorin' every moment of every day. But do you know the problem with that, Mr. Delano?"

I said nothin', so she went on, liftin' her right hand to wiggle her fingers—what was left of 'em—in the air.

"It makes ya sloppy," she stated flatly. "And desperate. And that's how I was able to use ya all this time, weren't it?"

"Boss..." her lieutenant spoke up abruptly. "Boss, we got an airship incomin'."

Airship? I almost looked, almost. But Nan was too close. And all the amusement had gone outta her face.

She held up a hand to her man again, curt and forceful this time. Tellin' him to shut up. And never takin' her eyes off me. "You wanna know where I got yer sister right now?" she whispered. "All right, sure." She shrugged like it weren't no big deal, but my breath caught in my throat, my thunderin' heart skipped a beat, and I forgot all about the incomin' airship.

Nan took another step forward. "I sold her off a long time ago, you damn idiot fool. She's gone. She's gone, you understand? You lost her."

Fer what seemed like an eternity I stood there and stared at her, and the world suddenly felt like it might be underwater. Everythin' muffled and slow, shiftin' and blurred. And then it all snapped back into focus, and I pulled iron.

XLIII

SALVATION

Pain shocked through my chest even as I pulled the trigger; two reports ripplin' out over the hills nearly overlappin'.

I stumbled, hit my back on the gravel bank and gasped, choked. I couldn't fuckin' breathe. My lungs spasmed, but there didn't seem to be enough air.

I heard more noises now: somethin' big crashin' through the underbrush, the thrummin' of that airship loud, competin' with the roar of the mill fire, and Nan's lieutenant sayin' somethin' frantic to her, and her snappin' somethin' back.

But I couldn't sort the words. The pain drowned 'em all out, my whole chest burnin' white-hot, and all the little rocks of the riverbank diggin' into my back as I laid there gapin' fer breath like a goddamned fish...

My pistol ... it was still in my hand. I closed my fingers around it just as Nan's face eclipsed my view of the sky. Her right hand was pressed to her left side. Blood seeped between her fingers.

I coughed a laugh, then cried out and choked again. Tasted blood myself.

Well, least I'd got her. Least I'd shown her Nine-Fingered Nan could bleed.

Nine-Fingered Nan could die.

I shuddered, and a cold sweat prickled across my skin. Fuck, but she'd got me, too. She'd got me good.

Her boot stepped on my right wrist, and then she leaned down and pried the gun outta my hand. "Like I said, Mr. Delano. Sloppy."

I wanted to say somethin', but every inhale was a struggle, and the words wouldn't come. My left hand fumbled fer my second pistol with numb, heavy fingers. I couldn't seem to grasp it ... and all the effort sent new hooks of agony tearin' through me till I had to stop tryin'. Till the pain was like a vice, slowly crushin'.

Nan straightened and shook her head. "When ya get to Hell, tell yer pa hello fer me. You tell him I was the one who destroyed his life. Destroyed his family. Took everythin' from him and his children both. Tell him I got my revenge, all right, despite his best efforts." She smiled. "And don't you worry about the Oracle or yer doctor friend. I'll find 'em both soon enough. I always get what I want in the end. The benefit of patience, Mr. Delano."

She touched the brim of her hat with her bloodied fingers, turned, and walked away.

I shifted, wantin' to sit, wantin' to pull my other pistol and fill her back with bullets, but all I succeeded in doin' was to make my heart seize up and black spots scatter across my vision so I thought I might die right then and there.

But I didn't. I only fell back into the gravel and blinked the blur outta my eyes, tried to breathe around the blood wellin' in my throat.

Gunfire cracked suddenly from the edge of the woods on the tail of thunderin' hooves, and answerin' fire sounded from off to my left. There was too much smoke and fire and pain to see what was happenin', but I heard boots runnin' off and a set of hooves chargin', and shots goin' back and forth.

And then there was the belly of that airship. Right above me. Huge and dark and floatin' soft as a butterfly. Part of me wondered if it was even real. Maybe I was hallucinatin'. My last dyin' wish ... gettin' to the ship that took Ethelyn...

"Attention, outlaws," a voice boomed from the sky. "By the authority of the East Republic, you are hereby under arrest. Cease fire and surrender your weapons or we *will* shoot to kill. We have you in our sights and I repeat, we *will* shoot to kill."

The airship ... the airship was talkin'. But the shootin' on the ground didn't stop. Not surprisin'. No one out here cared anythin' about the Republic's laws. We weren't even in the Republic; they had no jurisdiction here. The hell were they doin' so far out from their own borders, anyway?

"This is your last warning," the boomin' voice said again. "Cease fire and surrender your weapons—"

The gunfire went silent all at once. The horse skidded to a stop beside me, sprayin' gravel.

Boots hit the bank, and I saw ... Holt? He dropped to his knees at my side, and from the look on his face I knew I weren't gonna make it. He spat the worst string of curses I'd heard him utter in a long time, and then he unknotted his bandana and pressed it up against the hole in my chest.

"*Goddamnit*," he hissed. "Goddamnit, Van. Look what you did this time you stupid sonuvabitch."

I managed to get my left hand over the top of his. There was a lot I wanted to tell him, like the fact his horse was safe and sound, tied up a distance away. And that I was sorry I'd lost his long rifle; it'd have been burned up in that fire by now, nothin' more than melted slag. And there was a lot I wanted to ask him, too, like had he managed to shoot down Nine-Fingered Nan and her lieutenant, and why the hell was there an airship from the Republic hoverin' over us ... but every time I tried to talk I only choked, and then shuddered and gasped.

Holt worked his left arm under my shoulders and propped me up a little, and some of the blood ran out my mouth and then it was a little easier to breathe. The evenin' had turned to twilight, but even the glow of the mill's remains seemed dark now.

Guess I'd find out if pa had ever found that salvation of his soon enough.

"*Van?*" Another voice rang out from above, but this one didn't boom. Instead, it was high and thin, carried from far away. "*Van!* Hang on, we're coming down!"

It sounded like Charlotte. But that didn't make no sense...

Holt glanced up to the airship, then gave a snort. "It's the girl. Where in the hell you think she found a whole airship, eh?"

I shook my head, then winced. He pressed harder on that bandana. I couldn't imagine how she mighta found an airship, or why she might be on one in the first place, but I guessed it didn't much matter now.

"If those Republic bastards coulda got here earlier ... think they were the ones to scare off Nan more than me." Holt looked around at the other bodies strewn across the bank, then twisted to give the burnin' mill a good look, and he shook his head again and whistled low. "You do all this yerself, kid?"

I gave the slightest inclination of my chin, not wantin' to risk a full nod.

"Damn." His left hand squeezed my shoulder. "But *damn*. We had a plan, Van. And a damned good one fer once. Why couldn't you just stick to the goddamned plan? Why'd you have to take my horse, huh? Took me *ages* to track down another one I could steal ... coulda been here *hours* ago otherwise!"

But he hadn't been. And that's how I'd wanted it.

Couldn't let Nan take anyone else from me.

Not Holt, and not Charlotte.

Least the two of 'em were still alive, and still free. Least I had that.

Holt was still talkin', but I couldn't understand him no more. I closed my eyes and let his voice lull me into the dark.

Fer a long while, I drifted.

Through darkness and light, comfort and pain, occasionally aware of other sensations and sounds, and sometimes lost in somethin' like fever dreams. There was the crow-headed Oracle with her huge black wings, tellin' me it weren't too late. But she was burned up by the fire at the old lumber mill.

No, it weren't the mill. It was our house.

Our house in Kansas, lightin' up the night.

And Nan was there, watchin' it burn with a grin on her face, the flames dancin' in those pale eyes of hers.

And I was stuck in the middle of it. In the middle of the fire lookin' out at her while my skin boiled and fell off my flesh. I think I screamed. Or, I wanted to scream. I tried to.

Blackness swallowed the fire all at once, and fer a time I had peace. Until an airship appeared, floatin' across my vision. On the promenade deck stood Ethelyn as a child, and she was reachin' fer me.

I reached back fer her, and a hand met mine. But it weren't Ethelyn's.

My sister was still out of reach.

I blinked, opened my eyes. They felt dry and gritty.

There weren't no airship, and there weren't no Ethelyn. Instead there was ... Holt.

Holt?

He grinned as my bleary gaze landed on him and sprang up to his feet, clappin' me on the shoulder hard enough that pain spiked all through my chest and I grimaced, lettin' out a choked cry.

He sobered at my yell, his hearty shoulder-clap softenin' abruptly to a gentle pat. "Damn, sorry, kid. Sorry. Just so surprised to see ya awake ... praise the Holy Mother herself, I ain't seen nothin' like it as I live and breathe!" He caught my face in his hands abruptly. "Yer *alive* you fuckin' *lucky sonuvabitch*!"

I winced as his exuberance jostled me again, and when he sat back I managed a slow, relieved exhale.

Fuckin' hell. That's right. I'd been shot.

I shoulda been dead.

Shoulda been dead and not layin' here in ... where the hell was I, anyway? Holt was here, sure, but I didn't recognize the surroundings. It was dark, only lit here and there with lanterns hung on walls or set on empty stools, and there was a small fire glowin' in a stone hearth.

The walls, what little I could see of 'em, looked like ... logs? A log cabin of some kind, maybe. And I weren't layin' on no bed. Though I had a pillow and blankets, and there was somethin' soft under the bare skin of my back, it was too tall fer a bed. And too hard, despite whatever paddin' had been attempted over the top of it.

I worked my mouth till some semblance of a voice came out, though it was hardly more than a croak after so long—how long?—of disuse. "Wh—where are we? What happened?"

Holt whistled and shook his head. "Ha! Well, it was a ride, I'll tell ya." He resumed his seat next to me. "As fer the where ... you won't believe it, kid. We are currently, right now, in the home of that crazy witch the Oracle, herself."

I didn't much like that idea. A strange mix of feelin's stirred through me and I glanced around at what I could see of the little house again. But fer all her strangeness and unexplained abilities, her home seemed regular enough. At least fer the time bein'. I remembered the way she'd loomed over me in my dreams though, crow-headed and dark, and shuddered.

"Hey, hey, take it easy," Holt prompted. "I don't like it neither ... you know how much I dislike that creepy old woman. But she's got a whole little village out here, and it seems they do pretty well fer themselves. And to be honest, kid ... well, she's been almost downright hospitable lately. Keeps preachin' about undergoin' Judgement fer anyone who wants to enter *the temple*, of course, and she's mentioned you takin' part in somethin' called a Great Awakenin' a time or two now, whatever that means ... so she's certainly still crazy. But she did offer us a place to stay while you heal, and she's been feedin' us decent, and none of her followers has murdered us yet, so ... so I guess in a way they're all right."

I let out a little groan, not so certain about any of that.

"And as fer *what happened*," Holt continued, "*you* thought you could take on Nine-Fingered Nan and her whole crew all by yerself, it seems."

"Yeah," I husked. "I remember that part."

"I gotta admit, you put the hurt on 'em pretty good. Coroner counted twenty-two bodies, the paper said. They're callin' it the Massacre at the Mill."

"Twenty-five," I said.

"Huh?"

"I got ... got twenty-five of 'em. Three ... three got burned up. In the fire."

Holt lifted his eyebrows. "Well. Anyway. Massacre at the Mill, that's what they call it. Think those Republic fellas see ya as some kinda hero. They came all the way out here to try and dispatch Nine-Fingered Nan fer good only to find you'd already laid waste to a good part of her crew."

I frowned, vaguely rememberin' somethin' about Republic folk, and wonderin' why they were so far outside their own borders.

"But you know how it ended?" Holt asked.

I closed my eyes, not wantin' to say it out loud.

I'd lost. Those twenty-five of her gang I'd managed to gun down didn't matter in the least. There was still no Ethelyn. Ethelyn was gone. I'd managed to hit Nan this time ... but her shot should have killed me. And not indirectly by leavin' me stranded and bleedin' out in the desert.

No, this time she'd been about as direct as a person could get. Straight fer the heart.

"Nine-Fingered Nan gunned ya down," Holt said, unnecessarily. "Put a bullet into ya and shoulda fuckin' killed ya. Four inches lower, Van, and you'd be six feet under right now instead of here talkin' to me. Hell, even where she got ya shoulda killed ya."

I tried to wet dry lips. "Nan ... I got her, too. I got her, Holt."

He grunted. "Yeah. You did. And yeah, that's somethin', kid. Ain't heard of anyone gettin' a shot on Nan fer a long, *long* time now. But she still walked away, didn't she? And you didn't."

I cracked my eyes open again. "Coulda still killed her."

He shrugged. "Maybe. I dunno. She was runnin' pretty good when I got there. Took some shots at her myself ... I mighta snagged her some but it was hard to tell. Think I got her man good once. But they both high-tailed it when that airship got there. Those Republic gents are still out there lookin' fer her."

"The hell they doin' all the way out here, anyway?"

Holt gave a snort and twisted on his stool to look over his shoulder briefly, though there weren't nothin' or no one there fer the moment. Then he turned back to me. "Yer girl," he said lowly.

"Huh?"

"Charlotte. Charlotte Harrison, daughter of Senator John Henry Harrison from the east, you remember her sayin' all that back in Copperwell?"

I frowned more, not seein' how any of this related to that airship. "Sure."

Holt leaned forward on his stool, closer to me. "Yeah, well, when she ran off, turns out she went to Blackbird. While we were settin' up the mill, she sent a wire to her senator father. Told him Nine-Fingered Nan was comin' to this area and to send the calvary. And I guess he did."

My mind felt disoriented, sluggish, and I had a hard time figurin' how Charlotte would have known where or when Nan might be comin'. I'd never told her. Hadn't told her on purpose.

"But remember how she also said her pa didn't know where she'd gone, back when we first found her lurkin' around at Grave Gulch?"

"Yeah..."

"When she sent the wire about Nan, her pa figured out where she must be, of course. He was real sore about her runnin' off, apparently. Ordered some of those men he sent after Nan to escort her home immediately. On that airship, no less."

My heart picked up pace at this news, pulsin' a heavy ache through the left side of my chest, and I took deep, slow breaths to try and ease it off. "Did ... did they...?"

Holt scoffed. "What do you think? Hell no, kid. She don't want to go home. Fer all that wealth she's got, her home must be an awful place with as certain as she is about not goin' back. They had her all loaded up on that airship already when they went to the mill to go after Nan, but when she saw you bleedin' out on the riverbank, she told her pa's men you were the one who'd helped rescue her from Whittaker, convinced 'em to take you aboard and bring you to yer doctor friend." He paused, and his shinin' blue gaze went distant fer a spell, his expression goin' slack before he blinked and snapped outta it. "Gotta tell ya, kid, yer doctor friend is somethin' else. I ain't never seen no doctor do the things he can do. Not in my life."

I glanced down to the shape of my metal leg beneath the blankets and twitched the metal toes. They moved just like I wanted 'em to. Just like natural toes. Maybe me and that leg were finally gettin' used to each other. "Yeah," I croaked. "Me neither."

"'Course, bein' that yer doctor friend was in that cave of yers—the *temple*, she calls it—and none of those Republic fellas had passed her Judgement, the Oracle made all that quite an affair. Thought you were a goner fer sure by the time Charlotte herself went in alone and brought out the doc ... thought we might have ourselves another massacre, but eventually Dr. Balogh got everyone calmed down and got to work on ya. And that's why we're here now, and not in that cave. Cuz of the Oracle's blasted *Judgement* and no one wantin' to partake of it. Which is just fine with me, mind you. Never wanted to go into that place myself, anyway. Not after all the things you told me about it. And the senator's hired guns are far more interested in findin' Nan than in the ravings of a crazy old woman."

I struggled to make sense of it all, tryin' to sort through everything he'd just said. But it was a lot. And I couldn't get my words to keep up with all my questions.

Holt kept on goin' before I could manage to speak, anyway. "'Course that means those Republic bastards are gonna stick around fer awhile, I guess. Till they find Nan, find her body, or are satisfied in some other way before headin' back east to report to Senator Harrison. I think a few of 'em mighta gone ahead and taken Charlotte home already though, 'cept their airship seems to be havin' some kind of mechanical difficulties." He glanced around the empty house again and then dropped his voice. "If ya ask me, I think the girl sabotaged it on purpose. But that means we got 'em millin' around here fer awhile, waitin' to drag Charlotte back home and ... well, I'm not entirely sure what they wanna do with you and me, kid."

I closed my eyes again. "How much do they know?"

I heard Holt shift on his stool. "Dunno. Don't think too much beyond what Charlotte's told 'em about us so far, which ain't much considerin'. So far I believe it's all been positive. And like I said, they seem to regard you as some kinda hero fer takin' out so many of Nan's gang. Guess they consider murder all right long as yer murderin' people they want murdered. If they don't do too much diggin', they shouldn't wanna hang us right off, at least. Although ... although there *was* mention of Sheriff Reeves sayin' somethin' to 'em back in Blackbird about you bein' wanted fer questionin'. Somethin' about the murder of Blackbird's long-time telegram operator Mr. Brown."

I grimaced.

Holt grunted. "So it *was* you."

I opened one eye just to be doubly sure there weren't no one else around besides Holt. But we were still alone. So I let out a breath and closed that eye again. "He saw the return wire from Nan. He woulda told Sheriff Reeves."

"Well maybe you shoulda let him. Then maybe you wouldn't be here now layin' on that table almost dead."

"She woulda got other people involved."

There was a heartbeat of silence, and then a creak as Holt shifted forward on his stool, his voice soundin' closer when he spoke again. "Yeah. That's the point. *Then maybe you wouldn't be here almost dead.*"

"Or maybe all of 'em woulda ended up like me," I countered. "Or ... or worse. Or maybe they woulda screwed up our ambush, or never ... never let us plan it like we wanted in the first place. Not ... worth the risk, Holt."

He grunted. "But it was worth the risk to take on a whole crew like that yerself, was it?"

I pulled my eyes open again, though with some difficulty now. All this talkin' and thinkin' was downright exhaustin', but I managed to hold his incredulous gaze. "Yeah. She was gonna ... she was gonna kill you. And Charlotte, if she woulda been there, too. She woulda done it outta spite. To get at me."

That look she'd given me at the end, when she'd been standin' over me as I was dyin' ... it chilled me to the bone. That carefully measured mask of hers had gone entirely, leavin' behind only raw, wild hatred.

That's when I'd known I'd done the right thing in goin' to that mill alone. No matter how it had ended ... if Holt or Charlotte or both had been there, she woulda taken them, too. No doubt about it.

"Tell him I was the one who destroyed his life. Destroyed his family. Took everythin' from him and his children both."

But not everything. Not quite.

Holt let out a heavy sigh and shook his head. "*Or* ... I coulda been there to take the long shot at Nan while she was distracted with you, and those Republic gents wouldn't have to be out there wanderin' the woods tryin' to find her right now."

"Maybe," I croaked. "But maybe she's already dead. Maybe we both got her, after all."

Holt shrugged. "Maybe. A mean ol' coot like her, though? Wouldn't bet on it."

A moment of silence passed between us as I pondered Nan's chances of bein' alive, and Holt dropped his eyes to his lap. "So. You ... happen to get any word on yer sister durin' all this mess, bein' that's the whole reason we set this trap in the first place?"

The mention of Ethelyn went through me hot and sharp as that bullet had and my fists clenched around handfuls of the blanket that covered me. I squeezed my eyes shut even as the rest of me blazed in a sudden swell of rage. But that only served to send a new burst of agony radiatin' outward from my wound, makin' me gasp and cry out again.

Holt stood fast from his stool. "Van? You all right?"

I ground my teeth and waited fer the pain to pass, clutchin' at the blankets fer all I was worth. Cold sweat broke out across my skin.

"Hey, take it easy." Holt reached over behind my head to grab a damp washcloth. He dabbed it at my face. "Doc says you shouldn't be gettin' yerself worked up. I'm sorry, I shouldn'ta asked—shoulda known better—"

I reached up to snatch his wrist with my right hand, makin' him stop pattin' at my face. "She's ... she's gone. Sold off."

His face fell and he lowered his arm, though I didn't release his wrist. "Fer sure? You don't think Nan was just fuckin' with ya again?"

I shook my head. It'd been hard to tell one way or another most times ... but not this time. There'd been a cruel certainty in her tone this time that hadn't been there before. Not even when she'd told me at first Ethelyn was dead. "Not this time." My voice was all gruff and I cleared it. I was gonna say more, but then suddenly I couldn't.

So I only laid there and tried to breathe through all the little hooks pullin' at my ribs, and all that rage still circulatin' in my blood. I let go of Holt's wrist, and he dropped that hand back to his side. "No mention of where? Or when?"

I shook my head again. "It's why ... why I ... why I shot her."

Holt looked to me sharply. "*You* pulled first?"

I nodded.

He hissed a breath through his teeth. "The hell were you thinkin', Van? Goin' up against Nine-Fingered Nan direct like that? No wonder you ended up on yer back with a hole almost right through yer heart..."

I glared at him. "I was thinkin' she kidnapped and sold my sister and deserved a bullet 'tween the eyes, that's what." I coughed, grimaced ... the pain worsened again, blood rushin' in my ears. I tried to calm down, tried to will myself into that patience Nan loved to preach about so much, but then that only made me angrier.

Holt motioned at me to settle down like maybe I were some riled-up, rabid dog. Even backed away slow, toward the vague outline of a door I supposed was the entrance to this particular little cabin currently servin' as my bedroom. "All right," he said soothingly. "All right, kid. Just take it easy. Don't get yerself excited, remember?"

He *really* weren't helpin' any here.

He opened the house's front door and leaned out into the darkness beyond, then yelled. "Doc? Hey, doc!" His voice echoed away into the night outside. "Think I might need some help here!"

Dr. Balogh appeared almost immediately, and he looked both surprised and dismayed at seein' me awake. He sent a pointed glare in Holt's direction. "You were supposed to alert me when he regained consciousness."

Holt shrugged. "It weren't too long ago he woke up. And anyway, I told ya just now, didn't I?"

The doc rolled his eyes and came to the left side of my makeshift bed. "He seems quite agitated ... did you upset him?"

Holt took a step back at the accusation, spreadin' his arms. "What? Naw, it weren't me—Nan's the one that's got him all upset."

Them talkin' about me like I weren't layin' right there was upsettin' me. "I can speak fer myself," I spat. Although in truth, speakin' was gettin' more and more difficult. Seemed to be takin' more and more effort.

"You should not be speaking," Dr. Balogh said dryly. "Or at least, only speaking at a minimum. You just went through a lot, young man. Came to me in an even worse state this time than the last time I found you almost dead. You certainly seem to have a greater affinity for death than anyone else I've ever met."

I only grunted.

"You got no idea, Doc," Holt offered.

I sent him another glare. Half the times I'd almost died durin' the last eight years were *his* fault.

"Well, Mr. Delano," Dr. Balogh said. "I suppose we meet again much sooner than either of us expected, eh?" He gently lifted the blanket from my chest and checked the bandage there. It'd been wrapped thick around my torso under my arms, and then up over my left shoulder. There was a little circle of blood leakin' through it high on the left side above my heart, but nothin' compared to what it'd been bleedin' like before.

The doc murmured somethin' and let the blanket down, then smoothed it over me gently. "I've managed to stabilize you ... for now. If Ms. Harrison had not thought to bring you to me immediately, it would have been a very different story. You required extensive surgery, and it will take you several weeks to recover, but you should be all right. *As long as* you do exactly as I say, Mr. Delano, do you understand? *Absolutely no* sneaking off before you are fully healed this time, do you hear?"

I grumbled, fixed my glare on the old wooden door across the room. I didn't like the thought of layin' here in this uncomfortable makeshift bed in the house of an old woman I didn't trust fer weeks, but I also didn't think I coulda sat up right now without blackin' out. Figured I didn't have much choice in the matter.

"I've arranged for someone to stay with you at all times, mind you," Dr. Balogh went on, movin' now across the tiny house to shuffle through various vials lined up on a roughly hewn wooden shelf. "Just to make sure you stay put. But for now, you need to rest. Minimize your movement, and your speaking. We will take it one day at a time and keep a close eye on that wound to be sure it does not catch infection."

He came back to my bedside with a bottle of laudanum. Poured me a spoonful and offered it out to me. "Here. Take this. It will help with the pain, and help you rest."

I turned my head away. "No thanks." But already it was feelin' like a weight was crushin' my chest again, and I was cold.

"I am afraid I must insist, Mr. Delano."

Holt reached down near the stool he'd been sittin' on and brought up a half-empty bottle of whiskey. "I got this."

Dr. Balogh sighed. "Mr. Haggerty, would you go and fetch another blanket please?"

Holt squinted at the doctor, but then shrugged. "All right. Sure." He glanced to me. "Do as the doc says, kid. He's a goddamn miracle worker far as I can tell."

Dr. Balogh pursed his lips and raised his eyebrows. "Not a miracle worker, Mr. Haggerty. Just very practiced at what I do."

"Seems like the same thing to me," Holt muttered on his way to the door. Then he pushed out of it and shut it behind him, and I was left alone with the doc.

XLIV

NOT EVERYTHING

In the end, I took the medicine. Mostly 'cause I didn't have enough strength left to offer any more resistance to it. And admittedly, I was awful keen to have the growin' pain dulled again. Then the doc took my temperature; seemed satisfied with the result and went about lightin' a few candles that put out a gentle, pleasant scent. Lavender and maybe chamomile, I think.

Despite everything, and all the questions I had crowdin' around in my head, I started to relax. Started to get sleepy. I drowsed as Dr. Balogh kept shufflin' about the single room. Didn't have a clue what he was doin', but somethin' about the quiet activity was calmin' in and of itself. I was only vaguely aware of Holt returnin', and they laid another blanket atop me, but then I couldn't keep my eyes open any more, and I slipped into a heavy sleep.

Next time I woke, the house was still mostly dark. Fewer lamps and candles were lit now, but the fire in the hearth burned brighter, givin' the place a soft, warm glow. The little table to my right had a plate and cup on it, leftovers from a recent meal.

The sound of a page turnin' caught my attention and I glanced to my left to see Charlotte herself sittin' there now. She wore a white blouse with ruffles down the front and at the end of the sleeves and a simple pink skirt, and had one leg crossed over the other. Atop her knee was one of that ancient dead fella's journals. She was skimmin' the yellowed pages by candlelight, and now and then she'd absently tuck a strand of hair that had escaped her loose braid behind her ear.

Fer a minute or two, I just watched her. Remembered what she'd said to me last time we'd seen each other proper. And swallowed.

She glanced toward me, then did a double-take as she realized I was awake and shut the journal.

I blinked, shiftin' my eyes somewhere else. Hoped she didn't think I'd been starin'.

"Oh," she said, standin' from her stool. "How long have you been awake?"

"Not long."

"Would you like something to eat? Dr. Balogh gave us the recipe for a good soup. Said you should eat something tonight if you're up for it."

I considered. "Sure. Sure ... that sounds ... nice."

"All right then." She moved to the hearth and took the lid from a small pot that sat near it. Dished some soup into a bowl, fetched a spoon, and brought it to me. "Here."

I took the bowl from her, usin' my right hand so as to not have to move my left arm. "Thank you."

"Let me help you sit up just a bit." There were more straw and down-filled pillows on the floor, and she managed to both help me sit slightly and wedge them one after the other under my shoulders till I was at an appropriate angle to eat without chokin'.

"Thank you," I said again. There was a lot more I wanted to say, too, but I was havin' a hard time gettin' it out.

"You're welcome," was all she said in return. Then she put a cup of water atop a stool to my right so I could reach it and resumed her seat on the stool to my left. She flipped open the journal again and went back to readin'.

The sounds of the forest at night had quieted since the last time I'd been conscious fer an evenin', and I found myself wishin' fer that thunderous chorus of insects again to fill the sudden void of silence.

I sat fer a minute waitin' to see if she might say anythin' else, but she didn't. I finally tried the soup, and it was good, and as soon as it hit my belly I realized how hungry I was, and I drank the rest of it down quick. And then gulped the water.

But Charlotte just kept on readin'.

Shit. Well, I weren't gonna sit here the whole night like this ... and I wouldn't be able to rest none, neither, till the air was cleared between us. So at last I took a deep, slow breath and exhaled quietly. The doc had told me not to talk too much, but some things had to be said. Or asked. "How ... how did you know where we were?"

She paused her readin'. Then she snapped the book closed and turned on her stool to face me. "You mean because you never saw fit to include me in your plan?"

I met her angry blue glare evenly. "I didn't include Holt neither, in the end. If that makes you feel any better."

Her gaze narrowed. "No it does not, Van. That's why you're here, like this. That's why you almost died. If you'd had Holt, and me, and my father's hired guns, we could have arrested all those people—could have had Nan, even—and brought them all to justice."

"I already brought 'em to justice," I growled.

"Except Nan."

Anger spiked, bringin' pain again. I tried to swallow it all back. "They ain't found her yet?"

Charlotte shook her head.

Goddamnit. Though I supposed there was still a chance she was out there dyin' miserable and slow and alone like her man Lowery had done. I could only hope. Though I woulda preferred a body to confirm it, certainly. "She had wagons with her," I offered. "Two of 'em. Those'll be ... slow and harder to hide. Maybe those hired guns of yer pa's should ... should start lookin' fer those. Find the wagons, and I bet they'll find Nan, too."

"Good idea," Charlotte admitted. "I will tell Mr. Eckerton in the morning. He's the one in charge, apparently."

"Still don't explain how you knew where we were," I said.

Charlotte straightened her shoulders and clasped the journal in her lap. "I followed you. You and Holt. Watched till you rode off from the

Temple ... the power station, I mean, and then I followed you at a distance. It was rather easy, to be honest."

I scowled. Despite her intense displeasure at me orderin' her to stay put at that cave, it'd never occurred to me she might try somethin' as simple as just followin' us. "Yeah well we weren't expectin' to have a tail," I growled. "And you shouldn'ta done that ... shouldn'ta been ridin' around so soon after gettin' those stitches."

She pursed her lips. "Like *you* should be one to lecture *me* about what to do and not to do after getting injured. It wasn't exactly comfortable, true. But I managed just fine, thank you. And once I realized you were fortifying that old lumber mill, I decided you must be planning some kind of a stand there. That's where you wanted Nan and anyone else she might bring with her to go. That's where the fight would happen. Or else you and Holt wouldn't have put so much effort into readying the area. Then I calculated travel time between Bravebank and there, since Nan was reported as being seen in Bravebank most recently, and assuming she would want to take the fastest route to the mill as possible. As soon as I was sure of that, I traveled back into Blackbird and sent a wire to my father informing him that I knew where Nine-Fingered Nan would be in seven days' time, and that he should send whatever men he'd managed to recruit immediately so they could apprehend her."

I dropped my gaze to my hands, which had clutched at the blankets. All of that sounded awful logical. And yet ... she had no idea how the arrival of all those law-abidin' guns coulda fucked everythin' up if the timin' had been different. Not to mention that accordin' to them, in most cases, I'd be just as much an outlaw as any of Nan's crew.

I lifted my eyes back up to Charlotte and gave a careful sigh. "I didn't want the law involved on purpose. Or any hired guns, neither. They don't know Nan like I do. What if ... what if they'd spooked her before I could spring the ambush? What if she'd brought Ethelyn along and my sister got caught in the crossfire? What if they'd gunned Nan down before I got any of my questions answered ... or worse, decided she needed a proper trial and denied me my own justice? Bringin' in more people just brings in more unknowns, Charlotte. And in a situation like that ... you can't afford more unknowns."

She looked at me evenly fer a long minute, and then her shoulders softened, and she slumped on the stool a little. "Why couldn't you have just told me all that before?"

I blinked, the question unexpected in its simplicity. "I ... I don't know." I suppose I'd been too wrapped up in my plan, in doin' things my way, and still unused to workin' with much of anyone outside of Holt.

Unused to fully trustin' much of anyone ... even Holt.

"I ... should have. I'm ... I'm sorry."

Charlotte turned to set the dead fella's journal on the shelf behind her, then smoothed her skirts over her lap and sighed heavily. "I thought I was helping. Thought I might prevent you from being killed and help end Nine-Fingered Nan too in the process. Though I did fail to consider that doing so would alert my father to exactly where I was, and that he would then demand my immediate return back home." One of her eyebrows arched. "I also did not realize that Sheriff Reeves wished to speak with you so keenly."

My heart jumped at the mention of the sheriff, and I clenched my jaw against the fresh ache in my chest. I was really gonna have to work on stayin' calm, at this rate...

"I had planned to return to the mill," Charlotte said, "had planned to even let you know I had figured out what you were doing and had help on the way. But I suppose the sheriff had put out word around town that I was an acquaintance of yours, and someone must have spotted me and informed her, because she found me soon enough. And ... *apprehended* me. For questioning."

That fresh ache deepened as my heart picked up pace again, afraid of what she might tell me next.

"Mostly about *your* whereabouts. Your history and tendency toward violence." She shifted on the stool. "I didn't exactly like her line of questioning, so I didn't tell her much. But she insisted on holding me at the sheriff's station until she managed to track you down. I think she thought you'd eventually come looking for me. Only my father's men arrived a few days later, of course, and they confirmed my identity and had orders directly from my father that I was to be escorted back home."

I frowned. "But this ain't the Republic. Sheriff Reeves don't have to listen to yer father."

Charlotte scoffed. "No, but my father has been working with the Commune's Council to form that new organization of his ... and since his hired guns came here to specifically apprehend Nine-Fingered Nan if they could, he had the Council's full blessing. And Sheriff Reeves *does* have to listen to the Council. Especially if she wants their aid in handling the current supply shortage."

"Huh."

"My father also took the liberty of voiding your bounty for Baron Whittaker's murder."

"*What?*" I was quite sure I'd heard her wrong. I struggled to sit up further on my pillows, but gave up quick when the motion only served to make everything hurt worse. I grimaced and sank back into 'em as Charlotte stood again and shook her head.

"No, no, stop moving around. Lay still. There you are." She adjusted the blankets over me. "He got some lawyers to plead your case. Given the baron purchased me illegally, and given your help in my escape, they said you were acting in self-defense when 'you' murdered him. Of course the Territories have no centralized ruling body, so it's really only void in the Commune and the Republic ... but it does mean any licensed bounty hunter won't be able to legally collect that bounty anymore."

"Legally," I grunted.

Charlotte pursed her lips. "If they were going to do it illegally, they wouldn't bother getting a license in the first place. At least that means that Duster fellow should leave you alone now."

I snorted. If her pa coulda done such a thing weeks ago, then maybe I wouldn'ta had to throw the man off a train. But Charlotte still didn't know I had done that. So all I said was, "Sure. Yeah, I suppose." Now if only her pa could void the rest of my bounties everywhere else, too...

"It only applies to that one specific bounty, though," Charlotte said, almost like she could read my thoughts. And then she fixed me with a very pointed look that made me highly uncomfortable, and I wished again I could manage to get up off this bed and leave. "What did you do in Blackbird, Van? Sheriff Reeves *deputized* us. And then I go back and she's holding me in a *jail cell* and asking me questions about how well I know you and about what kind of man you are. Why?"

I tried to hold her stare but couldn't bear it. So instead I closed my eyes and focused on takin' slow, deep breaths. Fer a second I considered tellin' her the truth. Opened my mouth to say it, even. To tell her I'd killed that helpful old man Mr. Brown, and that Sheriff Reeves had likely heard from witnesses about a fella lookin' somethin' like me comin' outta there right before he'd been found slumped in his chair with a bullet between the eyes. But when I spoke, it was a different truth that came out. "Some of Nan's men found me at the post office when I went to send a wire to her about findin' those Old World ruins."

"You said you weren't going to tell her about that!"

"I ... I wasn't. I didn't. I mean I was gonna tell her I found somethin', just to get her out here. But some of her crew had been followin' us all the way from near Bravebank turns out, and I ... well I ended up murderin' 'em all. And I suppose there were probably witnesses to all that. And I'm sure the sheriff had some questions about it."

There was a moment of silence. "I see."

I kept silent, kept my eyes closed. Didn't want to volunteer anythin' else about any of that business.

"That settles that then, I suppose." She breathed a soft sigh. "Perhaps I'll see if Mr. Eckerton can go speak to her on your behalf and explain the situation."

I winced, pretty sure that was a bad idea. "Does she know where I am now?"

"No. None of us have been back to town since departing for the mill three days ago. She sent a water wagon and some men to try and contain the mill fire after it was reported ... but no, she doesn't know where any of us are right now."

"Should probably ... probably stay that way fer awhile. She may not take kindly to murder inside her town, even if all those murdered were no good bastards. May not ... may not want her talkin' to Mr. Eckerton, anyway."

I heard Charlotte shift on her stool. "Why not?"

"What if she tells him she suspects me a murderer?" Maybe he'd passed off her first mention of it, but if the two of 'em happened to get into some kinda involved, deep discussion about me and what I had or hadn't done ... I was fair sure one of 'em would end up doin' that diggin' Holt and me both surely didn't want 'em doin'. "Didn't yer pa organize those men to clean up the Territories? Ain't ... ain't that their whole purpose here? And in the eyes of the law, a murder is a murder. What if they decide I'm no better than Nan or any of her gang? What if they wanna take me to trial ... or just hang me right off?"

Charlotte was silent fer a long minute. She must not have ever considered that side of it before. In the interest of my own neck, I was happy to enlighten her.

She shifted on the stool again. "Well. Perhaps I will not send Mr. Eckerton to speak to her, then."

"Wise ... wise decision." Words were becomin' difficult again, and I felt short of breath.

"You should rest," Charlotte said abruptly. "You're looking a little pale. I'm sorry, we've probably talked too much. Would you like any more soup, or water?"

I shook my head.

"I believe you are due for another dose of medicine. Let me get that for you." She bustled about briefly gettin' it ready, and I took it obediently, mostly 'cause I just wanted to sink back into that hole of nothin'ness again.

No more talkin', no more questions, no more thinkin' of Mr. Brown, murdered so I'd have a chance at gettin' Ethelyn and endin' Nan, only I hadn't done either. And how many others had been murdered along the way fer the same purpose? All to get me here, layin' in some makeshift cabin in the middle of the woods, almost dead.

"Get some rest," Charlotte said quietly. "I'll just be here reading for awhile longer if you need me."

I heard the scrape of leather bindin' against wood as she pulled that journal off the shelf, the whisper of paper as she opened it again, and then came the flick as she turned a page. And then another.

The laudanum sank in and warmed my limbs, took the edge off the pain, and then it was easier to breathe again. And I just laid there and listened to all the muted night sounds, and the soft crackle of the fire, and to the sounds of Charlotte readin'.

And I remembered layin' there dyin', chokin' on my own blood next to the river, and the thought I'd had then came back to me now, too.

Nine-Fingered Nan hadn't taken everything from me.

And she hadn't killed me neither. I was still livin', and so was Charlotte, and so was Holt. Fer all the folk I'd murdered, and all that had happened to me, least I'd done that. Least I'd managed to keep those two safe.

I reached my left hand out weakly, carefully, gropin' till my fingers brushed Charlotte's sleeve.

She caught my hand, and I wrapped my fingers around her palm and gave it a squeeze.

She squeezed back.

XLV

LIVE SO THAT YOU MAY LIVE

It took a good few weeks to heal, all right. Just like Dr. Balogh had said.

By the time I was able to get up and around without swoonin' or collapsin' into a mess of hurt, autumn had come and nearly gone in Akansa, and winter was drawin' nearer than I liked. The hired guns from the east had finally given up on bringin' Charlotte back to her father and departed on their mended airship two weeks past, though not without quite a fuss.

They'd been furious and appalled when they'd learned Charlotte had watched over me at the beginnin' of my healin' without a *chaperone*, as they said, and had thereafter insisted one of 'em stay with her at all times if she were ever gonna be sittin' with me.

It was the most ridiculous thing I'd ever seen, them watchin' over her carefully as a nanny might a child, and most times glarin' at me through narrowed eyes, too. No matter that I was mostly hardly conscious and couldn't get off the bed without feelin' like I'd got shot all over again.

And when she'd still refused to accompany 'em back to Pennsylvania later, I thought there might be another gunfight. I'd been half-healed at that point, able to hobble around fer brief periods, and all the shoutin' and arguin' had roused me enough to open the door of my temporary housin' and check on things.

In the end, Charlotte had hidden away in the power station's cave, and none of her father's men could find her. Neither Dr. Balogh nor the Seers nor myself would help 'em locate her, and their resultin' threats were not taken kindly. They were driven back to their airship under a whole lot of arrows, a few warnin' shots from pistols, and a flock of mechanical birds Dr. Balogh had been tinkerin' with. I'd been hopin' the doc had had some of those poisonous bees to use on 'em by that point ... but no such luck.

They assured Dr. Balogh—and anyone else nearby enough in the forest to hear their shoutin'—that Senator Harrison had promised to disown his daughter if she did not return with 'em, and that meant no more future estate and no more money.

Apparently, Charlotte cared not one bit.

I was beginnin' to see why she'd come back west now.

It was only later, after Charlotte had been informed that they'd finally departed and she'd rejoined us in the Oracle's little village, she told us she'd taken enough jewelry and other small valuables from her home on her way out here to provide her a decent livin' fer a good long while, anyway.

I imagined that was probably another reason her father had been so put out about her abrupt departure.

Holt had missed the commotion surroundin' the departure of the hired guns, bein' as he remained mighty uncomfortable with the Oracle and her people and spent most his time roamin' the woods in search of game and supplies, but he was there to hear Charlotte admit to stealin' from her own family, and he gave me a pointed look from across the fire.

Told you so, it said. *Told you she could be useful.*

I only pursed my lips and gave a little shake of my head.

I still didn't want Charlotte goin' with us anywhere, to do any of the usual things we did. I'd worked this hard to keep her outta any real danger again ... I weren't gonna willingly put her right back into it.

To my relief, Dr. Balogh and his family invited her to stay with them, and she was more than happy to accept their invitation. I didn't think she'd stopped porin' over those old journals since I'd woke up after thinkin' I was dead. And her eyes lit up any time the doc mentioned any of those metal contraptions he'd been workin' on. Given her upbringin', she already spoke what the doc called "the language of the Engineers", which was the language most of those movin' statues had been programmed to respond to. Apparently it was somethin' wealthy folk in the east often learned as children, though more as an academic curiosity than fer any practical use, but I'd never heard it used before. That's how she'd been able to talk to the demon-woman thing when it had first been comin' after us, and why Dr. Balogh had taken note of what was happenin' in that chamber in the first place.

She'd fit right in with the Balogh family. Would be happy stayin' with them. Happier than she ever musta been in the east.

Happier than she woulda been if she'd stayed to ride on with me and Holt.

I ignored the tightness in my throat at the thought. Tried to concentrate instead on figurin' out just what the hell I was gonna do now. I'd probably enjoyed these last few weeks a little too much, in truth. Despite all the pain, the frustratin' helplessness, the lengthy recovery, and the disturbingly close presence of the strange Oracle woman most times ... there was also almost a hypnotic, soothin' calm to the whole routine.

I usually didn't like stayin' in one place fer so long. Those three weeks waitin' on Nan in Bravebank had nearly driven me mad. But here ... this place was different. Tucked away far in the woods, away from outside pryin' ears and eyes, there weren't much chance of any law happenin' across us. Or any others who might be wantin' to collect on any of our bounties.

And despite the intense unpleasantness of her so-called *Judgement*, the Oracle and her people had been relatively benign and helpful durin' our stay with 'em. Holt remained highly suspicious, but I'd found myself beginnin' to relax.

Beginnin' to almost even trust 'em.

This place felt ... safe.

And that was a feelin' I didn't often have these days. Hadn't felt like I could afford to relax much ever since Mama and Pa had been murdered. There'd always been somethin' to concern myself with since: where the next meal was comin' from, where to find shelter, where to find work so I could earn some money fer travelin', who might be comin' to rob or murder me ... where was the next word about a girl named Ethelyn Delano.

And that was the worst part.

The fact I was feelin' safe at all. The fact I was here bein' tended to and patched up and fed ... and I'd even let myself enjoy it. I'd let that old sense of languid contentment slip in some days, especially lately when I was hurtin' less and wrapped in a fur blanket and set in front of the hearth to keep off the chill of the oncomin' winter. I'd let myself wallow in that feelin' some days.

But I didn't deserve it. None of it.

By all accounts, I shoulda died on that riverbank. That's what I deserved. Not to be resurrected to heal in relative comfort while Ethelyn was still a captive somewhere.

The news that she'd already left this continent had killed that obsessive, burnin' urgency once like a livin' thing inside me ... but now in its wake was only a cold vacancy. A feelin' of bein' completely lost. Overwhelmed at the notion of her bein' in a completely different country, at the number of possible countries she could have gone to, at how the hell I'd ever find out exactly where she might have gone, how I'd ever get there, how I'd ever find her if I did get there...

Senator Harrison's hired guns had never found Nine-Fingered Nan, either of her wagons, or her last remainin' lieutenant. There were accounts of more murders in the woods ... dead prospectors and travelers, and more robberies along the roads in the area as well. And Sheriff Reeves started sendin' out patrols and posses, but they were spread thin and nothin' much ever came outta 'em.

Coulda been Nan and her skeleton crew doin' the robbin' and murderin' ... or it coulda just been some desperate folk fightin' fer their chance at survival out here like all the rest of us.

Holt kept his eye on the papers when he could sneak up to the outskirts of Blackbird and snatch away a discarded one, but there was no mention of Nan appearin' in any nearby town. Or any town at all, fer that matter. In fact, after a few weeks, the *Blackbird Daily* started speculatin' that Nan's long-standin' reign of terror in the west might have even been collapsin'.

Seemed a few groups of her gang she'd left behind in various other footholds of hers were gettin' restless at her absence; had started fightin' amongst themselves and made the job of what law there was in the Territories a lot easier.

Maybe I'd killed her, after all.

Maybe she was nothin' more than bones even now, scattered by the wildlife and indiscernible from any of the other bones left behind by the *incident*.

I considered the notion as I helped gather firewood fer the village one chill mornin', all the dead leaves underfoot havin' a thin layer of frost atop 'em—the first frost of the year—and my breath cloudin' in the air. I was only gatherin' small stuff, no big logs and certainly no choppin' yet, doctor's orders, but it was a rhythmic chore that left plenty of time fer thinkin'.

And I was thinkin' it was time fer me to move on, whether Nine-Fingered Nan was dead or not. No matter what contentment I'd managed to find in this little cluster of haphazard log shacks populated by unstable, forest-dwellin' folk. No matter how safe it seemed.

That itch had started to come back now that I was feelin' more myself. The pervasive rot that always seemed to be eatin' away at me, no matter where I was or what I was doin'.

Guilt.

I shouldn't be here just livin' a simple life. I needed to be *out there*, doin' what I'd said I'd do nine years ago. Or at the very least, fulfillin' my promise to Nine-Fingered Nan.

I'd told her I'd destroy everythin' she had if she didn't give me my sister.

Seemed far past time to start deliverin' on that promise ... even if she weren't around to know about it.

A week later and I was saddlin' Joe up in the cold of pre-dawn, a lantern set on a nearby tree stump makin' just enough light fer me to see by. After almost a decade in the desert, I'd also forgotten how cold a winter could get. And it had only just begun.

I hadn't had any suitable warm clothes no more, so Dr. Balogh and the Oracle's flock had generously donated a coat to me and Holt both so we wouldn't freeze in the swiftly coolin' weather.

I pulled the wool-lined collar up to shield my neck and retrieved Joe's bridle, warmin' the bit in my hand before slidin' it into his mouth. The saddle had been a bit tricky to work with; throwin' it up onto his back had stretched muscles in my chest that were still tender and reluctant to work that hard just yet. But there were no more stitches, and the scars were only faint now, and there weren't generally any more pain unless it came from the nightmares.

Once Joe was ready, I re-checked everything to be sure it was all in order. It'd been a spell since I'd ridden out, and I almost felt outta practice already. Satisfied as I could be fer the moment, I caught up Joe's reins and grabbed the lantern, and turned to see a person standin' there.

He caught me so much by surprise I jumped backward and fell right into Joe's shoulder, blurtin' a few good curses under my breath. The mule blew a snort and then nickered softly, and I raised the lantern to better illuminate the man's face.

Holt squinted in the light. "Think sittin' around here so long has dulled yer senses some, kid. I weren't even tryin' to be all that quiet."

I gave a grunt, steppin' away from the mule to blow out a breath of my own and resume my walk toward the edge of the Oracle's small settlement. Holt had been campin' outside of the village, even despite the worsenin' weather, but he was suspiciously fully clothed and kitted up already, boots and guns and all. "Why are you even awake?"

He fell into step beside me. "Had to take a piss. Saw the light and figured no one who was up to any good should be up this early. Then I saw you saddlin' up, figured you thought you could sneak off without havin' to say any goodbyes."

I shrugged. "That ... that was the plan, yeah."

"Uh huh. Well come on, then. We'd better get goin' 'fore you wake up anyone else."

"*We?*"

"You think I wanna stay here with that crazy old woman any longer? Hell no."

I stopped walkin', considerin', then turned to face him. "I don't even know where I'm goin' or what I'm doin' yet, Holt."

He shrugged, a cloud of breath foggin' around his head. "And when exactly has that ever mattered? C'mon, I'm freezin'. I wanna get movin'." He turned to trudge back toward his camp, and I followed more outta habit than anythin' else. As we got closer, I saw he'd already packed up and saddled his gelding.

I frowned as he mounted up. "You were gonna leave today, too?"

He reined around to face me with a snort. "Naw. I just saw you fixin' to leave and packed up myself." A wry smile parted his scraggly gray beard. "Think sittin' around here so long has slowed you up some, too. Got myself ready to go in about half the time it took you to saddle the mule."

I scowled at him. "Yeah, well ... I almost got shot through the heart, ya know. That takes its toll on a fella."

"So I've heard." He sobered some and sighed, glancin' toward the ramshackle village we'd just left behind. "Look, kid. You seem awful happy here ... 'specially when you started feelin' better. Don't think I've ever seen you lookin' so peaceful. I know this ain't much of a life, but it's more than I could ever give ya. It's more like what you grew up with, ain't it? And I think ... I think it's more of what you really want. Seein' Death up close and personal like that tends to let a man know real fast what he really wants." He grunted and shook his head. "Trust me, I know. Seen it myself. So what I'm tryin' to say is ... maybe you should stay. Maybe this time ... maybe this time you don't need to ride off."

Maybe you don't need to ride off...

Fer an instant, the pull to stay put fer once was so strong it brought a sour taste to my mouth. To have a home, even if borrowed, and many more days around a roarin' hearth listenin' to the quiet sounds of Charlotte readin'...

But then I swallowed. Pushed through it. Shook my head. "I ... I can't. I can't stay."

Holt sat quiet fer a minute, and Joe nosed at my elbow, wonderin' why we were just standin' around. "You sure?" Holt asked. "I had to watch yer pa search fer his salvation, remember. He searched fer it awful hard ... but in the end I think he found it with yer ma, and with you kids. Think that's why he left everythin' else behind. And I was sore about it, sure ... but he was happy there. Just 'cause I ain't found my place yet don't mean he didn't find his. And don't mean you ain't found yers. If you wanna stay..."

"No," I said, quick before the temptation could rise again. I put out the lantern and set it over at the base of a nearby tree. Someone would find it later. Then I swung up onto Joe and gathered my reins. "I ain't stayin'."

Holt lifted one bushy eyebrow. "Still ain't punished yerself enough, eh? Fer Chrissakes, kid, ya almost took a bullet to the heart! You sure it's worth it? Sure it's worth leavin' all this behind?"

I glared at him steadily, then took one last look over my shoulder before nudgin' Joe forward. "It's a crazy old woman and her lot of backwoods folk. Ain't nothin' I can't do without."

Holt prodded his gelding after me. "*And* the doctor who saved yer life—twice."

Three times, in truth. There was the time in the cave he'd stopped the automatons from tearin' me and Charlotte apart. But Holt hadn't yet heard all of that story, and I didn't mention it now, neither.

"*And* the pretty girl you like. And I think she likes you, too."

That sour taste rose in my mouth again. "She deserves a lot better than me," I muttered.

Holt scoffed. "And yer ma deserved a lot better than yer pa, believe you me. But that didn't stop *him*, did it?"

I clenched my jaw and said nothin', dislikin' the route of this discussion.

Holt came to ride beside me, but at my continued silence got the hint, and finally let it go with a heavy sigh. "Fine. Fine. Well then, the least you can do is take this."

I glanced at him to see him holdin' out pa's sixshooter again. The silver platin' was impossibly bright even in the muted light of early dawn. I rolled my eyes, but he pushed on.

"I tried shootin' it, Van. It's what I used when I managed to track you down at the mill. Emptied it at Nan and her man … but it just don't feel right. It ain't mine. It's supposed to be yers." He extended his arm, so the thing was nearly in my lap.

I pulled Joe to a halt and Holt did the same, and then I sat there starin' down at the pistol. There was a phrase elegantly scrolled along the barrel that I hadn't noticed before: *Vive ut vivas*. I had no idea what that meant, but I knew sure enough what all the tally marks over the rest of it meant.

My right holster currently held the gun meant fer my left, and the left was empty. I'd put the smaller sixgun meant fer my leg holster back into its hidden compartment, and the doc had refilled those little bags of medicines again, bein' that they'd deployed when Nan had shot me. The leg was all put together and whole again like the rest of me, but I was still missin' a gun.

I'd planned to run through a town later, once I was far from Blackbird and Sheriff Reeves, and pick up another one.

But then, here was pa's. I swallowed again and lifted it from Holt's palm.

It was hefty, heavier than the pistols I usually preferred. I let my reins drop over my saddle horn and turned it over in my hands, studyin' it. Feelin' all the little grooves of the tally marks beneath my fingertips. There was some empty space along the frame.

Room fer more notches.

"Holt … was it Nan who came after us? Who murdered Mama and Pa and burned everything?"

He shrugged. "I dunno, kid. I weren't there. You didn't see her?"

I shook my head. I hadn't seen the person doin' the murderin'. I'd been in the back room with Mama and Ethelyn. We'd only heard the shot, seen the results of it. "Papers said it was some of Paul's gang," I said.

Holt nodded. "Coulda been. Or it coulda been Nan, too. Like I told you before … she hated him most of all, seemed like."

"She told me at the river she was the one who destroyed his life. Destroyed his family. Took everything from him."

Holt's face went hard. "Then it sure sounds like it was her, all right."

My right hand tightened around the pistol's ivory grip. "She said it was revenge."

"Fer losin' her finger?"

"She didn't specify."

"That's a lotta rage over a finger."

It was. A whole family and their livelihood destroyed. Well, maybe Holt was right. Maybe it was only right I finished takin' down all the rest of what Nan had built, and did it usin' pa's pistol. I pulled mine from the right holster and moved it back where it belonged on the left, then settled the big forty-four at my right hip. "I'm gonna take it all down, Holt."

"Didn't expect anythin' less of ya, kid. I knew what was in yer head just as soon as I saw you saddlin' up."

"Then why'd you try to get me to stay?"

"Ain't I always been here to talk some sense into ya? I had to try, at least."

I grunted. *Sense* is what he called it, huh? I tugged my hat down a little lower. "Right. Sure. All right, then. Let's go." I spurred Joe onward. He leapt into a brisk trot, headin' away into the woods.

Holt followed, and we made a trail through the frost goin' westward, our backs to the risin' sun.

EPILOGUE

THE SHADOW

They had been following her for quite some time. Four of them.

But the dark and the drizzling rain and the hood of the cloak she currently clutched around herself made it impossible to properly identify them. Some of Yamamoto's men, maybe, come to retrieve her despite the old man's claims she was not his property? Despite his assurance that she now had the freedom to roam about the city as she pleased—though he strongly recommended she take along one of his guides, of course.

But no. If they had been some of Yamamoto's, surely they would have caught up to her already and announced themselves. They wouldn't have been lurking around back there, slowly creeping closer and closer like maybe they thought she wouldn't notice they'd been tailing her since she'd reached the city's outskirts.

Ethelyn pulled her cloak tighter around herself and stole another glance at them in the reflection of a shop window. She'd been through enough rough territories in her life to spot when a person was following her; had been attacked and robbed and swindled enough to know when a person meant trouble.

These four meant trouble.

And all she had on her for weapons was a pair of those wooden sticks the people of this country commonly ate with and the single filigree butterfly hairpin currently nestled into the coils of her dark locks.

She cursed her impulsive foolishness. She knew better than this. She knew better than to walk into a potentially dangerous situation unarmed and unprepared. She hadn't been this careless in years. But the invitation of freedom, the chance to leave Yamamoto's manor, the opportunity to test all of his claims that she was not property, not a slave or even a servant, had been too much.

As soon as he'd announced to all of his newest arrivals that they were free to do as they wished, even leave if they wanted—while always having a home at his estate, should they wish to return—she had fled.

And sure enough, none of his black-clad guards with their ever-stoic expressions and double swords at the hip had lifted a finger to stop her. Or to stop any of those who had left along with her.

But they had all gone their separate ways not long after reaching the end of Yamamoto's long drive, and eventually she'd found herself in the depths of a strange and unfamiliar city, completely and utterly lost.

Now night had fallen, and darkness shrouded already unknown streets. There were more buildings and lights and people crowded together here than she'd ever seen before, and the reflections thrown back from rain-slicked edifices and pools in the narrow dirt corridors only made everything more disorienting and confusing.

This city, this place ... there were so many *people*. And so many *machines* ... they rumbled in the sky, growled down the wider roads, and whirred and clanked from the doorways of shops.

It was all nearly overwhelming. Oppressive. Suffocating.

She couldn't read any of the signs, couldn't understand or speak the language, had no idea where she was going or even where she was. She had no money, and hardly a thing to trade. And the more she kept twisting and turning down side streets and back alleys and dodging through the thick presses of people in efforts to lose the men following her, the more lost and turned around she became.

She shouldn't have left Yamamoto's place so soon. She should have stayed longer, even with as stifling as it was ... she should have stayed to *learn*.

Stupid, Ethelyn. You know better than this. Why didn't you think this through?

She'd have to deal with her tail. Better to get them out of the way so she could think clearly and maybe find a safe place to bed down for the night. Better to confront them on her own terms, rather than wait until *they* finally decided to strike.

She stepped abruptly off into another side alley, then threw back the hood of her cloak and turned her face to the sky, closing her eyes as the cold drizzle hit her bared skin like so many tiny, pricking needles. She pressed her back up against the wooden side wall of a shop. Inhaled deeply through her nose, then exhaled explosively through her teeth and pulled the hairpin free, shaking her head as her long locks tumbled free around her shoulders.

Here goes nothing.

She'd die before she let anyone else drag her back into captivity. It would either be her or them bleeding out in the rain tonight. Her right hand tightened around the end of the hairpin, the points of the butter-fly's wings digging painfully into her palm.

The first of the four men rounded the corner into the alley's shadows, hooded in a dark cloak, his face hidden.

But it didn't matter. Ethelyn still had a pretty good idea of where his eyes should be. She brought the sharp end of the hairpin up and around in a flat arc, sending a quick stab into the darkness beneath the rim of the hood.

She caught him completely by surprise, and the pin stuck into flesh, all right. The man shrieked and recoiled with a jerk, his hands flying up to cover his shrouded face as he reeled backwards.

The other three men rushed up behind him, drawing weapons that were much more deadly than Ethelyn's meager pin.

Her heart picked up pace at the dim glint of their long knives in the rain, and she took a few steps deeper into the alley as they looked quickly over their injured companion and then lifted glares in her direction.

One snarled something she couldn't understand, then lunged at her.

She ducked away from him, jabbing outward with her pin again. But she only snagged the wide sleeve of his *kimono* this time, and he caught her in the temple with the hilt of his knife.

Stars burst across her vision and Ethelyn stumbled, right into the arms of one of the other men. She felt strong hands around her arms, fingers digging painfully into her biceps, but she dropped down quickly to her knees and twisted her body violently, managing to wrench herself out of his grip. She rolled, jumped to her feet, and tore off her cloak, heavy and clinging with wet.

The three men encircled her. The fourth was leaning against a wall hunched over, one hand over his face, and in the guttering glow from distant lamps she saw the dark spread of blood all down his cheek.

Good. She pulled the wooden eating sticks from a pocket in her sleeve and circled to face the three remaining in turn, baring her teeth like some feral animal, wielding her makeshift weapons as if they were blades themselves.

The three men, all dressed in dark, simple garb, only laughed. One said something to the others, and though she couldn't decipher his words, his tone was clear enough. Derisive, dismissive, arrogant.

She caught a glimpse of his grin beneath his hood ... wanted to stab the haughty expression right off his face.

Only before she could make a move, something darker than a shadow dropped down soundlessly behind him.

He must have seen her expression change. His smirk faded, and he turned to follow the shift of her eyes.

Too late.

Another, much longer blade flashed, and the man's head separated neatly from his body.

Ethelyn jumped back as the other two whirled, and one shouted in alarm. They were dispatched as quickly as the first, spurts of blood staining the rainwater red at her feet as they fell.

The fourth man, still holding his face and woozy near the wall, never got a chance to see his death coming. The sword pierced his back and came out his front, right through his heart.

He sagged and choked on blood, and then the shadow planted a boot against his rear to yank the sword free, and the would-be assailant crumpled to the mud alongside his fellows.

The shadow turned to face her then, and she saw he wasn't really a shadow at all. Just dressed all in black, wearing the traditional garb most people here wore, only with pants instead of a skirt. His smooth black hair was shoulder-length, but half had been pulled back into a knot at the back of his head. And he wore proper boots instead of sandals. If only she could have had some proper boots herself...

In the darkness, his pale face almost seemed to glow, his dark eyes calm and quiet and not at all alarmed by the beheaded bodies at his feet, or by the streams of blood lapping at the soles of his shoes.

Ethelyn had braced herself to run, to turn and flee the alley and lose herself in the crowd of people again, not convinced at all this shadow had come to rescue her, but suspecting instead he was just another who meant her harm. Only then he sheathed his sword, and she realized with a start he had two. Two swords. On his left hip, and dressed all in black ... just like Yamamoto's guards...

She narrowed a glare at him. "I knew it. I knew Yamamoto's freedom was just a lie!"

He blinked once. "It is not."

His use of English took her by surprise and she rocked backwards, blinking herself. Only Yamamoto and very few of his staff knew English. She'd certainly never heard one of his guards speak it. She spluttered for a return retort. "Then ... then why are you here? Why are you *following* me?"

In answer, he merely spread his hands, indicating the corpses bleeding out beneath them.

Ethelyn swallowed. "I could have managed."

This time he tilted his head a fraction to the left, and one corner of his full lips twitched. "Certainly not."

She didn't need his skepticism. Or his protection. Or ... why-ever else he might be here. She whirled away from him and stalked back out of the alley, tucking both the eating sticks and the hairpin into her sleeve pocket, her sandals sinking and sliding in the muddy street.

She was soaked through now, having discarded her cloak, but she didn't care. It was chilly, especially with the rain, but nothing compared to the winters of Colorado or Kansas. She'd manage just fine till she found some kind of shelter. She only needed a safe, dry place to stay for the night. And in the morning, she'd decide what to do next.

"You should have taken a guide."

Ethelyn jolted to a stop and whirled again at the voice. It was him, the shadow ... but when she turned, he wasn't there.

She frowned.

"It is unsafe for you to wander alone."

She whipped back to the front only to see him standing there, so close she recoiled and instinctively reached into her sleeve pocket for her hairpin. But just as quick as she pulled it out, he caught her wrist in a grip like steel, and she gasped despite herself.

"Yamamoto can teach you," he said simply.

Ethelyn tried to yank her wrist free, but to no avail. "If it is unsafe," she finally said through gritted teeth, "then why did he tell us we could go? *Without* a guide if we so wished?"

Now he smiled, and the expression softened the severe lines of his face in a way that almost made him attractive. Almost. He let go of her wrist abruptly. "Yamamoto believes his students should learn their own lessons."

"I am not his student," Ethelyn snarled, and she stepped around him to continue on her way, marching briskly down the road.

"Are you not?" he asked at her shoulder.

She turned to snap at him, but he was gone again. Her steps faltered briefly, but she shook off the unease and kept on going, trying to recover her wits. She still gripped the butterfly pin in her right hand. Kept scanning the crowd for further threats. He *had* been real, hadn't he? Surely she hadn't imagined those other men getting their heads chopped off...

"My name is Takumi."

She yelped and jumped sideways as he appeared at her left elbow. And then, to her irritation, he fell into step beside her, easily keeping pace with her angry march.

"I know what you are feeling," he said quietly. "I remember it well myself. It is hard to know when you can stop running. Hard to know who to fight."

"I'm not running," Ethelyn snapped. "And I know exactly who to fight."

Takumi only let out a little grunt.

There was silence between them for a while, and Ethelyn wished he'd leave her alone already. She had half a mind to dodge off through the crowds and twisting side streets again, like she had before in attempts to lose those other unsavory men who'd been following her, but she had a good idea even her best efforts at losing this particular man would prove futile.

So she just kept walking, staring straight ahead, and decided to ignore him. Maybe if she ignored him for long enough, he would understand she didn't want—or need—his company. Or his opinion. On anything.

But eventually, he cleared his throat and spoke again. "My parents died when I was young. My uncle took me in after that, then sold me when I was ten. I ... I did not go to Yamamoto first."

Ethelyn slowed her pace, watching him from the corner of her eye. His jaw clenched, muscles rippling along his cheek. His dark eyes shifted away from her, into the distance. And she felt a pang of grief herself.

Ten. When her own parents had died ... when her own brother had abandoned her...

She swallowed back bile.

"Yamamoto saved me. Taught me many things. Gave me the skills to take back my life." Takumi's left hand went to rest atop one of his sword hilts, and his gaze lit with fire as he turned to look at her again. "To deal with men such as those who attacked you in that alley. Would you not like to take back your life?"

Ethelyn squinted at him. She wasn't entirely sure he was being genuine. Not entirely sure this wasn't some kind of elaborate ruse. Some kind of trick to lure her back to Yamamoto's manor, into some kind of captivity disguised as the greater good ... she'd seen such things done before to others. Had almost fallen victim to it herself a time or two.

And one of those times had got her cousin killed.

Ethelyn stopped walking and turned to face him. Around them, the rest of the pedestrians continued on their business, flowing like one great river of bodies back and forth and between. Overhead, a pot-bellied machine made of copper whirred by, making her momentarily flinch. But she kept her eyes locked on Takumi. "What do you think I'm doing right now?" she asked.

He arched an eyebrow. "Wandering in circles?"

She scoffed, rolled her eyes, and marched onward.

He followed.

"I'm taking back my life."

"How?"

"By getting out of here."

"How?"

She gritted her teeth, fingers tightening around the hairpin. "I'll find a way. I always do. I'm going home."

"You don't have a home."

The words seared through her like fire. Rage surged hot and sudden, and she struck out quick as a snake with that hairpin, aiming for his chest.

Her wrist struck his forearm instead, her hand going numb, the pin flinging from her fingers. His fist hit her in the sternum in the next instant and crushed the air out of her, and then she was rolling over wet cobblestones, the startled cries of passersby echoing out into the evening's bustle.

She laid there choking for air as the rain pelted her face; struggled up to her hands and knees as Takumi approached, but there were little black spots floating in her vision, and her lungs felt crushed.

She noticed how no one else seemed eager to come to her aid. Noticed how they all passed wide around her—and especially *him*—scurried by with averted eyes and whispers to each other.

She almost expected him to behead her now, too. But instead, he held down a hand.

She only glared up at him.

"This district is not safe for foreigners to wander unescorted," he said gently. "That is why Yamamoto sent me, and my brothers and sisters, to watch after his fleeing flock. But if you do not wish to return to him, he will not make you. And neither will I. You may send me away, continue on as you are, and see how long you last. Or you may come with me, and I will show you the way back. I will show you how to take back your life. I will show you how to walk any street, anywhere, without fear. That is the gift Yamamoto has given me. And I think it is a gift you would very much like as well." He took another step closer, reached his hand a little lower. The rain ran in rivulets down his face and dripped off his fingers. "You have no home," he repeated. "But you could."

Ethelyn eyed his outstretched hand. The tightness in her chest had begun to ease now, and she gulped air hungrily, her fingers digging into the cracks of the cobblestones. Could he possibly be telling the truth?

What if she *could* move like he did? Drop from the sky ... vanish and reappear seemingly at will ... wield a sword? She wondered if he might be any good at firearms, too. At least *that* she was fair skilled at already herself.

She had just scolded herself for her impulsive foolishness at leaving Yamamoto's manor too soon. Told herself she should have stayed longer to *learn*. Maybe she could still do that. Learn the language and the customs of this unfamiliar country, and maybe a lot more than that, a lot more *useful* talents, too, if Takumi could be trusted.

At the very least she would have a safe and dry place to stay the night, and more time to develop a smarter, better plan of escape if it turned out he was being less than truthful...

She hesitated for another long moment, but Takumi simply waited.

He watched her, deep brown eyes soft and patient, and made no other demands or arguments.

So at last she sighed, set her jaw, and reached out to take his hand.

THE END

THE
BLACKBIRD
DAILY

25c

MASSACRE AT THE MILL

BLACKBIRD, ARKANSA, OCTO-BER 8 – A scene of unspeakable horror has unfolded at the old saw mill a day's ride out from Blackbird as flames danced against the twilight sky, drawing the attention of lawmen and townsfolk alike. What they discovered upon arrival was a ghastly tableau of death and chaos: twenty-two bodies strewn across the forest floor and the riverbank, with several dead horses nearby, all victims of a violent shootout that sent ripples of fear through the community.

The charred remains of the mill, now but a smoldering ruin, were the site of what appears to be a calculated ambush against the notorious outlaw queen of the Western Territories herself, Nine-Fingered Nan, and her infamous gang. Authorities were left aghast at the brutal scene, with Sheriff Madeleine Reeves stating, "This is a tragedy of unimaginable proportions. We are fortunate the flames did not spread, but the loss of life is beyond reckoning."

Initial investigations suggest that the dead are likely members of Nan's crew, long feared and loathed throughout the region. However, the identity of the assailant – or assailants – remains shrouded in mystery, leaving the law at a loss. How such an audacious attack could be launched against the infamous outlaw Nan and her band of miscreants is a question that looms large. Sheriff Reeves is urging any townsfolk or travelers who may possess knowledge regarding this horrific event to come forth. "We must uncover the truth behind this massacre," she implored. "It is crucial to determine whether this murderer is a friend or foe to the good people of Blackbird." In a bid to gather information, the sheriff has announced a handsome reward for anyone who can provide leads related to the attack. As word of the massacre spreads, tension hangs heavy in the air of this fair town, with many fearing that a new and deadly player may have entered the game… one capable of taking down even the most terrible of outlaws.

As the coroner continues to examine the bodies, the people of Blackbird are left with more questions than answers. The shadow of violence looms ever larger, and the townsfolk can only wait and wonder who will strike next in this perilous game of survival…

READ ON

FOR A SNEAK PEEK…

THE LEGACY OF LUCKY LOGAN
BOOK 4

A PICK AND A SPADE

It took a good long while to dig a grave big enough fer a full-grown man ... took even longer when you were diggin' it all by yerself and had only a pick and a spade to do it with.

And even longer still when that grave you were diggin' was meant to be yer own.

But I'd always been more stubborn than impatient, and so I'd set myself on a nearby boulder, lit a cigarillo, and watched the man work under the light of the full moon. He could take all night if he wanted. I didn't mind. The grave would be dug and he'd be goin' into it one way or another, whether it took him hours or days.

Although I didn't think his friend was gonna last much longer.

The second man was laid out at my feet, all bloodied up and with wrists and ankles bound. I'd had to beat on him awful hard to get him and the one diggin' to share their secrets ... but they'd cracked eventually. Most did, in the end. I'd worked my way up Nine-Fingered Nan's chain of command a long way over the last few years, and these fellas here were some of the last few left.

Lieutenants.

The folks I'd been workin' toward trackin' all this time.

It was sometimes slow work, but it always paid off.

Just like this time.

I took a long draw on the cigarillo, and the end of it flared a bright, burnin' red in the darkness. I savored the taste of it fer a spell, then exhaled a cloud of smoke.

The fella diggin' his own grave kept eyein' me sideways. I had a notion he hadn't yet given up on the idea he might yet best me somehow, or maybe at least get away with his life. So the next time he glanced my way, I bit down on the end of my light and grinned at him, givin' him a little salute before pattin' the silver-plated .44 restin' on my right hip.

He scowled and went quick back to diggin'.

His only escape tonight was gonna be a fast death. I'd promised him at least that much fer all the helpful information he'd given me. And I'd let him have that, sure, long as he kept on diggin' that hole and didn't try nothin' stupid.

A ways off, coyotes yipped and howled, but they'd been gradually gettin' closer and closer all night. They smelled blood.

My mule Joe roused from where he dozed a few yards away and pricked his ears in that direction.

I lifted an eyebrow and shook my head, pluckin' my light from my mouth to cluck my tongue at the fella laborin' at the hole. "Might wanna hurry it up, Mister. You don't get yer friend here six feet under soon, those coyotes just might make off with him." I stuck the cigarillo back between my teeth and chewed on the end of it as I gave him another grin. "Course, if they *do* come fer him, well, I ain't gonna stop 'em. Are you?"

He was down on his hands and knees, scoopin' out handfuls of sandy dirt with the spade, but he paused at my question and sat back on his heels. Even in the moonlight I could see the shine of sweat and streaks of grit on his skin, the damp that soaked his shirtfront, and the glare he fixed me with now coulda flayed a man.

But I only kept smilin' at him.

Then, suddenly, he quirked a smile himself and snorted a laugh. "Look at you ... awful proud of yerself, ain't you? Sittin' there smug as a goddamn cat that's got the cream. You think you've accomplished somethin' here? Think you've made a difference?"

"Oh, I've made a difference, all right."

He laughed again. "That so? And what, exactly, have you accomplished then? Huh?"

I pulled my right pistol and he flinched. But I didn't plan to shoot him with it. Yet. Instead I just turned it over in my hands, my fingertips runnin' over the multitude of tally marks etched into it. There had been some empty space along the frame when the gun had first come into my possession, when I'd finally accepted it at Holt's repeated urgin'.

But now ... now there weren't no blank space left. "Well, let's see..." I pretended to count those dark etches in the silver, though there weren't no real need fer it. I already knew exactly how many there were. Exactly how many my own pa had put there, and exactly how many I'd added myself.

Fer the benefit of this particular discussion, however, I only counted the new ones.

"Seems I've put thirty-six of Nan's crew in the ground thus far," I commented mildly, liftin' my eyes to the fella by the hole again. "You'll make thirty-seven, and yer friend here thirty-eight." I kicked his boot, but he didn't so much as stir or even grunt. Unconscious ... or maybe already dead. "Not sure I got any more room on this here pistol to accommodate yer notches." I held it up fer him to see more clearly, and the silver gleamed in the moon's white light.

I always made sure to keep it polished. Just like pa had done, and then Holt after him.

"But then, I guess that's what I got this one fer, ain't it?" I patted at the pistol on my left hip. I'd sprung fer one to match pa's awhile ago, havin' disliked the imbalance of my old .38 sixgun alongside pa's old .44, so now I had two silver-plated, ivory handled .44s, and I guessed it was about time to start addin' notches to the second one.

The man's jaw clenched, and some of the amusement went outta his face. His throat bobbed as he swallowed. "Guess you're too young to remember how the Territories used to be," he growled. "Before Nine-Fingered Nan came along. You think things were bad under her rule here?" He scoffed. "Boy, you ain't seen nothin'. Boss brought order and structure and *economy* to the Territories, you understand? Things here used to be chaos. Petty thieves and bandits all over the roads. Hardly an honest trade to be made anywhere. Folk bein' murdered on the daily. You want to go back to that? That really what you're tryin' to do?"

I narrowed my glare at him, puffin' at my cigarillo a few more times before stubbin' it out against the side of the boulder I perched upon and then flickin' it at the unconscious fella at my feet. "Look, Mister, I don't give two shits about the Territories, all right? I couldn't care less what happens to 'em. All I know is I made Nan a promise ... and I promised her I'd destroy everythin' she'd built. So that's what I'm doin', and I'm gonna continue to do it until it's all gone. All of it. All her order and structure and *economy*—I'm erasin' all of it. You understand?"

He glared at me flatly fer a long, silent moment, and the frantic cries of those coyotes rose to fill the quiet.

"What you're doin' is suicide," he finally said, hardly audible over the coyotes. "You realize that? If Nan don't get you for this, then all the rest who's been waitin' for the Territories to open up again is gonna do it. Maybe the *demon* you pretend to be has had a good run ... but you can't fight 'em all."

I gave him another smile and stood from my seat, pa's old gun still gripped loose in my hand. "Now, now, Mister. You've really gotta work on yer threats. I won't *have* to fight 'em all. That's what those fine Eckerton fellas are for, yeah? I'll leave the clean-up of the rest of the Territories in their very capable hands."

The Eckertons. A full-fledged, federally backed organization these days, and very capable, all right. *Too* capable, if you asked me. More than once now they'd gotten in my way, spoiled my plans, hauled off one of Nan's people to face proper justice before I could enact my own kind. Even the thought of 'em now heated my blood, and my fingers tightened around my pistol grip, my left hand ballin' into a fist.

And then came the other thought that always followed my acknowledgement of that particular brand of lawmen: Charlotte.

Charlotte Harrison.

It was her senator father who had lobbied fer the Eckertons' creation in the first place, after all.

But I'd left her ... left her behind five years ago when Holt and I had ridden out from that makeshift village of so-called Seers. And I hadn't seen her since.

Had a pile of letters from her, ones she sent every now and then to the Grave Gulch post office, but those had been comin' less and less frequently of late.

And I'd stopped goin' to our camp in those hills a long time ago, too worried I'd show up there one day to find her waitin' fer me, demandin' to know why I'd left without a goodbye all those years ago, demandin' to know why I couldn't even be bothered to send a letter back.

But I couldn't risk it. Couldn't face her. Couldn't afford to have her along with me fer any of this business here, and didn't have the time or the energy to fight with her over it if she insisted. And I had a good idea she would insist.

I swallowed, flooded briefly by memories of my time healin' in that village, rememberin' still much too clearly the periods of comfort and contentment, two things I never shoulda allowed myself ... two things I surely hadn't deserved.

Not then, not now.

That sour taste rose in my mouth again and I scowled as I shook myself free of the memories, the regrets ... that goddamned *longin'* ... and turned the full of my attention back on the man kneelin' by the half-dug grave. "And as fer Nan," I growled. Sayin' her name helped me re-focus. Helped harden over that brief bubble of feelin'. "As fer her, well, I figure it'll be mighty hard fer her to do anything about me wreckin' her business, considerin' she's dead and all."

That grin of his came back, his teeth gleamin' dully in the moonlight. And then he threw back his head and laughed.

I waited fer him to expend his amusement. The higher-ups in Nan's extensive web across the Territories often reacted like this when I told 'em their boss was dead. The lower grunts, the expendables, and those less loyal, on the other hand, they tended to agree with me. Tended to think the once-infamous Nine-Fingered Nan was either dead or had abandoned 'em fer some other enterprise elsewhere, and they were mighty resentful of her fer either. When I'd first started out on this venture, it'd almost been too easy to get 'em to turn on her.

But now ... now it was gettin' more and more difficult.

I'd started findin' all her most loyal dogs now ... and they were loathe to admit the outlaw queen they'd followed all this time, had admired fer so long—worshipped, even, seemed like sometimes—was gone.

But gone she was.

Nearly five years now I'd spent eradicatin' her people, her deals, her trades, her establishments, her businesses ... if she were still alive, if she was anywhere this earthly news could travel to her waitin' ears, she woulda never let me get away with any of that.

She woulda found me after that first night I'd burned down one of her brothels and strung up the people of hers who'd been runnin' it, aimin' to finish what she'd started alongside that abandoned mill down by Blackbird.

But ... she hadn't.

Five whole years now, and not a peep from her. Not even so much as a note, or an indirect message from any of her other lackeys.

Nine-Fingered Nan was gone.

As unsatisfyin' as it had been in the end—and ever-lovin' *painful*, considerin' the bullet that'd almost gone right through my heart—it seemed I'd managed to end Nan's reign at the Massacre at the Mill, after all.

I stood a little straighter at the thought. Whatever else I'd done or hadn't done in my life, or couldn't have 'cause of this, or given up fer doin' this, or lost 'cause of that old hag ... that fact alone made all of it at least a little more bearable.

The man by the hole meant to be his grave was still laughin', but there was a high edge to it now, makin' him sound almost manic.

I sighed and took a few steps toward him, but he didn't stop laughin'. Now I was startin' to get annoyed. "I suppose yer gonna tell me she ain't dead?"

"She ain't!" he managed to choke.

"Uh huh. And I suppose yer also gonna tell me she's gonna come back someday? Come back with..." I waved my empty left hand in the air, tryin' to remember what the other lieutenants had claimed. "I dunno ... somethin' or other that's gonna make all the Independent Americas kneel at her feet?"

"She is!"

I rolled my eyes. "Right. I've heard it all before, fella. But you know what? All this time I've been tearin' down what she built and murderin' all her loyal dogs and she ain't yet raised one finger to stop me. You tell me … if she were alive … you think she ever woulda allowed any of that?"

His snickerin' finally subsided enough fer him manage a complete sentence. "Oh, she's got bigger fish to fry these days, Delano. Everythin' you've done, what you think you've accomplished here … it ain't nothin' compared to what she's got comin'! She'll give ya what's comin' to ya soon enough, don't you worry about that. You'll be squashed under her boot like a bug, just like all the rest! Hell, the only reason you're breathin' even now is 'cause she thought she already killed ya!" His amusement turned into a sneer. "Heard you tried to pull on her, and she plugged you right in the heart. Left you bleedin' out on the riverbank and gapin' like a fish. Lucky Logan's brat, they said, ended just as easy as his pa, even after all the stories we always heard told about the indomitable Lucky Logan Delano."

He had to stop talkin' to laugh again, and I took another step toward him, my finger curlin' around my trigger. If he kept this up, I was gonna take back my promise of a quick death.

"But maybe he just passed all his luck on to you, huh?" he went on, once he caught his breath. "'Cause here you are, still alive despite it all. Guess maybe the boss shoulda blown your head off, instead, like what happened to your pa. Ain't no comin' back from that!"

The crack of my .44 echoed out across the desert, and the man gave a grunt as the bullet punched through his gut, his right hand droppin' the spade quick to cover the sudden bloom of blood.

Well hell. I hadn't really meant to shoot him; it'd just happened. A reflex. I was gettin' better about bein' so impulsive, but I guess sometimes the temptation to shut up a no-good sonuvabitch with a bullet was too much to resist.

"She didn't get me in the heart," I said, slow and quiet, walkin' a little closer, but mindful of the pick he still had at his disposal. "She missed her mark. And maybe you didn't hear, but I got her, too. Got her right in the gut, just like I got you now. And no one ever saw her again. She's dead, Mister. She's dead, and Lucky Logan's *brat* is the one who got her."

He gave another choked chuckle and shook his head. His left hand moved. I took a step back and lifted my pistol again, but he didn't go fer the pick. Instead, his fingers went to the top of his left boot and then emerged holdin' what looked like a small metal ball. I couldn't tell what it was, but he didn't do nothin' with it, only held it loose in his fist.

Except I'd seen enough alarmin' Old World contraptions made of metal to stay wary of it, and I switched my aim toward his hand ... just in case.

"We saw her," he panted, his voice now strained. "Me an' Bobby." He nodded toward the bound, unconscious man I'd left near the boulder. "She came back from Akansa, alive and well. Heard Long-Eye Harry managed to open that lockbox you brought her. And inside ... oh, inside there was a mighty fine treasure, all right. It was the last piece she needed."

His words made my skin prickle, although I was fair certain he was lyin'.

Mostly certain.

Except fer that little cold snake of fear that crawled up my throat. Fear that he might *not* be lyin'. Fear that Nine-Fingered Nan had had five whole years now to plan who knew what from God only knew where.

But no. So-called *bigger fish* or not ... she still woulda never let me wreck her business like I'd been doin' lately. This fella was lyin'. Tryin' to rile me up; feel like he had some kinda victory in these last moments of his life.

I still had my pistol pointed in his direction, and now I thumbed my hammer back. "I told you once and I'll tell you again: lyin' is only gonna make yer end more miserable."

"Think I'm lyin', huh? How much you willin' to bet on that?"

"Maybe you forgot that deal we made was dependent on you bein' forthcomin' with any information I happen to request outta you."

He glanced down to the blood that soaked his shirtfront and seeped between his fingers. "Maybe you forgot our deal entirely, considerin' you just gut-shot me."

I smiled at him, but even I could tell from the way it felt that it was more of a snarl. "Tell me what was in the lockbox then, and I'll still keep my end of the deal. Put my next bullet through yer skull instead of through yer knee."

The chorus of coyotes rose abruptly again around us. They were startin' to circle. Still out of sight, but real, real close.

Joe whickered nervously from behind me.

I ignored all of it, never breakin' eye contact with the fella on his knees.

He held my stare fer another long minute, then closed his left fist tight around that little metal ball. Bright blue light flared out between his fingers, but it was his last, lop-sided grin that made me twist away from him and leap fer cover—just as an explosion tore him apart.

AVAILABLE HERE!

https://jrfrontera.com/books/demon-at-devils-deep/

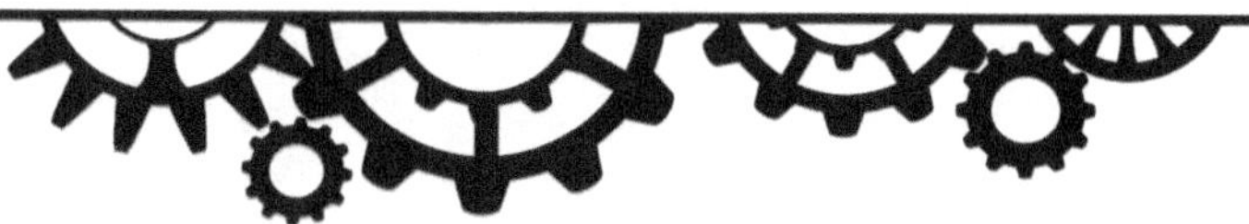

Don't forget, if you'd be so kind, to leave a review for this book on your favorite platform! The number of a book's reviews directly influences how visible the retail platform makes it to other readers! And leaving a few sentences about what you loved most about the book will help others decide whether or not this book might be for them, too! Also, you'll have my eternal gratitude!

The first three books of the Legacy of Lucky Logan series are also available in audiobook – narrated by none other than the amazingly talented Roger Clark (of Red Dead Redemption II fame)! Visit https://jrfrontera.com/allaudiobooks/ to learn more!

JOIN THE OUTLAW SYSTEMS...

EXCLUSIVE POSTCARD + PRIVATE GROUP INVITE

10% OFF
JRFRONTERA.COM/STORE

ABOUT THE AUTHOR

J. R. Frontera is an Outlaw Storyteller who dares to write the stories she personally loves most for the readers out there who are looking for something different, and not for the algorithms, sales numbers, or the most recent popular trend. She has been telling stories in some form or another since she could hold a crayon and draw, and her love of science fiction and fantasy originated with her early exposure to the worlds of Star Wars, Star Trek, Lord of the Rings, and Dune. Exploring the potential and pitfalls of humanity in future or fantastical worlds is a temptation she's just never been able to resist. She co-founded a local writing group known as The Wordwraiths in 2013 and is co-owner of their publishing imprint Wordwraith Books and their newly minted entertainment branch Wordwraith Studios, under which she'll be producing her first film in 2025. When she's not writing, filming, momming, or working at her full-time job, she's often horseback riding, playing videogames, or cosplaying. She lives in rural Missouri with her husband, son, and more animals than she'd prefer to disclose. You can find out more about J. R. Frontera, her books, and her films by visiting her website at https://www.jrfrontera.com.

www.ingramcontent.com/pod-product-compliance
Lightning Source LLC
Chambersburg PA
CBHW051421190726
48289CB00001B/1